DELUSIONS *of* CLARITY

A NOVEL OF INTRIGUE AND PERCEPTION

VERN BRYK

· MANDO FORTE BOOKS ·

Published by Mando Forte Books, Cleveland, Ohio

Manufactured in the United States of America

ISBN 978-1-7320496-2-8

0 9 8 7 6 5 4 3 2 1

Cover and interior design by Sheila Hart, Sheila Hart Design,
Strongsville, Ohio. www.hartsart.net

Constellations have always been troublesome things
to name. If you give one of them a fanciful name, it
will always refuse to live up to it; it will always persist
in not resembling the thing it has been named for.
Ultimately, to satisfy the public, the fanciful name has
to be discarded for a common-sense one, a manifestly
descriptive one. The Great Bear remained the Great
Bear—and unrecognizable as such—for thousands of
years; and people complained about it all the time, and
quite properly; but as soon as it became the property
of the United States, Congress changed it to the Big
Dipper, and now everybody is satisfied, and there is no
more talk about riots.

—Mark Twain, from *Following the Equator*

MONDAY, AUGUST 6, 2007

DAY ONE

RICOCHET

It was two beers past noon when the phrase "bystanders were hit" caught his attention like a fishhook in the cheek. Bullets fired by cops, or at them, always ricocheted into the world of Karl Jommers, police psychologist. In Grayton, Ohio, a city law required every cop involved in a critical incident to get a head check, and Jommers was the designated guy who popped the hood and took a look. Bullets flying either way qualified as a critical incident, whether or not any lead hit the mark.

More often than not, such assessments were routine, like a dental checkup for a scrupulous flosser. But the news that bystanders had been shot shattered any prospect that the next few days would be routine.

The ominous words crackled out of an old tube television hanging crookedly from a ceiling bracket over in the left corner of the bar. Few ever paid much attention to the TV. It was only there to give a solitary drinker at the bar something to stare at besides the backsides of beer taps.

Larry, the ever-present owner-bartender, was struggling to handle a busy lunch crowd with only one helper. The patrons were focused on their food, drink, and small talk. And Jommers himself was engaged in his cherished practice of eavesdropping, which he believed provided more insight into the human condition than any textbook or drama ever could. The raw, unfiltered, unguarded output of ordinary conversation provided hot-wired, unauthorized access to the private places in the psyche.

Spreckels Tavern was a perfect spot for such reconnaissance, as it was one of the few remaining social neutral zones with a liquor license. It drew a motley crowd and was among the last of places where one might hear a litigation lawyer debating sports with a limestone hauler, or a certified boiler operator grousing about the state of popular music with a podiatric intern.

The TV was at the periphery of Jommers's attention. Occupying his favorite barstool, he cocked his head slightly to aim a snooping ear and discreet glance toward the table where an office equipment sales rep was touting the benefits of a new automated letter opener, one whose exclusive tilt-and-tamp feature ensured that the top of the envelope was cleanly sliced without damaging the contents. It was the sales rep's show going on the sales rep's tab, but his performance was awkward, the banter slightly off. Tension in the voice. The forced chuckles. The tight face with occasional eye twitches. Jommers noted it all, even though the rep's clients seemed not to.

The noon news had already delivered its upfront serious stuff and was now in its warm-and-fuzzy segment, something about a soccer-playing dog. So Jommers covertly stayed tuned in to the sales rep's spiel about the tilt-and-tamp letter opener. But then soccer dog got interrupted, abruptly replaced by a live on-scene report about a police raid gone bad. Bystanders hit. Jommers jerked his head back to the TV and gave it his full attention.

Information at the moment was sketchy, and police were keeping reporters and everyone else at a distance from the scene. They had but the bare gist of it. SWAT had raided a meth lab on the East Side, and, as with war, the first casualty had been the plan. The TV reporter's urgent voice and her spotty information suggested that the calamity was still unfolding.

A SWAT cop had once told Jommers that a raid can go wrong in all kinds of ways. Some you've seen. Some you've only heard about. Some you couldn't even dream up. And sometimes it goes wrong in a way that can only be described using metaphors for flaming excremental deluge. Judging by the reporter's comments, Jommers sensed this misadventure was falling into the last category.

"We've heard a report that some bystanders were hit by gunfire, but we haven't been able to confirm that yet. The operation is ongoing. But . . . and this is strange . . . we've heard that the bystanders were not near the action. Which makes no sense. So it's not clear how. Not clear how they were hit, that is. We can't see much of anything from our position. We're not sure exactly what's happening. There's a lot of confusion. We just don't know . . . This is strange," the reporter repeated. "Makes no sense."

The words hung in the air like solid objects, and that was because, at some point, Jommers himself would have to make sense of it all. His interest was both professional and personal. Shots fired meant every member of SWAT would need to be interviewed separately within the coming days. His appointment calendar was suddenly fuller. But his personal concern was foremost on his mind at the moment. After performing the job for a number of years, he had seen all the SWAT guys before. They weren't just faceless badges, they were real people. People he knew. People he liked. And now, these people that he knew and liked were in the middle of a major hell puke.

Which was why Jommers got annoyed when the office equipment sales rep shuffled up close and distracted him. The sales rep had come up to the bar to pay his check, but it was clear by his proximity that he wanted to say something.

"Oh, hey, aren't you that psychologist guy?"

Jommers didn't wear a sign on his back indicating his occupation, but he was not surprised at the question, knowing how the bar's owner talked him up. In Larry's mind, having a psychologist as a regular was like a seal of approval that the place had good vibes, or at least nontoxic vibes. So Larry was fond of muttering about the honor to customers whenever Jommers was present. "See that guy over there? You know what he does?"

Customers given the scoop by Larry then turned their heads slightly and gave Jommers the once-over. What they saw was a burly guy with a casual, self-assured posture, a guy whose chevron mustache crowned but did not conceal a slight, knowing smile.

On this day, that psychologist guy was wearing navy-blue twill slacks and a light blue tattersall oxford-cloth shirt with a narrow blue tie. His simple attire varied little from day to day, and constant aspects included wearing the tie loose, with shirt open at the neck and rolled-up sleeves. It was the look of a down-to-earth guy who's willing to offer a nod to formality, but not a bow.

It wasn't only his bar look. Patients arriving in his office found him dressed much the same way, standing with feet apart and hands on hips, waiting to deliver a bearish handshake. The image conveyed seriousness without stuffiness, like a bowling team at a funeral.

On most occasions the affable psychologist was more than happy to chat with a casual inquirer, given that any one of them was potentially a future patient. He usually gave them two business cards, along with the suggestion that the second one be given to the acquaintance most likely to need it.

Though Jommers was only forty-seven, the deep timbre and slow cadence of his voice carried a tone of gently shared wisdom, like an old-timer telling an apprentice how things are done.

On this occasion, however, the sales rep did not receive the normal warm welcome. Jommers answered the man without looking at him, eyes locked on the TV.

"You're not depressed, my friend. You're just miserable. There's a difference."

"What?"

"Couldn't help but overhear your conversation, and I picked up on a few things beyond the features of your really cool letter opener. You didn't saunter up to this spot at the bar by chance. There's a discontent in your life, and you were wondering if I might be the guy to explain it. So here you go. You're miffed about the things you're forced to do to pay the bills and put food on the table, which puts you in company with billions of other people on the planet and most of the souls that ever walked it. Like almost everybody today, you think you're special, that you shouldn't have to endure the daily misery of an ordinary life. And when the world fails to recognize your specialness, you get all glum and pissy. You don't need a psychologist, friend. You need the ghost of an ancestor to teach you humility and gratitude. Gratitude that you have a job. A job that doesn't burn your flesh, break your fingers, or wrench your back. A job you can do in the shade, as they used to say in the country. You take your shower before work, while hardworking men take theirs after. That's the real divider in life. Be happy with the side you're on."

The sales rep was both surprised and irked by the instant analysis, but was too unnerved to dispute it. Without uttering a word, he paid his bill and walked away from the bar without giving Jommers another glance.

Jommers hadn't intended to sound so uncaring, and the rebuke he'd delivered was completely contrary to his normal response. But the TV news report about the shootout had upset him, and the sketchy details had a premonitory quality that briefly knocked him off his game. He didn't believe in omens, yet he sensed that the impact of the shots being fired on the other side of town would somehow rumble into his life in a bad way. It was a feeling he couldn't explain, though he understood that the subconscious sometimes forges ahead with calculations that the conscious mind has deferred. Whatever beast had been unleashed was not simply the product of this day, but the sum of many.

Feeling a bit guilty, and hoping to amend his comments, Jommers swiveled around to look for the sales rep, but the man was already gone. Jommers left some money on the bar, then strode briskly out the door, at a pace several notches above his usual gait, which lay somewhere between an amble and a trudge.

"Hey, buddy," Jommers called out.

The sales rep stopped and looked at Jommers warily. Jommers smiled, stuck his hands partly in his front pockets, and casually strolled over.

"You know you pronounced the name of that pitcher wrong."

"Yeah? So?"

"Easy to do if you just read it, since it sounds different from how it's spelled. But if you were a real sports fan, you would have heard it pronounced on the radio or TV. But if you're not a sports fan, how would you know it at all? You hate sports, but you know your clients are going to talk about it at lunch, so you give the sports section of the paper a quick skim so you can toss something into the ring without sounding like an idiot."

"It's part of the game."

"Right, but it's a game you can't stand anymore, not that you ever could. Your forced laughs, tense voice, and strained efforts at small talk tell me that you are not a gregarious person by nature. And there's nothing wrong with that, except when you have a job that demands it, like sales. You despise these client lunch things. You get a knot in your stomach before each one."

"Yeah, I do, but like you said, we have to do what we have to do. No free lunch and all that."

"True enough. But sometimes we can shift the load around, move it this way or that, make it easier to carry. I've got some tests I can give you that can nail down your personality traits. Then I've got some resources that help identify a job where those particular traits would be a plus instead of a minus. If you're willing to go through the process, and willing to consider a career change, I think we can find a way to make it easier for you to get up in the morning." Jommers handed the man one of his cards. "Give it some thought. Then give me a call."

"Okay. Thanks."

As Jommers headed back toward his wheels, he noticed a bad taste in his mouth. Part of it was his uncharacteristic snotty behavior, and part of it was from the half-finished walleye sandwich that had been slathered in a tartar sauce gone slightly south. Larry was a terrific bartender, but a lousy food service operator. He saw expiration dates as mere suggestions and put way too much faith in the reputed antimicrobial properties of hops.

Contributing to the sensory assault was Lake Erie's late-summer breath, which silently belched ashore about a half mile away, reeking of rotted algae. Erie was the shallowest of the Great Lakes, making it the warmest in summer. That distinction endowed its waters with more fish than the rest, but also more of the green glop. The temperature-dependent algae bloom visited predictably in late August, but a long heat wave had made it worse than usual, souring the city's tap water. When Erie got the fever, the city's water got sick.

As Jommers plodded onward, he grimaced and held his arms slightly away from his body, trying to cool his swampy pits. It was a futile effort, as the air was almost as thick as the viscous puddles of gum gobs melting on the griddle-hot sidewalk.

He knew he was acting wimpy about it, but like most Great Lakers accustomed to moderate summers, he did not well abide the siege of a Southern-style swelter that had audaciously slithered north. The blistering weather that a Southerner bears without much fuss wears on a Northerner like a hair shirt with matching hair underwear. During those rare occasions, a cicada-like whine arose throughout the region as if some great injustice had been inflicted. People proudly displayed their indignant torment and, unbidden, shared tales of brown lawns and withering plants. In a contentious society, the perceived offense of uncomfortable weather remained one of the few things that people could rally around.

Jommers walked over to his '97 Ford Taurus, whose sun-faded royal-blue paint job was further dulled by accumulated road dust. He slid inside and found everything he touched was close to grilling temperature, even though he'd left the windows open. The A/C had tanked a few years back and he was still waiting for a better cash flow position to invest in its repair. But it didn't matter, as it was only a short drive back to the office, which, like Spreckels, was down in the Bends. In fact, most of his trips were short these days, as he had unintentionally evolved into a creature of the Bends, where he lived, worked, and played.

That unofficial tag—the Bends—described the flat, low-lying strips of land that abutted the navigation channel of the lower Claybank River as it snaked its way to Lake Erie minus a snake's elegance. On a map, the large, uneven loops of the river's final stretch looked more like unraveled entrails. The area's moniker stemmed from the colorful names ascribed to some of the meanders— Fish Head Bend, Armory Bend, Bootlegger Bend, Grist Mill Bend, and Tangle Bend, which was so named because its once-narrow passage caused the riggings of passing sailing ships to become entangled.

That section of the river, the navigation channel, loosely demarcated the length of the Bends area, while the width of the flatland tract was determined by the short hills hemming it in on both sides. Grayton's business district gazed down from the east elevation. Peering down from the west was the Old Town neighborhood, the site of the original settlement, and a place where repeated efforts at gentrification had achieved only spotty results.

As a longtime dweller of the area, Jommers was well-versed in its history. He knew that nature continually reshapes meanders over time, but that once the river banks were lined with bulkheads, first of stone blocks, then later of steel, the river's course was locked in. The interruption of the natural process was necessitated by the arrival of industry, which required stable banks for its infrastructure and a deep channel for ships.

He also knew that, due to the clay subsoil in the region, the waters of the lower Claybank had been murky long before humans had arrived and started dumping crap into it. Farming had increased the soil erosion and the muddiness, making the river waters look like liquid earth, but it was industrial pollution that had transformed the waters from merely turbid into toxic, quashing aquatic life.

The Bends had once been the bustling heart of Grayton's industry, back in the days when cities wore smoky skies as a badge of honor, a smudgy proof of progress and prosperity, when the word pollution had not been in anyone's vocabulary or thoughts. So back then, no one had cared much about spillage of chemicals, sewage, or oil into the river. It would all wash out somehow.

Eventually, environmental laws and deindustrialization reduced industrial gunk, but the antiquated sewer systems of older inner-ring suburbs still allowed storms to wash raw sewage into the river's tributaries, along with a lot of other natural debris and garbage. So even though the river was a lot cleaner than in the past, its fetid odor still pervaded the air, and its brown frothy water remained grotty—a strange cocoa whose foam was topped with crud instead of marshmallows.

Ore boats still snaked their way up to the last remaining steel operation, but overall, the area had been ravaged by industry consolidation, increased global competition, and migration of factories to the suburbs. The smoke had cleared out, but so had the vitality.

But the zone wasn't dead by any means. The ball-bearing factory still cranked out gazillions of them. The construction supply company still produced mountains of concrete. The asphalt company still churned out an unending stream of it. And the manufacturer of rope and chain still rolled out miles of both.

In addition, a gradual influx of new, nontraditional players had been drawn to the Bends, infusing new life into the interstices. They included a recreational boat storage facility, a jet-ski rental operation, a rowing club, a craft shop devoted to custom iron work, and an artist who specialized in designing and fabricating novel neon signs. Also arriving were a variety of upscale boutiques and galleries that exploited the aesthetic charms of century-old brick architecture with its segmented arched windows. With a good sandblasting, some upgraded lighting and new windows, an old brick hulk could be transformed into a quaint little place oozing with antique allure.

So the Bends was an odd, patchwork quilt—clusters of vibrant commerce scattered amidst pockets of ruin. A thriving business might find itself lodged between vacant crumbling properties with broken windows and walls covered with weedy vines. And those ubiquitous green creepers were the markers that signified the quick and the dead. In some places they were so rampant, you could imagine having discovered a lost Incan city in the Ecuadoran rainforest.

The local infrastructure exhibited a similar patchiness, especially the roads, whose holes and craters conspired to transform ordinary driving into a slalom course. The regulars had learned where to zig and zag by muscle memory without thinking, but a first-timer had to approach the roads with trepidation, like an explorer on hazardous terrain, so a vehicle's speed quickly distinguished natives from wayfarers.

So the Bends was an odd place to launch a therapy practice, a healing mission ensconced in ailing environs. But for Jommers, it made perfect sense. The setting stood as a testament to tenacity. The ubiquitous grit that crunched underfoot wherever one walked in the Bends evoked the other kind of grit, that of character. It was a tough place. The people who had built it and had worked there were strong and resolute. They had a steely doggedness to survive and better their lives in the face of obstacles and harsh conditions. They had resilience. And if you're a clinical psychologist, that's the one big thing you wish you could instill into all your patients. Resilience. You wish you could dispense it, the way the blast furnaces dispensed salt pills to sweating workers. But you can't. For those who have lost it, or never had it, the trait must be taught, like touch-typing, tango, or ju-jitsu. And some people won't ever get it, just as some people won't ever master driving a stick shift. Their gears will always grind. But you have to try. Do your best to teach them. And where better to instill grit than a place where it abounds all around you?

One guy who had exactly that kind of grit was Pete Gerzny, proud owner of Gerzny's Truck & Trailer Repair on Nickel Plate Road. Gerzny was a grizzled sixty-seven-year old man with a tough, wiry frame and a tough old-school attitude. Life is hard. The only answer is to work hard. He walked swiftly and determinedly with his hands on his hips. His gait had a slight forward lean, like someone battling a stiff headwind. He inspected the work of his mechanics with an exacting eye, as if every dirty, beat-to-hell truck in the shop was a space shuttle that required perfection. That was old-school, too. But behind that stern visage lived a pretty nice guy, nice enough to help out a young psychologist who had desperately needed cheap office space years ago.

Gerzny was an old friend of the Jommers family and had made young Karl an offer. The offices for the shop were on the ground floor at the right end of the building, and there was an unused second floor above them that had once held a discontinued truck sales operation. The deal presented to the fledgling psychologist was this: cart out the junk that was up there, remodel it at his own expense, convert the fire escape into a separate entrance, get it set up for separate utilities, and he could use the space at no charge. And that was how a therapist had come to start a private practice above a truck-and-trailer repair shop down in the Bends.

Returning from lunch, Jommers had barely turned his Taurus into the parking lot when he saw Pete pointing to a car, wagging his finger with a sense of urgency. A woman, standing by the passenger side, was holding the door open and pleading with a man to come out. Jommers rode right up to her.

"I'm Karl Jommers. How can I help?"

"Oh, thank God you're here. Thank God you're here. I wanted to plan this, but he wouldn't come. I had to lie about where we were going. It's been going on too long. One of his old friends from the First District said you could help. I just don't know what else to do."

"What's the problem?"

"Kenny didn't go to work this morning. Said he felt sick, but wouldn't say what was wrong. Then, a little bit later, I see him staring at his gun and I think, okay, that's it, no more, this can't go on. Something has to happen."

"So he's been depressed for a while?"

"Months. It started out slow, so I kept thinking it would pass. But it just got worse."

Jommers looked inside the car. Kenny was hunched over and motionless, staring blankly at the dashboard. He looked borderline catatonic.

"Hey, Kenny, what's going on, man? Can you tell me?"

Kenny didn't answer or even acknowledge hearing the question. Jommers turned back to the wife.

"Has he shown any other symptoms? Fatigue, loss of appetite, memory or concentration problems?"

"Well, yeah, all of that, but that's like all part of depression, isn't it?"

"Often, yes. But his skin doesn't look right to me. I'm wondering if something physiological is going on here. Let me ask you this—can you think of any changes or events in his life that preceded his slide into this? Anything, big or small."

"Well, that's what's so confusing. For sixteen years he works the First District, on patrol, and you know what it's like over there. Terrell Avenue, Terrible

Terry. But it doesn't faze him. Just rolls off his back. Then he gets a cake assignment, and after a while, he starts to change. Just makes no sense."

"What's the cake assignment?"

"He was always one of the best marksmen on the force. So they offered him a position over at the range when someone there retired after getting sick. He does training, runs the requals."

Jommers frowned. "I think you should take him to the emergency room right now."

"What? Why?"

"I'm not a doctor, so this is just a hunch, but I think he has lead poisoning."

"Oh my God!"

"I've heard other cops complain about the lack of ventilation there. Every round fired puts more lead particles in the air. It builds up. And he's there breathing that stuff every day. If I'm right, this is very serious."

"Oh my God."

"Here's my card. Call me later. Let me know what's going on."

The woman jumped into the car and spun the tires as she sped out of the lot. Pete turned his head and raised an eyebrow. Jommers walked over.

"I think that guy has—"

Pete raised his hand in a stop signal motion. "I don't even want to know."

Jommers smiled and walked upstairs to his office. Upon arriving, he noticed a bad smell, which made him momentarily forget what he intended to do next. But that was all part of it.

A therapy practice operating over a repair shop did suffer from the occasional sensory distraction. The acrid odor of arc welder smoke drifting upward, the whining noise of a grinder, or the jolt of intermittent hammering. In addition, a heavy-duty impact wrench working on a rusted lug nut could sound unnervingly like a machine gun, not an ideal background sound when trying to calm an anxious cop.

On the other hand, the sounds and smells of hard work comforted the male ego and helped overcome the traditional male attitude towards psychological counseling, the idea that therapy was for pussies. Overcoming that resistance had already been on Jommers's mind back in his college days, and it was the subject of his thesis and dissertation research. Men were being underserved by available psychological resources due to their own reluctance to seek help, and the psychological profession was obligated to address the problem.

Jommers's big idea was that the whole notion of therapy needed repositioning for the masculine gender. Men understood the concept of repair. Things break. You get them fixed. Of course, he knew better than anyone that the human brain was a bit more complicated than a water pump with shot bearings, but that didn't matter for the purposes of reaching out. As any good bait-and-switch salesman knows, the trick is to get them through the door. You deal with the details later.

The guy-friendly decor of the office reinforced that message. It was not the full man-tacky stuff like swords, moose heads, cowboy art, and paintings of bullfighters. Instead it featured artifacts and photographs that related to the immediate environment, such as factories, ships, lighthouses and trains, all bounded by old brick walls and a scarred hardwood floor. The style wasn't obtrusive, but stood in definite contrast to the typical suburban medical center office with fluorescent lights casting a sterile glow over pastel wall coverings and budget prints of Impressionist paintings.

There was no couch either, not even an upholstered chair. Instead, seating consisted of several heavy Amish-made oak rocking chairs. The beauty of rocking chairs is that they could be positioned any way you want. Jommers usually had them facing a northerly window with a good view of the Bends. In therapy sessions, Jommers liked to sit in a rocker next to the patient, facing the same direction. That setup, along with the distinct creaky *ka-lump* sound made by a wooden rocker stroking a wooden floor, allowed the patient to imagine he was on a front porch somewhere, talking things over with an old friend or wise uncle. For more formal interactions, such as an interview or test session, Jommers might sit behind the old oak table that he used as a desk.

After dismissing the foul odor as familiar—burnt rubber bushing in a shock absorber caught in the flame of a gas torch—Jommers walked over to that table desk, looked at his appointment book and sighed. He'd seen two patients that morning, but none were scheduled for the rest of the day. Light days like this were becoming more frequent, which concerned him.

He couldn't refrain from thinking how the morning's disastrous police assault benefited him. Every SWAT cop on the scene would require a post-critical-incident review. And given that Jommers was a private contractor, not a police department employee, each one would be a separate billing. Along with that, the sessions would be categorized as administrative, so the bills would be paid directly by the department, not by an insurance company, meaning no negotiated discount of the kind that insurance companies forced you to eat to stay in their network.

He tried to block the thought because it was unseemly, his benefiting from someone else's trouble and misfortune. But there was no reason to deny it or pretend otherwise. Morticians benefit when people die. Are they supposed to feel guilty about new business? It's just the way it is.

He turned on his TV, waiting for the station's on-the-hour news update. The rundown was still sketchy, but more than what he'd heard in the bar. Police had been busting a drug lab operating on the second floor of an abandoned printing shop on Eggers Court off McKinley Boulevard. The action had ignited a gun battle. Three suspects were dead. Five bystanders had also been hit by gunfire. Two of them were pronounced dead at the scene, including a twelve-year-old boy. The other three were taken to the hospital.

The five were all residents of the Mentmore Manor apartments, one of those old inner-city buildings with fancy Anglophile names whose units had definitely been a step up at the time they were built, but, being rooted in earth, the structures could not follow the middle-class migration outward. Mentmore was another left-behind building housing left-behind people.

The five victims had been standing out on their balconies, watching the excitement. It was not yet clear whether the bystanders had been hit with bullets fired by the police or the suspects, as the apartment building was perpendicular to the line of crossfire. The reporters found the last part confusing, voicing the refrain heard in the earlier live coverage. *This is strange. It makes no sense.* Jommers was unfamiliar with the neighborhood, so he couldn't visualize the scene.

He sat down at his table desk and made some phone calls in an effort to find out exactly what had happened with the SWAT raid on the East Side. Unfortunately, the same official police contacts who might know something would be among those frantically managing the aftermath. So he decided to try an unofficial contact. He knew an older cop with a desk job down at Central who had provided some inside information in the past.

"Hey, Tom, Karl Jommers."

"Hey, Karl. Long time. How you been?"

"Still plugging. Yourself?"

"Not so hot. The knees got way worse. Feels like pieces of broken glass in there, just grinding away. Hurts like hell."

"Sorry to hear that."

"I shouldn't complain. Desk jobs are switching over to civilians now. So when guy like me can't do the streets anymore, he'll just have to go."

"I guess you heard about the raid on Eggers Court."

"You kidding? It's liked a kicked beehive down here."

"Yeah, I'll bet. Any idea what happened?"

"Hearing bits and pieces, half of which contradict each other. Everyone just hoping it wasn't the tank that nailed the bystanders."

"The what?"

"The tank the army gave us. It was in the paper."

"Oh, yeah. The mini-tank thing. I remember."

"Yeah, mini-tank, whatever. It was there. You know, I'm not a big fan of all this shock-and-awe crap. I know it's a rundown neighborhood and all, but there's still plenty of decent people who live there. Old people, women, kids. You don't treat a residential neighborhood like some goddamn battlefield in Iraq. Show a little finesse for Chrissake."

"Was it involved? The mini-tank?"

"Not sure. Those army guys would know."

"The who?"

"Whenever the army gives you something complicated, they send trainers with it. So they set these guys up in an unused office down the hall. They're not in uniform, but the haircuts give them away. That and the strut."

"Would they talk to me? Can you switch me over?"

"Brass would rip me a new one. Technically, I'm not even supposed to know they're here."

"Okay. But if you know the office, you can look up the extension. I wait fifteen minutes, call the switchboard and ask for that number, and I forget where I got it."

"Well, okay. But you have to forget really hard. If you read the article, you know the whole thing is a sensitive issue."

"Understood. Appreciate it."

Jommers waited about twenty minutes, then called back and asked the operator for the extension. He got through.

"Hello. My name is Karl Jommers. I'm a psychologist who works with Grayton PD and—"

"Who the hell put you through to this extension?"

"I don't really know. I called trying to get some information about the incident at Eggers Court and I got bounced around until—"

"Listen, Pajamas, or whatever your name is, you don't ever call this extension again. You stick with your designated points of interface. Do not deviate from your established protocol. Do you understand me?"

"Sure. I wasn't trying to be a buttinsky here. My job is to help police officers deal with the aftermath of these things, so I was just curious about—"

"Don't be curious. Curiosity is what got those people hurt this morning. If they had stayed inside and stayed low, they would have got through it just fine. You could learn from that."

"Stay inside. Stay low. Got it."

"Don't forget it."

TIME TO LET IT GO

Jommers realized that a fully detailed account of the incident was not going to be imminently available, that he would have to patiently wait for one like everybody else. So he went home, hoping to distract himself with some music. It was a short commute.

To get to his apartment in the back, he walked through his library, which consisted of several interleaved corridors of bookshelves containing psychology books and journals. The circuitous path created by the arrangement was designed to both separate and conceal the apartment behind the office. He preferred that patients didn't know he lived there. And if he happened to be in the apartment when someone entered the front office area, then it would appear as if he was emerging from a library when he went out to meet them.

More importantly, the serpentine library buffer established a separation that was psychological as well as physical, keeping the spheres of work and home apart. To that end, he enforced certain rules upon himself. He didn't carry patient files into his apartment to read, and didn't pay personal bills in the office. In that same vein, he had two pen cups, two calculators, two staplers, two tape dispensers, two pair of scissors, and so on, one for each realm. So the library corridors served as a force field that barred mixing of the two universes. Only three things were able to move through the intangible barrier: his person, his beer, and his music.

The apartment setup had not originally been intended as a permanent residence. He'd built it into his office plan primarily to have to avoid a long trip home after a late appointment. Evening appointments were often a necessary part of his stigma-reduction efforts. If a man says he needs time off for a doctor appointment, his coworkers will almost certainly ask about what's wrong. The man then has two choices: reluctantly admit he is seeing a therapist, or lie to his friends. Evening appointments circumvented the whole conversation.

There was plenty of space available, enough for both the office and the apartment. It wasn't fancy. The apartment side was one big room housing most everything, with only the bathroom constructed as a separate enclosed space.

The apartment wasn't used much in the early days of his operation, though it often proved handy after an evening of bar-hopping in the Bends. His marriage to Rachel had put an end to the pub crawls, and the trip home after a late appointment hadn't seemed quite so long once there was a woman waiting at the other end of it. Perception of task magnitude correlates inversely with reward magnitude, and things had been good between them at first.

When their marriage hit a rocky patch, the apartment acquired more utility. Occasional blasts of arctic weather on the home front made the Bends seem balmy by comparison. The rift grew slowly, but steadily, like a crack in a wall over a sinking foundation. You barely notice at first, but then everything seems to collapse at once.

The occasional encampments became more frequent and eventually stretched into the indefinite stay as the marital situation slipped into an informal state of separation. He'd believed for a long while that it was only temporary, but relationships, like trucks, do not repair themselves. Some effort is required on somebody's part, and neither party had made one.

So it did not come as a surprise the day she called to inform him that she was moving to Cincinnati and that it was "time to formalize the de facto status." Those were the words she'd used to request a divorce, and they left little room to dispute the suggestion. And they also formalized Jommers's status as a full-time creature of the Bends.

And now today, after the twenty-five-second walk home from front to back, he strolled over the shelving holding his CD collection. He grabbed one CD in particular without thinking. And ten seconds later that bugged him. He had this thing. A psychologist's thing. It wasn't enough to understand someone else's behavior. He needed to comprehend his own. And nothing piqued his curiosity more than acting without prior deliberation. So he constantly played detective with himself, which can be a demanding way to live. Fortunately, most of his personal mini-mysteries were easily solvable, as was this one.

He'd grabbed a compilation CD whose first track was "I Got a Strange Feeling," performed by Buddy Guy. As soon as he heard Buddy sing the first line, it all clicked. The song, written by Willie Dixon and Al Perkins, is better known by its alternate title, "When My Left Eye Jumps."

During lunch at Spreckels, he had noticed the salesman with the twitchy eye around the same time the TV reporter had said, "This is strange." Somehow, in the behind-the-wall wiring of Jommers's brain, this juxtaposition had wrangled him to a song about a man with a jumpy eye and a strange feeling. One more mini-mystery solved. If only the big ones were that easy.

And, of course, it was a blues song.

Everyone has their own preferred head-straightening music they use to comb out the tangles in their brain waves, their personal mood medicine that sets things right. For Jommers it was the blues. His jazz-loving ex-wife, Rachel, used to mock that bent, finding the blues stale, tedious, and simplistic. But familiarity is the whole point of a retreat, he thought. You want your comfort food to taste the same way it did the last time. Like coming home to the solid ground of certainty after a hard day sailing on the stormy sea of doubt. But more than that, the blues served up an attitude with protective powers. A reconciliation with life's vicissitudes. A musical Serenity Prayer with better licks. Resolution guaranteed, musically, if nowhere else.

While he liked all kinds of blues, he maintained a clear ranking of preferences. Acoustic over electric. Older over newer. North Hill Country over Delta. Guitar over piano. Slide style over standard. He especially loved those old field recordings, like the ones made by Alan Lomax and others, where the artists' music was often captured in their living room or on the front porch, where, if you listen closely, you might hear in the background a child laughing, a dog barking, or crickets chirping. He thought that the unvarnished authenticity of those recordings generated a raw power, an unimpeachable purity that stood in stark contrast to the music of modern times, which got cranked out like an engineered synthetic food product, like the cheese-less cheese snack.

His favorite blues artists included both the well known and the more obscure: Mississippi Fred McDowell, Lightnin' Hopkins, Mississippi John Hurt, Memphis Minnie, Sonny Terry, Brownie McGhee, Son House, Sam Chatmon, John Cephas & Phil Wiggins, Lattie Murrell, Guitar Frank Hovington, Barbecue Bob, Sylvester Weaver, Robert Johnson, Tampa Red, and Napoleon Strickland.

Each of them might have one or more labels attached, subjective and often indistinct style categories created by the bluesicologists. But before the record companies came calling, the old blues masters didn't play to type. They played to their time and place, to their friends and family, and to themselves. And really, how do you categorize Ed and Lonnie Young playing "Chevrolet" on fife and drum?

The only truly distinct separator is electric versus acoustic, and in Jommers's mind, the electric blues was like a young man who leaves his country family behind in order to make some real money in the big city. And then, when the young man comes back to visit, the family can't help but notice the louder voice, the flashier style, and the cock-of-the-walk strut. And they smile with quiet, amused pity at what the boy has become. Yet they welcome him to the table. He's still family.

But Jommers also knew that the dichotomy might be more of a listener thing, not a player thing. It's the followers who get fussy about it all. The players themselves don't see the fence. They can walk back and forth from one side to the other without thinking they've left the yard.

Buddy Guy was probably the best electric blues guitar player ever. Yet that same electric wizard collaborated with harmonica player Junior Wells to create some of the purest, sweetest, acoustic blues the world had ever heard.

Go figure.

As the music played, Jommers flipped a switch that ran it through the Philco, that being a classic Philco Model 90 cathedral-style radio from 1931. He'd snapped up the antique at a good price because neither the radio nor the speaker had worked, though the wood cabinet itself was mint. Speaker cloth, too. So he pulled out the guts and installed some decent speakers. Then he'd wired the thing to serve as an alternate external speaker for his CD player. There was something cool about having old blues come out of an old thing.

As he listened to the music, he turned around and did a slow scan of the apartment, taking in all the other things he thought cool, or at least had perceived so at the time of acquisition. But from the perspective of middle age, the place was taking on a different and discomfiting hue.

The first thing he studied was the dusty Native American blankets hanging on the bare brick walls. The motivation for buying them had not been primarily improving the decor. It was summer when he'd originally remodeled the space way back when, and he'd thought that the old bare brick by itself was aesthetically interesting enough to forgo any adornments.

Then winter came.

The cold weather brought with it a lesson in architecture history. In a building of that vintage, the brick wasn't just *on* the wall, it *was* the wall. One side facing indoors, the other side exposed to the great outdoors. Nothing in between. The wall got so cold that frost formed on the inside of it. Streams of chilled air cascaded off the wall's surface and enveloped the room like an arctic flood. The blankets went up on the wall as a way of temporarily mitigating the comfort crisis, and like so many other things in Jommers's life, the temporary became permanent through inattention and procrastination.

Jommers then shifted his gaze from the blankets to his various lamps, the driftwood lamps first.

Lake Erie was a sculptor whose favorite medium was wood. The rivers supplied the raw material in the form of storm-felled timber, then the great lake worked its art on the material with watery hands, fashioning exotic shapes no man could ever dream of. And when the works were completed and finely polished, Erie proudly presented her output on the galleries of the shore for all to admire.

In his younger days, Jommers had been in awe of such works and scoured the beaches for interesting pieces. After accumulating a number he found particularly captivating, he'd transformed them into lamps that he'd wired himself.

They were definitely distinctive, and he beamed with pride over his collaboration with nature.

It was only fairly recently that the driftwood lamps had started to appear peculiar to him. Weird, even. Likewise the railroad lanterns, the antique tools, the Mission-style furniture, and a whole bunch of other stuff that now poked at him like a high school yearbook picture.

When these doubts had first surfaced, he hadn't understood why he was starting to sour on his surroundings after years of faithful service. Then, ever the detective, he'd put it all together. It was a confluence of several things.

First was the bat.

A small section of mortar between the bricks had begun to crumble and permit a peek of daylight. It was only slightly less than an inch, but big enough for a bat to find it. The critter had dug out some of the loose mortar to make the gap bigger, then tried to squeeze through the gap to get inside. It got just far enough for its head to poke through the inside wall, then it got stuck. And that was the last thing the little critter ever did, except for maybe to mutter, "Oh, crap." It was long dead before Jommers noticed a strange ornament on his wall that he hadn't put there.

The second thing was a feature article in the newspaper about a proposed condo project for the Bends that would target young professionals. One of the paper's columnists sardonically suggested this would launch a Grayton version of hipsters, upscale cosmopolitans who would see it as fashionably ironic to live in the midst of postindustrial ruin.

Jommers, who had been living down in the Bends for years as an outlier, detested the idea of being trendy. It irked him to think that he, the man who abhorred fashion, might unwillingly serve it just by staying put.

The third factor was inadvertently hearing a song in a bar, Steve Winwood singing "Can't Find My Way Home." It happened to be one of those few songs he'd really liked when he was young and still listened to pop-rock music. That got him thinking about how much time had passed since then. And that in turn triggered one of those well-known midlife reflection-reappraisal episodes. Where have I been? How did I get here? Where am I going? Blah, blah, blah. It was the kind of thing he thought beneath him, being a psychologist and all. But as he had often learned, his profession did not immunize him against the standard human head crap any more than being a doctor protects you from getting sick.

The fourth and final catalyst was the day he was sitting at the bar in Spreckels when Larry silently got Jommers attention, nodding toward a customer at the other end of the bar, a paunchy, disheveled guy in his late sixties with a scraggly gray beard and long gray ponytail who was wearing a faded purple T-shirt, sandals, and well-worn jeans with ragged, frazzled hem. But it was the ponytail that made Larry roll his eyes. The guy was mostly bald, so it was a relatively small portion of his scalp that contributed to the ponytail, the parts around the ears and the back of the neck.

When Larry got a free second to come by, he leaned over the bar and spoke to Jommers in a muted voice. "I'm just dying to go over there and say to him, 'Hey man, it's time. Time to let it go. Do yourself a favor, and us, too. Just let it go.'"

The brief comment resonated with Jommers, but he didn't then know why. But now, while surveying his living quarters, the light came on. This place. The digs he had once thought so cool. This place was his gray-haired ponytail. And he could hear Larry's voice whispering in the ether. "Hey, man. It's time. Time to let it go."

The dispiriting reflection about his apartment was interrupted by a phone call from Chelsea confirming their meeting later in the day. Chelsea was a thirty-year-old grad student in psychology who had returned to college after logging in a few years as a social worker. He had met her at Grayton State University, whose campus clung to the eastern edge of the business district. He occasionally served as a guest lecturer for the psychology department, acquainting students with the field of police psychology.

When she'd approached him after their first encounter, it wasn't because she was interested in police psychology, but rather the process by which one decided to take the road less traveled, or not. She was a smart and inquisitive woman, fascinated by psychology, but not sure in which niche she belonged. She naturally had a faculty advisor for her master's research, but she also valued the input of psychologists practicing in the real world, those who engaged with patients daily.

Jommers had talked to her several times since that first meeting, always in the role of real-world mentor, and he expected this evening's conversation to unfold in similar fashion, even though this was their first time meeting somewhere other than a campus coffee shop. She surprised him by suggesting that they should meet for a drink down in the Bends.

The salient feature of the Bends was the multitude of bars and restaurants, particularly the concentration of establishments on the east bank near the river's mouth. They ranged from tony bistros to head-banger punch-and-puke palaces that sold cheap beer by the pitcher. Their shared lure was a venue that evoked the atmosphere of genuine old world crappiness, as opposed to the imitation old world crappiness found in suburban restaurant chains with their mass-produced bric-a-brac.

As an alternative to the intentional insipidness of suburban aesthetics, the Bends environment served as a grimy shrine to authenticity for those who felt the need to worship at one. The cratered roads, crumbling brick warehouses, vacant weedy lots, rusting decommissioned railroad spurs, soot-blackened lift bridges spanning a mucky river—they were all part of the charm. But charming to whom, an inquisitive psychologist might wonder. Wasn't this why we had suburban sprawl, people trying to get away from places like this? Who finds romance in industrial ruin? The half-wrecked brick structure that once was Vorisek Tool & Die did not exactly inspire awe like, say, the Acropolis or the Colosseum.

The answer depended upon your work. People who got their hands dirty for a living, like those who worked in a grungy, ugly factory, were more than happy to spend their free time in synthetic surroundings. They were perfectly content to patronize a suburban pseudo-Italian restaurant with plastic stucco walls and rubber grapes hanging from the ceiling, a place where the Ukrainian waiters mangled Italian greetings and where the precooked chicken Parmesan was rethermalized in its vacuum pouch. And it was all good so long as the place was clean and reasonably priced. If you spent all day working in a dirty, grubby place, you didn't spend your evening playing in a dirty, grubby place.

It was the affluent professionals trapped in their sterile, windowless, fluorescent-lit cubes all day who yearned to reacquaint themselves with harsh, bracing reality. It was the anesthetizing office cube, that archetype of artifice, smaller than the isolation cells used to punish prisoners, that numbed your spirit into a stupor and made you ache to be pricked back awake, to be revivified, and a jaunt to the Bends did exactly that.

As an entertainment area, it wasn't first rate, but good enough for out-of-towners to make a point of spending some time down there before going home. And as less-fortunate cities would admit, a second-rate entertainment area was better than none. A trip to the Bends was a cheap vacation, where you could get away from the rat race without leaving town. And on a warm summer night, the murmur of the throng and the flicker of the lights beckoned you. With music and laughter wafting through the air and pleasure boats drifting along the river, the scene could fool you into thinking you'd traveled to some exotic place, that your passport had been stamped. A night in the Bends offered a hint of adventure, a potential for passion, and the eternal pursuit of the ephemeral experience.

The place where Chelsea wanted to meet was Cafe Annique over on Old Levee Road, not far from the river's mouth. The melange of bars on Old Levee presented as a mix of gemstones spread over a table in a bazaar in some far-off land. Some were cut and polished. Some were dirty and rough. Some sparkled and flashed. Some were muted and subdued.

A common concern, however, was how to avoid the leveling effect, where every operation slowly slides down to serve the lowest common denominator. Each establishment targeted a specific clientele. But unless you operated as a private club, anybody who wanted to could walk through the door.

Some of the places tried to address the issue by posting a dress code policy at the door. The idea was to deter gangbangers, bikers, and hookers. But this proved problematic in an age where otherwise ordinary people inexplicably loved to dress like gangbangers, bikers, and hookers. How do you enforce a dress code for a place where every night is Halloween?

One popular strategy was to post a couple of large men at the door whose posture and menacing expressions screamed "short-tempered bouncer." But for those establishments operating at the upper end of the scale, the answer was much simpler. High prices. That strategy tended to keep out most of the riffraff most of the time. In these places, people dressed *up* instead of *down*, though it was a costume party all the same.

Cafe Annique was one of the last truly tony spots. The chichi joints typically followed a meteoric path. Initially, they soared brightly on the novel juxtaposition of a lively upscale bistro blooming in the midst of a decaying industrial landscape. But novelty has a short shelf life, and such places typically dimmed within a couple of years. And for customers, nothing diminishes novelty faster than tiptoeing through vomit on the sidewalks, witnessing a fight in the streets, and having your vehicle electronics stolen for the third time.

Cafe Annique hung on perhaps because of its ever-changing trendy foodie menu, its riverside position, and a spacious patio deck that crept up to the water's edge, providing a scenic view of the river and its grime-blackened bridges.

It was shortly after seven o'clock when Jommers arrived at the cafe. Before entering, he took a call on his cell phone from the desperate woman he'd helped earlier in the day.

"You were right," she said. "It was lead poisoning. They're starting something called chelation to clean it out. They say he should recover."

"That's good news. But I also want you to call his union rep and tell him what happened. For that matter, call OSHA, too. Do not let your husband return to that shooting range until they have fixed the ventilation issue."

"That's a promise. Thank you so much for your help."

The call made Jommers feel good about himself, thinking that he'd possibly saved the cop from dying, or at the very least from kidney failure. He owed himself a reward. As he was in an upscale bar, he deserved an upscale brew. He loved hoppy beers in the summer and was especially fond of Sharp Twinge Imperial India pale ale, produced by a local craft brewery. The IPA boasted five varieties of hops and a whopping 95 IBU (International Bittering Units).

And so while Chelsea ordered a glass of white zinfandel, Jommers went for a Sharp Twinge. He was aware that, like many craft brews, it had a higher-than-average alcohol content, registering a potent nine percent ABV (alcohol by volume), roughly double the percentage of an ordinary beer. But he wasn't worried. He had a higher tolerance for alcohol than most, given his brawny body mass and regular heavy consumption. Besides, it was a short drive home, and the work day was done.

Or so he thought.

His mood became even more elevated shortly into his conversation with Chelsea. The first time they had gotten together, she had off-handedly dropped the name of the guy she was living with. It was done in the manner that ringless women often use to post the off-limits sign, to confirm that the meeting was strictly business. This time, she casually worked in the guy's name in a different fashion, something about making faster progress on her research now that so-and-so had moved to Chicago. So he naturally wondered if the unsolicited bit of intelligence was a signal, knowing full well that an unattached man can interpret almost anything as a signal, including breathing.

She was a slender woman with short dark hair and the simple, unadorned prettiness one sees on a model in an outdoor apparel catalog. He knew from previous conversations that she was not only very smart, but had a curious mind, which tend to go hand in hand. Her lily-white skin in August suggested she also had the good sense to put health above fashion when it came to sun exposure. Most of the other women in the place were well tanned.

In previous meetings, she exhibited an intense expression and posture, as if the wisdom she sought had some urgency. But today, wearing a casual summer dress with a floral print, she displayed a more languid pose, accompanied by an inviting smile and easy laugh, as if she were some Southern belle beckoning a suitor to join her on the front porch.

Was this new body language another signal?

And that was when the age-gap issue popped into Jommers's head. He was forty-seven, she was thirty. He was aware of the popular rule-of-thumb equation, that half your age plus seven determines the minimum socially acceptable age of someone you should date. By that standard everything was copacetic, if barely. But, as a psychologist, he also knew that research on the matter didn't jibe with the popular rule. Real-world opinions are stricter, though they varied by region, social status, and values. This raised the obvious question—who the hell cares? He wasn't running for Congress. All that matters is the other person's view.

It wasn't like he was taking advantage of some weak and vulnerable woman. Chelsea was a confident, self-assured, intelligent, goal-directed woman. If she was okay with the gap, then so what? And what was the likelihood of this leading to anything anyway? It was only a drink and a chat.

He realized that his reflection was less about her age than his. Men in good health and good spirits don't normally sense they're growing older until something calls attention to it. Youth seeps away steadily, but the loss is noticed only episodically, like a sudden breeze from an open window whirling around the faded backside of a curtain. The sun-bleached paleness of the fabric shocks. When the hell did that happen?

So this meeting with Chelsea was another one of those moments where you glimpse that backside of the curtain and your face stiffens. The occasion reminds you—this is where you are now, in case you've forgotten.

After the first bottle of Sharp Twinge went down quickly, he shrugged off his previous concerns about their age difference. Chelsea had ostensibly sought the meeting to get career advice. She had become fascinated by the fashionable topic of Internet addiction. She was worried about how the problem might extract people from the social sphere, locking them into self-made isolation chambers. More importantly, she wondered if there would be enough people acquiring the problem to warrant making it a specialty as a clinical psychologist. And within that set of people, would there be enough of them who recognized the need to seek professional assistance?

Jommers's view was that an Internet addiction was not much different than a Häagen-Dazs addiction—a character shortcoming, perhaps, but not a disorder that required clinical intervention. But he was eager to discuss it anyway. He loved playing devil's advocate.

As on previous occasions, she spoke at a quick pace, shooting out lots of ideas, running fast across open field. He listened attentively while diving into another bottle of Sharp Twinge. Then, without meaning to, Jommers stopped her with a chop block.

"What about Internet porn?"

"What?"

"Is that a separate thing, or a subset of your thing? Or, let me put it this way. Person A spends six hours a night with Internet porn. Person B spends six hours with online games. Person C online shopping, and Person D online gambling. Are those four separate disorders, or four facets of the same disorder?"

"Um . . ."

"And how are six hours spent on a computer different from six hours spent watching old sitcoms on TV, reading romance novels, collecting stamps, restoring antique cars, or playing medieval music? What are your criteria for differentiating a problem from an individualistic lifestyle?"

"Hmm . . ."

"And, if in fact you want to categorize any solitary activity as an antisocial disorder, are they all separate problems, or are they all various manifestations of other, larger underlying problems? In which case, you should be spending your efforts diagnosing and correcting the underlying problem rather than its symptoms. And if indeed causality runs deeper than the surface indicators, then a therapist specializing in Internet addiction is as useful as a podiatrist specializing in the third toe on the right foot."

He hadn't intended to cut her short, he was only trying to contribute to the discussion. But the question stunned her, rendering her temporarily speechless. To his surprise, she tilted her head and smiled.

"You see, that's what I like about you, the way you do that. Reshuffling the deck. Forcing me to take a fresh look at what I thought I'd settled. I need to spend more time talking to you."

That remark, along with her coquettish smile and serious eye contact, made Jommers confident that he had gotten the signals right for once. And as he was about to say, "I agree, you should spend more time with me. What are you doing Friday?" his cell phone rang.

He could see from the display that it was Earl Tarburn, a police officer. In an effort to accommodate cops working different shifts, Jommers always told them that they could call anytime they needed to. Yet, he always said it with fingers slightly crossed, silently acknowledging exceptions, allowing himself the right not to take the call in certain circumstances, allowing himself the right to have a life beyond talking to cops. But Tarburn was on SWAT. He had most certainly been at the disastrous Eggers Court drug lab raid earlier that day, the one where bystanders had been hit.

Jommers had to take the call.

She smiled politely, not seeming to mind the interruption.

"Tarburn, what's up?"

"Hey, Jommers. I'm not feeling right. I don't know who else to call. Is this okay? Did I get you at something?"

"No, we're good. What's going on?"

"Well, I don't know. I'm feeling funny. Like something's wrong."

"You're feeling bad about what happened today. The bystanders."

"Oh, yeah. I feel real bad about that. More than I can even tell you now. But that's in my heart, you know? What I'm calling about is something in my gut, or my head, I don't even know where it is."

"What do you feel?"

"It's a weird feeling, a quivering, like I got ice in my belly. And then there's like, I don't know, vibrating all over. You know like how your hand feels after you use a drill or a saw for a long time, and when you're done, you still feel that vibration like an echo? It feels like that, only all over."

"Do you use any kind of stimulants?"

"No. Well, once maybe. I needed to stay up late for something. You know how I look at the sky."

"Right."

"I think it was the Leonid meteor shower. I took some of those caffeine pills you get at the store. Took too many. Got that same feeling."

"But not today?"

"No. Nothing like that today."

"You said you feel something in your head."

"Yeah. I'm feeling all antsy anxious. Like something's coming. But there's nothing going on. So I don't get it. You know me. I don't get like this. You know the stuff I've been through with SWAT. And I told you about Desert Storm in '91. I just don't get like this. Not ever."

"So you've never had this feeling before, ever in your whole life?"

"No, no. Maybe once. I was in the eighth grade. I had to give this speech in front of the whole school at an assembly. That was the most scared I've been in my whole life. So I don't know what's going on."

"Do you feel physically or mentally impaired? Like you can't function? Like you need to go to the hospital?"

"No. Not yet, anyway."

"Okay, Tarburn, don't get pissed at me, I have to ask you this. Have you smoked any marijuana or taken any kind of drugs?"

"You know I don't do any of that stuff. Never have. Ever. My faith . . ."

"Right, I had to ask. How about prescription medications?"

"No."

"Okay. This sounds to me like an exposure issue. Did you eat anything unusual?"

"No."

"Did you drink anything unusual?"

"No."

"Did you spill any chemicals on your skin? Any kind—paint, turpentine, rubber cement?"

"No."

"Did you come into contact with any chemicals at the meth lab raid today?"

"No, we dress for that kind of thing. Gas masks, rubber gloves and other stuff. Like a moon suit when we take down a lab."

"Okay. If nothing happened there, did you inhale anything out of the ordinary afterward?"

"No chemicals."

"Anything. Anything you don't normally inhale?" There was a long pause. Jommers sensed a reluctance to answer the question. "Tarburn? You there?"

"Yeah."

"Did you inhale anything you don't normally inhale? I can't help you if you're not straight up with me."

"I smoked a cigar."

"That's it? You smoked a cigar?"

"Yeah."

"So why didn't you want to tell me that? It's not a sin to smoke a cigar."

"It is for me. You know I'm religious. Old-time kind. I don't drink. I don't smoke."

"Then why did you smoke it?"

"I'm a loyal man. You know that. Loyalty is a virtue. But there are different levels, you know? Different ranks. One loyalty may rank higher than another. Sometimes you get them mixed up, out of order, you know?"

Jommers was confused. Didn't understand why Tarburn was holding back about smoking a goddamn cigar. But then, Jommers's mind was moving in a slower gear. When you suck down two high-powered craft beers with the ABV of four normal beers, slowness can happen. He frowned quizzically for a few seconds. Then it finally clicked. It was Tarburn's use of the word "ranks" that did it. He remembered that the chief of police, Derle Scubbetts, smoked cigars. Big, fat black cigars with a humongous nicotine content.

"Did you smoke a cigar with the chief today?"

"Yeah."

"Why didn't you just say so?"

"I don't know. A man's supposed to live by his code, you know? But sometimes, you also have to show respect for your leader. Sometimes you have to do things you don't want to do to show your respect, show that you trust him, you know? Show that you'll follow him. We're both from army. We both understand that. I know that's hard to get it if you haven't been in service."

"That's okay. I'm glad you told me. It all makes sense now."

"It does?"

"Yeah. The chief gave me one of his cigars once, too. And I don't smoke either. So that thing hit me like a nicotine bomb. I felt like I was flying around the room on a belt sander. What you're going through is just a nicotine buzz. It'll pass. Drink a lot of water and go for a walk. That will help your body process it and wash it out. You'll be fine in an hour or two. And if for some reason you aren't, you can call me back. Okay?"

"I need to see you. Can I come down there now? I really need to talk about some things."

Jommers looked over at Chelsea, who had a polite but uncomfortable smile on her face and was beginning to fidget. It was the kind of fidget that said, "Pay attention to me, or this catch will wiggle right off the hook."

"Tarburn, you know I have to give all you guys the old checkout tomorrow like I always do after some action. I'll slot you first. So I'll see you first thing in the morning. How's that?"

"I really need to see you now. There's bad things coming. Going to be a long, dark night."

"All right. Let's do this. Give it one hour, okay? One hour. Nothing is going to happen in an hour. You call me back then. My guess is that it's just a nicotine rush and you'll be feeling better by then. If not, then we'll do something about it, okay? One hour."

"Okay. I'll do that. But you're wrong, you know."

"About the nicotine?"

"About that nothing can happen in an hour."

"Call me then, and we'll deal with it, one way or another."

"Okay."

Jommers looked at Chelsea and recast the awkward interruption into a mentor moment, trying to regain the upper hand.

"I'm sorry about that, but in my line, I tell them they can call me anytime. I have to honor that commitment."

"No, don't apologize. That's actually kind of cool that you do that. Your commitment."

While he'd been on the phone, the waitress had stopped by to see if they wanted another round. Chelsea had simply nodded, and now a fresh bottle of Sharp Twinge Ale stood before him. He took a long swig and then finished his earlier thought about asking her out for Friday night. She eagerly agreed.

She was also curious about the phone call, hearing only one side of the conversation, but Jommers declined to discuss it, since it was technically confidential. In retrospect, he realized he should have stepped away from her so that she wouldn't have heard anything. His reticence intrigued her all the more and she started shooting him questions about his work. So he tried to shift the conversation away from the personal to the general, and seized the opportunity to expound on one of his pet ideas, that the president of the United States needs a Behavior Advisory Council comprised of psychologists, sociologists, and cultural anthropologists.

She laughed.

"No, seriously," he said. "Think of it. Most government actions are designed to influence human behavior in some way. Prohibitory laws and regulations seek to discourage certain behaviors. Tax deductions and credits, along with grants, attempt to encourage certain behaviors. And not just inside our borders. Diplomacy, sanctions, threats, and military actions are all meant to impact the behavior of foreigners. So if all actions of government are focused on affecting human behavior, then government should seek the advice of experts who understand how to accomplish that. Oh, historians should be on the panel, too."

"Historians?"

"Yes. They can provide examples on the positive results of getting it right, and on the negative consequences of getting it wrong."

She then took her turn at playing devil's advocate, punching holes in his notion. And so the banter went, like a tennis game, both sides having fun.

As twilight advanced, the Bends put on its flashy trashy evening dress, with lights and glowing signs beckoning one and all to come on down. Traffic grew dense as the target audience heeded the call. The legendary nightly hum on Old Levee Road had begun.

The bustle inside the cafe had gotten livelier and noisier as the couple gabbed away. She leaned closer to him to better hear, their shoulders touching. In this fashion, the hour passed quickly.

Then Earl Tarburn called a second time, precisely sixty minutes after the first call.

"Hey, Tarburn, you feeling better now?" Jommers asked.

"I understand it now."

"What do you mean?"

"I thought I was sick, but I was just suppressing it, you know, afraid to face the truth of it. But then it just burst through. I have to face the reality. They're coming. And it's my fault. And so I'm the one who has to deal with it."

Jommers jumped out of his seat and stepped away from Chelsea so she wouldn't hear anything more.

"Who's coming?"

"I can't bring you into this, man. They'll just get you, too. I can't do that to you. It wouldn't be right. I have to handle this alone."

"Tarburn, I need to see you. I need to see you right now."

"I can't do that. It's between me and them now. You can't help me with that."

Tarburn had clearly gotten worse over the hour, not better. Even more frightening was how he had changed his interpretation of what was happening to him. On the first call, he'd felt like something was making him sick, that it was a physical phenomenon. By the second call, he had justified his anxieties and saw them as real. He no longer felt sick, but hunted.

"Tarburn, I need to talk you face-to-face, now. I want you to meet me at my office. Okay?"

"I can't do that to you. You're a good man, Jommers, I can't put you at risk. You know, I actually liked going to see you. Got something out of it. The others, they saw it as a joke or something, you know, that they had to talk to you. But I took it serious. The fact that someone cared about what was going on inside us. That meant something. I wanted you to know that."

The tone of farewell in Tarburn's voice jolted Jommers into state of desperation. He had only seconds to cajole Tarburn into a meeting, yet Jommers had no idea where the man was. Once the call ended, Tarburn would be lost.

In the seconds he had left, Jommers could think of only one strategy, one he loathed to employ. He hated it because it was risky, and because it meant affirming delusions, making them harder to dispel later. But he had no choice. The clock was down to zero.

"Tarburn, I can help you. I can help hide you. Go to my office now. I will meet you there. Understand? Go to my office now."

"I can't put you at risk, man. I can't do it. I got no right."

"It's my choice. I accept the risk. It's not on you. Okay?"

"I don't know . . ."

"You'll be safer there. No one will think to look there. If you don't feel safe, you can leave, but at least go there first before you make a decision, okay? It will give you a chance to rest and think about what to do next. You can tell me what's going on and we can figure out the best way to handle this. Okay? Trust me, this is the best thing for you to do now. You with me?"

"I just don't know."

"Where else can you go? Who else can you trust?"

"Okay. I'll go. But I won't stay long. I have to keep moving. Got to keep moving . . . they're near . . ."

"I understand. I'm on my way. I'll see you soon."

After terminating the call, Jommers returned briefly to Chelsea.

"I'm sorry. I've got an urgent situation. I have to run. I'll call you about Friday."

THE SUN HAD MELTED over the horizon's edge, leaving behind a puddle of mixed berry sky, and Old Levee Road was having its usual evening stroke, clotted and clogged by more cars than it was designed to handle. Too many bars and too little parking turned traffic into a sluggish crawl as everyone cruised endlessly, desperately searching for a parking spot with the persistence of conquistadors seeking El Dorado, and with equivalent success. So Jommers's drive back to the office, which normally took ten minutes in the day, might take up to twenty or more at this hour. He hoped to get there before Tarburn.

He didn't get far when his cell phone rang. His faced tightened when he saw that it was Derle Scubbetts, the chief of police. The problem was about to get more complicated.

"Jommers . . . Scubbetts."

"You're working late, Chief."

"It's been one of those days."

"I heard about Eggers Court. What happened?"

"I'll get into that later. I have a more pressing concern. By any chance, have you spoken with Patrol Officer Earl Tarburn?"

Jommers had about one second to decide how to handle this new wrinkle. One second to choose his loyalties. Who had higher status, a cop in trouble or the chief of police?

"No, I haven't. Why? What's up?"

"I've got a situation, and I'm debating whether I need to involve you. Do you have any idea where he might be?"

"Well, I don't know him that well. I know he likes looking at the stars. Goes out to the park with his telescope a lot."

"Yes, well, that won't be on his agenda tonight. Listen, are you going to be around? Are you at your place?"

"Not at the moment, but I'm in the area."

"Okay. There's a remote possibility that Tarburn might try to contact you tonight, or even possibly show up at your place. In either case, I want you to call me immediately. Understood?"

"Sure. No problem."

"And just to cover all the bases here, I'm going to send an unmarked unit down to keep an eye on things. So I don't want you to get spooked when you see it. It's just my people. Okay?"

"Understood. You can't tell me what's going on?"

"I'll call you back later."

Jommers now had to quickly call Tarburn and change the meeting place, realizing he had about two seconds to figure out the best way to explain to someone having a paranoid episode why they needed to change their plan.

"Tarburn, where are you?"

"I'm here, outside your place. You going to be here soon? I don't know if it's safe here."

"Look, I'm stuck over on Old Levee. Some yahoo's got my car blocked in. I may have to hoof it. Can you meet me closer to where I am?"

"Okay. Where do you want me to go?"

"There's this bar over by the Willow Street swing bridge, the Lousy Pirate. You know which one I mean?"

"Yeah. I think so."

"All right. I'll see you there in a few minutes."

The chief obviously knew about Tarburn's state of mind, either by direct contact or indirect advisement, and wanted to get his man to a hospital before somebody got hurt. That was Jommers's preference, too, but he felt he could minimize the potential for confrontation better than uniforms jumping out of a patrol car. Jommers had repeatedly and futilely suggested that patrol officers receive better training on how to handle people with psychological problems. But that had never happened, so the standard response by a patrol unit was to treat a disturbed individual the same as someone who robbed a convenience store. Subdue by any means possible.

Everyone involved understood the stakes. Grayton was one of those cities where police department regulations required officers to carry their weapons and badges when off duty to effectively multiply the presence of law enforcement in the community.

Tarburn would be armed. Armed and itching to protect himself from imaginary pursuers. And now there were real pursuers out to capture him.

TENSE NEGOTIATIONS

The Lousy Pirate was on the east bank of Horseshoe Bend, near the Willow Street swing bridge. With traffic moving at a snail's pace, it took Jommers a while to escape the gridlocked zoo of Old Levee Road. After turning onto Chandlers Way, which was only slightly less jammed up, Jommers took another ten minutes to get near the bar. He deliberately parked on the west side of the river so that he could approach the bar by foot, which was congruent with his excuse for not being able to meet at the office. It also gave him the opportunity to observe Tarburn from a distance before approaching, which might yield useful insights.

He walked halfway across the swing bridge then stopped. Even though the bridge was lighted, his presence was less noticeable given the many pedestrians crossing the bridge in both directions, pub crawlers on a summer night in the Bends. Jommers looked in the direction of the bar, but did not yet see Tarburn. So he turned and leaned on the railing to gaze down at the river below. The essence of the water reached up into his nostrils. The heat wave had bumped up the river's odor from misdemeanor musty to felony fetid.

The Willow Street swing bridge had twenty-foot clearance, so smaller craft were able to pass underneath without the bridge opening. He watched as small boats cruised slowly in both directions heading nowhere in particular, just seeing and being seen, like young drivers cruising the main drag in a small city. With their engines on low, the boats made low murmur sounds as the water playfully slapped their hulls. As one of the boats passed underneath, a tipsy woman looked up at the people on the bridge and let out a "woo-hoo" whoop, and some of the bridge crossers responded in kind. A mutually understood language of nighttime partiers in the Bends. Although Jommers enjoyed watching the boats, he had no desire to board one. He had a disdain for confinement. A boat was a holding cell with a view.

He reeled his thoughts back in to the urgency of the moment—Tarburn. Jommers was puzzled by what might have struck Tarburn so hard and fast that it spun him 180 out of his normal disposition. The man was a rock, both physically and emotionally. And he had a long record of displaying courage under fire.

Jommers's first thought was environmental exposure to something toxic. They had raided a meth lab earlier in the day, and such places typically contain a witch's brew of noxious chemicals used to make meth. But neurological problems could not be ruled out either. A head injury can cause bleeding or swelling of the brain. A small stroke, or tumor occurring at specific spot in the brain, can also induce such behavior. Any of the physiological scenarios demanded urgent medical attention.

Jommers looked up at the sky above. Twilight had surrendered to night, but the street was brightly lit in front of the bar where they were to meet. He should have no trouble spotting the big man upon arrival.

Jommers looked back down at the river. The shimmer of lights reflecting off the water disoriented him for a moment, and he realized he was still feeling the alcohol from the Sharp Twinge Ale. He turned his gaze toward the solid river-bank on the right. There he saw a willow tree leaning sharply over the water, hanging in gravity-defying tension, as if one good windstorm might toss it in the river. But the firmly rooted willows knew how to perform this trick endless-ly, having performed such daredevil stunts for decades on end.

Then Tarburn bounded into view about a hundred and fifty feet away. He was walking in a herky-jerky fashion, flinching and stopping at sudden noises, and occasionally whirling around to see if anyone was following him.

He was wearing sneakers, blue jeans and an oversized Hawaiian shirt. There was also a small blue kit bag hanging from a shoulder strap, but it was the shirt that made Jommers uneasy. The requirement for cops to carry their weap-ons when off duty proved problematic in hot summer months, when people dressed lightly. How do you pack heat unobtrusively? One simple solution is an ankle holster, but that delays access in an unexpected urgent situation. The other choice was a horizontal belt holster worn at the small of the back, cov-ered by a loose, untucked shirt. Cops preferring this choice were often fond of oversized Hawaiian shirts. Tarburn was almost certainly carrying his Glock 17, a fear soon confirmed.

The Lousy Pirate had a mural painted on its outside wall, one that realisti-cally depicted several life-sized pirates who looked nasty and ready to rumble. In a joke on the bar's name, each pirate was scratching his head with one hand, while brandishing a cutlass with the other. As soon as Tarburn saw the pirates, he jerked back in recoil and pulled his gun, looking terrified of the pictorial menace. A second later, a couple of drunken revelers burst out through the bar's door. The energetic exit sent the door flying into its stop, making a loud whack. Tarburn jumped again, swinging his gun around to aim in that direction. For-tunately, the exiting patrons headed off in the opposite direction with no idea that a gun was aimed at their backs.

This was not good.

Jommers now wished he'd chosen a different meeting spot. The Lousy Pirate was a rowdy joint where beer was sold by the pitcher at state minimum prices. The kind of place where the sidewalks out front often glistened with the golden froth of beer vomit.

He began walking slowly toward the east end of the bridge, but was interrupted by his cell phone. Chief Scubbetts, again. Jommers had exactly four rings before the call went to voice mail, four rings to decide who to speak with first.

"Yes, Chief."

"I was hoping not to bring you into this. Hoping to keep it an internal matter. But the way things are unfolding, I have no choice."

"What's going on?"

"I've got a situation with Patrolman Tarburn. He's got the heebie-jeebies."

"He's got what?"

"Look, I don't know all your goddamn terminology and I don't need to. The son of a bitch is fucking delirious. Is that sufficient for you? He's raving about people chasing him. He's deranged, of unsound mind. He's—"

"I get it. Sounds like paranoid psychotic behavior. So you want me to evaluate him?"

"I want you to help find him."

"Well, you got a whole police department at your disposal. I just have me."

"We have no idea where he is. He's not at home and he's not answering our calls. But he might take one from you."

"Do you have any idea what happened to him?"

"I don't have time for speculation. You need to understand, we are in crisis mode here. There is a man out there exhibiting—what did you call it?"

"Paranoid psychotic behavior."

"Yes. And he most certainly is armed. You understand the gravity of the situation."

"I do."

"Then you will assist in an expeditious manner."

"What exactly do you want from me, Chief?"

"I want you to call Tarburn. Arrange a meeting place. Then you call me back. We will arrive at the meeting place and collect him."

"Collect him?"

"Take him into custody, then take him to a hospital for psychiatric hold and evaluation."

"Well, I agree he needs to get to a hospital. But I'm not sure I agree on your method to collect him, as you put it."

"We don't have time for an academic debate. His life and the lives of others may be at stake. You understand?"

"I understand perfectly. I absolutely want to minimize the risk to him and others. I would like the opportunity to get him to the hospital voluntarily, without departmental intervention."

"Jommers. I want you to listen to me. We are at a foundational juncture . . ."

While listening to the chief talk, Jommers keyed in on the phrase "foundational juncture." The chief often used big words incorrectly in an effort to sound intelligent or express a sense of importance. But sometimes he used big words exactly right. The chief had used the word "foundational" once or twice before when trying to persuade Jommers to perform his bidding. Jommers had interpreted the word as a veiled threat. Do what I want, or our business relationship is in jeopardy.

Jommers returned volley with some big words of his own.

"Chief, it would be a dereliction of my duties as a clinical psychologist if I failed to first attempt a low-risk passive intervention before assenting to a high-risk confrontational intervention."

"This is not your call. I'm telling you what I want you to do."

"In my judgment, I have a better shot at resolving the situation. Tarburn knows me, he knows I'm unarmed. That presents a much lower risk of escalation then sending armed strangers after him, which would only serve to confirm his worst fears in his current state of mind."

"This is not a debate. I'm telling you what I want you to do."

"I'm professionally and ethically obligated to give my approach a shot. I'll call you back and let you know how it goes."

"Jommers, I want you to listen to me—"

Jommers terminated the call, then resumed walking slowly across the bridge. He was proud of himself for standing up to the chief, who was also his chief benefactor. The business end of the relationship was most certainly at risk. But Jommers had no choice. The bigger problem at the moment was that he had no backup plan. He waved and called from a distance to avoid startling.

"Hey, Tarburn."

"Jommers. We shouldn't be in the light, man. We shouldn't be in the light."

Just then, bouncers for the Lousy Pirate ejected a couple of drunken miscreants. There was a scuffle, loud cursing, and a number of threats tossed out in both directions. Tarburn put his hand at his back, on his gun. His face showed unbearable tension, like a steel wire cable strained way past its load rating, ready to snap and slice anyone in its path of retraction.

Jommers pointed to a low-lying unlit grassy area near the riverbank. "Let's go down there, where it's darker."

Jommers led Tarburn down a small, but sharply angled slope. The small plot of land had been deliberately flattened and shorn to provide clearance for the swing bridge opening. Nothing was down there but grass and weeds. They took care to avoid getting too close to the water's edge, as there was no fence or railing, only a slightly raised rusty metal bulkhead serving as a knife edge between solid land and deep water.

"Okay," Jommers said calmly. "Let's take a breath now. Relax and look at the water. Nobody can see us down here. Nobody knows where you are. It's just you and me kicking back and shooting the breeze on a lazy, beautiful night, hanging out by the river, watching the little ripples dancing in the light. Okay?"

"Okay."

"All right. Now, you've been through a number of interviews with me before, you know I have to ask you a lot of questions, right?"

"Right."

"So I want you to answer them straight up like you always do, calm and steady, not getting offended or excited. Taking it easy, going through the drill, just like you always do. Okay?"

"Okay. But this isn't like always. No way like always."

"All right, then let's start with that. Tell me what's going on. Tell me in whatever way you want to tell me."

"I can't."

"Why can't you tell me?"

"I just can't."

"Well, you already mentioned before that someone was after you, and you are certainly acting like that's the case. So, can you tell me who is after you and why?"

"Jommers, don't make me do this."

"Relax, okay? Nobody can hear you. Nobody can see you. Nobody knows where you are. Right here, right now, there's nothing to be afraid of."

"I'm not just afraid for me. I'm afraid for you."

"What do you mean?"

"This is such a shame, that I can't tell you of all people, because you're the one person who can understand it. It's right up your alley."

"Then why can't you tell me?"

"Because then they'll have to get you, too."

"Why?"

"Because they have to remove all the traces. It's a black ops cleanup. That's what's going on. They know my code name. They know me now. That's why they have to clean me. If I tell you anything, then they have to clean you, too."

"Okay. Let's try a different tack here. Without telling me who is after you or why, tell me why you think that."

Tarburn anxiously rubbed his forehead, conflicted over answering the question. Jommers pressed, calmly repeating the question. "What makes you think someone is after you? Was it something you saw or heard? Or did somebody tell you that?"

Tarburn began pacing, still wrestling with it. Then Jommers eased ahead to his key concern. Gently as possible he pursued that line. "Did a person tell you that?" He paused. "Or did a voice tell you that?"

Tarburn abruptly stopped pacing and spun around.

"A voice? A voice? You think I'm hearing voices? You think I'm crazy? Oh, man. Oh, man." Tarburn put his hands over his face like he wanted to cry. Then, after a few seconds, he sighed and put his hands on his hips. "You know what? That's actually good. Good that you think I'm crazy. That way, they leave you alone. When they ask you, when they ask you what I said, you tell them straight up, that Tarburn dude was crazy, crazy as a loon, that you couldn't make heads or tails of what he was talking about. He was just babbling nonsense. That's what you tell them, that's what you say. Then you're free. Then you're safe."

"Tarburn, do you remember a couple of hours ago when you first called me?"

"Yes, yes."

"At the time, you said you felt sick. Remember?"

"Yes, yes."

"Do you still feel sick now?"

"I don't feel good, but I don't feel sick."

"Okay. I want you to think carefully about what I'm going to ask you next. Do you think it's possible that you are so sick, you don't realize it?"

"I don't get that. That's just, that's just . . . I don't know."

"Look, I'm not trying to mess with you, okay? I just want you to take an inventory of yourself. I can't get inside where you are. So I need you to show me around. I want you to ask yourself how you feel right now and then ask yourself if this is normal for you. Look at how your hands are shaking. Look at how your skin is sweating. Is this how Earl Tarburn normally handles hairy situations?"

"No. No, it's not. Definitely not."

"Then you agree with me that something is different tonight, that you aren't your normal self."

"Yes. This is not me. I don't get like this. Not ever."

"Then can you at least consider the possibility that what's going on here is maybe about things happening inside you and not outside you?"

"I suppose. It's possible. I just don't know, you know? It's all so confusing. Everything was so clear before."

"You've seen people hit before, haven't you?"

"Oh, yeah. I seen people go down. And sometimes, because I made it happen. Part of my job sometimes."

"Then you know that, when people are experiencing trauma, that they sometimes can't think clearly, right?"

"Yeah, I seen that."

"Then can you consider the possibility that you've been hit by something that you can't feel, an invisible bullet, and that maybe a doctor could get it out and patch things up, make everything all right again?"

"It's possible. Maybe. I don't know."

"Well, if you agree that it is possible, but not certain, then maybe the best thing to do in such a situation is to find out one way or the other. You want to know whether this problem is inside or outside. Me, too. So why don't we find out? Let me take you to the hospital. We'll get you all checked out. If something's wrong, we get it fixed. If not, then at least we've narrowed the possibilities and we'll have a better idea what's going on. It can't hurt. It can only help. What do you say?"

"Can't do that. Have to give up the gun. They'd find me there. I'd be defenseless."

"We'll get guards. We can protect you inside a lot better there than out here."

"No. You wouldn't recognize them. They would get right past you."

"I'll call your buddies on SWAT. They'll do anything to help you. You know that. They'll stand watch over you. You'll be protected by the guys you know and trust."

"Jommers, I just need a place to hide. A place to hide till morning. If I can make it until morning, then everything will be all right. I know it."

"Okay, now. I want you to think carefully about what you just said. Why do you think things will be better by morning?"

"I don't know. Something just telling me it will. Just a feeling, I guess."

"Let me suggest why. It's your unconscious mind telling you that you have an internal affliction, a temporary internal affliction that will pass by morning. Your unconscious mind knows what's going on. But we don't have to wait until morning. You don't have to suffer all night. We can take care of the affliction now. We can remove the threat now. You want it removed, don't you?"

Tarburn nervously tapped his forehead with his fist, as if it could somehow influence the outcome of the battle taking place in his head. And that gave Jommers an idea. If he could get Tarburn to increase the activity in the rational part of his brain, call forth the executive function, maybe it could overpower the raw emotions bubbling up like a hot sulfur spring.

"Tarburn, did you check your sky charts for this week?"

"Huh? Yeah, yeah. I always check them, even though I know them."

"Tell me what's up there now."

"Can't see much tonight. The clouds moving in. Too much light pollution down here anyway. You can't sky watch in the city."

"What if you were out at your favorite place with your telescope? It's a golf course, isn't it?"

"Yeah. The Metroparks course out in Crutchfield. It's nice and dark out there, dark and open, away from the tree line."

"If you were there, right now, and it wasn't cloudy, what would you see up there? Give me a tour."

Tarburn closed his eyes and shook his head. "Oh, man, I don't know. I can't even think right now. Everything is a jumble."

"Yes, you can think. You know the sky like your backyard. Concentrate. Focus. Tell me what you'd see out in Crutchfield. Tell me."

Tarburn took a deep breath, his eyes still closed. "Okay, okay. If I look straight up over my head, I should find Vega, second-brightest star in the sky, at least up here, Northern half. It's part of Lyra the Harp. In summer, that's my clarity check. If I can't see Vega real good, I won't be seeing much else. So if I get Vega okay, then I look nearby for Altair in Aquila the Eagle, and Deneb in Cygnus the Swan. Those three stars form the Summer Triangle. Now I've got my orientation, where I'm at in the sky. I look a little west for the Big Dipper, which is actually part of Ursa Major, the Great Bear. Then I follow the curve of the dipper handle south to Arcturus, the arc to Arcturus, which will be the brightest star in the sky where we are, looking kind of orangey. It's part of Boötes the Herdsman, though it really looks more like a kite. Then, a little lower to the left, I see Antares, a reddish star, the heart of the scorpion in Scorpius. And right above Antares is what I'm really looking for tonight—Jupiter, which'll be brighter than any of the stars. I'll look for its giant red spot, which is a huge storm. Then I'll look for the big four moons, the Galilean moons. I should be able to see Io and Europa at least, and sometimes after a moon's pass, you can see its shadow. Looks like black dot on the planet's surface. And, and . . . I don't know, is that enough?"

"That's terrific. That's excellent." The strategy was working. While talking about the sky, Tarburn had calmed down slightly and appeared more in control. So Jommers wanted to keep it going. "You really know your constellations."

"Yeah, I guess. That's what gets you into it to start, but, you know, they don't really exist, you know? I mean, the stars in a constellation aren't actually anywhere near each other, not in the same plane. The grouping is just your angle of perspective. Even then, the grouping doesn't really resemble anything. Just some ancient guy trying to make sense of the sky. Figuring out where he is. Ursa Major doesn't look anything like a bear. You connect the dots differently, you can make it an upright vacuum cleaner. But the powers that be tell you it's a bear, then that's what you see."

"But you're still into it."

"I'm fascinated by the patterns. The movements and conjunctions. The predictability in the mystery."

"Anything unpredictable ever happen?"

"The stars are always the stars. But you do get your meteor showers. And the big one is coming 'round the corner. I'm already psyched."

"Yeah?"

"Oh, yeah. August is the Perseids. Next week will be best. They should peak around Monday or Tuesday. And the moon will be dark then, so they'll be easier to see. Should be good watching. You should be able to see as many as one a minute if you get to a dark place."

"How do you know where to point your telescope?"

"You don't use the scope for those because they show up in different parts of the sky. You just kind of look up to the east, northeast and eyeball it. You got to bring something to lie back in or you'll break your neck looking, you know, if you're going to stay a while. I got this really nice folding reclining camp chair, goes all the way back. It's got this bungee suspension, it's super comfortable. So I grab that, some munchies, some soda pop, then I go—"

Before he could finish the thought, a motorcycle accelerated across the bridge, and its explosive, sputtering exhaust jolted Tarburn back into his psychotic mode. He simultaneously spun around, dropped into a crouch, and drew his gun, aiming it the bridge. And that's all it took to jerk the man right back to his hyperanxious state, the lucid moment totally undone.

Jommers tried to calm him.

"Stand down, man, stand down. It's just a motorcycle. Okay?"

Tarburn was breathing heavy now. He lowered his gun but, disturbingly, did not re-holster it. Jommers faced a dilemma. There was no way to pacify Tarburn in such a high-stimulus environment, but changing locations meant separating, with no guarantee of rejoining. With that possibility in his mind, Jommers knew any crucial questions needed to be asked now.

"Tarburn, what's in the kit bag?"

"You didn't see that bag, okay? If they ask, you didn't see any bag. You don't know what they're talking about. And that's for your sake, okay? It will be trouble for you otherwise. You did not see any bag."

"Fine. I didn't see the bag. But if I can forget seeing the bag, then I can also forget what's in it. Right? So what's in it?"

Tarburn held back, his face drawn tight into a pained grimace. He shook his head, like answering no, and kept doing it.

"Tarburn, what's in the bag?"

"It was supposed to save lives, but it did the opposite. Now they have to cover it up, like the test never happened. Clean up everything and everybody. No traces. Full clean."

"Cover what up? What test?"

At that moment, a car with open windows booming hip-hop music drove past the bar and turned onto the bridge. It was one of those cars with weaponized woofers, blasting out a barrage of thumping bass like artillery.

Tarburn swung around, again went into a crouch, and trained his gun on the car, tracking it as it made the turn, keeping the gun on it the whole time it went over the bridge.

Jommers realized that he had to get Tarburn away from people and stimuli immediately, even at the risk of separation.

"Tarburn, I know a place you can hide. A place where no one will find you."

"Where?"

Jommers pointed off into the distance.

"See that railroad drawbridge sticking up in the air?"

"You mean the jackknife?"

"Yeah. It's out of service, locked vertical, with no tender. On the left side as you approach is the bridge house. It's supposed to be locked up. But a couple of years ago, that bad winter, some of the homeless guys that hang around down here busted the lock to get out of the cold. Nobody's ever fixed it. You can get in there."

"But there's people in there."

"No. The homeless guys only use it in the winter. The bridge house is made of steel, like the bridge, so it's going to be real hot in there, which is why no one goes in there during the summer. No one will think to look for you there."

"Okay. How do I get there?"

"It's at the dead end of Dills Run. You have to walk around a fence, but it's easy to do. The house is mounted on pylons two stories high. The metal stairs are rusty and covered with vines, so you need to be careful going up."

"I'm sorry I put you through this, Jommers. You mean well."

"You didn't put me through anything. I just want you to be all right. Once you're safe in the bridge house, I want you to look out the window at the sky and imagine all the stars above the clouds. Don't think about anything else, okay?"

"I'll try, man. I'll try. Thanks for helping me out. Thanks for coming here."

"Everything's going to be all right."

～

JOMMERS'S ALCOHOL BUZZ was slipping away, but its inevitable aftereffects combined with the stifling heat to induce lethargy. He felt like a spent boxer who had gone all out in the early rounds hoping for a knockout, but now had nothing left for the rounds ahead.

And there were more rounds ahead.

He sat down on the grass and gazed at the still waters of the river. To his right, a patch of weeds and reeds near the river edge held so many crickets that their collective chirping sounded like a continuous trill blown on a mighty whistle. He closed his eyes and imagined himself out in the country somewhere, sitting on the front porch of a cabin counting fireflies, a sleeping golden retriever next to him.

Unfortunately, his rural reverie lasted only a few seconds before he was yanked back to his urban reality by his cell phone. He knew without looking.

"Yes, Chief."

"Have you made contact with Tarburn?"

"Yes."

"Where is he?"

"He's in a safe place. A place where he won't hurt anybody."

"Jommers, listen to me, I don't have time for games. This is a dangerous, high-risk situation. We're talking about a paranoid psychotic with a gun on the loose. I need to bring him in now. Right now. Where is he?"

"He's not going to hurt anybody where he is."

"I'm confused, Jommers. What the hell do you think you're doing here?"

"I'm trying to protect my patient from harm. I have an ethical obligation to—"

"You have an overriding ethical obligation to prevent an innocent person from being harmed by a dangerous armed individual who is no longer in control of his faculties. If you were to check the ethical guidelines of your profession, you will see that when a patient becomes an imminent threat to society, your larger obligation is to society. I shouldn't have to educate you on this point."

"I don't believe he's as much of a threat as you suggest. I think that—"

"You think? You think? You're not in a position to think. You're not in a condition to be making grave decisions with potentially tragic consequences."

"I'm not sure what you mean."

"Jommers, let's be frank. We both know you've had a few tonight. Maybe more than a few. And that's okay. A man puts in a hard day's work, he's entitled to kick back at the end of day and relax. He's earned it. But he does not have the right to clock back in and make life-and-death decisions while in an impaired state."

"I'm not drunk."

"Don't play semantics with me. You know better than anyone that it's not an either/or situation. It's a sliding scale, and we both know where you are on the scale right now. Crispness of speech, clarity of thinking, soundness of judgment, they all go long before motor skills."

"There's nothing wrong with my judgment."

"Really? Then what's your plan? Right now, tell me your plan."

"Well, I . . . uh . . ."

"You don't have one, do you? You've already tried to get him into the hospital voluntarily and he refused, didn't he? So now you're struggling to think of a plan B, but you can't come up with one because your head is clouded, your thinking sluggish."

"That's not true."

"Then what's your plan? Tell me your plan."

Jommers paused, trying in vain to think of one. He couldn't. The chief didn't let up.

"Look, Jommers, I'm not trying to beat you up here. I'm just trying to prevent a disaster. You know we need to pick him up. You know that, don't you?"

"Yes."

"Then tell me where he is."

"I will. But I want to be there when you do that."

"That's not a feasible strategy. I don't want you near the operation."

"I can help calm him. I can help prevent escalation of tension. My presence—"

"Your presence would be a significant hindrance to the operation. Instead of focusing on the objective at hand, the officers on the scene would need to be preoccupied with your safety. They might have to put themselves at risk to protect you from harm. Furthermore, there is the distinct possibility that Tarburn, in his current state, might use you as a hostage to elude custody. Your presence would be a wild card that would almost certainly lead to unnecessary disaster."

"I don't know that I agree with that."

"That's entirely my point. You don't know. Look, Jommers, I understand what's going on in your head right now. You're confused. You're worried about getting blamed for not making the right call if this doesn't go well. Well, here's how you eject that worry. Let it go, and put it on us. Cast your burden down, and let me pick it up. If things go wrong, it's on me, not on you. You've done your best, now it's time to hand it off."

"I just don't want him to get hurt."

"You think I do? He's one of us. He's family. We will do everything we can to avoid harming him. Now, I don't want to belabor the point, but it's just plain irresponsible on your part to be injecting yourself into the situation in your current condition. Your ethical obligation is quite clear now. You need to hand it off to professionals with a plan. We have the tools. We have the manpower. We have the experience. We have clarity of thought and purpose. You would be derelict in your duties not to defer to us. Hand it off before you get somebody killed. Hand it off now."

It had only been a short while earlier that Jommers had been confidently dueling with the chief, seizing the upper hand, brazenly defying him. But now, with his energy and concentration quickly ebbing, he felt the best he could do was to negotiate the terms of surrender.

"Okay, okay. But you send plainclothes for him."

"Yes. Department policy requires that whenever we pick up one of our own, we send Internal Affairs. They will be in plainclothes."

"You send only two people for the direct encounter. You put your backups nearby, but not in sight. He can't feel like some army is descending on him."

"Agreed."

"They must try talk to him first. If that fails, then Tasers. No guns."

"My people are professionals, not cowboys. Show a little respect. They're going to pick up a sick colleague. They will take every care. They will be aware of his condition. But if things turn ugly, they will have to use their best judgment in the field. And you understand there is a range limit on a Taser. The only guarantee I can give you is that they will use lethal force as an absolute last resort."

"They take him directly to the hospital, the psych ward at Saint Bridget's, not a holding cell."

"Agreed."

"Okay, then . . ."

Jommers explained where to find Tarburn, and how to approach the decommissioned railroad bascule bridge at the end of Dills Run, also known as the jackknife bridge for the way in which the counterweight arm folds into the stationary truss when open, now its permanent state.

And just like that, it was over.

With head down and hands in his pockets, Jommers trudged slowly back to his car and drove slowly back to the truck repair shop that was also his home.

As he parked the dusty old Taurus outside the shop, he found himself increasingly uncomfortable with his decision. He paced around the lot a minute or two, wondering if there was anything further he could do.

And that was when the sound of gunshots punctured the thick night air, echoing around the Bends. The startling sound halted him in midstep and seized his ability to move. He desperately wanted to think firecrackers. The Fourth of July was little more than a month past. People had leftover bangers and occasionally used them. But the patterned sequence shattered his wishful thinking.

He recognized the paired rhythm. Pop-pop, pop-pop. Pause. Pop-pop, pop-pop. Eight shots total. He knew but did not want to accept. It was a gun battle. And it was already over.

With the reverberation, he was not exactly sure where the shots were fired, but he could guess, and within a few seconds, he was racing out of the lot toward the old bascule bridge where he'd sent Earl Tarburn.

When he got to the dead end of Dills Run, he found an empty police cruiser with its door open and lights still flashing. He got out and ran around the hulking steel bridge toward the bridge house stairs on the far side.

When he got there, he saw a uniformed patrol officer leaning over a man on the ground. The man was writhing in pain, and his lower right leg was bent out sideways at an unnatural angle. A badge hanging around his neck suggested he was a plainclothes.

The patrol officer was startled by Jommers rushing forward in the darkness. He jumped up and drew his weapon.

"Stop where you are. Stop now!"

"I'm a psychologist. I'm looking for my patient. He—"

"I don't give a shit who you are. This is a police scene. Get the hell out of here now."

There was no point in arguing, given that Tarburn wasn't there anyway. Jommers went back to his car, trying to guess which way Tarburn might have run. And that's when he heard sirens.

With no good way to turn around at the dead end, he raced in reverse back to Beech Street, then followed the siren noise. Less than a minute later, he saw the pulsing reflections of flashers off in the distance. They appeared headed for Copperhead Bend. Jommers followed the lights.

As he arrived at the intersection of West Drain Road and German Hill Road, he saw an EMS unit parked with its back doors open, three black-and-white police cruisers with their flashers on, and an unmarked police car with its front grille flashers on.

One of the cruisers straddled the far side of West Drain, as if blocking passage to Crone Point. Such blocking was unnecessary, as the road was closed past the intersection. The paramedics needed to take their gurney on foot to go further.

When Jommers pulled up and got out of his car to approach the scene, a patrol officer ran toward him shouting with his hand on his weapon.

"This is a police scene. Turn around now!"

Jommers made a vain attempt to explain his interest in the matter, but the patrol officer, who was just following orders and feeling slightly threatened, kept repeating his command for Jommers to turn around and leave the scene.

As Jommers turned back toward his car, he could hear the loud crackle of voices emanating from the cruiser's police radio.

"Unit three-seven to comm two."

"Go ahead, three-seven."

"The five-one-two-two is down and critical. EMS will transport to Bridget. Unit three-seven will escort."

"Copy."

The Grayton Police Department, like many others across the country, was moving away from the numerical code systems traditionally used in police radio communications. The federal government had been encouraging the use of plain language communications a result of the jurisdictional interoperability problems that occurred during both 9/11 and Katrina. However, maintaining certain codes was deemed desirable. For example, if you were trying to corral a disturbed individual, you would not want that individual to inadvertently hear a query over a police radio about the status of the "mental patient."

The "five-one-two-two" mentioned in the radio transmission referred to Section 5122 of the Ohio Revised Code, which dealt with involuntary psychiatric holds. As a psychologist, Jommers recognized the number, and he knew immediately that the ambulance had been sent for Tarburn. The reference to

Bridget meant that they were taking him to the emergency room at Saint Bridget Charity Medical Center.

Jommers ran back to his car and then raced over to Saint Bridget's. He beat the ambulance by a couple of minutes, and was surprised to see it roll in slowly with no flashers or siren. He wanted to rush toward the wagon, but found himself standing still in the parking lot, as if suffering from some neural short circuit. As if he already knew.

The back doors of the EMS unit opened slowly, but no one came bursting out with a gurney. Instead, a doctor strolled out of the hospital and entered the truck. He emerged little more than a minute later and went back into the hospital. The doors of the ambulance closed, and the vehicle drove off slowly.

The conclusion was obvious. Tarburn had been officially pronounced dead and was now being taken to the county coroner.

Jommers remained motionless, stunned by the evening's events, bowled over by the rapidity at which they unfolded, and disturbed by his fitful role in them. It was but a short time ago he had been sitting in an upscale cafe, shoulder-to-shoulder with a pretty woman. He felt dumbfounded, like someone who had just stepped on a mine.

His thoughts were interrupted by the arrival of a second ambulance, carrying the plainclothes cop with the seriously busted leg. They pulled out the gurney and rushed him inside. He was obviously one of the two IA detectives sent to "collect" Tarburn.

The humid air was filled with questions, but there were too many missing pieces to assemble any answers. Then his cell phone rang.

"Yes, Chief."

"Things didn't go as planned," the chief said.

"What happened?"

"Tarburn was totally berserk by the time IA got to him. He threw the first officer off the bridge house, then bolted. The second officer chased him. He ran toward the river. When he found himself cornered, he turned and started firing. The second officer had no choice but to return fire. They took him to the hospital, where he was pronounced DOA."

"If I had been there, this might have had a different outcome."

"The only difference would have been a longer casualty list. I'm told Tarburn was unresponsive, unapproachable, belligerent, and threatening. The situation exploded immediately upon their arrival without even a chance for conversation."

"He might have listened to me."

"Well, people like you have the luxury of entertaining the whole what-if thing, don't you? Down here, we have to deal with the what-is. The outcome of this was predetermined the moment Tarburn went over the edge. Nobody could have reversed his descent."

"Do you have any idea what pushed him over?"

"All we have is speculation, which I don't have time to get into now. Tomorrow will be a long, busy day. I have meetings scheduled with the mayor and safety director, the district commanders, the Force Review Committee, Internal Affairs, the media, and so on. And now I have two shootings to explain instead of one. But I need to talk to you first, because I won't have time to squeeze you in later. I want you down at Central at zero six thirty sharp. We'll talk then. Also, plan on doing your SWAT interviews at the station office and concluding them quickly."

The chief terminated the call immediately after his instructions, leaving no further room for discussion. Jommers was too confounded to argue anyway.

After leaving the hospital, on his way back to the Bends, Jommers deliberately took the longer route in order to drive over the Trammel Street lift bridge. Once he'd crossed over it, he slowed, pulled over to the curb, and parked the car. He got out, walked to the back of the car and leaned back against the trunk, staring upwards, looking for the bridge's west-end counterweight.

The Trammel Street bridge was the vertical-lift type where the span rises at both ends while remaining parallel to the bridge deck. A massive elevated counterweight is employed at each end to minimize the force needed to raise the span. When the bridge goes up, the counterweights come down. The counterweights on this bridge were enormous rusted steel boxes that had been filled with concrete. When the bridge span was raised, huge electric motors strained and rumbled while winding the groaning cables that lowered the counterweights. In their down position, a couple of feet off the road surface, the counterweights presented the face of an immovable wall to the road. When the bridge came back down, the counterweights rose back up.

There was some history between Jommers and the counterweight on the west end of the bridge. He could barely see it up there in the darkness, but didn't need to. He'd stared up at it a hundred times before. He knew every inch of its face. Every inch of the wall that had absorbed his father's life.

Karl Jommers had been a young boy when his old man Vic had bought a Triumph TR6 Trophy motorcycle, not long after the movie *The Great Escape* came out in 1963. The bike was used and a bit banged up, so Vic Jommers had gotten it for a good price. He'd nicknamed it Tara, which only added to his wife's irritation over the purchase. ("I'm going out with Tara.") Karl was too young to remember his parents' first argument about the motorcycle, but it didn't matter, as the fight was regularly repeated. She thought the money could have been better spent on something for the home. But what really irked her was that the expense benefited Vic alone and not the whole family. It was a solitary indulgence. Instead of going somewhere in the car with his family, Vic went off somewhere alone on the bike, usually to a bar, leaving his wife and kid at home. And that was why, whenever Vic Jommers said he was going out with Tara, his wife seethed.

In *The Great Escape*, Steve McQueen's character, Virgil Hilts, a POW, steals a motorcycle from a German soldier and tries to jump it over the barricades at the Swiss border. The moviemakers had to trick it up as a BMW R75 bike, because that was what a German soldier rode in WWII, but real bikers knew it was a Triumph TR6, chosen because it had the power-to-weight ratio necessary for the gravity-defying stunts the film required and because McQueen, an avid rider, fancied that model.

In the movie, Hilts repeatedly fails at his escape attempts and is always brought back and thrown in the cooler, an isolation cell, for his punishment. Young Karl did not see how this resonated with his old man, nor could he have comprehended it. How can a mere boy understand existential despair coupled with clinical depression?

Sure, he knew his old man had a persistent dark mood and often made cryptic comments, when he spoke at all. But the boy presumed that all dads were this way. How could he know otherwise? It is the curse of children every-where to lack a point of comparative reference for their parents' behavior. Since you only have one set, whatever they do, good or bad, seems normative. So young Karl presumed every kid had a gloomy dad. It wasn't until that fateful night that the boy realized his dad was not like all the rest.

Vic Jommers was a steel worker who put in long hours at a blast furnace for one of the steelmakers situated upriver in the Bends. It was his custom to stop at the CZ Bar after his shift, a custom shared by many, then and now.

The name of the shot-and-beer joint was derived from the original owner, a man named Czarkovic, though the place had been sold a half dozen times since then. It stood at the intersection of three roads on an odd, pie-shaped lot and was designed in the familiar windowless speakeasy style that permitted the sin of drinking to be committed discreetly. The sagging, low-slung clapboard structure was surrounded by a small dirty gravel parking lot in which visitors parked at whatever angle they happened to drive in. Patrons included steel-workers, and guys from the rail yards, stone yards, steel-finishing operations, and other nearby plants. What they shared in common was a desire to tank up on cheap hooch the way the old B&O steamers stopped to tank up on water a little further down the road.

The CZ Bar's dark atmosphere did not offer much conviviality. It was the kind of place where no one knew your name or wanted theirs known. The post-shift numbing ritual was serious business, and personal. For some, the ceremonial consumption of cheap spirits was a reward for a brutal day of hellish work, a celebration of survival. For others, it was a transitional cleansing that prepared one for reentry into the normal world, the equivalent of a mental shower, because the grit didn't just get in your skivvies, it got in your head, too.

One night, on the way home from the bar, Vic Jommers was headed for the Trammel Street bridge on his motorcycle. The bridge span was up to accommodate a passing ore boat. The approach was straight for about a quarter mile, so he certainly saw the giant counterweight straddling the road, as well as the behemoth ship passing under the bridge. No one will ever know whether it was an impulsive decision, or whether he had rehearsed it in his head, but in either case, the old man saw an opportunity to make his own great escape in the only way he saw left to him—driving the motorcycle into the bridge counterweight at sixty miles an hour, leaving behind a wife and a young boy.

Most people said it was the booze. Everyone knew he was a drinker. They said that the man was too drunk to realize the bridge was up. But the few people close to him knew better. The bridge had a railroad-style wooden gate, flashing red lights, and a loud clanging bell. And the man had taken that way home from the bar countless times before in the same condition. There were no skid marks. And you can't ride a motorcycle while asleep.

For the sake of the boy, everybody painted it as a tragic accident. Only when the boy got older did he begin to understand. The clarity had arrived slowly, like the gradual emergence of a buried artifact whose muddy veil is incrementally washed away by rain. Even then, Karl Jommers did not make the connection between the past and his pursuit of clinical psychology as a career. He was almost finished with his education when a friend of the family complimented him on how he was turning tragedy into inspiration, committing himself to saving the fathers of other little boys.

He was shocked at the suggestion, and only later conceded an element of truth to it. The smart one in the family was the last to figure it out. No one wants to envision himself as a mere hockey puck, whose direction is determined by the violent whacks of external forces. Every man wants to believe that his every action is a deliberate, well-considered choice, that he is the captain of his own ship. It wasn't until Jommers finished his internships that he grasped that the dichotomy was not so simple, that men were neither hockey pucks nor captains, but some strange blurry thing in between, a thing his profession labored mightily to fathom.

At some point after recognizing the connection between his father's suicide and his choice of profession, Karl Jommers chose not only to accept the fact, but to embrace it, harness it. It was then that the Trammel Street lift bridge became somewhat of a shrine, a place with restorative powers, a North Star that helped him maintain a true course in times of doubt. But tonight, the shrine's dark magic was absent. He did not feel set aright, just lost. Night fog lost.

Off in the distance, a half-lit moon rose in the east as scattered clumps of elongated clouds floated in procession across the sky. Eerily backlit by the lunar lamp, the creeping, flat-bottomed billows displayed a ghastly glow, conjuring up the image of a ghost ship armada sailing at dead slow ahead.

DAY TWO

CRAWLING KING SNAKE

Jommers got out of bed before dawn. It wasn't a matter of getting up early for his meeting with the chief. He had never gotten to sleep to begin with and had grown tired of staring at the ceiling. After showering and shaving, he was struck with the notion of driving over to Copperhead Bend, named after the northern copperhead snake that populated that part of the west bank back when it was a low-lying marshy area in the early phase of the city's settlement.

He wasn't sure why he wanted to go there. Maybe he hoped the scene would speak to him, secretly whisper in his ear some clue to the inexplicable madness that had occurred there the night before.

He parked the old Taurus over on West Drain Road at German Hill Road, near the place where he'd been blockaded the night before. The intersection was familiar, as it was on his jogging route. To his right was the Telstar Lounge, shuttered long ago. Along the top of the bar's east-facing wall were the weathered remnants of a painted mural featuring the namesake sixties-era satellite, a couple of martini glasses tilted at opposite angles, and some dancing musical notes.

Across the street to the south was a former Sinclair service station, now occupied by a commercial flat-roof sealing service. The east-facing wall of this building displayed the flaked residue of an old painting on brick, in this case, the green ghost of the famous Sinclair Oil dinosaur.

Straight ahead was the continuation of West Drain, obstructed by a *Road Closed* sign, which, if ignored, would result in a very short, unhappy drive, as the crumbling, overgrown roadway sported fallen tree branches and impassable, axle-crunching chuckholes. The now dead-end street had once allowed traffic to Crone Point and a low drawbridge that had crossed the river long ago. As development had tracked upstream in the city's early days, increased ship traffic and the low height of the old drawbridge had meant that it was open more often than closed, so it was eventually removed. So West Drain past German Hill was now a path to nowhere, a destination best traveled on foot.

He got out of the car and started walking. In spite of the predawn hour, the humid air still felt pudding thick. The overnight temperature had not dropped below the dew point, allowing the ground-level atmosphere to jealously hoard all its moisture like a miser. He walked slowly in the dim light to avoid tripping over debris or stepping into a hole.

Crone Point was a hooked promontory that, as early settlers had noted, pointed across the river like a crone's crooked finger. As Jommers approached the midsection of the small, weedy peninsula, he saw that an area had been cordoned off with yellow Police Scene tape on stakes. He presumed the shooting had taken place there, and his first thought was why Tarburn had headed down a path of no escape—he surely knew the area. But the man was not in a rational state of mind. How could any of his actions be explained?

While ruminating on that riddle, Jommers noticed something moving at the tip of the peninsula, right behind a rowed pairing of tall, graffiti-splashed stone blocks that had once supported the now-truant bridge. Absent their mission, the rough-hewn columns represented just another urban Stonehenge, bearing cryptic witness to things long gone.

Jommers fixed his gaze on the place where he'd spotted movement. A few moments later, he saw it again, but only barely. It was still mostly dark at ground level, but dawn's vanguard had faintly lightened the eastern sky, which now reflected off the placid water of the river. With the aid of that reflection, he spied the silhouette of a skinny man at the river's edge.

Jommers crept to his left to get a less obstructed perspective. He moved slowly but not quietly as drought-browned weeds softly crunched beneath his feet. He quickly stopped, but had moved just enough to attain a better view.

The mystery man was dressed in dark clothes, possibly black or navy blue. Long pants and long-sleeved shirt. A small orange dot occasionally glowed near his face, suggesting he was smoking. He held a long stick and was poking around the water with it, as if trying to fish something out. A few seconds later, he snared his target and pulled it ashore.

The strange thing on the end of the stick was hard to discern. At first it looked like a trash bag, tied at the top. But for a brief moment, the dim light reflected off the river showed that the bag was colored neon lime green and had white reflective stripes on it, like a hi-visibility safety jacket worn by road crews, only with something wrapped up in it.

Jommers first wondered if the man was one of the River Dogs, a band of environmentalist volunteers who took it on themselves to clean up the river and pull junk out of it. But they usually worked in teams, and they were not likely to be working at his early hour. And in hot weather, they would likely be wearing shorts and T-shirts.

The dim predawn light must have made a silhouette of Jommers, also, because the peculiar man in the distance became aware he was being watched and disappeared behind a pillar of stone, as if hiding. Jommers waited a minute, hoping for the enigma to reemerge. He was about to walk out there to investigate when he looked at the time on his watch. The chief didn't just expect people to show up for meetings on time, he expected them to show up early. And Jommers knew he would be struggling for the upper hand in the meeting, and arriving later than expected was no way to gain it. So he turned around, walked back to the car, and then made the short drive to downtown, whose clustered commerce overlooked the low-lying Bends from the east elevation.

THE CENTRAL POLICE STATION on Astor Avenue was built in a Romanesque Revival style in the 1920s. The massive stonework, elegant arches, and high-pitched roofs had most certainly looked grand at the time, but the dated style and accumulated black grime streaked by acid rain now gave it a sinister sheen. Where yesterday's eyes had beheld a palace, today's eyes perceived a dungeon. Jommers, however, loved the place, as he did many other old things. He admired the heft of the materials, the design and detail, the whole ethic of its construction, the old-world attitude that things should be built well and last long, that you could and should combine art with function.

The chief's door was closed, and it was too early for his secretary, Rita, to be manning the anteroom outside his office, so Jommers sat down and waited. The chief's voice was loud enough to penetrate the door, and Jommers could tell that someone inside was getting chewed out. Cocking his head closer to the door, he determined that it was Sergeant Piebalgs receiving the reaming. Piebalgs headed up the department's public affairs office, and Scubbetts always referred to the man by his duty, PAO, as if that was actually his name.

Sergeant Piebalgs was getting blasted for his handling of the media regarding the Eggers Court raid where the bystanders had been shot. He was now receiving his orders for how to handle inquiries into the shooting of Patrolman Tarburn. Piebalgs had an impossible job. Chief Scubbetts's preferred strategy for dealing with the media was stonewalling, evasion, and outright deceit. Piebalgs had the unfortunate role of reminding the chief that the police were public servants who owed the general public some answers, if for no other reason than to stay on the good side of city council, which controlled the department's budget and staffing levels.

When the chief's door opened, Piebalgs trudged out, shoulders slumped, face glum. The poor man was already beaten for the day, and it had hardly begun. Jommers stood up, set his shoulders square, and walked in. During the few seconds of changing visitors, Scubbetts had picked up his phone and was busy yelling at someone else.

Jommers sat down and looked around. It had been a while since he'd been in the chief's office. Once the relationship had been established, they communicated mostly by phone, or through Rita. Once settled in the chair, he noticed a chemical-like odor in the air that was both sweet and sharp. He looked around and noticed a small beige plastic device sitting on the floor. It had a vent grille on the front and an electric cord that was plugged into a wall outlet. Curiously, it carried no brand logos or any other graphics.

He then turned his attention to the chief. Even as Scubbetts was on the phone, eviscerating an underling, he was staring at Jommers with his unblinking lancet eyes, locking on to his next target with a transfixing gaze.

Those eyes were blue, but not the bright blue of a summer sky or Bahamian sea. Instead, they were an unpleasant, disconcerting blue, the kind of blue seen on bruises and fruit mold. They were set in an expressionless masklike face whose chalky skin lacked the wrinkles or puffiness you expect in a man in his sixties. His coarse hair was grayish yellow, like weathered straw. He had an average build, and less than average height, but his erect posture and commanding pose made him seem bigger than he actually was.

He wore the chief's summer uniform: navy-blue pants, short-sleeved white shirt with epaulets, Grayton Police shoulder patches, badge over left pocket, nameplate over right pocket, and four gold stars on the epaulets to indicate rank. That much had been standard for years for the chief's uniform. But when Scubbetts had come to town, he'd added gold lapel pins in the shape of eagles with the word CHIEF, and heavy gold braid cord looped through the left epaulet and dangling over the shoulder. In the army, he was accustomed to wearing a ribbon rack, but without a history with Grayton Police, he initially had no ribbons. To remedy the situation, he soon began presenting himself with awards so that he could have ribbons to wear. He'd never explained to anyone what he'd done to merit the awards, nor did he have to.

His hat, which sat on the corner of his desk, had the Grayton Police emblem, a gold braid band across the front, and gold leaf embellishments on the visor, similar to the visor decorations on the hats of military officers, often referred to by grunts as "scrambled eggs." The new look of the chief's outfit inspired lower-level officers to refer to it as the Mexican General's uniform. Sticking out of the chief's left shirt pocket was a metal cigar tube. On his left wrist was an oversized black-faced watch displaying military time.

Holstered on his right hip was the fifty-cal version of the Desert Eagle Mark XIX semiauto with a six-inch barrel and titanium-gold finish, even though standard issue for Grayton Police was a Glock 17. Whether Scubbetts could actually hit anything with his uber-gun was another matter. Action movies gave the Desert Eagle a rep as a badass gun, but its arm-crumpling kick made it unsuited for police tactical work. The hand cannon might be good for shooting a bear, so long as the bear was right in front of you and sleeping.

Scubbetts sat in an oversized brown leather swivel chair behind a massive oak desk that, strangely, had very little on it, save for an inbox, a big telephone with lots of buttons, a decorative penholder, an antique bronze nameplate with his name, and a crystal ashtray set in a leather base.

The walls were wood-paneled and dark-stained. Behind him right flank was an American flag on a pole, and left flank was the flag for the state of Ohio. In a corner stood a simple oak umbrella stand. Poking out the top was the handle of a saber, allegedly a genuine Model 1840 U.S. Cavalry saber. Scubbetts liked showing it to visitors, claiming it was an original handed down through the family, though the good condition of the cutting edge and wire-bound leather grip suggested it was a modern reproduction. He was known to occasionally strut around the room carrying the saber like a walking stick, often while smoking a long, fat cigar. Periodically he struck a pose with his accoutrements, as if imitating a nobleman in a nineteenth-century painting.

On the wall directly behind the chief's desk hung a strange and disturbing photograph, enlarged and framed. Its position and content riveted your attention. Taken during the Gulf War in 1991, it depicted a blown-up Iraqi Soviet-made T-55 tank in the desert. Extending halfway out of a top hatch was a charred and blackened corpse. Its lips were burned away, revealing all its teeth, displaying the grotesque smile of death. Standing proudly in front of the tank was Scubbetts, hands on hips, as if it had been his kill, though it could not have been. Lieutenant Colonel Scubbetts had commanded a military police battalion whose mission was not combat, but managing Iraqi prisoners.

Upon retiring from the army, Scubbetts had sought a position in civilian police work, right around the same time the City of Grayton had been looking for an outsider to serve as its new chief of police. For decades, Grayton's mayors promoted from within the department, usually appointing a district commander to be the new chief when necessary. But at the time in question, Grayton Police had an image problem. Multiple cases of excessive force. Corruption charges in the Vice Unit. A scandal involving abuse of overtime. Sluggish responses to emergency calls. The department had come across as out of control. The public, the media, and city council had all screamed for change.

And so the previous chief had been sacrificed on the altar of public indignation, a time-honored Grayton ritual whenever the department came under fire. Because the mayor had the power to both hire and fire a police chief, the position was both the most powerful one in the department, and the most vulnerable.

This time around, the city council, the media, and the public had virtually demanded the hiring of an outsider to clean things up. They'd feared that the tradition of promotion from the ranks would simply lead to more cronyism, perpetuating a circle-the-wagons culture where everyone in the department, top to bottom, could be counted on to cover everyone else's back. Bowing to the pressure, the mayor had hired Scubbetts, promising that the ex-military man would restore order and discipline to the police department.

Jommers had not yet been affiliated with the police department at the time, but he'd heard about what happened next from a number of department sources who loathed their new leader.

Scubbetts's first problem concerned the six resentful district commanders, each of whom felt unjustly passed over for the job. They wanted Scubbetts sent back to Arkansas, where he came from. The long knives were out, as Scubbetts expected. So he employed a strategy straight out of the military textbooks, feigning weakness to lure the enemy into a trap.

Scubbetts perceived three of the six commanders as his biggest threats. Then, whenever he was with one of the three antagonists, he acted completely unhinged. Yelling loudly. Blurting incoherent ramblings. Suggesting bizarre changes. Pacing wildly. He even threatened them with physical harm, which he emphasized by whacking the top of the desk with the heavy saber. But he acted totally composed, rational, and genteel in front of anyone else, particularly the mayor and safety director, his civilian superiors.

Eventually the three rival commanders conspired against him. They drew up a list of allegations questioning the chief's competence and mental state and presented the charges to the mayor and safety director. But Scubbetts had already beaten them by warning his superiors that three insubordinate commanders were undermining his authority, collaborating on false accusations against him, and sowing chaos in the chain of command. He claimed that they were creating the very kind of disorder he had been brought in to clean up. They were obstacles to reform.

So when the three rebel commanders had shown up at the mayor's office to demand the firing of the new chief, they'd unknowingly affirmed everything Scubbetts had previously said about them. They had stepped into the trap.

Patrol officers were protected by one union, managerial positions such as sergeants, lieutenants, and captains by a different union, but district commanders had no protection. As a result, with the mayor's blessing, the chief was allowed to fire all three of his foes. It was classic maneuvering, and no one dared oppose Scubbetts after that episode.

It was shortly after that affair that city council had passed an ordinance requiring the department to employ psychological services as part of the reform effort. The idea was to establish formal methods to keep bad apples off the force and get rid of the ones already there.

The safety director, lacking previous experience in this area, turned to the head of the psychology department at Grayton State University for consultation. The professor helped establish policies and procedures for the use of psychological services and suggested that the department contract with an experienced clinical psychologist to provide them. At the same time, the professor recommended a former student named Karl Jommers, whose graduate studies had focused on overcoming the blue-collar male's resistance to psychological counseling.

When Jommers first interviewed with Chief Scubbetts in a bid to get the business, he struggled to contain his excitement. The chance to treat police officers regularly was a perfect opportunity to allow him to test and further develop his theories about the cultural inhibitions of men and their attitudes toward therapy. The macho culture found in law enforcement was second only to that found in the military. If he could figure out how to get cops to open up, he would have the key to reaching out to virtually any other therapy-resistant male.

Yet, Jommers also understood that the talk with the new chief was more than an interview, it was also a preliminary negotiation, and that eagerness weakens your position. So during that initial encounter with Chief Scubbetts, Jommers took the risk of presenting several conditions that were important to him.

One: He would not attempt any criminal profiling. In spite of films, novels and television shows that celebrated the concept of psychologists helping to catch criminals, Jommers considered it load of crap, comparable to back-alley psychics. He cited stats showing how the most notorious criminals were typically captured through the matching of fingerprints or DNA, tips from the public, or just plain dumb luck, noting the number of serial killers arrested during routine traffic stops.

Two: He would not engage in any interrogation of criminal suspects to elicit confessions or make judgments on truthfulness, as such interactions were better handled by detectives trained in proper techniques.

Three: He would have no involvement with polygraph testing. His view, shared by most scientists, was that the potential for false positives and false negatives rendered the device no more useful than a Ouija board. He knew he could not eliminate the use of the polygraph, given that law enforcement culture has a near-religious devotion to it, but he made it clear that he would not be a party to such tests.

Chief Scubbetts didn't appreciate anyone trying to get the upper hand with him, but he happened to agree that psychologists had no place in crime solving, a discipline better served by legwork than mind reading. In addition, Scubbetts was tired of backstabbers who acted like suck-ups in his presence. Jommers's open, upfront candor made him appear trustworthy by comparison.

So Jommers's gamble paid off. The two agreed that the psychologist's primary role would be focused on the men and women in blue, performing evaluations and providing counseling. Yet the accord quickly became complicated and strained.

Chief Scubbetts was irritated that Jommers, an independent contractor, could not be manipulated or controlled as easily as a department subordinate. And Jommers was disappointed to realize that Scubbetts had little respect or regard for the people who served under him. On top of that, the psychologist was irked every time Scubbetts suggested that the psychological evaluation process be exploited to drum out people the chief didn't like.

So the relationship quickly devolved into a tense accommodation. The chief was required by municipal ordinance to keep a police psychologist on retainer. So if he dumped Jommers, the chief would have to find another one who might prove harder to work with. And as much as Jommers disliked Scubbetts, the psychologist needed the business that was sent his way at the chief's discretion.

They were like two pencils pushed against each other at the eraser tips. When the forces exerted are in perfect alignment, there is stability. Contact is maintained. But if one pencil should be tilted off the common axis, contact is immediately broken. Both men understood this on an intuitive level and endeavored to avoid that event. Yet anyone who tries holding pencils in such a position soon discovers that they cannot be held that way indefinitely. The muscles tire.

While waiting for Scubbetts to end his phone call, Jommers looked down at the surface of the desk and noticed several long cut marks in the wood, suggesting that the saber-whacking legends were true. He knew that when Scubbetts got off the phone, there would be no etiquette observed, no polite greeting or handshake, just a blunt lurch into business, like someone letting out the clutch too fast on a stick shift car. But Jommers also knew there would be no saber-banging either. The last thing Scubbetts needed was a board-certified clinical psychologist telling the mayor that his police chief was crazy.

The chief slammed down the phone. And then it was Jommers's turn.

"Tell me how Patrolman Tarburn presented himself last night," Scubbetts demanded.

It was a strangely worded inquiry, but Jommers knew exactly what the chief was after.

"You mean his behavior?" Jommers responded.

"I mean everything," Scubbetts said with irritation. "How he acted, how he spoke, what he wore, what he had with him."

Bingo. That's what Scubbetts really wanted. The mysterious kit bag that Tarburn carried, its contents so important that Tarburn wouldn't reveal them to Jommers for fear it would put the psychologist in jeopardy. The fact that Scubbetts was asking about it meant that he didn't have it, desperately wanted it, and no one knew where it was.

Jommers detailed Tarburn's eccentric, paranoid behavior, his attire and appearance, and so on, but said nothing about the bag. Scubbetts appeared frustrated. He wanted to be more specific without tipping his hand.

"Was he carrying anything unusual? You know, like a bomb or anything? Strange weapon? Anything odd?"

"Not that I could see."

"You're absolutely positive?"

"Yes, absolutely positive," Jommers said. "Now you understand that Tarburn had to drive down to the Bends, so that if he did have anything unusual in his possession, he would have likely left it in his car."

Scubbetts gave Jommers a stare-down, looking for a twitch or a blink. Jommers returned the stare, offering neither. After about ten seconds of this, Scubbetts slapped his hands down on the desk and yelled in a strained voice.

"This is not cha-cha-cha, damn it! Don't you think we looked in his car?"

This is not cha-cha-cha. It was one of many peculiar expressions that Scubbetts had, phrases that revealed a difficulty in making ordinary conversation, which neatly complemented his social awkwardness. This particular exclamation was meant to emphasize the gravity of the situation but, like some of the others, sounded borderline comical.

Scubbetts knew he had to watch his behavior in front of a psychologist, so whenever he slipped and lost his cool, he quickly recovered and overcompensated by clumsily shifting to strained small talk. Mundane observations about sports or weather were meant to defuse tension, but the odd juxtaposition of threat and banality had the opposite effect and wound the temper of the talk ever tighter.

"I got an ozone generator," Scubbetts said, pointing to the little beige box on the floor. "The brochure says it bleaches the air. I guess that's technically correct. You know, oxidation and all that. I got it to eat the cigar smoke. Technically, you're not supposed to smoke in government buildings. But the mayor smokes in his office. Nobody says anything."

"Have you talked to the coroner?" Jommers asked.

"Why would I talk to the coroner?"

"You'll want to contact him before he performs his autopsy on Tarburn and request that it be as thorough as possible."

"Are you implying the coroner is not normally thorough?"

This was how Scubbetts kept people on the defensive. Responding to comments with questions, forcing people to justify their every utterance.

"I'm suggesting that, without explicit communication, he may not comprehend the full depth of our interest," Jommers answered.

"I don't get what you mean. Full depth of interest?"

"An explanation of causality."

"Causality? Tarburn was shot. Twice. One in the throat. One in the face. Are you proposing another cause of death?"

"No. I'm talking about the cause of the behavior that led to his death. People without a history of psychological problems don't suddenly have a psychotic episode. His brain, heart and thyroid should all be examined for abnormalities. His tissue and blood should be tested for chemicals and drugs, as well as the liver, since that's where toxins get processed. Stomach contents should be analyzed. Every inch of his skin inspected for hypodermic needle marks, rashes, or any other symptomatic signs of underlying diseases."

Scubbetts waved his hands dismissively. "This seems hardly a mystery here. The man took part in a raid on a meth lab earlier in the day, a place that typically contains some of the nastiest chemicals under the sun. I think it's fairly obvious he was affected by something he encountered there. Isn't it? Or are you suggesting it's just a really big coincidence? We should consider the obvious first, shouldn't we?"

"Yes, initially, but not exclusively. The autopsy will be your one and only chance to find a solid answer. You need to look at everything. If what happened to Tarburn was preventable, you'd want to know that, wouldn't you? You wouldn't want to lose another man the same way, would you? If your theory is correct, how was the contact with the substance made? Was he wearing inferior protective equipment? If so, that's a purchasing issue that comes back to your desk. Or was he not wearing his equipment properly? Or did he fail to follow established protocols? That would be a training issue, which also comes back to your desk. You'd want to be on top of this before fingers started pointing in your direction, wouldn't you?"

Scubbetts disliked having his own technique thrown back at him, which was why Jommers always looked for the earliest opportunity to do so, always reminding that he was not one of the intimidated subordinates. The chief's silent glare expressed his irritation with the intransigent tone, but already getting off track, he did not want to waste any more time on the issue.

"The coroner is an experienced man," Scubbetts said. "It would be insulting for me to tell him how to do his job. However, I will relay your concerns."

"Thank you."

Scubbetts then swiftly reasserted control of the conversation. "All right. Let's get to business here. Because of that stupid shit law about critical incidents, or whatever the hell they call them, my first-string SWAT team is sitting on the bench. Mandatory administrative leave until you clear them to go back to work."

"It's not just my end, as you know. Force Review Committee will have to clear them, also."

"You let me worry about fucking Force Review. You worry about your end, which is clearing my men, which you will do today."

"I've already cleared my schedule in preparation."

"Absolute fucking craziness that I have to be put in this situation, the whole city and its citizens put in this goddamn situation. The barbarian hordes are on the march as ever, and my first line of defense is on vacation because of some pissant bureaucrat's rules and regulations. I can't have this. I can't leave this city vulnerable and unprotected, the gates thrown open to attack. I can't have it, you understand? I need these men back on the line as soon as possible. You will perform your psych evals here in the downstairs office. And you will complete them by end of day. Do you have a problem with that?"

"If they are all made available to me, then it should be doable."

"Rita will make the arrangements and provide you a list of everyone you need to see and their designated times. She will also bring you the sign-off forms. Understand that they will only be able to discuss their physical and mental health with you, not anything that happened at the raid. As that incident is still under investigation, the details remain confidential until completion."

"Understood."

"Then we're done."

"Just one more thing . . ."

"We're done," Scubbetts said. "I have a busy day ahead."

"When you called me last night the second time, you told me that Tarburn was delirious and deranged, raving about people chasing him. I'm curious how you knew that. Did you have personal contact with him, or was this second-hand information you received?"

"What does it matter? The description was clearly accurate."

"As someone who must make such determinations, I'm curious as to who made the assessment, and how. Something, or someone, had to initiate the sequence of events. I'm sure the Force Review Committee will be pondering the same question, so it must be answered at some point."

Scubbetts gave Jommers a long, intense, pointed glare, the body language equivalent of an ice pick in the neck. The two faced each other in motionless, menacing silence, like mongoose and viper, with no clarity as to who was playing which role.

After a half minute or so of this, Scubbetts took out a big black cigar that was thick as a broomstick. He then grabbed a silver lighter, about the size of a thick pack of business cards. The lighter had a punch cutter in the bottom, used to make a hole in the cigar's drawing end. The piezo-ignition, double-jet device produced two thin but fierce spikes of blue flame. While lighting the cigar, Scubbetts took several quick, bellows-like puffs that injected a cloud of dense smoke into the air.

It takes a very big man to smoke a very big cigar without looking comical. Churchill could do it. Schwarzenegger can do it. Scubbetts could not. He looked like a man whose face had been impaled with a smoldering log.

The theatrical lighting of the cigar allowed the opportunity for delay, a means of reestablishing the sovereignty of his space, because Scubbetts knew that Jommers's last observation was correct. The question would have to be answered eventually. How did the chief know about Tarburn's condition?

"We had a talk," Scubbetts said. "We shared a cigar. I wanted his personal take on the Eggers Court raid. What went wrong from the grunt's end, getting that perspective, which is often different than what you get from the officer in charge who is covering his ass."

"The chief of police, sharing a cigar with a patrolman."

Scubbetts blew a billow of smoke Jommers's way with a look of contempt, irritated at the subtle assertion of deceit.

"Tarburn and I both worked for the uncle. Tarburn, just a few years. For me, a few decades. We both were part of Operation Desert Storm in ninety-one, though I didn't know him at the time. But the bond was there nonetheless, the common bond that transcends rank and position. You could not understand, never properly having served your country. Whenever I wanted an honest perspective of what was going on down in the trenches, with no intermediaries spinning and massaging the facts, I knew I could trust Tarburn to tell it straight. Just two old soldiers talking man-to-man. No bullshit. So that's why I called him in yesterday, as I had done before. But as we spoke, he slowly began acting strangely. I was concerned, so I followed up with periodic phone calls afterwards. Each time I talked to him, he sounded worse. Finally, I realized something was seriously wrong. Something that required immediate attention."

"So it was your assessment. Your call."

"Yes. It was my call. Unfortunately, I didn't call it soon enough. This is what happens when you let emotions get in the way of reason. Nothing but trouble."

"You lost a good man."

"Yes. And now the media are crawling all over it, before they've even finished salivating over Eggers Court. It's a goddamn PR nightmare. They're always attacking. I'm set on by jackals of every stripe. Do they think I can control every goddamn interaction between police and rabble scum? What do they expect? This is a war, damn it. Shit happens."

Jommers was perturbed that Scubbetts appeared more concerned about his own problems than the loss of a man. Jommers remembered an incident the year before in an adjacent county when an officer had been shot and killed during a traffic stop. The police chief in that city had been trying to explain to TV reporters what had happened, but he couldn't get through it without choking up. "I'm sorry," he'd said, "we've lost family here." Grief and remorse would be the expected reaction from a normal police chief after losing an officer. But Scubbetts was anything but normal.

"One more thing," Scubbetts said. "When we get past all this crap, there's a nervous Nellie I want you to evaluate. See if we can boot him without union troubles."

"Nervous Nellie?"

"K-9 officer. Somehow his damned dog got out in traffic and got run over. When other units arrived on the scene, they found the dumb son of a bitch crying uncontrollably over the dead dog. That would qualify as psycho, wouldn't it?"

"Not really. A normal grief. The K-9 officers form strong attachments to their dogs, not so different from the way another officer bonds with a human partner."

"That's what I'm talking about. It's retarded. It's just a dumb fucking animal. The fact that you can train it to do something for you doesn't make anything more. You can train a rat to run through a maze, but it's still just a rat."

"I'll be happy to talk to the officer if you send him my way and see if I can help him."

"You agree, it's crazy, right?"

"I'll be happy to talk to the K-9 officer."

Outside the chief's office, Jommers encountered two brawny men with butch haircuts, both wearing blue jeans and khaki T-shirts. One of them took Jommers's picture with a cell phone. Then they brushed by him as they walked into the chief's office.

As Jommers headed down the hallway, his mental jukebox cued up a blues song, and the selection was no mystery. John Lee Hooker singing "Crawling King Snake."

LISTENING AND ITCHING

The meeting had lasted slightly past sunrise. The reddish saffron sun was poised above the horizon like a branding iron, presaging another day of burning torment. Jommers had some time to kill before the scheduled interviews, so he walked several blocks over to Fleck's Diner, a joint whose streamlined moderne appearance exemplified the maxim that nothing becomes antiquated faster than the future. Built in the '30s, the design featured broadly rounded corners, with the entranceway centered on the right corner instead of the front wall. The exterior was shiny white except for alternating swaths of turquoise and pink at the top and bottom. The eatery's name was displayed in large, lighted letters in a roundish font, with each letter tilted in opposite directions, like they were dancing. Underneath was another sign that boasted about foods being prepared with real butter.

The layout inside was linear, with a single walkway separating the full-length counter from the booths lining the outside walls. The curvy counter seats alternated between white and lime green. The booths were cherry red. The wall covering, now yellowed and peeling, featured a cartoonish geometric pastel pattern of tableware chasing coffee cups.

The diner was only a block away from the Ledger Building, which housed the city's daily newspaper. The proximity to both Central and the daily rag ensured that both cops and reporters were steady customers. The pleasant chatter among regulars competed with the crackle and sizzle of things being fried quickly. In butter.

Jommers noticed the presence of the newspaper's police reporter, Yolanda Arroyo, whom he had met a few times before. With the botched Eggers Court raid and the shooting of Patrolman Earl Tarburn by another police officer, she would have a lot to write about in the coming days, with a lot of it ending up on page one. She would also have a lot of questions. When they made eye contact, she nodded in recognition.

On her way out, she stopped by Jommers at the counter.

"I was getting my driver's license renewed the other day," she said, "and when it was time for the picture, the woman said, 'Smile,' paused, then said, 'If you want to.' That's how they do it now. Apparently some people don't like being ordered around by the state. Interesting, though, don't you think? It's kind of Zen-like, you know, giving you a command followed by an opt-out. Or maybe it's another way of saying that your disposition is up to you, which is kind of your thing, isn't it?"

"You should put it on T-shirts and sell them. Maybe make enough to quit your day job."

"A lot going on in cop world," she said. "We should talk sometime."

"No. We shouldn't."

"I'll be in touch."

"Don't bother."

AFTER EATING A THREE-CHEESE OMELET with some Southwestern home-fried potatoes, Jommers grabbed a large coffee to go and headed back to Central to conduct post-critical incident psychological assessments of those SWAT members involved in the Eggers Court raid. These assessments would be distinct from the formal operational inquiry performed by the Force Review Committee, and the officers involved would be placed on paid administrative leave until both processes were completed.

The psychological evaluation performed by Jommers would be brief and narrow in scope, determining whether or not the officer was suffering from post-traumatic stress as a result of the incident, and, if so, whether or not it was of sufficient magnitude to warrant delaying the officer's return to duty.

By contrast, the mission of the Force Review Committee was to examine all incidents of lethal or injurious force exercised by the police in the line of duty and determine whether the level of force deployed by the officer was justified by the circumstances as measured against established department protocols. Originally it was called the Shooting Review Committee, but later, when pepper spray and stun guns had been added to the officer's utility belt, the scope of the committee had been widened. By city law, the Force Review Committee consisted of seven people holding specific positions. From the PD: the chief, the head of Internal Affairs, and the head of the Detective Unit. From city government executive branch: the safety director, the prosecutor and the law director. From the legislative side, the chairman of the Safety Committee in city council.

The time required for the committee to conclude its investigation varied from a week to several months, depending on the complexity and clarity of events. There was also an unstated but implicitly understood formula that the length of incident review time should roughly correlate to the PRT (public relations temperature) as measured by the DPO (degree of public outrage).

If a cop shoots an armed bank robber who just shot a bank teller and it's all captured on security video, then the absence of either ambiguity or outrage means the cop is going back to work soon. But if the cop shoots an unarmed teenager at the end of a car chase, claiming that the teen was attempting to use the car as a weapon, and there are witnesses who dispute the officer's account, then both ambiguity and outrage register high on the scale, and the officer can look forward to some lengthy time off, enough time to repaint the house, and maybe fit in a road trip to Yellowstone to see Old Faithful.

From a practical perspective, a cop should see admin leave as a bonus, an extra bit of paid vacation. But in reality, they resented it. They saw the prohibition from working as a pronouncement of guilty until proven innocent. The admin leave was a cloud over their head. And the longer it remained, the more they were irritated by it.

Jommers's end of things, the psychological assessments, was typically concluded within a few days, well before a cop's clearance by Force Review. So Jommers's part was rarely any cause for delay in return to duty. That was why he was surprised to hear Scubbetts ordering him to expedite the assessments. Given the ambiguity surrounding the Eggers Court raid, the SWAT team members who fired their weapons would not be cleared by Force Review anytime soon. So Scubbetts's instruction to hurry things along was mostly another example of him throwing his weight around.

The office provided for Jommers at the police station was in the basement with the old records. It was one of several offices in the room that had been formerly occupied by file clerks since laid off. The windowless place had a musty smell to it, and the unadorned concrete walls and floors gave it the ambiance of a salt mine. But the location did provide some advantages. It was quiet, with no distractions. And when it was necessary to talk with a number of police officers in succession, doing it at Central was more efficient.

The location had a positive effect on the cops, too, making them more relaxed. They weren't being sent anywhere, they were in their own home space. Central was also good to perform various tests. The environment of a workplace emphasized the seriousness of a test and of the tester. This was official business, not a game. No screwing around.

Actual therapy sessions, however, took place at Jommers's office in the Bends. For such personal interactions, it was necessary to separate the cops from their environment and colleagues so that they could feel free to speak openly and candidly. At the station, they were cops first, employees fulfilling an obligation, showing up in uniform. At the psychologist's office they were people first, showing up in their street clothes and with off-duty attitude. It made all the difference in the world in terms of communication.

Jommers opened up his weathered and worn tan canvas brief bag and pulled out some forms, checklists, and notepads, though it wasn't actually necessary. The questions he would ask, he'd asked a hundred times before. The signs he would look for, he'd looked for a hundred times before. But the presence of papers and files on the desktop conveyed a message of formality. It reaffirmed to the interviewee that they weren't just shooting the breeze, that the conversation had consequences.

Not long after Jommers had set up, Rita, the chief's secretary, walked in with the appointment list she'd created. She had a trim, youthful physique, which she maintained by long walks carrying hand weights. The only things that gave her age away were the gray hair she defiantly refused to dye and the reading glasses that hung on a gold chain around her neck. She dressed conservatively, and today that was a long gray skirt and white blouse. As usual, she was crisp and formal in speech and manner. All business.

"That was quick," Jommers said.

"I had already set up a schedule for each of them to talk to Internal Affairs for the Force Review. So I used the same sequence and told each of them to stop down here when they were done with IA. So they might be early or late with you, depending on how it goes, but the order will be the same. These are just the ones from the Eggers Court incident."

"He wants to clear SWAT first."

"Correct. The ones involved with the incident by the river will probably be tomorrow."

"Is that the chief's phrase or yours?"

"What?"

"What happened to Patrolman Earl Tarburn is a devastating tragedy. An inexplicable, horrible, bizarre tragedy. A good man, a good cop, getting shot to death by another cop. And you refer to it as 'the incident by the river.' Have you become the chief's alter ego?"

She flashed a look of resentment but retorted calmly. Formally. "Certain occupations require a degree of detachment. I presume someone in your profession understands that."

"Is that your secret? Is that how you've lasted longer than any of his other previous secretaries? Detachment?"

"Some people see challenges as hardships. Others see challenges as opportunities. It's all about one's ability to adapt, learn new things."

"And who did the learning, him or you?"

"Business relationships always require some accommodation on both sides. Even when they are superior-subordinate relationships."

"What you really mean is that the chief finally realized that he couldn't effectively function if he continued to alienate everyone around him. That he needed at least a few allies he could trust to tell him what the hell was going on. People who could see where he couldn't see, hear where he couldn't hear. People like you."

"I've got a busy day ahead. Good to see you again. Let me know if there are any problems with the scheduling."

CITY OF GRAYTON ORDINANCE NUMBER 893-96 was known informally as the Oakrift law, after Detective Gil Oakrift. In the summer of '95, Detective Oakrift and his partner had gone to a house on Beam Street looking for information about a homicide suspect, not knowing the suspect was inside. After ringing the doorbell, Oakrift stepped off to one side of the door in an effort to look through a window. At the same moment, bullets came flying through the front door, felling his partner. Oakrift fired back through the door, emptying his pistol. After reloading, he kicked through the door and found that he'd killed the suspect. The entire encounter lasted less than thirty seconds. Oakrift's partner was declared dead on the scene.

Afterward, Oakrift had acted strangely unaffected. Feigned nonchalance and false bravado are common male responses to strife in both law enforcement and the military, but there are some situations where it is clearly inappropriate, such as the loss of a partner and longtime friend. Colleagues knew something was wrong, but at the time there was no means for doing anything about it.

Oakrift showed up in the squad room the next day acting like nothing had happened. After about an hour, he looked over and noticed the empty desk of his deceased partner and asked if his partner had called off sick. The other detectives looked at each other, puzzled, not knowing how to react. When Oakrift was reminded of the previous day's events, he looked confused, and then said he was going out to grab some lunch, even though it was still early morning at the time.

Instead of grabbing lunch, however, he went home, dragged his old accordion out of an upstairs closet, then started driving. Hours later, for reasons unknown, he stopped in downtown Cincinnati, parking near an old hotel. There he took out his accordion and started playing on the sidewalk. To passersby and hotel staff, it was initially amusing, if peculiar. But when night fell and he was still playing, it had passed peculiar and fallen far short of amusing. Guests complained. Police were summoned. When questioned, Oakrift said he was filling in for the regular night accordion player who was out sick. When they told him he had to stop, he instead kept repeating his mission: filling in for the night accordion player who was sick.

When the two Cinci police officers tried to take him into custody, Oakrift pulled out his gun and shot one of them in the hip. The other returned fire, shooting right through the accordion and putting several bullets into Oakrift's chest, killing him on the spot.

Had a psychologist evaluated Oakrift that morning, the psychologist would have quickly surmised that Oakrift was suffering from some type of dissociative disorder, possibly a fugue state, but no such official procedure was required at the time.

To prevent similar incidents from occurring again, Grayton City Council had passed Ordinance Number 893-96, mandating that any law enforcement officer experiencing a critical incident receive a psychological evaluation before returning to duty.

The ordinance listed a number of circumstances that qualified as critical incidents, including interactions where force was used by officers or against officers, interactions that resulted in injury or death, and so on. Or as cops put it, anything that could be classified as hairy shit, which is why some of them referred to it dismissively as the Hairy Shit law, which they naturally loathed. The notion that a cop should have his head examined simply for doing his job was offensive and absurd.

Jommers thought it was a good law in principle, but recognized a couple of implementation issues. For one, people often exhibited a delayed reaction to traumatic experiences. Anxiety, depression, substance abuse, and other effects could emerge days, weeks or even months later. He'd suggested to the chief and the chairman of the Safety Committee in city council that two follow-up interviews at later dates also be required. The idea was shot down, and some accused the psychologist of trying to pad his business. He suspected that the law had been written more as a symbolic gesture of concern than a genuine corrective action. Still, the law allowed the realm of psychology to get its foot in the door at the station house, a place where no such foot had trod before.

The second issue concerned SWAT specifically. By definition, SWAT was the trouble team, the cops you sent for high-risk operations. They saw a lot of action, which meant they saw a lot of Jommers.

So each time they came in for the required head check, they knew the drill. They knew what would be asked and how they needed to answer to get back to work. They were elite warriors with an elite warrior attitude. Therapy is for pussies. Persuading them to open up was like trying to sell nursing home insurance to twenty-year-olds.

Jommers did not expect anything different on this day, even though they had lost a comrade. They would feel the loss, but not show it. Not to an outsider, anyway. They would be less jaunty than usual, possibly somber, but there would be no crack in their reserve.

Of course, he knew his part of the drill, too. First, put on the game face. They were used to being in charge of an interaction with a civilian, so respective roles must be established at the outset. Display enough assertiveness to remind them that it's your show, not theirs, but not so much as to generate confrontation. Adhere to the formality of the procedure, but with a relaxed, conversational style. Be cordial, yet dispassionate. Do not exhibit any emotional reaction to anything they say, as it might inhibit further response. Do not reveal what you are thinking until it's over. Be aware that they have mentally prepared for the encounter and it won't be spontaneous. And when their behavior strays out of bounds, you must gently tug them back in with silken rope. Offer the subtle reminder that they must get past you in order to get back to work. But don't throw it in their face either.

Usually, Jommers deftly balanced these objectives with few problems. To begin with, he had a natural affability. Being a steelworker's son, he hadn't needed to shed affectations, merely avoid acquiring them. And he had learned not to take it personally when presented with a display of attitude. He understood they were irritated with the principle of being required to see him, not irritated with him personally. They were annoyed by the process, the idea that trouble needed to be examined. Or, as one of them put it: "If there's shit in your path, you step over it and keep moving. You don't kneel down and smell it."

〜

THE MORNING APPOINTMENTS went mostly as expected, like the umpteenth performance of a long-running play. The only difference was the absence of the usual dark humor or wisecracks. They had lost a comrade and were in no mood for banter. They were filled with emotion, but determined not to reveal it.

One of them struggled to hold it back. As was standard practice, Jommers offered the opportunity for some follow-up counseling. The officer declined, which was standard practice on their part. Jommers then suggested that the cop consider taking a few vacation days. The man stiffened, his face indignant. "You honor the fallen by working harder," he said.

Most of them said little more than necessary, with the exception of the last morning appointment. When Jommers finished with his questions, the officer sat quietly in his chair for a few moments, shaking his head. Finally he spoke, his voice high, almost cracking.

"This is so weird. He's gone now. Yet I'm still mad at him, sort of."

Jommers was eager to know why but thought it best to be patient. Remain silent. Let it bubble up at its own pace. And that took another minute or so.

"He'd never go to the bar with us. And when I asked him why, he said he didn't drink. So I said, well, you don't have to drink alcohol. They got the fake beer, soft drinks, juice . . . and he still said, no, he can't. The wife doesn't like him going to bars. So this one weekend I had a barbecue. Invited all the guys on the team. And, except for those pulling duty, they all came, all except Tarburn. So I called him on it. I was really pissed. I said, what the fuck is your problem? We're your buddies. We're trying to be friends with you. And this is how you treat us. And I could see he was hurt by it. And he hung his head down, all sheepish and embarrassed. He said it was the wife. She didn't like his job. So when they got married, she laid down some conditions. And the big one was keeping the job separate from the rest of his life. She did not want cop world mixing with home world. She instructed him, the people you work with stay just that, people you work with. And when he told me that, I kind of lost it, and I say, man, how can a guy as big and strong as you be so goddamned whipped? Well, we didn't talk much after that, least not for a while. Then I got to thinking . . . you know, marriage is hard. Even harder with a job like this. Everybody's got to figure out their own deal for making it work. And so, when you get down to it, you got to respect someone else's deal, even if it's not a deal you'd make. Eventually, I apologized to him, and he said it was okay, that he understood, but I still had trouble shaking that off. I just wanted to be friends, you know? He was a good guy. I just wanted . . ."

He leaned his face into his hand for a few moments, then slowly got up. "I have to go."

"There's no hurry. You can stay," Jommers said.

"No. I have to go."

"If you want to talk more, I've got some time later in the afternoon, when these interviews are over. Or we can get together tomorrow, day after, later in the week, whatever works for you."

"No. I'm good, thanks."

Before the man got too far out the door, Jommers jumped up, and ran after him.

"Hey!"

"Yeah?"

"Look, I know you guys aren't ever going to open up with me, but at the very least, you have to talk to each other. Promise me you'll do that."

The cop nodded without looking up and hurried off.

Jommers sat back down, stunned at what he'd just said. "I know you guys aren't ever going to open up with me . . ." The admission of his failure. These cops needed help that he was eager to provide, but the connection wasn't happening. He'd never imagined it would be this hard. When he'd launched his practice, he'd had all kinds of ideas for breaking the macho walls, but the barriers had proven stronger than he'd expected. Was it them? Or was it him?

And that was when he felt the itch. That familiar tightening at the back of the neck, a hot tension that would be massaged out by two familiar hands, barley and hops.

He looked at his watch. It was only eleven thirty. The morning appointments had finished early. If he drove slowly and maybe made a detour or two, he could arrive at Spreckels Tavern about noon, his green-light time. Given his profession's lack of precise criteria for defining excessive drinking, Jommers had constructed his own criteria for permissible level: never get shitfaced drunk, never drink before noon, never feel impaired, never increase daily consumption, never suffer any negative consequences.

As long as he met those conditions, he felt he did not have a drinking problem, even though he recognized that he drank a lot. He was aware that the most insidious form of deception was self-deception, because it was the least likely to be exposed. He also understood intelligence did not confer immunity from self-deception, it simply made the language of denial more eloquent and convincing. He also knew that the body adapted to alcohol intake up to a point. The liver increased the enzymes that oxidize ethanol, which increased alcohol tolerance in a regular drinker. So as long as he was not increasing his consumption, he felt safe, believing that he had not yet crossed the line, a line yet to be quantitatively defined.

When he was young, he'd never imagined making such calculations. He'd been a diligent student in college, one who'd avoided the party scene and the college bars. He'd begun his higher education with both parents already deceased, so he hadn't had the luxury of living like so many other students, where the extension of education was a de facto prolongation of teenage life. Circumstance compelled the early adoption of an adult sense of responsibility. And he had taken it very seriously when a psychology professor had argued that drunkenness was the equivalent of temporary suicide, that heavy drinking arose from the desire to put a reversible bullet into one's head. "Until you understand that desire, you cannot uproot it." Jommers never forgot those words, and yet there it was.

It all started with the cops, and for much the same reason they started. The job. The cops saw some pretty awful stuff, and they often shared it with the therapist. Battered wives and children. Brutalized rape victims. Finding a ripe corpse at the maximal state of bursting putrescence. The dead newborn in a trash dumper. Collecting severed limbs in the street after a horrible motorcycle accident. The teenager tortured by a gang he tried to leave. The child deliberately scalded by a parent as punishment. The stabbing victim trying unsuccessfully trying to hold in his guts from spilling out his belly. The sight of a blackened burn victim from a house fire and the smell of burnt flesh. And on and on.

Each time Jommers listened sympathetically to one of these stories, he felt like he was sucking snake venom out of someone and taking it into his own system. And eventually the poison had accumulated to where he was desperate for an antidote.

Popular culture cuts you some slack about tossing back a few after a bad day. The problem with that dispensation arises when you start having multiple bad days in succession, when the bad days become the rule instead of the exception. And that was how the slide began, the slide that deposited you at Spreckels Tavern around noon.

AN ODD DETAIL

Jommers was a regular at Spreckels, among those who attended with church-like devotion. And like other such congregants, he was well-versed in the tavern's hallowed history. The establishment was founded in the late 1800s, and if layers of grime were like tree rings, you could date it in similar fashion. The brick building and its short sandstone facade had been darkened by the coal-smoked air of an earlier age, but nothing dimmed the splendor of its tall arched windows. Evidence of the establishment's vintage could be seen on a yellowed piece of paper protected by glass and mounted on a wall inside the bar's entryway. It was a notice from the city dated 1898, warning "proprietors, river bank dwellers, and river men" that operations to widen and deepen the Claybank River would soon commence "in order that the waterway may accommodate new styles of vessels with iron hulls."

The German lagers served at Spreckels were originally derided by a population accustomed to English ales, and the Germans themselves hadn't fared much better initially, particularly during World War I, when they were suspected of being spies or traitors. It was around that time a Molotov cocktail had come through the window one night. The flames had singed a section of the long oak bar before it was doused, and if you knew where to look, you could still find traces of the scorch marks where the wood was poorly sanded and refinished.

Things had eventually improved for the Germans, and while their old homeland lost the war in Europe, their lagers won the battle of the beers in America. The beers took a break during Prohibition, when the establishment converted into a bakery, or so it seemed. A false wall in the front area featured display cases full of baked goods, but when a patron in the know asked for a specific, obscure item, like say a pistachio elderberry cream torte, he was told it could be found in the back, whereupon a door was opened for him that led to an illicit barroom.

After repeal, the tavern gradually became more Americanized. As the Germans migrated out to the suburbs, the schnitzel gave way to cheeseburgers, though the garlicky bratwurst with sweet sauerkraut and hot mustard still held on. But even as times changed, none of the subsequent owners dared touch the faded, water-stained mural of a German biergarten on the wall behind the bar, nor, just below it, old German beer steins that shared space with top-shelf whiskeys. Those decorative touches had been added by the founder himself, Old Man Spreckels, and were considered sacred.

Over time, though, the half dozen or so different owners had felt free to add their own distinctive touches, a decorative graffito of sorts that said, "I was here." For example, one wall displayed a large banner with the Warsaw Falcon. A little red cardboard arrow was pinned to it, pointing to the crown on the falcon's head, and Eastern Europeans understood. The banner had been hung back during the Cold War, when the bar had been owned by a Pole wanting to show his solidarity with his anticommunist brethren back home. In Commie-era Poland, one could only display the falcon *minus* the crown, as the crowned falcon was deemed a symbol of the deposed monarchy. Displaying the falcon *with* the crown was how you flipped the bird to the Commies.

Another owner, a hunter, had added a boar's head and bear's head to the wall. Other adornments included original vintage tin beer signs from defunct breweries, a couple of old railroad lanterns, a streetcar fare box, an antique cash register, and more.

A small addition by Larry, the current owner, was a little sign offering inspirational wisdom: *Every day is a prize. Celebrate with beer!*

But Larry's greatest contribution was restraint. As the old bluesmen advise, it's not the notes you play, but the ones you don't. Neglect had bestowed a slight shabbiness on the establishment, but one that that fell within the tolerable. It was frayed but not ratty. Any sensible businessman could see that a bit of refurbishing and sprucing up, along with a menu upgrade, would permit price increases that would bump up revenue. But Larry didn't want to run a place that was classier than he was. Didn't want to narrow the crowd mix to a monoculture. He understood the lure of the tavern's inclusive vibe, which was why he'd bought the place to begin with.

The regulars found comfort in the diversity. They kept returning because it was one of the few remaining bars where one could hold a normal conversation without shouting. One of the last that was not an annoyingly noisy sports bar or part of a corporate chain with a formulized atmosphere. It was neither a punch palace dive nor a snooty bistro. It had no targeted demographic. It was not the product of some MBA's marketing strategy. Instead, it was a vestige of what taverns were prior to Prohibition branding them as dens of iniquity—a town square that served beer.

And so the sooty dust on the pewter lids of the old beer steins remained untouched, and also the cracked floor tiles, the damaged tin ceiling tiles, and everything else needing attention. And that was just fine with Jommers. The joint's lack of pretension matched his own.

He also liked Larry, the amiable, rumpled owner and ever-present bartender whose doughy form moved gracelessly but efficiently from task to task. The pace of the job had imprinted a perpetual harried look on the man's face that remained even when he was at rest. The other constant was a cigarette dangling from his mouth that rolled, bobbed, and weaved like a baton conducting an unseen orchestra.

"Hey, Larry," Jommers called out. "Am I seeing things, or are you walking funny? Almost like one foot is just a wee bit heavier than the other."

Larry came over and made that hand motion that says *keep it quiet.*

"Is the bulge that noticeable?" he asked. "I didn't think anyone would see it on my ankle."

"It's okay," Jommers said. "Ordinary people won't notice. But a cop would."

"That's all right. I got a CCP."

"Concealed carry permit."

"Right. I got my reasons, too. I'm not one of those paranoids arming up for some Armageddon."

"I wasn't implying anything. Just curious."

"There's some stickup guys out there specializing in bars at closing time, knowing the owner is going to be carrying a sack of money to the bank night drop. You know Finn, at the Shamrock, up on the hill?"

"Yeah."

"A few weeks ago, they got him after he closed, put one in his leg. Ripped an artery. Almost bled to death. He's still out."

"I hadn't heard."

"Yeah. So now that's all I think about when I close. Who's out there waiting for me? So when I walk to the car, it's like walking through—how does that thing go? You know, that valley thing."

"Even though I walk through the valley of the shadow of death—"

"Yeah, yeah, that one. Now it ain't a long valley, mind you, just out to the car, but I got to walk it every night, alone, in the dark. And my shepherd is an S&W M&P compact forty-cal, ten plus one. It's in my right hand as I walk out the door. I got no choice. You know?"

"A reasonable response to a reasonable fear. That's what it's all about. Just make sure you practice with it."

"It shouldn't have to be this way. It's the goddamned twenty-first century. We can figure out how to let people safely live in a space station, but we can't figure out how to let people safely run a cash business in the city."

"I agree."

Jommers wasn't sure how long the interviews would take, so on the way back to Central, he stopped and bought some beer and ice and put them both in a cooler he kept in the trunk, except for a few cans he put in his grungy canvas briefcase.

Not long after returning to the mildewy office in the police station's basement file room, Jommers received a visit from a balding, short man with a potbelly, wearing a short-sleeved shirt and tie and thick black-framed glasses. The toady-looking man reminded Jommers of his eleventh-grade math teacher.

"You Jommers?"

"Yes."

"I'm Captain Wifflyn."

"You're not on my list."

"No. But you're on mine. I head up Internal Affairs."

"Of course."

Jommers had expected this visit for two reasons. First, it was an Internal Affairs officer who had shot Earl Tarburn down by the river. And second, even if it had been an officer from another unit, Wifflyn would still be involved, as his position title made him a member of the Force Review Committee.

Wifflyn started, "About last night—"

"Can you tell me what happened at Crone Point?" Jommers interjected.

"Excuse me. I'll be doing the question part here. You'll be doing the answer part."

"I've got an interest in this—"

"Everybody's got an interest in this. But nobody outside the Force Review Committee gets anything until we nail it down and release the report, including you. Now, all I need to do is document your role in this, and then we can both get on with our day. Understood?"

"Happy to help."

Jommers confirmed his assessment that Tarburn had been exhibiting paranoid psychotic behavior and urgently required hospitalization. He also noted his disagreement with Chief Scubbetts on how that should have been implemented, suggesting that if the psychologist had been present, events would have unfolded differently.

"To your knowledge, did Patrolman Tarburn go by any nickname?" Wifflyn asked.

"No. Why?"

"Like I said, I'm doing questions, you're doing answers."

"I'm not aware of any nickname."

"Can you be more specific about some of the things he said to you, things that led you to believe he was suffering from a paranoid episode?"

"No."

"What do you mean, no? You have short-term memory problems? We're talking about something that happened less than twenty-four hours ago."

"He was babbling incoherently, making nonsensical statements, which tend not to register in the memory. And I was paying more attention to his behavior than his language."

"So you're telling me you can't remember a single specific statement he made less than twenty-four hours ago?"

"That's correct."

"I find that very peculiar."

"You asked a question, I gave you an answer. Or are we having a different discussion?"

"Look, I'm not on anybody's side here, I'm just trying to nail down the facts, all right?"

"I've given you the facts I have."

"Right. One last thing. Was Tarburn carrying anything with him when you saw him?"

"He was carrying a gun in a belt holster positioned at the back."

"Besides the gun."

"No."

"So you didn't see a bag of any sort?"

"No."

"You're sure?"

"Yes."

"Well, I guess that's it, then."

"I don't know if you have any influence in this area, but I had strongly recommended to the chief about contacting the coroner to encourage the most thorough autopsy possible to determine if there were any chemicals or physiological conditions that might have triggered Tarburn's behavior."

"The chief doesn't need or appreciate reminders."

"How about foot massages? Does he appreciate those?"

"You got a problem, Jommers?"

"I got no problems. Life is good. But I can't help but notice some things."

"Like?"

"Like how you can spy patrolmen taking free donuts, but when it comes to brass taking sugar, your glasses somehow fog."

"Everybody who works has to deal with conditions. If you ever had a real job in the real world, you would know that."

"In other words, because you report to the chief instead of an independent civilian overseer, he sets your boundaries of inquiry."

"If I think of more questions, I'll be back."

"It will be a pleasure."

⌒

THE EARLY-AFTERNOON INTERVIEWS also went largely as expected, with most of them ending before their allotted time, allowing Jommers to work on the beers he had stashed in the briefcase. However, things got unexpectedly interesting when the two-thirty appointment stayed to chat for a minute.

"Are you allowed to tell me?" the cop asked.

"Tell you what?" Jommers responded.

"You know, what made Tarburn go off like that, what put him over the edge."

"I don't actually know. I'm hoping the coroner's autopsy will find something that will explain it. They don't have the report yet. Do you have any insights you want to share?"

"Not that I can think of. Not someone who has insights much. Just getting it done, you know?"

"Sure. How about stories?"

"Oh, I got stories, lots of stories. I don't know that they count as insights."

"Just tell me a good story, then."

"You mean like a worst-day story? Where the day just kind of explodes on you?"

"Not necessarily. Something that sticks out in your memory because it's weird, or funny, or poignant, unsettling. Use your intuition, then pick one."

"Hmm. Well, there was this one day, don't remember how far back now, but we were called up about a guy who had threatened his neighbor with a gun. We get there, and this guy is standing on his front porch dangling a gun at his side, ranting and raving about the neighbors. He was high, drunk, or nuts, maybe all three, I couldn't tell. So there we are, pointing our assault rifles at him, yelling at him to drop the gun. And he's not dropping it, but he's not raising it either. He's pacing back and forth on the porch, yapping away, the gun swinging around at his side. And so we all got the same thought in our heads. How high does he raise his gun before we fill his body with bullets? Fifteen degrees? Thirty? Forty-five? What's the angle of death? If he raises it level at you, you shoot for sure. But he doesn't. And this goes on for like an hour or more. Everyone with their finger at the ready . . . you can feel the cramp setting in. Your finger, your hand, your arm, they all hurt, and you just want to pull to get it all over with, because you just know that's where it's going, right? And it's a really hot day, and we're in full gear, and we're standing in the direct sun, and the sweat is just pouring out every square inch of your body. He lifts his gun . . . it goes up about twenty degrees, and you almost shoot, but it goes back down. And this happens every five minutes or so. And you're going goddamned nuts already. You want something to happen. You want to make something happen. Then, finally, the son of a bitch drops the gun, and someone runs up, knocks him to the ground, and cuffs him. And Tarburn, he's right next to me, he bolts and runs in the house. I'm guessing he wants to secure it, make sure no one else is in there with a gun. I follow him in, but he's not checking out the house. He's running to the bathroom, dropping his drawers on the way. He gets in there and starts taking a volcano shit. So, later, I ask him, what the hell's going on, you have some bad potato salad at a picnic or what? And he asks me not to talk about it. Says he's going to take care of it. Won't happen again. So the way he says that, it suggests to me an ongoing problem, something he's going to get treated. And treatment today usually means drugs, right?"

"Right."

"So maybe he started taking something for it. Maybe something that interacted with something else. You know the way drugs are. I mean, my mom is taking blood thinner, and she has to watch what she eats, especially vegetables, because they want her to keep her vitamin K intake steady. Vitamin K? I didn't even know vitamins went up to K. How the hell you supposed to know all this shit? So, I don't know, did that help any?"

"It might. Thank you."

One of the later appointments in the day also offered an insight, although reluctantly. He gave predictable answers during the interview, but then, as he was about to leave, paused in the doorway.

"Something you want to add?" Jommers asked.

"I'm pissed off."

"You want to tell me about it?"

"I'm not supposed to talk about anything what happened yesterday."

"Understood. It won't be repeated or recorded."

"Well, I'm really, really, pissed off. There's word going around about how the department is going to officially explain Tarburn going flip. They're going to say he took off his mask at the meth lab site and inhaled something nasty. And that's just pure bullshit, because I was right by him the whole time. He never took off his mask, and he wouldn't ever do that. Some of the guys can be gonzo, but not Tarburn. He was nitpicky about procedure, did everything by the book. He was the kind of guy who wouldn't go through a red light in the middle of the night on a deserted country road. Know what I mean? So hearing what they want to put on him—I'm so boiling right now I could fucking strangle somebody. Whatever made him flip—it had to be something fierce. And it didn't happen at Eggers Court."

"Thank you. I appreciate your sharing that with me."

"Don't let them blame him, okay? Whatever happened to him, it wasn't his fault. I know that. I absolutely totally know that."

The last appointment on the list was Lieutenant Augie Dallabaco, the commander of SWAT. About fifteen minutes past his scheduled time, he briefly appeared in the doorway.

"Jommers, I'm up to my eyeballs in shit. I don't have time to do this right now. How about I stop by your place later?"

"Yeah, sure. I'll be there."

JOMMERS FINISHED UP filling out forms for the officers he'd talked to, then made copies for his own files. The originals were for the chief's secretary, Rita, who came down for them at the end of the day.

"There's three more you'll need to interview regarding the critical incident last night," she said.

"You're referring to the tragic shooting of Patrolman Earl Tarburn."

"Correct. There's two from Internal Affairs, Detective Ilona Voros and Detective Moe Balzer. Then there's a uniform by the name of Dwayne Biederbach, who was assaulted by Patrolman Tarburn, so he qualifies under the rules. Detective Balzer is in the hospital due to injuries sustained and won't be coming back to work for quite a while, so there's no urgency with him. I've scheduled Voros and Biederbach to see you tomorrow at your office."

"Who shot him?"

"Excuse me?"

"Which one of them shot Earl Tarburn?"

"That would be Detective Voros."

"Thank you."

"By the way, Chief Scubbetts wanted me to inform you that the coroner's autopsy has been concluded and the remains have been turned over to the family."

"What did the coroner find?"

"He found that Patrolman Tarburn had been shot to death."

"We kind of knew that. What did he find in regard to explaining Patrolman Tarburn's psychotic behavior in term of toxins or physiological abnormalities?"

"He didn't find anything in that regard."

Jommers clenched his fists. Felt like blowing a gasket. But he refrained from raging at Rita. She was only the messenger.

He was infuriated because he knew the coroner was an incompetent hack who likely had not performed any tests. In Claybank County, as in many across the country, the coroner's position was elected. And given that one party dominated the area, it was essentially an appointed position—whoever the party picked to run would win. There were no certification requirements for the job, and nothing in the law even mandated that the coroner have any medical training or experience. As a result, the coroner was typically a political operative who tailored his reports to provide whatever the police department requested of him. It was very likely no real autopsy had been performed at all. If there was any physiological or chemical explanation for Tarburn's behavior the night before, it was now beyond discovery. The answer might never be known.

It had been a long day, and the truck repair shop was already closed when Jommers got back to his office. He found a note on his desk from Claire Maroun, his bookkeeper, who had stopped by while he was out. Her note suggested that there were some important issues that needed discussing. She said she would try again tomorrow. Claire was actually Pete Gerzny's secretary and bookkeeper for the shop downstairs, but she handled Jommers's billing and accounting on a freelance arrangement as she was a longtime friend and wanted to help him out.

He pulled the files and forms from his briefcase, then walked over to his file room. In a busy practice, filing would normally be performed by a secretary-receptionist, but his practice never got busy enough to justify the expense of a staff employee. So he handled his own filing and appointment scheduling for his office practice, while Rita typically handled scheduling for official department business. And with Claire doing the books, all the bases were covered without the need for extra help.

Before leaving the file room, he turned back and dug out the file for Earl Tarburn. Excluding the night before, the last time the two had talked was a couple of months ago after a peculiar SWAT engagement on Juneberry Boulevard, an incident that some referred to as the Juneberry Jumper.

Jommers recalled having a curious conversation with Tarburn after the standard post-critical incident evaluation. He wasn't certain that he'd taken notes on it given that it was an informal chat they'd had while Tarburn was leaving. Jommers could still picture Tarburn standing in the doorway, shifting his weight to and fro, one part of him pushing to leave, another holding him to stay.

Jommers plunked Tarburn's file on the old table that served as his desk and sat down. He hesitated for a moment, half-afraid he might implicate himself for some kind of negligence, then opened the file quickly, the way one would yank a small bandage off a hairy arm.

In cases where a critical incident was written up in the *Ledger*, Jommers made copies of the newspaper article and placed them in the pertinent files for reference purposes. And so the first item in the file was a copy of an article written by Yolanda Arroyo, the police reporter he'd seen in the diner in the morning.

The trouble described by the article began when a woman called 911 from an apartment, saying that her ex-boyfriend was trying to break down her door, threatening to kill her. By the time a patrol car got there, the guy was already in the apartment knocking her around. The guy grabbed and held her as a shield, while pulling a gun. He said that if the cops didn't leave, he'd shoot her. In a flash, a simple domestic violence situation became a hostage situation. SWAT was sent to the scene.

They couldn't storm the place and risk the woman's life, so they tried first to talk the guy down with a bullhorn. The guy was irrationally enraged, and drunk as well. The situation dragged on. Then SWAT caught a break. The woman broke free and escaped. The guy didn't chase after her because he knew cops were outside waiting for him.

The SWAT commander, Lieutenant Augie Dallabaco, didn't wish to waste any more time, but he didn't want a shootout in such a densely populated area, especially given that his team hadn't been able to evacuate residents from the adjacent apartments.

So Dallabaco had tear gas shot into the specific apartment unit, hoping to flush the guy out, or at least diminish his ability to engage in combat. A few minutes later, the police in the street heard the sound of gunfire coming from the unit. Not knowing what or who the guy might be shooting at, they rushed up. But before they even got there, the crazy ex-boyfriend did something strange.

He jumped out the window. Headfirst. He broke his skull and neck and died immediately. The only plausible explanation anyone could concoct was that the cornered suspect preferred suicide over prison. But there was an obvious question that the newspaper did not raise, one which Jommers asked himself in a truncated note scrawled in the bottom margin of the page: "Why jump? Had gun. If suicide, why not shoot himself?"

Nobody else had pondered that conspicuous incongruity.

After rereading the newspaper article, Jommers looked at the evaluation form he'd filled out for Tarburn after that incident. No issues were noted, as expected. Like the rest, he'd been through such evaluations before and knew how to answer the questions to get it over with as quickly as possible. And that's why Tarburn had waited until he was almost out the door before tossing out his question, making it clear that this was a casual conversation, not part of anything official.

Jommers turned the page over, desperately hoping to find that he'd taken notes on that little talk. He had. They weren't extensive notes, but enough to jog his memory, enough to fill in the blanks.

One notable aspect about Tarburn set him apart—he was very religious and applied his beliefs to his daily life and job. There was none of the typical dark cop humor coming from Tarburn, no grim jokes or cynical observations. He genuinely pitied those lost souls who'd gone wrong. He came from a rough neighborhood himself, so he understood how easy it was to go astray. One wrong friend, one wrong party, one wrong ride, and everything changes, and your life goes another way.

"There but for the grace of God go I," was a favorite line of Tarburn, a man who never cared whether a quote was trite or corny. He wasn't writing an essay, after all. He was just a common man letting you know how he felt. So while some of the others on SWAT joked about the crazy ass who jumped headfirst out the window, Tarburn mourned the needless waste of a life, and recited another of his favorite quotes, the famous one from John Donne:

Any man's death diminishes me, because I am involved in mankind,
and therefore never send to know for whom the bell tolls; it tolls for thee.

Tarburn was a simple man, but also an educated and curious one. He had gone to Grayton State University and earned a bachelor's degree in criminal justice. Then there was his fascination with the night sky, which both delighted and troubled him. He once said: "I don't wonder why God made me. I don't wonder why God made us. I wonder why he made so much stuff that has nothing to do with us."

While in college, he had taken some psychology courses as part of the core curriculum, classes that gave him a passing familiarity with the classic experiments. As a religious man, he pondered those having moral implications.

As Jommers read his notes, more specific details from the conversation emerged from the fog of memory. He looked across the room, trying to conjure the scene, recall the conversation. The formal part of the interview was over, but Tarburn had stayed a few minutes at the doorway to shoot the breeze. Tarburn was looking for a good transition, but couldn't find it, so the question he asked Jommers came out of the blue.

"Hey, do you remember that guy who did the experiment with the electric shocks?" Tarburn asked.

"You mean the famous experiment done at Yale in the sixties by Stanley Milgram, where most of the test subjects were willing to administer shocks to another person when instructed to do so?"

"Yeah, yeah. That one. How'd that go again?"

"Milgram was testing the average person's willingness to defer to authority, to defer moral responsibility. No one actually got shocked. The person appearing to be on the receiving end was pretending to be in pain, but did not actually experience any. But the test subjects didn't know that. They believed they were delivering pain and did it anyway. The surprising results of the experiment suggested a capability for blind obedience to authority, to follow orders, even when ordered to do something awful."

"Right, right," Tarburn said. "Thing is, though, I don't think they got it right—the conclusion, I mean. It's not really like that, you know, the whole blind obedience thing. I've been to war, and I've seen people do bad things. I've been a cop in a tough city, another kind of war, and I've seen people do bad things. And I can tell you, nobody does stuff against their grain. They do it because they're on board with it. They do it because they think it's okay. And the bigger the bad thing is, the more they have to believe it."

"Believe what?" Jommers asked.

"That a bad thing can be a good thing."

"Are we talking philosophically here? Or are you wrestling with something?"

"Wrestling isn't the word. Not even close."

"Okay. Can you tell me about it?"

"You know that I'm a religious man. I go to one of those churches where they're always asking, what would Jesus do? My wife, too. I think I told you this before, but she doesn't like my job. She asks me, would Jesus carry a gun? And honestly, I don't think so. So you can see, I got conflicts from the get-go. But I can deal with that one. A gun is a bad thing. But if I use it to protect the people in my community, maybe not so bad. That's a weight to carry, but one I can handle. But now I got a boulder. A big one. Some days I can't hardly stand up straight."

"You're struggling with a moral quandary where you have to determine the higher good. And the fact that you brought up the obedience issue, I'm going to go out on a limb here and speculate. A superior has asked you to carry out a task in the line of duty, a task that conflicts with your personal moral code."

"Understand, I'm not confused about the big picture. God's law is above everything. Above country, above family, above me. I'm perfectly clear on that. It's the nitty-gritty level, translating it down to a specific situation, that's where it gets fuzzy. You know, like, if you hurt someone over here to save someone over there. That kind of thing."

"Right. Only it's hard for me to offer advice without actually knowing the details."

"Oh, I'm not asking you to help me decide anything. I wouldn't put that on you. I couldn't anyway. I swore to keep it in confidence, and when I do that, I take it serious. I'm just wondering how people in that situation deal with the stress. How do you carry that boulder?"

"You know, I don't think we can properly address this with you standing there with one foot out the door. Why don't we pick a time where we can have an unhurried chat, take our time, chew it over, do it right?"

"I can't make an appointment, you know that. A SWAT man can't have issues. I'd be done."

"Hear me out a second. I understand your concerns about the peer pressure. I don't agree with them, but I understand them. So I'm willing to do it informally. No billing, no paperwork. Nobody would know. Wouldn't even have to be here. We could go somewhere else. Just two guys sitting on a park bench somewhere, drinking coffee and shooting the breeze. What do you say?"

"I suppose that could work, maybe. Let me think about it. I'd have to check the duty schedule first anyway. Let me get back to you on that."

"Okay. Good. Please do get back to me."

TARBURN NEVER HAD RESPONDED to that suggestion, and now Jommers wondered if he should have done more. Should the therapist actively pursue the troubled soul? Or patiently wait until the person feels ready to talk? Sitting there with his notes, recalling the conversation, Jommers felt certain that Tarburn's inner conflict was connected to his demise, but there was no way to prove it now.

Was it possible for moral quandary to drive a man insane? Tarburn was a strong man, but people can be like materials, varied in their reaction to different stresses. Concrete excels at resisting the pushing force of compression, but fares poorly when handling the pulling force of tension. Adding rebar solves the problem because steel has high tensile strength. Was it possible that Tarburn could remain unmoved when pushed one way, but crumble when pulled another way? Jommers shook his head and dismissed the notion. Moral quandary can cause and anxiety and depression, but it's highly unlikely to induce paranoid psychosis.

And even if Tarburn had been more forthcoming about his dilemma, how could the therapist have helped? Does moral counseling lie within the realm of clinical psychology?

Jommers looked back down at the file, realizing it needed updating. He should add some notes about their final conversation by the river the night before. He should also include the patient's new status—deceased. But instead of updating the file, he closed it and placed it at a far corner of the table. He simply couldn't look at it anymore.

He walked over to a window and stared outside for a while, turning his back to work. A short while later he saw a black Ford Explorer coming up the road toward the shop. His face turned from pensive to quizzical as he wondered about the encounter ahead. He refiled Tarburn's folder and then grabbed a few beers from the back. He sat down and made ready as he heard heavy footsteps marching up the perforated metal stairs to his office.

THE BOXER'S TALE

Lieutenant Augie Dallabaco flung the door open and swaggered into the office with a fierce urgency, like a man late for a street fight. He was a short man, wiry and muscular. Though he was fifty-one, his physique was every bit as tough and lean as the welterweight boxer he'd been in his youth. Without saying a word, he strode over to the punching bag hanging in the corner and started pummeling it.

The wide-open space of the building's upper floor allowed Jommers to feature distractions not normally found in a therapist's office. In addition to the punching bag, there was a pool table, a dart board, a big-screen television, an aging upright piano, and a battered but still functional pinball machine salvaged from a defunct bar.

The various diversions had a greater purpose than providing a comfortable atmosphere. Jommers had learned early on that many men preferred to reveal sensitive things obliquely. A guy might start playing with the antique hand drill while talking about the new lawnmower he got with the really cool blade-clutch system that disengages the blade without shutting down the engine when the dead-man switch pops, but then he segues into his upcoming divorce and how it's all because of the job and he tells you all this while still cranking the antique drill because it's the only way he can talk about it. A way to open up without having it appear as gut-spilling.

But the only thing that Dallabaco ever touched was the bag. Usually it was to perform, to show he still had the moves. The finesse. The dance. That he could still throw jabs like a machine gun. But he wasn't performing tonight. He was displaying pure rage, as if killing a wild beast with fist blows.

Jommers observed quietly, already knowing he wasn't going to bother with the checklist of questions. Dallabaco was a team leader who'd just lost a good man and took it personally. Jommers's only thought was how he could help support a guy he didn't actually like. That was part of the job, too.

Dallabaco worked on the bag until he was exhausted and dripping with sweat. Then he walked over, grabbed a beer and sat down.

"What the fuck happened yesterday? Huh? What the fuck happened yesterday?"

Jommers stayed quiet, letting the rhetorical question hang in the air while Dallabaco gulped half a beer down.

"Bystanders get hit for the first time ever on my watch and two of them dead, including a twelve-year-old kid. For no fucking reason. They were nowhere near the action. And if that isn't fucked up enough, then, later in the day, one of my guys goes nuts for no fucking reason and gets himself shot by some Internal Affairs asshole. All this bizarre shit, all the same day, none of it making any sense. What the fuck is going on? What the fuck is going on?"

Dallabaco guzzled the rest of the beer, threw the can against a wall, then grabbed another one. Jommers remained still as Dallabaco's questions shifted from the rhetorical to the specific.

"They say you saw him before he got shot. Was he really that wigged out?"

"Yes," Jommers answered.

"I mean, it wasn't just a panic attack or something?"

"No. He really was psychotic. Split away from reality."

"I can't believe that. I just can't accept that."

"You know that bar by the Willow Street swing bridge, The Lousy Pirate, with the pirates painted on the wall?"

"Yeah."

"He went for his gun when he saw them, the pirates, flinched backward with fear. He was a hair away from pumping bullets into the bar."

"Holy shit. Holy shit."

"He was also going on about people chasing him. Out to get him."

"Who? Who was chasing him? And why?" Dallabaco asked.

"I don't know. I couldn't make it out. Maybe he was intuitively aware that IA was trying to pick him up and that got him all twisted."

"How does that happen? You're the goddamn expert, explain it to me. Tarburn was like the rock of Gibraltar, then he suddenly crumbles to sand for no reason. How the hell does that happen?"

"Well, I had a few theories, most of them physiological, not psychological, but the hack coroner we have didn't do a thorough autopsy as I'd requested, and Tarburn's remains have been turned over to the family. So we'll probably never know."

"Son of bitch. He did it. Whatever it was, he did it."

"Who?" Jommers asked.

"That fucking Ozark cracker. That piece of cow shit we have to call chief. You get along with that motherfucker?"

"Not really. We tolerate each other."

"There's a rumor going around that Tarburn stole something, something important, but no one knows what. But a lot of people are apparently looking for it. When you saw him last night, did he have anything with him?"

"Not that I could see." Jommers had already resolved that he was not going to tell anyone about the Tarburn's blue kit bag, not until he had some vague idea of what was in it, and who now had it. "But let me ask you something. Did anything unusual happen at the Eggers Court raid that could have triggered Tarburn's condition?"

"I don't see how. I mean, yeah, we were all upset about the bystanders, but no one else went psycho over it. But yet, there's got to be some connection, right? It can't be a coincidence, can it? Two weird things like that, the same day."

"The first one being . . ."

"The butthead meth cooks. The stupid bastards were shooting the wrong way. Made no sense."

"What do you mean?"

"Okay, this is between you and me, got it?"

"Got it."

Dallabaco grabbed a notepad and pen from Jommers's table desk and started sketching.

"Okay, look here. This is the intersection of McKinley and Eggers. McKinley is the main drag, Eggers Court is a side street. This is the old vacant printing plant where the meth lab was. It faces Eggers on the south side of McKinley. There is a vacant lot next to it where something burned down. So, on the southeast corner you have an open lot adjacent to the side of the building. On the northeast corner of the intersection, you have this tire store. It faces McKinley and the vacant lot. Right behind the tire store is this old apartment building, Mentmore Manor. The front of the apartment faces Eggers on the north. But it's six floors high, so the upper levels rise above the tire store. It's an old red brick building with some fakey gothic touches to it, so it was probably a classy place in its day, but now just your typical beat-to-shit inner-city rathole. But it still has these black iron balconies on the sides, with the south side balconies overlooking the tire store. So when the people who lived on this side of the apartment heard the action, they went out on these balconies to watch, which put them in direct line of sight with the north side of the printing plant. You with me?"

"Yep."

"Okay. The printing plant has only two points of entry—the front door facing Eggers, and back door and loading docks facing a rear parking lot. Now, the first-floor windows got burglar cages on them. The meth lab is on the second floor, but the first floor has a high ceiling, a typical industrial plant, so the second-floor windows are about forty feet up. So they ain't jumping out the side windows and walking afterward. So I position my guys front and back, the only ways out. Still with me?"

"Yep."

"So after we fire up some tear gas, the shit hits the fan and they start shooting, but not at us, not out the front or the back, which is where we are. The stupid bastards start shooting out the north-side windows here, in the direction of the tire store and apartment building, and they hit some of those apartment people out on their balconies. Why? What the fuck were they shooting at? Why would you shoot at people on their balconies more than a hundred yards away when you got a shitload of cops downstairs about to take you down?"

"What's the official explanation going to be?"

"I just found that out. They're going to say that the idiots were shooting at the windows to break them, to ventilate the place, hoping the tear gas would blow out. But that is pure bullshit. You know how you read about dumb shit SWAT teams in other cities raiding the wrong place, and someone gets hurt because those assholes didn't do their homework? I make sure that doesn't happen here. When we have an operation planned, I always scope it out before, every which way possible. Now, in this place, the windows in this building were already broken out, probably for years. Hell, that's likely why they chose it. You cook meth, you need lot of ventilation, because it makes some hellish fumes. It also makes a hellish stink, which is why they chose the second floor, hoping the smell would go out and up, that the neighbors wouldn't notice. But the neighbors did notice, and somebody called the tip line."

"Why did they have time to shoot? If I'm not mistaken, you usually just ram and rush."

"Excellent question, because it points to something else hinky-stinky about all this. Ram and rush would be my normal preference, as you astutely observed. But shortly before we're ready to go, I get a call from the chief. He tells me the entryways are booby-trapped, that if we rush in, some of my men will get killed. So he orders me to lay siege. Surround them, gas them, and make them come out, instead of busting in. So I ask him how he knows this, and he tells me that he was so informed by the Narcotics Unit. I tell him I find this strange, since I've been working closely with Narcotics on coordinating the whole goddamn thing. And, well, you know how he gets when you challenge him. Goes on a fucking tirade. So I figure, okay, I don't have time for this shit, I'm just going to do it his way and get it over with. Bad decision. I should have fought it. When we finally went in, there was no evidence of booby traps. I talked to Narcotics this morning. They never said anything about booby traps to anybody. They didn't know what the hell Scubbetts was talking about."

"Any chance that the tear gas made them fire blindly? You know, watering eyes, and all that."

"No. If that was the reason, they would have been shooting wildly in all directions. These were grouped shots on the apartment building. They were definitely shooting at something specific, but it wasn't us. And I can't for the life of me figure out what. I keep going over it. What could I have done differently? The media are already saying I should have cleared and sealed off more area. Shit. What the fuck do they know? Depending on the gun, the charge, and angle of trajectory, a bullet can travel maybe two miles. Am I supposed to clear sixteen square miles of inner city before every goddamn operation? I missed something, but what? What didn't I see?"

"It's not you. This is not your fault."

"My position makes it my fault, regardless. I am SWAT commander. I'm supposed to control the scene. That's what I do, and I failed. So, yes, it is on me. I fucking failed and people are dead because of it."

"Jumping to the second thing—you mentioned the need for ventilation in this place. Any chance that Tarburn removed his gas mask and inhaled something foul?"

"No. He would never do something that stupid. Besides, we had a briefing on this operation. From surveillance, we already knew that these crazy motherfuckers were using the Red P method."

"Red P?"

"Red phosphorus. They get it from road flares. Nasty shit. Produces phosphine gas, which is deadly and flammable. Phosphine shuts things down in the body. It doesn't stir things up. Phosphine doesn't make you crazy. It just makes you dead."

"How come it didn't kill them?"

"They had an illegal power hookup and used it to run fans to blow it out the windows. These guys were coffeepot cooks, buttheads, not pros. Real morons. If we'd let them alone, they would have likely killed themselves eventually."

"How come their fans didn't blow away the tear gas?"

"We cut the power before we shot it up."

"So you can't think of anything that happened there that might have affected Tarburn?"

"No. But at the same time, there has to be a connection, doesn't there? What are the odds that he freaks out for unrelated reasons the exact same day we raid a meth lab? What are the odds? None of it makes any goddamn sense." Dallabaco chugged the rest of the beer he was holding and then smashed it with his fist. "Shit!" He got up and paced angrily for a few moments. He stopped, took a long, slow breath, and turned to look at Jommers. "I shouldn't lose my cool here, should I? That would give you an excuse to bench me, wouldn't it?"

"Your reactions are normal."

"Thank you. And surely you know how much I hate that whole fucking concept of you judging me, you condescending to tell me whether I'm normal or not, every fucking time something goes down—you know how I feel about that, don't you?"

"I'm aware of your opinion on the matter."

"You remember how I had to submit to an interview with you to get this promotion? Had to get your fucking approval?"

"I do."

"I resented the hell out of it. And I let you know it."

"I remember."

"And you resented me. And you let me know it."

"I remember that, too."

"Then why the hell did you sign off on it? Why did you give me the thumbs-up when you can't stand me? Your teeth clench every time I walk in the room."

"It's fair to say we don't have congruent personalities. I'm a laid-back kind of guy, easygoing, open-minded, nonjudgmental. You, on the other hand, are an intense, domineering control freak with no tolerance for ambiguity. Everything has to be black or white for you. You are quick to act and quick to judge. These qualities do not suit you to be my drinking buddy. However, they do suit a position where one has to size up a situation quickly, take decisive action, and bring order to chaos on the fly. And that's why I recommended you for SWAT commander."

"I don't know if I'll be keeping that title after all this." Dallabaco paused a moment. "You know, an optimist expects a new day to be a good one. A realist expects that the new day will start out as a good one, then unexpectedly turn to shit in a way no one thought possible. My wife had this uncle, Gino. Nicest guy in the world. You know, the kind who would smile and wave when you'd pass by even if he didn't know you. He had this long, steep driveway, and so he used a snowplow service in the winter. And at the beginning of every winter, he'd put in a whole mess of those fiberglass marker sticks on each side of the drive to help the plow guy know where the drive is when it's covered with snow. Now one of these winter days Gino is walking down his driveway to get his mail, and he's walking down one side of the drive. He slips on a patch of ice and falls. And he just happens to be in the wrong spot, because he falls right on one of those driveway markers, which impales him through the neck like an arrow. And just like that, he's done. Everything he was, everything he was yet to be. Over."

He paused again for a moment.

"Now then, no normal person going out to get his mail ponders getting killed on the way. But that's exactly how I'm supposed to think, because I'm not a normal person, I'm a SWAT commander. I'm supposed to imagine every freak shit thing that can possibly happen and then be ready for it. And I did not foresee that some butthead meth cooks, when surrounded, would start shooting at something nowhere near the action, and that it would kill innocent bystanders."

"No one could have predicted that. Not you, not anyone."

"But it's on me regardless. So now, I have to figure out what the hell happened." Dallabaco walked over to Jommers and poked his finger into Jommers's chest. "Look, all the shit between you and me, the history, we got to put all that aside now. The only way to make sense of this out is for us to work together. You're going to hear things I won't. I'm going to hear things you won't. We need to talk. Keep in touch. That's the only way to figure it all out."

"Captain Wifflyn at Internal Affairs is already on it. Figuring it all out is kind of his job, isn't it?"

"Wifflyn can't find his own dick with both hands. If you and me don't get it done, it ain't going to happen. I lost a good man yesterday. And I'm not letting go of this until I know why."

DAY THREE

Jommers was a third of the way up German Hill when he found himself doubled over, gasping for breath, frustrated and baffled. Damn it. Had it been that long?

He kept himself in shape by taking a regular morning run around the Bends, a trek that included an arduous, steep ascent up German Hill Road. It cleared his head and kept his beer gut in check. He'd been good about it throughout the lousy winter. Even bought strap-on gripper cleats for his running shoes that allowed him to plow up the hill when it was snow-covered and icy.

The problem came in July. A smothering heat wave had enveloped the city a few days after the holiday. He'd expected it to be fleeting. And so, one morning that week, when the stifling mugginess was already present at dawn like a patient predator that had not budged in the night, Jommers chose to skip the run just that once. Just once.

But the beast refused to leave, and its rancid, steamy breath kept the runner inside a second day. Then a third. And a fourth. And now, here he was, more than a month without a run, disgusted at how fast conditioning could slip away, stunned at how quickly brief neglect reset everything to zero.

Head down, hands on hips, he plodded back down the hill in defeat, a dispirited soldier trudging home after surrender.

While limping back, he hoped to salvage part of the outing by walking over to Crone Point at Copperhead Bend, the place where Patrolman Earl Tarburn had been shot while fleeing a colleague from Internal Affairs two nights before.

The yellow Police Scene tape was still there, but it was already broken and lay draped over the drought-browned weeds, another item of litter, distinguished from the rest of the trash only by its bright color and cleanliness.

The depth of the river at this spot, coupled with the absence of rain, made the river seem almost still, its subtle movement hidden below like the ulterior motives of men.

Why? Why had Tarburn, knowing he was being pursued, fled onto a peninsula from which there was no escape? Was he disoriented and lost? Did he imagine he could swim across the river? Or was he so deranged that he wasn't even thinking at all?

And then, Jommers remembered how, when he'd stopped by the morning before, he had seen a skinny man dressed in blue, fishing something out of the river with a long stick, a strange man who had then hid behind the vestiges of the long-gone bridge. He walked over to where the old stone supports stood sentinel and gazed down at the river. The hook in the crone's finger pointed slightly downstream, which meant that water flowing around it created a slight backflow eddy on the inside curve of the hook of land. The effect caused flotsam and scum to gather near the bank, where it would likely remain undisturbed until the next rain swelled the river, purging old flotsam and replacing it with new stuff. Somebody could easily throw a floating object into that pool of debris and retrieve it at a later time, confident that, absent a rain, it would still be there.

He thought of the blue kit bag Tarburn had carried that night. He thought about all the people asking whether he had seen it. All the different players wondering where it was. And, again, he thought about the strange man fishing something out of the water right at this same spot yesterday morning.

And then his cell phone rang. He looked at it and sighed with disgust.

"Yes, Rita."

"Chief Scubbetts would like to speak with you."

"Yes, I do have a minute. Thanks for asking."

"One moment, please."

There was a long pause, for which there was likely no good reason other than for Scubbetts to demonstrate that his time was more valuable than someone else's. In the gap, Jommers imagined Scubbetts's command to Rita. "Get Jommers on the horn." His use of old military slang was more than a habit, it was his way of suggesting his superiority over non-vets. He had "worked for the Uncle."

"Jommers."

"Yes, Chief."

"I've looked over all the forms you submitted yesterday and see that you've cleared the members of SWAT to return to duty."

"You're welcome."

There was another long pause. Scubbetts had difficulty recognizing sarcasm. Jommers figured that it was either some neurological deficiency or the mere unfamiliarity with someone throwing it at him, given his years of being in a position of authority. In either case, Jommers occasionally found it satisfying to get in a dig without starting an argument.

"Rita has arranged for you to see two of the people involved in the Monday night situation," Scubbetts said.

"The Monday night situation. Where a cop got shot by another cop. Where a good man died before his time for no good reason. You mean that situation?"

"Yes. You'll be seeing Detective Ilona Voros and Patrolman Dwayne Biederbach. A messenger will deliver files on them."

"I've already got it down."

"Good. And take your time with these two. Give them careful scrutiny. If you find any issues or concerns, however slight, we need to delay their return to duty."

"I'm a little confused here, Chief. You're usually urging me to get officers back on the line as soon as possible."

"These two are different. Biederbach, for example. There's something squirrelly about him."

"Squirrelly?"

"I mean sinister. He's involved with some things that are potentially disruptive to the command structure."

"Such as?"

"I don't have time to delve into it now, and we're still trying to nail down the details, but in the meantime, the longer we can sideline him, the better."

"And, what's her name, Voros? What's up with her?"

"As you noted, a police officer shooting another police officer is a highly unusual event. It has put the spotlight on us. The media, the public, the mayor's office, city council . . . everybody is riled up about it. Returning her to duty too quickly could have some political fallout."

"Well, I will certainly give them both a very careful evaluation." He paused for effect. "Just as I always do."

"You're not getting the message here. Let me try again. There are valid reasons to keep these two off duty for a while—in one case, maybe even permanently."

"If you possess information that gives you a well-founded reason for keeping either of them off active duty, then it is within your authority as chief to make an executive decision to that effect. But that happens at your end. My role as psychologist is limited in scope and clearly defined, to determine whether they're psychologically fit to return to work. What happens after I make that determination is entirely in your hands. If you keep them off, it's your call for your reasons."

"You're still not getting my point."

"Yes, I am. You're not getting mine. I won't serve as an extension of your labor relations staff. You can't use me to skirt around their union."

"I don't know what's happened to you, Jommers. It seems like you no longer understand the concept of cooperation."

"I understand the concept perfectly. Enough to know that the word *cooperation* is not synonymous with *submissiveness*."

"We need to discuss this further, but I have a meeting coming up. Drop by later in the day and we'll talk."

"I've got a busy day."

"I'll swing by your place on my way out."

"Like I said, I've got a busy day."

"Me too, so it'll be late when I stop by. See you then."

As Jommers plodded back to the shop, his words with the chief stuck to him as uncomfortably as the sweaty T-shirt he wore. "I won't serve as an extension of your labor relations staff."

In fact, he had done exactly that back in the early days of their relationship. At the time, he'd lacked previous experience in working with police in general or with Chief Scubbetts in particular. He hadn't been quite sure what the rules of interaction were or whether he should create his own. He was eager to make it work. He was not yet aware of Scubbetts's manipulative tendencies and the danger of yielding. So in the beginning, when Scubbetts pushed, Jommers bent a little.

Scubbetts had been brought in to clean up the department and its image, the latter being more important to the mayor who hired him. The overzealous cops who had a habit of ending up on the front page of the *Ledger* were among the chief's first targets. But, as always, the patrolman's union fought for every cop's job regardless. As Scubbetts put it, if Jack the Ripper was a Grayton cop, the union would still fight to save his job, claiming that off-duty activities were unrelated to job performance. The wisecrack was only a partial exaggeration.

Under the terms of the union contract, any disciplinary actions related to performance were subject to arbitration, which always went in favor of the union, even in the most blatant of cases. However, the contract had an Achilles heel, which Chief Scubbetts was first to exploit, a provision that permitted the department to dismiss a patrolman for health or medical reasons with nothing more than the professional opinion of an accredited professional in the field. And psychological problems fell under the heading of health and medical.

Importantly, the process was not subject to arbitration. The union could still challenge the dismissal in court, but that required paying a lawyer and an expert of their own to dispute the decision. And if they lost in open court, the cop not only lost his job but got labeled a psycho, making it difficult to find another job in law enforcement.

Often in such cases, a deal would be offered first. Resign quietly, voluntarily, and you leave with a good recommendation that helps you get a job elsewhere. Put up a fight, and we label you a psycho and kick you anyway.

So the provision gave the department some extra leverage in prying a bad cop off the force, and Jommers was the crowbar that could make it happen.

At first, when Scubbetts sent Jommers those first few problem cases, Scubbetts didn't ask Jommers to portray a sheep as a wolf, only to depict an obvious wolf as a really bad one. And given that a psychological evaluation is by nature interpretative, there was plenty of opportunity to spin the report. Jommers initially had no problem with such fudging. He saw himself as helping a reformer police chief clean up a troubled police department and make it more professional.

And then came Nitchenko.

Complaints concerning excessive force are not uncommon at any urban police department. But few erupt into news stories because the complaints are mostly filed by low-income people who committed a crime or had a criminal history. The public has little sympathy for them, excessive force or not.

The Nitchenko case, however, was one of those few that made a big noise. Patrolman Nitchenko had beaten up a deaf guy who hadn't responded to commands or questions, for the obvious reason. Even more troubling was that the victim hadn't committed any crime and was the cousin of a city councilman. Both the press and the public wanted answers, but more than that, they wanted action.

Patrolman Nitchenko claimed he was attacked by the victim. The victim denied it. Two different stories, with no witnesses available to weigh in. The patrolman's union vigorously defended the patrolman, as it always did, regardless of the circumstances. That's what you paid your dues for.

So the chief had a problem. He was brought in to instill discipline and order, and now here was an embarrassing case that was destined to drag on and stay in the public eye for a long while. Jommers was the solution.

Scubbetts could toss Nitchenko immediately with a letter from Jommers saying that the patrolman was psychologically unfit for duty. No hearings, no union, no hassle. One letter and it's over. Then Scubbetts looked like a man of action. A man who got it done.

And so the chief called a meeting with Jommers, the department's officially designated psychologist. Scubbetts presented a thick file of complaints against Nitchenko and made a detailed case against the patrolman. The chief painted a bull's-eye on the cop and demanded that Jommers pull the trigger.

Based on what Jommers heard and saw in the file, he mostly agreed with the chief. But desiring to perform due diligence, the psychologist wanted the chance to personally evaluate the patrolman before signing off on the cop's dismissal. Scubbetts went ballistic and roared back that if Nitchenko was allowed back on the street and later killed an innocent citizen of Grayton, the blood would be on Jommers's hands.

Jommers held. He wanted a face-to-face with the cop. And he got it.

Nitchenko showed up for the evaluation with a rabid, self-destructive attitude. He was hostile and uncommunicative, answering every question with cursing.

Jommers wrote the letter. Nitchenko was canned. Chief Scubbetts thanked the psychologist for being a team player.

After the confrontation with Patrolman Nitchenko, Jommers was more likely to trust the chief's opinion on such matters, and that case set a pattern wherein Scubbetts would short-circuit the official disciplinary process and use the psych evaluation as a tool to dispose of cops he didn't like.

It wasn't until later that Jommers realized that he was being used, that some of the information he was receiving about bad cops was exaggerated or even fabricated. But instead of confronting the chief over it, Jommers simply became more circumspect and less pliable. He wanted to have it both ways. Do things by the book, but not lose the business. The wire he had to walk became increasingly thinner.

And so now, this morning, while standing at Crone Point, Jommers had gotten so riled by the chief's presumptuous request that he'd forgotten why he was there or what he was thinking about. He half wanted to turn back and make another attempt at running up German Hill to clear the irritation, but changed his mind after looking at his watch. In a few hours, he was scheduled to conduct a post-critical incident evaluation on Detective Ilona Voros, the Internal Affairs officer who had shot Patrolman Earl Tarburn at this location. He had not seen her before and wanted time to prepare.

Before leaving the place where the shooting had happened, Jommers turned and looked back at it one more time, wondering how it had all gone down. Where she stood. What she saw and heard. Why she fired her weapon.

The chain of events was so unbelievable, he could not even visualize the scene. The stage before him remained steadfastly empty, refusing to admit even imaginary actors. The tragic play was over, and there would be no repeat performance and no audience to review it. The unobserved prelude to its dark denouement was a secret held exclusively by its only surviving cast member, Detective Ilona Voros.

Voros strode into the room with a vibrant, confident step. She made eye contact immediately and beamed a broad salesman's smile. She had a solid, athletic build, evoking Rosie the Riveter plus gym junkie. Her file said she was forty-five, but she looked younger. She had wide green eyes and paprika-red hair, which was cut short. Her freckled face had natural color and was free of cosmetics. She wore a dressy tan pantsuit and a crisp white blouse. In her left hand she carried a tan attaché case made of soft leather. She sped toward him forcefully but smoothly, like a bowling ball toward a pin. She shook his hand firmly and spoke boldly and cheerily.

"Good morning, Mr. Jommers. It's a pleasure to meet you."

She did not at all present herself like a cop coming in for a psych eval, but rather like a corporate executive arriving to tender a business proposal. When she turned around to sit down and found only the sturdy oak rocking chairs, she smiled and chuckled. "Well, I guess rockers it is, then." After sitting down, she tittered briefly. "This is actually kind of fun. Puts one at ease. Very clever."

Once settled, she overtly reconnoitered the room. She smiled again. "This is great, what you've done here, it really is. But you did leave out something important, I think." She paused for effect. "You need a humongous painting of a bullfighter sticking the sword in." She gave another polite chortle, the same kind that a motivational speaker emits to signal the audience that a joke has been told, in case it hadn't been obvious.

"No, seriously. This is well thought out and percipient. You understand perfectly the character of the people you're dealing with, as well as the challenge of seeing inside them. You clearly grasp the need to bore a peephole through the wall of masculine ego to get a picture of the storm raging within."

She had a sonorous voice, well articulated with a practiced, modulated inflection, similar to a radio announcer for a classical music station. After a momentary pause in her patter, she displayed a look of revelation.

"You know, after saying that, it just hit me, we're in a similar position, you and I. Both outsiders looking in. We both have to address problems with police officers. We both have to ascertain who and what we're dealing with. Is this someone who just needs a reassignment to get back on the right track? Is this someone having trouble coping, who just needs some counseling? Or is he an irredeemable in need of a career change? We could probably learn a few things from each other. Perhaps when we're through here we can share some pointers."

The woman had only been in the room a couple of minutes, and she already seemed to own it. He had not expected a charm offensive, but then, every cop developed their own strategy for dealing with a psych eval. Apparently, this was hers.

A look of embarrassed surprise lit across her face as she put her right hand over her stomach. "Oops! You didn't hear that, did you? Forgive my tummy growling. It's used to seeing a Honeycrisp apple right about this time, and now it's yelling at me. Hey, where's my apple?" This was followed by another polite chortle.

She leaned forward and looked at him intently. "Well, why don't we begin with you describing this whole process to me, since this is my maiden voyage into your realm? Tell me how this goes. What exactly you expect from my side of the table."

On any other occasion, he might have marveled at her aplomb. But it was just too much. She'd just killed a man two nights before. According to her file, it was the first time she'd ever shot anybody. And it wasn't an ordinary person, either, it was a fellow police officer. And here she was, acting like she was here to discuss window treatments.

Her utter lack of emotion over the tragedy, the disrespect of it, stunned Jommers and ignited a slow burn inside him, but he didn't show a trace of either. He had realized long ago that the people sitting in that chair studied him as keenly as he studied them. He understood that the slightest reaction could be perceived as a judgment, one that clamps the conversation or changes its course. So he'd trained himself to refrain from reacting emotionally to anything they said, however interesting, funny, sad, awful, or infuriating. No shifting of weight to a different elbow or tapping of a pen or pencil. No arching an eyebrow. No tightening of the face. He was better than a sphinx. He was a sphinx playing poker.

"Well, Detective, it goes like this. I will ask you a series of questions based on a standard questionnaire specifically developed to assess the psychological impact of a critical incident on law enforcement personnel. And what I expect from your side of the table is cooperation and honesty in answering the questions."

"What if I'm not a standard person?"

"The standardized questionnaire helps to minimize variability and bias in the assessment. It also provides a means of comparison for research purposes."

"I see. Well, I presume that an experienced man such as yourself knows how to size up people pretty quickly without a lot of rigmarole. So if you care to use an abbreviated version, that would be just fine with me."

"I'll stick with the standard version. Thanks."

"I understand completely. You obviously have a keen grasp on how to navigate the byzantine protocols of government bureaucracy and satisfy the appetite of the red tape beast. I appreciate your patience and professionalism in dealing with all these formalities."

"Speaking of formalities, let me get a few out of the way. Regarding fees. Given that this session is administratively required, my fees for it are picked up by the department. There are no costs to you. Regarding confidentiality. There are different levels of confidentiality in this particular business based on the type of interaction and who initiates it. Given that this is an administratively required evaluation being performed contractually for the City of Grayton Police Department, I will be forwarding the results of the evaluation, along with my interpretation, to your human resources office. Is that understood?"

"Understood."

"The exception to that will be any digressions that don't relate to the purpose of the evaluation. Information revealed that is not pertinent to the objective won't go out of this room."

"Got it. You know, this is really kind of ironic, me sitting here for one of these."

"How so?"

"You know what they call these, don't you? An Oakrift. I'm getting an Oakrift. After the detective who lost a partner, then suffered a dissociative disorder, probably a fugue state, which led to a tragic end."

"I'm familiar with the case, but was not aware he had been officially diagnosed as such."

"Well, not officially. That's merely my interpretation. You see, I was with Internal Affairs at the time, and IA is always a part of any Force Review debriefing. I talked with Oakrift right after it happened. It was clear to me right off the bat that something was wrong. I consider myself somewhat of an amateur psychologist. I studied it in order to help me with my work. So the diagnosis was mine. Would you concur?"

"I hesitate to diagnose the deceased, someone I never met. But given the outcome, there clearly was some type of problem that needed addressing."

"Thank you. Unfortunately, I couldn't get anyone else to agree. I tried to alert anybody and everybody up the chain of command. 'Hey, guys, we got a situation here. There's a bomb that's about to go off.' But nobody listened. They resented the suggestion. 'Oakrift is a good man with a solid record. How dare you cast aspersions on him?' Well, when he ended up dead, then they all came to me, begging for my advice. I was the one who suggested establishing the constant availability of psychological services for the department, as well as the need for mandatory psychological evaluations after critical incidents. So this process we're about to go through, as well as your whole association with the department, is really all because of me."

"Interesting story. Perhaps we should begin now."

THE Q AND A PROCESS went smoothly. Too smoothly. Either she had presciently predicted the questions, or she had talked to someone who'd been through the evaluation before. All her answers were neatly wrapped and tied with a bow. When she realized how well it was going for her, she segued into a condescending, sympathetic tone, as if she pitied Jommers for needing to perform such a pointless exercise. That irritated him. But again, the sphinx didn't reveal a trace of his feelings.

Then came some questions on how she dealt with stress.

"I don't actually get stressed much. I'm kind of an easygoing person. I take things in stride. Just my nature. But if I do need to unwind, I just kick back, have some wine, listen to some bluesy jazz, or jazzy blues, whatever you call it, and take it easy. Life is too short to get uptight. All things pass. Right? Relaxing in some old, homey tavern will do more for you than a bottle of pills."

By now, Jommers was deeply troubled, especially with these last comments. To begin with, her self-description of being easygoing completely contradicted her initial behavior, that of an intense person determined to take control of the encounter.

More worrisome were her references to kicking back with a drink, listening to some blues, hanging out in a homey old tavern—she was describing him, not herself. She was mirroring. A classic manipulative technique employed by narcissists. It was evident early on when she said, "We are really in the same position, outsiders looking in," and again after, when she referred to herself as an amateur psychologist and tossed out some psychological terminology, such as "fugue state."

But the most disturbing part about the mirroring was that she could not have done it without first researching him extensively. For someone to engage in such extraordinary preparation to pass a simple psychological evaluation set off an alarm within Jommers. The only thing a narcissist fears is having the facade stripped away, revealing the naked, damaged psyche behind it.

From a strictly formal standpoint, the answers tendered, she passed the test with flying colors, but his intuition demanded something more.

It was not uncommon for people to prepare for an encounter with a psychologist—or with anyone else, for that matter. Everyone rehearses what they will say when they want to tell a doctor about a problem, return an item to a store, submit to a job interview, go on a first date, and so on. Mental rehearsal to facilitate communication can be a good thing. Mental rehearsal to disguise the truth is not. Either way, everyone performs. And Jommers knew it. So he had developed a number of techniques to cut through the performance and get to the actor behind the mask.

One inspiration came from reading about a famous photographer who asked his celebrity subjects to jump in the air while he took their picture. The photographer's reasoning was that celebrities concentrated hard on presenting an engineered persona, and that asking them to jump in the air would force them to allocate their concentration to the jump, briefly dropping their image and revealing who they actually were.

Jommers's idea was to design his own "jumps," tasks that required a level of concentration that would make it difficult to simultaneously deliver a performance.

When Jommers closed his questionnaire booklet, she queried immediately. "How'd I do? Do I get the hook? The padded cell?" Again with the smiles.

Jommers answered politely. "Can you draw?"

"What?"

"Can you draw? You know, illustrations."

"Oh, no. I'm terrible at that. I can't even do a stick figure."

"Good. Then I'd like you to draw something for me."

"I don't understand. Is this part of the test?"

"I'm doing research into how people approach unfamiliar tasks. Do you mind?"

"No. I'll give it a stab. But don't expect much."

"I'm not interested in the result. Only the process."

He handed her a pad of blank paper and a pencil, along with the illustration he wished her to duplicate. It was a drawing of a towering giant from a children's book, and the task was challenging because the viewpoint was from the giant's feet, looking upward. The image presented a difficult exercise in perspective, which is the hardest thing for a nonartist to grasp.

She laughed when she saw the challenge. "This won't even be close. You realize that?"

"Do the best you can."

While she attempted to draw the giant, Jommers engaged in casual conversation with her. How long you been on the force? What part of town you live in? What kind of wine do you drink? And while answering those questions, she managed to keep her pencil active, her smile alive, her warm cheeriness stoked.

Then he asked her: "Was Patrolman Tarburn still alive when you approached him, or was he already dead?"

Her pencil and her face froze at the same time. A brief look of panic flashed from her eyes. "You know, I don't think I can do this. I can't draw at all. I'm sorry."

She tossed the pad, pencil, and illustration on Jommers's table. Her expression shot from warm to icy, like something dropped into liquid nitrogen. There was a long pause as she stared at him coldly. He waited patiently to see if she would answer the question or leave. The extended silence unnerved her to the point where she was forced to answer.

"No. He was already dead. He'd been shot in the throat and face."

He noted that she used passive voice, as if someone else might have shot him.

"Is that where you were aiming?" he asked.

"Yes. Normally you aim for the heart, or upper torso in general. But he was a big man wearing a loose shirt. I thought he might be wearing a BRV."

"Bullet-resistant vest."

"Yes. In that case, you go for secondary targets, throat and head."

She answered these questions formally and matter-of-factly, and with a sense of unease. She had not prepared for this approach and had no script for it. She looked like she might bolt any second. So he gave her an opportunity to slip back into character. Give the narcissist a chance to shine.

"That was very courageous of you," he said. "Charging out into the darkness, knowing there was a psychotic with a gun waiting for you. Most would have waited for backup."

"Well, you said it, didn't you? Psychotic with a gun. You don't have time to think in a situation like that. Your training kicks in and you go on autopilot. You do what needs to be done."

"Right."

"A backup was there, by the way," she said. "But he was lying on the ground, whining about his back. Saying he couldn't move."

"That would be Patrolman Biederbach."

"Was that his name? I don't even remember. Only that he was a wormy little man. It's amazing how useless so many of them are. You got the wimps like him, then the fatsos who can't run thirty feet without sucking wind. Yet they still get to wear the badge. It's a disgrace. You can't count on them."

"You think he was faking? Biederbach?" Jommers asked.

"Almost certainly. Who wants to chase into the dark after a crack shot? That takes some cojones, you know? Plus, no cop wants to take on another cop. That takes a special something, a steeliness you only find in IA. There's no glory in it. Just the opposite. The better you do your job, the more they despise you. What's that saying in the Bible, a prophet is not honored in his own country? You have to be strong enough to deal with that."

"Where was your partner?"

"Balzer? Well, he was on his back, too. At the initial point of contact. That bridge house."

"Was he faking, too?"

"No. He was seriously hurt. But that's because he didn't listen to me. It was his own fault."

"What do you mean?" Jommers asked.

"We knew the fifty-one twenty-two was in the bridge house—"

"Patrolman Tarburn."

"Yes. Him. And there was only one way down. So I suggested we make an effort to talk him down and avoid confrontation. But Balzer wouldn't listen. He just wanted to charge up there. Use the element of surprise. I said, no, you don't want to surprise a paranoid psychotic with a gun. Again, he wouldn't listen. I tried to block him, but he pushed me down, then charged up the stairs. I got up just in time to see him being pushed over the railing at the top. I had to think quick. I tried to get under him to break his fall, even though I knew I'd get hurt."

"Did you? Get hurt?"

"No, fortunately. Just got my bell rung. But I probably saved his life. By the time I got out from under him, the subject was already on the run."

"Patrolman Tarburn was on the run."

"Yes. Him." She looked at Jommers suspiciously. "Is this part of the evaluation, or are we just shooting the breeze here? Because if we're done, I've got things to do."

"Yes. We're done."

"Well, this was interesting. It was good to see this side of it." She rekindled her salesman smile, picked up the attaché case, stood up and shook his hand. "It was a pleasure speaking with you. I appreciate your professionalism and thoroughness. You'll certainly get a good review from me."

"Thank you."

"So do I take the form with me, or do you send the approval directly to Human Resources?"

He paused to study her face while making her wait for the answer. "I won't be clearing you just yet. I'm going to suggest some follow-up discussions."

She turned to stone, as if paralyzed by a neurological event. Her face displayed panicked incomprehension, like a primitive observing a solar eclipse. She sputtered incoherently for a few seconds, trying to express several thoughts simultaneously with none of them emerging as the winner. Finally, she closed her eyes and tapped her forehead with two fingers as if she was pressing the restart button for her head.

In a flash, she reconstituted her counterfeit grin and rebooted her program of contrived cordiality.

"I'm not sure which specification you feel I momentarily strayed from, but I'm sure that any perceived brief misstep outside your normative values was merely a linguistic slip on my part, poor word choice leading to misperception. Whatever minutiae piqued your interest, as a judicious and discerning man, I'm sure you can readily distinguish the trivial from the critical. I'm sure we both agree that someone in my position needs to be restored to duty as quickly as possible. Someone with your vantage has clearly observed the shaky underpinnings of this department, and you certainly understand how Internal Affairs is the real glue that holds all together."

"Yes, I am judicious and discerning. And I discern a problem, something discordant, out of kilter. And my judgment is that I need to nail that down. As for the urgency of you returning to duty, you're already on administrative leave and will remain so until the Force Review Committee finishes its investigation, as is standard departmental procedure. Any supplemental inquiry on my end is likely to be concluded well before the committee's work is concluded. So, further sessions with me won't likely affect the date of your return. I think you know that. What really concerns you is the blow to your ego in being told that further sessions are necessary."

Her face grew cold and stern, her voice tinged with barely restrained anger. "I don't understand. What did I say to deserve this punishment? What did I do? I performed flawlessly. Flawlessly."

"Yes, with the emphasis on the word *perform*. You shot and killed a man for the first time in your career. Not just any man, either, but a fellow police officer. Yet you did not exhibit even the smallest trace of emotion over the incident, an incident that would be considered traumatic by every cop I know. A driver who runs over a cat or dog exhibits more emotion than you have exhibited here over the death of a human being. You've acted like we've been discussing nothing more than the damaging of a police vehicle against a utility pole. I'm sorry, that's really not normal. I'm very concerned that you're repressing your emotional response for fear you can't deal with it. That the longer you delay your reaction, the bigger it will be when it blows. I'm not trying to punish you for anything. I'm trying to help you."

"This is just so unfair. You don't have any idea what it's like for a woman to try and succeed in a macho man's world. You have to be twice as tough, twice as stoic as they are, or you're perceived as weak and unfit for the job. And when you manage to pull that off, your reward is to be called a heartless bitch."

"You're right, I don't understand what it's like, but I am aware of the difficulty faced by women on the force, and I'm aware of how they often overcompensate. But even still, allowing for all that, your lack of reaction is peculiar. Your inability to speak Patrolman Tarburn's name, to recognize him as a human being. The way you began a discussion about his death by joking about your tummy growling. These things trouble me. There's something wrong, and we need to get to the bottom of it. Together. It's for your benefit."

"This is all crap. You're an extension of their culture, where every male response is considered normal and every female response is proof she's a head case. It's discrimination, and I won't tolerate it. I'll go to the union rep, the union lawyer, and I'll have this challenged and overturned. This will not stand."

"You can do all that. It will involve them finding another psychologist to render a second opinion that contradicts mine, and then going to court over it, since health and medical determinations are not subject to the arbitration process. Even if you're lucky enough to ultimately win, the case would likely take a year or more, so you'd be out a good while. Alternatively, you can play ball with me, and if all goes well, you could be cleared by the time Force Review is finished, which is likely a few weeks. Your call."

Her face slipped into neutral as she struggled to shift gears, trying to find one better suited for the new terrain. There was a bit of gear grinding, engine shuddering, and frantic clutching. Finally she found a new sync. Or rather, a new act.

She hung her head down and spoke slowly with a penitent tone.

"I'm sorry. You're right. I did overstudy for this, over-rehearse. It's just the way I am. It's the same way I prepare a case against an officer. Relentlessly thorough preparation, going over every detail repeatedly. If you asked me to arrange a barbecue, I would be figuring out in advance exactly how many charcoal briquettes are need to form a single layer in a grill. And then I would test it to make sure. That's me. As you know, a distinctive trait can be a virtue in one context, and a flaw in another. I should not have brought that one here for this. It was a mistake, and I apologize. I saw it as an exam, and I got focused on passing. But, of course, I see the big picture. Of course I recognize the tragedy. And I think you're partly right, there is a delayed reaction coming. I'm not the cold person you think I am. It just hasn't fully registered yet. It happened so fast. And in the dark. I don't have a mental map of it. It's like it happened to someone else and I only read about it. So, yes, you're right. Something has to happen in me. And I'll take whatever help I can get. Where do we go from here?"

"I'd like you to come back here Friday, same time."

"Okay. I'll be here. And it will be just me. I'll leave Miss Fussbudget and her action plan at home."

"That's good to hear. I'll see you then."

Before she got to the door, she stopped and turned. "Oh my God. You knew him, didn't you?"

"Yes, I did."

"I'm sorry for your loss. You were clearly saddened by it. And you saw my dispassionate manner as insensitive, disrespectful. And so you were angry with me. That's what happened here. I'm so sorry."

"This isn't about me. I'll see you Friday."

"Yes."

With that, she exited, stage left.

Her closing lines left him creeped out. She was right, he had been angry, but he had been excruciatingly careful to conceal it. She had picked up on it anyway. And that scared the hell out of him.

THE CONSPIRACY THEORIST

Patrolman Dwayne Biederbach was strange, but not in an uncommon way. There was a certain type of cop—solitary with no social life—who was never off duty psychologically, and Biederbach fit the profile. He wore navy-blue twill slacks, dark blue shirt, and mirror sunglasses. He drove up in a dark blue Ford Crown Vic beater whose spotlight and blackwalls suggested it was a used police car that he'd bought at auction. He'd probably had the old Ford outfitted with a scanner and CB and very likely spent his time off patrolling his neighborhood, occasionally baffling teenagers on the street by warning them to "straighten up and fly right." And he most surely owned lots of guns.

He was a lanky man who moved like a lizard, perfectly still one moment, then jerkily changing position the next. He lit up a cigarette first thing. His file said he was thirty-eight, but the smokes had piled on another twenty to his pale, haggard face.

The smoking. That was hands down the most peculiar thing about him. The way he did it. An exaggerated style reminiscent of a flamboyant character in some old black-and-white movie. He had an elaborate sequence. To inhale, he first extended his lips into a fishlike pucker and tightened his face. The cigarette was inserted carefully, with the unused fingers extended upward. He then sucked on it slowly but heavily, and, as he did, his outstretched fingers curled inward as if being deflated. He held it for a moment or two, then turned his head slightly, wrenched his pucker to the left side of his face, and let the smoke out slowly in a tight stream. When the smoke was exhausted, he sniffed twice, wrinkling his nose first to the left, then to the right. He finished off by raising his eyebrows and tilting his head back. It seemed like a lot of work, but he unfailingly observed this ritual for every puff without tiring of it.

The other funny thing about him was his voice. Nature had bestowed on him a high, whiny tone, while tobacco had added a low, phlegmatic one, so his speech bounced between the two like a snap-action switch that has no middle position.

His opening remark was an instruction on the proper pronunciation of his last name—the first part rhymes with bead, not bide. He then apologized for not asking permission before lighting up.

"I noticed some guy arc-welding downstairs and just assumed that someone who puts his office over a truck repair shop isn't fussy about indoor air quality."

"Not a problem," Jommers said. "I keep it loose here for a reason." Jommers picked up the man's file. "I'm looking at the notes here, Patrolman, and I have to confess I'm a bit puzzled as to why you're here."

"I was physically assaulted by Patrolman Tarburn the other night during efforts to subdue him. Physical assault counts as a critical incident, which means I need my head examined, according to the rules."

"You don't appear injured. How did he assault you?"

"Perhaps we should begin at the beginning. Put it all in context."

"Whatever makes you comfortable." Jommers was not actually empowered to debrief someone for purposed of post-critical-incident evaluation. He was to focus on the emotional after-effects of the incident. However, if the subject wished to volunteer information, Jommers was not obliged to silence him.

"I was one of two units assigned to back up two plainclothes who would be attempting to take a fifty-one twenty-two into custody. That's all they told us. We didn't know until after it was all over that the fifty-one twenty-two was a fellow cop. They wanted us to be ready, but they didn't want to incite panic in the individual. So we were told to take positions near the bridge house on Dills Run, but not within sight of it, then wait for further instructions. I parked a half mile to the south of the bridge, West Drain and German Hill. The other unit parked somewhere north of it. So I'm sitting there in my cruiser waiting, when I see a big guy in a Hawaiian shirt running toward me—"

"Wait a minute—Tarburn is being chased by police officers, but he runs toward your black-and-white cruiser?"

"Affirmative. My theory is that he was unaware that the plainclothes chasing him were police, that he thought himself in jeopardy and was seeking assistance."

"So then what?"

"I get out as he approaches. He's in a highly agitated state and exhibiting coherence issues with his speech. I tell him he needs to calm down and go quietly. He gets angry with me and pushes me back against the cruiser. Unfortunately, it happens I have a trick back. So when he does this, it goes out on me and I fall down. Suddenly I've got a crippling pain in my lower back that shoots down my legs. I'm essentially paralyzed, almost blacking out."

"You seem in good shape now."

"Well, that's the thing about a trick back. It goes out suddenly, then recovers suddenly. That's why they call it a trick back."

"I see."

"So Tarburn—mind you I don't know who he is at that point, he's just a big guy in a Hawaiian shirt—he runs off into the field toward the river, to Crone Point. Just about the same time, an unmarked races over and screeches to a halt, its grille flashers going. Detective Voros jumps out and approaches me. She orders me to get up and accompany her into the field and assist in the pursuit. I inform her that I can't move. She utters some choice expletives at me, then goes after Tarburn by herself. A minute or so after that, I hear shots fired. She fired first."

"How do you know that? Did you see it in the dark?"

"No. But my ears can detect Doppler effect. I can tell whether a gun is being fired toward me or away from me."

"Well, those are some fine ears, indeed. But their relative positions could have changed once in the field. You don't know who was facing toward you or away from you, and since they carried similar weapons, you can't say for sure who fired first. More importantly is the logic issue. Her shots hit the mark and killed. If she fired first, Tarburn would not have been able to return fire."

"Unless her first shots missed."

"If that were the case, what's the point of your observation?"

"My point is that I am fairly certain that the final outcome of the evening's events was intended by those who initiated the chain of events."

"And what's your basis for that statement?"

"My experience-based intuition."

"I see," Jommers said. "Well, I think we're done here. I see no reason why you can't return to duty immediately."

"Aren't you going to ask me who would intend such an outcome? Or why?"

"No. It's not pertinent to the psychological evaluation. If you have concerns about how your colleagues handled things that evening, then you should express your concerns to your superiors and Internal Affairs."

"Not much of an evaluation. You didn't even ask me how I feel. So how can you say I'm okay to go back?"

"My experience-based intuition."

"I don't believe what happened the other night was simply a random, spontaneous chain of events. I believe Patrolman Tarburn was a victim of larger forces for reasons I cannot yet discern."

"Let me guess," Jommers said, "would those larger forces be connected to the federal government?"

"You are a perceptive individual, after all, aren't you?"

"Like I said, we're done here, Patrolman. Evaluation over. You're free to go. Have a nice day."

"What if I told you I had emotional problems that I felt needed further professional attention and additional sessions?"

"Then you should seek out an experienced board-certified psychologist, preferably someone other than myself, and make an appointment to discuss those issues. As a government employee, you have better benefits than most people. Your health insurance will cover a certain number of sessions."

"I have an unusual problem I think you might be interested in. You could write a journal article about it and become famous—you know, within your milieu, that is."

"I'm not your guy."

"I have a unique phobia. I'm afraid that my feces contain elemental sodium, and that they will explode upon hitting water. So instead of using a normal bathroom, I squat over a box of cat litter I keep in the garage. It's affecting my self-esteem and cramping my social life."

"I can refer to someone who specializes in phobias."

"I can't believe you're turning a deaf ear to a cry for help. How can you turn away business?"

"It is both unethical and illegal for a health care provider to accept insurance reimbursement for providing a treatment to someone who clearly does not need said treatment. Look, you're a man with some strong political opinions. I get it. And, like many such people, you're eager to share those opinions. I get that, too. I understand the proselytizing impulse, but that's what bars are for. If you don't have a favorite, I can recommend a few."

"When's the last time you had this place swept?" Biederbach asked.

"I straighten things up daily and have a cleaner come in on Fridays. Why?"

"Cute. I was referring to electronic listening devices."

"I don't have time for this. You need to go now."

"Would you mind walking me to my car? My back is starting feel kind of shaky. I'm afraid it might go out on me before I get there."

"If it will expedite your departure, then yes. Let's go."

Biederbach made it down the stairs without any apparent trouble, but then clutched his lower back when they hit the parking lot.

"Can we pause here a second?" he asked.

"Your car is only thirty feet away."

"Are you familiar with federal deputization of local law enforcement personnel?"

"No. I am not."

"A federal agency with law enforcement authority can deputize a municipal police officer and confer on him, or her, the authority of a federal agent. DEA, ATF, Immigration Department, they've been doing it for years. More recently, Homeland Security has started doing it, too."

"Fascinating," Jommers said.

"I'm glad you agree. You see, it's fascinating to me for the questions it raises. For example, police officers who have been federally deputized are not required to report it to their superiors. So the first fascinating question would be what percentage of municipal police officers have already been federally deputized. Is it three percent? Ten percent? Forty percent? The second fascinating question is how many federal agencies are engaged in this practice. The third and most fascinating question is this: If a federally deputized police officer receives conflicting commands from his federal and municipal overseers, where would his loyalties lie? Which master would he serve? And the question regarding those officers deputized by DHS is critical because DHS has set up so-called Fusion Centers in cities across the country, allegedly to coordinate with local law enforcement agencies on antiterror activities, but in reality these centers represent the thin end of the wedge by which the government will influence and ultimately subsume local law enforcement."

"So many worries, and so little time to fit them all in. It must be a hectic life."

"You may be right about my having little time. They know that I know. When I try to warn some of my fellow brothers in blue, I have to be careful. Some of them are clearly agent provocateurs, recording me, trying to trick me, set me up for a fall."

"You're obviously one of the many who don't like the way things are being run now. But over time, each side gets its turn," Jommers said.

"The guys running things now are only links in a long chain that goes way back. You can't see that because you're one of the many who slept through history class, which is why you fail to grasp that the past is the prime mover of the present. The hands of ghosts lie heavy on the wheel, but no one ever sees them."

"But you do."

"Absolutely. There's Jefferson on one side, there's Hamilton on the other, both grappling for command of the wheel. The battle between centralized control and local control lies at the core of our history, it is the fundamental dynamic. And nowhere is it more evident than in two centuries' worth of continued efforts of the federal government to exert control over forces that provide protection at the local level. You see it right in the beginning with the heated conflict over passage of the Militia Act of 1792, and the echoes of that clash reverberate through the Second Amendment, where Madison promises the states they can keep their militias. The issue smolders on and the smoke permeates the Insurrection Act of 1807, the Posse Comitatus Act of 1878, and the Militia Act of 1903, which replaced state militias with the National Guard and granted the federal government authority to mobilize said guard. Now in the present time we suffer under Lord Vile Veep, the malevolent machinator, and his presidential puppet, Flap Ear Feebleflub. Last year they pressured Congress to pass the John Warner Defense Authorization Act, which made it easier for the president to declare martial law whenever it suits him. But those are merely the naked attempts at control. The octopus has been stealthily and steadily working its tentacles into local law enforcement for decades while hiding behind the war on drugs, the war on illegal immigration, and, now, the war on terror. Hell, the people behind all this owe Osama bin Laden a blow job for his unwitting contribution to their agenda."

"Those people, the ones pursuing this agenda for two centuries, they must be getting pretty old now. How do they keep going? Do they drink acai berry juice or something?"

"I can't believe someone educated in the social sciences can be so naive." Biederbach held his cigarette high in the air. "See this? The companies who make these conspired for decades to conceal the truth about what they do to you. And even after it all came out, they're still selling them, like it's okay or something. Do you think it's been the same people the whole time? Of course not. There were different executives at different companies, and each of those positions have turned over dozens of times while the goals and practices of the companies remained the same. Bureaucracies, corporate or governmental, are living organisms that pass on their DNA to new members through their internal cultures. The inhabitants of an organization come and go, but its mission carries on, continually propagated by the culture. I really shouldn't have to teach this stuff to someone with your background."

"That must have been an interesting and gratifying conversation you had with Earl Tarburn the other night. There you are, stewing alone in your own little world, and then, out of the blue comes this guy talking your language. Must have seemed like a gift. Manna from heaven. And that's why you faked back pain and didn't help Detective Voros go after him. He was a kindred spirit. You wanted him to escape. Anyway, it appears your back has stabilized, so it's time for you to get on with your day. Good luck, Patrolman."

Jommers smiled pleasantly and turned to walk away. He got about twenty feet when Biederbach yelled after him, "Hey! You saw him that night, didn't you?"

Jommers stopped but didn't turn around.

Biederbach continued, "The way you just said that to me now, about him talking my language—how would you know? He came to you for help, didn't he? And what did you do? You handed him over like Judas."

Jommers immediately heard fast warning bells clanging both inside and outside his head. The outside bell was coming from a nearby lift bridge about to go up. It was alerting cars to stop and pedestrians to stand clear. Keep away. The inside bell was coming from his experience-based intuition, and it signaled a different message. Keep walking. Don't turn around. The man is baiting you, tempting you to dip a toe into his dark, Stygian waters. Don't do it. There are things swimming in there hoping to pull you in. You might never come out again. This is a crossroads moment. Keep walking. And above all, do not turn around. Do not turn around.

Jommers turned around.

He had planned to respond to the Judas accusation, but when he turned around, whatever verbal response he had formulated was blown out of his head by a blast of recognition. There was something about Biederbach's leaning posture as he stamped out a cigarette butt, something about the way he looked at that particular moment, and Jommers realized that Biederbach was the peculiar man he'd seen yesterday morning, the one fishing something out of the river at Crone Point.

Jommers walked slowly toward Biederbach, and the man assumed a defensive posture, as if expecting hand-to-hand combat. The psychologist stopped about two feet away from his tormentor and smiled.

"I'll bet they make you carry a lot of stuff in that cruiser, don't they?" Jommers asked.

"Yeah. Too much stuff, if you ask me."

"I'll bet that somewhere in all that stuff is a waterproof rain poncho. You know, in case you need to direct traffic around an accident during a storm or something."

"Yeah, I think there is one of those in there somewhere."

"And for your own protection, it's probably a hi-vis poncho. You know, neon green with silver reflective strips on it."

"You may be right. I don't recall ever using it."

"And I'll also bet that if you took that waterproof rain poncho, wrapped something in it, then somehow tied it tight with the hood strings, this thing would probably float if you threw it in the water."

"Maybe. Couldn't say, really."

"And if you threw this thing in a slow-moving river on the downstream side of a point where a looping backflow current causes a pool of flotsam to form, it would probably sit there in the flotsam for a while, not going anywhere until the next rainstorm. So somebody could come back at their leisure to fish it out."

"Possibly. I wouldn't know."

"A lot of people suggest Earl Tarburn was carrying something important that night, and they're very eager to find it. But you know, because you have it. As soon as he came up to you and started jabbering about mysterious forces out to get him, you were on his side. He explained the importance of what he had, and you quickly devised a plan to prevent its capture. You wrapped it up in your poncho and told him exactly where to toss it in the river so that it could be recovered later. That's why he ran down a dead-end peninsula with no escape, to hide the package. Then, the next morning, when all the commotion was over, you went down there to fish it out. And there it was, floating with the rest of the junk and scum. Nobody had bothered to look at the flotsam. I saw you, and you saw me. So you know I know. So now there are only two questions. What was it? And why haven't you turned it in?"

"Well, I can't answer those questions because I don't know what you're talking about. I was nowhere near Crone Point yesterday morning. I was down at Hulett Park doing Tai Chi. And if Tarburn had something important, he didn't tell me about it. But if this thing exists, and if someone has it, I might be able to creatively speculate on why they're keeping quiet about it—you know, on a purely hypothetical basis."

"Okay. Speculate away," Jommers said.

"Do you ever read those anthropology stories in the newspaper? You know, like how Professor Schmutz discovered an ancient ass bone in Ethiopia's Rift Valley. The journalists always write it up to make it sound like it just happened. But when you get to the end of the story, you find out it was discovered over a year ago and Professor Schmutz is just now talking about it. So why does he wait so long? Well, he's got to figure out whose ass bone it is, how old it is, whether it's a significant find, and so on. He doesn't talk about the ass bone until he understands the ass bone."

"You're playing a dangerous game, buddy."

"The game is already on. The danger is mistakenly thinking you can sit it out."

A long, awkward silence followed, broken only by the clanking and whirring sounds wafting out from the open garage doors of the truck repair shop. Finally, Biederbach spoke.

"I don't want to sound like the twitchy type, but I would greatly appreciate it if you could avoid disseminating your impressions on what you thought you saw at Crone Point yesterday morning."

"Don't worry about it," Jommers said. "My job is to solve problems, not create them."

"Which brings me back to my earlier request. I would still wish to become a voluntary patient of yours. Given your view of me, you could possibly classify me as having paranoid personality disorder for insurance billing purposes. Or, perhaps, since I'm clearly a highly functioning individual, you could code this as a persecutory type of delusional disorder. I'm flexible on it."

"Why do you want to do this?"

"It would allow us to share insights under the aegis of a confidential therapist-patient relationship. It's for your own protection. In doing so, we could jointly arrive at conclusions that we might not be able to achieve separately."

"If I were to take you on as a patient, I would not be encouraging your predispositions, but actively trying to dissuade you from harboring them."

"Fair enough. But if persuasion is the game, then let me propose a challenge of sorts. A dual track of meetings. Track one meetings take place on your turf in your office, where you try to convince me that my fears are groundless. Track two meetings occur at places of my choosing, where I will demonstrate to you why my concerns are genuine. A psychological slugfest. A polemical punch-up. The best man wins."

"That's lunacy."

"Is it? You're a psychologist. How can you walk away from a chance to cure someone of irrational notions? Might give you a case study to write up. You know, I'm pretty good at reading people myself, and I sense a certain funk. You're feeling a bit rusty right now, off your game. This challenge would help you tune it up, get your mojo back. How can you resist such an opportunity?"

The bells on the lift bridge had already stopped, but the ones in his head were still clanging. Don't answer, just turn around and walk away. Turn around. Walk away.

"Deal."

Jommers could hardly wait to get over to Spreckels Tavern.

"Larry, good to see you again."

"You just saw me yesterday."

"Yeah, I know, but sometimes it's really good to get back around normal people."

"I ain't normal, Karl. I just don't have time to be wacko."

"That's close enough. You know what I need."

"Coming up."

After he got his beer, Jommers ordered one of Larry's famous Burnerator Burgers—a titanic slab of blackened beef topped with hot mustard, raw onion, and jalapeno peppers, all served on fried garlic bread. The fiery burger helped to clear his head on those occasions when it needed clearing, and all that heat also gave him an excuse to have an extra beer before leaving.

Later, as the lunch crunch slowed to a less hurried pace, Larry strolled over by Jommers to shoot the breeze for a minute.

"Let me ask you something, since this is your area."

"Sure," Jommers said.

"How can people believe totally crazy shit?"

"You have an example in mind, I suspect."

"There was this guy in here last night. Starts talking about UFOs. Says they're real, but not from outer space at all. Says they're flown by these reptilian dudes that live in inner earth somewhere. At first, I think he's messing with me, but then I realize, he's like dead serious about it. What do you make of that?"

"I think somebody ought to look into it."

"Seriously?"

"Absolutely. Reptiles are edible. This could be the solution to the world hunger problem. In fact, you could even create a new burger from it. The Inner Earth Reptilian Burger."

"That's kind of long," Larry said. "How about just the Reptilicious? Or Reptilacious? I could put a bunch of green stuff on it—you know, like guacamole or something."

"I'm liking it already."

"Seriously, though. What's up with a guy like that?"

"Well, he got it from somebody else, who got it from somebody else, and so on. It's like a social disease. You will notice that whenever you hear one of these peculiar notions, there are lots of other people who believe the exact same thing. You rarely hear anyone express a truly unique peculiar notion. This seems to affirm the communicable disease model. And each of these cultural notions is of a classifiable type, like germs."

"So it's basically like catching a cold."

"Right. Only it's a cold that tends not to go away, so it's more like herpes. And with sociocultural transmission, just like other communicable diseases, you get clusters based on proximal contact. Take UFOs. In some countries, sightings are rare or nonexistent. In others, like ours, sightings are as ubiquitous as cheeseburgers and hideous tattoos. Further affirming the model is the fact that internal regional variations present themselves in similar fashion. It wouldn't surprise you to learn that UFOs visit California way more than Wyoming."

"Well, of course. California's got Disneyland."

"I'm more partial to San Simeon myself," Jommers said.

"So if it's like a cold, how come only some people catch it?"

"Excellent question. I suspect that susceptibility results from inherent predisposition combined with an accumulation of personal experiences over time. You'll notice you don't often hear this stuff coming out of kids. It's mostly adults, which suggests that such beliefs are acquired errors. For example, you hear pretentious people using the awful-sounding phrase 'an historic.' This is an error of affectation. They think they're sounding British or aristocratic, not realizing they sound like a character out of *Guys and Dolls*. But more important is that you never hear a fifth grader make the same error. A fifth grader knows how to use articles in front of *H* words. Only adults screw it up."

"I don't know about that," Larry said. "When I was a kid, there was this little girl next door who liked to entertain imaginary friends."

"Yes, children have active fantasy lives, but they still know the difference between fantasy and reality. This girl you mention, she was consciously pretending. She knew her imaginary friends were imaginary. She was not messed up. She was playing. I mean, you do the same thing every time you watch a movie. You temporarily suspend reality and pretend the characters and actions are real even though you know they aren't. So that girl was normal."

"Yeah. She actually grew up to be pretty smart, if I remember."

"But this inner earth reptilian guy you talked to, he isn't pretending. He truly believes it, and the critical thing for me is that he did not believe that as a kid. But somehow, he came to believe it as an adult," Jommers said.

"So what happened? Did he like walk into a utility pole one day and rattle his noggin, or did he eat too many magic mushrooms in his younger days?"

"I don't think either, but how people come to acquire strange beliefs remains a fascinating mystery to me. Part of it has something to do with cultural affinity, the desire to associate with an appealing image, or disassociate from an unappealing one. The mystery to me is why it's more common now. People are supposedly better educated than ever, but more susceptible than ever. Though I have a theory about it."

"Which is?"

"I think it goes back to the sixties," Jommers said. "The rise of the counterculture and the breakdown of social conformity. Society is now more tolerant of nonconformist behavior, and that includes peculiar and unorthodox thinking."

"So tolerance breeds irrationality?"

"I wouldn't say breeds so much as permits. Say you stopped mowing your lawn, stopped putting weed killer on it. It would become a different yard. There would be lots of new things cropping up. Some of those new things you would like, some you wouldn't like."

"So society is becoming an unmowed lawn."

"Or a pleasant wildflower meadow, depending on your perspective."

"Okay, here's the other thing I don't get," Larry said. "This guy—before we got to the reptiloids, we were talking about ordinary stuff. Sports, tools, cars, growing tomatoes. How he takes his family to Cedar Point every summer to check out the new rides. Perfectly normal guy, seemingly. And then, bam! He starts spewing this other stuff. How can he be normal all over but in one small part be nutterball?"

"Another excellent question. This guy, in order for him to afford your exorbitant prices, he has to have a good job somewhere. Whatever it is, he must be performing it well enough to keep it, which means he's a highly functioning individual, except for the one odd corner. This is actually very common, and also very perplexing. How can a sound mind hold unsound ideas? How can rationality and irrationality coexist peacefully within the same skull?"

"Well, it didn't coexist peacefully here. When I suggested he was spouting crazy shit, even though I didn't use those exact words, he got all hot and pissed off at me."

"I'm sure you were your usual tactful self," Jommers said. "But it wouldn't matter how delicately you put it. If the man truly and deeply believed the notion, then attacking it would be no different than attacking someone's religion. All beliefs reside in the same mental neighborhood. There's a second possibility, not necessarily mutually exclusive with the first. And it has to do with our stories. You see, the stories we tell help define us, become an integral part of our identity. So when you subvert someone's stories, you're undermining their very selfhood. You pose an existential threat. Attempted debunking is akin to attempted murder."

"Attempted murder? Huh. I guess that's why he didn't leave a tip."

"Among other reasons."

"But you know what? I'll bet you he doesn't talk about that crap with his boss."

"Because?" Jommers asked.

"Because he knows the boss would kick his ass out of wherever he is, not wanting a loony on board. And he doesn't mention it to his doctor, who might have him committed. And he doesn't mention it to the cop who pulls him over for speeding, who might arrest him and take him down to a psych ward."

"And your point?"

"He only talks about it when there's no consequences. When it can't hurt him."

"Which means that at some deeper level, he understands the belief is abnormal. And if we could access that level, we might correct his thinking."

"How do you do that?"

"Excellent question."

WALKING BACK TO HIS CAR, Jommers thought about reptiloid guy, how someone could compartmentalize irrational beliefs while still functioning normally in other spheres of life: staying healthy, holding a job, paying bills, raising a family, sustaining friendships, maintaining a house, avoiding run-ins with the law.

How was it possible for his new patient, Patrolman Biederbach, to suffer from conspiracy theories and paranoia, yet comport himself well enough to hold a job as a police officer?

Was the compartmentalization paradox nothing more than human vanity? After all, no one has a problem accepting selective sickness of the body, that the foot can hurt but not the hand, that the pancreas can be afflicted while the kidneys thrive, that the left lung can be damaged but not the right. Why is it more difficult to accept partial illness of the mind?

Jommers believed it was that self and mind appear as an integrated whole, not a mere assembly of parts, not some lowly engine where the water pump is shot but the rest works fine. Therefore, a bias toward the unified self makes it difficult to accept partial mental illness. One must be lucid or insane, with no middle ground allowed. To admit otherwise is to accept the compositeness of self.

Yet he knew that partial detachment from reality abounds, that roughly three-quarters of Americans have at least one paranormal belief. They can't all be deranged, but they're not completely of sound mind either.

Now that he had elected to take on Patrolman Biederbach as a patient, the theoretical question of how to explain partial irrationality must yield to the more imminent challenge of treating it. He considered how keyhole surgery could neatly remove an infected gall bladder and wondered if he possessed equivalent therapist tools to excise a small clump of unsound ideas from a worried mind. He would soon find out.

A DIFFERING TAKE

In their morning phone conversation, Chief Scubbetts had indicated he would stop by in the afternoon. In an effort to avoid him, Jommers did not go back to the office. Instead, he headed over to Saint Bridget's Hospital to visit the injured Internal Affairs detective who had been Detective Ilona Voros's partner the night of the Tarburn shooting.

Detective Moe Balzer was busted up pretty good on the whole right side. Shoulder, arm, wrist, leg, ankle, foot—all wrapped and braced. He'd spent the morning in another round of surgery, getting various pins and plates installed. His eyes had the fixed gaze of someone receiving lots of pain medication, but Jommers recognized something else in that vacant stare—the psychological aftershock of a life-changing trauma. One minute you're an active man doing a job. The next minute you're just an immobilized damaged lump warehoused with other immobilized damaged lumps. Like some big hook just yanked you into another dimension where nothing was the same, and might never be again.

"I can come back if you're not up to chatting," Jommers said.

"That's okay," Balzer said. "The conversation will help distract me. Besides, you're just the right guy for me to ask."

"Ask what?"

"If I told you I had an out-of-body experience this morning while they were working on me, would you think I was nuts?"

"No. It's not uncommon with anesthesia. It's strictly a neurological phenomenon. It was probably when you were going under or coming out. Different parts of the brain respond to the anesthetic at different rates and to different degrees. So in those transitional moments, the captain of your brain has trouble figuring out what the hell is going on because some sectors are reporting in and some aren't, and some are sending a garbled message. So your captain struggles to interpret the situation with incomplete information, a struggle that can lead to sensory illusion. The mind is driven to decipher everything, which is its blessing and its curse, because it will go ahead and produce a report, paint a picture, even when it lacks sufficient information to do so. And that's how we get false impressions."

"Well, that's good to hear. I got one less thing to worry about. I suppose it's good I'm all tied up here, or I'd be kicking myself in the ass."

"Why?"

"Rule number one when you approach a door—determine which way it opens. That's what did it."

"You're saying the bridge house door knocked you over the railing, not Tarburn."

"Right. Tarburn never touched me. He exploded out the door when I happened to be outside it. It was a steel door that opened out. So when it flew open and hit me, it sent me flying like a home run ball hit out of the park. I don't think he even knew it happened. I don't believe he meant to hurt me. He was just scared to death of something, like a man running from the devil. We were given some bad info. It set him off."

"What kind of bad info?"

"We were told that he was acting paranoid and antsy and all that, and they said we could maybe calm him down by using his nickname that his friends called him, Early Bear. If we called him Early Bear, he would see us as friends. So they said."

"Early Bear?"

"Yeah. Coming from his first name, Earl, and second part because he's big like a bear. So they said. So I used it, hoping to get him out of the bridge house without having to go in. But as soon as I said it, boom! Just the opposite. The words triggered something in his head and he went all berserko. Next thing I know I'm on the ground. You know how crumpled up Beetle Bailey looks after Sergeant Snorkel gets done working him over? That was me."

"Who provided you with the nickname?"

"Captain Wifflyn. Said he got it from the chief."

"That's curious," Jommers said.

"Yeah? How so?"

"I knew Tarburn and all the other guys on his team. Nobody ever mentioned a nickname."

"Just one more screwed-up thing on a screwed-up night."

"I suppose you know how it ended."

"Yeah. Wifflyn told me," Balzer said.

"Not your partner, Detective Voros?"

"What, are you crazy? She's not going to come to see me. That's the only plus about being wrecked up like this, I get a break from working with that psycho bitch. She could have got us killed."

"What do you mean?"

"She always wants to be the hero, grab the glory. She wanted to charge up the stairs to the bridge house and surprise him. I tell her how stupid that is. You got a guy with a gun having a paranoid psychotic episode, a guy on the edge of snapping, the absolute last thing you want to do is surprise him. You're going to have guns blazing all over the place. We need to finesse this. Talk him down. Take it slow and easy. Surprise wasn't going to be possible anyway. The metal stairs up to the bridge house were all grown over with that weedy vine shit, and the drought turned all the leaves on it brown and crunchy. Going up those stairs was like walking on cornflakes. Not a lot of surprise potential there."

"So I take it you won the argument."

"Not exactly. She didn't want to listen. So, as she was about to barrel up the stairs, I grabbed her by the collar from behind and yanked as hard as I could. Threw her to the ground. Probably saved the dumb bitch's life. How does she respond? She gets up and tries to give me some kind of karate kick. I manage to miss it and grab her foot and start twisting it. So how crazy is this? We're supposed to be calming down an agitated guy, but instead, we're fighting each other. So I twist her around to where she goes back down again, then she pulls her gun on me. Can you believe that shit? So I say fine, you go ahead and shoot, but it'll have to be in the back. Then I turn around and start slowly walking up the stairs. Tell you what, I was more scared of catching one from her than Tarburn. He was just psycho that one night. She's psycho every goddamn day."

"That's interesting. Then what happened?"

"Like I said, I go up real slow, crunchy noise all the way. I call out to him. Tell him who I am, what's going on. I promise him I won't try to get into the bridge house, that I'll stay outside and just talk. I mean, there wasn't any real hurry. There was no other way out. He was begging me to please leave him alone. Just leave him there. Everything would be fine in the morning. Told him I couldn't do that. Eventually he went from pleading to demanding. Then the demanding started sliding into threatening, and that's when I pulled out the ace up my sleeve, the nickname I thought would calm him down. Instead, as soon as I utter the words Early Bear, all hell breaks loose. Damn shame. There should be a better way of doing this. I know he had a gun, that something needed to be done. But there's got to be a better way. That shouldn't have been me up there. Should have been someone like you."

"I know it didn't work out well, but just for the record, your approach was the correct one, and I will back you up formally on that. What happened when Tarburn ran into Voros at the bottom of the stairs, or couldn't you see?"

"That's the other thing that pisses me off. She wasn't there covering my back like she was supposed to. She'd gone around the other side and started climbing a ladder on the bridge itself. She couldn't get in that way, but she might have gotten up high enough to see in through the windows. If you ask me, I'll bet she was thinking of picking him off that way. Get herself a trophy."

"You're not serious. She can't be that bad."

"Oh, yeah, she's definitely that bad. She lies, she cheats, she falsifies reports, undermines colleagues, anything to make herself look good and everyone else bad. She got rid of her previous partner by repeatedly claiming that the guy was hungover, even though he wasn't much of a drinker. He did start looking tired after he began working with her. Me and some of the others think she put something in his coffee to make him look that way. He was fine before her. He was fine after her. So I guess you could classify her as a disease. The other thing is how she verbally abuses our targets. I mean, we're investigating fellow police officers, not street trash. You just don't treat your own that way. They're innocent until proven guilty, and sometimes they really are innocent. People will call in a tip or file a complaint against a cop for no other reason than to get even. So you have to consider that. But she doesn't. She loves browbeating them. Like, when she knows she's going to make an arrest, she dresses up in a man's suit, then taunts the guy. 'How does it feel to be collared by someone who's more man than you can ever hope to be?' Stuff like that. Oh, and she also loves humiliating them where they live, showing up at the house and yelling insults and accusations loud so that his wife and kids can hear. Or confronting him while he's out washing his car, yelling at the top of her lungs what a rotten, stinking cop he is, so all the neighbors can hear it. One time she shows up at a cop's backyard barbecue dressed in leather like one of those—what do you call them, those punishing bitches?"

"Dominatrix."

"Yeah, one of those. And so she starts needling him, embarrassing the hell out of him in front of all his friends and family. She mocked him and told him how he would be crawling for mercy like a slug. He got so riled he nearly charged her with the barbecue fork, but his buddies held him back. Then she goes off, cackling with this evil laugh."

"How does she get away with it? Don't they complain?"

"Sure. But she denies it. She'll say, hey, who you going to believe, me or a crooked cop? Plus, she knows how to sweet-talk Captain Wifflyn. Always complimenting him on his leadership skills and shrewd advice. So all he sees is the sweet suck-up. He never sees the witch. That's how she gets away with it."

"Those are some fascinating and helpful insights," Jommers said.

"That's right. You're the one who has to clear her to go back, aren't you? Don't do it. Just don't. For the sake of humanity, don't do it."

"Let's talk about your road back to health."

"Let's not."

"It's going to be long and hard. Lots of pain. Lots of rehab. Lots of times where you'll be feeling helpless, hopeless—"

"Thanks for the rosy optimism," Balzer said.

"At some point, a pain management specialist will talk to you about various options, including biofeedback and meditation. Don't blow it off. That stuff works. A few other suggestions. Keep your mind active and distracted. Read books and magazines, do crossword puzzles. If you must watch TV, watch history and science channels. Keep your good hand busy with some skill-related activity that will help maintain a sense of control: draw, play a game, toss a ball, make things out of Silly Putty, fold paper airplanes, whatever. Use your social support network. Don't wait for friends and family to visit you. Call them first. Call them often. And if you feel yourself getting depressed, you have a couple of options. You can ask to see a staff psychiatrist who'll spend two minutes with you, then prescribe an antidepressant that may or may not work better than a placebo and for which this hospital will charge a three-thousand-percent markup, and his decision may or may not be influenced by all the gifts he gets from the pharmaceutical industry. Or you can call me. I have practicing privileges here."

"So those pills are just bogus?"

"The most commonly prescribed antidepressants, the SSRIs, do help many with severe depression, but mild cases are better served by therapy. I don't believe depression is a single disorder splayed across a severity spectrum. I think it's two separate problems, with the milder cases being psychological in nature and responsive to therapy. The severe cases are likely neurological in nature, and medications will work best there. But I won't bore you with our intramural arguments."

"It beats daytime TV."

"One more thing. When you're in the hospital, it's okay to fart at will."

"Yeah, I kind of do that anyway."

"Then we're set."

SMELLING A SKUNK

When Jommers got back to the shop, his nose was assaulted by a stabbing stench before he even got out of the car. Owner Pete Gerzny was standing outside with a scowl on his face, and some of the mechanics had tied red shop rags over their faces to block the smell, making them look like a bunch of grease-covered bandits.

Jommers walked over to Pete, who explained that a fleet customer had brought in a tractor-trailer rig that had run over a skunk, and the vile beast had "splatterized" across the undercarriage of the trailer. The rig was owned by a small local grocery store chain, which wanted the miasmic gunk cleaned off as soon as possible so that the odor would not affect any food hauled in the trailer. Technically, the job did not exactly fall under the heading of repair, but the grocery chain was a good customer, so Pete didn't want to turn away the business.

The rig was left out in the yard, and an unlucky guy in the shop was chosen to blast the undercarriage with a steam cleaner. The steamer had done the trick, but in doing so had aerosolized the skunk juice and created a large spreading puddle of overcooked skunk stew, both of which exacerbated and disseminated the foul odor.

Some of the mechanics were ribbing the poor soul stuck with the job, but Jommers didn't see any humor in any of it. He, after all, lived upstairs. He would have to smell it all night long.

It was right then that Chief Scubbetts pulled in the yard.

"Well, look who's here," Pete muttered, "The mountain zombie." Pete had noticed a peculiar social cluelessness about Scubbetts the first time he had shown up looking for Jommers. After that initial encounter, Pete had described Scubbetts's behavior as that of a pigeon with a concussion. While it was true that Pete disapproved of many people, he genuinely loathed only a few, and Scubbetts was among them.

The chief parked his black Hummer H2 SUV in the far corner of the lot, then, amazingly, walked across the yard right through the skunk broth without seeming to even notice it. Pete shook his head, rolled his eyes, then walked away to avoid contact.

Jommers led Scubbetts up the stairs to his office. As they sat down, Jommers apologized for the stink in the air. When Scubbetts answered that it didn't seem that bad, Jommers wondered if all those cigars had somehow cauterized the man's olfactory system, or if something else was at play. Jommers knew, for example, that sociopaths had a high threshold for disgust. You couldn't gross them out.

"Talk about stink," Scubbetts said. "I was raised on a chicken farm in Arkansas. We had this huge pond in the back. Only it wasn't filled with water. It was filled with chicken shit. So that's what you smelled all the time. That's what your clothes and your hair smelled like all the time. In the summertime, the heat made it bubble, like boiling pudding. The girl that lived there, she would shoplift bars of Lux soap at the pharmacy in town, and at night, she would sleep holding a bar of soap under her nose. I guess for the scent. She held it even when I was on her."

"The girl—you mean your sister."

"No. She was their girl."

"Whose girl?"

"The guy who owned the place. He was my old man's brother."

"You mean your uncle."

"Right."

"So the girl was your cousin."

"Right."

"Where were your parents?"

"They were already gone by then. The old man, he lost some fingertips at the lumber mill. The hand got infected, then his arm got all black. Then he died. It was about a year or so after that, the old lady, she gets some rotten teeth pulled, and she gets infected. Her whole head gets all puffy big and red, like a giant rotten tomato. Then she went crazy and died. So that's when I got sent to the farm. Losing fingers or teeth is never a good thing, but in the city, it usually isn't a fatal thing. But medical care out in the savage nowhere—good luck. You're just another critter in the woods as far as the world cares. I don't know how much it's changed since then, if any. Once I joined the army, I never went back."

Jommers always marveled at how a man with such peculiar speech patterns and stunted social skills could run an urban police department, or how he had even gotten through the interview process to begin with. To Scubbetts, the brief reminiscence constituted pleasant chitchat. To Jommers, the revelations were every bit as chilling as the recollections of a patient in a psychiatric hospital. In both cases, Jommers concealed his reactions behind the mask of an amiable sphinx. But he could not escape the troubling question in his head: why should such a disguise be necessary with someone who wasn't a patient?

Maybe it was the weirdness of the man, a cold, clever schemer who was also short-tempered, peculiar, and socially inept. A man who was preternaturally aware of threats and the weaknesses of others, yet blind to his own strangeness. He acted without hesitation or a clue. A one-eyed hawk swooping into the field, unaware of its missing view.

But the fact that Scubbetts was even making an ungainly effort at small talk was indicative of a phase change. The chief was not subtle about his carrot-and-stick approach to relationships. The hostility he had exhibited to Jommers yesterday was the stick part. Today's clumsy effort at camaraderie was what passed for carrot.

"It's good to see you playing ball again," Scubbetts said.

"What do you mean?"

"I heard from Human Resources. I found out that you declined to approve Detective Voros for return to duty as I requested. I also found out that, while you did clear Patrolman Biederbach, he unexpectedly put in for two weeks' vacation time. So he won't be right back either. Not sure what you did with him, but nice job."

"Just for the record, my decision on Detective Voros was based on my professional judgment, not on your personal request. And I had nothing to do with Patrolman Biederbach's vacation request. That was his decision."

"I don't care how you did it or what you need to call it at your end to feel comfortable. It was good work. Try not to screw up getting a compliment."

Jommers felt his blood simmer at the suggestion of compliance, but he kept his resentment behind the screen as he debated whether to argue the point further. The appearance of performing favors only elicited more such requests. On the other hand, the illusion of cooperation might keep Scubbetts off Jommers's back while he tried to sort out the issues with Voros and Biederbach. Less interference could yield faster progress.

Jommers let it slide. During his internal deliberation, Scubbetts had extracted one of his monster cigars, ceremoniously punch-cut a hole in the drawing end, then gotten the black rod smoldering with his double-jet lighter.

After fogging the room with the first few puffs, the chief held the grand cigar aloft with gravitas and authority, striking a Churchill-like pose. He clearly imagined himself regal, unaware that his graceless theatrics were borderline comical. The dark roll in his hand looked like a hardened turd afire. It smelled like one, too.

Scubbetts preferred potent, full-strength cigars, nicotine locomotives that were not for the faint of heart. He would brag about how expensive they were, how they were from Honduras or the Dominican Republic, made of tobacco grown from Cuban seed spirited out before the revolution. He also liked them thick and would point out the ring gauge, usually a 50 or bigger. He snorted that slender cigars were more for women yearning to be men or vice versa.

There were two reasons that the chief would occasionally condescend to visit Jommers. One was to project power and presence. He had summoned Jommers in the morning, and Jommers had refused to obey, saying he had appointments. The visit was the chief's way of saying he could not be avoided or ignored.

The second reason for visiting was more sinister. Whenever he desired a private conversation that could not be overheard, especially an off-the-record request for unethical action, he preferred talk away from the station, which preserved the option of deniability.

At the moment, it appeared both reasons were in play.

"I'm baffled here, Chief," Jommers said. "As I noted this morning, you normally want your people back on the line as soon as possible. But these two, Voros and Biederbach, you want them to stay out as long as possible. You were going to explain that contradiction to me."

"Voros . . . she's erratic, unstable. We believe that she has previously existing mental health issues that disqualify her for police work, issues that went undisclosed by her and undetected by us. Furthermore, she creates dissension in her unit, which undermines morale. She isn't fit for this line of work, and so our goal is to get her out of it. Understand, when we do that, we're doing that person a favor. We're helping them to find their true calling sooner, enabling them to make faster progress with it. Don't you agree? What was your take on her?"

"The initial evaluation is more a checklist format designed to detect a potential problem. Identifying the problem and its dimensions will require additional sessions."

"I need to be kept apprised of those. Everything you find out."

"What's your problem with Patrolman Biederbach?"

"We've been building a case against him for some time. Security cameras inside the station have caught him covertly placing subversive literature in locations where it can be found by other police officers. I've had some patrolmen pretend to be sympathetic and engage him in conversation while secretly recording his diatribes. We're hoping to get him past the general ranting and onto inciting something specific so we have a tighter case. Any assistance you can provide would help us expedite matters."

"What do you mean by subversive?"

"There's a radical wacko element embedded into law enforcement, and not only here. I first heard about them at a police chief's conference. They are working peace officers who believe that the federal government intends to implement martial law at some point in the near future and it is their duty to defend against it. So they have secretly sworn amongst themselves not to cooperate with any federal troops or any federal agents deployed to their jurisdiction. Even worse, some of them promise to attack federal troops or agents in such a deployment. So try to envision a bizarre scenario where the National Guard has been called up to deal with a natural disaster or race riot or something, and suddenly you have cops shooting at National Guardsmen. And you have to deal with that on top of the original problem, be it a disaster or riot. Can you imagine the chaos? The anarchy? These people are a cancer on law enforcement. They are seditious, bordering on treasonous. They need to be identified and excised before they spread further into the body."

"Well, I'm not familiar with that particular group, but I have talked with Biederbach, and I recognize his type. In most cases such as his, the inflammatory rhetoric is merely a symbolic fist-shaking. Often it's just impotent rage, a reaction against feelings of powerlessness against changing economic conditions. Sometimes they're people with a victim mentality who feel they've been screwed by a bureaucracy—a bank, insurance company, hospital, or government agency, like the VA. But most often, these views are a means of projecting a persona or identifying with a subculture. Viewpoints are acquired like clothes, selected to complement a particular image. The rhetoric is mostly fashion, the social equivalent of wearing a shoulder patch to identify one's unit or division."

"That's the scary part," Scubbetts said. "That these types are banding together for concerted actions."

"In some cases, perhaps, but increasingly what you see are people who are merely virtual members of a group."

"What do you mean, virtual members?"

"The Internet makes it possible for a loner to subscribe to groupthink without having the face-to-face social interactions that typically occur with traditional groups. So what you get is this paradoxical phenomenon—the solitary disciple. Most of these people are like praying mantises, scary but harmless."

"Most, maybe, but not all. How do you tell them apart? Do you have a magic brain scanner that tells you which guy is just a loopy yapper and which one is a ticking time bomb?"

"No, I don't," Jommers said.

"Can you look at a mob of militia mopes and determine which ones are just the usual brain-damaged cow-humpers and which one will be the next Timothy McVeigh?"

"No."

"Then you implement the mushroom policy," Scubbetts said.

"Mushroom policy?"

"When you walk through the woods, do you personally know which mushrooms you see are edible and which are poisonous?"

"No."

"So you avoid eating or touching any of them. You presume that they're all dangerous until you know otherwise. And that's the sensible thing to do. And people are even harder to figure out than mushrooms. You agree?"

"That's a good point," Jommers said, while glancing at the skunk gunk on Scubbetts's shoes. "By the way, in your efforts to get Voros declared unfit for duty, you may wish to consult with the city law director."

"About what?"

"There have been some localized court decisions around the country that place psychological disorders under scrutiny of the Americans with Disabilities Act. Somewhere down the road, an appeals court decision could set a precedent that limits the scope of psychological evaluations being the basis for dismissal."

"What are you saying, that we can't fire loonies anymore?"

"The law is trending in a direction that requires evidence of occupational pertinence. Meaning that a specific disorder must be identified and then shown how it interferes with a specific job function. For example, if a man develops a fear of heights, then that would disqualify him for a job as a window washer, but not for a job as a barista in a ground-floor coffeehouse. Just something for you to consider."

"In that event, we'll obviously need your assistance in the matter."

"I'll do my job . . . as I see it," Jommers said.

"Speaking of which—your duties include counseling the bereaved families of fallen officers, do they not?"

"Yes, they do."

"I want you to talk to the wife," Scubbetts said.

"You mean Patrolman Tarburn's widow."

"Yes. Sooner is better than later."

"Not a problem. I can go tomorrow."

"Good."

"Will she be expecting me?"

"No. There's been minimal communication at this point."

"I don't understand."

"She's got an attitude problem. She won't talk to us."

"Understandable. Her husband was a decorated police officer who got shot and killed by a fellow police officer."

"Yes, there's that. Then there's the funeral thing."

"Tarburn's funeral."

"Yes. You understand that he was not shot in the line of duty. In fact, he was shot as a felon. By firing his weapon at Detective Voros, he was committing assault with a deadly weapon. So he doesn't get a police funeral."

"You mean he doesn't get the parade. No bagpipers playing 'Amazing Grace,' no line of uniforms saluting as he goes by."

"Correct."

"So in addition to being confused and devastated, Mrs. Tarburn is totally pissed off and not answering any questions from your people."

"Correct."

"So this request isn't really about me assuaging her grief or anger, it's about intelligence gathering. You can't get anything, but maybe I can, right?"

"Bereavement counseling is part of your job function. If, in the process, you should inadvertently acquire information pertinent to our inquiry of the evening's events, then we expect you to so advise us. We all want clarity on this, don't we?"

"Like I said, I'll go see her tomorrow."

"I'll be interested in your report."

Scubbetts then got up and walked out, and just in time. Jommers's sphinx had dissolved and the psychologist was ready to explode. Instead, he grabbed a beer to douse the fuse. When he returned to his desk table with the foaming can, he found his friend and bookkeeper, Claire Maroun, sitting in one of the rockers.

"We need to talk," she said.

THE BOOKKEEPER ALWAYS KNOWS

Decades ago, Jakub Plotska had emphysema so bad he could hardly walk around the truck repair shop he owned and managed, so he'd promoted his best mechanic, Pete Gerzny, to foreman. Pete had supervised the shop while Old Man Plotska passed his time doing paperwork and coughing his brains out.

Pete knew the shop would come up for sale soon and hoped to buy it. Plotska couldn't possibly last much longer, and his two college-educated kids had professional careers and zero interest in owning a truck repair shop.

To make some extra money, Pete took an evening job as bartender at the CZ Bar, not far away. It was a regular stop for a lot of the guys at the mills, including Vic Jommers, Karl's father. Vic always sat at Pete's end of the bar, and the two men became friends. It was Pete who had served Vic his last drink the night he'd rammed his motorcycle into the bridge counterweight.

Back in those days, nobody blamed bartenders for serving someone who drank too much. It was a time when drinkers were held responsible for their own actions. So nobody blamed Pete for what happened that night. Nobody except Pete himself.

He never said it, never even hinted at it, but others around him sensed it and whispered about it. And young Karl heard the whispers.

Pete took an interest in young Karl after his father's death, and took the boy fishing and to ball games. Karl didn't actually like fishing or ball games, but he did like Pete and was happy to see him regardless of where they went. Unlike Vic Jommers, who was moody all the time, Pete had an unflappable steadiness about him that Karl admired. One day when they were driving home from somewhere, the engine blew up on the car. Blew up with such force that it threw the hood open and wrapped it backwards over the windshield. After stopping the car, Pete calmly announced that getting home would take a little longer than usual. If you were on a ship in a storm, Pete would be the guy you'd want at the helm.

Sometimes, when they went to the beach in the summer, Pete brought along his niece, Claire Maroun, so that Karl would have someone to splash around with. She was a girl who had a wise way about her. She was two years older than Karl, and when you're a kid, two years is huge, a different league. At the beach, Karl and Claire debated weighty matters such as whether a humongous Lake Erie carp could bite your toes off and whether it would be inclined to do so while you were wading near it.

By the time Old Man Plotska finally coughed up the ghost, Claire was grown up and Pete begged her to run the office. He wanted someone he could trust to handle the money side of things. She'd agreed to do it for a little while, but then never left.

Karl and Claire had fallen out of touch as they'd grown older, but then reconnected when he'd opened his practice over the shop, now owned by her uncle Pete. And in spite of Karl's fancy college education, she still seemed wiser, excluding the fact that she'd married a jerk who cheated on her. Recalling how she used to beat Karl in their races across the hot sand at the beach, she joked darkly that she'd beat him to divorce court, also.

When Jommers first started the practice, Claire agreed to temporarily handle his billing and books in her spare time for a reasonable fee. She said it would only be until he got established, but this clearly had a floating definition, given that she was still at it years later.

Claire was like vodka—intensely plain. Her porcelain face was framed by flour-white hair cut in a blunt bob, both highlighting her vivid blue-gray eyes. She was an ordinary woman made distinct by a sharp, lively spirit. She would have made a great kindergarten teacher, which was what she had once wanted to be. But sometimes life can be like a drive through the Bends. When the bridge in front of you starts to go up, you have to finagle another route, and heaven knows where you're going to end up.

Claire was wearing her work outfit, navy chinos and a light blue shirt, a uniform look. She wasn't required to dress that way, she just didn't want to wear nice things in a dirty shop environment. Or so she said. Jommers suspected that the real reason behind the unvarying appearance was that she didn't want the goobers in the shop looking her over every day. Nothing to see here, boys, so don't bother looking. While she spent most of her time in the office, when things got busy, she didn't hesitate to hop in a truck that needed moving in or out of the shop. A pair of reading glasses hung around her neck on leashes.

Jommers set his beer down on the table and noticed a stiff paper plate covered with foil.

"I was baking last night," Claire said. "Saved you a few. I know, baking in this heat, crazy. But it's comforting, you know? The idea that if you do everything right, it turns out good time after time. You don't get that from life."

Jommers gingerly lifted up an edge of the foil to peek. "Ooh! Are these those pineapple cheese thingies I love?"

"Yes."

"Oh, you're an angel."

"Perhaps, but at the moment, I'm one of those messenger type angels bringing you news. And it is not the glad tidings kind. There will be no trumpets."

"This would be about the revenue."

"Yes, or more precisely, the absence thereof."

"Well, things have been a bit slow lately."

"Slow?" she said. "Turtles are slow. You're in the speed range of rust. And it hasn't been just lately. I could make some really cool multicolor charts for you, but I think you already know what they'd look like. So what's going on?"

"The health insurance companies are killing this business. Their plans are now structured to favor pharmaceutical solutions over counseling. People are going where they get better reimbursement, not where they get better help."

"So you're saying that all private practice psychologists are tanking?"

"Well, I wouldn't say they're all tanking, but it's fair to say that they're all challenged."

"And would it be fair to say that some are more challenged than others?"

"Okay, I admit I'm not that stellar in the marketing department," he said.

"Don't you think that's kind of a necessity when you're self-employed? What would you say to a pearl diver who admits that he's not that stellar in the swimming department?"

"You're right. I need to crank that up. And I will."

"Here's my other concern. The services you provide to the police department have become the dominant source of revenue."

"Is that a bad thing?"

"Not so much a bad thing, as an iffy thing. You don't have a signed long-term contract with them. It's an at-will arrangement that can be terminated at any time by either party for any reason. From the perspective of municipal government, you're just another vendor, like the guy who stocks the paper products for the city hall johns."

"Thanks for that uplifting observation."

"My point is the fragility of the relationship. Police chiefs come and go in this town. If the next one doesn't like you, you're toast. If you tick off this one, you're toast. Then you'll be begging Pete for a job fixing trucks."

"I'm aware of that."

"Which is my other concern. Will the importance of holding on to the police business affect your judgment in handling cases?"

"That's kind of beyond the realm of finances, isn't it?"

"I'm not just your bookkeeper. I'm your friend. Remember? And I'm not sure how many of those you have."

"I've got lots of friends."

"You've got lots of acquaintances. Lots of drinking buddies. But if your head got in a dark place and you were having trouble coping, how many of them could you call for help? If you broke your leg tomorrow, how many of those buddies would be willing to go to the grocery store for you? You know lots of people in lots of places, but you're not rooted. You're a rambling man who doesn't go anywhere. You lead the same life, only without racking up the miles."

"I think you're overstating somewhat."

"Am I? That guy who was shot down here the other night, you knew him. He's been here. I know that because his name is in the books. You knew before it hit the news. So somehow you were involved. And ever since then, you're walking like you got a cement truck on your back, yet you don't say boo to me about it, you don't say boo to Pete. Are you talking to somebody somewhere about it? I hope so. Because where I'm sitting, that weight looks pretty damn heavy. If you need to talk, you know where to find me."

She got up to leave, but before walking out the door added one more thing. "And if you should break a leg tomorrow and need someone to get you a stack of your favorite crappy microwaveable meals, I can do that too."

After she left, he stewed about the strangeness of the day and its unusual conversations. More specifically, he fretted about the deal he'd made with Patrolman Biederbach, wondering what event engine he had just fired up. And when he was done with all the pondering, he grabbed the plate of pineapple cheese thingies and wolfed them all down, leaving not a crumb.

DAY FOUR

THE WIDOW AND THE DEVIL

"They ain't letting men in today."

The man making the announcement was slouched over to one side on a wooden porch swing painted robin's-egg blue. He had short hair and a pencil-thin mustache and wore a white collar shirt and navy-blue dress pants, both of which looked like they'd been owned for a long time. His left hand held a brown paper bag with an open bottle of something. The man had obviously stated the entry restriction as a general proposition to avoid admitting that it applied to him specifically.

The Tarburn house was an old, small wooden bungalow that appeared meticulously maintained. Fresh paint. Spotless windows. Carefully designed flower beds with plants arranged by color and height and bounded by red round-top edgers. The tiny front yard boasted lush green grass at the tail end of a hot, dry summer, suggesting a nightly watering with a garden hose that was neatly stored away.

The homes in this part of the inner city were built in the 1920s, but not many looked as good as this one. The area was a patchwork quilt that defied easy categorization. One neighborhood was as well maintained as an upper-middle-class suburb. But a few blocks away, another neighborhood looked like a war zone, a checkerboard pattern of vacant lots and surviving houses in disrepair. Then there were streets and blocks that fell somewhere between the two extremes. A one-minute drive could take you to a different planet with a different civilization.

It was the sociological equivalent of varying microclimates existing within a larger ecosystem. And each microclimate had its own culture and rhythms, its own values and aesthetics, with each easily discerned. In one place, flowers and fresh paint shouted out a defiant song of hope. In another, uncut lawns and sagging gutters grumbled a surrender to despair.

Everybody knows that a cop living on an inner-city street can positively affect its character, help sustain its security and dignity. Jommers wondered how much the presence of Patrolman Earl Tarburn had influenced this well-kept street, and what would happen to it now that he was gone.

Jommers had enough sense to call before coming. During the phone call, the widow, Becca Tarburn, seemed puzzled by the offer of city-paid counseling services, confused as to why she would want to talk to a stranger in such a dark hour, when people normally turn to family and friends. He was about to give up, but then there was a long pause on the phone, after which she asked him to repeat his name. When he did so, she curiously changed her mind and suggested he should stop by.

After Jommers rang the doorbell, two women appeared at the door, holding corn brooms like guardians wielding poleaxes. He identified himself, and a woman's voice from behind them approved his admittance. The guardians opened the door only slightly, forcing him to squeeze through sideways. Immediately after, he understood why.

The man on the porch swing seized the opportunity by jumping up and trying to follow Jommers inside the door. The intruder quickly came under assault by the two women with brooms, who jabbed and poked the intruder with the hard end of their broomsticks. They were not gentle warning pokes, but vigorous spearing jabs intended to cause pain. The interloper yelled and protested, but eventually retreated. He shouted his complaint.

"Becca! Why do you do this to me? I'm your brother-in-law. Earl told me that I should look after you if anything ever happened to him."

"He never said any such thing."

"I came here to help, Becca."

"You came here to mooch. Go home."

"I ain't a moocher. That ain't right."

"You are a moocher. Now, go home."

"Aw, Becca."

The brother-in-law stepped back from the door, but instead of following instructions to leave, he parked himself back on the porch swing, then took a swig from whatever bottle was in the brown paper bag.

Jommers stood inside the door, carefully choosing not to advance a single inch until invited to do so. The two women with corn brooms gave him a stern gaze and maintained their guardian posture. Then Becca Tarburn approached and gave a silent nod, and the two guardians withdrew to the sofa.

The widow was tall and sturdy and stood with a stiff, formal posture. She wore a long, traditional-style gingham dress. Jommers guessed that her fitness and lioness poise came not from a gym, but from the daily activity of a traditional, hard-working life. He discerned an old-school sensibility about her, one that held that easy chairs are for company, that decent people kept busy in their waking hours.

Her demeanor was predictably somber, but her face betrayed a hint of curiosity about the man who stood before her.

Speaking softly, he again advised her of the availability of bereavement counseling provided at city expense, the ostensible reason for his presence. The words sounded hollow and dry. He suspected that, given her character and social support network, she would no more need a therapist than she would need a butler or a chauffeur. After a long pause, she confirmed that suspicion, but declined the offer graciously, and thanked him for the business card he gave her.

Jommers again offered his condolences, then as he turned to leave, she read his name aloud off the card.

"Karl Jommers."

He stopped.

"This name," she said. "This name and number was on Earl's cell phone. He called you that night."

Jommers nodded. "Yes."

"There's so much I don't understand about what happened," she said.

"Yes. There's much that puzzles me, as well."

So there it was, hanging in the air, the unstated negotiation, the real reason for him being there. They each wanted answers that only the other could offer. It was her move. If the conversation continued, it would have nothing to do with counseling, but an implicitly understood mutual intelligence-gathering opportunity.

"You serve the police department," she noted. "You are its emissary, I gather."

He understood perfectly what she was really asking. Can I trust you, or are you a stooge for the chief?

"I'm not part of police department staff. I'm an independent psychologist who does counseling work for them as a private contractor. With the exception of job-related personnel evaluations, my conversations are kept confidential." He paused, knowing he had not yet sealed the deal. "I can't pretend that Earl and I were close friends, but he was more than just some man who passed through my office. We talked of many things, including his love of the stars. My expression of sympathy is not just a polite formality, it is deeply felt."

She stared at him intently with test-probe eyes, cold and sharp, checking the continuity of his soul. She then slowly raised her right hand, inviting him to step into the small living room. He walked in gingerly, as if the floor were fragile and might break beneath his feet. But he did not sit down. He would do nothing without invitation. He was on trial.

"This is my cousin Althea and my friend and neighbor Velma. We were going through some old pictures, looking for things to put on the board at the funeral home."

Jommers smiled and nodded at them. He subtly scanned the room, moving his eyes, but not his head. The interior of the small house was spare, but comfortable. Everything was as traditional and tidy as the exterior. The coffee table had several magazines neatly arrayed in his-and-hers fashion: his issues of *Sky and Telescope* and *Popular Science* on one side, her issues of *Family Circle* and *Good Housekeeping* on the other. In between was the thing that they both shared: a well-thumbed leather-bound King James Bible. Wall hangings were few but included framed prints of a cornucopia and a lighthouse, a decorative piece of cloth embroidered with the Serenity Prayer, and some family photos. Then Jommers's eyes fixed on the telescope.

"There she is," he said.

"Yes, there she is, the mistress who lured him out into the night." Her tone revealed a trace of scorn, but the fact that Jommers knew of the telescope confirmed that he did know her husband. "What else do you know?"

He knew what she meant. He was to go first.

"Earl was having a bad night," Jommers said. "There was something wrong with him. He was highly agitated, almost in a state of panic, terrified that someone was after him. I'd known him for years, known him to be the steadiest man I'd ever met. This wasn't him. There was something in him. I suspected some type of chemical exposure. It was the only thing I could think of. He had participated in a raid on a meth lab earlier that day. Perhaps he encountered something there. It was the only thing that made sense to me. I wanted to take him to the hospital and tried to talk him into going with me. He refused. It was agreed that he needed to be taken to the hospital as soon as possible, involuntarily, if necessary."

"It was agreed by whom?"

"By myself and Chief Scubbetts."

"I see."

"We couldn't leave him loose in that condition. He was armed, grabbing his gun every time he heard a noise, every time a person walked by. His condition was worsening. It could not be allowed to continue. Detectives were sent to bring him to the hospital."

"And you assisted?"

"I did not. Police procedures and regulations are very clear on the involvement of civilians in such actions. I'm allowed to advise before and after, but I am not permitted to participate in the action."

"So you didn't see what actually happened?"

"No, I did not."

She did not appear satisfied with what she heard, but Jommers went for his part of the deal nonetheless.

"Can I ask you if you observed any unusual behavior in Earl prior to that evening?"

"He was fine until that day. The weekend before it, he was almost giddy, talking about how the cherry tomatoes were about to come ripe in the back. He couldn't stop fussing over them. Like a boy shaking wrapped Christmas presents. He was still fine when he went off to work Monday morning. But when he got home . . . that's when things were wrong."

"Wrong in what way?"

"He was all jumpy and antsy, upset about something. I already knew about the raid going bad. He called after to tell me he was all right. I should have asked what was troubling him. But I was selfish. I surrendered to my anger."

"What were you angry about?" Jommers asked.

"As soon as he came in the door, I could smell it on him, the cigar smoke. It was strong, so it wasn't just secondhand from someone else. I knew he had smoked. You understand, no one smokes in this house. We consider it a sin. We are to be good stewards of the life we have been so graciously given. So we had words. Unkind words. Words I now regret. He said he felt obliged when his commanding officer insisted they share a smoke while chatting."

"You mean the chief."

"Yes, the vassal of the void. Earl was loyal to a fault, but I reminded him of the higher loyalty. Jesus said that a man cannot serve two masters. When earthly rulers veer off God's path, you must choose who to follow. I could not know that my scolding would be our last words."

She hung her head down, eyes closed.

"What did you mean by that phrase, the vassal of the void?" Jommers asked.

"I met the chief only once. Before he even spoke, I sensed a preternatural malevolence. I'd felt this only once before in my life. Many years ago, I'd gotten off a bus and was walking down a main street at night. Shops and stores were already closed. And as I walked by a vacant storefront, I had the sense that somebody or something was in there watching me walk by. I turned my head to look. It was mostly dark inside, but some of the streetlight spilled inside. All I could see was shadows, but I could feel its presence. It isn't a slithering beast like in the movies, not some dragon in a fairy tale. It is the endless maw of emptiness, the nothingness that has a name."

"You think the chief is evil."

"You don't?"

"He is peculiar, to be sure," Jommers said. "And he presents a confrontational posture that he imagines necessary for a command position. But I don't know him that well. Our discussions are formal and business-related. My job often requires a sense of detachment, like a prison dentist, who must focus on the teeth and not their owner. I must deal with Chief Scubbetts in order to help those who work for him."

"A noble sentiment. I hope it isn't detached from reality."

"If we could go back to that day for a moment . . . the idea of possible exposure to something . . . had he done anything that involved chemicals? Painting, gluing, spraying insecticide on the lawn, putting fluids in the car?"

"No," she said.

"Was he the type to take folk or herbal remedies?"

"No."

"Was he the type who might pick and eat something wild in the woods? Wild berries? Wild mushrooms? Wild carrots?"

"No."

"Was he suffering from any infections? Or had he recently exhibited a fever?"

"No."

"Any sleeping trouble or fatigue issues?"

"No."

"Was he taking any medications, either prescription or over-the-counter?"

"He was taking some pills prescribed by a gastroenterologist. He wouldn't say specifically what for, just a problem down below was all he said. He'd been taking them for some time now. I suppose you want to see them."

"If it's not too much trouble."

She stepped out of the room and returned a minute later, handing Jommers a small brown plastic pill container. He could see by the original fill date and the refill number that she was right, Earl had been taking it for a while.

"Scopolamine," Jommers said. "It's commonly prescribed for irritable bowel syndrome, which is maybe why he didn't want to talk about it. In a very miniscule number of cases, scopolamine can cause severe side effects, including agitation, confusion, delusions, paranoia, and even hallucinations."

"But he'd been taking it for some time with none of those problems," she said.

"Here's the thing. Multiple drugs or chemicals in the body can have synergistic effects, meaning that the combined effect can be different from and greater than the effect of any one substance by itself. We know that he smoked a cigar, which may not sound like a big deal. But I happen to know that the particular kind of cigar the chief smokes is gigantic and packs a potent amount of nicotine. For someone who doesn't normally smoke, the effect of the nicotine surge would be fierce and dizzying if he smoked the whole thing. It has also been suggested that Earl's gas mask came loose briefly during the raid on the meth lab and that he may have inhaled some noxious fumes there. If that's true, then it's possible that those three substances working in concert could have caused Earl's altered state that night."

"Is that what you believe?"

"It's my best guess given the limited information I have. We likely won't ever know for sure. I know that's not what you want to hear. But you were wondering what happened and why. This may be as close as you get to the why. When he called you after the raid to tell you he was all right, did he say anything else about it, the things that happened at Eggers Court? The bystanders?"

"No, but he wouldn't. We had an arrangement. I approved of a public service career that maintains order in the world, but I knew he would see and hear ugly things on the job, and I did not want those ugly things brought into my home. I wanted our son to grow up in a wholesome environment. So we agreed that he would leave the job at the door, like a pair of muddy work boots."

"No shoptalk."

"That's right."

"So you wouldn't know if his cop buddies had a nickname for him."

"I wasn't aware of any. Why?"

"The detectives that were sent to bring him in, they were told to call him a nickname—Early Bear—that it might calm him, signify the approach of friends, not enemies."

"I've never heard that." She left the room briefly, then returned with a pen and a small rose-tinted lined notepad that featured an illustration of a rooster at the top of each page. She wrote down the name Early Bear on the pad, and then froze as she stared at it.

"I'm sorry. I can't look at this anymore. A while back, I'd read this magazine article about how you can only hold seven things in your working memory at one time, and if you try to add one more, something else falls off the shelf. So one day when I was in one of those closeout stores, I happened to see a pile of these notepads going for some ridiculously low price. I think I bought the whole pile. So I got in the habit of using them to write things down. Things to do, things to get. It got to be funny after a while. Earl would kid me and say, there she goes again, rapping with that rooster. On Monday night, after I got the call that he wasn't coming home, I sat down, numb, not comprehending. Alone, so utterly, completely alone. If you had put me in a hole on the moon, I could not have felt more alone. I don't know how long I sat like that, but then I snapped to. And suddenly, my head was filled with all the things I had to do. Arrangements to be made. People to call. How to get Eric home from band camp. I reached for one of these notepads, and I swear I heard Earl's voice say, there she goes again, rapping with that rooster."

Her eyes closed and her face tightened into a grimace of pain. Her body flinched as she tried unsuccessfully to stifle sobbing.

Jommers's instinct as a person was to say or do something to comfort her. But his training as a therapist reminded him: you cannot imagine what she is feeling, you cannot know what she needs or wants. So he chose to offer a respectful silence, knowing that sometimes grief is a prayer that should not be interrupted.

In the brief quiet moments that passed, her face reshaped from a grimace of pain into a scowl of anger. She looked up with barely controlled rage.

"They shot him in the face, so I have to keep the casket closed at the funeral home. Somebody from the department calls me the next morning. I'm expecting them to express regret or sympathy. Instead, they ask me if there is any police property in the house that they need to pick up. I get another call later. I think, okay, this will be the expression of sympathy. But no, there is no sympathy. They call to tell me bluntly that they won't be giving him an official police funeral because of the circumstances. So I am on my own with arrangements. All those years of loyal service, and that's how they treat him at the end. They are soulless, heartless creatures. They are not the second family as he saw them. They are false allies, betrayers. They will not be welcome at the funeral. They will not be welcome in my home. They will not be welcome in the house of honor."

Jommers began to feel like he was no longer welcome either. He again expressed his condolences, apologized for the intrusion, and thanked her for her time. She responded coldly.

"You would do well to remember the lesson that Earl forgot," she said. "A man cannot serve two masters."

Jommers nodded politely and walked out the door. As he did, the brother-in-law got up off the porch swing, seeing another opportunity to gain entry. Jommers stood in his path and spoke in a low, threatening voice.

"Step back."

The man gave Jommers an indignant look, but obeyed.

As Jommers drove away from the house, he thought about the phone call Becca Tarburn had gotten Tuesday morning, the one asking about police property. Whoever had called clearly wanted the bag that Earl Tarburn had carried with him that night, but they didn't want to make it obvious. Jommers had considered asking her about it, but figured if she had seen it, she would have mentioned it on her own. There was no reason to put any more unanswered questions in her head.

He also thought about her subtle, but not unreasonable, allegation that he was the chief's emissary on a reconnoiter. And the juke in his head started playing Eddie Boyd's "Third Degree," where the singer bemoans a string of false accusations.

He looked at his watch and put it all out of his head. It was Spreckels time.

Larry was puzzled.

"Pomma what?"

"Pomegranate juice."

Yolanda Arroyo, the police reporter for the *Ledger*, had slid onto the bar-stool next to Jommers at the bar and was trying to order some pomegranate juice from Larry, who was not comprehending what it was, but fairly certain he didn't have it. She eventually settled for orange juice. The color and thickness of it suggested that it had been around almost as long as some of the wall decorations. She looked at it, sniffed it, and refrained from trying it.

"If I recall, your predecessor was more of a whiskey man," Jommers said.

"That's what I hear," she answered. "Maybe that has something to do with why he's in hospice now, dying of esophageal cancer."

She was a short, young, dark-haired woman, with large dark brown eyes and an alert, kinetic demeanor. She wore a turquoise skirt and a white blouse. He wasn't surprised to see her chase him for a comment, but this was the first time she tracked him down to Spreckels. In the past, she had always dropped by his office. It was kind of like a ritual or dance. She would politely make inquiries. He would politely decline to comment. But a good reporter, like a good sales-man, keeps going back, because maybe, just maybe, on that forty-seventh cast of the line you get a bite.

"You can save your breath," he said. "I have no comments."

"How about off the record, or background only, just to give me a place to start?" she asked.

"Sorry."

"There's something going on. A police officer participates in a botched raid that ends up with bystanders dead, and that same night, he himself ends up dead, shot by another police officer. Is that a coincidence?"

"You should direct that question to the police department's public affairs officer," he said.

"He says they can't say anything until they finish their investigation."

"Sounds prudent to me."

"But that's always their tactic. Delay, and more delay, hoping we'll lose interest."

"Or, maybe they understand that releasing incomplete versions of events leads to erroneous conclusions that become impossible to erase in the public's mind. You can't unring a bell."

"The people have a right to know what's happening," she said. "And they want to know now."

"They want to know now because your trade has created the false expectation that they can know now. You have conditioned them to be like children demanding instant gratification. Unfortunately, the world is not a vending machine that dispenses all desired information at the touch of a button. Sometimes knowledge emerges slowly, and you just have to wait for it, like an archeologist gridding off a site and patiently brushing off one thin layer of earth at a time because the position of a fossil in three-dimensional space will prove crucial in understanding its significance."

"Oh, wonderful. My managing editor will love that as an excuse. Look, you don't have any idea how hard it is to get straight information out of PD. When I first asked the public affairs sergeant about the shooting at Crone Point, he flat-out lied to me, pretended not to know who the victim was yet. So I asked him if he wanted me to write the usual in such cases, that you want the public's help with any information they have, and so on, and he says no. That's when I know he knows, that he is lying to me. I confront him on it, and then he says, they think they know who it is, but they haven't made positive ID yet, and when they do they'll have to notify family first, yada yada. They didn't want me to know. So you know how I find out? By going to Fleck's Diner and walking up to the first cop I see. Everybody on the force knew the whole story at that point by word of mouth. Now then, scanner traffic that night mentioned a Code 5122, and you know what that means. And since the Code 5122 referred to a cop, the situation almost certainly involved you somehow. So you're saying that's there's absolutely nothing we could talk about here?"

"Well, we could talk about the abysmal state of health reporting by media today, how they sound false alarms one day, promote false cures the next. We could talk about how they play up stories about meaningless observational studies. Or we could talk about how most journalists continue to carelessly misuse psychological terms like schizophrenic or split personality, stupidly suggesting it means dual personality, when in fact it refers to a split from reality."

"Sounds interesting, but not my beat."

"Too bad."

Arroyo looked down at her cell phone, read a text message, frowned, sighed, then shook her head.

"I have to go," she said.

"You're looking more stressed these days," he said.

"There's been another round of layoffs, and another round of pay cuts. So we're all working longer hours for less pay. Nice career choice on my part, huh? Yet we're told to be grateful, because this time next year, the paper might not even be around. So what's it going to be like when there's no reliable source of information anymore, and all that's left is rumors, rhetoric, and thirty-seven flavors of bullshit?"

"It'll be like today, only with more flavors."

She scowled as she rose to leave. "You can have my orange juice."

After she'd gone, Larry strolled over.

"Hey, did you know that a bull has cartilage in its schwantz?"

"I did not know that," Jommers said.

"Yeah. I'm guessing that if guys were packing cartilage in their pokers, they wouldn't need those boinga boinga pills much."

"I'm guessing you're right."

"Animals got all the cool ideas," Larry went on. "Owls have night vision. Bats got that sonar thing. Sharks are always growing new teeth, so they don't have to worry about flossing—"

"Somebody's been watching the nature shows again."

"Then there's these ocean birds called shearwaters that have a desalinization thing in their noses that allows them to drink seawater. And vultures. Talk about leftovers. They can eat all kinds of rotten dead stuff because their stomach acid is so strong it kills bacteria, even anthrax and botulism."

"That could be a beneficial attribute for patrons dining at this establishment. By the way, have any of those shows ever explored the formation of biofilms in keg lines and their deleterious effect on beer flavor?"

"And cockroaches. Those suckers can go a month without food. And whales. A sperm whale can hold its breath for over an hour—"

"Another potentially useful feature for Spreckels patrons, particularly when using the restrooms."

"But look at us. We don't even have fur to keep us warm. Well, except for that Dion guy who comes around. He's got a good coat going. But the rest of us—it's like we're nature's losers."

"Except for the part about there being six billion of us crowding all the rest of them off the planet."

"Yeah, except for that part," Larry said.

"But, hey, you want to talk interesting creature capabilities, how about one that can exert mind control?"

"What? No way."

"Seriously," Jommers said. "There's this parasite, *toxoplasma gondii,* that infects mice. But it can only reproduce in the gut of a cat. Now then, if you're a sane mouse, you've got a healthy fear of cats and you run like hell away from them. So this parasite gets itself into the mouse's brain, the part that controls fear, and makes the mouse unafraid of the cat. So that makes it easier for cats to catch and eat the mouse, which then puts the parasite back where it wants to be, in a cat's gut."

"Whoa! That is creepy. I wonder if the mice I got here got that thing in them. They been acting pretty ballsy lately."

"Get a cat."

"Hey, what if it turns out that everyone with a loose lug nut just has some bug in the brain and all he's got to do is take some deworming pill to get normal? Wouldn't that be cool? Of course, you'd probably be out of a job then."

"Yeah. You too."

Jommers was neither a mind reader nor a fortune-teller, but such skills were occasionally expected in cases where he was asked to predict the likelihood of a police officer using excessive force in the future after an incident.

His early-afternoon appointment, Patrolman Ongskew, was one of those cases. The cop had two serious complaints lodged against him, and after the most recent one, disciplinary hearings were scheduled. But the department wanted Jommers's opinion as well. Specifically, they wanted advice on whether the officer could be rehabilitated with some anger management courses or whether he should be kept off the streets altogether by either reassignment or termination.

Patrolman Ongskew wasn't making it easy. He recounted the incidents with an impassive voice and demeanor, exhibiting neither defensiveness or regret. Just the facts.

Jommers, as usual, avoided any hint of judgmental tone that might inhibit candor.

So it was a sphinx interviewing a sphinx.

"Okay," Jommers said. "Tell me about the first one."

"Sure. I answered a call about a belligerent drunk hassling people for money outside a nightclub. I think he was both drunk and stoned. I gave him the option of simply moving on, but he gets belligerent with me, too, so I thought he needed a night in the tank. Right after I get him in the back of the cruiser, he passes out. At some point later, he wakes up and doesn't know where he is. He sees the separator between front and back and thinks he's in a taxicab. So he starts looking for the driver ID and permit like you would see in a cab, and when he doesn't see it, he starts yelling, 'Where's your tag, man? Where's your tag?' I tell him to shut up. But instead he starts screaming louder. 'Where's your tag, man? Where's your tag?' And then he starts kicking the separator behind my head. So, after a few minutes of this, I'd had enough. I pulled over somewhere, opened up the back and used the stun gun on him."

"Once, or more than once?"

"It was multiple times. I don't remember the exact number."

"And what was going through your head at the time?"

"He was like a wild animal that needed to be tranquilized. So I tranquilized him."

Ongskew said it matter-of-factly, with neither pride nor shame.

"Okay," Jommers said. "Tell me about the second one."

"Sure. I arrested a rent boy for soliciting down in front of the bus station. I had arrested him several times in the past for the same thing at the same location. So there were no formalities. We both understood the process. So I'm taking him back to Central, but on the way he said he needed to use a bathroom and real quick. I told him we were just a few blocks away from the station, that he could just hold it. But he doesn't. Somehow he able to wriggle his pants down a bit and just splatters the whole backseat of the cruiser. You know, when they take too many loads up the chute, it acts like an enema. So you have that whole mess all over the back. And the smell was horrific. Like it wasn't even from a human. It's the drugs that do that. The drugs make it smell like that."

"So how did you handle that?"

"I didn't go right back to the station. I drove down to the Bends, pulled the cruiser under a bridge, one of those places where no one is around. Then I put on some rubber gloves, grabbed my pepper spray, opened the back door and just started spraying him."

"For how long?"

"Until the can was empty. Then I got another one and emptied that."

"And what was going through your head at the time?"

"It was like I'm using disinfectant to clean a public bathroom. You got to use maximum strength. You got to disinfect."

He described the second incident with the same dispassionate attitude as the first, with no trace of judgment on his own behavior.

Jommers was perplexed. The level of detail that Ongskew had included in the accounts was surprising. Normally a cop in this situation tries to downplay what he did while playing up the justification for it. Was he trying to curry favor by a display of honesty? Or was his stark candor just his way of saying he didn't see anything wrong with what he did?

Also unusual was Ongskew's dress attire. It's common these days for people to visit the doctor or dentist or therapist in casual clothes, even blue jeans and T-shirt. And in Jommers's work, he occasionally got the defiant cop wearing one of those cop T-shirts expressing a cynical attitude with dark humor. On one such occasion, a cop had come in wearing a T-shirt that said, "My favorite ammo is double-aught turdshot." Underneath the words was a drawing of a dead man riddled with holes.

But Ongskew, who was only thirty-six, looked old-school in a navy-blue suit and tie with freshly polished black dress shoes. He sat straight and answered all questions respectfully. And that made him an enigma. He seemed to understand the seriousness of the interview, but not the seriousness of what he'd done.

Jommers knew from experience that there was always an X factor. If a cop was accused of being bad twice, he'd likely been bad two plus X times, with the two representing only the number of formal complaints. Most victims of police brutality don't bother to file a complaint unless there are witnesses. So Jommers asked his usual question, paying close attention to the cop's expression when he answered.

"Were there any other incidents of a similar nature that maybe didn't make it into the files?"

"There may have been occasions where I was overly enthusiastic in handling a situation, possibly, but I don't recall any other specific ones at the moment."

It was a too-clever answer, one that didn't add to the evidence, but one that didn't constitute an outright lie that could be confronted later.

"So there might be more incidents of this nature, but you don't recall?"

Ongskew paused, as if calculating his response.

"You know, I'm not one of those cops who goes looking for this. I don't seek opportunities to do it. I go to work hoping to have a normal day."

"You don't have a normal job, so you don't get to have a normal day. You were trained to deal with the abnormal day, which includes the proper handling of provocation and confrontation."

"What I mean is that I'm not the one who makes it happen. They make it happen. They initiate the chain of events that lead to the incidents."

"So it's all their fault?"

"Mostly, yes. I mean, you know what I look like in uniform. I'm wearing a badge. I got a radio clipped on my shoulder so I can call for backup in a heartbeat. I'm carrying a gun. I got a stun gun. A nightstick. Pepper spray. Handcuffs. And you can see all that stuff in full view. So when you can see all that potential hurt standing in front of you, why on earth would you even think of messing with me? Why? It's like they want it to happen. They do everything possible to make it happen. What's wrong with their head that they would do that?"

"Well, we could ruminate about that, but this chat is not about them. It's about you. Dealing with provocation is part of your job. If you can't handle provocation, then you can't handle the job. So are you saying you can't handle the job?"

Ongskew paused again. Recalculating.

"I'm not a bad person, I'm not a bad cop."

"But you have done bad things."

"I had a couple of bad days where bad things happened. Everybody does. Some of it gets logged, some of it doesn't."

"So you're saying everybody does it, you're just the one who got caught."

Pause. Recalculate. "I've put in over thirteen years, and these are the only two marks against me."

"Do you recognize the gravity of those two things?"

"They were obviously considered important for me to be here."

"Do you recognize that what you did was wrong?"

"It was definitely improper procedure."

"Do you recognize it as morally wrong, that it's wrong to harm another human being unnecessarily?"

"I agree, I should not have done it. You're right."

"The department wants my advice on whether you will do something like this again. What should I tell them?"

"Well, no. I won't."

"Why not? What specifically will you do differently to see that it doesn't?"

"Well, I'll practice changing my response, show more self-discipline."

"That's it, change your response? This isn't just a bad habit like cursing or eating too many donuts. You can't just put a little note on your dashboard that says 'don't hurt anybody today.' You have to recognize on a fundamental core level that it's morally wrong. You don't refrain because you've read five tips for boosting willpower, you refrain because it's just plain wrong, because it's against your internal moral code."

"Yes. You're right. I'll do that."

"The first time this happened—what did you do when you got home?"

"I don't remember."

"Did you discuss it with a wife or a friend?"

"I see lots of bad stuff. It's not good to drag the day home with you."

"Did you cry?"

"No."

"Did you get drunk?"

"No."

"Did you stew about it? Go into a funk?"

"No."

"So it had no effect on you emotionally?"

Pause. Recalculate. "I'm sure it had some effect, I don't remember the specifics. You know, I've got a lot of experience here. I've dealt with a lot of things. I've learned how to handle them. Much like yourself, I imagine. You hear a lot of stuff every day, but you don't go nervous Nellie every day. Your experience teaches you how to deal."

"Why did you want to be a cop? Go after bad guys? Bust heads? Somebody hurt you or your family when you were young?"

"No, no. Wasn't anything like that. It was Old Man Mooney."

"Who's he?"

"He was a guy lived on our street when I was a kid, but everybody on the street looked up to him because he was a cop. They would go to him for advice. Ask him to mediate disputes between neighbors. Be their kid's godfather. Serve as a reference on a job application. It's like he was some tribal elder or something and the street was his village. Thing is, he was just an ordinary guy, that's all. But the badge, it made him special. I guess I wanted to be special like that."

"So it's about the respect. You put on a suit and shined your shoes today to show respect for my position. And when it's your show, you expect people to respect you."

"Yes."

"And when they don't show proper respect, they need to be given a civics lesson. Isn't that the term?"

"I'm not familiar with that term."

"Have you ever hit your wife?"

"No."

"Have you ever cursed at your wife in anger?"

"No. We don't do that."

"You never fight with your wife? You're Ozzie and Harriet?"

"I mean we don't take it that far. We've learned how to fight without going nuclear."

"So you're able to control your temper."

"Yes."

"That proves my point, then, doesn't it? This isn't about anger management. In the pepper spray incident, you were coolheaded enough to put on your rubber gloves before you took care of business. It wasn't an act of impulsive rage. It was a calm, calculated administering of the lesson. And you felt totally justified in doing it."

"Look, I don't do public speaking or community theater, so I can't give you some eloquent spiel to convince you that I get your message. All I can do is tell you . . . I get it. It won't happen again. I understand the trouble I've caused the department and myself, and it's forced me to do a lot of thinking about it."

"And do you understand the pain you inflicted on your victims?"

Ongskew sighed with frustration. "What do you want me to say? What is it you want to hear?"

"Almost anything but that. But maybe you can come up with something better in a different setting. So here's what I want you to do. Take some paper and a pen. Go to a park, bar, coffee shop, or wherever you feel comfortable, and write two letters, one to each victim, in which you both apologize for your actions and attempt to explain them."

"Seriously."

"Yes, seriously. You won't have to worry about them being used against you. When you bring them back, I will look at them briefly and hand them back to you immediately. No one else will ever see them. I want them within three hours."

"How long do they need to be?"

"As long or as short as you feel necessary to achieve the stated objective."

"Okay. I can do that."

～

PATROLMAN ONGSKEW DIDN'T NEED the allotted three hours. He was back in less than forty minutes. He hadn't made much effort with the project. The letters were short, formal in tone, and insincere, like a letter from the city service department apologizing for snowplow damage to your mailbox.

"I know it's not what you wanted," Ongskew said. "But I'm not good with words. I'm just a cop. But a good cop. Yes, I lost it. Lost it twice in thirteen years. I am not a bad cop."

Jommers gave him back the letters, and Ongskew shook his hand politely as if it had been only some minor business meeting.

So now Jommers had to make a recommendation one way or the other. Was it likely true that the patrolman had only lost it twice in thirteen years and that he was basically a decent guy? Could he be trained to better handle disrespect? Inner-city high school teachers and customer service reps get just as much disrespect as a cop, maybe more, and they have to handle it every day. Could he learn from them? Would role-playing sessions help?

Or was he a bad actor who needed to leave the stage as soon as possible? Was he one of those who had gotten away with way too much for way too long and the department should seize the opportunity to be rid of him?

Jommers could request further interviews, administer certain standard tests, but there was no magic in either. Everyone imagines that psychologists have predictive powers in such situations, but they don't. Education and experience make psychologists more perceptive, but not psychic, their judgment no more than an educated guess.

How to lean. Which was the greater error: ruining a redeemable man's career, or putting a monster back on the street?

In voluntary cases, where the police officer sought out the therapist for help with a problem, the first duty was to serve the patient. But in administrative cases, where the officer was compelled to submit to an evaluation, Jommers served the police department and the city and, by extension, the good citizens of Grayton, Ohio.

As a result, it was not unusual for Jommers to switch between serving two masters several times over the course of an ordinary day. And for any given case, it was usually clear who that master was. Usually.

It was after six when Chief Scubbetts called. Jommers looked at the caller ID and declined to answer. Scubbetts left a message wanting to know what Jommers had learned from Becca Tarburn, no longer bothering to disguise intent behind the request to visit her. Jommers decided to return the call the next morning, that his service to Grayton PD was done for the day.

He then drove over to Spreckels, where he was pleased to see a fellow regular and old pal, Connor Quirke, sitting at the bar. Quirke was a corpulent, ruddy-faced middle-aged man with longish white hair that hung over his forehead at a jaunty slant. He was an attorney who specialized in criminal cases and was on a first-name basis with more miscreants than any sane person would care to be. They ranged from the merely mischievous to the frighteningly malevolent, from impulsive idiots to ingenious careerists. Many had simply grown up in a near-feral environment where the illicit was normative, where the letter of the law was a distant abstraction and all that mattered was the law of the street. These types often reacted to their arrest with puzzled annoyance, like a cat being scolded for chomping on the neck of a bird. Regardless of their mindset, they were all just customers to Quirke, and like anybody else, they expected good customer service, which he ably and amiably provided.

Quirke's conviviality belied his astuteness and broad conversance. A typical chat might jump from jocular badinage to a weighty debate, then touch on some local scuttlebutt, then finally alight on a raunchy tale that might or might not be true.

They both had occupations that required professional detachment, that capacity to engage in dispassionate discourse in the face of the bizarre and outlandish. The repeated practice of such skills inevitably induces a worldview that lies somewhere between a serene smirk and plain numbness. The two men had once hatched an idea for a private club called The Wry Bred. But after generating restrictive criteria and reviewing their respective acquaintances, they realized that they were the only two people qualified for membership, making further pursuit of the idea unnecessary. After all, they already had a clubhouse in Spreckels, at which they both shared a nearly perfect attendance.

"Mr. Jommers."

"Mr. Quirke."

"I'm glad you're here. I have a problem that may require your services."

"I already know what it is," Jommers said.

"It's that obvious?"

"The orange powder on the front of your shirt. The orange fingertips on your right hand. You got a cheese puff monkey on your back."

"I thought I could handle it. Then it just slid out of control. I don't even remember how it happened."

"It's the cheese puff paradox. You pick one up, it looks substantial, solid. You try it. But as soon as you start to chew on it, it just dissolves away like it never existed. A palpable something turns to nothing. It's incongruous . . ."

"Yes."

"And your mind, it has evolved to dislike mysteries, so the puzzle must be resolved. Which means you have to take another one in order to figure it out. But the same thing happens again, which only deepens the mystery."

"Yes."

"So you eat another, then another, desperately searching for an unobtainable answer."

"Yes, yes."

"And you keep searching, eating more and more, searching and searching."

"Yes, yes, yes."

"And before you know it, you've been drawn into the cheese puff vortex."

"Oh, God, is there any hope for me?"

"There is no known treatment. The only chance of escape is to relocate to a place where they don't sell cheese puffs."

"Do such places exist?"

"Yes, but they are few. The higher elevations of Nepal, the desert plains of Mongolia, the outlying forested regions in Botswana."

"Damn. I can't relocate now. I just put in a new stamped-concrete patio."

"What pattern?"

"The fake cobblestone."

"I love that look."

"Yeah, well, if you ever do it, pick a darker color than you actually want, because the sun will fade it. I know a guy who went with the red brick look. The sun faded it to pink. Now his neighbors give him shit. The guy with the pink patio."

"Must be hell."

"I'll tell you hell. I have to make closing arguments for a rapist tomorrow. I must pretend to sincerely believe in his innocence, drawing deep upon my thespian talents in a futile effort to convince the jury it was a case of mistaken identity. Throughout the trial, this bug-eyed halfwit has been staring at the female jurors, mentally undressing them and jumping their bones. He was toast from day one. I will be exercising my vocal cords, nothing more."

"But the bill will be paid. You've identified resources beforehand."

"Of course."

"A paid performance requires no applause."

"True enough. Though there is the matter of reputation."

"You do have a reputation. Nobody fakes it better than you."

"Thank you."

"Do you ever get any innocent clients?"

"Occasionally, but, ironically, they are the most difficult to vindicate. The whole experience is so humiliating that the expression of shame on their face makes them look guilty."

"The facts of the matter are of no assistance?"

"Generally, no. Jurors just stare at the defendant and try to divine the truth from his appearance and manner. Everyone imagines themselves a psychic when judging someone else's character. Amusing, given that they rarely have a clear picture of their own."

"You advise your clients on how to dress, comport themselves?"

"Of course. SOP. But they're not professional performers. I'm asking them to hold a certain posture and demeanor for hours on end with no prior acting experience. It's like taking somebody off the street randomly and asking him to perform gymnastic routines on the parallel bars. Success will be limited. If we were truly serious about justice, we would strip out jurors' impressions, force them to focus only on the facts."

"How would you do that?"

"Easy. You remove gut instincts from the equation. You don't let the jury actually hear anyone's testimony. They are only allowed to read transcripts after the fact. They don't even get to see the witnesses or the defendant. All they get to see is text. You take away their opportunity for subjectivity. A jury is meant to be a trier of fact, so the facts are all it requires."

"Interesting idea."

"It's a goddamn excellent idea, but it will never happen. In law, as elsewhere, tradition trumps reason. The inertia of flawed systems makes it impossible to derail them. Criminal justice in this country is so hidebound, it barely surpasses the medieval. A nation that every July celebrates its independence from monarchs should not replicate their regal capriciousness. Injustice delivered from the jury box is no less onerous than injustice delivered from the throne."

"I suspect that such a method would render fewer convictions and that prosecutors would oppose it."

"Naturally. If those crazy bastards had their way, they'd bring back trial by ordeal and summary execution. All they care about is reelection, and the more people you lock up, the more votes you get. And speaking of crazy, what's up with that shooting the other night? Cop shoots another cop, that's some wild stuff going on. Didn't that happen close to you?"

"Yes," Jommers said. "Very close."

"I suppose it will involve you at some point."

"Yes, that it will."

"Any idea what the hell happened?"

"It's too early to tell."

"Well, at least it shouldn't scare off any investors in the Sentinel Bluff project, given that it wasn't a crime actually," Quirke said. "I assume you're aware of the plans?"

"Yes. Some type of humongous upscale condo development with shops and restaurants on the ground floor."

"You don't sound too fond of the idea. In fact, your face just twisted all up like you got a mouthful of Larry's rancid coleslaw and you don't know where to spit it. You should be happy someone wants to invest down here, improve things, give you a better class of company. And don't call it gentrification either, because no one is being displaced. No one lives down here, except a few oddballs like yourself, so it's more like pioneering. Or would you rather see the Bends deteriorate further until nothing is left but a cluster of punch-and-puke palaces?"

"I'm not against redevelopment down here," Jommers said. "But I'd rather see it happen on a smaller scale, you know? In a way that preserves the variety, the whole hodgepodge that makes the place unique."

"The whole Jane Jacobs thing. Small is beautiful."

"Not smallness, per se, but rather a mix of old and new that preserves affordability and diversity."

"You're worried about losing a few starving artists. But maybe they'll get more business."

"Here's the thing," Jommers said. "New construction is expensive, as Jacobs was fond of pointing out. What kind of tenants will you get on the ground floor of this place? Upscale chain stores and upscale chain restaurants, the same kind you find elsewhere. So it becomes a clone thing, with maybe a few token architectural flourishes incorporated as a nod to the locale. But in the end, it becomes just another sterile, upscale theme park. A steel-town version of Epcot Center. Chic kitsch."

"You want the natural ecosystem analogy. Things popping up or disappearing on their own without massive intervention. An unmanaged system."

"Exactly."

"Sounds great, only here's the thing. Have you heard of phragmites?"

"Bugs?"

"No. It's a type of wetland reed grass. Around here it's considered an invasive species that crowds out native vegetation. So there's this marsh out where I live, and the phragmites have taken over. So every year, the park system enlists legions of volunteers to go wade in the muck to help remove phragmites. And it's a constant losing battle. You see the irony here, that the diversity of a desired natural ecosystem cannot be achieved without massive human intervention. Now translate that example to the Jacobs urban ecosystem model. This isn't the '50s anymore, where goods and services are provided by mom-and-pop operations. This is the age of big chains and mobile capital. The pizza chains are driving local shops out of business and the hair-cutting chains are sending Nick the barber into early retirement. Out-of-town money is phragmites. It comes in and takes over your little urban marsh, and Mom and Pop get steamrollered. In other words, the diversity of a Jacobs natural urban ecosystem cannot happen anymore without intervention."

"So then we intervene."

"Sounds simple. But to intervene is to choose a vision. What's the vision? Who gets to choose? And so whichever way you go, there's nothing natural about it. It's somebody in authority somewhere saying this is how it will be. Regulated randomness. It's a non sequitur."

"So you're okay with urban phragmites."

"Aesthetically, no. But if that's the way the world works now, and it is, then I'd rather have the out-of-town money come here than go somewhere else. It'll boost the economy, create jobs. So what's more important, prosperity and revitalization, or preserving the aesthetic integrity of post-industrial ruin? It's a city, not some hellacious open-air museum."

"You know, everybody uses those terms as a justification for getting all orgasmic over new development. Jobs, prosperity. But it's a ruse."

"How so?" Quirke asked.

"Look, aggregate demand in an urban economy is a function of population. A specific quantity of people need a specific quantity of residences and a specific quantity of retail space for goods and services. If the population is stable, or declining like Grayton's, then it's a zero-sum game. Increasing supply does not increase demand. A new thing can only succeed by taking away business from an old thing. For a new house to be occupied, an old house must be abandoned. For a new restaurant to survive, an old restaurant must die. Without any increase in population, development does not increase economic activity, it merely shifts it from one place to another. It's not revitalization. It's a shell game. A con."

"If I may draw attention to a fallacy or two. One, aggregate demand in an urban economy is not solely a function of population; income also matters. Two, population isn't just about body count, but demographic composition. For example, a population loss of two thousand over a year does not necessarily mean that two thousand people departed. It may mean that five thousand people left here and three thousand people came here, and that the two thousand figure just shows the net change in bodies. So let's say that the five thousand who left were low-wage laborers looking for better jobs in the South, and that the three thousand who came here were well-paid professionals with money to spend and an upscale lifestyle that inclines them to spend it. In that scenario, your aggregate demand can increase even though you have lost bodies."

"Is that actually happening?"

"The point is that it can. Look, I know you're a traditionalist and recalcitrant preservationist, but there is no such thing as stasis. Everything moves. Things get better, or things get worse. One way or another, your world is about to change."

DAY FIVE

A PAST REVEALED

Drilling was devised for combat. Specifically, to combat fear. For ages, well-drilled armies have marched steadfastly into the bloody, mangling maw of battle. The drilling instills a conditioned response so that advancing becomes reflexive, bypassing both reason and emotion. You just do it without thinking about it.

Practice drills also benefit athletes and musicians. And fire drills are meant to help children escape burning schools.

Police officers drill to practice for crowd control and riots, and SWAT teams drill for all kinds of hairy situations. Jommers believed that drilling could also aid cops in withstanding provocation. He had once proposed a series of training sessions where actors would realistically attempt to incite police officers, with Jommers providing several routines for the patrolmen to practice resistance. That idea was shot down, but he did get the green light to develop a brief training spiel that could be presented at roll call.

To capture their attention, he began with football video, specifically, video where players were miked, giving the viewer the opportunity to hear the face-to-face trash talking that occurs on the field. Trash talking in football serves a deliberate tactical objective, to break the opponent's concentration so that he makes a mistake—a false start, blown assignment, dropped pass, and so on. In the best-case scenario, the provocation incites a physical response that draws a penalty flag.

Jommers had assembled a number of clips showing the negative consequences of succumbing to taunts and explained how the head game is a separate subset of the overall game. He emphasized the proper response by hitting the mute button in the middle of an on-screen taunt-fest.

"That's what you do. Hit the mute button in your head. Put the image in there. Your finger on the button. Next time someone is giving you crap, you press it, turn off the sound. You don't hear him. It's just a mouth moving with nothing coming out. Remember, it's a head game. He's trying to pull you over the line. Don't be suckered. If you lose it, you lose the game, and maybe your job. You mute, you win. When you control yourself, you control the situation."

Initially, Jommers was proud of his little presentation. By now he'd given it a number of times at the different district station houses and also at the police academy. But the presentation today sounded dry and airless.

He looked around the room at the faces watching him. They were all smiling politely, no wisecracks or sneers. But it was the polite smile you give while attending a wedding or funeral at a house of worship where you don't belong. You display quiet respect for the sacred utterances streaming from the pulpit, but at the same time, you let the words waft on by, like so much cottonwood fluff on the breeze. They are not your words.

He understood why it felt different today—the encounter with Patrolman Ongskew the day before. The conclusion Jommers had arrived at was still echoing in his head. The incidents of violence weren't about controlling the anger impulse, but rather moral character. Each of the faces staring politely at him was unresponsive for one of two reasons. The majority of them who behaved didn't need the lecture. And those who felt it was acceptable to occasionally administer a civics lesson would be unaffected by the lecture. So what was the point, then? Why bother?

The question trailed him out of the room like a troubling odor picked up on clothes. As he started down the hallway, he saw a small figure at the far end, its head wreathed in smoke, standing and staring in Jommers's direction.

Chief Scubbetts was an imposing person only by virtue of his authority and behavior, not by his size. To subordinates, he appeared as a menacing dragon, but to those outside his ranks, the dread he exuded was not that of a hulking beast, but that of a hairy black spider darting in the shadows. The creepiness of venom skulking.

It was nervy for Scubbetts to smoke a cigar in a city building where it was prohibited, but nerviness was part of his uniform. Jommers knew he owed the chief a return call, but was determined not to apologize for it. He strolled down the hall nonchalantly and pretended not to see Scubbetts until he was practically on the man's toes, then, once there mumbled a casual greeting.

"Morning, Chief."

Scubbetts glared back for a few moments before speaking. "The widow."

"Oh, yeah," Jommers said. "You want to know how Becca Tarburn is holding up. She's doing okay. She's a strong woman. Much like her husband was. I think she'll be all right."

"What did she say?"

"Well, she's pissed off. She doesn't understand how or why her husband got shot. Why a good cop isn't getting a good cop's funeral."

"I meant, what does she know?"

"Not much. She's as confused as the rest of us."

"What did she say about me?"

"You didn't come up."

"Did she say if anything had been troubling the man? Particularly about the job?"

"She didn't mention anything."

"What did Tarburn say to her that day about what he was doing, where he was going?"

"He apparently didn't say much," Jommers said. "She had no idea."

"What, the man leaves his house in a tizzy and doesn't tell his wife where he's going? What were their exact words?"

"I don't know, I wasn't there. You need to understand something about their marriage. They had an agreement that he wouldn't talk about the job at home, that he would leave it outside the door like muddy boots. If something was bothering him, he kept it to himself. We'll never know."

That was exactly what Scubbetts had hoped to hear, and his posture loosened slightly, revealing his relief. Jommers declined to tell Scubbetts that Tarburn had been taking scopolamine because Jommers didn't want the department pestering Becca Tarburn. Jommers's objective for this conversation was to ensure that nobody bothered her again, to insulate her from whatever might lie ahead.

"I'm surprised she didn't get hysterical with you," Scubbetts said. "Those people can get really carried away."

"Those people—you mean wives?"

For Scubbetts, sarcasm was like a bullet whistling overhead, not connecting, only hinting at its passage. His vanity prevented him from acknowledging he'd missed something, so he typically dismissed it and kept moving.

"I don't understand why she's upset about not getting the show funeral," Scubbetts said. "I don't get why we even do them. Why all the drama? Where I grew up, when someone dropped, you buried them in the woods. You covered it with rocks or logs so the coons wouldn't dig them up. Then you went back to work."

"Formalizing the grieving process helps people cope with the sense of loss," Jommers said. "It's a path back to normalcy."

"That's circular logic. You learn to get sick over it so you can learn to cure the sickness. If you skip the first part, you don't need the second part. I blame it on the movies. That's where people learn it. People didn't behave this way in the past. All the drama. People carrying on, crying, laughing, screaming, acting crazy. I just don't get it, why anyone would want to watch all that."

"Getting into someone else's head in a movie or a book allows you to take a brief vacation from your own head. Don't you ever feel the need to escape your own thoughts, Chief?"

"I never run. Not from anything. Or anyone."

"Well, I've got to run. Busy day—oh, wait. One more thing. I've got an idea for adding another training session."

"I'll bet you do."

"In light of the tragedy the other night, I think more training is needed on how to properly handle people who are suffering from emotional disturbances, psychological disorders, or cognitive disabilities. First and foremost, how to recognize the situation. Distinguishing between the lack of comprehension from noncompliance."

"You're becoming quite creative in finding new ways to milk money from us."

"I would think that humanitarian concerns would be at the top of your mind. The safety of the citizenry. But if money is your only concern, then think of it in terms of liability. You recall the incident where one of your officers repeatedly used a stun gun on an unarmed autistic teenager who had committed no crime. He was minding his own business, riding his bike. For some reason the officer suspected the bike was stolen. When the boy was unable to process the questions, the officer knocked him off the bike and onto the ground, then ordered him to stand up. The boy curled up into a ball, paralyzed with fear, unable to move. So the officer repeatedly stunned the boy for refusal to get up. The boy suffered head and face injuries, burns and permanent nerve damage. The family's lawsuit against the city ended up being settled for something in the six-figure range, if I recall. Not to mention, it didn't make you look good. You want to look good, don't you, Chief?"

"What I want is a solid explanation I can give to the media and to city council as to why Tarburn went off the rails Monday night."

"Sorry, conducting a postmortem psychological assessment doesn't fall within my certification. I have no insights, and I'm not likely to acquire any. Whatever happened with Tarburn, your people will have to figure it out."

Jommers said it with an air of finality, as if by mere tone he could shut the door on any further use of himself as an intelligence agent, but Scubbetts quickly stuck his foot in that door.

"Let me know what you learn from the red loopy today. I'll be waiting for your call."

Before walking off, the chief tightened his mouth into a small circle and jetted a dense cylinder of smoke. The gray plume curled upward and coiled into a nautilus shape that crawled into Jommers's face.

The "red loopy" referred to Voros, who was on Jommers's appointment list for the day. Jommers had said nothing to suggest she was "loopy." Scubbetts used the term to convey the assessment that he expected.

LIFE IS A WINDY DECK where everyone needs a lifeline. And when a customary one is not at hand, you grasp at whatever is available, however ill-suited it might be. So when you encounter someone with peculiar passions, the mystery is not what is present, but absent.

That was Jommers's first thought as he mentally prepared for his first session with Patrolman Dwayne Biederbach. While doing so, Jommers found himself inadvertently thinking about the writer Jack London. Jommers had written a paper on the author for a required freshman English course in college. The assignment was to compare and contrast *White Fang* with *Call of the Wild*, the former about a wild wolf dog who becomes civilized and the latter about a house dog who returns to the wild and leads a wolf pack.

The teacher was interested in literary themes and symbols, but young freshman Jommers took his own tack on the assignment, analyzing the effect of such stories on the male psyche. He mused about how male readers of adversity stories generally absorbed the wrong message. Instead of being inspired to heroism or resilience, men often used tales of survival to justify their behavioral shortcomings. It was, the young freshman had written, a central problem with male mentality, the belief that when life was hard, a man was entitled to act like a jerk. And given that most men perceived their life as hard, even when it wasn't, they granted themselves perpetual license to be jerks. Young Jommers had titled the paper "The Call of the Riled." The teacher had awarded the paper a grade of D minus and scrawled on it with big red letters: "This is an English class, not a psychology class!"

The college paper suggested insights that Jommers would later confirm through direct observation of patients, and those insights now resurfaced with the paradox before him. Jommers had already sensed in Biederbach a survivalist mentality, a man who feels under siege. Attacking that disposition has the unintended effect of affirming it, driving the man ever deeper into his antisocial personality. So how does one discreetly excise a diseased worldview from someone who stands poised to defend it, sword in hand at the battlements? What Trojan Horse can the therapist use to get inside that well-guarded gate?

A short time before the patrolman's scheduled appointment, Jommers positioned himself at a window overlooking the parking lot so that he could observe his patient arriving. The therapist found Biederbach's elaborate style of smoking curious and wanted to determine if there was more to it than mere performance. The best way to find out was to see if Biederbach smoked in the same manner when by himself, sans audience.

He did.

As soon as Biederbach emerged from his old dull-finish Crown Vic in the parking lot, he hiked up the waist of his pants, a routine necessity for a man with a hipless, beanpole physique. Then he tossed the butt of the cigarette he'd been smoking and promptly lit up a fresh one. He puffed it with the same sequence, tightening the face for inhaling, turning the nose and grimacing while exhaling. Whatever its origin, the ritual was now a reflexive habit.

The skinny man paused to study the other vehicles in the lot and survey the general area, then he slowly marched toward the metal stairs.

He entered the room with a practiced casualness designed to conceal his discomfort. He sat down in one of the rockers and Jommers sat in the other. The chairs were angled toward each other in a way that allowed the men to look at each other while talking, but not in direct opposition.

Biederbach did not relax after sitting down and kept the rocker motionless. He held himself with a tense stillness, which takes effort in a rocker. His eyes stayed fixed, his feet planted, his posture at the ready, like a grappler waiting for the whistle.

"Before we start," Jommers said, "given that you've returned here as a voluntary private patient, we're under a different set of rules than the first time. Everything you say here from now on will be held in strictest confidence and no one will even know that you've been here, with the exception of your health insurance company. Which means I need to make a copy of your card before you go."

"How are you going to code it?"

"I'll make that decision after our first session concludes."

"Doesn't matter. Just curious."

"Now then, I don't like to impose informality on my visitors. Would you prefer to be addressed by title and last name, or by your first name?"

"Whatever. A rose by any other name is still a prickly thing."

"Okay. I'll call you Dwayne, then."

"I'm more concerned with your conversational posture than form of address," Biederbach said.

"Meaning?"

"Meaning I'd prefer that we treat this as a parley of peers as opposed to the usual superior/subordinate, doctor/patient thing. I assume you have plenty of experience with that kind of dynamic discourse given your large Jewish clientele."

"Can you elaborate on that?"

"I mean that Jews have a nonhierarchical religion where they're encouraged to debate and challenge authority rather than be passive receptacles of wisdom like sheep. So I'm sure you're used to having spirited arguments with them."

"What I meant was, what makes you think I have a large number of Jewish patients?"

"Really? You're seriously asking me that when the signs are so conspicuous?"

"I'm curious about your thought processes, yes."

"Now I know how Sherlock Holmes felt needing to explain the obvious evidence to Watson all the time. Okay, so here goes the walk-through. More than half the men working in the shop below are wearing yarmulkes, and each headpiece bears the name Zedek, indicating they all belong to the same temple. What makes this curious is the religious calendar on the wall of the office, which is from a Maronite Catholic Church. So why does the Catholic owner of a repair shop favor hiring Jews from a particular temple? Because the owner is clearly only part owner. To swing the deal, he needed a silent investor. So he found a Jewish rabbi, the one from the Zedek temple, who might be interested. The rabbi probably already had some investment in a trucking firm that uses the shop for repairs, and that's how the connection was made. Part of the deal included Gerzny's hiring of men who belonged to the temple."

"Interesting inference. But how would that affect me?"

"Simple. It means that the rabbi is your true landlord who you pay rent to for this space. So he made a deal with you, too. You treat members of his temple at a discount rate, and you get a discount on your rent. And so to let your Jewish clients know that they were welcome here, you hung that iron Star of David over there on the wall, one featuring the shape of a Kiddush chalice in the middle of the star."

"You have unusual powers of observation," Jommers said.

"I am refraining from using the word elementary."

"If your elegant deductive reasoning was meant to be reminiscent of Holmes, I'd have to say it more resembled Holmes on cocaine."

"Did I leave out something?"

"Yes, reality. Unfortunately, your keen powers of observation are not matched by equally keen powers of interpretation. Okay, so here's the walk-through. Pete is not a Catholic. He's not a member of any organized religion, nor even a disorganized one. He believes that, if there is a deity, said deity would look more kindly on men who fix things rather than break them. So, as the owner of a repair shop, he feels he's got it covered, theologically speaking. The church calendar was put on the wall by the woman who does the books, Claire, to help her keep track of billing due dates and repair appointments. Also, there is no mysterious silent partner, Jewish or otherwise. Pete is the sole owner of this fine restorative enterprise. The headwear you see on the men in the shop are not yarmulkes. They are welders' caps, worn to prevent errant sparks from setting one's hair on fire. The bill-less beanie style is so you can easily wear a welder's face mask over it. Zedek is the name of the industrial gas distributor who delivers the oxygen and acetylene tanks and picks up the empties.

The company passes out the beanies to their customers as a way to promote the company name. As for the iron hexagram hanging off my wall over there, while it looks similar to the Star of David, it is in fact the Brauerstern, or brewer's star, a symbol for tapping beer and for the brewer's guild, which originated in Bavaria in the late Middle Ages. Years ago, when I was still married, my wife went to a conference in Germany and spent some time touring there. She went to a small Bavarian town that has maintained its medieval flavor for tourist purposes and saw the original version of the brewer's star hanging from a chain outside a centuries-old tavern. She bought a replica in the souvenir shop and gave it to me for a present. The shape in the middle of the star, by the way, is meant to be a pilsner glass."

Biederbach enacted another theatrical puff of his cigarette and shrugged off the elaborate misread. "You have to admit, it was a well-constructed hypothesis."

"Yes, except for the complete absence of foundation."

"The linkages were sound. I just got thrown by the beanies."

"Yes," Jommers said. "Which raises the obvious question, what else has thrown you? What other intricate models do you lug around that are nothing more than concretized vapor?"

"I'm normally pretty good at it. This was a forced error because I was eager to set the tone. Give and take and all."

"Yes, you are allowed to argue with me, so long as your argument has grounds. Rejection without rationale is not argument, it's just denial, and I will call you on it."

"That's cool. I always have a rationale."

"I'm actually glad you made the forced error, because it illustrates a key point," Jommers said. "We all have an innate desire to comprehend our environment, and when we see something we don't understand, we attempt to fill in the blanks, even when we lack sufficient information to do so. Being unfamiliar with welder's caps, they were a curiosity to you, one that demanded explanation, so you labored to construct one, because even the most convoluted, outlandish interpretation is more palatable than an unanswered question hanging in the air. This is why people enjoy reading about Holmes and his literary descendants. We yearn for a world where all puzzles have unambiguous solutions."

"So what you're saying is that my theorizing is perfectly natural, which means that I am completely normal."

"Your temptations are normal. Your eagerness to yield to them less so. But your opening salvo raises another crucial point I need to stress. While I welcome robust discourse, its outcome will not be fruitful if you envision this as nothing more than a joust, a zero-sum game with points won or lost. You need to jettison the notion that I am an opponent to be defeated, or this won't work."

"Easy for you to say. You're not the one about to get sliced and diced."

"That's not what's going to happen here. I don't intend to ridicule your fears, but rather relieve you of them, the same as if you were afraid of heights, elevators, or spiders. Unfortunately, the big difference here is that phobics want to be freed from their fears, where you wish to cling to them. That will make this interaction more challenging. But, again, I don't want you to view me as an opponent, but as a guide. You're a man who has misread a map, made some wrong turns, and gotten lost in the boonies. And now you've spotted this guy on his front porch and stopped to ask for directions. He's a nice guy who will help you get back to the main road. Help you get back home."

Biederbach nodded affirmatively, but with some reluctance. He was an intelligent man and desperate to be perceived as such. For Jommers, this presented both obstacle and opportunity. Intelligent people are much more adept at defending peculiar beliefs, but their desire to appear analytical leaves a chink in their armor by which the sword of reason might find its mark.

But before Jommers could hope to repair the focusing mechanism on Biederbach's mental camera, the therapist needed to quantify the magnitude of the problem. To what degree did the man possess paranoid tendencies? How vast were his conspiracy theories in both breadth and depth? How much life impairment resulted from his distorted view of the world?

Jommers began by asking him questions to gauge the presence of hypervigilance in his lifestyle and how he interacted in various surroundings. Those were followed by questions to ascertain tendencies to perceive and forgive insults, the ability to deal with setbacks and understand their causes, the propensity for combativeness, the ease or difficulty of maintaining relationships, the sense that he felt betrayed or undermined by other people, and so forth.

Biederbach's answers were quick and neat. Too neat. He wisecracked: "If it helps, I do have a T-shirt that says: There are no strangers. Only enemies I haven't met yet."

The joke, along with the near-perfect answers, confirmed Jommers's fears. Biederbach had prepared for this encounter and researched how it would unfold. He knew what he would be asked and how he should respond. But Jommers found an incongruity and used it as an opening.

"When I asked you a minute ago about whether you felt anyone was watching you or taping you, you answered no. That stands in direct contradiction to what you said to me the other day when you suggested that your conversations with colleagues at the station were being recorded, that some of them were acting as agent provocateurs, trying to set you up. Explain."

"Must have slipped my mind," Biederbach said.

"An extremely vigilant person just happens to forget about being followed by agent provocateurs trying to set him up? Don't think so. You're performing here. And that's not going to fly if you want this arrangement to continue. You need to be straight with me. Starting now."

"Fine. But are you going to be equally straight with me?"

"Yes," Jommers said.

"I mean, I can't help but wonder why you brought that one up and why you aren't trying to talk me out of it. And that's because you know it happens to be true, and there's only one way you would know. They told you they're watching me, didn't they?"

"My conversations with other people are as confidential as you would expect this one to be with you."

"You don't have to be specific. You can just nod."

"Let me say this. There is a concept in my field known as the self-fulfilling prophecy. An example of that might be where someone who thinks people are spying on him begins to act in such a manner that his behavior kindles the very attention he suspects, attention that would not have otherwise been drawn. You should ponder that when interacting with your colleagues in the locker room."

"Your caginess on this issue makes me wonder whether you're genuinely interested in treating me as a patient, or whether you're acting as an intelligence agent for Chief Scubbetts."

"Now we're getting to the real Dwayne, aren't we?"

"Yes, the inquisitive, perspicacious Dwayne."

"If you really believe that I'm acting in the chief's interest and not in yours, then you need to get up and leave right now."

Biederbach didn't respond, but he didn't move either.

Jommers's next move to unpeel the real Dwayne was to administer a number of projective tests, personality tests where revelatory responses were expected from ambiguous prompts. The most well-known example has the patient describe inkblots. The determination of results relies on the interpretation of the psychologist. By contrast, objective personality tests have more standardized interpretation of responses and are often structured as multiple-choice exams.

Jommers declined to use the established versions of either projective or objective personality tests and had instead devised his own unique variations of them. The reason was simple. Some years ago, he had discovered that some cops in the detective unit were selling guides for passing the psychological tests required for getting on the force, getting a promotion, and so on. They had obtained most of the standard tests along with scoring and interpretation methods and were turning a nice profit by selling the inside information. Jommers knew who they were, but couldn't do anything about it without hard proof. So his response was to design his own tests.

The first task presented to Biederbach was to complete a series of sentence fragments, adding an end to the beginning to make a complete sentence. The list of snippets related to childhood, occupation, emotions, likes and dislikes, significant events, and other topics that might yield emotional or insightful responses. Some related directly to police work.

> I wanted to be a police officer because____
> The thing I hate most about police work is____
> The thing I love most about police work is____
> The worst shift I ever worked____

After that battery, Jommers then showed a series of photographs. Biederbach was asked to tell a brief story about each one: what was happening, what led up to it, how it ended up. Jommers had selected the photos himself. Some were cut out from magazines, others from stock photography catalogs. Some were taken by Jommers.

The goal of projective testing is to slip underneath the subject's conscious defenses. Find out what's going on down in the boiler room. It wasn't working today. When Jommers showed the final photo, he knew for sure that Biederbach was working mightily to game the process. The last image in this set had been taken by Jommers just the day before. He had posed someone on the riverbank down at Crone Point, given the person a stick and asked him to pretend he was fishing something out of the water. It was the exact same position Biederbach exhibited on Tuesday morning.

When shown the picture, Biederbach didn't flinch, hesitate, or even display a trace of recognition. He simply and calmly invented a story about a man who had lost an expensive Australian Army slouch hat. The wind had blown it off his head and into the river, and now he was trying to retrieve it.

"It was a present from his girlfriend. She thinks it looks really cool, even though he thinks it's dorky. It's not so much that he cares about hurting her feelings, it's just that he only gets laid when he wears the hat. He is literally trying to rescue his sex life. Hence, the anxious look on his face."

The next test involved showing a different set of photographs and with a different intent. Biederbach was instructed to indicate when he perceived something recognizable in a series of complex images. The goal was to gauge his tendency to make nonexistent connections, see patterns that weren't there, a propensity known as pareidolia, a type of apophenia.

"So this will be like whether I see Jesus on a tortilla, or the monkey face rock on Mars," Biederbach queried.

"Yes, exactly. Only I'll be showing you images you haven't seen before. It has to be a first look. Once somebody primes you to see a monkey face in a rock, then that's how you will see it thereafter, even if you aren't normally so predisposed."

"Like seeing those three stars at night and trying not to think Orion's Belt."

"Yes. Or like the figure/ground illusion in the Rubin vase. You miss the faces at first, but once they're pointed out, you cannot fail to see them thereafter. The coolest version of that, by the way, is the Pittsburgh Zoo logo. You ready?"

"Let's do it."

Jommers exhibited images of natural and man-made objects whose textures or forms were peculiar and potentially suggestive. They included shots of clouds, smoke, burled wood, gnarled tree roots, rock formations, rotted tree stumps, butterfly wings, pork chops, rusted metal, dirty windows, yams, peeling paint, greasy shop rags, and various items of pastry.

While everyone has a natural inclination to discern patterns, those who too readily envision patterns in randomness may have their thinking altered by that proclivity. And perceiving malevolence in the pattern adds another worrisome dimension. If you add the flour of apophenia to the waters of grievance, then infuse it with the yeast of paranoia, you get a twisted loaf.

But Biederbach was still employing the dodge, pretending to see nothing unusual, even when Jommers prodded.

"Are you sure on this one?" Jommers asked about a picture of a jagged, rotting tree stump. "A lot of people see a wizard casting a spell. See, this is his pointy hat, these are his outstretched arms and cloak . . ."

"Sorry. Not seeing it."

It's hard to argue with imagination, which was why Jommers set him up with a ringer. He watched closely as Biederbach gazed at the last image, a close-up shot of a grilled pork chop that had been seared.

"See anything in that one?" Jommers asked.

"Nope. Sorry."

"You're lying. I have a friend in graphic arts, good with Photoshop. I had him embed a faint but clearly recognizable image of Willie Nelson in there. Importantly, I had him place it at a certain angle. When people see it, they reflexively cock their head to that angle. That's when I know they've seen it. So the question is why you're lying about not seeing it."

Biederbach shrugged. "I guess he just dropped out of my mind after he went all fusiony. I mean, that reggae wreck of a thing he did two years ago. Jesus, what was he thinking?"

"All right, listen to me. This is my last warning about fabricating your responses. This next set of questions gets to the heart of why you're here—conspiracy theories. It is imperative that you are completely open and candid about which ones you believe. You should not fear that I'm going to pass judgment on your intellect or your politics based on your responses. People of all stripes and education levels hold such beliefs. There are many highly educated liberals, for example, that believe the Twin Towers were blown up by the government, in spite of all evidence to the contrary. So there's no reason not to be perfectly honest. This isn't an intelligence test. This isn't a political screening. Understood?"

"Got it."

"Okay, then. I'll start with the big one. JFK. A lot of people believe that Oswald didn't act alone, that he was part of a larger plot. Your take."

"Ridiculous."

"Explain."

"There's a hundred reasons, but let's just look at a couple. First, Oswald's strategy for fleeing the scene is to walk several blocks to catch a city bus, then later hail a cab. He stupidly goes home, then even more stupidly decides to go for a stroll, which doesn't end well. Does that sound like a brilliantly conceived getaway plan of some well-organized conspiracy to you? Even a crackhead from the projects knocking over a 7-Eleven knows to have a car running outside. This grand nefarious web of conspirators together can't cough up a few hundred bucks for a beater that runs? Second is all the timing. Oswald didn't initiate the idea to seek a job at the book depository. He serendipitously hears about a job opening from a friend who hears about it from a neighbor. More importantly, he gets hired there on October sixteenth. The decision to run a motorcade through Dallas isn't made until after October twenty-eighth, when a college cancels plans to give Kennedy an honorary degree, creating an empty spot in the schedule. The idea for the motorcade is Kennedy's, by the way. Others were opposed to it. The route for the motorcade isn't planned until November fifteenth and isn't publicized until November nineteenth. Bottom line—if Oswald takes a job at the book depository as part of a plan to shoot Kennedy on November twenty-second, then somebody in the conspiracy has to be a psychic, because the day Oswald is hired for the job, October sixteenth, no one in the world knows Kennedy will be passing by a month later. And if you want to believe a psychic was involved, then you have to ask why the psychic didn't foresee how it ends."

"Okay. Roswell. Area 51. Government concealing visitations by extraterrestrials."

"Oh, please. You've got to have goose shit for brains to believe that. We could talk physics, like how it would take a half million years for someone to get here. We could talk common sense, like why they don't seem to do anything here after making such a phenomenal effort to get here. What's their purpose? See the Grand Canyon? We could talk about the impossibility of such a massive cover-up, an effort that would involve thousands of people in dozens of countries across multiple generations, and how not one single son of a bitch ever says to his wife on his deathbed, 'Hey, Marge, did I ever tell you about the aliens?' But let's just cut to the chase, the absurd notion that the government would *want* to keep it secret. Governments love to scare the shit out of their own people, as often as possible, by any means possible. Scaring the shit out of people is how you turn them into quivering pissing sheep that surrender their constitutional rights, like Americans did when approving the Patriot Act. Scaring the shit out of people is how you get the media to roll over and lie down like a sick old dog with loose bowels, just like our media flopped over in the run-up to the Iraq War. And this crew we got in charge now, they know how to bang the gong better than anyone. Let me tell you, if Lord Vile Veep and Flap Ear Feebleflub had a spaceship somewhere, they'd be parking it on the White House lawn and holding regular press conferences in front of it to explain why all future elections will be put on hold until this here alien sitch-ee-ay-shun is taken care of."

Jommers tossed out a list of other well-known conspiracy theories, including those about the Illuminati, New World Order, FEMA concentration camps, faking of the Apollo moon landings, the creation and spreading of diseases by pharmaceutical companies, and more. He included theories from different ends of the political spectrum and some so far off the charts they weren't on any spectrum. Biederbach shot them all down with facility. Yet, when confronted with his own personal pet theory—the notion that the federal government was intent on infiltrating and subsuming law enforcement agencies—he held to it steadfastly.

Personalities that are susceptible to conspiracy theories typically embrace them in multiples, as the impetus is the same. It is not uncommon for them to adopt theories that contradict each other. So it was unusual and perplexing to encounter a man who fervently espoused a single conspiracy while ridiculing a host of others. Of course, there was the distinct possibility that he was lying about the rest, concealing a broader belief in such notions so as to bolster his reasonableness in touting the one he felt most important.

Jommers took another tack and reviewed Biederbach's responses to the picture story exercise and sentence completion test, looking for clues.

The first thing he noticed was the complete absence of the word "home" in any of the responses, even where the setup begged for it. For example, the sentence fragment:

There's no place____

For a large percentage of people, the phrase triggers Dorothy's line from the *Wizard of Oz*: there's no place like home. For Biederbach it was: there's no place to get a decent steak around here.

Jommers detected a similar lack of connection to parents in the responses. Nothing about Mom or Dad, even when the prompts clearly steered a response in that direction. There were many possible reasons for a sense of detachment to both parents and concept of home. Maybe when he was a child, his parents were in the military and they moved around a lot. Maybe he spent most of the year away at boarding school and summers at camp, rarely seeing parents or home. Or maybe the parents and the home were unpleasant memories.

But Jommers saw another clue in Biederbach's apparent disassociation with the concept of lineage. In the picture story test, Jommers included a photo of an old man talking to a boy in front of a fireplace. The old man is pointing in the general direction of the fireplace mantel, which holds framed black-and-white photos of people from a different era. Above the mantel is a family coat of arms. The picture almost always inspires a story that involves ancestry. But Biederbach saw an old man telling a boy how to build a fire.

The capper was Biederbach's earlier twist on Shakespeare's line from *Romeo and Juliet* about a rose by any other name, a wisecrack that suggested ambivalence about his own name. Altogether, they provided Jommers with a hunch.

"Were you a foster kid, Dwayne?"

"Is it pertinent?"

"If you'd said simply yes or no, then maybe not. Your reluctance to answer directly suggests it might be."

Biederbach nodded in the affirmative, showing no emotion.

"Did you have multiple placements? They move you around a lot?"

Another affirmative nod.

"The system kicks you out at eighteen, doesn't it? Literally and figuratively."

Another nod.

"So there you are, on your eighteenth birthday, standing on the street with no place to go, no one to turn to, clutching a plastic trash bag that contains what few belongings you have, utterly alone in the world. Happy birthday."

Biederbach reflected a bit before answering. "It was an instructional moment, telling me with bracing clarity what to expect from life. Like ice water in the face, or vinegar in your mouth. It's not fun, but it sure as hell wakes you up. And I am more awake than most. So in that sense, it *was* a gift."

"And that explains the seeming incongruity of someone who resents power structures joining one. You had a string of different of foster care fathers, total strangers who told you how it was going to be. They laid down the law. And all that created a resentment and distrust of authority. In spite of that, you seek out a job in law enforcement, which has a hierarchical structure. Why? For one, it gives you a family you never had. Every uniform is a brother. And, two, it also gives you a security you never had, security on multiple levels. It's the financial security of a good government job that won't move to Mexico, but it's also physical security. At least one or more of your foster fathers slapped the crap out of you for no good reason. Now you get to carry a gun all the time. Nobody is ever going to slap the crap out of you again."

"Yeah, all that," Biederbach said. "Plus, the uniform thing eliminates fashion anxiety. And blue is my favorite color. But what the hell does any of that have to do with anything?"

"Maybe something. Maybe nothing. We're exploring here. Creating a map. Trying to figure out where you are and how you got there. That's the process."

Biederbach chain-smoked throughout the whole session, grabbing the next cigarette like Tarzan reaching for the next vine while swinging through the trees, as if any gap would result in a fall. And all the facial calisthenics involved with Biederbach's smoking steered Jommers toward another hunch.

"The foster care system wasn't your only hardship, was it? You had another affliction, one that followed you from stop to stop, because it was in you. The tics started before puberty, didn't they?"

Biederbach no longer bothered to nod, providing confirmation with an annoyed expression and flick of the hand.

"It was humiliating," Jommers continued, "the way they laughed at you in school, wasn't it? And your fake parents weren't about to spend money on a doctor for you. So you had to deal with Tourette syndrome on your own. You didn't even know it had a name yet, but being a very smart kid, even then, you discovered something on your own. An alternate, competing movement could deflate the tic. Maybe you chewed on a pencil or pen when you felt one coming, chewed it like a dog on a bone. Or maybe you pretended to have an allergy and did fake repressed sneezes. The formal term for it is Habit Reversal Training. Later on you discovered smoking, and it was a godsend. Teenagers smoke to look cool, so all the motions and expressions accompanying it are exaggerated. Smoking is a form of theater when you're young, which made it a perfect solution for you. At some point, you might have even imagined that the nicotine cured the problem. Thing is, most cases of Tourette syndrome that occur before puberty resolve themselves as you get older. It's probably long gone by now, but you're still clinging to the cure. A cure for something you no longer have."

Biederbach didn't refute the assertions, but maintained his silent gaze of annoyance. Jommers continued his assessment.

"So you've had a past where you've been oppressed by forces beyond your control, both internally and externally, creating feelings of powerlessness. Do you think those experiences might have contributed to your current worldview?"

Biederbach took a long time before responding.

"Okay. So I got issues. Everybody's got issues. It doesn't change objective reality. When the storm hits, it rains on everybody, issues or not. And the storm is coming. So when someone with issues tells you there's a storm coming, it doesn't mean he's wrong. Now you can tell me I got this or that condition, but so what? This isn't about me. It's about what's going on out there. If I didn't exist, it would all still be happening."

"Yes, well, we're not out there, we're in here, and in here, it most certainly is about you. And you're going to get something from me that you maybe never got before—undivided attention. Now then, I'm going to give you a home-work assignment. Get a small notebook, something you can put in a pocket and take wherever you go. For the next several days I want you to record all your idle daydreams. What's happening in them, regardless of how trivial. And, even more importantly, what transpires right before them."

"You want a log of my daydreams. All of them."

"Yes. Some people see themselves having fun somewhere. Some envision per-forming heroic deeds, or committing evil ones. A lot of people fantasize about having sex with somebody. Some play out little dramas in their head where they're performing somehow, being entertaining or clever in a group setting, winning admiration with displays of humor or logic. Some people with strong opinions dream about telling somebody off, handily winning a fierce debate, deftly spar-ring with a lawyer in a courtroom, and so on. Your interior dialogues."

"You want cranial exhaust fumes. A whole day's worth."

"Everybody builds castles in the sky. I want to know what's taking place in yours and how they connect to the ground. Which is why I also want you to record what's happening in the real world just before the daydream enters your head."

"This sounds rather cumbersome."

"You're on vacation. Shouldn't be a problem."

What Jommers had in mind with the assignment was Thurber's Walter Mit-ty, whose compensatory heroic fantasies act as counterpoint to his existence as a meek and henpecked husband. The reactive fantasy reveals the active reality, just as the antibody identifies the infector. But it only works when the patient acts honestly, already a problem with Biederbach.

At the end of the session, Biederbach departed without the slightest acknowl-edgment that anything significant had taken place, even though he had just re-vealed more about his inner self to Jommers than he likely had to anybody else in his entire life. He walked out with the same rehearsed nonchalance with which he'd entered, like someone dropping into a store to buy a newspaper.

The revelation about foster care was certainly illuminating, but Jommers resisted the temptation to see it as singularly elucidating. The mind is a strange and motley goulash that has been improvised without recipe. To stick your fingers in it, pluck out a chunk of something, and then proclaim, 'Aha, this is what it's all about'—well, that is almost always a mistake.

And yet, he could not help but recall research examining tameness in animals. According to the studies, the physiological and neurological factors behind the fight-or-flight response take a while to mature. If you habituate an animal to humans during the brief window of opportunity beforehand, you can make the animal tame, unafraid of people. After the window of opportunity closes, after the fight-or-flight response matures, it is difficult or impossible to tame an animal. It remains permanently wild and fearful of humans.

When Jommers read reviews of such research, his obvious first thought was whether that might also apply to humans. That is, if you fail to provide proper socialization and interaction within a given window of opportunity, will a child develop a feral fearfulness, become a wild child? It was a troubling thought, because it suggested irreversibility, and reversing problems was the underlying premise of therapy.

The mental jousting with Biederbach had left Jommers feeling a bit edgy, desperately wanting a beer, but he denied himself. He needed to prepare for the upcoming encounter with Ilona Voros, the Internal Affairs detective who had shot Patrolman Earl Tarburn down at Crone Point. He had declined to clear her after her first visit.

She sauntered in about twenty minutes late for her appointment, suggesting a calculated contempt for the process, confirmed by any lack of contrition. She wore a man's suit, solid white, topped with a white fedora trimmed with a black band. She carried an ebony walking stick with a brass raven's-head handle and thumped it loudly on the old wooden floor as she walked.

Jommers was already seated in one of the rockers waiting for her. When she approached, she swung the adjacent rocker around so that it was directly facing him. She sat down with her knees wide apart, planted the walking stick between, then leaned forward, both hands on top of the raven's head, chin on top of the hands, staring into Jommers's face.

This wasn't the performance he was expecting, but it at least confirmed one thing—the tales of her eccentric behavior were likely true.

Before he could even process the visual surprise, his olfactory system was overwhelmed by the scent of her cologne. It was woody, like fresh-cut cedar that's still dark and moist. There were also hints of ginger and cider. The earthiness of it was ambiguous, something suiting either a man or a woman. She had applied it liberally, and the engine-hot air revved up the scent's power so that it enveloped him like a sweet, sultry cloud.

He was puzzled, but didn't reveal it, remaining the unimpressed sphinx. He'd expected that after accusing her of acting abnormally, she would on the second visit appear to behave quintessentially normal, bleached of imperfection, exhibiting an unnatural naturalness that would easily clear his bar.

So what was up with this shtick? Whatever message she was trying to convey, he was certain that she had formulated it as meticulously as Eisenhower planned D-day.

"The old farts can't process a woman in police work," she said. "They think only a dyke would want to be a cop. Is that what you think, too?"

"I do not."

"Should we start by exploring my sexuality?"

"No, we should not. It's not pertinent."

"How do you know? The mind is a seething cauldron of juices, intermingling with each other, oozing into something new. All those little perky ganglia, knotted and twisted together. Everything is connected up there. Down there, too."

"Again, it's not pertinent."

"Don't you want to examine the whole of me? Go down deep? Or are you afraid to get that close?"

Then it clicked. She wasn't trying to convey anything. The puzzle was the point. Cognitive load distraction. Take him off his game.

"Are you done yet?" he asked. "Or is there more?"

"Oh, much more. Here, I wrote you a poem."

She held out a piece of paper toward him, but he refused to take it.

"You're right," she said. "It's much better if I read it to you. So here goes. It's called True Love:

> *Pity the woman too eager to please*
> *When she rightly foresees the hurt.*
> *It's just like having pica disease*
> *Where you can't stop eating dirt.*

"I have another, but perhaps later. You look overloaded. Poor dear."

He didn't respond.

The poem was interesting on several counts, in a few words displaying both defiance and a wit worthy of Dorothy Parker. But also a message. The reference to pica, a psychological disorder, along with her display of intellect, was a plea to be taken seriously. *I may be troubled, but I'm not a fool. Don't talk down to me.*

Jommers had two strategies for dealing with a performance. One was to deflate it as quickly as possible, puncture the balloon. The other response was to let it play out until it exhausted itself. Follow quietly but steadily until the actor runs out of steam and lies spent and helpless on the stage. Then move in. For this new performance from Voros, he chose the latter approach.

"You expected me to crawl for your blessing, didn't you?" she asked. "Well, I'm not good at crawling. Or bawling. So don't expect to see that either."

As the sphinx remained still and quiet, she looked slightly unnerved by it. She had prepared for a battle, not a siege. She leaned back in her rocker and scanned the room. Her gaze fixed momentarily on the old oak upright piano off in the corner and immediately jerked her head in the other direction, as if she didn't want to be caught looking at it. He wasn't taking written notes, only mental ones, so he was able to track her gestures, expressions, and eye movements without any interruption. Nothing missed.

The second thing that caught her eye during the reconnoiter was a photo of General Ulysses S. Grant on the wall. She smiled. This was what she had been looking for. He already knew where she was going.

"Is he your hero?" she asked. "Is he up there to inspire your patients, or you?"

It was a well-known photo taken by famed Civil War photographer Matthew Brady at the Battle of Cold Harbor. In it, Grant is awkwardly trying to look casual, leaning against a tree. But his face is shot with anxiety and dread, like a man who wants to put his head through a wall. Or, more likely, a man who needs a drink.

Jommers had been motivated to find a photo of Grant after reading a Lincoln quote, possibly apocryphal, but widely repeated. In the midst of civil war, the nation torn asunder, some aides had approached President Lincoln with sober news. General Grant had taken back to the whiskey again. They suggested the general be relieved of command. Lincoln noted dryly that Grant was the only one of his generals who was winning any battles at the time. That being the case, the aides should find out what brand of whiskey Grant was drinking so that the president could send a barrel of it to his other generals.

Jommers had put it on the wall as a reminder for his patients. Imperfect people can still do good work. Flawed men can still accomplish great things.

She seemed to know that, which meant that she had spent the intervening days tracking down others who had been treated by Jommers. Grilling them. Doing intensive preparatory research. Her motivation for doing so smacked of desperation. Or fear. Why did she need an edge? Why couldn't she just show up?

"Let me guess," she continued. "Old Uly baby is there to reassure your cop buddies that it's okay to be a drunken fuckup, because you can still win the war on crime. And he's there to tell you that it's okay to pop another beer because you can be a fucked-up police psychologist and still keep your business with the city. Nice idea, but it might work better if you found more successful drunks, though. Maybe create a gallery. Drunks who done good. You like candor in your interviews, don't you? So let's be candid. You're a lathe operator. You know what I mean, don't you? No? Let me explain. When I first got into Internal Affairs, Captain Wifflyn told me that the biggest problem wasn't cops who were corrupt, but cops who were drunks. And he said that there were two kinds. Type one is the over-the-falls drunk. They delay having that first drink of the day as long as possible because, once they take it, they dive into it, like going over Niagara Falls in a barrel. Those kind are easier to boot. They tend to mess up in a big way. They don't even fight it when you take them down.

"Then there's the second type, who carefully doses his hooch to control the buzz, like a lathe operator who periodically adjusts the cutting tool to shave off the optimal amount of reality. Controlling the lack of control. Those are the worst. They deny they have a problem and fight like hell to keep their job. They rarely screw up in a big way, just in a hundred little ways. So, like I said, let's be candid. You don't clear me to go back to work? I will challenge it in court. And I will make your boozing exhibit one. A man in a constant state of low-level ine-briation is not possibly capable of rendering a sound judgment on my emotional state or anybody else's. Your buzz-bomb defect and incompetence will become a permanent part of the public record, which makes its way to the media, too. You'll never work for this city again, nor any other. So let's just cut the bullshit and get this over with. You know what I'm capable of. You're no Grant and there is no Abe Lincoln to cover your back. You fuck with me, and you're toast."

The sphinx remained expressionless, inscrutable. A damp fuse that would not light. It was a good routine that she delivered. Among the better he'd seen. But she could not know that it was nothing compared to what he'd endured from the likes of Augie Dallabaco.

Jommers's lack of reaction rattled her. Her voice grew tenser and louder, less self-assured.

"Is this a tactic, or are you napping?" she asked. "You don't really care, do you? You're just as burned out as the cops you treat. This is just a show. You maintain a captive clientele and the city pays the bill. So you stretch it out as long as you can, pump up the revenue stream. Nice gig. Corrupt as hell, but nice."

He maintained his silence.

She struck the floor with the walking stick. "Answer me, damn it!"

Jommers paused for a few moments, then spoke calmly and slowly. "You've brought more than this. So I'm simply waiting for you to use it up. Then, when it's all over with, we'll begin the session. So go ahead and finish up. I'm in no hurry."

"Session? This isn't a therapy session, it's a psychological lynching. You were involved that night, weren't you? I can tell. And now you feel guilty for how it turned out. So you want to pin your guilt trip on me so you can cast it off, walk away from your own fiasco-level fuckup. You think if you can make me cry, then it's on me, an admission of responsibility, my tears washing away your sin. Not going to happen. No matter where you poke or what you poke with. You need a thick skin to be a woman on the Grayton PD, and when you're in IA on top of that, you need even better. You need rhino hide. So don't even dream of penetrating it. I run over guys like you every day without breaking stride."

"Rhino hide," he said. "All right. Now we're getting somewhere."

"We're not getting anywhere."

"Oh, I think we are. You sashayed into the room here all cocky and cooing, and now you've totally lost it."

She leapt up from the rocker. "I have not lost it. I am in total fucking control!" She slammed the walking stick against the floor so hard that it broke free from her hand, bounced up and whacked her in the knee. She hobbled a few steps away and started screaming the word *shit* in rapid repetition, like an automatic riveter.

Then, she abruptly launched into some kind of recovery routine. She straightened up, took deep slow breaths, and did a finger exercise in which each finger sequentially tapped the thumb, index to pinky, pinky to index. She did this with both hands simultaneously. After a few cycles of this, she slowly raised her right hand with forefinger pointing and others curled inward, then touched her forehead as if hitting a reset button. She held it there for about a half minute.

When she was finished, she calmly sat down as if nothing had happened.

"Before we begin," she said, "I need to understand the confidentiality level."

She uttered the sentence as if she had just walked in the door.

"That's a fair request," he said. "The session is officially considered to be a continuation of the initial administratively mandated evaluation. As such, I will be submitting to your human resources department my best professional assessment of your emotional state as it relates to the ability to perform your job function."

"So you tell them everything I say."

"No. I give them only my interpretive conclusion. The specific things you say, the details, do not go past me."

"So when we're talking about what happened that night . . . if I should say something that could be interpreted as accusatory . . . about someone . . . it doesn't get back to that someone. Nobody will know."

"Correct. And let me elaborate further. This has nothing to do with the Force Review Committee investigation, of which I have no part. It is not the purpose of this session to investigate what happened that night. The purpose of this session is to explore your emotional reaction to what happened. Are we clear?"

"Yes. Thank you."

"Okay, then," he said. "Let's continue where we left off. It has been my experience that when a police officer has to shoot someone for the first time, there is a strong emotional response. They are shook up, no matter how justified the shoot. You exhibited no such reaction, which I find disconcerting. Especially given that the person you shot was a fellow police officer, which should amplify the emotional distress. How do you explain your apathy?"

"You're making this more complicated than it is. When shit hits the fan, you go into duty mode. Dealing with the situation is your first priority. Doing what you have to do. Emotions get put on the back burner until everything is handled. Only then do you allow yourself to process it, let the emotions flow. This isn't just a cop thing, it's an everybody thing. I'm surprised you find it so perplexing. My father died of a heart attack when I was still a little girl. Died right in the shop after lunch. There was no big scene, clutching of the chest, tremendous pain . . . he just said that he was tired and needed a nap. He sat down on the floor right where he was and never got up again. I remember how my mother went into duty mode, handling everything that needed handling. She was solemn, but strong. Showing no trace of grief. And then, when it was all over, the funeral, the paperwork, the phone calls, the lawyer, nothing left to do, that's when she collapsed into grief. That's when the wave hit her. Cried for days and moped for months."

"So it's not a lack of emotion, merely a postponement of emotion."

"Exactly," she said.

"Fill me in on what's furthering the postponement," he said. "Today is Friday. The shooting took place Monday night. Your duties—debriefing, reports, paperwork, being interviewed—would all be over by now. On top of that, you're on admin leave. Why hasn't the wave hit you yet? What's left for you to handle?"

"You."

"Me?"

"I mean, this process. Getting cleared. Obtaining your seal of approval. It's my last hurdle, my last duty, as it relates to the incident. It's been occupying my brain to the exclusion of all else. I can't process the incident emotionally, experience catharsis, or whatever you call it. None of that can happen until I get past this. Past you."

"So I'm the barrier. I'm responsible for your lack of emotional response."

"Yes."

"So the normal emotional response doesn't come until after I clear you, which I can't do until I see the normal emotional response. That's a bit of a dilemma, don't you think?"

"Yes—yes, it is. One you can solve by trusting me. I have a good history with the department, which I'm sure you already know. If I was a head case, it would be evident in the record. It isn't."

Jommers thought a moment about the reference to her father's death. She couldn't just say that the father died. She'd provided a tale to go with it. And that would be the tipoff with her, the tipoff for a lie.

"Let me back up a second," he said. "How did your father's death affect you?"

"Me? Well, I was devastated, of course. I didn't understand."

"What were you doing when you found out? And what did you do after?"

"Doing? I, um, don't actually remember. I was a little girl. It was a long time ago."

"That's interesting. You remember with great detail how it affected your mother, but not how it affected you. How do you explain that?"

She paused before answering. Gears clicking and grinding in her head. "Is cross-examination the preferred therapist technique these days?"

"It's not the preferred technique, but in the case of an involuntary subject engaged in evasion, it can be a necessary technique. The longer you hide the ball, the longer the game takes. The length of this process is entirely in your hands."

She got up from the rocker and walked over to a window. She put her left hand on her hip and rubbed her forehead with the right. Pondering. Or, acting like she was pondering. Hard to tell.

She returned and spoke with a subdued voice. "Okay. Okay. Here's the thing. It's no secret that it's tough to be a woman in a man's world, even tougher when it's a macho man's world, like the military or a police department. When a man cries, he's showing his sensitive side, his humanity. When a woman cries, it means she can't handle the job. So you have to act twice as hard to be taken seriously. I realized long ago I couldn't wait for that to gradually happen, that I had to actively work at it, train myself to be stoic. I remember reading this account of a navy pilot shot down over North Vietnam. I can't remember his name . . ."

"Stockdale."

"Yes, that's it. Anyway, he had studied ancient philosophy and admired the Stoics. And as he was floating down in his parachute, sensing what suffering was ahead, he said to himself, 'I'm leaving the world of technology and entering the world of Epictetus.' You know him?"

Jommers nodded affirmatively, and she continued.

"So I practiced that, you know, getting that emotional detachment. I studied photos of homicides and abused children, watched autopsies at the coroner's, spent time in the pediatric intensive care unit at Saint Bridget's . . . anything that would normally trigger a woman's emotions. And for each encounter I prepared a set of mental exercises to shunt the expected emotional response. I did this for a long time. Other things, too. Skydiving, bungee jumping, motorcycle riding . . . things to conquer fear. Training for discomfort and pain . . . running in hot weather with a sweat suit, going out in the cold soaking wet and not coming in until just before hypothermia sets in . . . I know you think that's nuts, but doing all that made me what I am. And after years of doing it, I can't just turn it off like a switch. It's what I am now. I can't give you the weepy Wilma you want. She left the building a long time ago. So where do we go from here?"

Jommers had no doubt she had read James B. Stockdale's account of his eight torturous years as a prisoner of war, but he wondered when she'd read it—years ago as claimed, or yesterday. Forgetting the man's name was too neat.

He had no doubt she had read up on Stoicism, as well. He was familiar with the topic. Some credit the Stoics as the true originators of cognitive behavioral therapy, given the similarity of principles in several areas. Both emphasized that it was not external events and stressors themselves that cause emotional disturbance, but rather our interpretation and reaction to those experiences. Restructuring one's internal judgment of externalities can protect against their negative effects. Some argue that Reinhold Niebuhr's Serenity Prayer represents stoicism in a nutshell. Another similarity is the emphasis on mental rehearsal and the repetition of sayings as a means of achieving that mental restructuring.

The question before Jommers now was this. If both sociopaths and stoics exhibit similar resilience and emotional detachment on the outside, how then can you tell them apart?

He could try various diagnostic tools that were both widely used and widely criticized, but a crafty subject such as Voros would likely be familiar with them and be armed with prepared responses. Besides, he'd already acquired insights about her from the sessions thus far.

Sociopaths are great liars and manipulators. Check. Her strategy in this session was clever. She'd opened with a halfhearted assault. The feint. She'd followed with a staged retreat to fallback position one. Since this would appear too easy, she'd followed with a staged retreat to fallback position two, which would seem more believable than if presented initially.

By contrast, a stoic would be straight up. No bullshit. A genuine stoic would have no reason to fool or fear a psychologist. A genuine stoic would engage the therapist in philosophical discourse, perhaps even offer advice on the business of offering advice.

There was one quick test he could try, however. Accuse her outright. A true stoic shrugs it off. A narcissistic sociopath blows up.

"Well, that's a nice little tale," he said. "But I don't believe any of it. I don't believe you're a stoic either. A real stoic is calm and steady. You're a skittish chameleon. Bobbing and weaving like a boxer on speed. You are a classic sociopath. You're not fit for police work, here or anywhere. I'm going to recommend your termination. We're done."

"What?" Her face showed alarm, like when a driver sees an oncoming car on the wrong side of the road.

"I said we're done. You can go."

"No, we are not done."

"Yes. We are done. And you're done, too. Given your antisocial personality, your callousness and contempt for humanity, I would suggest you seek employment as a customer service rep in cable TV. You'd be a good fit there."

"You don't get to tell me I'm done."

"I just did."

"No. No. No. You don't get to tell me I'm done. You don't get to tell me anything. You don't get to screw me over."

"I just did. I just did screw you. And it was fun."

"You son of a bitch. I could shoot your fucking head off right now and no one would care. All I have to do is say you were drunk and groped me, tried to rape me. No one would question. No one would care. I'd be doing the world a favor."

"So soon? You just killed somebody on Monday. Now you're ready for the thrill again on Friday. You're an ambitious sociopath, aren't you?"

"Stop calling me that!"

"Sociopath? Why? You are what you are. And you are, most definitely, a sociopath."

She leapt up and leaned close into his face, her hands on either side with fingers extended, as if holding an invisible watermelon. "I don't even need a gun to kill a piece of shit like you. You're a goddamn slug I can squeeze between my fingers. I can twist your head right off your body, pull your rancid brain out with my hand, then play soccer with what's left."

"Sounds like an interesting game. Now then, would that be more likely the sport of a stoic or a sociopath?"

She stared at him for several seconds, trembling with rage, huffing short intense breaths. Nostrils flaring with pulsing rhythm. She stepped back, turned around and did her little reboot ritual with the finger exercises and pressing the imaginary reset button on her forehead. After that, she collapsed back into her chair, realizing that she had just proved his point.

She sat awkwardly, knees tight together, shoulders slumped, arms folded over her breasts, as if she were sitting naked. Her face was blank, eyes staring at the floor.

Jommers acted as if nothing had happened and asked the next question casually.

"Have you visited your partner in the hospital?"

She jerked to life again as if jolted by an electric shock.

"That son of a bitch. What did he say about me? Is that where you got all this crap? Let me tell you about that jerk. He's a pathological liar. He's constantly trying to sabotage my career, make himself look like the hero . . ."

She went on for a minute or two, essentially saying every negative thing her partner had said about her. A mirror set of accusations, and only one could be true. When she finished, she reverted to the slumped position, belatedly realizing she had again proved his point.

"Your partner is busted up pretty bad," Jommers said. "He's in a lot of pain. His career may be over. Most people in your situation would be able to put their disagreements aside, stop by and wish him a speedy recovery, show a brief interest in his condition. Kind of like going to a funeral for someone you didn't really like but where you're expected. You suck it up and do the right thing."

"He wouldn't want to see me anyway. My presence would only agitate him. I'm doing him a favor by staying away."

"That's very thoughtful. I presume he was the one you wish to accuse?"

"What?"

"Earlier, when you asked me about confidentiality of the session. You expressed concern that if you uttered something accusatory about someone, it would get back to them. Your partner?"

"No."

"Someone else?"

"It was a general question. Stop trying to mine every little thing for hidden meaning."

"Of course, it's not your partner. I would have no reason to tell him anything, and he already dislikes you. You're worried about somebody higher up. And I report to management, the top. It's the chief you're worried about, isn't it? You want to accuse him of something, put the onus for the evening on him somehow, but you're afraid I'll tell him. Because he sends business my way, you think my first allegiance is to my benefactor."

"Well, isn't it?"

"Are you afraid of him?"

"I'm not afraid of any of them."

"Them. There's that word again. Them. I find your previous reference to the POW interesting. Is that how you feel, like a prisoner of war, being tormented by your captors?"

"You're twisting everything I say."

"No, I'm untwisting."

"This is past absurd already."

"I'm catching a whiff of persecution complex here."

"All I smell is a sweaty low-life loser panting in a grunge hole, laughably pretending to be a health care professional."

"Why are you so terrified of revealing your true self, so terrified that you painstakingly prepared for this session by meticulously crafting a parade of disguises? What is it that you don't want me to see?"

"Nothing, damn it!"

"Exactly. Your first honest answer, though inadvertent. You're afraid of me discovering the nothingness behind the mask. You can't show me who you really are because you don't even know yourself. But wearing that mask is a lot work, isn't it? It's a humongous, heavy mask, and it takes all your strength to hold it up. And your arms are getting tired. They're burning with muscle fatigue. At some point, they just go numb, and the weighty mask goes crashing to the floor."

"Perhaps. But will you be sober enough to hear it?" She turned her head away and glanced in the corner with the piano again.

"Do you play the piano?"

"No, why?"

"That's about the fifth time you glanced over at it. Each time with a wistful look."

"Again with the big deal over nothing. When I was a kid we had an old upright in the basement. Lots of people do. My dad used to play it at parties. Okay? Happy?"

"Was this before or after he died on the shop floor?"

She glared back at him. He didn't wait for an answer.

"Okay," he continued. "Here's where we stand. You have two conflicting goals here. One is to get back to work. The other is to remain an impenetrable enigma. You need to understand that those are mutually exclusive goals. You're not going back to work until I know who you are. So you need to decide which goal is more important to you. You have the weekend to think it over. And you'll also have plenty of time to complete your homework assignment."

"My what?"

"Your homework assignment. I want you to write an imaginary dialogue. Pretend that—you know how to pretend, right? Pretend that Patrolman Earl Tarburn did not die that night, but survived his injuries. You've gone to see him in the hospital. He is now awake, rational and clear-headed. What does he say to you? What do you say to him? Be specific, be detailed. Don't worry about spelling, punctuation or format. Just the words. Make it as long as necessary. No one else will see it. I will hand it back to you immediately upon reading it. I'll expect to see you back here Monday."

Her glare hardened into a scowl, her face creased with sulking resentment. She trained it on him like a weapon, as if the physical expression of her contempt might incinerate her nemesis. And when her withering glower failed to reduce him to ash, she slowly got up and trudged toward the door in defeat.

"Oh, don't forget your walking stick," he said. "That is really cool, by the way. Where do you get something like that?"

She picked it up off the floor and tucked it under her arm like a newspaper, then walked out without saying a word.

Only after her departure did he start taking copious notes while the memory of the interview was still fresh.

The most interesting observation about Detective Voros was that she and

Patrolman Biederbach had witnessed the same event yet had entirely opposite views on what had transpired. Strangely, that made him think of Salvador Dalí.

Jommers's ex-wife, Rachel, had a print of Dalí's *The Great Paranoiac*, which served as a focal point of their living room when they were still married. In the work, the grouping of figures in the foreground can also be perceived as forming the image of a human face. It was one of many double-image paintings by Dalí meant to exemplify his paranoiac-critical method that forces viewers to establish unobvious connections in the mind in order to see the secondary image. Another classic example is Dalí's *Paranoiac Face*, where the obvious image consists of African tribesmen sitting around a hut, but when viewed from a ninety-degree angle, it appears to be a large face on its side. The concept is analogous to the invisible connections made by conspiracy theorists, with one important distinction: in the double-image paintings, the invisible connections are implicit by design, so in that sense, they are real by virtue of intention. In the case of a conspiracy theory, the connections are purely imaginary, nonexistent.

The Dalí in their midst had been an occasional source of argument. Rachel was quite proud of owning it. Jommers, ever the traditionalist, had nothing but disdain for the surrealists in general, and Dalí in particular. As for the whole double-image thing in *The Great Paranoiac*, to him it was nothing more than the visual equivalent of a puzzle or joke, and once you have solved a puzzle or heard a joke, you need not bear it again. Likewise, the Dalí need not be looked at more than once. She, however, saw it as a great work of art that demanded regular appreciation and reflection.

"You don't value it because you fail to understand it," she would suggest.

"I understand it perfectly, I just don't think it's art," he would reply.

"That's because you don't get it."

"I get it. I just don't like it."

"Because you don't make any effort to grasp it."

"There's nothing to grasp. It's sheer contrivance."

And so it went. Two different people, two different perspectives.

<hr>

IT TOOK A LONG TIME for Jommers to complete his notes, and when he was finished, he looked at his watch and sighed. He mentally added up the time he'd spent on Biederbach and Voros—not only the sessions themselves, each of which had gone way over the intended time, but also the preparation and post-session ruminating and note taking. He then did the quick arithmetic on how little he would earn from it all. He could only bill for the time of a standard-length session, not the overage time, prep work, or follow-up. All in all, the day would have been more lucrative if he'd spent it working as a plumber. He shook his head in exasperation, knowing that his bookkeeper and friend Claire Maroun was ready to give him another lecture on his unprofitable business practices.

Business practice. The phrase grated on him. So antithetical to the concept of counseling. Yet he didn't have the luxury of ignoring the numbers. If he went under, he wouldn't be able to help anyone. He wondered if there would be any viable business model for providing therapy in the future, or if the concept would fade away or diminish into relic status, like slate roofs and hand-carved fireplace mantels. Social necessity and market necessity are two different things, and in some areas, the two diverge rather than intersect. Therapy just might be one of them.

A CLOUD ROLLS IN

On Fridays after work, Spreckels Tavern hosted a roiling frenzy of humanity in which supplicants came to the shrine to mend their occupationally induced psychic injuries. It was group therapy Spreckels style, and the healing was well underway.

Jommers normally avoided those times when his favorite tavern turned into a shaken hive, a place where the buzz drowned out the music and one must bellow to be heard, but sometimes he needed to reconnect to the world of the normal, whatever that was anymore.

Larry in particular often served as Jommers's reset button, an ordinary, guileless, easygoing, even-keeled man whose few hang-ups were worn plainly in the open like the bar rag on his belt. Shooting the breeze with Larry reassured Jommers that the world was not going to be swallowed by a black hole just yet. Maybe tomorrow, but not today, and that was good enough.

Larry used extra help for the weekend rush times, but the crowd still kept him hopping. Knowing his favorite bartender would be busy as hell, Jommers sat at the bar near the taps, the only place he could catch the man briefly standing still, working the myriad tap handles like some strange musical instrument.

"So there was this guy in here before, telling me about issues with the wife," Larry said. "They got a kid who's getting too chubby too soon and has really big feet."

"They all have big feet today."

"Tell me about it. I ran out to a mall for some underwear a while back and found myself in the middle of a pack of kids. All flopping around with big feet. Like I was in one of those penguin movies. I think it's the hormones in the water or something. But here's the thing . . . she blames him."

"For what?"

"She blames him for the kid being chubby with big feet, but it's the feet obsessing her."

"How is it his fault?"

"Somewhere she gets the notion that hubby dropped acid when he was young and it toasted some of his genes and that's why their kid turned out that way. The guy says no, he never did drugs of any kind, but she gets a bug up her butt about it. Just admit it, she says, then at least I can understand it, at least I can have closure, whatever the hell that is. But he says no, I'm not going to admit to something I didn't do. Things will go better for you if you do, she says."

"Sounds a lot like a police interrogation. And people don't understand how suspects can make false confessions."

"You're jumping ahead on me. So, in spite of his denials, she keeps on him about it, clamped on it like a Rott on your leg. Then she forbids access to the region until he confesses. So now it's getting to him, and the unscratched itch is warping his reason, making him think unwise thoughts. Just tell me the truth, she says, admit you've been lying about not using LSD, then we can put everything back to normal. Just tell me."

"I can see where this is going."

"Right. He caves. He thinks if he tells her what she wants to hear, it will all be over. They can move on."

"But it only makes it worse."

"Bull's-eye. And I won't get into the various ways of worse just to keep it brief. But, you know better than me, anytime you find yourself saying that you lied about having lied, well, things can only go downhill from there."

"Trust is an eggshell."

"Right. And he just rolled it under the wheel of a beer truck. You ready for another?"

"No, I have to go. I've got a date."

"Whoa! Stop the presses. Divulge the details. Disgorge every morsel."

"Next time. I'm already late."

⌒⌒

THE TRENCH WAS APTLY NAMED, given the bar's inky, dingy ambiance and lower-level location, beneath an old six-story dirty brick office building. The entrance was down a stairway at the back-alley side, as the front side was occupied by an office supply company.

The Trench was mostly a college bar, being two blocks from Grayton State University downtown, but it drew an eclectic crowd when it featured a blues band, which it did a few times a month. Grayton had once had a lively blues scene, but times and tastes had changed. There were only a couple bars left now that booked the blues, and only occasionally at that. Jommers liked to take advantage of those dwindling opportunities. Like tonight.

The last time he'd met with Chelsea it was at a tony bistro of her choosing. Her world. Now they would meet in his, and he wondered how that would go. This one was officially a date, where the first time was merely an informal get-together. It seemed like weeks ago, but it had only been days since that chaotic, catastrophic Monday. So much had happened since then, at least in his world. But he would avoid mentioning any of it to her. He wanted to get past their difference in position, the whole practitioner versus pupil thing. He wanted to see how it worked peer-to-peer, just a man and a woman. Also, he was thinking how Becca Tarburn had told her husband to leave his job outside the door like muddy boots. There was wisdom in that. Something to ponder for a guy who lived where he worked.

Chelsea had said she would be working late at the campus, doing research, so they'd agreed to meet at the bar, given its proximity.

She dressed simply. Blue jeans and a short-sleeved salmon blouse. No jewelry. She ordered a beer, even though she'd mentioned previously she didn't like it. Maybe she felt the need to fit in. He wanted to say that she needn't have bothered. The blues are like street fairs and graveyards. Everybody is welcome. But he let it slide. It's not polite to point.

"You know I didn't mean to be so blunt about shooting down your Internet addiction ideas Monday," he said. "It's just that I'm worried about disorder creep, and how that plays into the tentacles of the psychiatric-pharmaceutical-industrial-complex. Today's DSM has three times as many mental disorders than the first edition in fifty-two. And it has about seven times as many pages. God knows what the next one will be like. If the pharm-flunkies who write it get their way, we'll all be judged to have a set of disorders. In the future, we'll all begin our day consuming a personalized packet of pills custom-formulated by our personal pharmaceutical consultants. We'll all be perfect package cookies. And all those mom-made cookies, uneven and out-of-round, slightly burnt at the edges, those will all be forbidden."

Chelsea smiled and waved her hand in a gesture of dismissal. "Let's not talk shop. Tell me how you got into the blues."

He smiled back. "It's more like how did the blues get into me."

"And?"

"It was the work, actually. So to answer that, we do have to talk shop briefly. I started working it into some therapy sessions where I thought it was a fit, certain patients, certain situations."

"Counterintuitive, isn't it?"

"You know there's an old Mother Goose rhyme, supposedly written around 1700—'For every ailment under the sun, there is a remedy or there is none. If there be one, try to find it. If there be none, never mind it.'"

"Sounds like a precursor to the Serenity Prayer," she said.

"Yes, and there are many such precursors going back to ancient times, Epictetus, various religious texts. That Corinthians passage about love that's the big fave at weddings. Hopes all things. Endures all things. It's a common theme throughout history. Coping with suffering demands an acceptance of suffering. Now I can explain that to someone in philosophical terms and it will go right over their heads like a soaring red-tailed hawk. But the blues, they're saying the same thing on an emotional level that you can grasp intuitively and immediately. Life isn't fair, but I can deal with it. I can handle it."

"So we're not actually necessary, then. Psychologists can be replaced with a box set of essential blues CDs."

"It's only another tool in the toolkit. We can't make people happy. We can only help them cope with the things that make them unhappy. We can't ward off the storms of life. We can only sell raincoats. You do whatever works. And different things work for different people. I'm not into dogma. I'm into results."

"Okay. I get that part. But back to you, the music. Don't you ever get bored with it? The sameness of it all? The repetitiveness?"

"It's obviously repetitive in the chord progression, but it's the improvisation that keeps it fresh. Take a popular piece, done by a hundred musicians. Each one does a different take. And the best, they do a different take every time they do it. By contrast, you look at pop-rock acts, the solo part that poses as improvisation is in fact orchestrated beforehand. They play exactly the same way they did on the album, and play it the exact same way at every stop, on every stage. The performers hardly need to be there. They could just play the recording and no one would know the difference. So I would argue that it's pop-rock that suffers from mediocre sameness. It's all the same stuff but with different stylistic flourishes. Like a box of tofu burgers that comes with different flavor packets. Here's your country seasoning packet, here's your Cajun seasoning packet . . . but underneath, it's the same bland lump of glop."

"So that's why you prefer acoustic blues over electric. It's only rock and roll and you hate it."

"Rock screams down the highway in overdrive. The blues rumble down a rutted back road. When you smash the two together, there's a sense of discordance, of artifice. Like a veneer that attempts to make a countertop laminate look like rough-hewn granite."

"So your beef is about authenticity," she said.

"When you get a minute, listen to Skip James singing 'Hard Time Killing Floor Blues.' That's unbeatable authenticity."

"I'm sure it is unbeatable. It's also unduplicable. Authenticity doesn't exist in the ether. It's pegged to a time, place, and culture. Creative works must be expressed within the idiom of their age. You can't write in the style of Shakespeare. You can't write in the style of Raymond Chandler anymore without sounding silly, like a parody. But, back to music. Say you were into classical. It would be impossible for someone today to compose something authentically baroque. And in that same vein . . . why today's country is faux country."

"Maybe authenticity is not the right term. Maybe it's engagement. Or integrity. On the blues scene today, I see a lot of focus on technical proficiency at the expense of emotional content. Musicians showing you what they can do rather than telling you how they feel. Saw a band here a few weeks ago. Bunch of young guys. Mind-blowing musicianship. But I had the sense they were playing their guitars the same way they play their video games, with robotic soullessness. There's that old line, it's not the notes you play, but the ones you leave out."

"I like that line," she said. "It applies to relationships, too. If I may shift gears."

"You may."

"Everyone is always harping on communication as the key to a good relationship. Tell me what you're feeling. Let it all out. All that whole thing. You know? But in my experience, it's really about the things you refrain from saying, the firebombs you don't throw."

"An interesting analogy. A relationship is an instrument that must be well played."

"Do psychologists play it better?" she asked.

"Well, as you probably heard, I was once married . . . married to another psychologist, no less. So you're probably wondering how a psychologist screws up a marriage. Isn't he supposed to know about such things? Isn't that like a botanist getting poison ivy?"

"I guess it would be harder for two psychologists. I mean, they'd always be analyzing each other."

"All couples analyze each other. Psychologists just do it with bigger words. That's not the real reason the marriage failed."

"I didn't mean to pry."

"That's okay. I'll keep it general. It's reductionist and cliché to say that we just grew apart, but a more creative phrasing doesn't change what happened. Thing is, people today are always trying to reinvent themselves. And now that we're living longer, we have plenty of time to do so. Over the years I've seen people change their values, their politics, their lifestyle, even their appearance. I've seen an atheist become an evangelical, and vice versa. I've seen a barbecue hound become a vegan, and vice versa. And they don't limit themselves to just one transformation. I've seen people change their lives multiple times. Each time becoming a different person. So the thing you need to understand, if you're a young person getting married today, you are in fact marrying three different people, two of whom you haven't met yet."

"That's scary. Almost like a horror movie."

"Yes—yes, it is, and the horror movie analogy is more apt than you know."

"But suppose one of them is older, say a young woman marrying an older man, a solid, centered man who already knows what he's about; that would reduce the risk somewhat, wouldn't it?"

"Well, yes. I suppose it would."

He smiled. She smiled back. Harmonious mind meld. Somewhere the lost chord had been found and was being played at the right volume.

But then she'd just had to bring it up. She hadn't meant anything by it. No hidden motive. She didn't know. She was only pulling the conversation out of the awkward stall of mutually adoring, glowing gazes.

"You know, I thought about you Tuesday when I heard about that shooting down by the river Monday night. I know you live down that way. I was wondering if it was near you."

He sighed involuntarily. "Yes, it was."

"And then, what was really wild—when was it, the other day, the news reports said it was a policeman who had been acting psychotic. I remembered that you treat cops, and I thought, wow, I wonder if Karl knew that guy."

"Yes, I knew him." He said it slowly and deeply, sounding like a recording slowed to half speed.

"Was he like an active patient? Somebody you were treating? Or are you not allowed to talk about it?"

He didn't answer, nor need to. Given that he had prepared for a date, not a patient session, he had left his sphinx mask in a drawer back at the office, so even as his mouth was muzzled, his face was blaring.

"Oh," she said. "Was he the one who called you when we were at Cafe Annique?"

His silence roared the response.

"Oh, my," she said. "I'm sorry."

Her face registered an ambiguous astonishment, both comprehending and puzzled simultaneously. In just a few seconds, she fully grasped the entirety of events on Monday night, but appeared unsure how to react. Would she show empathy and concern for what Jommers had gone through, and might still be going through? Or would she look inward and ponder her own indirect involvement? Would she feel that her presence had influenced the outcome by holding Jommers at the cafe when he might have otherwise left upon getting the first call? And, if so, would she feel tarnished by extension? Guilt by association? Would she resent that the taint had been involuntarily thrust upon her?

Her demeanor deflated, and a coolness swept over them like the shadow of a cloud moving across an open field. She took a sip of beer, and the condensation from the glass wetted her hand, which she then wiped on her jeans.

He tried valiantly to restart the conversation, but the engine had died, the fuel pump shot. He could twist the key and turn it over, but it wasn't going to fire up. Not now. The short, sweet ride was over.

A brief while later, she complained about a sinus headache and that her allergies were acting up on her. She apologized weakly as she departed. The date was over and the band hadn't even started yet.

He had not expected a spectacular unforgettable evening with her, but neither had he foreseen disaster. The collision with an iceberg while at full cruising speed left him dazed and confused. He then chastised himself for being optimistic in the first place. At this point in life, he should know better. He got another beer and stared glumly into space.

And then the band came out—Max Ballroom. They started doing their sound checks, getting ready to play. Time for the blues to prove his thesis, the one about how when life knocks you down, the blues cushion the fall. He had known these guys for years, and they never failed to entertain.

The band took a novel angle by focusing on songs that had dance-like rhythms, pieces like "Cha Cha Cha in Blue" by Junior Wells, "Help the Poor" by B.B. King, "All Your Love" by Otis Rush, "Slow Drag" by Taj Mahal, and W.C. Handy's classic "St. Louis Blues." And when the band ran out of those, the guys rearranged blues standards to shake, skip, and sway to their own eccentric beat.

As part of their shtick, the band members wore shabby, mismatched tuxedos, as if they had been stolen from a trash dumper outside a two-bit formal-wear rental warehouse.

Jommers strolled over to say hello, and after exchanging greetings, he got some bad news from the band's leader.

"Stevie is selling the joint. Says he's too old to handle it anymore. Once the deal closes, we're out. The new owner is going with an all oldies format. Going to do a different decade every night of the week. Can it possibly get any pukier than that?"

"Don't tempt fate by asking," Jommers said.

"I don't know, man, I look around, and people look like they're grown up, but their heads are still in high school. It's a sad, strange thing that no one wants to plug into the real anymore. But I guess it keeps you busy."

"It keeps the pill pushers busy. I just sit and whittle little wooden whistles all day."

Jommers stayed till the very end, not knowing if he'd ever see the band again. And they held the last note of the last song way past the bounds of sanity, not knowing if they'd ever perform it again.

SATURDAY, AUGUST 11, 2007

DAY SIX

MYSTERIOUS GAS

Cemeteries come alive on Saturday. It's the preferred day for funerals—you get a higher turnout. The day is also prime time for visitors coming to see the stones of those who already had their send-off. To a primitive unfamiliar with it all, the behavior must appear odd. People staring at polished stones. Some blankly, some smiling, some weeping. Some talking as if the departed were sitting right there, nodding. The unfamiliar primitive stranger might be forgiven for thinking that the stones are possessed by spirits, drawing people near, transfixing them.

And this Saturday found one Karl Jommers at Myrtle Haven Cemetery, gently laying some flowers down in front of a headstone that watched over the remains of George and Ethel Banks. He pulled some untrimmed grass from around the edges of the stone while avoiding touching it, as the searing sun had imbued the granite with the heat of a glowing ember. He then stood up with hands clasped in front, as if praying, and stared reverently at the gravestone.

He had absolutely no idea who those people were, but the place of their ultimate repose was a conveniently optimal distance from the funeral being held nearby for Earl Tarburn.

Becca Tarburn had made it quite clear that police colleagues, or others from that side of his life, were not welcome. It was a private ceremony, for family, friends, neighbors, and fellow congregants at his church.

Jommers could not allow himself to stay away, but he didn't want to create a scene either. So he pretended to be visiting a grave, one far enough away to be inconspicuous, but close enough to barely make out the words of the pastor.

"Earl Tarburn was a devoted and loyal servant to his wife and family, to his friends and neighbors, to his community, to his nation, and ultimately, to his God and Savior."

The indirect reference to Tarburn serving his community was the one and only nod to his career as a police officer.

Jommers wore a wide-brimmed boonie hat and kept his back to the proceedings. Only occasionally did he turn slightly to take a quick glance. And each time he did, he noticed another man looking at a grave some distance from the funeral, only on the other side of it. That man also had his back to the crowd, but also turned occasionally to take a furtive glance from underneath the brim of an outback-style straw hat. It was if he was employing the same stratagem of covertly paying respect. His face was not visible, but there was something familiar about him, even from a distance. A short, wiry frame, held in a ready stance. Coiled energy waiting to be released by a tripwire. Like a boxer.

When the funeral crowd began to disperse, the mystery man walked slowly toward Jommers, head down. The distinctive gait yielded an ID long before the face came into view. It was Lieutenant Augie Dallabaco, SWAT commander, refusing to be AWOL when one of his own fallen was being laid to earth.

"I should have guessed you'd be here," Jommers said.

"I couldn't fail him today. He was one of us. The wife, she never understood. He had a second family. Us. But I don't blame her. She got treated shabby by the department. She has a right to be pissed. The whole thing . . . it's just not right."

"We the only ones?"

"Inside, yeah. But I was watching the road outside the gate. I could see the guys drive by, one by one. The car would approach, stop for a few seconds, paying their respects from a distance, not wanting to make a scene, but needing to say goodbye. Then each would slowly drive on. Couldn't keep a count, but it was a lot of them. I know it tore them up to have to do it that way. But all you can do is all you can do, right?"

"Right," Jommers said.

"You know, after we talked last time, I thought we had an understanding. I know you talked to those two this week. I'm presuming you heard things. Was hoping to hear from you. Did you lose my number?"

"If you're talking about evaluations of Biederbach and Voros, you know I can't repeat anything said in their sessions. It's against the code of ethics, which you would most certainly want me to observe if you were a patient."

"Ethics. Ethics. There's a good man over there being lowered into the ground. What about the ethics of ignoring how he got there? What are the ethics of forgetting him? You must care or you wouldn't be here, right?"

"When you do your job, you have to operate under rules of engagement. So do I. We all work under conditions. But before we get too philosophical, I don't have any new insights to share anyway. I don't understand it any better today than I did Monday night."

"No new insights. Well, then, maybe we should get some. You doing anything now?"

"No."

"Okay. Follow me."

JOMMERS FOLLOWED DALLABACO over to Fire Station No. 17, where he looked for an EMS paramedic named Orlando Houps.

"Hey, Lieutenant," Houps said. "Sorry I missed you last time. This Death Valley weather keeping us busy. Heatstroke and dehydration. Older folks, mostly. Lot of them live in a harsh place. You know those end-of-the-world kind of movies? Everything gone to hell, danger everywhere. In certain parts of the city, there's people living like that right now. Right here. So the old folks in those places, you know, they got no A/C, but they're too scared to open the windows, even when it's brutal hot like this. So they just sit and get cooked. Some of them got fans blowing on them, but it's just blowing hot air. Just turns an oven into a convection oven. They cook faster. Then they end up on the floor. Then off we go in the wagon to pick them up. And sometimes it's too late. Sad shame they got to live like that. Sad shame. So what can I do for you?"

"We won't keep you long," Dallabaco said. "This is Karl Jommers, a psychologist who works for the department as a contractor. He's helping us investigate the incident on Eggers Court Monday. We understand that your EMS unit was one of several on the scene, and that you were tending to one of the suspects briefly before he died."

"Yeah. And brief would be the word, which was fine with me, because he went dark before we got a chance to load him in. So I just left him there and said let the coroner take him with the others. And then one of your people, Narcotics, I think, started giving me shit about it. He wanted me to rush him over to Bridget. Says, maybe they can bring him to for a bit. Maybe I can get something out of him. And I say, bring him to? Bring him to? Let me tell you something, man. Jesus don't work at Bridget ER and EMS don't haul slab. This here is not red wagon material. This here is black wagon, and the lump is staying here until the black wagon come get it. Now I'm not normally such a prick about it, but this one was a butthead meth cook, which means he got nasty chemical shit all over him. And that triggers the decontamination protocol we got to follow anytime we haul a cook. So if I put the lump in the wagon, even for a minute, then, when I get back, I got to go through this whole clean-down procedure for the wagon and everything in it, which takes a couple of hours. And I did not want to have to go through all that for no reason. So we get into a tussle over it, me and the Narcotics guy. And he starts getting in my face, and that just don't worry me at all, because, you know, while cops get to wear lard, we got to maintain tone, because, like we may have to haul a shamu down six flights today. So I can take a badge belly. Anytime, any day. So he sees where I'm at on it and stands down, but says he's going to get me written up, but I know my report got my back, which he always does, so I don't worry about it. It's going to be cool in the end."

"Did the suspect say anything to you?" Dallabaco asked.

"Not anything that made sense."

"What do you mean?"

"Son of a bitch bleeding from six or seven different holes, shaking and trembling, pissing his pants, looks up at me and asks, did we get him? And I thought he said them, did we get them. So I say, no, asshole, they got you, because I think he's talking about the cops that raided the place. And he shakes his head and says no, I mean the giant. Did we get the giant? I don't know what the hell he's talking about. I say, what giant? He says, maggot man. Maggot man. Did we get him? And I just say, yeah, whatever, you know? And then he powers down, lights out. But it was freaky, you know? Here he was, just a few ticks left, and he's still scared of something. Scared shitless."

"I assume you've seen a lot of ODs," Jommers said.

"Oh, yeah."

"You think he was just wacked out on his own stuff?"

"Maybe. But, you know, I been on more than one run where the ghost bails the wagon and leaves me with the hide. And I tell you what, dying make you crazy, too."

Before leaving the fire station, Jommers gave the paramedic a few of his business cards. Dallabaco observed it and snickered.

"Since when did you become like the window replacement sales guy?"

"My bookkeeper is on my back. She says if I don't bring in new business soon, I'm going to be the window replacement sales guy."

"We need to talk. You heading back to your place?"

"Yes."

"I'll catch up with you there."

~

JOMMERS ARRIVED FIRST, grabbed a couple of beers, and sat down in one of the rockers. When Dallabaco showed up, he was carrying a large brown clasp envelope.

"By the way, my hat is way cooler than your hat," Dallabaco said.

"Good thing. You have a hotter head," Jommers replied.

Dallabaco sat down, opened a beer, looked at Jommers, and started thrumming his fingers on the big brown envelope. Dallabaco was trying to incite curiosity about the envelope's contents, force Jommers to ask about it so that something could be demanded in return for answering. Negotiation by body language.

Jommers didn't bite. The shop downstairs was quiet, as it was Saturday. So the only sounds were the rockers creaking, beer slurping, and fingers thrumming on an envelope.

Eventually Dallabaco broke the silence.

"If I'm someone trying to figure out what happened with Tarburn down here Monday night, I am definitely interested in Detective Ilona Voros, the person who shot him. But should I also be interested in Patrolman Dwayne Biederbach? On the one hand, he's just this squirrelly, noodle-nuts kind of guy who was there by happenstance. On the other hand, there was some kind of interaction between Biederbach and Tarburn before Voros got there. So you have to wonder what they talked about."

"I assume Internal Affairs has already asked Patrolman Biederbach that very question," Jommers said. "Which means that the people officially charged with investigating those events presumably have the answer."

The silence returned, except for the rocking, the slurping and the thrumming. And, again, Dallabaco broke the silence first.

"Word around the station is that Biederbach is one of those conspiracy nuts. Would that be your take?"

"We don't use that *N* word in my business," Jommers said. "But if he held some unorthodox views, it's not something I would get into for a critical incident follow-up."

"Hmm. But you know, people like that, they tend to volunteer a lot regardless. And, you know, given the strangeness of everything that happened that night, I imagine a guy like Biederbach would probably have cooked up some wild-ass theory to explain it all. You know, sinister forces hatching dark plots, all that. Probably would be eager to share that idea with a good listener, you know, like a therapist or somebody."

"I'm sure Patrolman Biederbach has shared his concerns during his interview with Internal Affairs. I understand they are good listeners."

"IA wouldn't ask for his opinion, they would just focus on the facts."

"And that's a good policy, isn't it? Focusing on the facts."

Dallabaco paused a long minute before continuing.

"I understand that one of his wild-ass theories is that the army is coming to take over the police."

"There are some out there who suggest that it has already happened," Jommers said.

"You talking about that asshole *Ledger* columnist foaming about our tank? First of all, it's just a mini-tank, a surplus LAV-150. And secondly, we replaced the gun on it with a ram. Thirdly, it proved indispensable on Monday. That old printing plant on Eggers Court had brick walls and steel doors in steel frames that open out, not in. Since steel is ductile and brick is brittle, we just punched the sucker right through the wall. Without that damn thing, the shooting would have gone on a hell of lot longer."

"If I recall, the *Ledger* writer wasn't only concerned about the tank, excuse me, the mini-tank, but all the military-type weapons and ammunition in general."

"And what of it? This isn't thirty years ago, where you're rousting some solo street shit with a snub .38 in his pocket. We're taking on armed gangs that have better hardware than we do sometimes. It's all we can do to keep up."

"I think he was also concerned about the regular presence of military advisors."

"Well, fuck yeah, and we're happy to have them, too. What the fuck does that numbnuts think SWAT stands for? Special weapons and tactics. If you have special weapons, you need special training in how to properly use them. And if you have special tactics, you need training in how to execute them. Look, let me tell you . . ."

By this point, Dallabaco was shouting, leaning forward and pointing his finger in Jommers's face. Then, suddenly, he stopped, leaned back in his chair, relaxed and smiled.

"You are fucking good. I will give you that. I'm on a track, you push my hot button, get me off my track. You are definitely fucking good."

The sphinx was officially off duty on Saturday, but Jommers denied himself any victory grin as a matter of habit. This was not a billable bout, but it was a match all the same. Dallabaco resumed thrumming his fingers on the brown envelope, and Jommers resumed ignoring it.

Another long, silent minute passed.

"I'm hearing that the Force Review Committee will clear my guys on Monday," Dallabaco said.

"That was fast. I expected it would take weeks or more, what with the questions."

"Yeah, well, you can't keep your best SWAT guys out for weeks. Not here, anyway. We don't have that size of a force. We don't have the luxury of dicking around and stretching out those reviews. Besides, it was an easy call. The TV crews were already at the perimeter before the fireworks started. Their videos clearly shows the butthead cooks firing first before we went in.

"As for the bystanders that got hit in the apartments, all those slugs were nine mil, fired from the Brazilian semis the cooks had. My guys carry Colt AR-15s, which use a .223 Rem. round. Different shape and size altogether, and our slugs were all accounted for at the scene or in the stiffs. So there are no real questions about the actions of my men, only questions about the buttheads."

"Did the Force Review Committee venture any speculation as to why your butthead cooks were shooting at the apartment building instead of you?"

"No, and that's not their bailiwick anyway. Their inquiry was narrow and specific—did Augie Dallabaco fuck up at Eggers Court? Answer—no, he did not. Inquiry over."

"Congratulations."

"Yeah, thanks. I'm warm all over about it. But it doesn't answer your question, does it? What those dipshits were shooting at and why." He kept his fingers thrumming on the envelope. "By the way, getting back to those military advisors, contrary to what that newspaper shithead thinks, these army advisors are not sinister storm troopers from the evil empire. They're just ordinary guys. Like anybody else, they got whiny families and disapproving in-laws, they got bills and credit card debt, they got bad knees and bad backs, they own shitty products that break right after the warranty expires, they got leaky faucets and clogged drains, they got crabgrass and dandelions in their lawn—in short, they deal with the same shit everyone does. They're just guys. Honestly, I think if all the antigovernment paranoids just spent some quality time with the people they're so afraid of—yeah, that's it. Both sides go bowling. Losing side buys pizza and beer."

"Like exposure therapy for phobias."

"Yeah, whatever the hell that means."

Thrum. Thrum. Thrum.

Finally, Dallabaco opened the envelope. He spent some time poking around through, clearly stretching out the suspense. When he was finished playing it up, he pulled out a brochure for car tires and handed it to Jommers.

"You in the market for some new tires?" Jommers asked.

"Yeah. I was thinking of a good set of all-season radials. Any recommendations?"

"The brand shown there is one of the better ones. Truth be told, though, I prefer a dedicated set of winter tires over all-seasons. You can't escape the Bends without going up a steep hill any way you turn. Ice and snow makes that pretty hairy, and salt trucks hit this place last, if at all. Seasonal changeover is a cinch, seeing as how I have access to a lift and air wrenches downstairs."

"So there is an upside to living over a repair shop. Who knew? Did you take note of the tire store address on the brochure?"

"I did," Jommers said.

"That tire shop is on McKinley, which is in front of the Mentmore Manor apartments and faces the north side of the printing plant on Eggers Court, the side that the cooks were shooting from."

"Okay."

Dallabaco reached back into the envelope and pulled out two enlarged photo prints and handed them to Jommers. "Like I told you before, when an assault is planned ahead of time, I personally reconnoiter the area. I take a lot of pictures. I study the pictures. When I come back with guns, I want it to be a place I know. I want to know it like I grew up there. I want to think of everything that can happen there. What I gave you there—those are two different pics of the tire store in front of the apartment. The one in your left hand, I took three days before the raid. The one in your right hand, I took the day after the shit storm. What do you notice different?"

"In the before picture," Jommers said, "a giant inflatable on the tire store roof. Not there afterward."

"Very good. Now I was curious about that, so I went in and asked the tire store manager about it. Said that he was holding a special on a particular brand of tires and put up the inflatable of the brand's mascot to promote it. But it got shot full of holes during the incident Monday and wouldn't hold air, so he took it down and sent it out for repair. Now then, let's rewind a bit, thirty minutes or so, back to our friendly paramedic who says that the dying words of a meth cook was to wonder whether they got the giant maggot man." Dallabaco pointed to the before picture. "If you were making a horror movie about a giant maggot man, would you make him look something like this?"

"Possibly. Though I wouldn't have him smiling and waving like that. What you're suggesting is that your bad guys were shooting at an inflatable on a tire store roof, not at the apartment dwellers on their balconies who just happened to be in the same line of fire."

"You got it. So the question is why they would they shoot at an inflatable mascot on a tire store when they're surrounded by cops with AR-15s."

"I guess the answer lies in the product they were cooking."

"Right. That's the easy answer, isn't it?"

"One begins with the simplest explanation, moving up the scale only if it proves inadequate," Jommers said.

"It's inadequate."

"How so?" Jommers asked.

"That inflatable had been up there more than a week. The cooks had been in their lab off and on almost every day over that time. They saw it every day without apparently imagining it as any giant maggot man. It was only after we shot the gas up that they started shooting at it. The goal was to get them to come out, because we were given some bullshit about booby traps. That's why we gassed. Only after the gas did they start shooting, and only after that did we bust through the wall. You know, with our tank."

"Obviously the gas combined with whatever else they had in their system to produce the psychotic reaction. When chemicals are combined in the body, they can have unpredictable synergistic effects."

"Another easy answer."

"Again, you have a better one?"

Dallabaco leaned back and with a mischievous look thrummed his fingers on the brown envelope again. There was clearly more inside it. "You're going to share with me, too, when I'm done, right?"

"I don't know what you want, so I can't tell you if I can share it," Jommers answered.

"Are you pretending to be disinterested as a bargaining ploy, knowing I have no one else to talk to about this, or do you just genuinely not get it yet?"

"It would be fair to say I don't know what it is that I don't know."

"Don't fuck with me, Jommers. This isn't a pissing contest. They put a good man to soil this morning. He was one of mine."

"He was one of mine, too."

Dallabaco paused for half a minute or so before reaching back into the envelope. He withdrew another enlargement and handed it to Jommers. The photo depicted the interior of a run-down apartment. Pieces of glass from a broken aquarium lay on a wet floor along with a handful of dead tropical fish.

"You remember couple months ago, incident over on Juneberry Boulevard? Shithole apartment over a thrift shop. Of course you do, given that we all had to file through here again after it, get the blessing from Father Jommers in order to get another payday. Anyway, some asshole got tossed out by his girlfriend he'd been living with, came back a few days later to threaten her. She calls 911 and mentions a gun. By the time we get there, it's evolved into a hostage situation. We distract him with a bullhorn and she manages to escape. We don't want to charge up there and start the lead flying just yet because there are several units up there and we don't know how many people might be on the floor. So we shoot some gas up through the window hoping he'll come down. And, boy, did he. A few minutes after we gassed him, we heard gunfire inside the apartment. Before we knew what was going on, we see him leap out the window headfirst. It was a pretty nice dive. I would have given it a nine point two, except for the fact that it was onto a concrete sidewalk, not into a pool. Broke his neck and died instantly."

"If I recall, the newspaper referred to him as the Juneberry Jumper."

"Yes. So, anyway, we wondered what he was shooting at, since he obviously wasn't shooting at us and the girlfriend had already blown. Now take a real close look at the picture. See the bullet holes in the wall by the broken aquarium frame? See the holes in the floor by the fish?"

"He was shooting at the fish," Jommers said.

"Correct. Now why in the fuck would he do that?"

"Ichthyophobia? Fear of fish?"

"You're not paying attention. Recall that I mentioned that he'd been living there before the girlfriend booted him. So he'd been with the fish every day, presumably with no problem."

"Tox screen?"

"Yes, PCP and marijuana."

"Well, there it is."

"You don't see any parallel with Eggers Court?"

"Sure I do," Jommers said. "I see drugs and tear gas in both cases, and apparently in some people the combination causes severe adverse reactions that include psychotic episodes."

"CS gas is just a chemical irritant. It's not psychoactive."

"Okay, fine. But meth, PCP and marijuana are. And those are sufficient. Look, in my younger days, I worked in a psych ward for a while. I saw lots of ODs, bad acid trips, all kinds of drug-induced psychosis. Some of the things I saw and heard would make your hair stand on end. All right? So you tell me that somebody high on meth shoots an inflatable, or somebody on PCP shoots some fish, I'm sorry, this is not raising my eyebrows much. On a one-to-ten scale of bizarre, I'd give it about a six point three."

"You like those easy outs, don't you?"

"SOP," Jommers said. "You start with the simplest explanation and escalate when new information justifies it."

"Okay, then let's escalate. You want to guess who my gas man was at both places?"

"Tarburn?"

"You're getting better at this. Yeah, Tarburn. You remember those arms on him . . . like those giant cables that hold up suspension bridges. A gun in those hands was the same as a gun in a vise. His nerves were like steel cable, too. No matter how much shit flying around, he'd be as calm as someone flipping burgers on the grill. He did not miss what he was shooting at. Not ever."

"Until Monday night, when he missed Voros."

"That's right. It appears he did fire first. So you do know some things, don't you? She's a very lucky woman. Does she appreciate that?"

"Go on."

"All right, let's talk about CS gas, what you call tear gas. Technically, it's not a gas. It's a solid chemical that's typically dissolved into a solvent then dispersed as an aerosol. The actual chemical name is ortho chloro something something. I don't remember because it has more syllables than I have years. But it's the same shit that everyone uses everywhere. And like I said, it's just a nontoxic chemical irritant. It does not make you fucking crazy. Okay?"

"Understood."

"Now, you can spray it, you can hose it, you can lob a grenade of it, or, if you want to put some distance between yourself and the cloud, you can shoot a gas grenade from a launcher. Now let's say you want to get it into an enclosed space. They make a penetrating round with this shit that can be fired from a twelve-gauge. We call them harpoons, and you can punch one through a window or a wooden door that isn't too thick. It's the most accurate delivery method. It doesn't have the same quantity as a grenade, but for an enclosed space, you need less than open air anyway. I remember a few years ago, I needed to put a couple of these through a window with a tight set of burglar bars on it. I ask Tarburn if he can do it, and he says no problem. So he grabs the Mossy—"

"Mossberg."

"Yes. So the first one goes through right between the bars, and I'm thinking he got lucky. Then he puts the second one through the same two bars, through the same hole in the window. And right then I know, this is my go-to guy for this shit. And so when I needed harpoons thrown at Juneberry and Eggers Court—"

"He was your guy."

"Correct. Now here's where it gets weird. Given that we have special weapons and all, I got to keep close track of this shit, right? Plus, whenever we go to a hoedown, Force Review makes me account for every round fired—how many, what type, who fired them, and where they ended up. So when it comes to inventory control, I am fussier than a pucker-puss librarian. Now I had Tarburn fire exactly two harpoons into that apartment over the thrift shop. So, when I do my counts after, I should be down two. But I'm not. And it gets weirder, because the spent shells from those two rounds that would have been ejected from the Mossy . . . they're nowhere to be found."

"Did you ask Tarburn about it?"

"I had to. I mean, it's not like a neighborhood softball game where you bring your own ball and bat."

"What did he say?"

"He couldn't explain it. He was hemming and hawing . . . I could tell he was lying. I'm sure you know he was a real religious man. And I mean real as in not fake. Not someone who puts on the church show to please the wife."

"Like yourself."

"Exactly. Tarburn was the real deal. And when you're the real deal, you're not good at lying, because you haven't had anywhere near the practice the rest of us have had. So the talk with him makes me double confused. Why is this otherwise honest man lying to me? And what is he lying about? I can see lying about something missing. But what's going on when you lie about having some extra?"

"There's only one reason an otherwise honest, loyal man lies to his immediate superior officer," Jommers said. "He's suffering from conflicted loyalties and he's siding with the higher authority."

"Very good. Now you're tracking me, now you're tracking. I think we both know who that higher authority might be. When you add up all this freaky-deaky shit, you got Tarburn bringing his own goodies to the party. Whatever he fired into those buildings at Juneberry and Eggers Court, it wasn't CS gas. It was something else he brought."

"Did you end up with extra after Eggers Court?"

"No, but another excellent question, though. I think he learned his lesson after our first talk. First time was an oversight because he wasn't aware how closely I monitor the stock. So whatever he was using at Eggers, he made sure to pocket an equivalent number of CS rounds. Now then, I know he was a smart man, a man who could name the stars in the sky, which I can't, but I'm pretty sure he wasn't a chemist. So these extracurricular rounds . . . who gave them to him and why? What was in them? Why is it secret? I mean, we don't hesitate to change products or vendors when we find something better. But it's not a big deal, not hush-hush. So what gives?"

"I don't know," Jommers said. "But if I were that newspaper columnist we were just talking about, the one worried about stuff you get from the army, maybe I'd be looking in that direction."

Dallabaco laughed. "You like irony? I mean, really big honking irony?"

"Sure."

"The military's not allowed to use CS gas on the battlefield because it violates an international chemical weapons convention we signed. Cops can use it on some unruly kids protesting the price of yogurt, but the army can't use it on the enemy. You can blow the shit out of combatants with everything you got, turn him into fucking hamburger, but you can't make him cry. Seriously. The treaty prohibits any compound that activates the trigeminal nerve. So a soldier can shoot an RPG into a house full of people, shred them into bloody pieces, and that's all copacetic. But if he tosses in a few cups of minced onion, he's a war criminal."

"Well, maybe that's your answer, then," Jommers said. "If the army wanted to test a chemical irritant that it's not permitted to use, then they get cops to test it, because cops are allowed to use it. So they find a police department run by a former career army man like Scubbetts, and he's probably happy to oblige. Tarburn was also ex-army, so he gets on board with it. It violates department rules, but Tarburn sees service to his country as the higher good."

"Sounds plausible, but why test something you can't use? More importantly, it doesn't explain circumventing the chain of command. When the military advisors have something new to talk about for SWAT, the conversation involves me, a captain, a commander, and the chief. So why does Scubbetts, a man who spent a lifetime observing chain-of-command protocol, take this straight to Tarburn, bypassing several layers of command structure?"

"Maybe it was a request by the military advisors. Keep personnel involvement to absolute lowest level. Minimize exposure."

"But I don't see getting all this antsy over a new flavor of tear gas," Dallabaco said. "Tears are tears. Snot is snot. Who cares how you get them flowing? Unless it's something more than just tear gas."

"Like?"

"Based on these two events, Juneberry and Eggers Court, it appears that anyone who inhales this stuff gets scared shitless psycho. What if that's not just a side effect? What if that's the intended effect?"

"I don't have a military mind," Jommers said, "but if I was engaged in combat, I don't think I'd want to use a weapon with such unpredictable effects on the enemy. Would the chemical make them afraid to fight? Or would it make them afraid to surrender?"

"Another excellent question. All the more reason you would want to test it before deploying it. So you get some cops to test it on lice from the hood and see what happens. You test it on real people facing some real shit and you observe real reactions, something you can't duplicate in a laboratory."

"But you said it's a violation of international law for them to use chemical weapons."

"Yes, and as we all know, people sometimes violate the law if they think they can get away with it. Look, any other shit you might use, whether it's mustard gas or tear gas, would have observable physical effects. You get caught. But if you can surreptitiously deliver a chemical that has only psychological effects, who would know? The only observable result would be fighters surrendering. So if you're considering breaking international law, you probably want to be subtle about it."

"Let's say you're right," Jommers said. "Let's say that instead of shooting CS gas into these two places, Tarburn popped in some strange, experimental chemical. Why didn't this chemical show up in the tox screens on the bodies?"

"It depends what they did or didn't do. If you got a body and you don't know how it got dead, you're going to run the kinds of tests that look for anything and everything. Mass spectrometry, spectrophotometry, shit like that. But if you got a guy who jumped out a window headfirst, all you want to know is what he was hopped up on. So you run a battery of simple up-or-down drug screens that are substance-specific. He was high on this, but not that. That's all you get from those. The other issue is the guy doing the tests."

"Our friendly county coroner," Jommers said.

"You know about him?"

"I've heard things."

"He's a political hack with no medical training," Dallabaco said. "His two main assistants are his cousin, who was an X-ray tech, and a sister-in-law who was a dental hygienist. All three supposedly have certificates in forensic training that they got online. More importantly, he's extremely cooperative with law enforcement."

"The department gets the report it wants."

"Most of the time."

"Doesn't he ever get tripped up in court?"

"He might someday, but in most criminal cases, the forensic report is used to squeeze a plea, and once you get it, the report becomes irrelevant, and often gets lost."

"Sweet."

"So, in our case here, if the chief should call his pal the coroner and say, there's a body coming your way, we suspect the guy was on PCP, guess what the report says."

"Interesting theory," Jommers said. "Bizarre as hell. But interesting."

"Thank you. Now what have you got for me? And don't say nothing or I will be really, really pissed."

"As I told you Tuesday, I saw Tarburn before it all went down. He was carrying a blue kit bag at the time. If he was in possession of extracurricular rounds, as you put it, they were likely in that bag."

"You didn't mention that before."

"I'm mentioning it now."

"What happened to it?"

"I don't know. He didn't give it to me."

"How about noodle balls Biederbach?"

"I don't see how. The whole area was searched, including his cruiser, before he was released from the scene."

"So then where the fuck is it?"

"Tarburn either hid it or disposed of it, and I suspect the latter. I find it curious that a man being pursued runs toward the river rather than away from it, runs to a dead end. My guess is that he tossed it in the river, and it's either at the bottom, or it washed out into the lake."

"Wonderful."

"The point I was going to make," Jommers said, "he was behaving paranoid, borderline psychotic. As I mentioned to you last time we talked, he pulled his gun on the pirates painted on the wall of The Lousy Pirate bar. That made no sense to me at the time, but in light of what you just told me, his behavior seems consistent with your two cases. So if your mystery chemical actually exists, and Tarburn was in possession of it, then his behavior suggests he became inadvertently exposed to it. So you tell me, would something like that leak? Blow up in the heat of car trunk in the sun?"

"A commercially made product . . . not likely. But with something experimental, hand-loaded . . . who the hell knows? Without knowing the active ingredient or the delivery medium used to aerosolize it, I can't even speculate.

Interesting, though, that you assume inadvertent exposure."

"You're suggesting it was deliberate?" Jommers asked.

"You got a guy conflicted about keeping a secret. Innocent bystanders get killed as a result of this big secret thing he did. He's a moral man, he feels guilty. He wants the whole thing to end. He wants to spill . . . get it off his chest. His handler senses this and decides to prevent that from happening. So the handler uses it on Tarburn, turns him into a raging psycho. And because this particular raging psycho carries a gun, it forces an unaware IA cop to shoot him. No link back. A murder that doesn't look like one."

"Handler. Singular. What about the military advisors? You suspect the secret stuff is coming from them."

"Yeah, they're doing something secret, but it's in service to their country. They're straight-up guys. They would never be party to a murder. This is Scubbetts all the way. Scubbetts likely never told them about anything going wrong."

"And I thought the first part of the theory was bizarre," Jommers said. "Now you're suggesting that the chief of police conspired to kill one of his own men to cover up a botched experiment and save his job."

"Yes. Now what do we do about it?"

"How the hell do I know? You have a wild theory that few would find credible. And you have no evidence or witnesses to support it. All you have is vapor."

"Let me rephrase the question," Dallabaco said. "What will you do to help me with it?"

"I don't know what you want from me."

"Word is you didn't clear Voros, that she'll be coming back here. She knows something. I feel it. You need to find out what."

"By your own theory, she was an unwitting pawn. What could she know?"

"She was the last one to see him alive. Maybe she knows or can figure out where that kit bag is. Also, you have access to Scubbetts, and as the official head checker, you have cause to discuss the situation with him. And I've just found out you're the only one that Becca Tarburn has talked to, which means you have access to her, as well. And I heard through the grapevine that Biederbach asked the benefits rep about therapy coverage, which means he's planning on seeing you even though you cleared him. Apparently the benefits person found it so hilarious—a shudder nutter asking about therapy—she just had to tell someone. So you're tied in to all the people who might know something about this clusterfuck. Which means you may be the only one who can untangle the knot."

"I'm a psychologist, not a secret agent."

"Well, then, damn it, you're about to learn a new skill." Dallabaco crushed his now-empty beer can on the arm of the rocker. "Somebody knows something and I want to know it, too." He then tossed the crushed can across the room.

"I said this before, didn't sink in apparently, so I'll say it again. You and me. We're the only ones who can unravel this. We got to put our attitudes aside and get it done." He hopped to his feet and pointed his finger at Jommers. "I made a promise to that man they threw dirt over him this morning, and I intend to keep it. So I'll be hearing from you soon, understood?"

JOMMERS HAD WITHHELD from Dallabaco the fact that Tarburn had smoked a cigar with Chief Scubbetts that day and that the two Internal Affairs detectives were given a nickname by which to address Tarburn, a nickname that inflamed rather than calmed. Jommers wasn't yet sure those facts meant anything, and was worried how Dallabaco might act on them. So he kept them in his pocket. Bargaining chips for the next time.

He tried to shake off the conversation, shake it off like a stiff muscle after a bad run. But long after Dallabaco had departed, the novel notions he'd deposited were still clattering around Jommers's head like the rattle in his old Taurus that he could never locate. Dallabaco had constructed an expansive implausible narrative to explain minor anomalies. Jommers had entertained the notion during the conversation to see where it was going, but in reality he found it unbelievable.

Jommers had no problem imagining Chief Scubbetts as a cold-blooded killer, but could not envision Scubbetts being such a terribly clever one. As for someone shooting an inflatable or a fish, Jommers had seen and heard about wigged-out people doing far worse when their brains are heated to a drug-fired boil.

The only thing he couldn't kick out of his thought path was Tarburn, the rock who was reduced to trembling terror and later ended up dead. That part was not a fuzzy theory, but a hard fact. A solid thing stuck onto the whole affair that could not be peeled off or removed by the solvent of rationalization.

If Jommers wanted to dismiss Dallabaco's concoction, flush it down the tube with other foul things, he would have to unearth an alternative explanation for what had happened to Tarburn Monday night. And at the moment, he couldn't.

Sure, he'd told Becca Tarburn it was probably the scopolamine that Tarburn had been taking for his IBS, but Jommers hadn't believed it even as he was saying it. He thought it might help her move on. But how would he move on? How could he keep barreling ahead when unanswered questions littered the path like unexploded bombs?

Jommers absolutely despised the concept of "closure," a phony and harmful approach to processing tragedy. As defined by pop culture, the acquisition of closure requires specific external events to happen, things generally beyond a person's control—a wrong righted, a debt paid, a mystery solved. Pegging serenity to external events denies the individual the opportunity to achieve the internal adjustments that represent the only true route to healing and coping. With the closure nonsense, you place the attainment of peace in the hands of fate when you need to be grabbing it with your own.

Yet, at the same time, he understood that sometimes there were dangerous things you just didn't detour around. You defused them. If not for your own sake, then for the sake of others who would pass that way.

Reluctantly, he grabbed a notepad and began taking notes on the strange conversation. Dallabaco was right about one thing at least, that Jommers had inadvertently become a locus of information, and at some point, the therapist might be the only one capable of discerning the pattern in the bits.

There was another compelling reason for taking notes—he had been selective about what he had revealed to different people. He was already having trouble remembering what he'd said to whom and who had said what to him. He had to keep track of all the inputs and the outputs so he didn't slip up. An honest man forced into a game of duplicity.

The irony was not lost on him. The therapist taking patient notes on his own life. Paradoxically, the more he wrote down, the murkier it became. Just like that crooked river off in the distance, which only got muddier after a clarifying rain.

It was not typical for Jommers to dive into the throbbing chattering whirl of Spreckels on a Saturday night, but after a troubling day that capped a troubling week, he craved a large side of white noise to go with his evening libations, which came not long after his afternoon libations. As he had hoped, the tavern racket helped drown out clamoring questions percolating in his head, questions that grated his nerves like the sound of steel wheels braking hard on rail.

After he was there a while, he smiled upon recognizing the bellowing, roguish voice of Connor Quirke piercing the din. Somewhere in the crowd, the gregarious lawyer was regaling acquaintances and strangers alike with jokes and amusing tales of the trade involving various rascals, morons, and malcontents. For those patrons lucky enough to be within earshot, it was free entertainment, and likely better than paid entertainment found elsewhere.

Later in the evening, when the roiling racket cooled slightly to a simmering rustle, Jommers was better able to engage his hobby of eavesdropping.

To his left were two concrete guys:

"No, you don't need an expansion joint in an unconstrained linear strip.

Only when it's up against a constraint."

"No, you do. The ends constrain the middle."

"No, a strip expands and contracts as a unit."

"Jesus Christ, man, have you never looked down at a buckled sidewalk?"

"That's frost heave."

"Jesus."

To his right were two aficionados of baroque music:

"If they composed it on a harpsichord, it should be played on a harpsichord. Playing a Scarlatti sonata on a piano is just as perverse as playing it on an accordion."

"That's ridiculous. Just look at how Bach cannibalized his own stuff. If he were around today, he would want to hear it played on the best instrument available, the piano. But he wouldn't mind hearing on an accordion either. You celebrate music, you don't strangle it."

Behind him, two mystery fans were discussing the meaning of the "Flitcraft Parable" in *The Maltese Falcon*:

"All that existentialist horseshit . . . you're just way overthinking it. Seeing things that aren't there. Look, Hammett didn't have an MFA, and thank God, too. He was a real detective, so it's really much simpler. Spade is a professional boasting of his skills to a client. He's telling O'Shaughnessy that he understands human behavior, and cautioning that he will eventually understand hers. That's all."

And somewhere nearby, another man was shouting:

"No, no, no. Barbecue is pork. Period. There's no such thing as barbecue chicken. Period."

It was around this time that Connor Quirke sauntered over to engage the psychologist in mirthful banter.

"Mr. Jommers."

"Mr. Quirke."

"A good evening to you, sir."

"And to you, sir."

"I wonder if you might indulge a technical inquiry into a matter."

"It would be a privilege to serve such an esteemed counselor at law."

"Given that you are a healer, of a sort anyway, how would you assess this challenge to orthodoxy known as alternative medicine? Would you embrace its promise, or flee from it as you would a disreputable carny? What do you know of it?"

"A smidgen, perhaps, more of a fragment found at the lower end of the smidgeon scale, but one that, like a landscape or portrait painted in miniature, may portray a larger picture when observed through a proper lens in proper light. I must warn you, though. This miniature rests not on survey or thorough study, but on a personal experience, a mere episode, as it were, but one that, like many anecdotal episodes, may be gleaned for meager insight. I'll offer it, if you'll have it."

"By all means. A meager insight betters an absent one."

"Well, then, I'll begin. Not long ago, I was approached by my aged uncle Helmut making inquiry in this very same topic area. After a lifetime of geniality, the man has been driven into a state of cocklebur crankiness by arthritis pain. A concerned and well-meaning friend gave him some advice on home remedies for said affliction. This would be the same friend who claims that using a cell phone causes his eyes to cross. But, I digress. In any event, the gist of the suggestion was that a certain quantity of raisins be soaked in a certain quantity of gin for a specified length of time. It was reputed that eating raisins treated in such fashion would impart curative compounds capable of alleviating joint pain."

"Indeed. I myself have heard that very story told. What of its veracity, then? Can such a concoction genuinely minister to such pain?"

"As you no doubt know, pain is a subjective thing, as is the memory of it. And both are influenced by many voices within and without. The flames of pain, then, are alternately fanned or quenched by fickle winds. In this particular case, however, my uncle Helmut's concern was less with efficacy than for the effect of chewy raisins on the aging amalgam in his molars, fillings installed back in the old country during the last days of the Kaiser. This is where he sought my advice, though I must admit that in the realm of dentistry, the only wisdom I can offer is that a dentist does not eliminate pain so much as simply relocate it from the mouth to the wallet. That said, I took my poor uncle Helmut's concerns seriously enough to put forth a novel proposal."

"And the content of that proposal?"

"I offered this solution to his dilemma. Given that the area of discussion was alternative medicine, it should be perfectly acceptable to seek an alternative for the raisins, so long as some grape derivation remained."

"A perfectly sensible assertion. Pray tell, what did you suggest?"

"Wine."

"A logical progression if ever there was one. And which wine did you recommend?"

"I wanted to maintain the focus on healing, so I selected a wine that was fortified with various herbs said to have curative properties, a wine that was originally formulated as a medicinal libation."

"And what is this wine called?"

"Vermouth."

"Your dear uncle Helmut is fortunate to have a nephew possessed of such far-ranging knowledge. Did he take your suggestion of employing vermouth with the gin?"

"Indeed he did. With great vigor."

"And how did he feel afterwards?"

"I can proclaim without equivocation that, after imbibing a certain quantity of the described potion, he was feeling no pain. Unfortunately, the same cannot be said for his dear wife, my beloved aunt Wiltrud, who tripped over him on the floor and broke her hip and now suffers horribly."

"Ah, so there are side effects with this alternative medicine."

"Indeed, as with all problems, one must ensure that the remedy is not more injurious than the ailment."

"To their health, then."

"To their health."

DAY SEVEN

THE HIDEAWAY

Trespassers don't ordinarily bring reading materials, but then Jommers was not an ordinary trespasser.

East Lake Park was as busy as one would expect on a hot August Sunday, but the park was just a pathway to his ultimate out-of-bounds destination. The drought had turned the grass so brown and dry that it crunched beneath his feet as he walked toward the park's far northeast corner. With each step, a handful of startled grasshoppers leapt aside, shooting this way and that like insect popcorn.

He was wearing a loose Hawaiian shirt and his wide-brimmed boonie hat, but he was already sweating, partly because of his load. Slung over his right shoulder was a folding camp chair and a soft cooler full of beer. Hanging from his left was a knapsack full of psychology journals. Sunday was his designated day to catch up with his reading. It was also his designated day to get out of the Bends for a spell.

His slow trudge took him to a chain-link fence, which he then followed to the water's edge. A weathered metal sign wired to the fence declared *No Trespassing, County Property, Violators Will Be Prosecuted.* He looked down at the water, a six-foot drop. Then he grabbed the fence's terminal post with both hands, planted his right foot firmly close to it, then swung around, planting his left foot on the other side. He used his momentum to swing his right leg around the post. The maneuver was accomplished smoothly, as he'd performed it many times before. On either side of the post, the grass had been worn away to hard earth, revealing that many others traveled this route.

The warning to stay out of the forbidden zone seemed amusing given that the place contained nothing but wilds. The official name was Grayton Harbor Confined Disposal Facility, but everyone just called it the Dike. It had begun life as a dumping place for river dredgings. Nearly a hundred acres of water were enclosed by corrugated steel pilings reinforced with stone and gravel on the inside and massive stone blocks on the outside. After a few decades the space had filled up, and the dumping continued elsewhere.

And that's when Mother Nature had taken over. The sun dried the muck to solid earth. Breezes and bird droppings brought the seeds that transformed the barren earth into meadow. The wetter parts sprouted marsh grasses and reeds. Later, shrubs and trees took hold, too.

To the untrained eye, the thick vegetation appeared no different than that found in any other nature preserve in the region. A naturalist, however, would note the slender diameters of tree trunks, the lack of old growth, and the absence of fallen giants slowly rotting. All clues betraying the youthful unnaturalness of a place reclaimed from the lake, a recent intrusion of land onto water.

The dense thicket at the core of the area would require a machete and trailblazer's will to penetrate, so Jommers hugged the path worn around the perimeter by other illicit visitors—bird-watchers, fishermen, and partying teenagers.

It was about a half-mile walk up to Jommers's favorite spot up at the northern edge of the site. A stand of aspen and a high wall of dense reed grass obscured the city behind him, and nothing but lake water lay before him. Tucked away in visual seclusion from the urban environment, he could pretend that he was touring a faraway coastal wilderness. It was a poor man's vacation, which was better than none at all.

To the right of where he set up his chair, a half dozen white butterflies fluttered around a cluster of purple wildflowers. To the left was a small patch of wild strawberries whose tiny red fruit looked ripe. He picked a few and ate them. His face puckered at their untamed tartness, but the recognizable sweetness was there, too. It was still strawberry.

At that particular spot, the rust-coated steel piling rose about a foot above the ground. A sloping cascade of stone blocks lay on the other side. Erie was calm today, and its unruffled blue-green surface looked like broccoli gelatin. While the still waters declined to provide any white noise, aural compensation was provided by cicadas, crickets, and the intermittent chattering and chirping of birds whose names he did not know. He soaked it all in for a few minutes. The pleasures of his private retreat. Then he got to work.

The primary goal of the academic reading was to keep abreast of what interventions had been shown to work best for specific problems. For example, numerous clinical trials had shown cognitive behavioral therapy to be effective for depression, post-traumatic stress, and a number of other disorders.

By contrast, the only thing improved by dolphin-assisted therapy was the wealth of the scammers running such operations. Jommers clearly had his own ideas on best practices, but keeping abreast of current research was essential to avoid the trap of being misled by personal experience and falsely attributing success to a personal approach, given that a third of patients were likely to improve regardless of treatment.

Yet such reading sessions also provided a pointed reminder of the undeniable squishiness of his field. Psychology is not cartography. Its publications do not provide unassailable instructions like repair manuals for mechanical Swiss watches. Certitude is in short supply.

Part of the problem lies in the inherent murkiness of the subject matter—human behavior and all its individual permutations. General principles do not always translate to specific circumstances due to multiple variables. You can understand the science behind sunsets, but you cannot predict how tonight's will look.

The realm of psychological research itself adds to the imprecision. First there is the replication problem, where the results of an initial psychological experiment cannot always be affirmed when the experiment is repeated by others. Long-held tenets may not really be true, and experts in the field cannot even agree on the breadth of the problem.

Then there's publication bias, the preference for publishing only studies with positive results over those with negative results. On top of all that are various questionable research practices found to be commonly used.

So there you are, running a therapy business, trying to follow best practices. You crave a detailed map, but receive only a rough sketch. You accept that the imperfections of the field do not invalidate it, yet you also understand the suspicions of the outsider, looking you over, wondering if you really have any scientific expertise or whether you're just a better-dressed shaman. How do you reassure that outsider when you cannot reassure yourself?

The inevitable arrival of that question caused Jommers to rub his eyes, stop reading, and throw the journals back into the knapsack. Long ago he had naively hoped that therapy could be performed as methodically as dentistry, but he soon learned otherwise. And nothing affirmed that rude awakening better than the crazy week he'd just had.

The peculiar demise of Patrolman Earl Tarburn and the enigma surrounding it raised questions Jommers could not answer, yet Augie Dallabaco, the SWAT commander, expected Jommers to help clear it all up. Jommers was not so inclined, and it had nothing to do with his dislike of Dallabaco. Rather, he understood the need to stay focused on his own job. While listening to cops every day, he often heard tales of mystery, but resisted the temptations of curiosity. The mysteries were theirs, not his.

He let out a deep sigh. It was time to put all of that away and relax. It was Sunday, after all, a day of rest. He shifted his gaze toward the hazy horizon and saw a slow-moving powerboat several hundred yards off shore. He trained his eyes on it, making an effort at self-hypnosis, hoping to quiet his mind, make his thoughts as calm as the lake before him.

Keep your eyes on the boat. Nothing else exists but the boat. Breathe slowly, deeply. Think of nothing but the boat. There is nothing but the boat.

It worked for about a minute. Then a text message arrived on his cell phone. "RLF2210."

The message from Patrolman Biederbach had been expected. They had struck a deal. There would be a series of formal therapy sessions held in Jommers's office in which the therapist would attempt to disprove Biederbach's quirky and baseless anxieties by examining the psychology that had given rise to them. Then there would be a parallel set of informal meetings where the patrolman would defend his positions and persuade the therapist that the suspicions were well-founded. A contest of sorts. One more than likely headed for a draw.

Biederbach, fearing tapped phones and inconspicuous tails, had provided Jommers with a coded list of meeting places for their secret talks. No one else would understand it. RL stood for rendezvous location. The F referenced a particular location on the list. The numbers gave the meeting time on a twenty-four-hour clock.

The opportunity for Jommers to relax was now shattered as he girded himself for the verbal duel that lay ahead.

On one hand, Jommers regretted the decision to stage it as a competition, as it created a false equivalency, granting equal weight to positions of unequal validity. But once the deal was struck, he was determined to stick with it, win the game. He knew that reasoning by itself was a wimpy tool for dislodging unreasonable views that had been emotionally encoded. It would take time to track down the hot leaky hose that had steamed up Biederbach's mental windshield. By showing respect for the man, Jommers could maintain access. It would also serve as an interesting psychological experiment. Was it even possible to exorcise the demons of a conspiracy theorist?

Besides, going ahead with it was consistent with his general treatment philosophy—toss the cookie-cutter approach and do whatever works.

～

ON THE WAY BACK HOME, he stopped in Spreckels for a quick one. The place was relatively quiet, which was typical for a late Sunday afternoon. Larry wiped some sweat off his brow, then frowned as he sniffed his shirt.

"Heat getting to you?" Jommers asked.

"It ain't the heat, it's the putridity," Larry said. "But I'm glad you're here."

"What's up?"

"Okay, you know way more stuff than I do."

"That's debatable. I know different stuff."

"Whatever. I got into an argument last night about planets."

"Well, that's a good thing. Usually the arguments are about your food."

"Guy trying to tell me we only got eight planets, when everybody knows we got nine. I cut him off."

"Actually, he was right. We used to have nine. But now only eight."

"Well, what the hell happened to number nine? It get hit by an asteroid and blow up or something?"

"Worse," Jommers said.

"What?"

"It got redefined."

"Huh?"

"Pluto was the ninth planet. It's still there, same as it ever was. Big icy chunk in a distant irregular orbit. But a few years back, they found two objects similar to Pluto in size, composition, and orbit. That meant they would have to include those as planets, giving us eleven. The alternative was to redefine the criteria for being a planet to exclude the two new ones, but doing so would also exclude Pluto. So the astro-fizzy folks had two choices: add two or subtract one. They chose the latter path."

"But Pluto is still there doing its thing," Larry said.

"Correct. The physical thing hasn't changed, just our perception of it. At least in terms of how we categorize reality."

"So we just get to invent reality."

"No, we get to invent our description of reality," Jommers said.

"So do we have designated people who get to do that?"

"Yes, they're called scientists. At least when talking about physical reality. When talking about psychological reality, it gets more complicated. Which is where the DSM comes in."

"You mean that stuff you smear all over for arthritis?"

"No. I mean the *Diagnostic and Statistical Manual of Mental Disorders*, published by the American Psychiatric Association."

"So it's like the dictionary of head cases."

"An inelegant definition, but it serves the present purpose. More to the point, just as with language dictionaries, the DSM periodically gets updated and revised. And with each revision, some new disorders get added and some old ones get tossed out."

"Like Pluto," Larry said.

"Exactly."

"So when a new one of these books come out, some people who were considered wackadoo are all of sudden now normal. And some people who were seen as normal are now wackadoo. Just because you guys change the definitions."

"More or less, yes," Jommers said. "What do you think about that?"

"I'm thinking I'd rather be the guy writing the dictionary than the guy who's in it."

"Indeed."

"So how do you define normal?"

"Interesting question," Jommers said. "Formally it would mean statistically prevalent. But then by that standard, running red lights is normal, since a majority of people do it. Informally it would mean 'that which meets with cultural approval.' But that approach has problems, too. There was a tribe in Papua New Guinea that used to eat the brains of their deceased as part of the funeral ceremony. Practiced that up through the fifties. By the standards of their culture, it was perfectly normal."

"Most people I know, eating their brains wouldn't be much of a meal. Not even an appetizer. Like a couple of clams maybe."

"Now let's say that instead of being a small, isolated tribe, these people constituted a nation, and that over time they became the most powerful nation in the world. Who would be in a position to tell them that eating brains was abnormal? The people who didn't eat brains would be the abnormal ones."

"You're giving me some ideas for new sandwiches here," Larry said. "You know, you could make ground pork look like brains if you didn't mush it together."

"I can hardly wait."

"But, hey, as long as we're talking psychological stuff. There was this other guy in here, Friday I think, and he was telling me that birth order makes a big difference in how you turn out, you know, whether you're the first kid, or the second, and so on. Supposedly affects your personality, intelligence, other stuff. That true?"

"Well, there's a lot of theories out there supporting that proposition, but the evidence is weak and hotly disputed. So it's still not definitive. However, anecdotally, I do know of one family where birth order made a huge difference."

"Seriously?" Larry asked.

"Yes. There was this couple that fell in love at first sight. And there was a particular song playing in the background at that exact moment, the old ballad 'Scarborough Fair,' the version sung by Simon and Garfunkel. So this couple ascribed a near-mystical significance to this conjunction and became obsessed with the song. So much so that they decided to have exactly four children and name them in order: Parsley, Sage, Rosemary, and Thyme."

"Wow. So I guess Rosemary was the lucky one."

"He didn't think so."

You can feel you're being watched, but it's just your imagination. There is no extra sense for it. Jommers knew that. And yet, that was precisely what he felt as he walked down Market Street on his way to meet Biederbach at the Baldwin Avenue Bridge. So he stopped and quickly swung around. He saw an unkempt man peering out of the shadows behind Saint Andrew's Church. Jommers was actually annoyed at being right since he could not explain the feeling.

It was a few clicks past ten. Jommers had parked his car by the church so that he could approach the meeting place on foot. The man in the dark was likely homeless. It was known among street people in the area that, during certain hours, one could obtain a baloney sandwich by knocking at the church's back door. It was long past that time, so maybe the guy wanted to be first in line in the morning. Or maybe he felt less likely to be mugged if he spent the night behind a church. Maybe Saint Andrew would watch over him. Or not.

As a resident with no fixed address, the guy would know that there was nothing open in the direction Jommers was walking and perhaps wondered about the stranger's destination. Upon catching Jommers's gaze, the man's curiosity vanished, and so did he, retreating quickly from the light.

Jommers resumed walking north a short distance, then turned right on Kerry Hill Road, which sloped downward toward the Bends. After another short walk, he arrived at the designated spot, a small, windowless structure built from stone block. In another context, it could easily be mistaken for a mausoleum, except for a commercial-style gray metal door on the front.

He turned to his left, and looking down the hill, he spied a small orange dot in the darkness, the glow of Biederbach's ever-present cigarette. The man was no doubt waiting to make sure Jommers had not been followed. Eventually, he strolled up, looked back over his shoulder, grabbed a ring of keys from his belt, and unlocked the door.

"The door used to be bronze. Somebody stole it," Biederbach said. "Twice in the last year I've responded to calls about someone trying to steal the copper roof tiles off Saint Andrews. It's like some goddamn postapocalypse movie down here. I'm waiting for cannibals to show up next."

"How do you have keys for this?"

"I've got keys for a lot of things on my beat."

"Right."

Biederbach carried a large spotlight-type flashlight with a handle on top. He flicked it on after swinging the heavy door open. The light revealed a wide stairwell down to a tunnel. The stairs were concrete with red brick edges. A tubular metal railing divided the stairs down the middle. A musty odor crept up the stairs to greet them as the light played over mold, grime, and various insect webs. They stepped inside and Biederbach closed the door behind them.

Jommers had never been down there before, but he knew where they were headed. The century-old Baldwin Avenue Bridge carried traffic over the Bends between downtown and the near West Side. In addition to its stunning, massive concrete arches, the double-deck bridge was notable for its lower level, which had once carried streetcars in both directions in the old days. Four sets of tracks, two for each direction. The streetcars entered and exited the bridge through tunnels at either end. The boarding stations were in the tunnels, and riders accessed them via stairways, such as the one the two men now descended. The last of the streetcars had rumbled and swayed over the span in the early '50s. The entranceways were then sealed off and the lower deck consigned to bats and pigeons.

As they trudged through the tunnel toward the platform, occasional crunching noises echoed around them as their feet trod over broken tiles and stonework that had fallen off the crumbling walls. Down at the platform, the decay of the decorative arches and columns created the illusion that they were exploring some ancient catacombs, an illusion betrayed by the empty light boxes in the columns and by the rusted streetcar rails lying before them.

They followed the rails toward the bridge and were soon walking its lower deck, which was framed by elegant arches on either side. The ambient light from the nearby city lights and the streetlights on the upper deck cast a bluish glow over the white arches and made the flashlight unnecessary once their eyes adjusted. The open arches offered a superb panoramic view of the Bends.

Jommers gazed upriver to the south, his eyes fixing on the eternal fire in the Bends' skyline, the flare stack down by the steel mill that burned off gases from the coke ovens. The rough, shape-shifting blue-orange flame was barely noticeable in the daylight, but its glow grabbed your attention at night, appearing as a bright ghost dancing crazily in the darkness.

While most of the bridge's length was supported by the reinforced concrete arches, the section directly over the river was fixed into a giant steel truss arch. In this section, the lower deck consisted of an open-mesh steel grid, which permitted a view of the river directly below.

The quiet water at that spot reflected the blinking lights from a strip club hugging the river's edge. That reflection was joined by the red-and-blue flashing lights of a police cruiser. Biederbach looked down at the joint and shook his head.

"I don't why the city doesn't padlock that place."

"Trouble spot?" Jommers asked.

"Nonstop. I remember responding to a call down there one night. The action is over by the time I get there, but here's what happened, according to the witnesses. Most of the dancers there are pipe heads. They can barely walk a straight line, much less dance. So they just slosh around like rancid pudding. So on this night, there was this one, she was so high, she walked right into the pole and knocked herself out. So she's lying there at the edge of the stage out cold and her bladder unleashes. The flood gates open. Now, the edge of the stage there functions like a bar. It overhangs and they got the high barstools lined up against it. So there's this guy sitting there, and he's so drunk that he's mostly out, too, his head facedown on the edge, with the warm puddle advancing toward him. Soon his head and face is awash in pipe-head stripper piss. He comes to. And when he figures out what happened, he jumps up on stage and starts punching the stripper, even though she's still unconscious. By this time, the bouncer has come over. He tosses the guy off the stage and drags him out the door. Then the bouncer beats the shit out of the guy in the parking lot. By the time I get there, the bouncer has gone back inside and the guy is lying in the handicapped parking space in a bloody heap. He doesn't even remember what happened. He thinks he was mugged." Biederbach shook his head slowly. "Just another glorious night in the Bends."

"Definitely a mélange of experiences available in the Bends."

"I assume mélange is a ten-dollar word for hash. So this is my turn, right?"

"Go for it."

"Are you familiar with the term *schreckstoff*?"

"No, but let me guess," Jommers said. "A German stew made with rabbit and sauerkraut."

"Not exactly. Back in the thirties, an Austrian scientist named von Frisch injured a minnow in a tank and noticed that the other minnows in the tank suddenly started acting panicky, darting around as if there were a predator in there. When von Frisch explored this effect further, he discovered that when a minnow is injured, it releases a chemical that warns the others of danger. In other words, the chemical is how a minnow tells his buds to get the hell out of here or you're going to get chomped like me. Von Frisch named the chemical *schreckstoff*, German for *fright stuff*. Since then, similar chemicals have been found in other species. It is theorized that humans may also have a *schreckstoff*, something you smell that makes you piss-pants scared."

"You're talking about alarm pheromones," Jommers said. "While commonly found in social insects such as bees and ants, at this point in time, there's no conclusive evidence that humans can produce or detect them. But even if it were so, what's it got to do with things going on here in Grayton, Ohio?"

"I suspect that someone has found a way to synthesize the human version of *schreckstoff*."

"Someone?"

"The federal government," Biederbach said.

"Surprise, surprise. And why would the federal government want to possess such a thing?"

"You put fear in a can, dispense it like air freshener. Push-button panic. When you scare the hell out of people, they become easier to manipulate and control. You really think that's so wild with the paranoia peddlers in charge these days?"

"I'm not a chemist, so I can't address the technical aspect of your hypothesis. I do know that scientists have been able to synthesize and mass-produce many naturally found chemicals, and that has led to all kinds of things, from artificial flavorings to aspirin to prescription medications. So if a human *schreckstoff* actually exists, it would not seem incredible that someone could synthesize it. What seems implausible to me is that anyone would need to. We live in an age where more people have more access to more information than ever before in history, and yet in spite of that, people today are more gullible and manipulable than ever before. When you can legally and effectively poison people with words, why would you bother to illegally and ineffectively poison people with chemicals? Why go to the trouble of creating and dispersing some exotic substance, when all you need is a soulless copywriter with a weaponized thesaurus?"

"Because what you've seen so far is only phase one. The next phase will require stronger stuff. *Schreckstoff*."

"Since this is your turn, I presume you're going to tell me about phase two whether I ask or not."

"I'm glad you asked," Biederbach said. "Lord Vile Veep and his puppet Drawling Doofus are going to trash the Bill of Rights far more than they already have with the warrantless phone tapping and other things. Have you actually read the Patriot Act? Do you understand all the things they're allowed to do now? You aren't at all worried?"

"I think the body of this nation, having been hit with a small infection, is now suffering from anaphylactic shock, where the body's response to a threat is actually more dangerous than the threat itself. I am, however, optimistic that reasonable people will show up at some point and deliver a much-needed dose of atropine."

"Let me tell you what will happen if and when reasonable people show up. They will be marginalized, accused of being unpatriotic. And those who are not prominent will simply disappear. And then you'll see reasonable but naive people take to the streets, thinking they can change things by making a big fuss, by making a lot of noise. The regime will have to quell the disturbance. But they can't just roll tanks over them like it was Tiananmen Square. Because here the cameras capture everything with live feed. You spill blood, it fuels the fire. So you need to be more creative. So instead of killing or harming the protestors, you hit them with a gas that fills them with a deep, inexplicable fear. On TV it will look just like ordinary tear gas. No one will know what it really is. Those who inhale it become terror-stricken. They run away screaming and crawl back into their little holes, and the situation is defused. No blood. No arrests. And, most importantly, no fired-up joiners, because cowards don't inspire joiners. Resistance wilts. Big Brother wins without a battle. It's elegant, simple, and unassailable, because no one knows what really happened."

"I think I know the answer," Jommers said, "but I'll pose the question anyway as a matter of formality. What is the humongous violation of the Constitution that is being plotted?"

"Federal takeover of municipal police departments by the Department of Homeland Security using the war on terror as a justifying pretext. The DHS has already established so-called liaison Fusion Centers in cities across the country, supposedly for coordination of threat analysis. They are in fact the launching pads that will facilitate the takeover. Ordinary crimes get attributed to terrorists. An ordinary bank robbery becomes terrorists gathering resources. This then triggers DHS involvement. Eventually they start taking over everything. They even have a code name for it—Operation Cobalt Quell."

"That's a familiar song. I think I've heard you sing it before."

"And I'll keep singing it until somebody listens, if it's not already too late. Here's what you need to understand. It's a scheme to get around the Posse Comitatus Act. Americans have an inherently wise reluctance to use the boys in green for domestic issues unless there's an insurrection. But thanks to TV, Americans have nothing but unconditional love for their boys in blue. So here's the plan. First militarize the police in terms of operations, tactics, equipment, philosophy and attitude. Then quietly transfer the line of report from the local to the federal level, justifying it as a necessity in the war on terror. The result is a federal police force, with the police an extension of the army, but no one has a problem with it because they're wearing blue instead of green. Liberty surrendered to more acceptable attire."

"Just for the sake of argument," Jommers said, "what would be so bad about the federal government running local law enforcement operations? This country has more than eighteen thousand local jurisdiction law enforcement agencies of varying sizes and sophistication. Some of those are Andy of Mayberry operations with no computers and a couple of guys carrying six-shooters they haven't fired in twenty years. A federally controlled system would provide standardized training, procedures, technology, resources, and communication, all leading to enhanced cooperation, improved efficiency, and greater professionalism. Why would that be such a bad thing? For example, look at how the creation of the National Guard was a vast improvement over the hodge-podge of poorly trained volunteer militias."

Biederbach shook his head and let out a great sigh of exasperation. "Do you have brain parts missing? The reason you don't want to go down that road is that it makes it easier for the government to implement martial law. You would, in fact, already have it, without the necessity for decreeing it. It is the natural tendency of any centralized state to maximize its degree of control. It's part of the DNA. Government is an organism, which, like any other organism, is pro-grammed to grow and prosper. It doesn't even need an ideology or a mission. It grows for the sake of growing, like a mat of fungus. It has no purpose other than to expand. Jesus, that I would have to explain this to an allegedly educated man."

"Okay, okay. Let's say all of what you say is true, including the whole big conspiracy thing. How does any of that connect with events happening here in Grayton, Ohio? You know, the mystery chemical and all that. What did you call it?"

"*Schreckstoff.* And this is how it relates. You want to use something like that, you got an unknown, because you can't simulate how real people will react when exposed to a psychotropic drug in a real-world confrontation. And you need to know that before you roll it out in a big way. So you want to test it in a small way, maybe a small place. Do it in a way that won't attract a lot of atten-tion if it all blows up on you. So you look for a loyal flunky, a police chief or commander somewhere who is ex-military and maybe nostalgic enough about it that he shows more loyalty to his old bosses than his new ones. The flunky tests it on some low-life ghetto scum that no one will miss. Then he reports back how it went. Maybe this test happens in multiple places. Then, when they collect enough data, they're ready to roll."

"Interesting theory. Extraordinary theory, actually. Which brings to mind a favorite saying of skeptics—extraordinary claims demand extraordinary evi-dence. What have you got?"

"I'm a bit thin in that department at the moment."

"So it seems."

"I've only been looking into this a few days, you know. I'll have more details as I get into it."

"Maybe you want fewer details," Jommers said.

"What do you mean?"

"Embellishments create a finely woven narrative that appeals to people on an emotional level, helps it all make sense, which increases plausibility in that type of mindset. For someone approaching it rationally, the opposite is true. Connecting all the suppositions requires that they all be simultaneously true. Logically speaking, increasing the number of elements that must be simultaneously true lowers the overall probability that they are all true. Every added detail raises the threshold for proof. Knowing how my mind works, do you think the construction of an expansive narrative best serves your objective of convincing me? Or would you be better off by focusing on a few linchpin contentions?"

"All right, then. You tell me, what do you find most improbable?"

"The idea of government covertly exposing American citizens to experimental chemicals for research purposes."

"Seriously? I expected you to be better informed. If you want some fun reading, check out the final report of the Advisory Committee on Human Radiation Experiments, which details how the government performed radiation experiments on thousands of Americans. Usually done by Atomic Energy Commission or the military. They fed radioactive food to mentally disabled children, injected pregnant women and babies with radioactive chemicals, irradiated the balls of prisoners, and dispersed radioactive materials over cities. And a whole lot more. You can look it up. Then there were the CIA experiments with LSD. In Project Bluebird, more than seven thousand soldiers were given LSD without their knowing it. Our soldiers. You can look that up, too. That program was later incorporated into a bigger one called MK ULTRA that experimented on hundreds of people to develop techniques for mind control and psychological torture, some of which are still used today you know where. The experiments were done at dozens of institutions, including schools, hospitals and prisons. I could also go into all the medical experiments, the injecting people with hepatitis and malaria, the Tuskegee syphilis experiment, and a hell of a lot more, but I know you want to get home at a reasonable hour. The most scary thing about it all is how the government enlisted the assistance of medical professionals, university professors, and other civilians to help perform the experiments, showing how easy it is to co-opt ordinary people into doing evil in the name of patriotism."

"Yes," Jommers said. "I'm aware of those things, they're well-documented. But they were exceptions, not the rule, and they were done some time ago. I'd like to think government is better behaved these days."

"Better behaved? Or better at concealment? Keep in mind that these things weren't exposed until decades after the fact. The stuff that's going on now . . . people might not know about it for another fifteen or twenty years. Think about it."

"Here's the thing. What you're suggesting would involve a large number of people to implement, with even a larger number being aware of it. The idea that so many could keep it a secret in an age where there are more leaks than a film with the Three Stooges as plumbers . . . I'm still sticking with highly improbable."

"It's also highly improbable that anyone would ever get hit by a meteorite. Yet in November 1954, it happened to a woman in Talladega County, Alabama, while she was taking a nap on the couch."

"If I recall, it wasn't a direct hit. It bounced off her radio. Do rebounds count?"

"Let me ask you something. Let's imagine that you and I are standing right here at the same time of year, only in 1986, during the reign of Cowboy Ronnie. And I'm telling you a wild, unbelievable story that our government was secretly sending arms shipments to Iran, which two years earlier had been designated a state sponsor of terrorism for its support of Hezbollah, which blew up and killed two hundred and forty-one U.S. Marines in Beirut. You would laugh me off this bridge. No way, you'd say. You're on drugs. Can't possibly happen. But as we know now, it did happen. Improbable is not the same as impossible. Because sometimes, the improbable happens."

"Yes," Jommers said. "My agreeing to meet a patient in an abandoned trolley car tunnel late at night to hear bizarre theories is evidence of that."

"Think of it as breaking new ground in therapy."

"You left something important out of your tale. How does the death of Earl Tarburn fit into your theory?"

"He was the guy they tapped to shoot the experimental gas, because he's the best gas man on SWAT. He would report back on what happened. Like how it all hit the fan at Eggers Court and Juneberry Boulevard. Another ex-army guy who put his old boss over his new boss. Then, for reasons unknown, they decided to terminate his involvement by terminating him."

"If they're using a SWAT guy, then Dallabaco is in on it, too, right?"

"No. He's a stooge. They went around him."

"What is your basis for saying that?"

"Just a hunch."

"How do you know that Tarburn shot the gas at Eggers Court and Juneberry?"

"I heard it through the grapevine, I guess."

"You're lying to me."

"I might have heard it somewhere else."

"Dwayne, did you bug my office when you were in there?"

"I might have. Sometimes I just do it out of habit."

"So you heard everything Dallabaco said to me on Saturday."

"Possibly."

"Where is it?"

"Stuck under the rocker."

"Listen to me closely," Jommers said. "If you ever, ever do anything like that again, I will cut you loose and feed you to the lions. Do you understand me?"

"No need to get all bent about it. It's just the times. Everybody does it."

"No. Everybody does not do it. And if you piss me off again, I'm going to tell Dallabaco you were eavesdropping on him Saturday, and he'll turn you into a pizza topping with his bare hands. Do you hear me?"

"I did warn you to sweep the room, didn't I?"

"Did you hear what I said?"

"Message received."

"Good. Now, how much of your theory comes from eavesdropping on Dallabaco, and how much comes from Tarburn himself? You were the last person to talk to him while he was alive. What did he say to you?"

"He said a lot, but only a small portion was comprehensible. He was in a state of panic. Talking fast. Marginally coherent. He says he's a cop. Says he's being chased by military intelligence. They want to kill him—"

"All right, now hold it right there a second," Jommers said. "Did he use those exact words? Did he say they want to kill him?"

"Exact words? It was something like, I'm done, I'm toast. Said it a few times."

"Let's get serious. You know phrases like that can be taken literally or figuratively. He might have just meant that he was in trouble, or that his career was over."

"The man was absolutely terrified, as if the jaws of hell were opening under his feet. You don't get that terrified about losing a job."

"And military intelligence . . . did he use those words?"

"He used the abbreviation MI," Biederbach said.

"Exact phrase, please."

"Said that MI was to blame. Several times."

"Are you sure he used the word *was* in the phrase?"

"I did mention he was yammering semicoherently, didn't I?"

"My point is," Jommers said, "could he have been rhetorically asking the question, 'Am I to blame?'"

"I suppose if you want to spin it that way . . ."

"And that's the nub, isn't it? How you spin it. How you interpret what's happening. And because of your perverse spin on the interaction, you blew the last chance to disarm him and prevent the shootout. He approached you because he trusted a fellow uniform. You could have promised to protect him at the hospital. And that was your assigned mission, wasn't it? Assist in getting an emotionally disturbed individual over to the psych ward at Saint Bridget's.

But you listened to your demons instead of your orders, and so you failed to perform your assigned duty."

"When two duties conflict, you choose the higher good, no? A fellow police officer was being hunted by assassins—"

"Serving a paranoid delusion is not a higher good," Jommers said. "You had but one duty that night—help get a sick man to a hospital. You were derelict in that duty, with disastrous results."

"Oh, so now you want to put it on me? You were his goddamn shrink. You're the one who failed him."

"I tried to talk him out of his fears; you juiced them up. That's the difference. And now he's dead."

"Yes," Biederbach said. "Now he's dead. And neither of us could have saved him. And the only way we can do him justice now is to figure out why he's dead so we can save the next one."

The two men glared at each other in the near darkness. Biederbach took a deep drag from his cigarette, held it, then slowly released, the resulting cloud enveloping his head. Framed against the background darkness, with a dim bluish light cast over the slowly swirling smoke, Biederbach appeared as a wraith in the night, delivering a warning. The long silence was broken only by the low hum of car tires speeding over the bridge deck above. Jommers was ready to go home and call it a night, but there was one loose end nagging him. One last question for the edgy, smog-spewing doomsayer.

"Tarburn wanted to give you the bag with the shotgun shells, didn't he?" Jommers said. "But you guessed your cruiser would be searched. So you gave him the rain poncho. Told him to wrap them up so they would float, then toss them in the flotsam pool where you would fish them out the next morning. So if you're so damned worried about some conspiracy, why don't you turn in the one piece of physical evidence that supports your theory?"

"Again, for the record, I don't have them, if they exist, which I can't speak to. However, I can ruminate about the motives of someone coming into possession of them."

"That line is getting old."

"First of all, who would you give them to? Given that both feds and local brass are deep in all this, what uninvolved, reliable law enforcement authority could you trust? Park rangers? Transit cops? Secondly, there's no verifiable chain of possession. A person turning over such shells couldn't prove where they were made, what they were used for, or who had them. The person might even be accused of manufacturing the shells himself as a hoax, like the guy who sneaks a pig prick into a package of bratwurst so he can sue the manufacturer. Then, of course, there's the obvious fact that we've already noted. The last person with knowledge of that bag and its contents got shot and killed. That would certainly be cause for reflection by whoever has the bag now."

"When are you going to stop with the denial nonsense? I know you have them."

"You suspect I have them. There's a difference, legally and practically. So if anyone should ask you point-blank about it, you can look them in the eye and honestly say you don't know, because you don't know. And that leaves you out of the loop of suspicion, which is where you want to be, since the person who last held the hypothetical bag is dead. We're in a situation where knowing certain secrets can be fatal, so you want to be very careful about what secrets you acquire. In other words, if I did have them, I would be doing you a favor by not admitting it." He paused. "You're welcome."

Jommers didn't respond. He merely pointed toward the tunnel end of the bridge, indicating it was time to go. Biederbach led the way back, having the big flashlight. Jommers briefly turned around to take one last look, knowing he'd likely never visit the closed transportation tomb again. He imagined a streetcar approaching from the other end, seeing its headlight in the darkness, hearing its creaking clickety-clack reverberate through the span. He smiled at the thought of his parents or grandparents maybe riding across, looking out the window, viewing the Bends from a now-forbidden vantage. Then his reverie was interrupted by Biederbach shouting.

"Hey, you! Stop! Police!"

Biederbach took off running and Jommers had no choice but to follow, as he had not brought a flashlight and didn't want to be lost in the darkness. They ran across the old station platform, through the access tunnel, then up the stairs to the street entrance. By the time they got out the door, Biederbach collapsed to his knees on the sidewalk, spent and gasping for breath. Jommers looked off in the distance and could barely see a running figure disappearing into the darkness. He looked down at Biederbach.

"This is what the smoking gets you, Dwayne. Look at you. A couple of flights of stairs and you're winded, wheezing, and whipped. You're running on empty before you even start. How the hell you supposed to catch bad guys?"

"You were supposed to make sure you weren't followed, damn it."

"It was probably just that homeless guy I saw behind the church."

"How do you know he was just a homeless guy? Was he wearing a sign? They're not going to be wearing trenchcoats and fedoras, you know."

"You're right. I should have asked him if he was a secret agent."

"Idiots," Biederbach muttered to himself. "Nobody gets it. Nobody sees."

When he finally caught his breath, he got up, locked the door, and started walking away without saying another word. Before he got too far, Jommers shouted at him.

"Remember you have a therapy session tomorrow. Don't be late."

When Jommers got back to his office and home, the first thing he did was locate the bug stuck on the underside of one of the rocking chairs. He then smashed it to pieces with a hammer and placed the fragments in an envelope.

He should have gone to bed after that, as the next day would be challenging—both Biederbach and Ilona Voros on the agenda. But the weirdness of the conversation at the bridge was too much. His brain needed deceleration. So he grabbed a beer and listened to some blues while kicking it all around.

He thought about Biederbach on the ground, muttering with disgust, "Nobody sees." *Wrong*, Jommers thought. *People see just fine. The problem is that they see different things.*

Jommers remembered the old days of black-and-white photography, where a pack of color filters could serve as a bag of tricks for a good photographer. When a film camera was loaded with monochrome film, a color filter would lighten similar colors and darken complementary colors. In a portrait shot, the right filter could make red acne all but disappear, while a different filter could turn the blemishes into dark blotches. Take a pleasant blue sky with white clouds. One filter could make the sky look bright and clear, another deepened the contrast and rendered the sky dark and angry.

People also use filters on their mental lenses, constantly altering the images registering in their brains. Every mind is a cipher, and you can't crack it until you figure out which filter is on the lens.

DAY EIGHT

Jommers got up early Monday morning, hoping to get in a good run before the heat became too oppressive. When he stepped outside, he was surprised to see a man sitting on the lowered tailgate of an aged Ford F-150 adorned with Almost Heaven bumper stickers and Yosemite Sam mud flaps. He was a big man, but not like a muscular linebacker. More pudgy-lunky kind of big. Looked to be in his late twenties. He had prominent ears, and freckles splayed across pale skin. He was wearing work clothes and a confused expression. The truck's radio was playing, but it wasn't music. Somebody talking, and the fervent intonation and cadence of the voice suggested it was a religious program. Jommers strolled over.

"You look lost. Can I help you?"

The man jumped off the tailgate and stood straight, as if snapping to attention.

"Oh, no, sir. I'm waiting for Mr. Gerzny. I am to start here today. I wanted to get here bright and early, but I guess it was a bit too early. Sorry if I caused a fret."

The man's voice was high-side soft, with a distinct Appalachian accent. His tone was polite and deferential.

"Not at all," Jommers said. "Just wasn't aware Pete had hired a new guy."

"It was all kind of quick like. I heard through word of mouth that he'd lost somebody, and I was looking, took a chance and just stopped by on Friday, and was surprised as heck when Mr. Gerzny said for me to show up Monday."

"So you're experienced in truck-and-trailer repair?"

"Well, not directly, but I've done lots of mechanical-type things, and when you do lots of those things, then you can pick up similar things. Had a good job in Weirton, but lost it when the mill closed, and there was just too many of us showing up when a spot came open. A hundred hounds chasing the same rabbit. I figured I'd go up to Michigan, see if maybe some car plants were hiring. Stopped off here in Grayton to get some chicken, and right across the street there was a muffler shop with a help wanted sign, and, well you know what they say, a bird in the hand . . . so I walked right on over, didn't even wait to eat the chicken, and they took me right in. Everything was fine for a while, but it was a chain, and

I guess the location wasn't making enough, so they closed that one down, and I was back to looking. Ready to leave again when I heard about this. So here I am."

Jommers introduced himself as the psychologist who worked upstairs, and the man identified himself as Norb Hobber. Jommers gave the man a copy of his business card, but Hobber looked stumped.

"So you're something like a scientist?"

Jommers tried to concisely explain the job function of a clinical psychologist.

"So if you know anybody who might need some emotional help," Jommers said, "somebody having trouble dealing with a death, or a drinking problem, or a marital problem, or anyone who needs any kind of emotional support, those are people who could benefit from psychological counseling."

"Well, everybody I know has family and a church," Hobber responded.

There was a long pause. Jommers looked in vain for a trace of a smirk that would signify the remark as a brilliant put-down of his profession, suggesting that only a godless loner loser could possibly need a psychologist for support. But there was no smirk. Only a seemingly genuine, head-scratching confusion as to what a psychologist was and why any ordinary person would ever need one.

Jommers noticed that strapped in the bed of the pickup was a banged-up greenish multidrawer toolbox on casters. Both sides of the toolbox displayed the same large decal, a purple head of a crazed bird with a bright yellow bill. Underneath it was the word *Thrush*. Jommers pointed to it.

"Who's that? Woody Woodpecker?"

"Oh, no, that's the famous Thrush emblem. Thrush is a brand of high-performance mufflers."

"So that was your favorite muffler?"

"No, sir. That was my favorite muffler decal."

"I see. Well, then. Welcome to the shop. Best of luck in your new job."

"Thank you, sir."

By the time Jommers got back from his run, Pete had arrived and opened up the shop. The new guy was hard at work, even though the clock had not started.

"I didn't know you lost somebody," Jommers said to Pete.

"I fired Lupu," Pete said. "He was getting too sloppy, safety-wise. First, he cuts a compressed air line, which then starts whipping around and whacks him in the face. Then, after he caught his hair on fire with a torch, I gave him a final warning. So, last week, he's jacking up a trailer, and he wants more height, and so he—you know how many times I've told these knuckleheads, you don't ever use a chunk of four-by-four to extend the range of a bottle jack. The slightest bit of shear force and, wham, it's airborne. Those blocks are lying around for one reason only, to block wheels. So what does this idiot do? He uses not one, but two—two pieces of wood on top of the jack. So, as you expect, the trailer wiggles a bit, and the blocks go flying, like out of a bazooka. One of the blocks hits him square. Fortunately, it hit him in a place where it could do no harm."

"His head."

"Correct. And that was his last day here."

"So the new guy just stopping by out of the blue was a stroke of luck."

"I guess. Nice guy, but he's got a television brain."

"Meaning?"

"It's on a five-second delay. But he seems conscientious, so I guess that's good enough. You don't get many Einsteins interested in truck repair."

"You would be the only one."

"That's exactly right."

THERAPIST CONUNDRUM: if a person who is definitely not normal starts behaving normal, are you witnessing progress or performance?

Detective Ilona Voros arrived for her appointment dressed simply in blue jeans and a casual light blue blouse. Missing from the entrance was her usual posturing, strutting, and theatrical gestures. Without any noticeable facial expression, she sat down quietly, clasping her hands around a paper cup of donut shop coffee, like someone waiting for her car to come out the other end of the car wash.

Was this the real Ilona? Or, more importantly, was there a real Ilona? Did she even have a true self, or was she nothing more than an emotional mannequin, defined only by costume?

He caught her looking at the old upright piano in the corner again. She knew it and quickly glanced away toward something else. Clearly annoyed with the silent observation, she spoke first.

"I just heard through the grapevine that you evaluated Patrolman Dwayne Biederbach. So apparently faking a back injury now counts as a critical incident also."

"I neither confirm nor deny speculation about who is on my patient list or why."

"I hope you didn't clear him to go back. You do realize that he's battier than I could ever dream of being."

"We're here about you."

"I'm not trying to start anything. I just thought I might help you with him."

"Help me?"

"Yes. Figure out where his head is at, in case you didn't know yet. I mean, it's like off the map. You know the place on old maps where it says 'here there be dragons'? He's way past that. He's in a place that makes dragons look warm and cuddly. And we've got the tapes to prove it."

"We?"

"Internal Affairs. He's under investigation for subversive activities. He keeps trying to recruit fellow officers to his cause. Keeps talking about the day when cops will have to disobey their superiors and do battle with federal agents to maintain local autonomy. Total wackjob. This is not a guy you want carrying a badge and a gun. We're giving him enough rope to hang himself, then, when we get enough on tape, we can get rid of him without hassles from the union. Freaking union. They try to protect everybody regardless, lunatic or monster. The devil himself if he wore a Grayton badge. Anyway, I can't get you copies of the tapes, but I could tell you what's on them if you want. Then you'd know what you're dealing with."

"No, thanks," Jommers said.

"You sure? I'm just trying to help here."

"Let's turn our focus to your situation, the reason you're here. I gave you a homework assignment last time. Do you have it?"

"Oh, yeah. You wanted me to write something."

She leaned forward and fished for a folded piece of paper in her back pocket. She straightened it out and then handed it to Jommers. It read:

> *I am worn out weary, when I should be alert,*
> *Ready as something spring-loaded, set to trip.*
> *But I've barely the will to move,*
> *So I use what I have,*
> *Use my stillness as my caution.*
>
> *Like a homeless soul*
> *In an alley of broken glass*
> *I clear a small patch,*
> *Then curl up in the safe spot,*
> *To rest in my unrest*
> *Forgetting my pursuers*
> *While remembering not to stretch or roll,*
> *Closing my eye to the light*
> *While the eye's memory*
> *Surveys the jaggedness around me.*
>
> *Both awake and asleep.*
> *Huddled in cold twilight.*

Jommers was stunned and troubled by the piece but, in usual sphinx fashion, refrained from showing it. The assignment he had given her was to write an imaginary dialogue with Patrolman Earl Tarburn, pretending that he had survived the shooting. She had completely ignored the specific instruction and instead written about how *she* felt. Her disregard of the instruction, her producing something so off the mark, was both irritating and instructive. The poem, or lament, appeared to confirm Jommers's initial assessment that she was a narcissist.

And that raised two questions for him. The first was gauging the level of her narcissism in an age where the trait had become so common that some argued it should no longer be considered a disorder, but the new norm. An age where schoolchildren expected awards for showing up, where people exhibited the minutiae of their lives on social media as if they were movie stars. An age where people wrote memoirs before turning thirty. So, was her narcissism merely the garden variety so prevalent in contemporary culture, or was it severe enough to be considered a disorder?

The second question was how to respond. She had submitted something revealing, and she was anxiously awaiting judgment, her hands squeezing her fingers white in anticipation. For a fleeting moment, the door to her psyche would be open. Should he express his disapproval and risk slamming the door shut? Or should he seize the opportunity for access?

He put the piece of paper down without showing any reaction, then calmly asked her:

"Are you into the blues much?"

Her mouth fell open slightly, as her face registered confusion and surprise that Jommers's question appeared unrelated to her composition. No praise, no sympathy, no curiosity. Baffled, she simply shook her head no, not saying a word.

"Well, I've always liked them," he continued. "Especially the early stuff, the acoustic blues. One of the things I've found interesting, maybe curious is the word, is how these guys, these blues masters, could crank out these profoundly moving songs full of passion and pain, play them with eloquent anguish, which makes you figure that they must have been deeply sensitive men. But then you look at the lives they led, full of drinking, gambling, mistreatment of women, violence—some of them served time for murder—you look at that and realize that many of them were scoundrels and miscreants. One of them told a story about this woman he'd been living with, how she was sick, and how this one day he finds her dead in the outhouse. He said he just walked away and moved on, just leaving her sitting there. Now, that's pretty cold. Yet this same guy wrote a searing song about the pain he felt in losing somebody he loved. How do you make sense out of that, that seeming contradiction, sensitive and insensitive?"

She didn't answer. She already saw where this line was headed. Her face was twisted into that peculiar kind of scowl that expresses both pain and resentment simultaneously. She was breathing heavy, ready for detonation, needing only a nudge.

And Jommers provided it.

"Now you can find this contradiction in other art forms, as well," Jommers said. "Critics and writers tend to romanticize it, saying that so-and-so was possessed by both angels and demons, and all that poetic piffle. But I think it's a whole lot simpler than that. Creative people often retain a childlike imagination, but unfortunately often also retain a childlike egocentricity, where they're acutely sensitive to their own feelings, but oblivious to the feelings of others. In adults, we refer to it as narcissism."

She jumped to her feet, pushing off the arms of the rocker with sufficient force to knock it over backwards. She was now in full threat mode. Tense, panting, nostrils flaring. But she said nothing, letting her savage glare say it all.

Jommers continued, pretending not to notice the noisy leap to her feet.

"I gave you a rather specific homework assignment. I asked you to imagine that the man you shot and killed had lived and that you were having a conversation with him. What would he say? How would he explain himself? You totally blew it off. You were utterly incapable of ruminating about what he might say, about what he might be going through. And the same shortcoming would be true for any other situation we might conjure, because you are incapable of thinking about anybody but yourself. It's all about you, one hundred percent of the time."

She grew ever more agitated and moved closer to him as if preparing for a physical assault. He calmly continued.

"I sought an exercise in empathy. But what I get instead is a self-centered, poetic pity party from Ilona the martyr. And the little princess expects me to praise how eloquently she has whined about her own pain. Princess expected comfort and sympathy. So now Princess is shocked an enraged by my insensitivity."

"Stop calling me that. Stop . . ." The words caught in her throat with a growling gargle, as if she were stifling a vomit.

"Princess bared her soul, showed her wounds, and the beast pours salt in them, while mocking her. Poor, poor Princess. How unfair it all is. How awful it must be to suffer so much, always the victim . . ."

At this point she let out some kind of primal yelp and kicked the overturned rocker, sending it sliding a few feet across the old wood floor. And this time she could not stifle the vomit. She leaned over and launched a small volley that hit the floor with a splat. She wiped her face on her sleeve and pointed her finger in Jommers's face and shouted, her whole body atremble.

"Fuck you. You don't know. Fuck you. You don't know. Fuck you . . ."

Jommers sat there calmly, waiting for the rant to conclude.

"What don't I know?"

"Fuck you."

"What don't I know?"

"You don't deserve to know. It's none of your goddamn business. And you're a fucking pig."

"What don't I know?"

"Shut up, you fucking pig. I told you it's none of your business. You fucking pig."

"Well, then. I'm afraid we can't move forward until we have that talk."

She grabbed her head in frustration and started pacing furiously. Tears leaked out her eyes and trickled around the contours of her face. The drops then held at the line of lip and jaw, awaiting a quick wipe of sleeve.

"Shit, shit, shit, shit . . ." She blurted it repetitively like machine gun. "I swore I would not let this happen. Would not let you take me here . . . not let this happen . . ."

"Well, it has happened. And here we are. So, do you want to stay here, or would you prefer to get through it and move forward?"

"Shit, shit, shit, shit . . ."

Jommers got up and righted the overturned rocker. He went in the back and got some paper towels to clean up the puke on the floor. Fortunately, it had not been a liquid torrent, but more of a semisolid glob. More patty than puddle. It picked up as easily as a clump of uncooked hamburger. When he was finished with the cleanup, he sat back down.

She had already seated herself and was drinking from a water bottle. But had turned her rocker away so as not to face him. Having agitated enough for one day, he remained quiet, patiently waiting for her to speak. After a few minutes of awkward silence, she did.

"It's not like TV, you know."

"What isn't?" he asked.

"The way guy cops and women cops get along. On TV, they respect each other, work together, focus their contempt on the bad guys. Even the corrupt ones are enlightened and politically correct in fantasyland, as if the battle for acceptance was long over with, as if Cagney and Lacey had put it to rest decades ago. Well, news flash. TV cops are the kind you *want* to have, but they're not the kind you *do* have. At least not in Grayton. You'll never see a TV cop grabbing the tits of a female rookie, then threatening to turn in a bad performance review if she tells. You'll never see a bunch of TV cops surrounding a red-haired rookie and debating whether she is red all over, and then pantsing her to find out. And every incident is followed with the warning about not telling. What happens if you do. But eventually, I did tell. Which just made it worse. I started reporting every incident to Internal Affairs. But IA said that without proof, they couldn't do anything. My word against theirs, as if I would make up this crap. So I wired myself. And the next time something happened, I had it. Turned it in to IA, then leaked it to TV news. They had no choice but to boot the son of a bitch."

"Was that the end of it?"

"Oh no, it just made me more of a target, but it was all anonymous after that, so no one would pay a price. Getting threatening phone calls. Finding gross things in your locker. Finding the word 'cunt' spray-painted on the side of your car in a secure, gated police parking lot with video cameras. I was too embarrassed to take it to a body shop, so I bought a can of spray paint and painted over it. It wouldn't be the last time. I got to carrying cans of paint in my car as a matter of habit, so I could cover it before even hitting the road."

"And how did that affect you?"

"Initially? I am totally upended, second-guessing myself. What am I doing here? I got into this to take bad people off the streets, but the bad people making the most trouble for me are wearing badges. I kept at it because I'm not a quitter. As long as it remained psychological warfare, I felt I could handle it, acclimate to it. But then it jumped that fence."

"How so?"

"I got in a dicey situation one day. I called for backup. But backup never came. I had to handle it on my own. And that's when I realized, this conflict with them isn't just a head game anymore. This is something that can get me killed. And that scared the hell out of me. And that's when I went to Captain Wifflyn at Internal Affairs and asked if I could get transferred to his unit. I figured if I was going to be at war with my fellow police officers, it might as well be formalized warfare. Take a position where the adversary relationship was open and understood. On the table. More importantly, the leverage would change. I would now be the one after them. I'm the hunter and they're the prey. The edge is now with me."

"How did that work out for you?"

"It was better in one sense. It made it easier to deal with hatred, because it's the accepted situation that cops hate IA. So I could pretend that the hate wasn't about me, but about my position. I could depersonalize it. But I still had trouble fitting in."

"How so?"

"Most of the guys in IA don't have their heart in it. There's a timidity, a reluctance to go after other cops. Too much professional respect. Deep inside, they miss their old gang. They actually apologize when bringing someone in. 'Sorry, Joe, sorry I have to do this.' And that totally pisses me off. Why the hell are you apologizing? This guy besmirched the badge, disgraced the department. He's a scumbag. You don't apologize to a scumbag. He should be apologizing to you for betraying his oath."

She paused to take another swig from the water bottle, then continued.

"Police departments are like hospitals the way they protect their fuckups.

Something bad happens and the people in charge promise to review policies and procedures. But nobody thinks to ask the obvious question—how do we make it easier to get rid of our fuckups? Because it's almost impossible. Being a cop is a Teflon gig. Nothing sticks. First of all, people are scared to death of retaliation if they file a complaint or testify against a cop. And not without cause. But the biggest problem is the union's contract. Everything goes to arbitration, and the arbitrators always side with cops, because the ones they use are always ex-cops. We've got cops with dozens of complaints about use of excessive force who have never been disciplined in any way and usually get promoted. Same with the tit-and-crotch grabbers, guys who pull over a woman for going five miles an hour over the limit, then make them get out for an extremely intense pat-down. No matter how many complaints, they're still here, they still get the promotion. And even when you get something serious enough to kick it into a court, you still have a problem, because juries tend to be pro cop, because TV has turned them into mythic heroes who can do no wrong. And even if you get a conviction, it gets tossed on appeal because judges are elected and they all want the union endorsement. And in those rare instances where you hook a bottom-feeder who is so bad that everybody agrees he has to go, there's this insidious practice of negotiating a quiet resignation or early retirement to avoid prosecution, allowing them to leave without disgrace. They even get a letter of recommendation that helps them get a job on a burb force."

"So even when you win, you still lose."

"Yes, and it burns the shit out of me the way they are all protected. It's exactly opposite of what you should be doing. You should be making an example of these scumbags. Make it as humiliating and painful as possible. That's how you create deterrence. That's how you clean it up. Unfortunately that's not how it's done. So I don't fit in well with IA either. I'm too gung ho on destroying careers, as they put it. Well, I'm sorry, some careers deserve to be destroyed. Cops exist to protect and serve the public, not themselves. So even though I am good at what I do, I'm still a pariah because of the way I handle things."

"And that riles you, not getting the respect of your peers, either on the force in general or in IA particular."

"You're goddamn right it riles me. It would rile any sane person. I'm better than all of them. I work harder than all of them, yet they have the nerve to look down on me. Making their smug little comments just out of earshot, sniggering like snotty little children. I tried to resign myself to it. Thought I could deal with it so long as I could leave it all behind me at the end of the day, retreat to my sanctuary, my home, my lovely little home. God, how I miss it. You know how most people have some vision of a dream house, but never find it? I found mine. You know that old neighborhood near the lake on West Side they call Tudor Town?"

"Yes, a very nice area."

"A gorgeous area. Incredible, charming houses with all their gables and turrets, high-pitched roofs with tall chimneys, the intricate brickwork and stone trim, the sandstone walks . . . I lived in the part where they had built the smaller houses in the cottage style. But mine was built with all the same craftsmanship and materials as the rest. It had one of those heavy wooden doors and sidelights with stained glass. Inside it had hardwood floors, oak trim, a wood-burning fireplace, built-in china cabinet, decorative iron railing for the stairs . . . all the fine little details you found in those old houses. This old couple selling it . . . it's like they had spent their whole lives preparing this place just for me. They'd planted pine trees in the front yard, which had since grown tall, so even though you were in this packed grid development, you could look outside the front window and imagine you were in a forest. But it was in the back that they had built my paradise. They tore out the lawn and turned the whole backyard into this exotic garden with stone pathways, vine-covered trellises, a little reflecting pool, Japanese lanterns, and all kinds of different shrubs and plants. And a bunch of bird baths and bird feeders, too. Oh, they loved birds. A lot of the plants were ones that attract birds. Right by the back porch, there was a line of tall lobelia, both red and blue. The hummingbirds love lobelia, though they liked the red better than the blue. The hummingbirds got so used to people sitting on the porch, they wouldn't get spooked. They would hover right there in front of you, doing their thing. It was so cool. You watched them work, and it took you to a different place. But my greatest comfort was my lovely little baby who shared it all with me."

"You had a child?"

"No. I mean my cat. An exuberant orange tabby full of affection. I'm not even going to tell you her name. You'll just mock it as silly."

"No, I won't. I only laugh at silly names for people. Pets are supposed to have silly names."

"Squeegee. I named her that because, when she was a kitten, she made this squeaky little meow, like the rubber edge of a squeegee rubbing a window. She was fascinated by the birds, but she never chased them, just watched. So I felt it was okay letting her roam out there. She didn't wander. She loved the place as much as I did. She would . . ."

She stopped suddenly, trying unsuccessfully to stifle a brief bout of sobbing.

"Okay," Jommers said. "The use of past tense . . . something happened. Paradise lost."

"More like paradise stolen. Serenity, too. It was right about the same time I got hit with another spray paint job that I came home and found that they went into my backyard and smashed the ceramic birdbaths when I wasn't home. Not long after that, they tried to break into my home, breaking the stained glass sidelights by the front door with the intent of unlocking it. But I knew that sidelights are a security risk, which is why I had a double-cylinder deadbolt installed—you need a key from either side to open it. Then, it was a few weeks after that, Squeegee didn't come home. I went looking across the street, where there was this like drainage ditch that snaked through the block. And that's when I found her. She'd been bludgeoned to death. She . . ."

She hung her head down and started sobbing again, her torso making those jerky movements from trying to hold it in. He refrained from telling her to let it all out. He refrained from telling her how to cry.

Instead, he quietly ruminated on the incongruities of the moment. She was no Derle Scubbetts, who had no more emotion than a block of wood. She could cry. She could cry for herself. Cry for her cat. But she had no tears for the man she had shot just seven days ago. She was like particle physics, where every new revelation brings new mysteries.

He waited silently while she gathered herself enough to continue.

"Obviously, that changed everything," she said. "The violation of personal space. The invasion of sanctuary. The idea that you have no refuge. You expect to deal with threat as a cop, but you also expect to be relieved of it when the shift is over. But this assault on my home space eliminated the separation. They could be anywhere now. I couldn't sleep, imagining them out there. I hear a squirrel in the bird feeder and I'm grabbing my gun. I knew I couldn't keep living that way, feeling unsafe. So I sold my dream house. Put my furniture in storage. I started living in efficiency apartments, moving to a new one every five or six months, like someone on the run. Too funny, huh? I'm with the police, but I'm on the run."

"Did you have any further harassment incidents after you moved?"

"No," she said. "I'm trying to stay two steps ahead of them."

"Any further harassment incidents at the station?"

"Well, there's always the muttering . . . the dirty looks . . ."

"But no more vandalism . . . spray paint . . . gross things in the locker."

"No. Why, what are you suggesting?"

"Not suggesting anything, just trying to get the whole picture, past and present. But my knowledge of harassment cases is that many times it's a small number of harassers involved, sometimes only one or two, and often, after a while, they lose interest in it, having already made their point. I'm just throwing out the possibility that it's all over, that your—"

"It's never over," she said. "How can you be so goddamned blind?"

After snapping back at him, she jumped out of her chair and turned her back on him, her arms tightly folded. As he thought about her story, he faced a challenge. How do you address a persecution complex in someone who truly has been persecuted? How do you mitigate a victim mentality in someone who was genuinely a victim?

He gave it his best shot.

"Everyone has been victimized at one point or another, in a variety of different ways, and to varying degrees," he said. "Obviously, some people get a heavier dose than others. Now, we can debate whether one form of abuse earns more victim points than another, argue about victim status rankings, but that would be off the mark. What really matters is how we respond, how we respond to our treatment by other people, and by life in general, given that we often have little control over it."

She was listening, but still with her back to him, staring at the floor. The movement of her torso betrayed heavy breathing. She had briefly wound down, but now appeared to be winding back up. He continued, in a low, calm voice.

"There are several pitfalls to avoid," he said. "The most obvious is becoming obsessed with vengeance, using injury to justify retaliatory inflicting of injury. Another is overreacting. Allowing the degree of our response, whether internal or otherwise, to be disproportionate to the degree of affliction. A more enduring and damaging danger is permitting the experience to infect us, letting it become a parasite that changes our very being, letting it change who we are and where we're headed. You had made previous mention of Stockdale's POW account, his drawing on the wisdom of the stoics. It seems that you perused it rather than absorbed it. Stockdale, channeling Epictetus, said that it is impossible to be a victim of someone else, you can only be a victim of yourself. It is your choice to live as a victim, you must allow it. The irony here is that, on one level, you're a control freak, yet by embracing victimhood, you surrender control to others. You let others determine how you live, how you think, how you feel. But the worst danger is permitting victimhood to alter your perception, imagining that there is a deliberate agent behind everything bad that happens, that you're a perpetual target. You begin to see connections that don't exist. You lose touch with reality, seeing threat everywhere. If my car gets keyed tonight in a parking lot, I will interpret it as a random act committed by vandals who I don't know and who don't know me. If your car gets keyed tonight, you will almost certainly interpret it as a targeted act by someone who wanted to get you. And that is the beginning of the downward spiral. The departure from sanity."

She turned around slowly to face him, and put her hands on her hips, breathing very heavy. It was obviously not what she wanted to hear. After revealing the injustices heaped on her, she had clearly expected comfort and solace. Concurrence with her grievance. Instead, she'd received instructions, as if she were a wayward child, as if the situation were all her fault. She was indignant, and she stared back with seething contempt, radiating the quiet menace of a nearing soldering iron.

"Well, that was a nice little helping of shrink-light," she said. "But I can get that from a magazine, one dishing good recipes for pasta salad, too. Do you offer recipes? No? Ah, a pity."

Jommers nodded. "I fully understand that it's easier to speak wisdom than to receive it, but that doesn't diminish its inherent simplicity. Wisdom isn't improved with neon or glitter, or by coming out of a cannon with colored smoke flares. Wisdom is more like a common sparrow, repeating the same simple song, but with few paying any notice."

"My, that is so touching, so inspiring," she said. "I swear there were butterflies floating out your ass."

"I'm sorry. I gathered at the start that you liked poetry. Apparently, only your own. Let me be more prosaic, then. The things we most need to hear are often simple things that we already know at a deeper level, but we need someone else to redirect our attention to them. This process, what we're doing here now, isn't about having earth-moving epiphanies that solve everything in an instant. This is about changing the way you interpret your experiences and your environment. It's about gradually changing your habits of thought, which is as slow and difficult as changing any other habit. Learning to think anew requires patient practice, like learning to play a musical instrument. Like, say, a piano."

"What the hell is your deal with the fucking piano?"

"The more pertinent question would be, what is your deal with the piano?"

"Who gives a shit?"

"You do, apparently. My guess is, the reason you keep looking at it is that you had one in your dream house, and it was important to you. Part of your escape, your self-healing process. And now, it's in storage somewhere, unable to help you. Am I close?"

"Okay, fine. So I know how to play the goddamn piano. So what?"

She stomped over to the old oak upright and started hammering out a deliberately sloppy version of "De Camptown Races," accompanied by some deliberately awful singing.

"There," she said. "You happy? Did you like it? You want more? How about the 'Beer Barrel Polka'? Hey, that would give you an excuse to crack one open, wouldn't it?"

She launched into that piece, but didn't get too far before stopping suddenly. Then, in frustration, she put her face into her hands and let her elbows fall to the keyboard, striking discordant notes. After a long pause, she shook her head and mumbled sadly to herself.

"I should have known better," she said.

"What's that?"

"I should have known better. Known better than to confide in you. That you would be on their side."

"Whose side?" he asked.

"They come through here often, don't they? You're probably good buds with all of them by now. That's why you're dancing around the obvious, pretending not to see it."

"Good buds with who?"

"You know who. Dallabaco's Divas."

"Is that your term for SWAT?"

"One of the nicer ones, yes."

"What's your beef with them?"

"That they exist. The entire concept."

"Explain."

"Look," she said, "here's the problem with that whole band-of-brothers mentality, aside from the fact that they don't want sisters. When you militarize law enforcement, you transform your police into an occupying army, and the citizens respond accordingly. They see you as the enemy. They don't trust you and they don't work with you. They stop reporting crimes, they stop being cooperative witnesses. They fight you. Criminals become freedom fighters, idolized instead of stigmatized. It's just gotten way out of hand now. There's maybe a handful of threatening situations all year that justify the use of SWAT, but now it's used all the time, even for simple arrests on outstanding warrants involving nonviolent crimes or simple searches for small quantities of drugs, and half the time they don't even find any after wrecking somebody's house. The level of force deployed is way out of proportion to the level of threat. Not surprisingly, the SWAT mentality has seeped into the rest of the force, as well. First we replaced revolvers with semiautomatics. Then we replaced their shotguns with military-style assault rifles. Gave them stun grenades and now even a freaking tank. What's next? RPGs? Flamethrowers? Blackhawk helicopters with Hellfire missiles called in on some schmuck selling a dime bag of weed?"

She paused, emitting a sigh of disgust before continuing.

"And the media, who should be questioning all this, instead, they glorify it. They show us a squadron of guys in black jumpsuits and helmets carrying assault rifles, swarming and storming some place just to grab some small-time mope, and we're supposed to find that cool. What's happened to land of the free and home of the brave? Not so brave, apparently. The white middle-class weenies have become increasingly paranoid about crime even as it's declining. That's why the public is okay with this crap. And they're okay with it because the abuse affects mostly the poor, and mostly black poor. So some black guy gets his house wrecked in the middle of the night, flash grenades thrown into a room with children, on no other basis than an undocumented rumor. Nobody cares. Because he's one of *those* people. And they're all guilty of something, aren't they? But you wait. This militaristic MO will spread into the burbs eventually. And then they'll care. When it starts happening to them, then they'll realize the monster they created."

"So your motives are purely philosophical," Jommers said. "Your indignation about injustice."

"You have to connect the dots between police behavior and societal attitudes. Cops do what society permits them to do. What are those attitudes? Just turn on your TV some night. What do you see? You see forty-seven flavors of lock-'em-up, but not one Perry Mason. This land of the free has the highest rate of incarceration in the world, with Russia and China trailing far behind us. You think that's the America dreamed of by Madison and Jefferson? We spend more money on prisons than on higher education. Average annual cost is over thirty thousand dollars per prisoner. So, I've got a cost-cutting idea for you. Instead of locking them up, pay them fifteen thousand a year to stay home and watch TV and stay out of trouble, and you can cut costs in half."

"Interesting observations," he said. "Many of which I would agree with. But they're off the point. I have a sneaking suspicion that your issues with SWAT are of a more personal nature."

"When you elevate and ennoble a group of people as an elite and special unit, then that's how they'll see themselves, as elite and special—and above the rules. The rules are for everybody else. Not for the special."

"And when rules are broken, Internal Affairs gets involved."

"There was this raid they did," she continued. "Nighttime raid. Small-time piece-of-shit weed dealer. But they send this storm trooper horde, like it was fucking Iwo Jima or something. Guy hears some noise and looks out the window. Sees a swarm of guys in black, carrying guns. He has no idea what the hell is happening. He's completely terrified. He grabs his cell phone and calls 911. They burst in, and there's the guy with the cell in his hand. And you should know that, when the trigger-happy boys from SWAT come calling, if you got anything in your hand bigger than a baby carrot, you're toast. So they drill him. Empty everything they have into him. By the time the poor guy hits the floor, he's got more holes than a cheese grater. So now they have a problem. There's no gun. Not even anywhere in the house. So, of course, someone produces a drop gun."

"Drop gun?"

"You serious? You don't know what that is? It's a non-traceable gun that you confiscate from a previous arrest, only instead of turning it in like you're supposed to, you carry it with you inconspicuously. Then if you happen to shoot an unarmed suspect, you take out the drop gun and press it in the dead guy's hand. So when Homicide shows up to work the scene, everything is cool. You're covered. I can't believe you don't know how this works."

"How do you know it went down that way?"

"Number one, we have a snippet of the 911 call. You hear him say there are guys with guns in his yard, then you hear shots, then nothing. Somebody shoots the phone. But we know from that snippet he was holding a phone in his hand, not a gun. Number two, I talked to everybody who knew the guy, and they all said the same thing. He hated guns, was scared of them, would never own one. And three—you know the old saying about the dog that didn't bark in the night? Something missing that should be there. If you own a gun, you also own ammo, even if it's only one small box. But not this guy. I searched that house so thoroughly, not even a lone bedbug would have escaped my attention. But there was not a round to be found anywhere. So why would you have a gun but no bullets? With those three points, I push hard for charges, but I'm denied. They stick together with their story. The code of silence. So they beat it, like they always do. The band of brothers. After that, they know me. And they don't forget me."

"So you assume that they're at war with you as a result of that investigation?"

"I don't assume, I know," she said. "And it wasn't only that one incident. There were others. Like the beanie boys."

"The beanie boys?"

"Two SWAT guys, good friends, both live on the North Side of Penn Line Yard neighborhood. You know it? You got a switchyard in the middle and a set of tracks cutting it in half. North Side was an old Slovenian neighborhood. South Side was Italian once, but is now mostly black. Over the past few years, some blacks start moving over the tracks. So eventually you get this one street corner where black kids start hanging out. And some North Siders don't like that, blacks hanging out on a North Side street corner. Happened to be a corner near the old Slovenian Hall where the old folks go to listen to polkas on the weekend. They saw it as an in-your-face kind of thing. Everybody talking about it. What to do about it. So these two guys in SWAT decide to get involved. So they get hold of some bean bag rounds—you know what those are? They're nonlethal rounds meant for riot control. A little bean bag in a shotgun shell. You fire them out of a twelve-gauge pump. But nonlethal doesn't mean harmless. These can cause some serious hurt. They can break a rib. Damage the liver. Rupture the spleen. Take out an eye. Anyway, these two guys, off duty, start periodically driving by this street corner at night, and one of them shoots bean bag rounds out the window at the black kids. Sending a message. Some of the parents file citizen complaints. But this is the Fourth District, where citizen complaints tend to get misfiled in an alternative universe, never to be seen again. I get wind of it. I talk to the people there. I tell them to get it on video. Get a license number. I tell them, when you have something, do not go to Fourth District station. Come to me. They do. I nail them, I nail the beanie boys. But, again, there's a negotiation. They get to resign without prosecution. I am totally furious. But the SWAT-holes are now totally infuriated with me. I finally dinged them."

"And how do you know this?" Jommers asked. "I mean, that members of SWAT are infuriated with you?"

"Well, it's rather obvious, isn't it?"

"Not to me."

"Either you can't see, or you don't want to see."

Jommers was genuinely confused. He tried to imagine what she might be thinking. What connections she might be making.

"Patrolman Tarburn was on SWAT," Jommers observed. "Are suggesting a connection here?"

"Duh! You think?"

"Okay. Let's pretend I'm really slow and need everything spelled out for me."

"That will be pretty easy," she said.

"Then go ahead."

She paused and took a deep breath.

"I am not supposed to be here. I was the one who was supposed to get shot at Crone Point that night. It was all an elaborate setup to take me out."

Jommers was stunned by her appraisal of events, but refrained from showing it. He responded impassively.

"That's how you see it?"

"How could I not? I mean, look at it. I just happened to be assigned to bring in the best marksman on SWAT, who just happens to be experiencing some temporary mental issues. My partner just happens to fall off a stairway and pretends to be injured. My backup, Patrolman Biederbach, just happens to injure his back and pretends he can't get up. So there I am, by myself, running onto this little dead-end strip of land in total darkness, where the best shot on SWAT is waiting to ambush me. And you think that's all just a big coincidence."

"There are a number of improbable conditions contained in your scenario, but let me start by noting that there would have to be a lot of people involved in this plot, a lot of people at multiple levels."

"Yes. And they all played their roles faultlessly, except for the hit man. He missed. I didn't."

"And that's why you have no sympathy for him. He was part of an elaborate plot to murder you."

"Why would I have sympathy for an assassin? That would be crazy. Any sane person would be expressing their sympathy for me. I've been sleeping in motels ever since that night. Moving to a new one every day. And you wonder why I'm stressed out and irritable, unable to engage in amiable banter."

"Backing up to the point about people involved . . . the order to Internal Affairs to bring in Tarburn came from Chief Scubbetts, so he would have to be part of this plot."

"Well, of course," she said. "I would expect that. There were several matters I had investigated about him, as well, matters I was instructed to drop. And in case you didn't know, his appetite for retribution is legendary. Nobody dares cross him. Ever. You might want to tuck that away for future reference."

Mystery solved. At least one, anyway. Jommers now understood why Detective Ilona Voros felt no remorse over shooting Patrolman Earl Tarburn. In her mind, he was part of a plot to murder her. If true, her lack of remorse would be perfectly understandable. But it wasn't true, and her interpretation of events presented a whole new problem for the therapist to handle.

There was a long, awkward silence. She had slumped back into her chair, arms folded, legs crossed, staring at him with hurt and resentment. How could she not? She was living a life on the run, believing herself to be a target for assassination. And here he was suggesting that her only problem was an excess of vanity.

The discordance in perspectives was a chasm that could not be leaped. They would have to both climb down slowly and meet somewhere at the bottom.

He could start by discussing his own involvement in the affair. He could tell her that it was he who had directed Tarburn to the bridge house and informed Internal Affairs of the location. But that would only spook her. Make her think that the psychologist himself was part of the plot somehow.

He could share with her information gleaned from other sources, such as Biederbach and Dallabaco, but that would require violating the confidentiality of those conversations. Besides, presenting her with more accurate information would not likely change her mind. That would be knocking on the wrong door. The beast of irrational belief was down the hall, hiding behind the Door of Emotion, and that was where it would need to be seized and dragged out.

But not today.

Jommers felt drained, like he'd been trapped on an hour-long roller-coaster ride with a rabid bobcat. She wasn't looking too perky either.

"We've made a lot of progress today," he said. "But we'll have to pursue it further at the next session."

"Progress? Progress at what?"

"The issue we need to deal with."

"The issue? The issue? You mean the fact that people are trying to kill me, but you think the only matter that needs attention is that I'm a princess with an attitude problem?"

"We obviously have significant differences in how we are interpreting events. And we are both going to work hard to bridge those differences. There's a lot of ambiguity here, a lot of fog. But we are going to cut through it. And when we're finished, we will achieve a unity of vision. We will both see things clearly, both see the same reality."

"The only way you're going to see reality is when they find my body."

He scheduled another appointment with her and also inquired about the address of her former dream house in Tudor Town and the time frame that she'd lived there.

She shuffled out slowly, looking listless, hopeless, helpless. He worried that she might disappear and never return.

He then grabbed a pad of paper and started writing down his observations on the session. It was his practice to take notes afterwards rather than during, so that note taking would not break the connection with the patient and interrupt the flow of conversation. When he was finished, he wrote something at the end and circled it:

Next time. The piano. The job. Why?

THREAT ASSESSMENT

The lunchtime eavesdropping at Spreckels Tavern was particularly entertaining today, providing exactly the escape Jommers needed after a disturbing session with Ilona Voros. Four women who worked at the Landfall Title Agency up the hill and were semiregulars for lunch were discussing their incompetent husbands. Not so much discussing as competing to see who had the best story. It had started inadvertently, when one of them had reminisced about her marriage and combining households with her new husband. Moving themselves, they had rented a truck, but the only vehicle left had a manual transmission. She had to drive the truck because her man didn't know how to drive stick. A simple tale, but it opened the floodgates.

The next woman recalled a recent barbecue where her husband, ignoring her warning, put the grill too close to the house, got distracted, and ended up half-melting a section of vinyl siding.

"Now it looks all droopy gloppy," she complained.

"That's nothing," said the next woman. She told how her husband was mowing the lawn one day, got hot, took off his shirt, foolishly laid it down on the grass, and then ran over it.

"The shirt got all wound around the blade shaft and stalled the mower," she said. "Instead of coming inside to get some scissors, he tried cutting it off with the trimming shears, which didn't work well, so he started stabbing it with the points and ended up stabbing his hand. So then we had to take him to the hospital for stitches."

"Well, at least he didn't wreck anything in the house," said the fourth woman. She related how her husband fancied himself Mr. Do-It-Yourselfer, the kind who thinks he doesn't need to read instructions. So when they needed a new clothes washer, he insisted on going up to the home center to get one and bringing it back in his pickup truck. She said they got one of those fancy new front-loading models, and explained how front-loaders need this exotic system of springs and shock absorbers for the drum when it spins, and how they use shipping bolts to lock up the drum during shipping so it doesn't bounce around, and how you need to remove the shipping bolts before you use it or the springs and shock absorbers won't work, and how you won't know that unless you read the instructions.

"So when it gets to the spin cycle, the damn thing starts hopping around like a kangaroo on amphetamines. It yanks the hoses right of the couplings, and now there's two streams of water, hot and cold, shooting across the laundry room. So he runs in there and promptly slips and falls on the wet vinyl floor, hurting his back. Then he starts screaming because he's getting hit by the hot water stream, which is scalding him. Meanwhile, water is starting to flow into the other rooms because it's a first-floor laundry . . ."

Jommers smiled at the amusing chitchat unfolding behind him, but his grin diminished when he noticed a troubled look on the face of Larry, the normally convivial tavern-owner. Jommers waited until the lunch business died down a bit before inquiring.

Larry leaned on the bar with his left elbow and took his ever-present cigarette out of his mouth with his right hand.

"This," he said, holding the cigarette in the air. "This is the problem."

"How so?" Jommers asked. "Other than the obvious fact that it's going to kill you?"

"You know that smoke-free workplace law that went into effect in January?"

"You mean the one that bans smoking in bars and restaurants and that you have been ignoring? That one?"

"From what I hear," Larry said, "four out of five bars in the state are ignoring it, and I know for a fact that most of the bars down here in the Bends are ignoring it. And you can get away with ignoring it so long as no one files a formal complaint."

"And somebody did."

"Yep. County Health Department guy came out at some point to verify the complaint, then sent me official warning, which I got today. If I ignore the warning, I get fined. And for every new occasion after, the fines double. If it keeps happening, they take away your liquor license."

"Maybe that's a good incentive to stop," Jommers said.

"It isn't just a habit with me, it's my support system. I know they're not good for me, but they give me energy and serenity at the same time, which sounds like a contradiction, but there it is. I don't know how I'll cope without them. I don't know what I'll do."

"I might be able to help you with that."

"I'm scared. I'm really scared."

"Seriously?"

"Yeah. You don't have any idea how consuming all this is. Don't get me wrong, I love this place. Had my first legal beer here. Thought it was the coolest bar in the whole damn world. I remember the night I was in here at the bar when Old

Man Kaz casually mentions that he's thinking of selling, that his bones were tired. I jumped on it before he could put it on the market. Begged and borrowed from everyone. Took out a second mortgage. I couldn't believe my luck when it went through. I owned my dream bar. But then, you know, you got to make the big decision right up front. Hire managers to run it when you're not here and accept that you're going to have fifteen to twenty percent shrinkage, or simply be here all the time. I went with the latter, because I couldn't take that amount of shrinkage and still pay on the loans. So I'm here day and night, seven days a week. After closing, I stay late to clean up and restock the coolers. But I have to get here early in the morning for deliveries. So I never get enough sleep and I have no home life. When Janie finally got fed up and left me, it took me a week to notice. I'd already been sleeping in the extra room. The dream, it costs you. And that's okay, I'm willing to pay. But I can't make it without these. Just can't."

He took another drag off the cig, then stared at it again as if it were a magical object that someone was about to steal.

JOMMERS WALKED OUT of the tavern pondering his friend's impending crisis, but his thoughts were interrupted by the sight of a young woman sitting on the hood of his car off in the distance. When he got closer, he recognized her.

Yolanda Arroyo, the police reporter for the *Ledger*, was finishing up a cup of yogurt, scraping the bottom with a plastic spoon for the last little glop. Her knees were pushed together awkwardly in an effort to hold an open bottle of water between her legs.

"I need an update," she said.

"It's still hot out."

"My editor is nagging me to write a follow-up on the policeman shooting. I need something new to say."

"He's still dead. And my work with Grayton PD is still confidential."

"It doesn't have to be confidential information. It could be some general observations on such matters, commentary, background, anything."

As she made her plea, her cell phone emitted a low, undistinguishable sound. She grabbed it with her right hand while juggling the yogurt container and spoon with her left. Whatever it was, she decided to ignore it.

"The pointless news update is as stultifying as the pointless cell phone call," Jommers said. "The false sense of urgency creates a false sense of importance. Meaning is no longer found in the content of communication, but in its frequency. The signal has been drowned by the noise."

"That's it?" she said. "That's all you got for me?"

"I thought that was pretty good for off the cuff."

"Bromides are not substitutes for insights."

"Tell that to your op-ed columnists."

"Look, I'm not the enemy," she said. "I'm not out to hurt anybody. I'm just trying to do my job."

"A guy shows up at my door trying to sell me a vacuum cleaner, he's just doing his job, too. That doesn't oblige me to buy one. What serves his interest does not necessarily serve mine."

"Someday you're going to need me."

"I think there's a song in there. Keep working it."

As Jommers prepared for his upcoming session, he mused about Patrolman Biederbach's faulty risk assessment. Worried that big government was coming to get him, while seemingly oblivious to the fact that big tobacco already had him and was strangling the life out of him.

Yet in some ways, Biederbach was not all that different from most people in their habit of misperceiving the magnitude of risks. The parents who are worried about their children getting shot at school don't think much about swimming pools, even though the number of children who drown in swimming pools is many times greater than the number of children shot at school. An unfortunate misperception, given that swimming pool deaths are more preventable. But you don't see news magazines featuring cover stories on killer swimming pools.

The usual reason for warped views on risk can be found in uneven weighting of emotional content, and there is no more powerful emotion than that of grievance, the indignation arising from a sense of injustice or victimization. Risks initiated by human malevolence bear an enormously heavier emotional weight than those risks voluntary assumed or assigned randomly by fate.

That issue was more than academic. To treat Biederbach's irrational fear of government, Jommers must first defuse the indignation that fuels the fear. And the biggest problem in disarming indignation is the overwhelming power of the occasional negative example that confirms suspicions while rendering the positive examples invisible. When people are mistreated by government, they reflexively see malevolence in what is more likely incompetence.

A large police force can effectively serve and protect its citizens with a high level of performance day after day, month after month, then overnight have that solid record mooted by an incident of excessive force that changes public perception. The police are out of control. Like a drop of ink in water, the stain of injustice pervades the whole.

A similar effect is observed in the attitudes toward the federal government, which effectively serves and protects its citizens day after day, month after month. Overseeing the safety of food, water, medications, vehicles, airplanes, workplaces, highways, waterways, railways. The FBI protecting citizens from organized crime and white-collar crime. The FDIC protecting bank accounts. The warnings from the National Weather Service that help save lives from severe weather. The Centers for Disease Control protecting citizens from deadly epidemics. The Coast Guard regularly rescuing people. The food stamp program helping struggling people feed their families. The Medicaid program allowing Granny to stay in the nursing home after her money runs out. And on, and on, and on.

But let the government commit one breach of trust, one perceived injustice, and boom, the ink drop falls. Beware! Evil Big Brother is out to get you.

So you're a good psychologist. You understand all this. Great. Now how do you get ink out of water?

JOMMERS DEFINITELY DISLIKED Patrolman Biederbach, and that was a good thing. It would be a great help in treating him. Provide the necessary detachment to sort through his issues. Jommers had learned long ago that getting too chummy with the cops diminished his effectiveness as a therapist.

In the early days of working with Grayton PD, Jommers had done a lot of patrol car ride-alongs. He wanted to see what they saw. Experience what they experienced. Understand what they were feeling. Share that apprehension a cop feels when making the lonely walk from a cruiser to a vehicle just pulled over, wondering whether that driver's reach into the glove compartment was for the car registration or a gun.

It was that unpredictability that bothered them most.

"It ain't like it's a steady stream of shit," one cop said. "It's more like infantry, where you have these long droughts of boredom occasionally interrupted by cloudbursts that drop extreme quantities of shit. You can spend half a shift just toodling around like a goddamn ice cream truck, then all of a sudden you're pedal to the metal, racing to the corner of hell and bedlam."

It was on these ride-alongs that Jommers learned cops also like to embellish a bit.

Eventually he realized the danger of over-empathizing with them, automatically taking their side. When you become too eager to listen, and less reluctant to teach, at that point, you're no better than a bartender.

While Jommers was waiting for Biederbach to show, the patrolman called. He was downstairs in the parking lot. He wanted to say something privately before the session began and still felt that Jommers's office was not secure. Jommers sighed, then went outside.

"First of all," Biederbach said, "would you consider it an act of chutzpah for me to request the return of the bug I put in your office?"

"No problem," Jommers said.

He then handed Biederbach the envelope full of pieces left after smashing the bug with a hammer. The patrolman looked inside, then tucked it into a pocket without reaction.

"Last night," Biederbach said, "the guy by the bridge. Maybe he was just a homeless guy, maybe he wasn't. Either way, the point remains. By talking to me, you have become an adjunct surveillance target. They will be watching you. So keep your eyes peeled. Don't expect them to be wearing black suits and sunglasses, either. They'll appear to be ordinary people going about ordinary business."

"Then how will I know them?"

"They'll be new to your environment."

Jommers realized they were standing near the pickup truck of Pete's new mechanic, but immediately dismissed the thought.

"They'll be listening to you, as well," Biederbach added. "I strongly advise you to have your office swept for bugs regularly, but also be aware they don't always need them."

"What do you mean?"

"There's this thing called laser interferometry. The sounds of your words are nothing more than modulated vibrations in air, and they'll induce matching modulated vibrations into hard surfaces, like windows. When a laser is shined onto the window, the vibrations slightly alter the reflections of the laser. So you can then take the modulated reflection pattern, run it through a computer and voice synthesizer, and convert the patterns back into speech."

"Interesting. How would I defend against that?"

"Long-term? Replace your flat glass windows with pebbled or rippled glass and stick sound-damping foam to the windows. Short-term, play some modulated low-frequency noise that will set the windows rattling and disrupt the technique. Didgeridoo music will work quite nicely. It's also very relaxing."

"Good to know. Any other top secret stuff we need to cover?"

"One more. The big red dog—Ilona Voros. I know she's seeing you as a patient and that you can't confirm or deny it. But you need to know, in addition to being Earl Tarburn's assassin, she's also functioning as an agent provocateur. She'll tell you outlandish notions that you will want to dispel with hard information, and that's how they'll keep tabs on what you know."

"Okay, then. You ready to go up?"

"Sure."

Before starting the talk part of the session, Jommers gave Biederbach a test to complete.

"The test presents five hypothetical criminal cases," Jommers said. "For each one there is a list of items. The items consist of known facts, physical evidence descriptions, and statements of individuals. You are to rate each item on a scale of one to five in terms of its value in identifying which of the suspects committed the crime. Five means the item has a high value in identifying the right suspect, one means it has a low utility in doing so. There is no time limit, so take as long as you need."

"Is that how you pad out the clock?"

"Just do it."

Biederbach spent about twenty-five minutes on the test. Jommers then took out a test key to evaluate the answers. He took some notes, then put it all aside temporarily.

"Did I pass?"

"It wasn't pass/fail. But we'll get to it in a little bit. First I want to talk about threat assessment. Would you say you are pretty good at that?"

"Probably better than Joe Blow on the street, given my occupation."

"You're a cop, and a cop has to confront people, some of whom may be criminals, some of whom may have a predisposition to violence."

"Correct."

"So how do you proceed? How do you make the assessment?"

"Well, the first thing is whether you know who you're dealing with. I mean, if you're being sent to pick up someone specific, you want to know why, and you want to know everything about that person before you get there."

"Because hard information beats an educated guess," Jommers said.

"Correct."

"So how about when you don't know? You're approaching some guy for whatever reason. How do you size him up?"

"You look at his eyes, facial expression, body language. You want to figure out if he's hostile or friendly, anxious or relaxed, high or straight. You look for bulges in the places where people might carry a gun."

"Do clothes matter?"

"You look at them, sure," Biederbach said. "A guy in a suit is less likely to be a gangbanger than some diddy-bopping dingleberry with his pants half-down showing ass crack. And a bum, excuse me, a homeless gentleman, is less likely to have a gun, but he might have a knife or a piece of pipe."

"How about race?"

"Yes, within the realm of context."

"Meaning?"

"A black guy in a white neighborhood strikes me the same way as a white guy in a black neighborhood. They're both out of place and I'm wondering why."

"But these subjective methods aren't foolproof, are they?"

"No," Biederbach said.

"The fidgety guy just may be one those people who gets anxious around cops for no reason. Lots of people like that."

"The blue butterflies. Right."

"And the sociopath who's willing and ready to whack you, he's dead calm, not blinking an eye."

"Right."

"And the guy in the suit, maybe he is a mobster, one coming back from a wedding, and maybe he's high as a kite and pissed off about something that happened there."

"That's possible, too."

"So even as you're making your threat assessment, you recognize that you could be wrong."

"Correct," Biederbach said. "Which is why you always watch the hands."

"Because the hands are observable. Their movement reveals the actuality of intention. The hands signal reality. And reality beats imagination."

"Correct."

"Now then, are you familiar with the case of Ali al-Marri?"

"I am not."

"Well, then, I'll brief you," Jommers said. "A week after the 9/11 attacks, Congress passed the Authorization for Use of Military Force, which gave the president broad powers to deal with terrorist threats. Ali al-Marri was a citizen of Qatar, but was a legal resident here. In 2001 he was arrested on criminal charges in Peoria. Federal agents looking at his computer determined that he was a sleeper agent for al-Qaeda who was planning some type of follow-up attack. In 2003 he was classified by the administration as an unlawful enemy combatant, a status that deprives you of normal legal rights available under criminal law. He was then transferred to a navy brig, put under military custody. His lawyers have challenged the enemy combatant designation and want him put back into the civilian criminal justice system. Now, this case will almost certainly go all the way up to the Supreme Court before the issue is resolved one way or the other, but the aspect that makes it legally significant—momentous, even—is the government's position on its powers to classify people as unlawful enemy combatants. Ali al-Marri happens to be a legal alien, but government lawyers argued in the Fourth Circuit Court of Appeals in February that the executive branch also has the authority to designate American citizens on American soil as enemy combatants without interference of the courts. Do you understand the implications of what I just said?"

"Yes, but I'm sure you will overexplain it for me."

"If the high court upholds the government's position, then it means that the executive branch of government could arbitrarily and unilaterally determine that anyone, including you, Dwayne Biederbach, represent a threat to the United States, and classify you as an unlawful enemy combatant, and could do so without evidence, due process, or a judge's permission. Once you were so classified, the government could send a contingent of army soldiers to pick you up and drop you in a military prison and hold you there indefinitely without charges or trial. They would not need the approval of any court to do this, and you would have absolutely no legal recourse, no way to challenge either your detention or classification. You would have fewer rights than a serial killer has, because you would have no rights at all. Imagine in the future we get another paranoid president like Nixon, seeing enemies everywhere. Imagine what he would do with such power. You see where I'm headed here?"

"You're about to make some really big point in your usual roundabout fashion."

"Yes," Jommers said. "And that point gets back to threat assessment. The very thing that you fear might be happening secretly in the shadows, the attempted transfer of civilian law enforcement powers into the hands of the military—martial law—that very fear is in fact unfolding in the bright light of day in an open, public court, and you are utterly oblivious to it. The one guy who should be on top of this is no more informed than his fellow Americans who, instead of expressing outrage that their civil liberties teeter at the precipice, are prattling about the new *Harry Potter* movie or the latest *Pirates of the Caribbean*."

Jommers said those last few words slowly and dramatically, and let them hang quietly in the air awhile before resuming. The look of concern on Biederbach's face indicated that the dart had struck its mark.

"So, how does this happen?" Jommers asked. "How can you be so obsessed with an improbable, imaginary threat, while ignoring a threat that is both real and at hand? Why is your capability for threat assessment so faulty?"

Jommers paused again for emphasis.

"One reason has to do with the level of emotional content, the dramatic element. Fear is an emotion. Explanations involving emotions have greater hold on us than those that don't. This is why people are always worrying about being the victim of a violent crime even though they're much more likely to be injured by a vehicle accident or simple fall. Crime has a higher level of emotional content. Likewise with your paradox. Lawyers engaging in dry debate over legal principles does not resonate emotionally, but the idea of sinister forces fomenting a conspiracy trips the alarm. So you get distracted by impressions when you should be watching the hands. On the street, that gets you killed."

"You may have a point," Biederbach said. "But that court case, other people are aware of it, even if I personally am not. Somebody is handling it. Fighting it.

You can't fight something if you don't know it's there. The things in the shadows are more important because no one sees them coming. Alarms are for the things you don't know about. Listening to the stories is how you learn what's going on."

"Perhaps, if you listened to all stories equally," Jommers said. "But you don't. You only listen to those spoken in your language. Which leads me to another cause of your distorted views, something we call confirmation bias."

"I don't have any political bias," Biederbach said. "Both sides are equally dangerous when it comes to expansion of government powers. The right hand promises to protect you from various enemies. The left hand offers to protect you from the fickleness of fate. And at the end of the day, both hands are wrapped around your throat, because it takes two to strangle."

"It's comforting to hear you're a political moderate. But that's not what I meant. I wasn't talking about political bias. The term confirmation bias refers to the selective filtering of information and ideas, taking in only things that confirm your existing views, while pretending that contrary information and ideas don't even exist."

"Everybody does that. Including people who are right and people who are wrong. So even if I were guilty of that, it wouldn't necessarily prove me wrong."

"Clever response," Jommers said. "But it's not a trivial matter when serious consequences are involved. Example: One of the biggest problems with criminal investigations is the inability of detectives to suspend judgment and examine the facts objectively in a scientific manner. They feel the need to have a working theory. Unfortunately, having a working theory also entails the targeting of a preferred suspect. Once that decision is made, it influences everything that happens thereafter. Specifically, it causes detectives to doggedly pursue evidence that supports their theory, while ignoring evidence that contradicts the theory. One can only guess how many innocent people have been sent to prison this way."

Jommers reached over and picked up his notes on the scoring of the test he'd given.

"That test I gave you earlier—I developed that with the help of a criminal defense lawyer I know. The facts in each of the hypothetical cases were carefully designed and weighted so that they might equally point to one of two suspects. When the test is administered with only those facts, the utility ratings given by the test subject for each item do not favor one suspect over another. However, when you insert disparaging comments about one of the suspects, comments that contain no useful information whatsoever but merely reflect the commenter's gut feelings, the test subject invariably rates evidence pointing to that suspect as having greater utility. I gave this test to a roomful of detectives once. All had the same hypothetical cases with the same facts. There was only one difference. Half the tests contained irrelevant, but disparaging comments about suspect A, and the other half contained irrelevant, but disparaging comments about suspect B. Unsurprisingly, subjects taking the first version rated more highly evidence that pointed to suspect A, and subjects taking the other version rated more highly evidence pointing to suspect B. When I revealed this to the detectives, they were mildly surprised and amused, but not chastened. I doubt that any of them have changed their methods. In the test I just gave you, in each case, you rated evidence more highly that appeared to implicate the suspect receiving disparaging remarks, which reveals your tendencies toward confirmation bias."

"Good," Biederbach said. "You've just told me I'm like everybody else, which means by the standards of your profession, I'm normal. I agree. Thank you."

"You are normal in your flaws, abnormal in the peculiar beliefs those flaws have spawned. What's interesting is that, much like a religious hypocrite, you can easily see a fault in others while blind to the exact same fault in yourself. Last week we briefly touched on the notion that the government was covering up evidence of alien visitations. You correctly noted that it would take the co-operation of scores of people at multiple levels of government across multiple generations and that it is highly improbable that not one of them would ever leak it, especially in an age where government leaking is rampant. Yet you're unable to apply that same reasoning to your own pet theories."

"Because mine have more validity."

"No," Jommers said, "that would not be the reason. Peculiar beliefs vary greatly in different individuals, both by type and intensity, and those variations are generated by differences in our experiences and backgrounds—who we are. Reports of UFO sightings are relatively high in some cultures, virtually nonexistent elsewhere. Presumably some alien tour packages are more popular than others. The nurturing gender, believed to have more empathy, is more inclined to believe in psychic powers than the warrior gender, which is more inclined to imagine monsters and enemies that need to be battled. The big conspiracy is a subset of things needing to be battled. And your conspiracy theory is about you. It was not simply plucked off a shelf like a candy bar. It grew organically out of who you are and what you've been through. Which brings me to your homework assignment. Did you bring the journal in which I asked you to record your daydreams?"

"No," Biederbach said. "I daydreamed that I had already done it and given it to you."

"So you blew it off."

"I didn't see the point."

"Wrong. You saw the point all too clearly. But you didn't want to reveal the content of your daydreaming, which is, in essence, a never-ending montage of confrontations. Some of them minor verbal skirmishes. Winning an argument or getting the last word. Ranting about poor service. Berating an unjust superior. Outwitting a lawyer in some imaginary courtroom. Getting the last word with some woman who dissed you. Some of the daydreams get physical. Overpowering attackers who get the jump on you. Defying the odds when outnumbered in a gunfight. Like James Bond, everyone misses but you. Your dreams are populated with conflict. Your head is the battlefield where you always get to win."

"Again, this is all very common, isn't it?"

"Yes," Jommers said. "But the question is to what degree? The tendency exists on a continuum, like most problems. How deep does it run? To what extent does it alter your personality, shape your worldview? Perhaps we all engage in fantasies that compensate for minor frustrations. But when the frustration becomes persistent and outsized, there's a danger that the reaction becomes outsized as well. Graffiti, rape, mass shootings—they're all connected in part to impotent rage. Feelings of powerlessness that get projected outward. And your anger gets projected outward, as well, toward your environment. So what is the source of your frustration? The thing you can't control. The thing that mocks your weakness day in and day out. The answer screams out of the quiet furls of smoke curling around you like tentacles. Last night, at the bridge, you collapsed after chasing that homeless guy up the stairs. That's not the first time something like that happened, is it? In fact, you probably begin every shift hoping and praying that you won't have to chase anyone on foot. Am I right?"

After a long delay, Biederbach surrendered a small nod of confirmation and slightly shifted his slumped position. The change in posture was physically minute, but psychologically broad, spanning the distance from defiant indifference to resigned enervation.

The room stayed quiet for a long time, except for the sounds of the shop echoing up. The whirring of an air tool. The crackle of an arc welder. Finally, Biederbach responded, speaking slowly, quietly.

"You know what the coolest thing in the world is?"

"What?" Jommers asked.

"An orange. Yeah, I know. I live small. But an orange is just, you know, just this remarkable thing, so sweet and tart and juicy, so intense. You know how you put a piece in your mouth and it just kind of explodes and all the lights go on. The fullness of it. Life is supposed to be like an orange. When I was a little kid, I used to dream about having a beautiful ripe juicy orange. Stupid, huh? All the crap out there a kid could want, and I dreamed about oranges. Of course, I didn't get much fresh fruit in the foster homes I passed through. Occasionally a few slices of canned peaches if I was lucky. So maybe that's the reason. Or maybe it wasn't even about the orange itself. Maybe I just wanted somebody somewhere to give me something to show they cared. Anyway, imagine you're that kid, that simple kid who dreamed about oranges. And now you're an adult with a good job, and you can buy as many goddamn oranges as you want. But you don't bother. Because now when you put one in your mouth, it tastes like wet newspaper. Your taste buds, your sense of smell—all of that has been cauterized. You don't get to live in the same world as everybody else. You live in an old, ash-littered fire pit. And you can't get out, no matter how hard you try. And so, at some point, you just give up trying. You asked me if I collapsed before—yes, last year. Only I wasn't running, and I wasn't out of breath. Just walking. Just fucking walking. And I just passed out. Dropped. Somebody found me and called 911. When I came to, I was in a hospital bed. The doctors and the nurses were staring at me in disbelief. You know why? I was dying of malnutrition. Middle-class guy living in America, dying like he was an abandoned child in the sub-Sahara. You see, these things don't just kill your taste, they kill your appetite. You don't want to eat. You don't remember to eat. I use timers and alarms now, set for certain times, and when they go off, I force something down. Either that or slug another bottle of that nutritional supplement stuff that they make for the old people. That stuff will keep you alive, but you ain't going to shit right, I'll tell you that. And don't tell me how goddamn sorry you are about it. I didn't tell you to get sympathy. I was just answering the question."

"I'm not offering sympathy," Jommers said. "I'm offering help. You don't need tears. You need a hand. So, we've got two issues here. The smoking, and its corollary effects, how the frustration over it impacts your personality and attitudes. Both are addressable. And both will take time and effort. Have you tried the patch?"

"Yeah. Didn't work."

"The gum?"

"Yep. Didn't work either."

"Hypnosis?"

"Those guys are quacks."

"They help some people."

"Yeah, so does Madame Esmeralda the fortune-teller. But in both cases, you got to believe or it doesn't work."

"Okay, I want you to try something for me. Starting now. Every time you feel like lighting up, I want you to wait two minutes before doing so. Time it. When you find that you can do that easily without agitation, I want you to add a minute, and time it. And when you find that you can comfortably wait three minutes, then increase it to four. And continue in this fashion. But don't push it. Make sure you get comfortable at each level before proceeding to the next. It's like running. You don't start out trying to run ten miles when you've never run before. Start small. Increase by little bits. Understand?"

"I'll give it a shot. Sounds cheaper than the goddamn gum."

"And do something with your face, too."

"You don't like my face?"

"I mean during the waiting period that you're postponing the smoking. Find an alternate means of using your mouth and facial muscles that will substitute for the expressions you normally make while smoking. Chew bubble gum and blow bubbles. Chew on a toothpick or drink stirrer. Or do the Kojak thing with the lollipop."

"Got it."

"Okay," Jommers said. "Now then, for the other issue, the larger one. I want you to start practicing mindfulness. And before you get a bug up your ass about it, thinking I mean some new age loony stuff, I'm not talking about anything weird, not talking about assuming painful yoga positions while listening to sitar music. What I mean by mindfulness is this—focus on what you are doing at any given moment. And you're going to say, well, I already do that or I couldn't get anything done. And no, you don't already do that. Like everybody else, you're doing one thing while thinking about something else. This is why we spill things, drop things, get in car accidents, misunderstand conversations, fail to read someone else's emotional state, and screw up life in general. The body is one place, the mind in another. And disunity is never a good thing. It's how we get detached from reality. And staying attached to reality is the essence of emotional health. So when I say you should practice mindfulness, it means that, if you're drinking a cup of coffee, then focus your attention on the coffee. If you're walking down the street, then focus on the experience of walking down the street. What do you see? What do you hear? What do you smell? What do you feel on the bottom of your foot with each step? This isn't mystical or exotic. It's about living right. Living awake. It also means being mindful about the little self-produced movie clips we run in our head all the time. Why did you just run that particular clip? What does it mean? And when the little clip contains a rant, what is the rant really about? What is the anger really about? And the key word here is practice. You won't accomplish mindfulness overnight."

Biederbach looked skeptical. "You're telling me this will change my attitudes and my theories."

"Yes, it will," Jommers said. "Because your attitudes and your theories are rooted in your emotional state. And when your emotional state settles down, your attitudes and theories will settle down, too."

"Well, I'll give that a shot, too. Maybe it will work, maybe it won't. But you need to understand, it doesn't change anything out there, because what's happening out there isn't about me. So it doesn't much matter if you turn me into Mr. Sunshine. Doesn't matter if I start planting wildflowers and start playing guitar in the park. It isn't about me. And you need to start getting mindful about that."

Jommers was frustrated. Biederbach refused to accept any linkage between his problems and his theories. The therapist tried another tack.

"Do you believe in fairies?"

"I assume you mean the Tinkerbelle type," Biederbach said.

"Yes."

"That would be a big negatory."

"What would you think of someone who did?"

"I would say he's got some serious issues that need dealt with. Way worse than mine."

"And what if I told you that this person who believed in fairies was a very intelligent, highly educated man, well versed in the sciences, and that he was a trained physician?"

"I'd guess that he had some psychiatric disorder that could benefit from psychotropic medication."

"In fact," Jommers said, "he was a highly functioning individual. Very successful and well respected."

"You're really into this whole trap-setting thing, aren't you?"

"Have you ever heard of the Cottingley Fairies?"

"No," Biederbach said, "but I guess I'm about to."

"There were these two young girls, cousins, who lived in Cottingley, a small village in England. In 1917, they copied some illustrations out of a children's book, cut them out, propped them up with hatpins outside in the garden, then took photographs of them. The pictures eventually created quite a stir, as many people believed them to be authentic images. One such person was Arthur Conan Doyle, who used the photos in a magazine article about fairies. Conan Doyle suggested that the photos provided clear evidence of psychic phenomena. He would later expound on that, writing a book called *The Coming of the Fairies*. So how do we process that? This very smart guy, the writer who gave us Sherlock Holmes, the paragon of logic and reason, this same writer believes in fairies. How is that possible?"

"I guess he just wanted to believe."

"Precisely," Jommers said. "He wanted it to be true. He was a spiritualist who delved into such matters frequently. He believed in spiritualism, psychic phenomena, that mediums could communicate with the dead. He had already conditioned himself to believe such things. He desired to. So when the opportunity to believe in fairies came along, he embraced it reflexively. It wasn't a leap at all. Just fulfilling his desire. So let me ask you—imagine you are me, a therapist, only back then. And you have this patient who believes in fairies—what do you do? How do you talk him out of it?"

"I guess my first question is, why bother? As long as he's not taking potshots at fairies in a crowded place, who cares?"

"Again," Jommers said, "you're me, a therapist. It's your job to care. It's your job to set people straight."

"Well, maybe that's not always possible."

"Why?"

"Well, if he believes it, if it's up there in the belief attic, all locked up where you can't get at it—well, then, there's nothing you can do. It would be like trying to talk the pope out of being Catholic. Ain't going to happen. So you just let it go. Accept that different people are going to believe different things. If he's paying his bills and he's not shooting people, not burdening society, then he's not a problem."

"So it's okay for us to have different views of reality, okay for us to live in different worlds so long as we don't shoot each other?"

"Why not?" Biederbach said. "Live and let live."

"But yet, you feel it imperative to convince me of your view of reality, convince me of the dangers you envision. How do you square that with what you just said?"

"I guess the operative word is danger. You have to be on the same page to deal with a threat."

"Because we need to cooperate to deal with threats, so we need to agree on what constitutes a false positive or a false negative."

"Yeah, whatever."

"This makes a nice transition to your next homework assignment."

"You're shitting me. We're not really doing this again, are we?"

"This one's easy," Jommers said. "I want you to do some research. You like doing that. I want you to examine how ancients and primitive peoples explained lightning. And give me a report."

"That's it?"

"Yep."

"We still have our deal, right?"

"Yes."

"So next time is my turn."

"Right."

"How's Wednesday night?"

"Sounds good to me," Jommers said.

"Good. It's going to be an eye-opener. Be ready to concede."

As soon as Biederbach left, Jommers began recording his notes on the session. While doing so, he began to doubt his own assessment of the patient. But then, this was standard operating procedure. The post-session reassessment, riddled with doubts, was precisely how he arrived at fresh insights. The doubts forced him to keep asking questions and not accept the easy answers.

Was he wrong about the connections? Was it possible that Biederbach's conspiracy theories would be exactly the same if he weren't a former foster child with a tobacco addiction? Of course it was possible. Biederbach's childhood certainly played a role in his outlook—in every recipe for justification, grievance served as the core ingredient. On the other hand, there were legions of people with strange theories who had normal upbringings and who did not suffer from any addictive behaviors.

And recognizing that point led him back to the question that always haunted him—how could people be selectively delusional? How could they be normal and reasonable in every other aspect, but have only one little crazy corner? You could classify it as monosymptomatic delusional disorder, in the same fashion that nineteenth-century psychologists had employed the now-outdated term monomania. But that just provided a label, not an answer. And the corollary riddle was how such a thing could exist in an extremely intelligent person.

And Biederbach certainly was an intelligent man, capable of sound reasoning. But the quality of one's reasoning can never exceed the quality of one's sources. You can be a well-read person, but be reading the wrong things. You're not stupid, just misinformed.

Carl Sagan pondered the issue in his book *The Demon-Haunted World* and concluded it is a failure of culture. But who controls culture? Is culture even controllable? Or is it just another multivariable phenomenon? In which case, blaming culture is no different than blaming the weather.

Culture helps explain why the creator of Sherlock Holmes could believe in fairies. Belief in Spiritualism was widespread in England at the time. But why did this particular person dive into that particular cultural current while others declined? Why did Conan Doyle pursue Spiritualism, but other literary contemporaries did not? Was it the death of Conan Doyle's son and the death of his brother? Had they both lived, would Conan Doyle still have attended séances?

Each person possesses a unique assortment of experiences, which again summons the analogy of weather being an unconquerable multivariable problem. And if you were a mere philosopher, you could leave it there and call it a day. But if you are a psychologist, charged with clearing clouds and bringing forth light in a person's life, then leaving it there is not good enough. Not by a long shot.

SOMEBODY IS WATCHING

Not long after Biederbach left, Jommers got a call from a Reverend Elvis Truly, who said he was the pastor at Evergreen Baptist Church on Hawthorne Boulevard, where Patrolman Earl Tarburn had been a member. It was the voice of Truly that Jommers had heard presiding over Tarburn's burial rites. The pastor wanted to speak with Jommers about Tarburn, but declined to be specific. Jommers sensed that the pastor's reluctance to elaborate on the phone was not due to any paranoia about the phone being tapped, but rather the reticence of an old-fashioned sort who believed that important conversations should be held face-to-face. They agreed on a meeting time for the following day.

As he finished the call with the pastor, Claire Maroun walked in.

"Is now a good time?" she asked.

"Your very presence turns bad times into good."

"Right."

"I'm hoping the books will look a little better next month," Jommers said. "I'm seeing a slight uptick in business."

"I'm not here about the books. Just wanted to check in on you to see if you're all right."

"I'm doing fine, thanks."

"It was hard not to hear this morning—even over the shop noise—that woman screaming and swearing at you. Then suddenly she's playing the 'Beer Barrel Polka.' Then she's screaming at you again. I thought, my God, how does he deal with that? How does he deal with crazy people all day?"

"Well, I wouldn't say they're crazy. I'd say they're troubled."

"A rose by any other name—either way, it's got to take a toll on you at the end of the day. How do you come down from that?"

"Well, I've got my music, for one."

"I don't see how that helps," she said. "Not the stuff you listen to, anyway. The blues are so depressing. It's just more people complaining about bad things happening to them, only with a guitar. Why do you want to hear more? You should be listening to happy music—you know, like calypso or something."

"Calypso. Now that would definitely drive me out the window."

"You used to like Jimmy Buffet."

"You remember my Parrothead days."

"I do, vividly. Especially the shirts."

"I still like Jimmy, but I settled down with the blues because it relates to the business of coping. The blues teach you acceptance. They're saying, yeah, the road is hard and the road is long, but you can wear better shoes."

"You should trademark that line and then license it to Timberland. That would solve the revenue problem. More importantly, you should get out more, too. I mean, you know, outside more. I remember how you used to ride your bike all around the Bends like a crazy man."

"Yeah."

"You'd hop the tracks and ride to the lake."

"Yep."

"You should be like that again."

"You're right."

"You know what I'm really worried about," she said.

"Yes. It's under control."

"And you would know better than me that anyone with such a problem would say exactly that."

"Yes," he said. "And some of them would be right, and some of them would be wrong."

"Just take better care of yourself, okay? Promise?"

"Promise."

⁓

NOT LONG AFTER the shop went quiet, with the mechanics gone home, Jommers got a call from Chief Scubbetts. As he sometimes did, the chief began with an inept attempt at small talk, as if casual conversation was a foreign language and he was still in his first year of learning it.

"I was in the latrine today here at the station," Scubbetts said. "Standing at the pisser. And there was this captain standing next to me. And as soon as I got there, he started flushing the damn thing over and over. And so I yelled at him, 'What the hell are you doing?'"

"It sounds like he has a common phobia called paruresis," Jommers said, "which makes it difficult to urinate when someone else is present or listening."

"Well, I won't tolerate that. Won't tolerate a nervous Nellie in my command standing in the latrine flushing the toilet all day. He's a captain, for chrissake. How the hell can you command forces when you can't even command your bladder to take a proper piss? So I ordered him to appear in that same latrine tomorrow morning at zero nine hundred hours and drink plenty of coffee beforehand, because at exactly that time he will be required to drop his drawers to his ankles, and in the presence of myself and other senior staff members, he will then either produce a steady stream of piss or a letter of resignation, one or the other."

"Well, before you do that, you might want to take a swing by Human Resources and have a chat."

"Fuck Human Resources!" He paused. "So how are things?"

"Things are going fine, Chief. How about with you?"

"Do you need any help getting the woman off your tail?"

"What woman?"

"The reporter."

Jommers was momentarily stunned. How did Scubbetts know that the police reporter had been hounding him outside Spreckels Tavern?

"She's just doing her job, Chief. Checking in with potential sources like she's supposed to. She knows I have nothing to say, but she's obliged to make the effort. It's just a ritual."

"There are things we can do to reduce her enthusiasm. You know, when you find that your car gets towed to the impound lot whenever you go to a certain neighborhood, maybe you stop going there."

"That's not necessary or advisable. You would be giving her another story to pursue. Please leave her alone."

"Well, we appreciate your solidarity with the department."

"It's standard procedure. If she were asking about a mechanic or janitor who was a patient, she would get the same response."

"Is everything okay with Lieutenant Dallabaco?"

"Yes," Jommers said. "Why do you ask?"

"According to HR, you cleared him, yet you've had multiple conversations with him."

"He is shaken and saddened by the loss of a good man who was also a good friend. He wanted to talk about it informally. He has the normal grief of a normal man. He'll be fine."

"And the red-haired detective . . ."

"Ilona Voros."

"Yes. Has she dropped any bombs?"

"Meaning?"

"Said anything radical. Offered any revelations on what happened last week."

"As you know, I don't do operational debriefing. That's your job. My purview in her case is post-critical-incident evaluation, to determine if the incident has affected her frame of mind such that it would interfere with her ability to do her job effectively."

"And the status of that evaluation."

"The evaluation is ongoing, with the outcome as yet to be determined."

"So you don't want her back on the job yet. That's good. That's what I want."

"That is my assessment at the moment," Jommers said. "That could change after the next session."

"I don't want it to change."

"Whether it does will be determined by what I see. I don't understand your concern with my end of it. Force Review will take weeks before they clear her to come off admin leave. I'll be done with her long before then."

"I don't want her back. Ever. Force Review can't accomplish that. You can."

"You need a reason," Jommers said. "You're running a government agency, not a truck stop."

"She's a loose cannon. She behaves erratically. She fails to follow proper procedures, and she's a loner who is incapable of cooperatively functioning with fellow officers because of hostile attitude. She's insubordinate to superiors, generally disruptive, and files false reports. Somebody like that does not meet the standards for police work."

"To the extent that those assertions were true and associated with a psychological condition, I would need some documentation and some paperwork from you officially expanding the scope of my inquiry to encompass a general job fitness evaluation based on performance issues."

"You have the authority to make that expansion when warranted based on your own observations," Scubbetts said. "You could do this."

"Yes, I could, if I had a legitimate reason for doing so. At this point in time, I do not."

"You understand that your contract with the city can be terminated by either party with thirty days' notice without cause."

"I do. You can sever the relationship at any time, as can I. But I don't see much value in raising that as a threat every time we disagree on procedural and policy matters. That is not conducive to a good professional business relationship. But if you think now is the time, with everything that is going on, if you think that it's prudent to place another decision under public scrutiny . . ."

"Now is not a good time. I was merely reminding you of the tenuousness of things."

"Hard to forget when it's tossed out routinely now in every conversation."

"I simply don't understand your need to butt heads on everything these days," Scubbetts said. "People can have different values and objectives but still cooperate when they have a common cause. We cooperated with a lot of greaseball generalissimos back in the Cold War because we had a common larger enemy in communism. And that cooperation proved successful. I think the difficulty here is that you have is a vision problem, the inability to see the larger common cause we both have. I think we both want to see a well-functioning police department comprised of well-functioning individuals."

"I agree."

"Then you should want to help me jettison individuals who do not function well and whose behavior inhibits the department from functioning well."

"I'll be happy to help in such efforts when there is a proper justification for doing so. This is government. There are rules and procedures. I would think a man who spent his entire life in government service would understand that."

"I can't help but be curious as to when such a free spirit such as yourself became enamored of bureaucratic red tape. This is new."

"The gravity of the situation is new," Jommers said. "This is not small potatoes. As you noted with the reporter, everybody is watching—the media, the public, city council. Whatever the outcome, there will be intense scrutiny. It's quite possible some parties may initiate litigation. It's entirely possible that you and I could find ourselves in a courtroom somewhere down the road, being sworn to testify about our conversations—including this one. I would recommend you keep careful records. As will I."

There was a long silence on the line before the chief spoke again.

"For the record, this was not an official communication. This was just casual conversation. Two acquaintances catching up and shooting the breeze. Okay?"

"Sure."

Jommers wondered how Scubbetts knew about the conversations with Lieutenant Dallabaco. He briefly entertained Biederbach's notion that the office was bugged. But if that were the case, then Scubbetts would not need to inquire about things revealed by Ilona Voros—he would already know. When Scubbetts stopped asking what Voros said, that would be the time to worry.

It was a nice evening for baseball.

After talking with Chief Scubbetts, Jommers called Dallabaco, suggesting the need for a brief meeting. Dallabaco directed him to Crabtree Park, where a boy's league baseball game was underway. Dallabaco was not hard to find. He was yelling advice to his son, who was about to enter the batter's box.

"Remember, keep your eye on the ball, keep your eye on the ball."

Jommers was mildly amused by the father's need to give obvious instructions. What else would you be looking at while standing at the plate? An airplane? A dog?

In spite of the repetition of paternal wisdom, the boy swung hard and missed the ball—three times in a row. The boy hung his head down, dejected, while the father offered a halfhearted consolation that barely concealed his disappointment. When Dallabaco saw Jommers standing near, he motioned with his head that they should step away from the crowd to talk.

"You know what his problem is," Dallabaco said. "He closes his eyes just as the ball arrives."

"A natural reflex to protect the eyes," Jommers said. "Baseball didn't play much a role in evolution."

"Okay, then, you're the witch doctor, what would you do about it?"

"I would create an exercise that focused exclusively on resisting the reflex. Put him in a chair. Put shop goggles on him. Then throw ping-pong balls at his eyes repeatedly until he learns not to blink."

"I like it. Unfortunately, this was the last game of the season, so I'll have to try that next year."

"Of course, there is another factor possibly at work here."

"Such as?"

"Maybe the kid hates baseball, and he only plays to please an overbearing father."

Dallabaco gave Jommers an acid look. "You didn't track me down here to offer advice on child-rearing."

"I got a call from Chief Scubbetts not long ago. He wanted to know what we talked about on Saturday."

"How does he know we talked on Saturday?"

"That's what I wondered, and I don't have an answer. But I thought I should let you know. There's a possibility he is watching you."

"Maybe he's watching you."

"I'm not interesting enough to be watched."

"You underestimate yourself . . . and him."

DAY NINE

Shortly after Jommers got up on Tuesday morning, he looked out the window and saw, off in the distance, somebody putting something on a tripod, a camera possibly, in the line of sight of his building. He planned to investigate indirectly by changing the route of his morning run so that he could just happen by without appearing nosy.

When arrived at the location, he stopped, put his hands on his knees, and pretended to be winded. At this point in the run, it did not require much pretending.

It was the backside of an abandoned brick building that faced Helmick Street. There was a bit of open space behind the building meant to accommodate a rail spur that was now unused and overgrown with weeds.

A compact hatchback car was parked nearby with the hatch open, revealing a fiberglass stepladder and a clutter of spray paint cans. A young woman was adjusting a tripod that was set up about thirty or forty feet behind the building. The tripod supported two cameras aimed at the back wall. She was a slender woman with short dark hair who looked to be in her midtwenties. She wore blue denim shorts, a baggy black T-shirt with the sleeves cut off, and a teal kerchief around her neck.

She looked over at him, shook her head and smiled.

"Don't be crazy," she said.

"Is that general advice, or did you have something specific in mind?"

"It's too hot for running. You'll get a sunstroke or something. I mean, you know, even if you were still game, it's still not healthy."

"Sometimes I need a little self-flagellation. What are you up to?"

"I'm separating."

"From?"

"Like, everybody else."

"You lost me."

"The writers down here. Bombers and taggers, mostly. Same old lame. Can't tell fresh from gramps."

"You mean graffiti. You're a graffiti artist."

"Abso-latte. You know that wall on the Brick Strip of South Mill, like where the big metal door takes you to the steam tunnels? Have you seen the scape to the right of that? The one where the river is a serpent?"

"Yes. I've seen it."

"Well, that's like my piece, my production. You can see my tag, Veena C. That's my burn. It's absolutely huger than anyone. Was just so totally stoked after it. Then the chatter starts dissing me, saying I couldn't have done that by myself, that my boyfriend helped, which pissed me off. And he like kind of didn't douse it enough in my view, so like, he's totally toast now. No way he gets to come around for wink anymore. So now I'm using two cameras. One for video, to prove my act. The other for the frames. When they see it, they'll have to definitely respect it."

"Frames?"

"For animation. Redrawing scenes, running them together. You know, like cartoons. Writing's like bush when all you do is throw-ups and tags. Lazy kicks. I'm going to tell stories. I'm going to burn them all. Then they will absolutely have to take me for real. I'm going to be like that Greek guy, Asap."

"Aesop."

"Yupperz, him. Only with the paint talking, not a toga guy. This is totally perfect weather. It'll dry fast. I can definitely slap one after the other."

"Why'd you pick this place?"

"The sun hits this wall totally perfect. Definitely lights it up. You mean the building? The broken windows. Totally ghost open, so no hassle. Plus, I like working safe."

"Safe?"

"I don't hang with the thrillers—you know, they like go hop the yard fence and do throwies on the freights. They get off on that whole bandit-rush thing. I'm absolutely not into that adventure. I mean, like the RCs are totally psych. They will rubble you to bag, even a girl."

"RCs?"

"Rail cops. And since 9/11, they're like double. I'm in it totally for the art. I want to have a voice. So, you know, you work on a ghost in the Bends, nobody bothers you. You can focus on the work, and not have to freak every time you hear something."

"It's still technically illegal, though, right?"

"Technically. Besides, the thing about animation—I mean after, I put the wall absolutely back like it was. See, it's not meant to live on the wall, but on the tube."

"The tube?"

"YouTube. It'll like live forever there. Which means I will, too."

"That's the website with the videos and stuff."

"Uh, yeahhh. You don't surf much, right? Fogey tech-phobe type."

"I wouldn't say I'm a technophobe, just more of a techno-utilitarian. My computer is just a tool, like my drill-driver. Happy to have it when I need it, but I don't play with it. Other things to do."

"Other things. So, like, what do you do?"

"I'm a clinical psychologist. I have an office over thataway."

"So, like, what's the difference between a psychologist and a psychiatrist?"

"Well, a psychiatrist functions more like a pharmaceutical distributor, whereas a psychologist actually helps people."

"Whoa. Serious 'tude."

"Perhaps a bit."

"It's okay, though. It means you're absolutely into it. Or you wouldn't care."

"So what story will you tell here?"

"Nope. You'll have to watch it roll, or catch it when I post. I mean, you know, catch it on your drill-driver."

"All right, then. Good luck with your project."

"You look so totally faded. You should maybe walk it on in."

She smiled impishly, then pulled her kerchief up over her mouth and nose and started spraying.

Jommers headed back to the office, heeding her advice to walk it on in. And as he walked, the jukebox in his head started playing didgeridoo music. It baffled him for two reasons. First, he had no idea how such music ever got into his head. He could not ever recall deliberately listening to it, and he was pretty sure the didgeridoo was not much used in the blues. Perhaps some long-forgotten *National Geographic* television special about Australia had deposited the musical nugget in some cranial crevice.

But the larger question was why it started playing at that moment. So the self-detective went to work, knocking on doors inside his head, hunting for clues. It didn't take long. Within a minute or so, one of those doors opened to reveal a nervous Patrolman Biederbach warning Jommers about an electronic eavesdropping technique known as laser interferometry which can be defeated with didgeridoo music, or so he claimed. And there was Biederbach advising Jommers to beware of new people in his environment. "Don't expect them to be wearing black suits and sunglasses, either. They will appear to be ordinary people."

And so here was this seemingly ordinary person, new to his environment, with electronic devices on a tripod, and of all the places in the Bends she could have set up, she chooses a spot a couple of hundred yards away from Jommers's windows. Coincidence?

On the other hand, if she was just pretending to be a graffiti artist, she was a damn good actress. Her speech pattern encompassed a confluence of at least three different social dialects, including Valspeak. Then there was her use of uptalk, or high rising terminal, where the end of a statement was intoned as a question.

Her speech was also sprinkled with vernacular terms from graffiti artist subculture, as well as some location-specific terms that Jommers had not heard anywhere outside of the Bends. Brick Strip was a term that described an old section of South Mill Road. "Ghost open" described the status of vacant buildings in the Bends that had been seized by the county for tax delinquency. Given that the county now owned an extensive collection of such ghost buildings, nobody ever went out to check on them, which meant that they were open to squatters who could take over the space without fear of being bothered.

There was also the mispronunciation of Aesop. So if she indeed was the kind of nefarious agent that kept Biederbach up at night, then she excelled at disguise and was very good at tradecraft.

AFTER ARRIVING BACK HOME, Jommers took a fast shower, then drove over to Grayton State University. At least once a semester, the head of the GSU Psychology Department asked Jommers to speak to students about life as a clinical psychologist in general, and as a police psychologist in particular.

Jommers was always eager to do so. He relished the opportunity to dispel the Hollywood-inspired myth that someone in his profession spent most of his time chasing and outwitting serial killers. He explained how the therapy side of the business was devoted to helping law enforcement personnel cope with occupationally induced emotional problems, and how on the administrative side he provided evaluations of candidates for employment and promotion, performed assessments of personnel involved in critical incidents, and presented training sessions to improve job performance. He was fond of noting that he had not once been asked to divine the mind of a serial killer and that on a personal level he was thankful that such a burden had never been placed on him. Thus far.

He discussed the challenges of maintaining a dispassionate professional temperament while listening to affecting stories that ranged from gruesome to heartrending. He cautioned against overestimating one's capacity for empathy. You could understand what they experienced, but never fully understand how they felt. He also warned about getting too cozy with the law enforcement subculture. He underscored the necessity of preserving a clear, unbiased perspective, which required maintaining a proper distance.

Standard procedure after such a talk was to entertain questions from the class. He enjoyed responding to their inquiries, even when they were occasionally challenging. On this particular afternoon, the class was smaller than usual, as it was summer semester. He was slightly concerned someone might ask an awkward question about recent events at Eggers Court or Crone Point, but was relieved when the first question turned out to be fairly typical and more generally related to clinical psychology than his particular specialty.

"Do you rely heavily on the DSM, see it as an important tool? Or do you rely mostly on your own experience?"

"The DSM is a deeply flawed and overly complicated guide, but sometimes a flawed guide is better than none," Jommers said. "We need some kind of diagnostic reference to identify conditions so we can determine how to best treat those conditions. An internist facing a patient with a seriously stuffed and runny nose needs to figure out whether it's a viral cold or a bacterial sinus infection, because the latter can be treated with antibiotics and the former can't. We have a similar imperative to differentiate among possible alternatives, so some type of categorical reference is necessary. But the problem in our field is that conditions are rarely discrete. In therapy, it's not always a situation where someone has this but not that. You may have a little of both. And the various conditions are not binary in nature, not fully present or fully absent, but present in varying degrees. So we can't, at least shouldn't, try to emulate physiology as a paradigm. We have to resist the notion that we can ever fully understand the workings of the mind the way we understand skeletal structure. There's too much emphasis on deep theories behind problems when there should be more emphasis on what works to solve them. The goal of research should not be to fill bookshelves, but to establish best practices for making people well."

"What's your batting average?"

"By that you mean what is my success rate in solving a patient's problems. The question is as crucial as it is unanswerable. It's not like being an orthopedist. You set somebody's broken arm, put a cast on it. They come back in so many weeks. You take the cast off and x-ray the arm to make sure everything is hunky-dory. You pat yourself on the back and chalk up another win. In clinical psychology, we don't get to do that. What happens in our field is that often the patient simply doesn't return and you won't know why. In some cases it will be because you have helped them sufficiently such that they don't feel the need for further assistance. You did good. In some cases their issues resolve themselves irrespective of your contribution. Then there's the negative possibilities. They don't feel any better after talking to you, so they conclude it's a waste of time. Or maybe they just don't click with you, don't like you, and they go find a different therapist. But you won't know that. Then sometimes it's not a voluntary decision. Wealthy people can afford to have indefinite relationships with their therapists, but ordinary people typically pay for therapy with health insurance, and the insurance company often authorizes a specified number of sessions depending on the diagnostic code and the specifics of the plan. In that case, you will know why they didn't return, but you won't know if the time together was sufficient."

"So you don't ever know for sure if you're making a difference? You do it on faith?"

"I wouldn't phrase it that way," Jommers said. "We know from research that in the aggregate we make a tremendous difference. But you won't always know whether you made a difference with a specific patient."

"Shouldn't we, though?" the student asked. "You're basically saying that out of sight and out of mind should be our professional posture, that patients matter only inside the office, and that once they walk out the door, they don't exist. What if the reason a guy didn't come back is that he committed suicide by jumping off a bridge? Wouldn't you want to know that?"

"There should definitely be more follow-up than currently exists. Patient surveys, and so on."

"Dead people don't do surveys."

"True. And the response rate from the living isn't much better. So how do you get that information?"

"You could call them up. Go see them. Show an interest that you care. Isn't that the ethical thing to do?"

"We could do that," Jommers said. "But there's an ethical case to be made on both sides. The voluntary patient has rights. The right to choose if, when, and where therapy is sought. The patient has a right to privacy. The right to be left alone. So let's say you call that patient to follow up without being first invited to do so. Is that perceived as genuine concern or hounding? Do you appear no different than the home remodeling contractor who's pressuring a prospect for the business?"

"So we don't invest emotionally at all in the patient?"

"You invest emotionally in your role. You invest emotionally in the time you spend with the patient to optimize it. But you maintain a certain professional detachment from the patient at the personal level. You care about their progress, obviously, but you're not their friend. There's a balance. At the end of the day, you're still a fee-based service provider, and it is the patient's prerogative to determine for themselves when such services are needed and from whom."

"There's this TV show about a brilliant doctor," the student said. "He's kind of a medical detective, dealing with mysterious cases. Sherlock Holmes set in a hospital. Anyway, his basic premise is that patients lie, so you have to snoop around, investigate their lives, even break into their house to find the truth so that you can cure them. Should we be like that, too? Don't therapy patients lie, also?"

"I wouldn't characterize it as lying, necessarily," Jommers said. "I see it more as the strategic withholding of certain bits of information to avoid personal embarrassment. In the presence of a stranger, psychological nakedness is every bit as uncomfortable as physical nakedness. Your goal is to establish a proper, professional, nonjudgmental rapport with the patient, so that they feel comfortable confiding in you without embarrassment. As for the housebreaking and various snooping methods of your fictional doctor, they are clearly and grossly unethical, which is why you will only find such methods employed in the fantasy world of TV. But let's just say for the sake of argument you were allowed to do that and you uncovered an important piece of information about your patient in that fashion. Then what? What would you do with it? You aren't in the business of picking a curative potion. Your curative arises from discourse, an interaction that requires trust. If you confronted your patient with a bit of surreptitiously acquired information, you would destroy that trust. You would be useless from that point on. We have a variety of tests, tools and techniques at our disposal to acquire the insights we need without skullduggery. Yes, sometimes it is a chess game. You have to be the better player."

"Okay," the student said. "I get your point. But what about when patients deceive themselves? How do you find out what's going on in their lives from the confines of your office? At some point, don't you have to get out of the office and look around?"

"You're posing an atypical situation," Jommers said. "Curious cases populate the literature because they are curious cases. In a typical clinical practice, you will be dealing with common conditions that you address with established procedures. Your focus won't be on solving mysteries, but helping people get back on their feet. The proper paradigm more closely resembles a physical therapist rather than a detective."

"So you're saying we should avoid innovation and just stay inside the box."

"I'm suggesting you utilize tools and techniques that have proven efficacy."

"Stay inside the box."

After the formal conclusion of the talk, the conversation spilled into the hallway as a handful of interested students expressed further curiosity about his work. He was happy to oblige, and as they chatted, he wondered if Chelsea might walk by at some point, further wondering whether he desired that prospect or dreaded it. The thought proved immaterial, as the event failed to occur.

GORILLA WITH A TUBA

It was late morning by the time he left the campus. He stopped nearby at Conchita's Deli Wok and picked up a turkey reuben burrito, which he took back to the office.

After lunch, first up on the afternoon schedule was an appointment with a retired cop who had come in with his wife. The man was in his early seventies, hauling a portly figure. He had short, wiry gray hair and a neatly trimmed gray mustache. He rested his folded hands on his ample gut and looked calmly ahead with a cheery expression and bright eyes. With the proper outfit, he could easily pull off a department store Santa.

The wife was probably the same age, but her deep-red-dyed hair, slim figure, and fidgety vigor belied it.

"I can go somewhere if I'm in the way," she said. "I'm just playing chauffeur."

"It's not a problem for me if it's okay with your husband," Jommers answered.

The husband smiled and nodded affirmatively. She could stay.

While Jommers looked over the information sheet the man had filled out, the couple talked to each other softly.

"You see how the red oak darkens with age," she said, rubbing the arm of the rocker. "That's why I wanted the white oak for the table."

"Yes," he replied. "But I still like the grain contrast in the red oak. It adds interest."

"This place reminds me of Jerry's basement," she said. "All the guy stuff."

"I was about to say the same thing," he said.

"But it works better here," she said. "Jerry's basement is kind of stuffy, crowded."

"Well, there's more room here, so it's more spread out," he said. "Better light, too."

"Yes," she said. "I think Jerry has too much furniture down there, too. Though this place could probably use a bit more."

The man shot his wife a disapproving look, as if to say *don't be impolite*. She responded with an apologetic *oops* look.

"But it works, though," she added. "It works."

Then Jommers piped in. "So what brings you here today? How can I help?"

"Well, I'm pretty sure I'm going crazy," the man said. "And I want to know if there is anything I can do about it."

He said it matter-of-factly, like someone complaining about deer eating his hosta.

"Why do you think you're going crazy?" Jommers asked.

"Well, I'm seeing things. What do you call it—hallucinations?"

"What are you seeing exactly?"

"Critters. Critters and bugs. Sometimes birds. Depending on where I'm looking," the man said.

"What do you mean?"

"Well, if I'm seeing them on the floor, it's mice or beetles or something. But if it's on the wall or ceiling, then it's butterflies or birds."

"Interesting," Jommers said. "Your mind is still putting things where they belong. Things that fly are up, things that crawl are down."

"Does that make me less crazy?"

"You recognized that these things weren't actually there, didn't you? That it was some type of illusion?"

"Yes," the man said. "That's why I kind of didn't worry about it much. But lately, things have gotten really weird. It's kind of freaking me out now."

"Example."

"We've got these lawn chairs set up in a circle out back, under a pin oak. Sometimes I look out the window and see gorillas sitting in the lawn chairs."

"And what are the gorillas doing? Just chewing the fat?"

"I wish. They have instruments. It's a gorilla band. But there's no music. They're just sitting there."

"What are the instruments?"

"Accordion. Banjo. Tuba."

"And you find this really weird because everyone knows that gorillas don't have the lips for tuba."

"Exactly," the man said.

The wife appeared shocked that Jommers made light of the situation, but he had an ulterior motive. He knew that grasping sarcasm required a lot of quick mental processing. People with cognitive impairments had trouble with humor. They didn't get sarcasm. This guy didn't miss a beat.

"I'm going to ask you some questions to get an idea about your mental state," Jommers said. "Try not to be offended by any of them. They're just standard questions that will help me figure out where things stand. Okay?"

"Sure."

"Do you ever hear voices inside your head?"

"No."

"Do you ever experience lost time or lose track of time?"

"Well, when you're retired, every day is like Saturday, so you sometimes forget what day it is."

"Do you have any unusual urges or desires that you've never had before?"

"I have to pee more now than I used to."

"Any strange thoughts or weird ideas?"

"Nope."

"Have you exhibited any strange behaviors?"

"I still go to the same place fishing, even though I know I won't catch anything. Does that count?"

"Have you experienced any unexplained emotional swings? Suddenly sad? Suddenly mad?"

"Nope."

"Any unexplained fears or anxieties?"

"I'm scared that someday I might end up in a nursing home. But so is everyone else my age."

"Around the time this all started, were there any significant changes in your health?"

"No, the decline in health has been gradual and steady. But nothing sudden."

"Around the time it started, were there any changes in any medications you were taking, either prescription or over-the-counter?"

"Nope."

"Changes in diet?"

"Nope. Well, except for the softeners, you know . . ."

"Any herbal supplements or alternative folk remedies?"

"Nope. But I use more hot sauce now. Can't seem to taste anything anymore."

"Around the time it started, were there any significant experiences in your life, or any significant changes in your life?"

The wife chimed in. "You got the new snow thrower about then, didn't you?"

"Yes," the man said. "But I don't think that's what he had in mind."

Jommers continued. "Is there a particular time of day when you're more likely to see your backyard visitors?"

"I guess early morning and evening, mostly."

"But not in the middle of the day?"

"Not generally."

"Would you say you're more or less likely to see them on a bright summer day versus a dark winter day?"

"Yeah. Dark days more."

"Okay, good," Jommers said. "Now then, your wife mentioned that she was playing chauffeur. Why is that?"

"I'm not allowed to drive anymore. Can't pass the vision test."

"General vision decline or specific conditions?"

"Well, they fixed the cataracts, and the eyeball pressure is under control with the drops, but the big problem now is the macular degeneration. I got both the wet and dry kinds. You can't do anything about the dry, but you can hold off the wet a bit with these shots they give you in the eyes every so often." The man laughed. "How would you like that for a fun day? Needles in your eyeballs."

The wife cringed. "I can't even watch when they do it," she said. "Can't even watch."

The man smiled. "And to think I used to get the willies over getting blood drawn."

Jommers smiled back. "I think you should have this conversation about the visions with your eye doctor."

"My eye doctor?"

"Yes," Jommers said. "I don't want to step outside my field here, but I think what you have is Charles Bonnet syndrome, which is fairly common among people with impaired eyesight."

"I don't understand," the man said. "You're saying eye problems can cause mental problems?"

"No. Here's what happens with Bonnet syndrome. Because of damage to your macula, your brain is not receiving good information about what your eyes are seeing. Your brain is getting a distorted message. But your brain is also structured to make sense of things. It doesn't want to accept the fuzziness. So it tries to interpret the bad information, takes an educated guess at what it might be."

"Like guessing the phrase on *Wheel of Fortune*."

"Exactly. And sometimes you guess right, and sometimes you don't. So say your eyes see a shadow pattern on the ceiling that your brain can't figure out, but it wants to. So it takes a stab at it. That has to be butterflies, it says. And so that's what your brain tells you. You are seeing butterflies. Your mind is not comfortable with an unrecognizable abstraction. It wants something more concrete. So when your mind gets imperfect information from the eyes about the complex shadows beneath your pin oak, a gorilla band actually makes more sense than an indiscernible pattern. In addition, what often happens is that your brain saves the misperception in memory so that it doesn't have to start from scratch the next time it is faced with the same scene. In other words, your brain says to itself, well, since it was gorillas last time, it's probably gorillas this time. The misperception becomes memory that affects future perception. The gorillas take up permanent residence in your backyard."

"So I'm not crazy."

"No," Jommers said. "This is a vision-processing problem."

The wife put her hand on the man's arm. "See, I told you that you weren't crazy. I would know. Don't you feel better now?"

The man smiled. "Well, it confirms the biggest lesson, the biggest thing I ever learned spending a life as a cop, the true meaning of luck."

"Which is?"

"Luck isn't about the good things that happen to you, it's about the bad things that don't. I guess my luck is still holding—so far, anyways."

"I should warn you," Jommers said, "and I'm sure your eye doc will tell you this, that there is no cure for this condition. You can't take a pill and make it go away. But you can maybe mitigate it by avoiding low-light situations that aggravate it. If you're up and about, keep illumination bright. All the lights on. If you're sleeping, keep the room totally dark, no nightlights. Wear a sleep mask. Avoid the in-between."

"Avoid the twilight."

"Yes. Avoid the twilight."

The Reverend Elvis Truly was a sausage.

There are heavyset people who accept the weight gain and buy new clothes to accommodate their extra inches, then there are those who resist because they intend to take off the added padding starting first thing tomorrow. For the latter, the clothes are tightly filled, no slack, the fabric strained like sausage casing.

They had arranged for a late-afternoon meeting, and the reverend arrived precisely on time, marching in at a deliberate pace. He sat upright but relaxed, with both his posture and face expressing a calm intensity. His attire was business casual—dress slacks and shirt, but no tie or clerical collar.

After introductions, Jommers made an offhand remark about the reverend's attire, a probing remark designed to appear conversational.

"I suppose it's too hot for the collar," Jommers said.

"I don't do the collar thing," Truly said. "No clerical garments either. At my church, we discourage the notion of a pastor as an intermediary, or that anyone needs one. It's not about me. I'm just a guy at a gas station giving you directions on how to get where you're going. The driving part is up to you. No pulpit or stage either. I stand on the floor at their level, walking among them. I am them. And they are me."

Reverend Truly had a deep voice and spoke in a cordial tone, like a neighbor dropping by for a chat. But the tone was also somber. A neighbor with bad news.

"As you know, Earl Tarburn was laid to rest Saturday," Truly said. "He was part of our church family, and a finer example of a God-loving man you won't find anywhere. He was a model Christian. And by that I mean he lived his faith, didn't just talk about it. He embodied both strength and humility, both discipline and joy. He showed his dedication to service in both his career and volunteering. But he was more than a dutiful congregant. He was my friend."

"I'm sorry for your loss, Reverend. I didn't know him well enough to speak to his faith, but well enough to agree with you on his strength, humility, and commitment to service. There are many saddened by his passing."

"Yes. Though that word, *passing*, sounds a bit too tame for the manner of it, don't you think?"

"Yes, I agree," Jommers said.

Truly studied Jommers's face with a stern interest, suggesting that he was not so much trying to peer into the psychologist's soul, but rather determine if the psychologist even had one.

"Becca Tarburn saw you at the cemetery, in spite of your effort to be incognito," Truly said. "You see, she's from the country originally. Out in the country, you learn to recognize people from a distance. Their shape, their posture, their gait—you look off afar at someone and you know that it's Elmer coming on over long before you ever see Elmer's face. She'd watched you come up the walk when you visited her. She said you step like a man who is in no hurry to get things done. She tries to discourage that in her son. Tells him you must always stride with determination and purpose, even when you don't know where you're going."

"Hurrying is not always appropriate, Reverend. Hurrying to judgment, for example. Correct me if I'm wrong, but patience is still a virtue. It certainly remains so in my work, as a lot of people who sit in that chair definitely try my patience. Marathoners take a different pace than sprinters. Unhurried does not mean unpurposed."

"Anyway, she was just curious," Truly said. "Why you were there. Wondering if she pegged you wrong."

The pastor was trying to have it both ways. One part folksy, down-to-earth, nice guy, the other part superior and judgmental. But Jommers would have none of it. Inside he bristled at the notion that both Becca Tarburn and her pastor were judging him and that now he was obliged to defend himself. He could have maintained his usual sphinx demeanor, but Truly wasn't a patient. So he made no attempt to conceal his resentment.

"Earl Tarburn had many friends beyond the circle you circumscribed," Jommers said. "He was admired and respected by many more than were permitted to attend his funeral. You prevented their physical beings from attending, but they were all there in spirit, honoring a man they cared about. Do you honor a man by choosing his friends after he's gone? How shall those friends peg you?"

The slight raising of an eyebrow suggested that Truly was surprised by the verbal counterattack.

"The restriction was Becca's decision, and she had her reasons," Truly replied. "I honored her wishes. In delicate situations such as these, you see, I am the servant, not the master."

An awkward silence followed. The reverend had come expecting deference to his profession, expecting the advantage. But Jommers was not giving any ground. Whatever objective Truly brought with him, his original plan would now require some improvisation. During the silent pause, Truly gave the office a casual reconnoiter. His eyes came to rest on a blues CD that Jommers had left on the table that served as his desk. The pastor smiled.

"So, you're a blues fan?"

"Yes," Jommers answered.

"Lot of gospel in the blues."

"Yes. Lot of drinking, screwing and killing, too."

"You familiar with 'Dark Was the Night' by Blind Willie Johnson? You know what that was about, don't you?"

"Yes."

"I believe they sent that into outer space. The golden record on the Voyager."

"I like the slide work on 'Dark,' but as songs go, I prefer 'Good Morning Little Schoolgirl.'"

The comment was meant to provoke, but the reverend was also pretty good at summoning the sphinx.

At this point both men understood the dilemma before them. Both were accustomed to giving counsel rather than receiving it, and so neither was willing to cede the high ground and don the role of subordinate. The pastor had come with information that he clearly wanted to share, but on his own terms. And Jommers wanted to gather that information, but on his own terms. Who had a greater need for the transaction to occur? Who would surrender first?

Truly looked at the arms of the rocking chair he sat in, ran his finger along one of them.

"Amish?" Truly asked.

"Yes," Jommers said.

"I thought so. Heavy-duty. They always make it twice as sturdy as it needs to be. Things that could be passed on for generations. I've always admired their furniture, but must confess, I was less enamored of their theology. To be honest, I used to think them silly folk, fools who took the whole simplicity thing a bit too far. But now today, I look at how technology has removed the guardrails from the road, made the path more perilous. Now, suddenly, they look like geniuses."

"Your religion advocates candor and forthrightness, if I'm not mistaken."

"That is correct."

"So you didn't come here to discuss music and furniture construction," Jommers said.

"Perhaps we got off on the wrong foot here. When I said that Becca thought she had pegged you wrong, that wasn't meant to be a disparagement of your character."

"Thank you. Appreciate it."

"She is aware of your respect for her late husband, but she's also aware of your close work with the police department, Chief Scubbetts specifically, about whom she has some concerns, and that he is the one who decides whether the work comes your way, and so her concern naturally was about your hierarchy of loyalties. So what I meant was . . ."

"You need to get some new drawers," Jommers said.

"Excuse me?"

"Your pants. They're about to blow. Big-time. Someone could get hurt."

The pastor's sphinx crumbled in an instant. His mouth fell open.

"I did not expect this from you. I suspected you weren't religious, but you are a professional. An educated man. I expected some basic respect."

"Well, then," Jommers said, "let's compare grievances, shall we? You invite yourself to my house, and immediately upon arriving insinuate that I'm a wicked person because I have some business association with another individual you also deem to be wicked, even though you have no grounds for either insinuation. I turn around and note that you are overweight, an observation for which there is ample evidence. Now then, we could spend time arguing which is the greater insult, but it would miss the point. And the point is that both of our observations are reductionist in that they strip away our respective humanity. There is much more to you than your physique. There is much more to me than my business associations. So, we have a choice here. We can both continue to address each other as objects, or start addressing each other as people. Your call."

And *call* was the right word, had it been poker. The psychologist had just reprimanded the preacher. There would be no more bluffing, no more dancing. The preacher would either lay his cards down or leave.

"She has some legitimate concerns about Chief Scubbetts," Truly said.

"Again, let's at least make a minimal effort to be candid here, okay? Becca Tarburn perceives the chief to be evil in the biblical sense of the word. She as much told me so in our brief conversation. Since I work closely with the chief, she assumes that I must be evil, too. Or, at the very least, a knowing accomplice to evil. So she sent you to make the assessment. Now, why would you care? There could only be one reason. You have information you wish to share, but only with a good person, not an evil person. So make up your mind. Am I evil?"

"You don't share her concerns about Chief Scubbetts?" Truly asked.

"Chief Scubbetts is cold, callous, creepy, obnoxious, and pompous. A mean, nasty son of a bitch. But all of that is irrelevant to what I do. I'm helping cops keep it together so that they can better serve their community. Police chiefs come and go in this town. I'm serving the department. I'm serving the community. That's all I care about."

"So you agree, the chief is evil."

"I said he was a nasty son of a bitch," Jommers said. "He is arrogant, egocentric, ruthless, devious, manipulative, and conniving. But that also describes most CEOs of major corporations and half the members of Congress. The designation of evil demands a higher threshold. Simply being an asshole is insufficient. Evil demands something above and beyond the standard depravity of autocratic managers in bureaucracies. If you're a businessman and take the position that you will never transact business with assholes, then your only recourse is to live on a deserted island and survive by foraging for coconuts."

"Chief Scubbetts's management, if that's the term, resulted in the killing of a good man. Does that meet your threshold for evil?"

"Do you have information suggesting that the chief intended that specific result or that the chief engaged in actions to bring about that specific result?"

"I do not," Truly said.

"Then all you have is a complaint about his style," Jommers said. "Unfortunately, style does not conveniently correlate with substance. The world is full of amiable crooks and snarly saints. Intuition does not substitute for information. You need facts."

"When I was a small boy, my parents had a troubled marriage. They competed for my favor, each persuading me how the other was at fault. But I was too young to understand adult arguments. I was confused. But my heart could still see things clearly, could see that one of them emanated love and the other evoked fear. And that provided the clarity. In my world, fear is the opposite of faith. Elevating one diminishes the other. Anyone who tries to instill fear in others, whether it's to manipulate, manage, dominate, or rule, is working the dark side of the field. So when I'm forced to judge people in situations too complex for me to understand, I often fall back on that childhood memory. Who speaks the language of love? Who speaks the language of fear?"

"And I would agree with you perfectly if all we were talking about is who I want to have a beer with or who I want to vote for," Jommers said. "But if we're talking about linking a specific individual to a specific act of wrongdoing, then more is required."

The pastor frowned and thrummed his fingers on the rocker arm. He was still holding back, dancing at the edge of his objective. He wanted to reveal something, but needed to hear something first. He was looking for a sign and had not yet seen it.

Again, he circled around, looking for an indirect approach.

"We talked of the Amish a bit ago," Truly said. "There's a particular gravesite in an Amish cemetery down in Middlefield that bespeaks a poignant tale. You see, there's this commandment—thou shalt not kill. And somewhere along the line, we put an asterisk next to it—thou shall not kill except under the following circumstances. Now the Amish, you see, they don't do asterisks. They are pacifists, conscientious objectors when it comes to military service. But back in World War II, there were some Amish men who thought that the evil of Nazism was so horrific, so threatening, that the imperative to defeat Nazi evil took precedence over the pacifist tradition. One of them who chose to fight was killed in action—came home in a box. And that presented a dilemma for his community. He had defied their principles, broken their rules, yet he was still one of them. So they buried him in their cemetery, but in a distant corner, away from the others. And that's where he rests, all by himself."

"The question of justified killing haunts many, both religious and secular," Jommers said.

"I hope it haunts everybody," Truly said. "You know, there was a saying that became popular in my faith some years ago, a question really. What would Jesus do? It was meant to be a reality check. Are you living your faith or just professing it? So let's apply that test to war. Would Jesus have helped fight the evil of Nazism? Would he have carried an M1 carbine while storming the beaches of Normandy? Would he have served as a sniper? Would he have helped firebomb Dresden? And what about unconventional wars? Say the Cold War. Would Jesus have helped the CIA carry out coups and assassinations in the fight against the evil of communism? And what about the war on terror? What role would Jesus accept in that? For many outside my faith, those sound like silly questions. But for Earl Tarburn, those questions were fundamental. They burned inside him like a wildfire advancing toward his soul. They arose first when he served in the Persian Gulf War back in ninety-one. Those concerns carried over into his service as a marksman for SWAT. I should add that, to some extent, these conflicts were fueled by Becca, who leans toward the pacifist end of the spectrum on such matters."

"Well, as a clergyman trained in theology and philosophy, you are no doubt perfectly suited to help people solve moral dilemmas, how to choose the higher good or the lesser evil."

"You would think," Truly said. "I must confess, I was not a stellar student in seminary. I'm more of a hands-on person less suited for theoretical discussion. If someone falls overboard into the sea, you try to save them. You don't discuss the physical properties of fluids. You see, this thing we now refer to as a religion, it all begins with the recruitment of some simple fishermen. So that's the test for me when I preach. Is what I'm saying comprehensible to a simple fisherman? Now intellectuals have been writing about moral dilemmas for centuries, and I can tell you from experience that if you read a table full of books on the subject, you will finish more confused than when you began. When congregants come to me for help, they aren't looking for philosophical discourse. They want a clear answer. What should I do?"

"So what do you tell them?"

"I have boiled it down to this. When two moral principles are in conflict, I ask which principle has the greater weight, which is more important? If that doesn't answer it, if the two principles seem to be of equal value, then you get pragmatic.

Which path yields the better outcome? Of course, throughout the process, you pray for guidance. With that approach, I had been able to get Earl through most of his conflicts. Until recently, that is. You see, most of our discussions on conflicts were retrospective. Was it right to have done something, after it had already been done. Putting it to rest. Within the past year, he was presented with another conflict, but stated in the present tense. It was something ongoing."

"And what was that conflict?" Jommers asked.

"He wouldn't tell me, at least not in specific terms. He would present the dilemma as a hypothetical. I have to confess, I was at first offended by this. I felt that he didn't trust me to maintain confidentiality. Only later did I realize that his reluctance was due to promises he'd made to someone else. It wasn't that he didn't trust me, it was that he'd promised not to reveal it to anyone, and being a man of his word, he took the promise seriously."

"What was the hypothetical?"

"It was vague, something to do with conflicting loyalties. Somebody being asked to do something that would be wrong under normal circumstances, but heroic under special circumstances. I wasn't getting it, and asked him to try another example. He came up with something about spies—you know, if a spy does something bad to serve his country, that kind of thing."

"What did you tell him?"

"I'm sure you understand as well as I do that it's risky to advise someone with nothing more than a presented hypothetical, because you can't ascertain the level of fidelity the hypothetical has to the real issue the person has. So you could end up giving a person bad advice simply because that person is not good at creating analogies. Without knowing the real issue, you can't give specific advice."

"What makes you think his conflict involved Chief Scubbetts?" Jommers asked.

"His analogies always regarded somebody at the top of the food chain, above immediate superiors. It was clear to me he was talking about the chief and I straight out asked him. He didn't respond verbally but his face answered for him. So then I asked him, why you? And he said he was chosen for his special talents and skills. You see, vanity is the back door that lets the devil in, and it's always unlocked. Who among us will argue when told that we are special? So whatever favor he was doing for the chief, it felt right to Earl in the beginning, and only later did he see it as wrong."

"And why do you think it was something wrong as opposed to being secret for legitimate reasons?"

"I asked him if he was at risk. I meant his life, but he thought I meant his job. He answered that he would be taken care of if he lost his job. There was an implicit suggestion that the chief has other irons in the fire, businesswise. But the answer shocked me. Why would a decorated police officer lose his job over a task his superior asked him to do? It had to be something well out of the mainstream, something unusual. Why, then, would he do it? Risk a career he loved, a career that supported his family and paid for his house? What was the perceived higher good compelling him to take such a grave risk?"

"Did he give you any more details?"

"No. And regrettably, I didn't push. As you noted earlier, patience is a virtue. I felt he would tell me when he was ready. I had no way to know that time was running out."

"Are you suggesting a connection between his inner conflict and his death?" Jommers asked.

"I'm not normally one prone to conspiracy theories and dark plots hiding behind the scenes. The multitude of evils that strut defiantly out in the open are more than enough to consume my attention. But when a man comes to me with a moral crisis over some secret thing, and then shortly afterward is inexplicably shot dead, it is very difficult for me to resist the notion of a linkage."

"I understand the inclination," Jommers said. "And there may indeed be a correlation. But if so, you would want to discover the mechanism of causality. For example, maybe the ongoing moral crisis you just described built to a crescendo that led to the panic attack that precipitated the events of that evening."

"Panic attack. Is that your diagnosis?"

"It's all I have, given the limited interaction. I only saw him for a few minutes. I can only speculate."

"I am pained that I was not able to help him that evening," Truly said. "He called me and left a message while I was out. I was visiting a shut-in congregant residing in a nursing home down in Dirkston. He urgently wanted to see me, but by the time I got back, it was too late. His voice on the message was scarcely recognizable. He was gripped by some unholy terror, like a man gazing into the maw of hell. This was more than a mere panic attack."

"Discerning the line between panic attack and psychotic episode would have required more time than I was given," Jommers said. "In any event, the reason for him having either one remains a mystery."

"Well, perhaps my visit today will help you solve it."

"Just to be clear, Reverend. I have no formal role in the investigation. I have been asked about my conversation with Earl that evening, and whether he exhibited any signs of emotional problems prior to that evening, and my answer was no. And that's it for me. Establishing the big-picture view, the formal investigation, will be handled by the Force Review Committee."

"We think, Becca and I, we think you owe it to Earl to take the bigger view and look deeper into the matter. She and I are no longer in a position to obtain answers. You are."

"If I may make a suggestion," Jommers said. "Instead of steering her down the adventure road of mystery solving, you might better serve her interests with more familiar counseling along the lines of acquiring the serenity to accept things that cannot be changed."

"I am, of course, well-acquainted with Pastor Niebuhr's famous prayer. In fact, I have given sermons suggesting it has been improperly named. Being familiar with the writings of the theologian, I think he would have preferred it be known as the Courage Prayer, with the emphasis on that line. You see, what he's really saying there is that you are obliged to pursue every possible avenue of change and that only after exhausting all the possibilities, only then are you entitled to the serenity of acceptance. His prayer, like his work, is a call for moral action, not an excuse for inaction. You must push the limits before you acknowledge them."

"You know, theology and all its lofty moral imperatives thing is not my strong suit," Jommers said. "I'm more about helping people get through the day without imploding."

"Well, then, if moral imperatives fail to inspire you, perhaps this will." Truly removed a photograph from his pocket and handed it to Jommers. "That was taken last year in their backyard. That's Earl showing his son Eric how to set up a telescope. You see, Earl didn't just teach his son to be good and stand tall, he taught the boy how to wonder, how to pursue, how to be more. I think you owe it to that boy to at least try and find some answers about what happened to his father. You weren't able to help Earl that night. Maybe you can help him now."

Jommers resented the less-than-subtle insinuation that he was partly responsible for the fiasco and was now obliged to redeem himself, but he let it slide. He let the reverend get in the last word, then, after the man was gone, Jommers offered a silent rebuttal inside.

Jommers not only took offense at the accusation of negligence, but was also irritated by the suggestion that his easygoing style made him a slacker. In fact, the laid-back manner was not inherent, but was deliberately cultivated to put patients at ease and help them open up. Nobody wants an antsy therapist.

As he rehearsed what should have been said but wasn't, his interior monologue grew louder. The rebuttal raced around his head, getting more indignant with every lap. It grew into that toxic type of outrage, the kind that lingered, percolated, and ultimately brewed into a storm. He knew better than to permit such foul mental weather, but he was only human like anyone else, and he was dimly aware that the reverend's snide accusation had touched a nerve because it echoed his own self-recrimination about that night. And that realization only fueled the tempest within, which now thrashed like Erie's winter waves slamming the outer breakwall.

So he headed over to Spreckels Tavern, hoping to quell the turbulence. But on the way, he found himself detouring toward the Trammel Street lift bridge where his father died. He took the detour every once in a while, usually when something vexed him. He would then park the car nearby, walk over and gaze at the structure.

The bridge fell short as a genuine shrine, lacking statues and architectural ornamentation. And while it did provide a shrine's opportunity for reflection, it failed to offer any comfort or serenity. In fact, it delivered exactly the opposite—disturbance. The place where his father had killed himself on a motorcycle still needled with its nagging question—why?

Technically, it required no answer. Some people suffer depression, and some of them commit suicide. It happens. In the previous year alone, more than thirty thousand Americans had killed themselves. As an adult, as a psychologist, Jommers understood this. But the boy in his memory demanded a better answer, one that would never come.

Though the bridge provided no peace, its silent mystery nonetheless made it an appropriate place to ponder other troubling questions. The query now on the table was Reverend Truly's assertion that Jommers was obliged to take the big picture perspective on the Tarburn tragedy, a view that extended beyond his own immediate professional domain. In addition, Truly implied that Jommers had a duty to assume an active role in solving the riddle, not merely pass on tidbits that accidentally fell into his lap.

Jommers first reflex was to reject that position, though he did allow it to briefly roam free long enough to interrogate himself. Was his reluctance simply the reasonable response of a cautious, level-headed man? Or was he guilty of omission bias, where inaction was favored over action? Or worse, was his hesitance rooted in fear of jeopardizing his relationship with the police department and dealing his faltering therapy business a fatal blow?

While some might have been stimulated by the opportunity to play detective, Jommers found the idea repugnant. Distraction is the enemy of utility. Heroic delusions are what lead good men astray. The good soldier stays at his post. The expert stays in his field. You best serve by doing the thing you are best equipped to do. There were plenty of capable, experienced people investigating last week's shooting. If there were something unusual to be discovered, they would most certainly find it.

And even if he accepted the contention that he owed something above and beyond his duties as a psychologist, what would that be? What more could he possibly do?

In the middle of that thought, he heard footsteps behind him, but he did not turn around. The slow trudge of the aimless combined with a slight shuffle and limp told him it was Gabriel, and Jommers remembered that Gabriel did not like being looked at. You could talk to him, but only by looking off in another direction. If you looked directly at him, he perceived it as a threat and would swing something at you, then run. Like many of the homeless that nomadically inhabited the Bends and adjacent areas, Gabriel had untreated psychological problems.

In spite of the steamy weather, Gabriel wore a long wool coat, ragged and covered with grime. That was less a symptom of his mental state than it was the reality of homeless life. A coat on your body is harder to steal or lose than a coat you carry. And if you expect to be around in winter, you will need that coat.

With his left hand he carried three blue plastic shopping bags containing his few possessions, some of which provided utility, and some only fascination. His right hand clutched a length of tree branch that looked like it was fished out of the river, then broken to length. He carried it like a hiking staff, but its real purpose was likely defense.

Like many of the homeless, Gabriel cast an invisible cloud of sour stench that seemed like a material extension of his being, like a hedgehog spreading out invisible quills. The odor was foul enough on an ordinary day, but when cooked by a summer swelter, the pungency was startling. How was it possible for a human being to smell like that and still be healthy enough to move about?

Jommers spoke without turning his head.

"Hello, Gabriel. How are you?"

"It's hot."

"Are you doing okay?"

"Too many dogs down here now. It's like Africa. Worrying about wild things eating you at night. You can't sleep. You hear them."

"Some of what you hear may be the coyotes. I know, it's weird, coyotes in the city. But I've seen them. They generally avoid people. So you shouldn't worry too much about them."

"It's not safe."

The brief conversation was interrupted by the clanging of the bridge bells and the lowering of its warning gate. A ship was coming upriver. Soon the bridge emitted loud, screechy metallic sounds, the creaking of cables being pulled taut and the groaning of steel trusses as their internal stresses changed direction.

A flock of cliff swallows that had huddled under the bridge deck took sudden flight, as the commotion disturbed their tranquility. They chattered noisily and flew around in large, swirling circles, displaying their objection.

Jommers never tired of watching the ships ply the river. No matter how many times he'd caught such scenes, it still amazed him how a massive, vast plateau of steel could smoothly maneuver around the tight turns of the Bends. He would shake his head. *No way that humongous ship is going to wiggle around that tight little bend. Just no way.* And yet, it always did.

When he was a boy and his father brought him down to watch river life, a ship's passage was sometimes more troublesome, as some of the older ships in service then still needed the help of tugboats to wrestle the bow this way or that. The tugs strained furiously to wrangle the hulking beast at the end of their leashes, their engines whining and roaring, hot black smoke shooting out their stubby stacks. But now, the later generations of ships, even though much larger, weaved their way unaided, their bow thrusters steering the bow left or right.

Jommers looked down at the river and watched the bow thrusters churn up a cocoa-like froth in the murky waters. His eyes then followed the ship's waterline to the stern, where the rotation of the screw generated a flurry of fleeting vortices.

Men with radios stood fore and aft, gauging the ship's proximity to the riverbanks, giving the leviathan eyes in all directions. Indeed, it seemed more a living thing than a machine, a serene creature that moved with self-assured grace.

Years ago this dance had been preceded by a song, an antiphonal exchange of horn signals between the ship and the bridge house. Rusting metal signs tacked on both sides of the bridge served as the song sheet. A boat requesting this bridge to open would blast its horn one long, two short, one long. If the bridge agreed to open, the operator in the bridge house would blast in return one long and one short. In the day, a red ball at the base of the bridge would rise to confirm opening, and a red light at night would say the same. A sequence of short blasts indicated bridge closing, the same signal being used to indicate occasions where it could not open. Different lift bridges on the river had different horn signal patterns. And sometimes they had to decline a request, say in the case of a railroad bridge expecting a train.

These days that conversation took place over marine band radio found on almost all vessels. Even the scullers carried portables to warn ships of their presence and avoid accidents.

As Jommers watched the spectacle with awe, Gabriel watched with fascination also, his eyes riveted on the lumbering vessel.

"I lived on a boat once," Gabriel said.

"Really?" Jommers asked. "What kind?"

"It was long, fast, and gray. It had guns and missiles. I saw Spain."

"So you were in the navy."

"I should not have left the boat. Had all good days on the boat. Things were clear. Everything I saw was there. There was always food. I saw Spain." He paused. "I should not have left the boat."

That insight caused Jommers to walk a few steps away, out of earshot, where he then called Joel Fishback, a colleague and friend who worked as a therapist at the VA hospital in Grayton. Jommers told him about the troubled soul who wandered the Bends and that he was likely a vet. Could he come down, talk to the man, get him into a treatment plan?

"You're not serious," Fishback said. "You have any idea what's going on out here?" He went on to explain how there were two wars going on with troops going through multiple rotations that were grinding them down, and how the government had not increased VA resources to deal with the upsurge in vets needing help.

"We're running an assembly line, basically, and yet we're still working hellacious hours to keep up. The idea that I would have the time to go chasing someone down in the Bends . . . look, even if you could promise me that you could hog-tie and drag him over here, we're talking a wait of weeks, maybe months. And, of course, you're not allowed to do that. You would have to gently persuade him to come voluntarily, and we both know how well that works with his type."

Jommers frowned. "If a man was walking around delirious with a screwdriver sticking out the side of his head, would anyone in their right mind suggest that we leave him be, that it's his constitutional right to walk around with a screwdriver in his brain? But when that screwdriver is invisible, everyone thinks it's a perfectly reasonable argument."

"You're preaching to the choir, Karl, preaching to the choir. But if you can't get him here voluntarily, there's nothing I can do."

The two talked on the phone another few minutes. By the end of the call, the ship had passed and the bridge was back down. Gabriel was already more than halfway across to the other side. Jommers watched with dismay as the man trudged steadily ahead. After Gabriel cleared the bridge, he turned to the right and disappeared behind a green tangle of brush.

THE DOORBELL IN THE NIGHT

Upon arriving at the tavern, Jommers was pleasantly surprised to find Connor Quirke, who provided relieving distraction by delivering a rant of his own.

"Stay the hell out of Chestnut Grove, in case you didn't already know." Quirke was referring to the suburb renowned for its speed traps, which provided the greater share of that suburb's revenue. "It should be renamed Gestapo Grove. The mayor out there is dirtier than dog shit in a mud hole, and everyone knows it. So there's a reform movement underway trying to recall and replace him. Residents who are part of it sport yard signs and bumper stickers that say 'Restore Trust.' So what's happening now is that the cops out there, who all support the mayor who gives them an under-the-table cut of the action, the cops are targeting people with these bumper stickers, citing them for minor infractions, you know, like a rolling stop at a stop sign, going three miles an hour over the speed limit, and so on. And when the cop hands over the citation, the driver gets a lecture on what an excellent city government they have and how the driver ought to reconsider displaying that slanderous bumper sticker. So my new client is one of those who gets pulled over for a rolling stop. But when he gets the lecture, he tries to record it on his cell phone. So the cop blows a gasket, drags him out of the car, throws him facedown into the street, and handcuffs him. And they are legally allowed to do that, handcuff you on a traffic stop if they feel like it, which you probably knew. So then the cop gives my client a pat-down and finds a small folding pocket knife in his front pocket. Now, what do you know about knife-carry law?"

"Not much," Jommers said.

"Like most everybody else," Quirke said. "State laws in Ohio are vague and general on it, which leaves the door open for municipalities to define things the way they choose as to what constitutes carrying a concealed weapon. So the various city laws on knife type and blade length are all over the place. In Gestapo Grove, they set legal blade length limit at a ridiculous two inches, so as to maximize their capacity to fuck with you. Blade length on my client's pocket knife was only a measly two and one-quarter inches, shorter than a standard folder a scout might take on a camping trip. But since it's one-quarter inch over the limit, they charge him with carrying a concealed deadly weapon. Now then, Gestapo Grove, not surprisingly, is one of those places with a mayor's court, where the fines go to the city. I could go on all day about mayor's courts. Aside from lack of impartiality, the obvious conflict of interest, they're rife with corruption. They ought to be abolished statewide, but it won't ever happen because when it comes to legal reform, Ohio is still stuck in the log cabin era. Anyway, the kangaroo court fines him a thousand smackers, which he wisely contests. Contesting it throws it into a real court system where I can get it kicked, since they can't show intent to use it as a weapon. Thing is, though, by the time it's all over, the total costs and aggravation may be greater. On top of all that, the motherfuckers posted his mug shot and charges on the city website in order to humiliate him. Did I mention he's a math teacher at a Catholic school? I mean, *was*, past tense. They fired him after they saw the mug shot. All that for sporting a bumper sticker that said 'Restore Trust.' I mean, Jesus. This shit is happening right here where we live. The birthplace of liberty, home of flags and fireworks on Fourth of July. You know, most people just don't have any idea how easy it is for government at any level to fuck with you at any time. Not a clue."

The two men discoursed at length on the matter until Quirke had to leave. By then it was late afternoon and action had slowed. The beer-after-work crowd had yet to arrive. Having a free moment, Larry wandered on over with a question.

"So, if you're hearing something you know ain't real, and it's at night, how do you know if it's a dream or an auditory hallucination?" Larry asked.

"Well," Jommers answered, "as a general rule, you want to start with the simplest explanation, then work your way up the complexity ladder only as needed. Since dreams are common and hallucinations are rare, I'm going with dream. What exactly are you hearing, if I may ask?"

"The doorbell," Larry said.

"The doorbell?"

"Yeah. So I get up to see who's there, and nobody is there. But I can't let it slide, or maybe there's trouble."

"What do you mean?"

"I read somewhere that burglars ring the doorbell before breaking in to make sure nobody's home. If there's no answer, then they bust in. So let's say that happens, and there you are. He's as surprised to see you as you are to see him. You get scared and grab your gun. He sees you going for your gun, so he pulls his. And so now you got Dodge City inside your house, all because you were too lazy to answer the doorbell."

"Yes, I can see how that's a problem," Jommers said. "Have you considered the possibility of a prankster?"

"Yeah. That ain't it."

"And how did you eliminate that possibility?"

"With a hammer."

"Applied to the doorbell?"

"Correct."

"Disconnecting the wires might have been a neater, more elegant solution."

"The hammer was a faster solution."

"But you still hear it from time to time?"

"Right. Only now I know it can't be real. That it's in my head."

"Interesting."

"Yeah. But what does it mean?" Larry asked.

"Well, as I have mentioned in the past, I don't find much merit in divining dreams. I understand the natural desire to find sense in the senseless, but it's a pointless endeavor that leads to false interpretations. Dreaming is the mental equivalent of flatulence. It's best not to stick your nose into it."

"Yeah. You're probably right. Funny thing about it, though . . ."

"What's that?"

"Last night, when it happened again, I realized something. The doorbell I was hearing in my head was not the doorbell I have. I mean, had. But it was still familiar. Like it was a doorbell from some other place I once lived."

⌒

JOMMERS LINGERED AT THE TAVERN till evening, talking with other acquaintances and regulars, but left in time to catch the sunset at West Shore Lakefront Park, where he went for a walk. Given the slant of the shoreline, he could stroll out to the end of the fishing pier and gaze leftward to watch the evening sun slowly quench itself in the lake. And the water itself was part of the display as the elongated cone of reflected sunlight sparkled on the rippled surface, gradually changing hues with each passing minute, presenting a slow but vivid animation that ran through the yellows, oranges, reds and purples, until the last frame when the reflection disappeared with its source, leaving behind a dim, plum-colored expanse.

And when the light show was over, Jommers intended to go home, but felt like something was holding him there. He found a bench facing the lake to the north, sat down and slouched down enough so that he could comfortably angle his head upward, but he didn't know why. After a while, the spreading ink of night completed its westward bleed, blotting out the last traces of twilight. The sky was clear and full of stars, but the lake waters were dark as the moon's new phase left its light absent from the scene.

He had stayed to look for something, but could not remember what. As always, he queried within, but this time, it was the sky that answered. Off in the distance at high elevation, a thin streak of light flashed like a spark off a grinding wheel. A meteor. A shooting star. He then recalled Earl Tarburn mentioning how Tuesday night would be optimal for viewing the Perseids. So he maintained the vigil a bit longer, hoping to see another burning arrow fly. But the heavens were not in a generous mood. All he got was the one.

DAY TEN

Early Wednesday morning, GG was already hard at work on her wall. That was how Jommers had reflexively labeled her in his head—GG, Graffiti Girl—even though she'd mentioned her tag name. After the first conversation with her, he'd dug out an old pair of binoculars and set it by the window with a notepad. He was interested in her animation project, but wasn't sure he'd find it on YouTube afterwards, or that he would even remember to look. So he wanted to monitor it in progress. Or maybe monitor her. He wasn't quite sure.

Over the course of the previous afternoon, she had painted a simplified rendering of a bend in the Claybank River. A title had appeared—*A Tale of Wonder*—then was painted over. In following scenes, four characters had emerged: a carp, a chipmunk, a crow, and a cat, with the cat hiding unseen by the others.

This morning, she started painting a thought bubble over the head of the carp, which was poking its head above the surface of the river. The first words were, "I wonder . . ."

Jommers needed to be at the police station soon to conduct a training session with detectives, but he was curious about what came next, so he waited until the thought bubble was finished.

"I wonder how it all looks on land," the carp thought.

PERSUADING POLICE DETECTIVES to change their established methods is like teaching cats to box. It can be done, but not easily or quickly. Some resistance can be expected.

Jommers's topic for the day: interview techniques.

"Face-to-face interviews with key suspects are obviously an integral part of investigations," Jommers said. "And when your intuition tells you that the suspect is guilty, you use certain techniques designed to elicit a confession. Some of these methods involve high-pressure interrogation, manipulation, bluffing, exhausting the suspect's will to resist—I don't need to describe those methods, you already use them every day. You've been assured that those methods are tried and true—field-proven. Needless to say, social scientists have conducted a lot of research in this area, and there are some things you need to know. First of all, your intuition regarding guilt is very often wrong, and the longer you've been in the field, the less likely you are to consider that possibility. Secondly, the more aggressive your questioning, the greater the probability you will get a false confession. And your first reaction to that statement is no way, innocent people don't confess to crimes they didn't commit. And you're wrong. It happens every day. Why? Because people under extreme duress will be focused on the short-term goal of ending that duress, rather than the long-term consequences of confessing. They tell you what you want to hear to end the torment. They assume that, because they are innocent, a lawyer will somehow, someway, get them out of the mess somewhere down the road. Think of it as a person jumping out the window of a burning building. To escape the heat of your interrogation, he will jump out the window by confessing and hope that there's a lawyer with a net below. Needless to say, false confessions aren't good for anybody. Best-case scenario, the innocent suspect is acquitted, but by then the trail will have gone cold for alternative suspects. Worst-case scenario, you get a conviction and send an innocent person to prison, which leaves the real criminal out on the street to commit further crimes. Extracting a false confession is a failure on your part, not a success."

Jommers paused to see how they would react to that comment. As his eyes scanned the room, he saw only impassive faces, as if he was lecturing them on laundry detergents. But he continued.

"Now, then, let's back up a second. I mentioned that you often use your intuition to determine if a suspect is guilty. Very often that determination is based on the deliberate or unconscious observation of body language and suspect behavior. You say to yourself, oh, look, he's fidgeting and blinking, avoiding eye contact—he must be lying. Let me tell you, that approach is flawed to the point of worthless. There have been studies performed where experienced law enforcement officers were asked to view videos of real suspect interviews and then afterward guess which ones were lying. Those officers who relied on observation of behavioral cues did no better than the flip of a coin in guessing correctly. Why? Because it's perfectly normal for an ordinary innocent person to become anxious when falsely accused. He's scared to death and sick to his stomach about possibly taking the fall for something he didn't do. We know from research that a driver's blood pressure and respiratory rate will rise when seeing a police car in the rearview mirror, even when they aren't speeding and have not committed any violations. Just the very sight of the cruiser behind them is enough for them to freak. So how do you think they're going to react when you put them in an interrogation room and accuse them of a serious crime? You're damn right they're going to fidget. Conversely, the experienced criminal who has been picked up and questioned before, he knows the drill. He's as cool as a cucumber. So the only thing body language tells you is how well someone handles pressure. It says nothing about honesty or guilt. So how do you find the truth?"

He paused and scanned the room again, trying to find even a single face interested in the answer to such an important question. No luck. He carried on anyway.

"You focus on the content, that's how. Concentrate on what they say, not on how they say it. We know that a detective reading the transcript of an interview has a better shot at detecting falseness than the detective that conducted the interview. Why? Because the one reading the transcript is focused exclusively on the content of what was said and is not distracted by emotional impressions. There are differences between what you get from honest and dishonest suspects, but it won't be found in sweaty hands. It's found in the stories they tell. And it's all in the details. You know the old saying—'Oh, what a tangled web we weave, when first we practice to deceive.' The practiced liar knows that line, too. Knows it all too well. Knows that it will be details that will trip him up. So he follows the advice of another old saying—'Keep it simple.' So when he fabricates a story, he'll keep it clean and simple, minimal detail. A bare outline. And he won't deviate from it. Because he will have rehearsed his lines many times before his performance, and he will avoid improvising. So what you get is the broken record. Rigidity. You get something different from the innocent person. You get more details. And you get them easily, because they are real. Unlike the bad guy who has to fabricate details and then calculate how they mesh with his narrative, the innocent person plucks his details easily as fruit off the vine and does not hesitate to share them. Because they are abundant and actual. So that's what you want to pursue in the interview—details. Even totally irrelevant details. The weather. The time. The sounds. The smells. The color of someone's socks or carpeting. Whether something was dirty or clean, cold or hot. The innocent person can easily remember such details. The liar must either fabricate them or pretend not to remember, and that difficulty creates a different type of speech pattern. As a result of these insights, some newer interview techniques have been developed to exploit these distinctions."

Jommers then distributed handouts describing these new techniques and the philosophy behind them. He also showed a video of a police officer using such a technique on a real suspect. After the video, he wrapped it up.

"Bottom line—gear your interviews toward obtaining information, not confessions."

After his summation, he solicited comments and questions. As usual, there were none. Only silent, polite, condescending smiles, all conveying the same message. What do you know about it? We're the ones who do this every day. Getting it done. Go back to your books. We've got work to do.

He sighed his usual sigh of disappointment at their lack of interest, then dismissed them. There would be no cat boxing today.

CHIEF SCUBBETTS WAS WAITING for Jommers out in the hallway, standing at parade rest, his usual large dark cigar clenched in his mouth. Sheer hubris, Jommers thought. Defiantly smoking the cigar in a city building against the law, out in the hallway in full view, unafraid that anyone would dare file a complaint. Assured that everyone was scared of him. A sense of invincibility bordering on reckless.

Jommers approached without hurry. He looked the chief straight in the eye, which was the therapist's way of conveying that he was not among the cowed.

"Good morning, Chief."

Scubbetts brought his hands around to the front, revealing a file folder in his left, as he grabbed the cigar with his right.

"So, did you teach them the mind meld, telepathy, or whatever? Give them the third eye? The mystic voodoo?"

"I reviewed some techniques that would help them ferret out the truth in face-to-face suspect interviews."

"Ferret? The truth is something the suspect vomits after you punch them with humiliation. You should be teaching techniques that will break the will without physical contact, how to extract a confession that will hold up in court."

"Extracting a confession and discovering the truth can be two different things."

"What? Jesus. You're like some crazy-ass abstract poet. I don't even know what the fuck you're saying half the time. And the other half I don't even want to hear it. I don't know even what the fuck you do. Why we need you."

"Well, as a refresher," Jommers said, "there are municipal ordinances that require—"

"Who the fuck cares? Does city council have a militia I need to be worried about?"

"How did things go with Captain Shy Bladder?" Jommers asked.

"He's in the hospital. He started screaming like a city kiddie, then doubled over and collapsed. Something happened. He'll have to go. Speaking of removal—this is for you."

Scubbetts started to hand the file folder to Jommers, but then deliberately dropped it before Jommers got his hands on it. Jommers bent down and picked it up, pretending not to notice the slight. The top sheet in the file was an official letter to Jommers from the department's director of Human Resources, but the bizarre introduction suggested it had been dictated by the chief.

> Dear Mr. Jommers:
> IN ORDER to protect the integrity of the department,
> IN ORDER to foster departmental esprit de corps,
> IN ORDER to advance the department's mission,
> IN ORDER to maintain departmental efficiencies,
> IN ORDER to promote high performance standards,
> IN ORDER to restore the respect and trust of the public,
> IN ORDER to shield the department from malfeasance litigation,
> IN ORDER to quash internal threats to the department's function,
> IN ORDER to quell insubordinate actions,
> IN ORDER to preserve order within the department,
> IN ORDER to secure proper procedural approvals,
> IN ORDER to expedite termination proceedings,
> You are hereby requested to change the designation and purpose of your psychological assessment of Detective Ilona Voros from post-critical incident evaluation to occupational fitness evaluation. Supporting documentation for this request is enclosed. You are directed to expedite this process so that it can be concluded in a timely manner and the department can focus its attention on more pressing matters.

The introduction read like some instructional sign at a military training camp, and Jommers knew from experience that the use of repetition was Scubbetts's way of expressing irritation. Jommers started looking through the papers in the folder, skimming them before speaking. Scubbetts spoke in the interim.

"So now that we've dotted and crossed the whatevers, you need to get to it, get it done. Everything you need is there. You know where I want this to go."

"I'm not seeing anything consequential in here yet," Jommers said, "though I'll give it a more thorough review when I get back. Understand, this process you're requesting, it's a formal process with criteria. It's not about style or likability. The fact that she's a bitch who doesn't get along with coworkers is not sufficient in and of itself to render a recommendation of termination from my end. We have to demonstrate psychological unfitness for duty, show that she has some issues and that those issues significantly inhibit her performance of assigned tasks and responsibilities."

"She's out of step with the organization. She interferes with unit cohesiveness. She is a hole in the perimeter."

Jommers found it ironic to hear about unit cohesiveness from an outsider who was despised by everyone in his command.

"As I understand it," Jommers said, "her purpose in Internal Affairs is to perform investigations into unethical, unprofessional, or illegal behavior by members of police force, then submit the results of those investigations to her superiors in timely fashion so that they might pursue disciplinary actions. Number one, you need to establish specifically how has she failed that mission. And number two, I would need to establish that those failures can be attributed to psychological disorders."

"Her eccentric personality and behavior inhibits cooperation into investigations."

"Yes, I'm guessing it's not a big surprise that police officers aren't eager to co-operate with investigations into their own misbehavior and that their buddies got their backs. What distinguishes her failure/success rate from her colleagues in Internal Affairs?"

"She is a fucking wacko who fails to get it done."

"Yes, well, we need to establish that connection. Poor performance in and of itself is an administrative issue for you to deal with. For me to weigh in on a dismissal, the poor performance has to stem from emotional issues. If your strategy here is to—"

"Strategy? Strategy? You don't need strategy when you outrange."

"Excuse me? Outrange?"

"When you have a longer range than your enemy," Scubbetts said. "In Desert Storm, our M1 Abrams tanks had a significantly longer range than the cast-off crap tanks the Russians gave Saddam. So in a lot of the armor battles, we didn't need to employ any brilliant tactics. Just sit outside their range and pick them off one by one. A turkey shoot. That's what this is, a turkey shoot. Why are you fighting for her? You bonking her?"

"I'm not fighting for her. I'm fighting for the process. I'm curious. Most of the stuff in here looks likes small potatoes. Last week she shot and killed a fellow police officer. And I'm not seeing anything on that in here. I would think that if you were looking to hang her, malfeasance resulting in death of a police officer would certainly would be a nice length of rope. Did she do what she was supposed to do that night?"

"She was supposed to take a disturbed man to the hospital. Instead, she shot him."

"Okay, fine," Jommers said. "Show me specifically what she did wrong from a procedure perspective, and how that mistake was due to emotional problems. Then we've got a case."

"The Force Review Committee hasn't completed its investigation into the shooting. I can't include anything on it until the report is formally submitted. What the fuck is your problem all of a sudden? Why can't you get with the program?"

"The mayor brought you here to impose order over chaos, to instill rules and procedures into a disorganized bureaucratic structure. That was a good move. You've done a good job. And my adherence to rules and procedures demonstrates that I'm totally with the program."

Scubbetts gave Jommers a long, silent glare before concluding.

"You know what I want. Get it done."

PATROLMAN HELFETTER LOATHED MOVIES that portrayed outlaws as romantic heroes. And the one he detested most of all was *Butch Cassidy and the Sundance Kid*. So the night he came home and found his wife watching it, his blood boiled. He tried to hold it in, say nothing. But at the end, he just burst. That was when the surrounded outlaw duo charged out at their pursuers with pistols blazing and got cut down in a hail of bullets. And that was when the wife began crying over the scene. When the cop saw the tears rolling down his wife's face, he went over and slapped her, then started yelling at her.

"You cry over cop killers? You dumb bitch. If I die in a shootout, you going to cry for me or the motherfucker who shoots me?"

Afterward, Patrolman Helfetter had the sense to realize there was a problem, and that was why he was now sitting in one of Jommers's rockers. He felt bad about hitting his wife. It was the first time, though he'd come close to it a dozen times before. He was sorry and didn't want it to happen again. But he wasn't backing down on his complaint about Hollywood romanticizing Old West outlaws.

"Those uniformed Bolivians that Butch and Sundance were shooting at, they were the authorities, the equivalent of cops for that place and time. If you're a sane, civilized person, you should be rooting for the guys in the uniforms, not the criminals shooting at them. I mean, those kind of movies, they're no different than the rap music glamorizing the gangbangers selling drugs in the projects. Making heroes out of scum. Why would you do that? I thought people were afraid of crime, why they moved to the suburbs. So why would you glamorize it?"

Like all therapists, Jommers instinctively knew that a disproportionate eruption over something small was merely an iceberg tip, that something larger was lurking underneath. The sonar must be activated.

Helfetter blamed his anger on the stress of the job, just like every other cop. And there was truth in that for a lot of them. But for many others, it served as an all-purpose excuse, a free pass that let them avoid taking ownership of their problems and behavior. Jommers suspected this guy fell into the latter category.

Law enforcement was an undeniably dangerous occupation, and the potential for being shot unexpectedly created a unique anxiety. Yet Jommers knew that the threat was often over-dramatized and overestimated. Statistically, there were more than a half dozen occupations with higher death rates, including loggers, fishermen, roofers, electrical linemen, and farmers. But no one ever produced heroic TV shows about those guys. Additionally, police officer fatalities on the job had been declining steadily over the years, and now roughly half were due to traffic accidents.

But Jommers also knew that the fastest way to infuriate a cop with a martyr complex was to point out that he had one. So Jommers approached the inquiry obliquely, hoping to outflank the patient's defenses.

In this case, he handed the cop a sheet of paper listing the time at thirty-minute intervals—8:00 a.m., 8:30 a.m., 9:00 a.m., and so on. Jommers then asked the patient to estimate his stress level, on a scale of one to five, for each period of time covering the previous day. Jommers then asked the man to do it again for the day before yesterday.

Only after the two sheets were completed did Jommers ask Helfetter about occurrences or conditions correlated with the particular times. In doing so, Jommers discovered that the cop's stress was not arising on the job, but popping up later at home. The only time it jumped while working was on lunch break—when he called home.

The next step was to determine the onset of elevated stress levels in the larger timeframe. Helfetter guessed that the stress had started to creep up on him a little over a year ago, when he'd started pursuing more overtime, which was why he associated it with the job.

"I started grabbing any OT that was hanging out there. And I got a lot of seniority now, so I got a longer reach."

Pushing further, Jommers asked why Helfetter suddenly was hot for the OT. Was there a financial problem? The patrolman said no, they were just thinking about buying a better house and needed some extra money to make that happen.

Jommers then asked if the couple's desire for a better house was shared equally by both of them. Helfetter paused, then sighed.

"It's mostly her idea."

Ping.

Jommers pressed for more info from the patrolman.

"I know what we got is small, but it's fine with me. It's easy to take care of, the yard especially. I mean, yeah, it's a postage stamp, but it's not like we need bigger. We got no kids, no dogs, don't have big parties. You got room for a grill and a small garden, what the hell else do you need? It's just right. You know, when that place was first built, it would have been like a mansion for someone moving out of an inner-city tenement. In its time, that was the suburbs. You were doing good to get there. And now . . ."

"So it's an old house in an old neighborhood," Jommers said. "Is it the house, or the neighborhood?"

"Yeah, you hit it. The neighborhood. Everything was fine until the house across the street got robbed. She went totally fritz after that. We got to get out of here, we got to get out of here, over and over. Like we we're living in Somalia or something. You know what? Break-ins happen. They can happen anywhere, even low-crime affluent neighborhoods. It's not like there's muggings and shootings on the corner at night. It's a decent place to live. But she won't let go of it. We got to get out of here. We got to get out of here."

"So you're working a lot of OT that you really don't want, for her."

"Yeah." Helfetter laughed and shook his head.

"Okay," Jommers said. "That laugh, that head shaking, there's more."

"Well, yeah. Now she bitches that I'm never around. How lonely she is. How she doesn't feel safe being by herself all the time. Drives me up a wall."

"So that's the real source of the anger. Feeling a double bind. You feel she's forcing you to work the OT and simultaneously making you feel guilty for doing it."

"Yeah. How's that for thanks? Ungrateful bitch."

"Do you say those words to her?"

"Sometimes."

"But you say them to yourself all the time, don't you?"

"Yeah," Helfetter said. "Sometimes I can't even look at her without those words screaming in my head."

"And it keeps winding up, winding up . . ."

"Yeah."

"So when you are with her, you're a cocked weapon, just waiting for an excuse to pull the trigger."

"Yeah."

"Then you blast her. And the words rip her apart like double-aught buck."

"Yeah."

"Okay," Jommers said. "We've got two things here, two issues to deal with, one immediate, the other longer term. First up is your anger. More specifically, how we're going to work on defusing it. It's clear that you spend a lot of time mentally rehearsing the fight you'll have with her. And, as you've already discovered, when you rehearse the fight, you most certainly will have the fight. So what we need to work on is changing the rehearsal, rewriting that mental script that you practice over and over. We're going to write you a new one to practice so that you will no longer enter your home as a cocked weapon. The second issue is that the two of you need marital counseling. That means the two of you in the room together with a therapist as mediator, trying to find a resolution of the conflicting goals, or, at the very least, a mutually agreed-on approach for accommodating the issue. The underlying causes that trigger your arguments aren't going away, so you both need to identify and avoid the triggers. If you flag a minefield, you can safely walk through it every day. While resolving the core conflicts will take time, you can start flagging the mines today. I'll be happy to help you with that part, also, but if you prefer a therapist who specializes in marital counseling, I can provide some referrals."

Helfetter put his head in his hands and groaned. "What a mess. What a fucking mess."

"Now don't get all spooked by this," Jommers said. "You had the good sense to come here, which means you also have the good sense to handle it. We're at the bottom of the hole now, about to start the slow climb out. It gets better from here."

"Way back, right before we got married, my old man says to me, did you have the money talk yet? And I said what? He says, did you talk about money yet? How much you will want and need, and how you'll get it. How you'll spend it and how you'll save it. I looked at him like he was crazy and just laughed. We don't need to talk about money. We're in love."

Jommers was poring over the menu at Spreckels Tavern, pondering what to eat for lunch, when Larry approached.

"Hey, you know how they say we all need more fiber?"

"Yes," Jommers said.

"Well, they got this new kind of fiber supplement now, dissolves invisible in any liquid, and you can't taste it either, so you don't even know it's there. So I was thinking, they ought to make a beer with it, then they could market the beer as healthy."

"What would you call it?"

"Never Fail Ale. Smooth from top to bottom."

"You have a brilliantly warped imagination. Speaking of which, what happened to the Hot and Horsy Hair Raiser? I don't see it on the menu anymore."

"Yeah, that was my favorite burger, with fresh-ground horseradish, hot mustard and paprika. Lot of people liked it. Then some asshole, never found out who or why, started spreading a rumor that the real reason it was called Hot and Horsy is that it was made from horsemeat. Boom! Just like that it was dead. Nobody ordered it. So I took it off the menu, afraid that the ones next to it would suffer guilt by association. Nothing I said made any difference. A stinking lie is like a stinking fart—once it's out, you can't get it recalled. Why are people so eager to believe bullshit?"

"You know, out in the wild, where we once dwelt, food was of uncertain and inconsistent availability. As a result, nature inclines animals to conserve energy, both physical and mental. And that means not engaging in any unnecessary activity, including nonessential thinking."

"Nature made us lazy."

"It would be more precise to say that nature predisposes us to shortcuts, particularly in our mental processes. If we pondered everything we heard, read or saw in the course of a day, we wouldn't have time to get anything done. So we reserve our ruminations for important matters, and use shortcuts to quickly dispense of less important matters. A person quickly accepts or rejects a rumor about a hamburger because they have more important things on their mind—their job, their marriage, their finances, a house they want to buy . . ."

"So what you're saying, then, is that bullshit rules forever and ever, amen."

"I hadn't thought of it quite that way, but I'd be hard-pressed to refute the proposition."

"That's a yes, right?"

"Yes."

"Well, then, that sucks the big one."

"Yes."

ON HIS WAY OUT of the tavern, Jommers ran into an acquaintance who also lived and worked down in the Bends. Eddy Lynxclaw was a self-employed artist, craftsman, and contractor who specialized in custom iron work—creative designs in iron fences, railings, burglar bars, and so forth.

"Hey, Eddy, how you doing?"

"Hey, Karl, I was just thinking about you the other day."

"Yeah?"

"Yeah. I'm kind of jittery these days. Can't seem to shake it."

"What's going on?"

"Well, I got this call a couple weeks back. Guy wanted an estimate for sectioning off the top floor of this big old three-story house, turning half of it into a cage. It was like a third-floor attic, only finished. He said he was going to start collecting tropical birds and wanted an area for them to fly around without constraints. So initially I'm thinking this is cool. So we start talking about spacing of the rails, and what he wants is not tight enough to hold birds, but he says he's going to put chicken wire on the inside of the rails so it won't be a problem. So I don't think anything about it. Then, while we're talking, the mailman rings the doorbell for some package he has, so while the guy goes downstairs, I go down one level to the second floor. Since I have to bolt the rails to the floor, I want to know what's underneath the floor, you know, what I have to work with. And when I look in this one room, I see the wall is plastered with pictures of a woman. Every picture, the same woman. And it doesn't look like she knew her picture was being taken. Suddenly, I get this chill all over me. It ain't birds he's looking to cage."

"So what did you do?"

"I hear him coming back up, so I return to the third floor, pretending I didn't see anything. I tell him I'll send him an estimate and then go. I get back to the shop and next thing I do is call the cops. Some detectives go out there.

But he doesn't let them in. They tell me there's nothing they can do. Even if he did let them in, it's not against the law to take pictures of someone in a public place. Paparazzi do it all the time. He hasn't broken any laws. So I get kind of pissed off that they don't seem to give a crap about this. And so I go to my councilman and he raises a stink with somebody somewhere and they put a detective on it. The detective tails this guy and figures out who he's stalking. They still can't arrest him, but at least they warn the woman what's going on, and so she files for a restraining order and takes precautions, so that thing that was going to happen probably not now going to happen, at least not with her."

"You did the right thing pursuing it," Jommers said.

"Yeah, maybe, but now I'm paying the price. That guy knows it was me who called the cops. So now I'm getting threatening phone messages. I know it's his voice. Says I'll pay for what I did. I call the cops again. They track the call to a gas station pay phone. No way to prove it was him. They say they can't do anything. So now I'm kind of spooked. Looking at every car that goes by. Flinching at every sound. I'm not in a good place right now."

"Would that have something to do with why you have a railroad spike hanging from your belt loop?"

"Yeah, I know it's dumb," Lynxclaw said. "I'm not going to do battle with a railroad spike. But carrying a gun or something, that's not me. So it's just sort of symbolic, but it makes me feel better, you know?"

"Sure. Plus, I like the look. It's you. You work with iron. It's a statement. You should keep it even after this is over."

"Now I know you're going to tell me to put it all in perspective, that the risk he's actually going to come after me is low."

"True. But I understand that the threats make it feel very real."

"Yeah, exactly. I mean, I'm not stupid. I know he's just trying to get in my head, but—"

"No, you're not stupid," Jommers said. "Though it might be better if you were in this case."

"I don't follow."

"You're an intelligent and creative person. An intelligent person is motivated to find solutions for problems. You have a problem and your intellect is demanding you solve it, so that has the unhelpful effect of keeping you focused on it, continually reminding you of it. And because you are creative, you have an active imagination. And that imagination is entertaining all the possible scenarios for how this might play out. So both your intellect and imagination are fueling your anxiety by keeping this at the top of your action list."

"Yep. That's exactly what's happening."

"Okay, a few things. Obviously take reasonable precautions, increase your vigilance, but not obsessively. Accept that there are things in life beyond your control, and this is just another one of them. You drive around, you can get rear-ended. And down here in the Bends, it might be a gravel truck that does it. But you don't spend time thinking about getting rear-ended because you can't prevent it, can't control it. It will happen or it won't, so you get on with your day. And so with this. You have no control over whether this guy shows up or not. It will happen or it won't. It's not a problem you can solve. So you get on with your day."

"Yeah, I know I shouldn't get all worked up over it."

"True, but don't beat yourself up, either. Accept the reality of your anxiety. You're a normal human being. Any normal person would have the same reaction. So accept that you can't make it go away by snapping your fingers. Now then, while you can't make it go away, you can get it off front and center stage in your head. Keep busy, active. Avoid downtime. Importantly, keep busy with things that demand your full mental attention. You want your cognitive load to push this other thing off the stage. Work on new designs for your customers. Read a complicated book. Try writing an essay or a poem."

"Yeah, I've been trying to do that."

"Good. Now, I know it's real easy for me to say all this, demand that your rational brain take control over your emotional brain, but we're still just people. Sometimes emotion is so strong that it fights off reason and rationalizing. Sometimes the only thing that can take on a negative emotion is a positive one. So focus on positive things that make you feel good. Your work obviously is the big one. Next one is people. Keep in closer contact with friends and family. See them more often. See if you can get a buddy to stay with you for a while. Play music that you like. Rewatch your favorite movies. Stock up on your favorite comfort foods. Visit your favorite places. Recall pleasant memories from the past. Be good to yourself. Remember, you had the guts to quit your job and do your thing, the guts to come and live down here back when hardly anybody else did. So you can handle this, too."

"Yeah, yeah."

"Finally, consider your daily performance, I mean your behavior, your expression, the way you carry yourself. There's some evidence that people who force themselves to smile will feel slightly happier. That people who exhibit a domineering pose will feel slightly stronger. People who display a fearless demeanor will feel braver. The mind follows the body's lead. So here's a performance suggestion for you, given your trade. Make an iron triangle, something that'll really ring out when you whack it. You set it up out in front of your place hanging from something. Make yourself an iron rod, or better yet, a poker or sword. Then every morning you go out and start your day by sticking that rod inside the triangle and banging it around as hard as you can. Make an unholy racket. Like a crazy man. And what you're doing there is making an announcement. I am here. I am not hiding. I am not afraid. Come get me if you dare."

Lynxclaw smiled. "Yeah, yeah. I like it. Only I can do something way cooler than a triangle. Way cooler. I'm already drawing it in my head. This is good. I got this. I got this."

"Call me tomorrow. Let me know."

"Will do. Thanks."

A KEY PROBLEM with a post-critical-incident review is not having a comparative frame of reference when seeing someone the first time. If an unusual personality trait is observed, there is no way to know whether the person had it all along, or whether the trait emerged spontaneously as a result of the incident.

Ilona Voros presented some peculiar behavior patterns, but without prior contact, Jommers could not discern which of those aspects, if any, had been caused or juiced by her shooting of Earl Tarburn. And now that Chief Scubbetts had changed the designation of her evaluation, Jommers felt a greater urgency to discover the undercurrents driving her behavior.

He was pondering that issue while driving back to the office when an idea struck him. He made a quick U-turn in the street after spontaneously deciding to pay a visit to the Reverend Elvis Truly.

THE EVERGREEN BAPTIST CHURCH was on Hawthorne Boulevard in an old neighborhood with old trees that loomed tall and broad. The church was set back enough to give it a front lawn that featured a towering sycamore tree whose broad branches spread upward like giant fingers holding a handful of leaves. Facing out from that lawn was the church signboard that announced service times with a message: If God seems far away, who moved?

The building itself was a small, unassuming brick structure with a pitched roof and rectangular sash windows. No stained glass. The only architectural flourishes that betrayed its calling were a short steeple and a small portico over its double doors.

Jommers found Reverend Truly at the back end of the building in the church's cramped office, talking with a woman who held a sheaf of spreadsheets, presumably the church's bookkeeper.

"The contractor said it's better to fix the roof while it's still warm," Truly said. "I don't remember all the reasons. Something about getting the shingles to lie flat."

"Yes," the woman said, "but we need to consider the long-term cost of this continual fix-and-patch approach. When you look at the cumulative total cost of all the roof repairs we've made over the last six years, and compare them to the cost of a new roof—"

"I'd love to get a new roof. Can we swing it?"

"No," she said. "Not with the other anticipated expenses. We'd need a special fund drive—"

"And we know how well those go."

"I mentioned this last year—if we could recruit a new member who had a truck and a plow, we could cancel the plowing service for the lot and pick up some funds there."

"That's a new twist on evangelism, isn't it? Go forth and save the soul of a man with a plow." At that point, Truly noticed his visitor and looked up. "Mr. Jommers, what's a tactful way of telling a congregation that God needs a new roof and it's time to pony up?"

"That sounds pretty good right there," Jommers answered.

"I'll come back later," the bookkeeper said, leaving the office.

"I assume you've come with news," Truly said.

"No. I have not."

"Oh."

"I've come with a request," Jommers said. "An outlandish request. One that will likely anger you and get me thrown out of here."

"That's either the worst possible introduction for a request, or the most brilliant."

"I have this patient—I'm having a problem deciphering her, and circumstances require that I do so quickly. So I need to lob one deep, even though it's ill-advised and reckless. So I was wondering if you would be willing to arrange a meeting between my patient and Becca Tarburn."

"Becca? I don't understand."

"The patient in question is the person who was required to use lethal force against Earl Tarburn."

Truly raised his eyebrows and shook his head in disbelief. "You're serious? If so, the word *outlandish* doesn't begin to describe the request. And *outrageous* barely scratches the surface."

"I'm sorry. I had to try. I'll let you get back to work."

"Hold on a second . . ." Truly rubbed his forehead, assuming a distraught and contemplative expression. "I have been talking to Becca almost daily since it happened. Trying to do my best to provide spiritual counseling, help her through this ordeal. But my best is not proving good enough. My words fall flat in the air, drifting to the floor like paper streamers. What are mere words against a crashing sea of pain?"

"I often have that challenge in my work also," Jommers said.

"I think that some of it is the strangeness of it all. I think if Earl had been killed by a criminal or died in a car accident, these things, however tragic, are at least comprehensible, they are things that happen. But this situation, where he was killed by a fellow police officer and where he was deemed the criminal in the matter . . . it's just all too much for her to grasp or accept. So now you've got me thinking, maybe I need to lob one deep." He rubbed his forehead again. "I need to ponder it. I need to pray on it. And I'll get back to you."

"Fair enough," Jommers said. "I appreciate the consideration. It's more than I had a right to expect."

"Before you go, let me ask you a question, a behavior question, since that's your specialty."

"Sure."

"You may have seen this in the news yesterday. Two men were standing in line at a fast-food joint, and one yells out loudly, questioning what's taking so long. His question begins with a vulgarity that journalists abbreviate with the letters WTF. So we can assume journalists find it amusing rather than rude. I don't understand their seeming delight in the walls of civilization crumbling. In any event, the second man was offended by the term, told the first man to watch his language, and so forth. They got into an argument about it. The second man, the scolder, ended up getting stabbed, though fortunately not fatally. It just so happens that the stabbing victim is a member of my congregation. So I have to address this issue from the pulpit Sunday. I cannot ignore it. Yet I need to find a way to expound on it in meaningful fashion, find the lesson."

"Right."

"You know," Truly said, "I understand longstanding feuds. I understand infidelity, hatred. I understand men fighting over women or money or because they're drunk. But I don't understand two sober men who don't know each other standing in line in a shop and one stabbing the other over a trifle. Help me comprehend that. Everybody on such a short fuse these days. Am I correct in seeing that as new, recent? Or am I guilty of viewing the past with rose-colored glasses? I just don't remember seeing these kinds of things happen so much when I was younger. Now you see them almost every day. People blowing up over nothing. Are the pressures of modern life that great that we're all on a tripwire?"

"I agree about the rage issue being more prevalent," Jommers said, "but I don't buy the excuse about modern life as the cause. You look back at the difficulty of life in preindustrial times. You want to eat dinner? You got to go out and kill something in your livestock pen, skin it or pluck it, then gut it, then build a fire to cook it—that's after you chop the wood for the fire and turn a crank fifty times to draw water from a well. And that's every time. And if predators had taken all your livestock in the night, then you'd have to go out and hunt for something, while your family is waiting for you with empty bellies. And if the summer was bad to your crops, you'd have nothing to eat come winter. And even if you had food stored, a good share of it would be eaten or fouled by rodents and bugs. Medical and dental care was primitive and scarce. Most people had a toothache or two at any given time, along with some other untreated chronic condition. And with no vaccines or antibiotics, if you were a parent, odds were better than even that you'd watch at least one child die slowly and painfully from an infectious disease. So no, I don't believe that traffic jams beat hunger and pain as stressors. I think people have less resilience these days. Their psyches are too fragile. Where people once were like granite, they're now like crystal stemware."

"Interesting," Truly said. "And would you classify resilience as strictly a psychological trait, or a moral virtue, an aspect of character?"

"Obviously, you can argue that, but either way, you have the same problem. You can't compel either virtue or mental health in a democracy. People are free to be weak and stupid, both individually and collectively as a culture."

"So it falls on men and women of influence, people with powers of persuasion and the power to change behavior. People like us."

"Interesting conjunction," Jommers said. "Had not thought of it that way."

"You had not seen the connection between moral virtues and mental health, or had not seen the connection between our two occupations?"

"Occupational specialization is a modern phenomenon. Two hundred years ago, eighty percent of men were farmers and eighty percent of women farmers' wives. But the contemplation of human behavior goes way back, back to the Greeks, Aristotle . . ."

"I remember getting lost in Aristotle," Truly said, "and I don't mean lost in a good way. To tell the truth, I prefer things reduced to pithy quotes. Simple instructions work better than abstract ruminations. You see, if you are approached by a hungry man, then you give him food, not recipes. Likewise, if you want to nourish people hungry for wisdom, you must give them hot pizza to go. And my favorite pizza is a quote about character that I have seen a dozen different ways with just as many attributions. My version goes like this: Your thoughts incite your actions. Your repeated actions create habits. Your habits define your character. And your character determines your destiny. Change your thinking and you change the course of your life."

"Yes, a common observation. The causal connections in it constitute the better part of my work."

"Good part of mine too," Truly said. "The best advice doesn't change much over time, does it? Of course, that's also the problem with dispensing it, isn't it? You keep saying the same things over and over, and people become numb to the repetition. Sometimes I'm at a loss how to write a fresh sermon anymore. I must confess, sometimes I bore myself, sounding like a record player. But what am I to do? Tell jokes? I'm a preacher. That's what I do."

"Yes," Jommers said. "People habituate to a frequently heard aphorism the same way they habituate to a frequently seen object in their visual environment—it ceases to register. Sometimes I want a patient to start the day by thinking or saying something to get themselves in a proper mental posture. I often advise them to post a note on their bathroom mirror with the reminder. But I'm aware that they habituate to the note within a couple of days, cease to notice its presence as it becomes part of the ambient visual field. So now I tell them to make a new note every day, in a different style or color, and post it in a different place. Otherwise it won't seize their attention."

"Yes, yes, that's what it's all about, seizing their attention. But how do we do that in an age of constant distraction, an age where everyone expects to be entertained? Maybe people in the advice business will need to learn to sing and dance in order to beguile their audiences."

"Well," Jommers said, "if that's where my business is headed, then I'm definitely going to need a new line of work."

"Me too."

THE KGB CHEMIST

The Bends was full of haunted places. Not haunted in the scary movie sense, but in the historical sense—abandoned places that had once had a life and purpose. Untouched for decades, they served as unofficial, unattended museums. Quiet and ignored, they whispered tales of long ago to those willing to listen.

The old Erie Railroad roundhouse on Union Street was just such a place. Like most roundhouses, the crumbling brick building was built in a semicircular design, and its primary purpose was to service steam locomotives. Roundhouses varied in the number of service stalls depending on their design. This one, built in the early 1900s, had originally had seventeen, though five had since collapsed.

The key feature of a roundhouse was its turntable, a rotating section of track. Once the steamer was on the turntable, the track rotated to direct the engine into a particular repair stall. When repairs were finished, the turntable would orient the steamer back into a forward direction, given that the original steam locomotives were not designed for reverse operation.

The property was cordoned off by a rusted chain-link fence with a gate. Normally the gate would be locked closed with a loop of chain and a padlock. But as Jommers approached it, he could see that the shackle was open. Biederbach, who seemed to have a key for everything, was already in there waiting.

It was dusk, but there was just enough light for Jommers to survey the scene. The grounds were a scraggle of weeds, but the turntable was still there. It was most likely locked in place now due to corrosion of its pivoting mechanism. The sunken circle in which it had once rotated was full of organic debris, and its brick floor sprouted grass in the gaps.

The doors on repair stalls were either missing or open, so the roundhouse appeared as a semicircular row of murky caves, with total blackness forestalled by glass block windows that captured the waning orange glimmer of the setting sun. The shadowy spaces were still and quiet, but for a man who lived above a truck repair shop, it was easy to envision the activity the place once supported, to hear the hammering and grinding, to smell the odors of grease, smoke, and molten metal. He imagined the old turntable creaking and groaning under the weight of a massive steamer, dialing the locomotive into its slot. Then his reverie was interrupted by the familiar sight of a small glowing dot in the darkness, the smoldering ember of Biederbach's ever-present cigarette.

Biederbach had warned in advance that he had acquired a great deal of information about the government plot. It would take some time to get through it all, so it might be a long meeting. In anticipation, Jommers had brought his folding camp chair, a small soft cooler full of beer, a bag of pretzels, a reporter's notebook, and a combination flashlight/lantern.

"Way to be inconspicuous, Jommers," Biederbach said. "Why didn't you just bring a boom box while you were at it?"

"I thought of that, but I ran out of hands."

"So we still have our deal, right? This is my turn to convince you. I talk and you listen."

"Yes," Jommers said, "though I assume I'll have the opportunity for Q and A."

"Correct."

The brick floor of the repair shop was covered with grimy dust, and the air smelled of rust and mold. Off toward the back walls were strange-looking and barely visible silhouettes—shafts, pipes and unrecognizable train parts punctuated by occasional piles of junk.

Jommers set up his chair and put the notebook in his lap. He took out a beer and offered one to Biederbach, who declined.

"Okay, shoot," Jommers said.

Instead of talking, Biederbach tensed up and scanned the darkness outside. He put his forefinger to his lips, indicating Jommers to remain quiet. Biederbach then withdrew a pistol.

Initially, Jommers didn't hear anything. But eventually he did—the slight crackling noise of something or someone outside walking across the crunchy dried weeds outside. Jommers slowly turned his head. A second later, he saw a dog charging him out of the shadows. He completely froze.

The shot rang out just as the dog was leaping. Biederbach's shot was true, but the dog's forward inertia was enough to keep it tumbling toward Jommers, who got knocked out of his chair—beer, pretzels and all. Biederbach quickly put two more shots in the dog's head.

"Another fucking Rott," Biederbach said. "Slum scum assholes, they get their Rotts and pits because they think it's cool having a badass dog—until they get bit. Then they dump them down here in the Bends. They go feral, living off cats and rats."

"I thought we were fenced in," Jommers said.

"The fence only goes back to the tracks. There it's open. We should move. They often hang in packs. His buds might be nearby."

Biederbach hiked up his pants, then led the way over to two rows of abandoned rail siding, one of which held three old passenger cars and a caboose from an earlier era. They were historic pieces that someone had intended to restore, but at the moment, they were but vandalized ruins with broken windows. They chose the battered caboose and climbed aboard. Biederbach sat at a small table where a train crew might have done paperwork or eaten their lunch.

"I'll take that beer now," he said.

Jommers handed him a can, then sat down in one of the bay windows, looking forward, the way a crew member would have long ago, watching the side of the train for shifting loads and overheated axles.

"You're going to need to keep an open mind here," Biederbach said.

"Consider it open . . . for the moment. But remember, a window stuck open is no better than a window stuck closed. In both cases, you've lost the use of a window."

As Jommers made that observation, he stuck his arm out the broken window of the caboose and waved it around for effect. Biederbach sniffed and squinted, demonstrating his lack of appreciation of the gesture. He lit another cigarette and began his saga.

"You recall last time I proposed the existence of a human version of *schreckstoff*, a synthesized chemical that would induce intense fear in someone exposed to it. Since then, I've been doing a lot of research, trying to figure out where it might have originated. And now, I know—the notorious Laboratory 12 in Moscow, also known as Kamera. Back in the Cold War days, Lab 12 was operated by KGB's Department Viktor. The lab employed a whole slew of neuropharmacologists who specialized in developing poisons and mind control agents. It was the gang at Lab 12, by the way, that developed the concentrated ricin that the Bulgarian secret police used to assassinate the exiled writer Georgi Markov in 1978. They jabbed him with a special umbrella while he was waiting for a bus by the River Thames."

"Yes, I remember hearing about that," Jommers said.

"Our story begins earlier, however, back in the sixties, when the Kremlin came up with a new approach for dealing with dissidents—diagnosing them as schizophrenics and locking them up in psychiatric hospitals like the infamous Serbsky Institute. The strategy provided two benefits. The first was legalistic. A psychiatric patient can be locked up indefinitely without charges or trial. You can't complain about a sham trial when you don't even get one. The second was propaganda value. You can say that only a crazy person would complain about the government, then validate your logic by showing that all the complainers are diagnosed schizos. See, we told you! They are all crazy! Don't listen to them. Many of these dissidents in the psych wards were also given massive doses of drugs against their will. Sometimes it was a megadose of aminazin, which put them into a depressed stupor. Sometimes it was a megadose of sulfazine, which caused excruciating pain and high fever. Torture by pharmacology."

"Yes," Jommers said, "I read about that in a psychology journal."

"Good. Then the rest of this shouldn't surprise you. Somewhere in the late sixties, an apparatchik in the Ministry of Internal Affairs, which ran these special psychiatric hospitals, came up with a diabolical idea. If we're going to label these troublemakers as paranoid schizophrenics, why not create a drug that will make them act like paranoids? The concept provided three advantages. One, you could release dissidents back into the population and get the West off your back for jailing them. Two, since they would be acting crazy and saying crazy things, no one would listen to them anymore. Three, since they'd be genuinely terrified, they'd be afraid to make any more trouble. They'd imagine themselves being watched even when they weren't. By putting minders in their heads, you wouldn't have to bother with real ones. They're leashed from within. So they assigned this mission to the gang in Lab 12. It was code-named Project Ghost Wolf. That's the English translation anyway, I can't pronounce the actual Russian term. Ghost Wolf, the idea of something that can terrorize you but remains unseen because it isn't actually there. They came up with a number of different formulas, testing them one at a time on dissidents. And with the thirty-seventh formula, they got the result they wanted. So they called it Ghost Wolf 37, whatever that is in Russian."

"Now that part is new to me," Jommers said. "Where did you find that?"

"I came across some samizdat, dissident literature, written by someone who experienced it. He described being overcome with a paralyzing fear and dread. He recalls how he cowered, tense and trembling, whimpering like a child. Imagine how you would feel, he wrote, if you are afraid of heights, someone who cannot climb a simple ladder, and you somehow find yourself clinging to the top spire of the Ostankino radio tower in Moscow, which is 1,772 feet high. That's what it felt like, according to him. He also noted how long the effects of the drug lasted. He said the only good to come of it is that he no longer feared death. He had already died a thousand times. There was an old psychiatrist in the facility who didn't approve of drugging the dissidents, but went along with it, kept his mouth shut to save his own hide. He felt sorry for the dissident, so before the dissident was released, the old man told him about the drug, what caused the terror, told him to get the word out, so that it would stop being used."

"I'd love to get your sources on this," Jommers said.

"Don't have them with me, but I'll get them to you later. So now you're asking yourself, how does a drug developed to torture Soviet dissidents in the Cold War era end up in Grayton, Ohio, today?"

"You read my mind."

"I think I've got a handle on the first part of the journey, but I'm still working on the rest of it. I started searching for academic journals and conference proceedings relating to the field of neuropharmacology to see if I could find any reference to such a drug. I'd almost given up. Then I found a copy of a preliminary program for a conference held in Zurich, Switzerland, in 2002. And one of the scheduled paper presentations was titled 'Bidirectional Pharmacological Regulation of Central Amygdala Neurotransmitters Related to Fear and Anxiety Behaviors.' Now, did you note that amazing word in that title? *Bidirectional.* What he's saying with this title is that he has the chemical secret to either reducing or elevating the level of neurotransmitters involved in the fear response. He can amp it up or tamp it down with drugs. What it also means is that you poison a room full of people with fear but spare yourself with the antidote. Everybody else would be scared but you. And it just so happens that the author of this paper has a Russian name. First name is Zoran and his last name is longer than a freight train and has mostly consonants, so I'll stick with just Zoran for now. So now I'm thinking, this has to be the guy, the guy who invented GW-37. Even more curious, the guy never shows for the conference, and the final program for the conference says that the paper was withdrawn."

"So this part is inference, then," Jommers said. "The paper was withdrawn, so you never read it. And you can't be certain the author was a chemist from Lab 12."

"What are the odds that someone else knows how to pharmacologically manipulate the fear response and just happens to be Russian?"

"Hmm. Let's accept it for the moment and move on. What's next?"

"Thinking that this Zoran is the guy, I start searching for him every which way possible. Journal contributors, staff listings at institutions, association memberships, phone books, lists of house transfers and county property listings, and then bingo. I find him in Maryland, near the Chesapeake Bay, but more importantly, within commuting distance of the Edgewood Area of the Army's Aberdeen Proving Grounds. Did you ever read anything about Edgewood in your psychology journals?"

"Yes, and it wasn't good," Jommers said.

"You got that right. And I'll give you the recap in case your memory is rusty. The Edgewood Area was formerly known as the Edgewood Arsenal, notorious for its chemical experiments on U.S. soldiers. Between 1950 and 1975, close to seven thousand American soldiers were part of experiments involving more than two hundred and fifty chemicals. Some were given psychotropic agents like LSD and PCP. Some were exposed to irritants and blister agents and even lethal nerve agents like sarin and VX, tests that inflicted a horrific amount of pain. Some had CS gas shot directly into their eyes. These guys were never told up front what they were in for or what they were getting. A lot of them got permanently messed up, physically and mentally. And that was our own government doing it to our own guys."

"A dark chapter, to be sure."

"Indeed. And the question is whether a newer, darker one is being written. Today, that place is where the Army's Research Development and Engineering Command operates the Edgewood Chemical Biological Center, which is where they research chemical and biological agents. So back to Zoran. Let's say when the Iron Curtain falls down and the Soviet Union falls apart, our man Zoran thinks to himself, I possess knowledge that the Americans would love to have. Knowledge that they would pay a lot of money for. Maybe Zoran harbored a secret dream of being sub-franchisor for Taco Bell, then buying a condo in Key Largo. And now he sees his chance at making his dreams come true. So he comes here. Finds the right person. Shows his wares, so to speak. Makes a deal to work for our side. Edgewood is exactly where he would end up doing that. So that's how GW-37 makes it across the ocean. I'm still working on how it made the final leg of the trip to Ohio."

"Of course, that's another inference," Jommers said. "Even if this Zoran is your guy, the fact that he lives within commuting distance of Edgewood could be a coincidence. Maybe he likes living near the Chesapeake for the crabs."

"That's a lot of coincidence to swallow. At some point you start to gag. Our government has a history of using harmful chemicals on its own citizens. And since they have done it in the past, I have no doubts they would do it again, or that they are doing it right now. So it would be both logical and ironic for Zoran to bring GW-37 to Edgewood. Ironic in that a chemical that Russia used to torment its own people is brought to a place where America used chemicals to torment its own people. Land of the free indeed."

Over the course of the talk, dusk had yielded to night, dim to dark, and Biederbach's features faded into silhouette. Strangely, the smoke from his cigarettes was still visible. Nightfall had not brought even a wisp of breeze, so the humid, heavy air remained perfectly still. Even though the broken caboose windows were no more than jagged pieces of glass clinging to the frame edges, the flat cloud smoke made no move to escape. The fog hovered motionless in the air with an eerie persistence, as if smoke could somehow petrify into permanence.

Jommers let silence reign for a few moments to suggest he was seriously considering the proposals put forth, then gently poked at the soft spots.

"You've woven what appears at first glance to be an interesting, seamless tapestry," Jommers said. "But I see some snags. Now then, I already knew about the drugging of Soviet dissidents. And I already knew about Edgewood. That stuff is documented. But when it gets to that specific drug you mention—"

"GW-37."

"Yes, that. How much of the information you have on that is documented and available?"

"I'm still trying to nail it down," Biederbach said.

"You said it was referenced in samizdat, Soviet dissident literature. Who was the author?"

"I don't have that yet. All I saw was an extract."

"And did you see this extract in a journal at the library, or was it something anonymously posted on an Internet forum?"

"The Internet sources I use are deemed highly reliable," Biederbach said.

"By whom?"

"By me. And the conjectures are reasonable conclusions drawn from available evidence."

"Reasonable to whom?"

"Look," Biederbach said, "scientists say that eighty-four percent of the matter in the universe is comprised of dark matter, even though they have yet to capture a single particle of it. Its presence is inferred by the math, the logic. Almost all exoplanets are discovered by indirect methods such as star wobble. They aren't actually seen. Their presence is inferred."

"That type of inference may have some validity in the realm of astrophysics, but in the realm of human activity, missing pieces of information make inference more problematic. In epidemiology, for example, the study of a disease spreading must also examine the role of human behavior. Say that you have an outbreak of an entirely new strain of influenza. Say that a hundred people become infected with this new strain. Now, most people who contract the flu try to ride it out before seeking medical attention. They only go to the doctor or hospital if it gets very bad. So the hundred people who contract this new strain, thinking it's everyday flu, try to ride it out. And say that eighty of the hundred are able to do so. But twenty of them seek medical assistance. And of those twenty, half them are in such bad shape that they die. Now then, if you're analyzing the data you have on this new strain, you're prone to making two errors. One, you underestimate prevalence. You get to see only twenty people with the new strain. You don't see the eighty who didn't seek medical treatment because they got better on their own. They aren't in your data set. Two, because half of those who did seek medical treatment died, you overestimate mortality rate. You think it's fifty percent, when in reality it's only ten percent. And yet, you think your conclusions are perfectly reasonable based on the data you have. You don't know what you don't know."

"Which is why the Internet is a useful tool for filling in missing pieces," Biederbach said. "It allows you to find and query people you might not otherwise be aware of."

"Revealing comment," Jommers said. "You're saying that your Internet-sourced information is not merely passively acquired, not just fruit you picked from a web page. You solicited that information by actively engaging in queries in chat rooms and web forums."

"Of course," Biederbach said. "That would be standard procedure for someone seeking answers. If you were a reporter or a detective, you don't just sit there and wait for information to just flow your way, you go out and ask questions."

"Okay, but these Internet sites where you launched your queries, they're sites typically visited by like-minded people, people with whom you share a similar view of the world, people with whom you feel a sense of affinity. Correct?"

"Well, if you're interested in trains, you don't go to a website about boats, do you?"

"Point taken," Jommers said. "But the correspondents at these sites, they all go by creative nicknames and have clever email addresses that conceal their identities, so that you don't really have any idea who they are or whether they have any credibility. Correct?"

"The credibility can be inferred from the content of their communications. They make references to things that an ordinary person would not know. Insider information. Personal experiences."

"But are they firsthand references?" Jommers asked. "Or are they synthesized, culled from other sources by a wannabe pretending to have done interesting things, or by a hoaxer who gets a laugh out of other peoples' gullibility? Your allegedly authoritative source could be a sharp teenager who's punking you. Look, you have a logical mind, but you need to be more discriminating with your inputs. You need to understand that the quality of your reasoning can never exceed the quality of the information you feed into it."

"If we all waited for perfect information before we acted, then we would all be functional catatonics, since perfect information is never available."

"There's a threshold . . ."

"Who sets it?"

Biederbach had gotten testy by this point, his voice rising with each challenge. He stood up and looked out the opposite bay window, turning his back on Jommers.

"My concern," Jommers continued, "is that you are employing various cognitive biases to confirm preexisting views. We've already talked about confirmation bias. But there is also in-group bias, where you ascribe greater value to content generated within your group than from outside it. I'm also sensing an anchoring bias, placing an overemphasis on one aspect—in this case, the chemical, which is the anchor on which you've linked the entire narrative—a chemical which may or may not exist. And I can't help but wonder if your anchoring on the chemical has something to do with the contents of the kit bag that Tarburn carried that night. If so, you need to remember that Tarburn wasn't behaving or thinking rationally at the time. The importance he attached to that bag could have been purely imaginary. It may be that the contents are ordinary and unenlightening. But you won't know unless you turn it in and have it examined."

Biederbach spun around and pointed his finger at Jommers. "We've been through this. I don't have the goddamn bag. And if I did, it would be suicide to turn it in. And as for biases, I think you suffer from the ultimate bias."

"Which is?"

"Thinking that your familiarity with various biases makes you immune to them."

"Okay," Jommers said. "We should probably wrap it up here, call it a night. So let's review, I want to make sure I have the correct overview of your theory of what you think is going on here. You believe that a chemical exists that can induce extreme fear in humans exposed to it and that the chemical was originally developed by the Soviets to suppress dissidents. That chemical is now possessed by the U.S. Army and has somehow found its way to Grayton, Ohio, where the chief of police, a former army officer, has his SWAT team test it unknowingly on criminals in siege situations. Earl Tarburn was exploited for this purpose, and when he realized the implications and wanted out, they gave him a dose of the chemical, inducing the psychotic behavior that resulted in his death. Is that an accurate nutshell summary of your hypothesis?"

"It is an accurate nutshell summary of what has in fact happened," Biederbach said.

"And the reason for testing the chemical on criminals first is that the federal government intends to take over local law enforcement agencies, and when local populations rise up against the move, this chemical will be used to quell the disturbances. That's your take?"

"I've actually revised my view on that part," Biederbach said. "I now project a somewhat more restricted application."

"Interesting," Jommers said. "What's the new version?"

"I don't believe the chemical will be used on the general public. I believe it will be used against my kind."

"Your kind? Meaning?"

"I'm reluctant to use specific labels at this point, given that we're likely targets of investigation. Let's just say there are other cops who see this takeover coming. I don't mean only here. Other local law enforcement people around the country—cops, sheriffs and deputies. It would be fair to say that we discuss the issue regularly—how we might prevent it, or more importantly, resist it."

"And how would you resist it?"

"I don't wish to get into specific details at this juncture," Biederbach said. "Let's just say the feds would have an incentive to use nonlethal methods for suppressing such opposition. Everybody knows a cop somewhere—friend, relative, neighbor. Images of federal agents shooting local cops wouldn't win many hearts and minds. But if you could quash the resistance through fear, without firing a shot, then your path is much easier. Maybe you identify and expose your targets in advance before resistance efforts even get mounted. Then the battle is over before it's begun. The conquest is quiet and imperceptible. Maybe there'd be an oblique announcement about enhanced cooperation agreements between the Department of Homeland Security and local law enforcement requiring temporary suspension of some aspects of home rule, all to better facilitate the war on terror. But terror isn't a country or a people, it's a strategy, one that will always be with us. Which means the war on terror will be indefinite. So any temporary suspension of rights that we permit becomes a de facto permanent suspension. But nobody gets that. They are all caught up in the humdrum of their trivial lives. They're obsessed with celebrities, sports, television, food, gadgets, but they're totally oblivious that their freedom, the thing they celebrate on Fourth of July, is being slowly siphoned away. By the time they notice it gone, it'll be too late to get it back."

ARRIVING BACK HOME, Jommers reviewed the notes he had taken in the caboose, then immediately started making new ones, which included both observations and ruminations. He had mixed feelings about this latest bout with Biederbach. On one hand, the therapist was encouraged that Biederbach had scaled back his conspiracy theory slightly. Originally, the federal government was going to unleash the mystery chemical on the general public. Now it was only going to be used against local law enforcement. This was progress of a sort, and perhaps suggestive of a strategy. If the conspiracy theory could not be imploded, maybe it could be whittled down to a less threatening dimension.

On the other hand, Jommers was disheartened to have one suspicion confirmed, that Biederbach's theories were fueled in part by his unquestioning acceptance of material extracted from dubious sources on the Internet. The prevalence of this habit was an infectious disease, in Jommers's view, one worse than many others. Most people recovered from influenza or norovirus, but the habit of reflexive acceptance of in-group views was an affliction that bent toward semipermanence. He understood the process, the susceptibility. One disease that cured another—anomie. Biederbach didn't prowl the web for information so much as affirmation.

In the old days, traditional forms of social control discouraged the expression of eccentric views. In those times, for better or for worse, outliers like Biederbach learned to conform or keep quiet. The practical effect was quarantine.

Then one day, a magical device appeared with a joyful message—you are not alone. There are others like you, others who think like you, out of sight, over the mountains. And through this magical device, you can find those fellow members of your lost tribe, dispersed by some unexplained Diaspora. You can now dwell among your own kind. There's no place like home. Only instead of clicking the heels of your red shoes like Dorothy, you click your mouse.

In the connected world, it doesn't matter how strange a person's ideas or tastes might be because there is always someone else out there who shares them. Aberrant views or behavior appear normative when a sufficient number of people hold them, and with billions of people interconnected, there is always a sufficient number. Everything is normative where everything is practiced. Chasing the fantastic and bizarre runs equal with knitting, stamp collecting, and growing heirloom tomatoes. Outliers never need change in such a world, they only need to find like-minded people. On the Internet, you never bowl alone.

As Jommers scribbled away, his ruminations evolved into questions of strategy. When proximal community is replaced by online community, and peculiar beliefs are rooted in affinity with such a community, then reforming someone's distorted thinking requires removing them from their village. And what you perceive as rescue, they see as abduction.

As he jotted down that insight, he immediately thought of Cynthia Ann Parker, whose plight had inspired the novel *The Searchers* and subsequent film with John Wayne. Abducted by the Comanche in 1836 at the age of eleven, Parker gradually became one of them, eventually marrying a Comanche chieftain and bearing him three children. But after about twenty-four years living with the Comanche, she was recaptured by Texas Rangers and taken back to the white culture into which she was born, but where she was now a stranger. She considered herself Comanche and tried unsuccessfully to escape and go back to them, back to her family, back to her tribe.

For Jommers, every true believer in conspiracy theories, aliens, ghosts, psychics, or any other peculiar and unfounded notion, every one of them was a Cynthia Ann Parker, an abductee refusing rescue. Yet Biederbach was an intelligent man, and more importantly, wished to be respected as one. And that was the chink in his armor, the point of potential access. He would at least listen. If Jommers had any chance to chip away at the conspiracy theory, he must demonstrate the proper procedure for evaluating one.

First you examine history. Had something similar already happened in the past that suggested possibility? The Watergate Scandal had become emblematic proof for many that bad things could and did happen in high places, but its revelations did not offer any general tools for evaluation of subsequent plots, real or imagined.

One useful metric was the general rule that the probability of a conspiracy theory correlated inversely with the scale of the theory, with scale being measured in several dimensions.

> What is the degree of difficulty in executing the plot?
> How many people would be required to execute the plot and thus keep it a secret?
> How grand is the size of the objective or motive behind the plot?
> What is the geographic scope of the plot? What territories or realms does it encompass?
> What is the chronological sweep of the plot? How many years has it been pursued without exposure?
> What level of resources would be necessary to execute and conceal the plot?

The larger the value assigned for each question, the lower the probability for the plot as a whole. The scale of Biederbach's theory incorporated both large and small components, but it had linearity and focus. The grander overview was highly improbable in its entirety. But was it possible that some of the smaller pieces held greater validity?

Like the proverbial stopped clock that was inadvertently right twice a day, Biederbach might be accidentally right about some of the little things, and that his error was simply in overestimating the size of the matter, taking something real and making too much of it. If so, then what were the real parts, and what were the imagined parts?

One of the things Jommers had learned from studying the urban legends at Snopes.com was that many of the tales were seeded with particles of truth to make the story more palatable and more likely to be swallowed whole. So while blindly biting on the whole of a story was a blunder, reflexively rejecting something in its entirety committed the opposite and equivalent error. There was no substitute for the tedious labors of threshing and winnowing the grains of truth and casting the chaff to the breeze.

But such fact-sifting would involve more than just labor. Discovering the truth would require investigating the particulars of the theory, which would force Jommers to step outside the therapist's domain. Was that advisable? Was that prudent?

DAY ELEVEN

THE PIANO AND THE PAST

The killing was swift. The carp never saw it coming. But Jommers did.

He had been following the progress of GG's animated graffiti fable, looking out the window with binoculars and taking notes. The fable was coming along at a good clip.

Yesterday, the carp in the river had wondered what life was like on the land. He had then crawled out of the river to find out. The fish marveled at all the wondrous new sights, how much more interesting the land was compared to the monotonous and muddy vistas underwater. But he complained about mobility, how difficult and tiring it was to move about on land by flopping around with his fins. As he stopped to rest, he was spied on by the cat.

So when Jommers checked back in the morning, he was not surprised to see the cat make a meal of the carp. At this point, the rest of the fable appeared fairly predictable. But he intended to follow it through, curious about the inevitable moral at the end.

After catching up with the tale, he forced himself to take a quick run, even though the heat had not abated. On this run, he made it three-quarters of the way up German Hill, better than last time, but still not back to normal. He took it slow coming back but still had to stop for a minute, and while catching his breath, he heard an interesting sound off in the distance. It was a rapid, metallic clanging sound, somebody beating on iron or steel. It emanated from the direction of Eddie Lynxclaw's place. Jommers recalled the advice he'd given the man the day before and smiled at the distant noise, the sound of a man defying fear.

The satisfying sound briefly improved his outlook, made him more hopeful about the challenging morning session that lay ahead.

⌒

Ilona Voros entered the room with the comportment of a mediator. Serious, but cordial. Businesslike, but not brusque. Confident, but not confrontational. She initiated the hello handshake.

"I hope we can meet your goals today so that we can both move on from this and both get on with our work," she said.

"This is my work," Jommers said. "But I also hope we will make progress, and I'm optimistic we will."

She nodded and smiled politely, then sat down. She was smartly dressed, with ocean-blue dress slacks, a sky-blue blouse, and an understated turquoise pendant with matching understated turquoise earrings.

She stared directly at him, acknowledging that it was his game, yet with a posture of expectation that it would be over soon. Perhaps that was why she had arrived twenty minutes early for her 10:00 a.m. appointment.

"Before we begin," Jommers said, "I need to inform you, in case you've not yet been apprised, that HR has officially changed the nature of this assessment from post-critical incident review to occupational fitness review."

She closed her eyes and visibly slumped. The air of cordial confidence flew off like a startled bird and was replaced by a deflated countenance.

"He doesn't quit, does he?" she asked. "Like a terrier. I should have seen it."

"As far as I'm concerned, it changes nothing at my end," Jommers said. "I was already assessing your ability to return to work, I now have a different bureaucratic reason for doing so. It doesn't change what I do or how I do it. More importantly, it doesn't change my final decision."

"Oh, please. We both know how dependent you are on PD business. You're going to give them what they want, one way or the other. This whole thing of stretching it out to make it look legitimate is a charade. The determination is a foregone conclusion."

"You're wrong, and I'm both sorry and disappointed that you feel that way. I thought by this point we had built up a level of mutual trust. If your accusation were true, I would not be making such a concerted interest to understand you. If the outcome of this was preordained, I would just go through the motions with you. Acting lackadaisical and disinterested, asking a lot of rote questions with no follow-up. At some level, you surely must recognize that I care about your well-being and your career. I'm treating this matter with the utmost seriousness. You would know if I didn't, wouldn't you?"

"Sorry if I offended you, but I'm a little PO'd right now. Like I don't have a chance in hell. Should my attitude surprise you?"

"No. But what's going on out there is out there. In here, it's just me and you. And you have to trust me to be fair, or we don't have a prayer of getting anywhere."

"Fine, but you have to admit, this proves my point, that he is out to get me. I'm not crazy. He clearly wants me gone. So I'm kind of right about that, aren't I?"

"Let's say that you are. There's a big difference between being killed and being fired, don't you think? We ended the last session with you believing the former. Now then, if he indeed intended to kill you, he would hardly waste time trying to terminate your employment. In fact, pursuing this course of action would help implicate him, which means he would be doing the exact opposite. He would be praising your performance, pinning a medal on you. Making it seem like he's the last person in the world responsible for your death."

"You overthink it sometimes," she said. "You think logically, so you mistakenly assume other people do. In the real world, people don't act logically when acting emotionally. People who hate aren't clever enough to disguise it. Their actions in all areas are consistent with their hatred. And the chief hates me." She paused. "Like everyone else on the force."

"Why do you think he wants to be rid of you?"

"He has his reasons."

"Can you be more specific?"

"No," she said. "You have your rules of confidentiality, and so do I. I'm not going to discuss ongoing investigations with someone outside the department. Especially with someone in close contact with the person being investigated."

"So you're investigating the chief about something?"

"I'm not confirming that, though it would seem obvious to any casual observer."

"Okay," he said. "Let's move away from that for now and get on with the session."

"Fine."

"You mentioned goals earlier. An important goal for me, for this session, is to understand how and why you got into police work."

"Why does that matter?"

"People dream," he said. "They dream about their ideal mate, their ideal job, their ideal house, their ideal place to live. These dreams carry with them expectations. As a general rule, reality almost always falls short of those expectations. It is in that gap that the thistles of human discontent grow. And it's that discontent, that violation of expectation, that flays the spirit and causes so many emotional problems. Nowhere is that more true than in the field of law enforcement, where people enter motivated by optimistic idealism, to help humanity, only to find that their days consist of the routine corralling of lowlives. As one cop put it to me, he had hoped to be a knight, but ended up feeling like a garbage man. So, when I understand why someone became a cop, I understand a lot about why they're sitting in that chair."

"Well, I don't fit that construct at all," she said. "I never dreamed of police work. Never planned it. It was all serendipity."

"Can you elaborate?"

"I was in college on a prelaw track, double major in business administration and political science. I had a good friend who was majoring in criminal justice. She was the one who dreamed of being a cop. Right after we graduate, she tells me that Grayton PD is hiring for the first time in years and that she's going to take the prelim exam. She talks me into going with her for moral support. So I go. I take it. Just for the kick. Ironically, I get offered a spot in the next police academy class and she doesn't. I feel bad about it, but she urges me to go for it. She said it would be good experience. Be a cop for a couple of years, then proceed to law school. Then, when I graduate from law school, I'll have some experience that the others won't, an edge. It made sense at the time. So I did it."

"Interesting. What kind of lawyer had you wanted to be?"

"I dreamed of working in the U.S. Attorney's Office. I wanted to prosecute white-collar crime, government corruption in particular. So I guess that, even though I never made it there, I'm doing something conceptually related in Internal Affairs, going after people who abuse positions of authority."

"What inspired you to that original goal?"

"My dad," she said.

"How so?"

"He was one of those guys who always wanted to be involved and connected. You know, a player, a mover and a shaker, whatever the term is today. So he belonged to lots of associations and organizations, a lot of civic groups, too. It was in those civic groups that he learned a lot about how cities are run, the influences behind the scenes. He would complain about how certain business interests actually ran the city, developers in particular. Political decisions were made to serve the needs of the special interests rather than the people. Some of the influence was legal, you know, campaign donations and endorsements, but a lot of it was out-and-out bribery. He was disgusted with what he saw. He compared it with communist regimes."

"Really?"

"Yes. You see, he was a 56er, one of those who fled Hungary after the failed revolt and subsequent Soviet crackdown. He saw how communists operate. The thing that baffled him initially was how bureaucrats would so easily cooperate with the machinery of oppression, instead of throwing sand in the gears. He realized that it was all about self-interest. If you cooperated, lived the lie, life would be better for you than for the rest. A corrupt politician in a democracy has the same mentality, putting his own self-interest ahead of the people. So as far as Dad was concerned, corruption wasn't just a criminal thing, it was philosophical thing. A corrupt democratic government was only one short step away from a totalitarian government because the politicians and bureaucrats had already forsaken the will of the people. So he eventually withdrew from the civics arena and occupied himself with Hungarian cultural societies."

"I'm guessing your dad was well-to-do, based on what you said about his interests."

"Yes, he was," she said. "And I'm proud of how he made it, too."

"How did he make it?"

"Short version? He was very smart and an extraordinarily hard worker. He had been through a lot, seen a lot. He often said to me, don't try to make sense of life. Just work as hard as you can to make the best of whatever position you are in."

"He does sound smart. What's the long version?"

"Seriously? We could be here a while."

"I've got nowhere to go," he said. "And I like stories."

"It's not a happy story. Not in the beginning, anyway. He was still a boy in World War II. In forty-four, his parents were executed by the Arrow Cross Party for hiding Jews at a time when they were being deported to Auschwitz. He and an older sister went to live with an uncle. When the Red Army came, they were like enraged barbarians. The Czechs and Serbs no better. Women and young girls were raped and killed. Thousands of men executed. Men and children sent to slave labor camps. My father's sister was gang-raped by Soviet soldiers, then beaten to death. His uncle and aunt were later murdered by Serbs. He fled again, taking refuge with another relative. Honest to God, I don't understand how people live through such horrors without going insane."

"The survival instinct can often mitigate the psychological effects of tragedy," Jommers noted. "Unfortunately, the effect is often a temporary one that simply delays the emotional reaction. So paradoxically, the emotional problems often arise after the individual has secured safety and comfort."

"He never actually talked about it with me personally," she said. "I heard it all secondhand from Mom. And even she didn't tell me until I was grown up. Anyway, this other relative took Dad in. Sent him to university, where he eventually studied law. It was there he fell in with a group of like-minded students, talking quietly about reform. Then a friend of his, someone from that circle, was arrested by the AVO, the secret police. Everybody dreaded the AVO. They had a reputation for torture during interrogation and sending people off to labor camps without trial. And above all was their relentless recruitment of informers using threats and intimidation. My father suspected his friend had been turned after release. So he was careful for a while, then he eventually moved to a different area. But he sensed that he was being watched wherever he went. Not long after that came the uprising, which my father was part of. But then the Soviet Army came in and crushed the rebellion. Hope was gone, and he was in danger. Like many of them, he had no choice but to leave. He managed to sneak across the border to Austria. After some time in a refugee camp, he found his way here. Of course, his Hungarian education didn't count for much in a new country where he could barely speak the language. Just another unskilled immigrant. He used connections in the Hungarian community to get a job in a machine shop. He picked up skills very quickly. Like I said, he was a smart man, a curious man, always wondering how things work, why things are done a certain way. Eventually he started tinkering. You know there are people who invent end products, and there are people who invent the exotic parts that go into those products, and then there are people who invent the machines that make those exotic parts. Dad fell into the latter category. He's one of those people you never heard of who made a lot of money inventing things you never heard of. So, yes, there was money after that. I'm proud of what he accomplished. He came off the boat with nothing more than some clothes in a duffel bag."

"And your mother was proud, too."

"Oh, she was more than proud, she was ecstatic. Her family came over in the early thirties, as soon as they realized another war was brewing. They had lost a lot of family in World War I and its aftermath. They wanted no part of another war. They were well-off in Hungary, but as is often the case, emigration resets the game. You start over at the bottom. Mom was working in a bakery when Dad met her. Part of why they clicked was that they both had that sense of being dispossessed. Both born into affluence, but leading working-class lives. So when his earnings started to climb, she saw it as a restoration. She was determined that we would live as a refined, upper-class Hungarian family. We moved into a proper house in a proper neighborhood. We had fine furniture, Hungarian lace and embroidery, porcelain, crystal. The finest Tokaji wines . . ."

"And a fine piano."

"Oh, yes. An absolutely gorgeous 1936 Blüthner Grand, six-three long with mahogany case. Dad got a deal on it from an estate. The people had used it as a showpiece and hardly ever used it, so it was mint."

"And you had private lessons?"

"Yes."

"And dance classes for proper poise and posture."

"Yes."

"And private schools for a proper education."

"Yes," she said. "I was raised to be a proper princess. But I should add that I was expected to work hard at it. There wasn't much slack time when I was growing up. The money didn't diminish their old-world work ethic, the sense that one should always be busy with something."

"You know, I kind of had a feeling about your upbringing, the breeding as they call it."

"Is that so?"

"Yes," he said. "There's the way you carry yourself. Your posture. The way you sit upright in a chair without slouching. The way you dress. Your intelligence. The way you speak, clearly enunciating everything without slurring. Always pronouncing the *Gs* on progressive verb tenses. Your vocabulary. And even when you curse, it sounds awkward, accentuated for effect. It's clear that casual cursing is not part of your normal discourse."

"I didn't realize my tiara was so conspicuous."

"In an earlier time, it wouldn't be. But in this day and age, where pop culture has everyone racing to the lowest common denominator, classy people stick out. They can't help it. Which may be another reason you didn't fit right in when you joined the force."

"Oh?"

"Traditionally, police work is pursued by people from a nonprofessional background. It's a way of earning good money and social respect without needing to be a college-educated professional. It's the ticket out from wherever. It's unusual for someone with your background to go that route. People like you go on to law, medicine, accounting, science, teaching, and so on."

"Well, like I said . . ."

"Yes, I heard. Serendipity. But a strong woman like yourself doesn't typically get blown about by the zephyrs of serendipity. You had a clear goal in mind when you entered college. Something knocked you off course. Something hard. The fact that it knocked you into police work suggests a crime was involved. A crime against you or someone you were close to. And because in all our sessions, you've exhibited a strong victim mentality, I'm guessing it was against you. Am I right?"

"What if you were? What does it matter? I already know my past. It would only be revelation to you. Why dig it up?"

"So I am right," he said.

"It was long ago. It doesn't matter. The past is just a bunch of stuff that happened. That's all."

"No. You're wrong. The past coaches the present, for better and for worse. In some cases, the past can misguide us, even debilitate us, even many years after the fact. You know, when I see you look at the piano, it's almost like you're seeing a ghost there. The ghost of what you once were, or were meant to be. Tell me what you see."

"What is it with your type? Do you get some kind of sick kick out of making people relive painful experiences? Does it make you feel superior to reduce someone into some squirming, bleeding, crying thing? What is the point?"

"The point of revisiting the past is not to reopen wounds or relive the pain, but to understand how the past influences present behavior. And just to be clear, I'm not talking about closure, whatever the hell that is. There is no closure. There is no upside or silver lining. There's no grand meaning to be found in it. A horrible thing is simply a horrible thing, no more, no less. It will always be horrible. It will always be there. We can't undo the pain or remove the scars, but where the pain has distorted perception, we can still correct our vision. Where the pain has knocked us off course, we can correct our heading. You are a smart woman. You take good care of yourself. You have self-discipline. You value strength and self-control. You more than anyone should resent subjugation by external forces, and that includes the past. Something or someone put a drag line on you. You more than anyone should want to cast it off and live free."

"I don't understand what this has to do with my job."

"You're right, you don't understand, and you need to."

"This isn't fair. I shouldn't have to—this goes beyond occupational fitness."

"You're right, it does," he said. "I'm guilty, guilty of caring about your welfare. I got into this business to help people, and sometimes that nudges me over the boundaries of narrow bureaucratic objectives. But if you want me to back off, I will. You want to walk around this, that's fine. You want me to play it by the book and just focus on the standard line of inquiry, I can do that, and I promise you it will not affect the outcome of the assessment. So I'll leave it up to you. Which way do you want to go here?"

She put her head down and grabbed her knees with her hands. She took in a long deep breath, then let it out slowly. She rose up and walked sluggishly over to the piano and then sat down on the bench. She wiggled her fingers for a while, as if exercising them. Then finally, she began to play. It was a buoyant piece of music that lasted several minutes.

"I assume you recognize that," she said.

"No," he said. "I don't actually know anything about classical music. I heard that thing with the cannons once on the Fourth of July, but that's pretty much it."

"What I played was a piano arrangement of a song by Franz Schubert, 'Die Forelle,' 'The Trout.' One of mother's favorites. She would have these little tea parties for the ladies in her circle. And I would perform for them. I would dress up in my finest, like I was going to church on Easter. She would announce the pieces with a grand voice: And now our young Ilona will play the 'Venetian Gondola Song,' Opus 30, Number 6 by Felix Mendelssohn, from his *Songs without Words*."

She played a few bars of the piece, then stopped.

"They were always light classics, what the critics call the old warhorses. 'The Maiden's Prayer' by Badarzewska, Dvorak's Humoresque Number 7, things like that." She paused. "And now our young Ilona will play an arrangement of the famous minuet from Luigi Boccherini's Quintet for Strings in E major."

She played a few bars of that, too.

"They couldn't be too gloomy, but they couldn't be too raucous either. They had to be just right." She paused again. "And now our young Ilona will play an arrangement of the Emperor Waltz by Johann Strauss, Junior."

She played a bit of that.

"And, of course, they couldn't be too hard. I wasn't exactly a prodigy. I had the head and heart for music, just not the hands. I think that's why she always inserted the word 'young' in the introduction, even though my age was obvious. I think it was her way of saying please excuse the mistakes and mechanical playing. And now our young Ilona will play Ludwig van Beethoven's famous Bagatelle in A minor, 'Für Elise.'"

She then played a longer portion of that.

"It was all good fun for a while. But I grew weary of it as I grew older. Part of it was a new teacher they put on me. She pushed me to play more difficult pieces. A good Hungarian is expected to play Liszt, or at least make the attempt, especially the Hungarian Rhapsodies. But they are fiendishly difficult for amateur."

She played a little bit of one.

"That was part of the second one, the one everyone knows. People who don't play, they don't realize the physicality of playing difficult works. It's gymnastics from the elbow down. And it's not just about practice, it's about what nature gave you. There's a reason you don't have lunky gymnasts. For piano, your fingers need to be a certain length, your hand a certain breadth. You need fast-twitch muscles in them, not slow-twitch. Yet they need endurance, as well, to keep going and going without tiring or cramping. I could close my eyes and play the piece perfectly in my head. In there, in that imaginary place, my fingers are long and elegant, scurrying across the keys like a millipede on the run. Then I open my eyes and try to play it for real, and I see my short, stubby fingers galumphing along like an arthritic woodchuck. I can't tell you the frustration. At that point, the music stopped being my friend, and became my enemy. I remember Mother asking me when my piano instructor would have me tackle the Rhapsodies. Father beamed and announced: 'She will play them with fire, like Cziffra.' Mother shot back: 'No, she will play them with art, like Horowitz.' Here they were, debating which virtuoso I would emulate, when I didn't have a prayer of playing the pieces at all, even at a turtle tempo."

She started playing more of the piece, but then stopped after hitting a wrong note.

"Still can't." She sighed. "Going to college was a relief. No, an escape. Escape from a programmed life, from expectation. I was exploring new things, meeting new people. I was free to breathe. It was exhilarating. That first year,

God, it was the best year of my life. But it didn't last. A short while after I'd started first semester of sophomore year, I was jogging in the park nearby. It was a college town. You're not supposed to have to worry about assault in a god-damn college town." She turned and gave Jommers a sour look. "You've already figured this out. Do you need to hear all the gory details?"

"No."

"Well, that's good, because I don't have many. He came up behind me and started punching me in the head. I didn't realize what was happening. By the time I became conscious, it was all over. I never even saw his face. The bruises healed by the next break, so I chose not to tell my parents. I didn't want to disturb them. At least, that's what I told myself. But the truth? I was afraid they would blame me somehow—you know, leading the wild coed life."

"Did they ever find out?"

"No."

"Did you ever seek counseling? Talk to anyone?"

"No," she said. "I told my best friend, but that was it. And that's when I returned to my oldest friend."

"Who?"

"The music. The college had a good music school. They had recently built a new conservatory with modern practice rooms. So the practice rooms in the old building were going mostly unused. I could lock myself in a room with a piano and hide from the world, and I did so regularly. And I mastered every gloomy piece I could find, or rather that my short stubby fingers would let me play. Funeral marches and nocturnes. Anything dark or sad. It wasn't therapy so much as retroactive wailing. I had been robbed of my humanity. I felt like one of those worms that gets caught by the sun trying to cross the sidewalk, and it's stuck there, writhing, desiccating into nothingness. There's a Liszt piano ar-rangement for the second movement of Beethoven's Seventh Symphony. It just drips with pathos. To me, this piece suggests a soul leaving earth and turning around for one last look."

She played a portion of it.

"I played that one a lot. Later, I turned to a piano arrangement of the Pre-lude to Act 1 of Tristan und Isolde by Wagner. It doesn't work all that well for piano, all those pauses and held notes. But it worked for me emotionally. The tension in it. The restlessness. The way it searches for an elusive resolution."

She played some of that.

"I don't know how the hell any of this relates to police work."

"Does it?" he asked.

"No. Maybe. I don't know."

"But you suspect?"

"You want to make the obvious easy connection. That I went into police work solely because of the rape. That I could get even with the bad guys. It's more complicated than that. Life isn't like some physics equation, like bullet impact being a function of weight and velocity. I think I saw it as a way to get back my confidence and inner strength. To force myself out of hiding, to confront life. Then, I think my friend's advice had merit, also, that a few years on the street as a cop would provide valuable insights that would help later on as a federal prosecutor."

"Okay, that all makes sense. But then why did you stay? You were being harassed on a job you only intended to be temporary anyway. Why not stick with the plan and go to law school?"

"Again, these big decisions in life, it's not like buying a blender. So after a few years on the force, when I started thinking about the original plan, chaos descended. Mom was diagnosed with breast cancer. She knew something was there, but was in denial about it. By the time she faced up to it, it was too late to save her. It was a long, drawn-out, draining experience. Not long after that, communism in Eastern Europe started collapsing. And that was both good and bad for Hungary. The people were now free to run their own affairs, become a democracy again. But with the loss of Soviet subsidies, the country was desperate to increase exports to keep its economy from collapsing. As I mentioned, Dad was a player, involved in all the Hungarian associations. Since he was a successful businessman who understood the American economy, a Hungarian trade group approached him about a position to promote Hungarian goods here. He jumped at it. But there was a catch. Part of his duties included lobbying, which meant he had to move to D.C., which he did. So here I was, suddenly all alone. I was in my mid-twenties, but felt like an orphan. So you want to know why I stayed on the force with all the trouble that came with it. It was my new family. Even though it was a dysfunctional family, and even though I was a pariah, it was the only family I had left."

"I'm sensing you don't have a strong social support network," he said.

"I've got friends."

"What kind of friends?"

She laughed plaintively. "You've already guessed. If I meet a nice guy, he comes off as anemic and insipid to me. If I meet a strong, gregarious guy, I immediately suspect a macho beast within and I want to clobber it. When I meet women who aren't cops, they don't understand what I do, and why on earth I want to do it. The things they talk about seem trivial to me, almost silly. So where does that leave me? The chick cops club."

"Have you ever considered seeking counseling about the assault? Or considered joining a support group?"

"It was more than two decades ago."

"And yet it's still right there, like something on the back of the back of your hand."

"You can't possibly understand."

"You're right," he said. "I can't and never will. But I can refer you to someone who can. In therapy, like much of health care, there are generalists and specialists. In my opinion, you would benefit greatly from seeing a woman therapist I know who specializes in this area and who once was a victim herself. She has helped many women, and I think she can help you."

"Another hoop I have to jump through."

"No, you don't have to do this. It's not a requirement and won't affect my assessment either way. I'm merely strongly recommending it because I think it would help you lead a better life. But it's your call. I won't push it. And I won't mention again. Now then, there's one more thing I need to address with you, but I think you've been through enough today. I know this is short notice, but is there any chance you can come back tomorrow around the same time? I'd like to wrap this up."

"I'm still on leave, obviously," she said. "So it shouldn't be a problem."

"Good."

Before she left the room, she remarked matter-of-factly, "Your piano needs tuning."

"It's the humidity," he said. "It'll sound fine in October."

"No, it won't. Not without help."

LIGHTNING STRIKES

Jommers stayed in for lunch, first taking notes on the session with Voros, the most productive one thus far. He wondered if her doting parents had inadvertently left her ill-prepared for the roughness of the world. Perhaps by overcompensating for their own hardships, they primed her for indignation. She'd entered the world expecting the same royal treatment, and when the world knocked her around, she was outraged. How dare you treat me this way? I'm so special!

Ironic, Jommers thought. *She grows up with too much love, and Biederbach too little. And both end up at odds with the world.*

And with that, Jommers switched to planning his afternoon session with Patrolman Biederbach, where to take it. If you pushed that type too hard, attacked their distorted perspective, they withdrew. Shut down. Ceased listening.

On the other hand, showing too much respect for their views inadvertently legitimized them. You strengthened their position, while weakening your own hand.

The middle way required finesse.

Right on time, Biederbach walked into the room with his customary affectation of aplomb.

"If we're going to rehash the things we debated last night, I would prefer to do it outdoors," Biederbach said. "I don't think you take seriously the idea of maintaining a secure environment."

"We won't be addressing the specifics of your ideas here today," Jommers said. "Instead, we will poke around the soil from which they spring."

"I can't help but notice the binoculars by the window."

"Yes. I'm following the progress of a young graffiti artist who is doing an animation sequence."

"Yes. I saw her. And her cameras. All of which just happen to be in direct line of sight of this place, which I suppose you see as just another coincidence. You recall me warning you about new people in your environment, and that they won't be men dressed in black with sunglasses. It's a well-established tactic, the idea of doing something secret in plain sight by disguising your intentions. You remember the Glomar Explorer ruse, don't you?"

"I've talked with her," Jommers said. "Seems like an ordinary person for her age and place."

"The fact that she's brazenly doing something illegal in broad daylight, out in the open, without fear of arrest—what does that tell you?"

"It tells me we're in the Bends."

"Humph."

"Besides, she really is a good artist. That's tough to fake."

Biederbach took out a cigarette, but instead of lighting it immediately, waited while looking at his watch. He chewed viciously on a toothpick while waiting, making various grimaces while doing so. He was clearly trying Jommers's suggestion and clearly wanted Jommers to see it. The patient was attempting to please the therapist, and Jommers took that as a good sign.

"How's that working?" Jommers asked.

"It's early," Biederbach answered with a shrug.

"The important thing to remember is not to get discouraged if you backslide, which will happen at some point. I know this sounds trite, but it's true. One step backward for every two steps forward is still forward progress. It still gets you where you want to go."

"We'll see."

"So, did you do the homework I assigned?"

"You mean the thing with lightning and the ancients?"

"Yes," Jommers said. "That thing."

"The Hurrians believed thunder and lightning were tossed out by an angry deity dude named Teshub, who was also known as Tarhun by the Hittites. The Hindus blamed thunderbolts on the god Indra getting pissed off. The Slavs attributed it to Perun, who was very similar to the Norse god Thor. At least they both had the same tailor. The Chinese split the duties, thinking that thunder came from Lei Gong, but that lightning itself came from his assistant Dian Mu. Japanese mythology blamed the god Raijin. The Incas fingered Apocatequil as the culprit. The Australian Aborigines put it on Mamaragan. Then, of course, there's the ever-popular Zeus from Ancient Greece—how many more of these do you want?"

"Do you see any common thread?" Jommers asked.

"Well, most of them seem pretty irritable for one. And strangely, they also appear to be mostly cast as males. In my experience, if you get hit with an unprovoked blast of highly charged negative energy, I'm thinking female. But that's just me."

"You're missing the big picture."

"Which is?"

"They were all wrong," Jommers said. "They created imaginary personal entities to explain an impersonal, random meteorological hazard. They could not accept the fact that bad things happen without a reason, so they invented one. They created supernatural personalities as fickle and disturbed as their own. They imposed their own personality on nature."

"They may have been wrong in their attributions, but they were correct in their observations. Take your lightning, toss in your snakes and tigers, diseases, floods and famines. The world really was out to get them—and us. Mother Nature is a psycho killer and she's still on the loose."

"Yes, generally, but not personally. There was no individual intelligence deliberately targeting a specific individual with a lightning bolt. So why would someone be inclined to think there was?"

"Scary stories help keep the kids in line," Biederbach said. "You know, like if you make out in the car in the park, the hook man will get you."

"You're avoiding it."

"Look, beyond natural dangers, the ancients lived in a world of human-induced mayhem. They were far more likely to be conked, stabbed, slashed, poisoned, or strangled by another human than to be hit by lightning. So adding thunderbolt gods into the rogue's gallery was just a minor error of inclusion. They understood how the world works. It wasn't Zeus who made Socrates drink hemlock, it was the government. What's going on today had already started then. Big people with power crushing little people without it. Their capricious pantheon of gods was just a natural extension of their capricious pantheon of chieftains, governors and emperors. Just another upper layer of government. They got the flowchart wrong, but the gist of it right. Washington is just Olympus with classier threads and decent barbers. I know that's not what you want to hear, but that's the way it is."

"You're conflating political populism with existentialism," Jommers said.

"That's entirely possible, but I can't say for sure, since I don't know what the hell you just said."

"Thinking that a specific power is out to get you in particular makes you important enough to be got. Understand? Being a target is scary. But not being a target is scarier, because it suggests an apathetic and impersonal universe where you specifically don't matter. In other words, your peculiar view of the world is very similar to the ancients' view of the cosmos. It represents a search for meaning, a fear of meaninglessness, a dread of accepting the bumper sticker view of reality—shit happens. And while that phrase is crude and cruel, it's also right on the money. And there's exactly zero difference between a thunderbolt god and a conspiracy theory. They're both mythologies constructed to combat that dread. So you're right. Your rant is not what I wanted to hear, but it's what I needed to hear. The assignment didn't teach you, but it taught me. It showed me that your unique perspective resides in that part of the brain that holds beliefs, the castle tower that's unassailable by facts. To use your own analogy from the other day, I can no more talk you out of your perspective than I can talk the pope out of being Catholic. In other words, I don't see any point in our having any further discussions with you. I think we're done here."

"Now, hold on, don't get all bent and prickly. We're just jawing about thunder gods. You're too sensitive sometimes. I'm still here, aren't I? I'm still listening."

"Then listen to this. People with your issue are the hardest to help because they refuse to recognize they have a problem that needs solving. A depressed person knows they're depressed and wants to be cured of it. An anxious person knows they're anxious and wants to be free of it. But people with paranoid inclinations have difficulty accepting the diagnosis. Can you? If not, then anything else I have to say will just roll off you like rain sliding off a hot-waxed hatchback."

Jommers had essentially issued an ultimatum. Accept the diagnosis and start listening, or take a hike. He gambled that Biederbach respected him just enough to want his approval and that the desire for approval would hold him in range a little longer.

Biederbach fell silent, allowing the sounds of the shop to dominate the air space, with the whirring of the air tools and the hammering of the impact wrenches providing a cartoonish metaphor for the calculating going on inside Biederbach's head.

After about a half minute or so, he finally responded.

"Okay," Biederbach said. "Let's just say for the sake of argument that I can occasionally be slightly overenthusiastic in expressing my views. What would be your suggestions for kicking it back a notch? What would be the homework?"

"First of all, let me say that I understand the need to feel significant in a cold, impersonal world where every organization you deal with treats you like crap. The banks, the consumer product manufacturers, the health insurance companies and hospitals, the various government bureaucracies at all levels, the way they all make you spend twenty minutes going through an automated phone menu to finally get a person who tells you they have no intention of solving your problem. I understand that frustration and the resentment it breeds. The desire to strangle somebody. I understand how modern life tries to dehumanize us at every turn. I understand how that instills a sense of powerlessness and anger. I also understand the need to fight those feelings and keep them from overpowering our reason. We are all buffeted by those same forces. Yet different people respond to them differently. You can't change how the world treats you, only how you respond to that treatment. No matter what happens, you control your response to it. If you accept the premise of self-mastery, then they lose power over you. It's your choice whether you will let yourself be defined by external forces, or whether you will define yourself. You can't stop the world from treating you like crap, but it's your choice whether or not you feel like crap. And when you acquire that sense of self-mastery, you won't feel the need to battle dragons—you'll simply ignore them. As much as we feel abused today, our forefathers suffered much greater indignations, at the hands of both nature and oppressive aristocracies. Yet they endured. They remained strong. They held their heads up high. They had resilience. And that's the key, resilience."

"We could debate how much resilience is just fatalism, but go on."

"I understand that it's our natural inclination to search for meaning in life. But there are healthy and unhealthy ways of satisfying that search. We all want to feel significant, that our existence matters. Unfortunately, nature is not going to provide that. As you have accurately noted, nature doesn't care about you, but people do. And that's a two-way street, by the way. It's not just getting people to care about you, but also you caring about them. We value individualism in this society, and that's a good thing most of the time, but it can be taken too far. You become the outsider. And when you spend too much time as an outsider, you develop an outsider mentality, a feeling of rejection by default. You start to perceive hostility where none was intended, where none exists."

"I've got a lot of contacts."

"Yes, I'm sure you do, and your reference to them as contacts rather than friends speaks volumes. There's a difference between genuine social relationships where people know and care about each other and enabling, exploitive relationships where the parties simply use each other to reaffirm eccentric positions or theories. The latter is like two addicts helping each other score drugs. No one would consider that a healthy relationship. It you wanted to get off drugs, you would have to avoid people using drugs, and start hanging around people who don't use drugs. It's a critical step to getting clean and staying clean."

"So what, then? I join a bowling team and all the bad things in the world just go away? No more storms. No more lightning."

"No, the bad things don't go away," Jommers said. "But you process them differently, you respond to them differently when you live in a more welcoming social environment. It's the difference between living inside or outside. People who live inside worry less about lightning than people who live outside."

Biederbach paused a moment. "Remember that movie, *The Big Lebowski*?"

"I do. Great flick."

"Those guys were on a bowling team."

"Yes, they were."

"They were pretty messed up, too, if I recall."

Jommers laughed. "I'm not sure there's much utility in analyzing fictional characters, but if I were imprudent enough to do so, I would suggest that they were living on the edge and that their friendship was the one thing that kept them from going over that edge."

Biederbach paused and looked out the window for a few moments. "It's not as easy as you make it sound, this business of going inside."

"I know."

"There are social skills involved," Biederbach said. "Sometimes people forget those skills. Sometimes they were never taught those skills to begin with."

"That's true. And if you bought a guitar today, I wouldn't expect you to sound like Clapton tomorrow. These things will take time. But you have to begin. Nothing changes until you start. So, you mentioned homework. First off, I want you to make a list of things that interest you. Doesn't have to be things you've already done or looked into. Could be just something hanging around the back of your mind. Start your list with this phrase: someday I would like to—then see what comes out. Then we'll talk about it. See how you might leverage that list as an opportunity for increased social connections. Understand that there will be some experimentation and serendipity involved with that. You don't just click with the first person you meet. If you typically like only one out of twenty people you meet, then you're going to have to meet twenty new people to find one you like."

"It might be thirty or forty in my case."

"Whatever it takes. One more thing. You need to realize that you've maintained your current disposition for a long time now, and that in doing so you have developed a certain mental reflex, a conditioned response to interpreting events. You must try to change that response. Break the habit. Retrain your brain. Now you know the reflex I'm talking about. You hear an account of something, and you find yourself saying, yeah, right, here's what's really going on. And you need to recognize that moment, and you need to resist taking it where you habitually do. Resist the spin. So here's what I want you to do. The next time that moment arises, the next time you feel that urge to spin reality, you stop, and you say to yourself the following: there are no fingerprints on thunderbolts. Okay? That will be the hook that pulls you out of the vortex, pulls you back to this conversation, pulls you back to reality. I want you to say that every time you feel that familiar urge. There are no fingerprints on thunderbolts. It'll be hard at first, as hard as resisting the smokes. One happy talk from me ain't going to make it happen. But if you work at it, you can do it. Initially, you should write it out and tape it to your bathroom mirror. And let me also point out the obvious: none of this works if you don't change your inputs. If you continue to immerse yourself in materials that drag you into the vortex, you won't have a prayer of resisting it. So you need to change more than one habit at more than one level. And it's entirely in your hands. I can't follow you around. I won't know what you've done or what you're thinking. It's up to you. How do you want to live?"

Biederbach paused and looked out the window again, then, after a few moments, looked back.

"Remember that final scene in the movie, at the bar with Sam Elliot's character, and The Dude delivers his famous line . . ."

"Yeah," Jommers said.

"And the music playing in the background, Townes Van Zandt doing that acoustic cover of 'Dead Flowers' by the Stones."

"Yeah."

"Best end-of-movie song ever."

"Without a doubt. Without a doubt."

Toward the end of the work day, as Jommers was finishing up his notes, Claire Maroun wandered upstairs and slumped into one of the rockers.

"Hey."

"Hey."

"So, wacky red-haired piano lady was here again today," she noted.

"Yes, she was," he said.

"You must be some kind of magician."

"What do you mean?"

"Well, she goes from screaming, swearing, and playing the 'Beer Barrel Polka' one day to being nice and quiet and playing beautiful, classical music. You must have worked some kind of magic on her."

"Nope. No magic in this business. Just the same old chipping away at boulders. And sometimes a bigger piece comes off than you expected."

"So that means she's getting better," she said.

"She's in a different place today. But her journey is not over."

"I saw creepy smoke-fiend guy was here again, too."

"Yes."

"Something tells me he's got a long journey, too. Like, really, really long. Like, all the way down to Tierra del Fuego long."

"Everyone's journey is different," he said.

"And what about yours? How's that journey?"

"Increasingly interesting, but not yet perilous."

"So things are going okay."

"Yes, everything is fine."

"Speaking of journeys," she said, "let's go downstairs for minute. Want to show you something."

Jommers groaned, but obeyed. When they got to the bottom of the stairs, he saw his old Huffy black cruiser bicycle.

"Pete and I dug it out, cleaned it up, oiled it and tightened the chain, and put air in the tires," she said. "You're ready to go now. No excuses. Maybe this will get your blood flowing again."

"Thank you."

"Don't thank me. Just ride. Go on, ride."

"Okay, okay."

Again, he obeyed. He mounted it slowly and took off cautiously, having not ridden it in years. It took only about a quarter mile before his sense of mastery of the thing came back to him, after which he started to pedal faster and gain speed. He smiled after rediscovering the simple joy of riding a bike.

He had bought the Huffy at a garage sale when he was in college, so the bike was already old then, probably dating back to the '60s, but it was in good condition and he kept it that way. Like the other cruisers from that era, it had fat tires, fenders, single-speed drive, coaster brakes, and handlebar design that allowed you to sit upright. This particular one also had a rear rack and small wire basket attached to the front handlebars.

He had bought it long after such a bike had gone out of style, but still decades before buying something nerdy would be considered cool in the ironic hipster sense. Back then, dorky was just dorky. Period. So it took some social courage to ride it around campus. And when his college buddies first saw it, they howled with laughter and dubbed it the granny bike.

But the teasing didn't faze him at all. He already had one foot into the future thinking about all the exciting things he would accomplish with his career. College was an exhilarating time, his mind awakened, his mere childhood curiosity blossoming into adult reflection and cogitation. It was like springtime in his head, with new ideas popping up like daffodils in April. It was easy when young to imagine himself as a prolific author of illuminating papers and articles that would be cited by others for decades to come.

So riding the laughably outdated bicycle back then was in part a statement of a confidence and self-assurance. I know who I am and where I am going. Or maybe it was also it possible that it made another statement, that the granny bike was a soft-spoken rebuttal to the staccato roar of his old man's motorcycle, a defiant denial of risk-loving machismo. Perhaps. But then again, sometimes a cigar is just a cigar.

Pete and Claire had done a good job fixing up the bike; it rode just like it used to. He'd forgotten how much fun it was. But after about a half hour, he headed back. He wasn't tired, just hot and sweaty. So much so that the handlebar grips had become wet and slippery. He resolved to ride it every day—just as soon as it got a tad cooler.

When he got back to the shop, Pete and his crew had gone home. Claire, too. But there was a black Ford Explorer sitting in the lot. As he rode his bike over toward the driver's side, out stepped Augie Dallabaco.

Dallabaco surveyed the bike.

"It's you. It's totally you."

"By that you mean simple, sturdy, functional, no-nonsense, timeless, and true."

Dallabaco laughed. "We should go upstairs, it's getting pretty deep down here."

They walked up to the office and Jommers grabbed a couple of beers.

"So how's the red-haired bitch?" Dallabaco asked. "Word is she's been through here a few times already. Not a good sign. She messed up? More than usual, that is."

Jommers smiled but kept it cryptic, reverting to sphinx mode. "Well, I'm not sure who you're talking about, but if she was a patient of mine, I would not even acknowledge that, much less give you a status report."

"You know, you can only play that card so long. This is not a game. There's some serious shit going down here."

"I agree. It's not a game. And I agree it's serious. I also know that when it's all over, there will be any number of people poring over everything that happened. Looking into who did what to whom. Who said what to whom. And some of those curious people will have subpoena power. I would recommend that any-one interested in this matter exercise caution in what they do and say, as will I."

"Always the wall with you," Dallabaco said. "I thought we'd gotten past that, but I guess not. What's it going to take?"

"There are skittish people who might argue that possessing certain knowl-edge can be a curse because it makes you a target, that you should be careful what you want to know."

"Yeah, well, I don't do skittish, as you probably know. Whoever or whatever is behind all this, they're the ones who need to be worried about me, not vice versa. So why are you still giving me all this evasive bullshit? We were going to work together on this, remember? Or have you already blown it off?"

"Look, let's say for the sake of argument I knew who you were talking about, and that she was a patient, my objective would be psychological assessment, evaluating her emotional state. And if I told you all about her emotional state, it would provide nothing useful for you. I don't do operational debriefing, as you know from experience. Which means that I don't have any information of value to an investigation."

"You see, I'm not buying that. If someone is messed up about something that happened, you can't talk about the messed-up part without talking about the thing that did the messing up, right? I mean, if A causes B, how do you talk about B without bringing up A?"

"If I had a patient who was messed up, my first priority would be to see that they don't become even more messed up by someone harassing them or by making them a target."

"According to the buzz, HR has changed your mission for Big Red from critical incident review to occupational fitness evaluation. Lot of people find that interesting. I mean, she's always been a psycho bitch. That's nothing new. So why, all of a sudden, is Chief Scumbutt so eager to give her the boot? The speculation is that she has something on him, you know, being IA and all, and that he needs to get rid of her before she can use it. What would be your take?"

"My take?"

"Yeah."

"My take is that you came here to horse trade," Jommers said. "You have something you want to share with me, but you want something in return. And you're pissed off that I don't have anything to offer. So now you're debating whether to tell me anyway. You don't want your ego to suffer from giving me something for nothing, but on the other hand, if you tell me, maybe it shakes something loose, gets me in your corner. So you're conflicted. What's more important to you? Keeping the upper hand with me, or solving your mystery? What ever will you do?"

"Someone in your occupation should be encouraging cooperation, don't you think? Why do want an adversarial relationship with someone who's trying to solve the same problem you are?"

"It's possible that we're defining the problem differently, which means that we would arrive at different solutions. I'm not trying to be your adversary. I'm just doing my job the way I was trained to do it, the same way you were trained to do yours. The same loyalty you show for your team is the same loyalty I have for my patients. You would do anything to protect your people. I will do anything to protect mine. So in a way, we're not so different as you think. We're both abiding by our respective loyalties."

"You're good, Jommers, but not in a good way. You're good like the guy who sells you a flood car." Dallabaco gulped the rest of his beer. "Okay. Give me another beer so that I can save face and pretend I got something out of this."

Jommers obliged. Dallabaco swallowed half of it before talking again.

"I was talking to a buddy in Homicide today," Dallabaco said. "Talking about Eggers Court. Homicide does all the initial site work on shootings, regardless who's shooting at who. Guns, bullets, trajectories—that's their thing, okay? So we're talking about Eggers, but I can see he's also working on Crone Point. Tarburn. So he agrees to tell me something, so long as I keep it under my hat. It'll all come out in the final report anyway, but for now, nobody else knows. It has to stay secret. You have to agree."

"Agreed."

"Okay. So Homicide goes down to Crone Point, first light, morning after that bad night. They're surveying the area where Voros shot Tarburn. And they find a dead rat. And so you might ask, so what? Well, it's an interesting dead rat. It's an interesting dead rat because it had been shot twice, and fairly recently, too. As they're looking down at the rat, they see two more holes in the ground near it. So they move the rat and dig for the bullets that went through it into the ground. Then they dig in the other two holes and find a bullet in each."

"Tarburn fired four rounds that night," Jommers said.

"Correct. See? You do know shit, even though you pretend not to. So they do ballistics on all four slugs they took out of the ground, and all four are from Tarburn's gun. The only four shots he fired. The son of a bitch wasn't shooting at Voros. He was shooting at a fucking rat. Now why would he do that? He's being chased by another cop, and he stops to shoot a rat."

"It's consistent with a paranoid psychotic episode. Irrational fears. Being afraid of whatever is dominating your attention at the moment. In those brief few seconds, he would have been in something like a bubble, where nothing existed but him and the rat, which would have seemed like a monster. In his state of mind, the monster was the immediate threat, and Voros was a million miles away."

"So that doesn't upset you? That she shot him for no reason?"

"I didn't say it doesn't upset me, just that it doesn't surprise me. She had no way to know he was shooting a rat. She was chasing an armed man having a psychotic episode, chasing him into the darkness of Crone Point. She hears shots fired, sees muzzle flashes, she assumes the obvious. She returns fire. She did what she was supposed to do. What any other cop would have done. What you would have done."

"I assume you're making the obvious connections here," Dallabaco said. "Tarburn shooting a rat. The meth heads shooting at a tire store inflatable. The pissed-off ex-boyfriend on Juneberry shooting tropical fish. Give me something. You know you got something you can give me. Don't make me despise you."

Jommers thought about it a moment.

"Moe Balzer," Jommers said.

"Who the hell is that?"

"He's in IA. He was working with Voros that night. I talked to him in the hospital, but since he's not yet a patient of mine yet, technically I could tell you what he told me without violating any confidence."

"Why's he in the hospital?"

"Tarburn was hiding in the bridge house for the jackknife bridge at the end of Dills Run. Balzer walked up the stairs to it, stood outside the door, tried to talk Tarburn into coming out peacefully. Balzer had been told that if he used Tarburn's nickname, it would calm him down, make it seem like a friend was talking. But the exact opposite happened. Balzer used the nickname and Tarburn exploded out the door. The door hit Balzer and he went flying to the ground. I forget all the different bones he has broken, but it ain't a good number."

"What was the nickname?"

"Early Bear," Jommers said.

"Early Bear? I knew Tarburn for years. I never heard anybody call him that. The only guys that get nicknames are the Slavic guys with umpteen-syllable names you can't pronounce. So where the hell did Balzer get that?"

"Balzer said the word came down from the chief's office."

"Holy shit," Dallabaco said. "This really stinks now. You don't smell it?"

"I do. But I don't know what it means."

"Then I would think you would want to find out. A good man was killed last week because he shot a fucking rat. If that doesn't piss you off, if that doesn't move you to action, then you're the one who is fucking messed up." Dallabaco guzzled the rest of his beer, then raised his arm as if he were going to crush the empty can on the table, just like last time. But instead, he set it down lightly. Looking Jommers in the eye, he spoke with uncharacteristic lightness, but in a way that expressed intensity.

"It's time," Dallabaco said. "It's time."

As Dallabaco stood up to go, Jommers offered one more tidbit.

"I have reason to believe that Tarburn smoked a cigar in Scubbetts's office that day," Jommers said.

"Tarburn didn't smoke."

"Exactly."

"So you're telling me that whatever got into him, Scubbetts did it with a spiked cigar that he compelled Tarburn to smoke."

"Possibly. Possibly not. Sometimes a cigar is just a cigar."

Later that evening, over at Spreckels, Jommers found himself eavesdropping on a conversation between two women. One of them was debating whether she should see a therapist for her unstated problem.

"Some days I think, stop whining and just accept it, you know, that it's just part of life. Pretend it's not there and maybe it will just go away in time. But then other days I think, why? Why put up with something if you don't have to? If a therapist can help, then just do it, stop futzing around. But then if I do that, formalize it and all, then it becomes a thing, you know? A solid thing parked right there in the middle of your life, and every day you have to look at that thing and say, oh, yay, I'm a therapy patient now. Do I want that? On the other hand, if it's already part of me—crap. I wish I could just talk to that guy who fixed my arm. Orthopedic doctors are the best. They understand broken."

Jommers's eavesdropping was interrupted by Larry, who had wandered over with a psychological question.

"So, do you believe in all this multiple personality stuff?"

"They're now calling it dissociative identity disorder, and it's another one of those controversial topics within the field," Jommers said. "There are some who think it's overdiagnosed, and others who aren't convinced it even exists. Personally, I tend to side with the skeptics. There's a tendency in this field to occasionally succumb to fads and fashions in diagnoses, a tendency that damages our credibility. When you're a bit too eager to find something, you shouldn't be surprised when you do. Then there's the wild card of popular culture and its influence on a highly suggestible population. In the '50s, you get this huge spike in diagnoses of multiple personalities after the publication of the book *The Three Faces of Eve* and the later release of its film version. It happens again in the '70s with the publication of *Sybil* and the showing of a TV miniseries based on it. So now, whenever we see something unusual, we have to ask, did this arise independently or was it induced by popular culture? Thing is, if you were to make up a completely new disorder, something nonexistent, and then feature it in a popular TV show, within weeks there would be thousands of people claiming to have it. I'm curious why you ask. Are you not feeling yourself today?"

"I feel the same as always," Larry said, "which is to say, just as miserable today as yesterday. The reason I ask, there was this guy in here last night sitting at the bar. I bring him his beer and he says to me, real polite like, 'Excuse me, I just want to give you a heads-up. I suffer from multiple personality disorder. So you might find yourself talking to several different people in this seat over the course of the evening.' So I says to him back, 'Okay, that's fine. Just make sure each one leaves a separate tip.' Funny thing. After that, I don't hear a peep out of any one of them."

DAY TWELVE

The past is a double-edged sword that can either darken or illuminate one's life, so it must be wielded carefully. Some of the past offers precious wisdom, heirlooms to be treasured, while other parts burden with curses, chains, and clutter that are best discarded.

Jommers was reflecting on a moment in his boyhood, but it was anything but nostalgic. It was about a week after his father's death when young Karl overheard his mother talking to a relative on the phone:

"I'm surprised he wrecked the motorcycle. It was the only thing he ever loved. I could have paid for the funeral with it."

The comment fell like a cluster bomb, delivering multiple shocks. So many things in so few words. Her tone suggested that she felt more insulted than stricken. More defeated than sad. Yet Dad's death still took its toll on her. It wasn't so much the emotional assault of tragedy, but rather the slow siege of absence, needing to handle the burdens all alone.

Of course, Mom had never been exactly chipper to begin with. It was as though she had to gear up to play the role. Like an offstage actor anxiously taking a deep breath before running out and donning a big smile. At some point after the crash, she lost interest in the performance. Oh, she remained a good mother in the formal sense—caring, nurturing, attentive, dutiful—but she stopped trying to hide her dreamy disconsolation, her distant expression. There is an unspoken manner possessed by some in which they reveal their belief that they were meant for bigger and better things. The way they stare at certain pictures in magazines. The way they gawk at a house where a large party is being held. The way they hear laughter with annoyed envy. And she had these ways.

As years went by, she became less robust, more susceptible to colds. In the spring of Karl's senior year in high school, she had the misfortune of contracting pneumonia on top of the flu. Her defenses were vanquished just two weeks after Karl's eighteenth birthday.

And, of course, everybody whispered the obvious. She was just hanging on until the boy grew up, eking it out until he was old enough to take care of himself. He believed it, too, initially. How could he not? He'd watched the long ordeal firsthand.

And in the immediate aftermath, his thoughts about her counting the days while waiting to die made him cry all the harder over her passing. But nothing made him cry more than the day he found the poems. He had put off going through her things all summer long. It was just too painful. So he closed her bedroom door and avoided it. But when he started college in September, he couldn't resist any longer. It was time. Time to be a man about it. Coming home to that closed door was just too damn creepy anymore.

He braced himself and entered. He saw a notepad on the nightstand next to the bed and went to that first. He found two poems that represented her final thoughts.

The first:

> *I will eavesdrop in the trees*
> *As the murmuring insects gossip with the wind.*
> *I will stay tuned to the river's endless drum roll*
> *That ceaselessly introduces the high-wire feat*
> *Of living the next moment alive in full.*
> *Or maybe I'll wait till tomorrow*
> *When I feel better.*

The second:

> *Nature's ballroom is humming and thrumming.*
> *The air is electric. Glowing and vibrating.*
> *The music incites my soul riot.*
> *I yearn to croon and do the stomp.*
> *But ghosts can't dance.*

Another cluster bomb. First there was the sadness of the words themselves. Then the realization that he had observed her scribbling on notepads often over the years, and that she typically crumpled the paper afterwards and tossed it. He never much wondered what that was all about. Mom stuff, he assumed. Grocery lists. To-do lists. Budgets. It never occurred to him that she was pouring her soul into poems, then just throwing them away.

The final wound was ripped open by a jagged question: Had the boy spent too much time pondering his father's death and not enough time considering his mother's life? Could he have done more for her?

The unanswerable query remained a sore point for years, and he had learned to stop probing and poking at it. But he had a special reason for thinking about his mother this particular day. It was that matter of the big coincidence, the timing of her death.

Education and the passage of time helped him realize that one could not choose to die by infectious disease. And one so infected could not schedule the time of departure. There was no way she could have been just waiting to die until he turned eighteen.

In more than one of his college psychology classes, he'd learned how the power of observed conjunctions could sway the mind. Ground-level astrology polluting the well of reason. Ruby whacking Oswald, spawning a ludicrous conspiracy theory that would never die.

It was the notion of coincidence that loomed in his mind as he prepared for an early-morning session with Ilona Voros. He had recently learned of a significant coincidence in Voros's life, one that had almost certainly influenced her in a negative way. He had planned to tell her about it the day before, but chose to postpone it after hearing her other revelations. Too much for one day. She would hear it today instead. He wondered how she would take it, whether she would believe it, whether it would even matter to her. He wondered because he understood.

The rational side of him knew the timing of his mother's death was mere coincidence. But he was still a human being, with human emotions, and few things in life carried more emotional impact than the death of one's mother. So his rational side occasionally had to put down rebellions on the emotional side regarding the issue. Even now, decades later, revolts against reason still flared up and had to be quashed.

So he definitely understood the battle. But he also knew that, when it came to persuading others, understanding the battle was no guarantee of winning it.

He put down his notes and rubbed his forehead. He then walked over to the window and picked up the binoculars. GG was already out there, hard at work on her graffiti animation.

She had painted a crow, perched on a bridge, looking down at the river below, and was now filling in a thought bubble over the bird's head. "It looks so mysterious! I wonder what life is like in water world."

Jommers put down his binoculars and shook his head. "No, my friend," he muttered. "Do not wonder. Stay in your own world."

He jotted down the latest development in GG's fable, feeling pretty sure how this episode would end.

ILONA VOROS ARRIVED EARLY for her appointment, dressed smartly as always. She smiled and said good morning, but instead of sitting in a rocker, she walked right by Jommers and went over to the piano. She sat down and played for several minutes.

"Beautiful piece," Jommers said afterward.

"That was the first of the three '*Gymnopédies*' by Erik Satie, another war-horse that is hard to screw up, my favorite kind. Though I think most pianists play the Satie pieces slower than intended. It was meant to be music, not a soporific. Anyway, I thought we'd just get the whole piano thing out of the way first so we can move on. Though to what, I'm not sure. You pretty much peeled me raw last time, left me bare and shivering. What more is there to see? What's left to biopsy?"

She turned slightly on the bench to speak, but did not rise, intent on staying there, rather than joining him on the rockers. This annoyed him at first, having to speak across the room. But he let it slide. As a vehicle for exhibiting self-mastery, the piano seemed to fortify her. Its proximity created a zone of comfort and safety. Jommers figured that was a good place for her to be at the moment.

"Would you please say the first half of the alphabet for me?" he asked.

"Seriously?"

"Seriously."

She raised her eyebrows, but then complied with the request.

"Did you hear it?" he asked.

"Hear what?"

"The alphabet song . . . in your head."

"Of course, it's impossible not to."

She then turned back to the keyboard and played the melody.

"It's also used for 'Twinkle, Twinkle, Little Star,' as I'm sure you know," she said. "But it actually comes from an old French folk song for children titled '*Ah! Vous dirai-je, Maman.*' Mozart helped make the tune famous by composing a set of twelve variations on it."

She played again briefly.

"That was the first variation," she said.

"Very nice," he said. "Now then, you said it was impossible to say the alphabet without hearing that tune . . ."

"Yes."

"But what if you had to? What if for some reason, it was absolutely necessary to split them apart, rip the melody off the back of the alphabet, detach it completely—how would you do that?"

"Gosh," she said, "I think the only way you could do that would be to write a different alphabet melody, and then learn that."

"But that would be hard, wouldn't it? You would have say your ABCs with the new melody over and over and over until it replaced the old melody in your head."

"Yes," she said.

"A lot of practice, a lot of work to establish that new association."

"Yes," she said. "I assume you're going somewhere with this."

"I'm always going somewhere. The point is that intractable associations are not just a musical phenomenon. Our experiences are also subject to linkages. If you had a special place you went in summer as a child, a place you loved, a place where you always had fun, it would be impossible to think of that place and not smile. Conversely, I knew someone in college who was fond of a certain coffee liqueur, and one night she drank way too much of it and spent a long time puking her guts out. She could never drink it again. Couldn't smell it or even look at it without feeling nauseous. Now those are some of the obvious emotional associations with experiences. But there are trickier, less obvious associations. Sometimes so tricky we're not consciously aware of them. We tend to think that a particular memory is a singular thing, when in fact it's a compound assembly. There's the memory of experience itself, and then there's your interpretation of the experience, which includes the meaning you ascribe to it and your emotional response to it. After time, that interpretation becomes welded to the memory in the same way that 'Twinkle, Twinkle' is welded to ABCs. And this isn't necessarily a problem, unless of course the interpretation is faulty. When the interpretation of past experience is faulty, it then distorts your interpretation of future experiences. Think of your memories as Hollywood docudramas. They both are recreations of the actual experience. They both play fast and loose with the facts. And they both have spin, a message. Sometimes an internal docudrama is so flawed, its message so wrong, that it distorts your perception of reality. It screws up your life. When that happens, you have to rewrite the script to that docudrama, correct the errors, then play it over and over in your head until the corrected version erases the flawed version. You with me?"

"That's quite a buildup," she said. "You definitely have my attention."

"I hope so. You recall telling me about your house in Tudor Town, about the vandalism and what happened to your cat. And I asked you for the home's address and the time frame that you lived there."

"Yes."

"I have some buddies who work over there in the Third District, which encompasses that neighborhood. Had them go through old police reports from that time. Found out some interesting things. You know from your police experience and training that when a neighborhood sees a sudden spike in crime, it's often due a small but highly active group of players, sometimes even a single individual. Around the same time you were having problems at your house there, others in the neighborhood also reported problems, including vandalism, break-ins, and missing cats. Had you filed a report, which you obviously did not, you would have been aware of that. But you presumed the things happening to you were committed by colleagues out to persecute you, so you saw no point in reporting them. In reality, what happened was that a bad kid had just moved into the neighborhood, a teenage troublemaker who quickly recruited a slightly younger accomplice. Over the course of a few months, the two generated a mini crime wave. When they were eventually caught, the instigator, the older one, kept a tight lip, but the younger follower spilled everything hoping for leniency. The two of them were responsible for just about everything that happened in that short time frame, including the killing of several cats. The things that happened to your house, including the death of your cat, all of it was almost certainly done by these two kids. You were not being harassed at your home by cops. You assumed that you were because of the harassment at work. You reflexively connected the two. But you were wrong. You sold your lovely dream house for no reason."

She was unfazed by the revelation.

"I expected you to try something like this," she said. "You are, if nothing else, a clever man. And you may even mean well by it. But you must understand, in my job, people are lying to me all the time. And they do it confidently, without blinking or hesitation, just like you. So I'm not easily duped at this point. It was a nice try, though. Just the right amount of detail."

Jommers rose from his chair and walked over to his desk table. He picked up a folder full of papers, walked over and handed it to her.

"I had him make copies of reports from the files," he said. "Presumably, you know what Grayton police reports look like. And while I have many skills, the technical competence to produce forgeries is not among them."

As she thumbed through the file, the expression on her face changed from unflappable to unnerved. As if some invisible stopper had been pulled, her self-assured composure quickly drained away. After a couple of minutes, she threw the folder to the floor and lurched to her feet.

"No. No. This can't be. It just can't be. It can't. It's a trick. I don't know how you did it. But these can't be real. They can't. They just . . . they just . . ."

She marched over to the open window and gazed outward with folded arms and a troubled face, trying to process the disclosure.

Jommers tried to play a one-finger version of "Twinkle, Twinkle" on the piano. He got about seven notes into it before hitting a clinker. He went back to talking.

"You know," he said, "there was this guy named Charles Mackay, a Scottish historian, generated a lot of famous quotes, and my fave is this one: 'Of all the offspring of Time, Error is the most ancient, and is so old and familiar an acquaintance, that Truth, when discovered, comes upon most of us like an intruder, and meets an intruder's welcome.' Kind of hits the mark, doesn't it?"

She didn't answer. Just kept staring out the window with a faraway gaze, like someone on the bridge of a ship, trying to spy land. He chose not to interrupt her reverie. Sometimes you had to take your thumb off the reel and let them run a bit. Wait till they turn back your way before taking in line.

After several minutes, she turned around, but she stayed at the window, arms folded, her face sporting a skeptical, pouty look.

"Let's say, hypothetically, what you just said is legit, which it can't possibly be. And let's say, hypothetically, it has affected me, how I feel about things. It doesn't change what happened that Monday night. My internal emotional state does not change external reality."

Jommers sighed. "Sometimes I feel like I'm riding a carousel horse, and the faster it goes, the sooner I get nowhere. Okay, remember the example I gave you a while back, how if we both get our cars keyed today, how you and I will process that offense differently. And I emphasized the point—not everything that happens to you is about you. Let me say it again for good measure. Not everything that happens to you is about you."

"What does it matter what I think or feel about it?"

"It matters a lot, personally and professionally. How you interpret an experience affects your decision on how to respond to that experience in terms of actions. Your framing of the past steers your future. If you get your past wrong, you get your future wrong. That's how it matters to you personally. But it also matters on a professional level. You're a detective. Your job is to investigate. Separate facts from fictions, truths from lies. And then sort out all the facts to gauge which are pertinent, which are irrelevant. If you let emotions distort your judgment, you will get it wrong."

"You've seen my file. You know I have a superior record of arrests and convictions. I don't make many mistakes."

"You're making one now. Your take on what happened at Crone Point that night is just plain wrong."

"You weren't there. I was."

"Refresh my memory. Your view of that night. Little picture and big picture. What happened and why."

"Fine," she said. "The rundown. I was selected for a detail to pick up a 5122 and take him to the hospital psych ward. Since the guy was a cop, it had to be IA handling it. Department policy. Anytime a cop has to be taken into custody for any reason, it falls to IA. So we know he's a cop, we know he's probably armed. So that notches it up. It's not just some guy singing in the street or ranting about aliens. Balzer is assigned to go with me. We're told that the target is in the railroad bridge house at the end of Dills Run. We go there. It doesn't go well. Balzer ends up on the ground, and the individual we're after is on the run. I chase him over to Crone Point. I corner the individual there. He turns and shoots at me. I return fire. He misses. I don't. End of rundown."

"And your big-picture view of all this?"

"It was supposed to end differently," she said.

"Meaning?"

"He wasn't supposed to miss. I was the one meant to die."

"So in your view, Tarburn wasn't really psychotic that night—it was all an act, all part of a plot to get you."

"Correct."

"Okay, let's start with the who."

"Chief Scubbetts."

"And why does Chief Scubbetts want to kill you?"

"I was investigating a few things about him. I suppose you want to know."

"I won't lie and say I'm not curious, though officially I'm not supposed to inquire about ongoing investigations. So I'll leave it to your discretion."

"I don't have a problem telling you," she said. "Maybe it will help you believe me. You remember that incident with the comedian a few years back?"

"Vaguely."

"Okay. You know who Commander Mungfreud is? Second District?"

"Yes," he said.

"Some years ago, Mungfreud was running a security business on the side, which, at the time, was allowed. His angle was to employ only off-duty cops for jobs. He put a tagline on ads and business cards: If you're going to rent a cop, rent a real one. The agency was called True Blue Security. So anyway, there's this B-list comedian who graduated from Madison High and he's coming back home for his ten-year reunion. Maybe he's worried about the neighborhood, maybe he just wants to impress, whatever reason, he hires True Blue to provide a bodyguard for the evening. Now, the alumni who organized the reunion, they think it's a good idea to have some security presence, but they want it discreet. So they also contract with True Blue. So, you have this big party where there are two off-duty cops in plain clothes who don't know each other, both working for True Blue, but each with a different client. So, as the night wears on and the booze flows, the comedian gets too full of himself, gets a little rowdy. Somebody suggests he settle down a bit, which just jacks him up more. So the organizers ask their True Blue security guy to toss the comedian. When he attempts to do so, the comedian's True Blue bodyguard steps in to protect his client. So now you have two off-duty cops fighting each other, neither realizing the other is a cop. Eventually, one pulls out a gun, which panics the other, and just like that, you have an absurd situation where two Grayton cops are shooting at each other. In a tribute to the marksmanship of Grayton PD, nobody was hit, though there was a lot of ceiling tile damage."

"I remember that now," Jommers said. "It was a big news story for a couple of days."

"Right. So then city council jumps on it. Passed an ordinance forbidding any member of Grayton PD to be involved with private security work in any fashion. So that was the end of True Blue. Or so we thought. Instead of divesting the business, Mungfreud decides to hold on to it, but keep below the radar. He stops using Grayton cops and shifts to using off-duty cops from the burbs to get around the city ban, but his own personal involvement was still a violation. So he ran it from the sidelines, kept his name and face out of it, but it was still his. He was still managing the business. I caught wind of it. Put together a good case. I was excited. This was going to be a huge coup for me. I'd never taken down anybody that high up before."

"But he's still there."

"Yes, unfortunately. Captain Wifflyn, my superior at IA, took it to Scubbetts before acting. Chief said he'd handle it. Nothing happens. We follow up. Scubbetts says that Mungfreud was just acting as a silent investor, which was bull. But, you see, we're stuck with this stupid circular setup where the head of IA reports to the chief. We should be an independent agency, but that's another story. Anyway, Commander Mungfreud is told to sell the interest in the business. And because Mungfreud is so close to retirement, Scubbetts says he'll cut him some slack and not fire him. Well, that's bull, too. Scubbetts never cuts anybody any slack. And you don't need to make deals with commanders because they're not union. A chief can kick a commander anytime for any reason. So it all stinks to me. So I keep probing, but in a silent running mode, for obvious reasons. Eventually I hear things. What I hear stuns me. Scubbetts essentially blackmails Mungfreud. He demands a controlling interest in the security business in return for letting Mungfreud keep his job. When you look at the generous retirement package for commanders, you can see why Mungfreud caves. So now Scubbetts is running the show, and he's a lot smarter about it. He hires a slick salesman type to work as front man, be the face of the business. Guy named Wolf Stonecipher, who sold security and surveillance systems. So that dimension gets added to the business, along with other things. Scubbetts builds it up and dresses it up. It goes from bouncers and bodyguards to full-service security services and consulting, and Wolf Stonecipher is now calling on corporate accounts. But Scubbetts is good at keeping his fingerprints off the whole business, so I can't prove his involvement. If I could, Mayor Cheeks would have to fire him. Scubbetts knows that I know, and that it's only a matter of time before I can prove it."

"Interesting," Jommers said. "So that's why you think he wants to kill you. To keep his job and his business."

"There's more, if you want it."

"If you wish to transmit something you feel is important, I cannot help but receive it."

"What the hell, why not?" she said. "Educate you about the guy you do business with. There's the high-end hooker, too. Raven. Upscale call girl working out of a luxury condo on the lakefront. Somehow Raven catches his eye. He sets her up for a phony drug bust, then puts the screws to her. In return for regular freebies, he'll make the drug case go away and offer her protection from any other legal troubles. So what choice does she have? She confirms this to me with a nod and a whisper, but won't formally admit it or file a complaint. She's scared of him. She told me that she's not the first, and when the last one tried to get out of the arrangement, she disappeared. So I have to work on her, slowly build her trust. I think eventually she'll relent and help me nail him. Scubbetts probably has his suspicions about that, too."

"Even more interesting," he said. "And if all of that were true, you believe that's sufficient motive for the man to arrange a killing."

"Yes. Scubbetts has a passion for retribution. Strange things happen to people who cross him. Everyone knows that. And he likes indirect methods. It never looks deliberate or planned."

"Okay, let's say for the sake of argument that he does want to kill you, which I don't believe. How does he pull all this off? How does he get you and Tarburn in a dark place together?"

"Well, first he sets up the phony 5122 pickup and makes sure I get on the detail. I know for a fact that someone high up requested my presence on it."

"Okay, stop there for a second. Someone high up requests that you be on the Tarburn detail. Why do you automatically assume something nefarious? Is it not possible you were requested for more benign reasons? You mentioned you had a superior record. If I had a delicate situation, I might want it handled by someone with proven capabilities. Or maybe someone thought that a woman's voice might have a more calming effect on a psychotic male. Or maybe someone knew that you're in better physical condition than a lot of your colleagues, that you're a good choice where some running and chasing on foot might be involved."

"I know therapists are supposed to be all Pollyanna and everything, but this is ridiculous," she said.

"There would have to be an awful lot people involved this plot in addition to the chief. Your boss, Wifflyn. Your partner, Balzer, who ended up on the ground. Patrolman Biederbach, who was also briefly on the ground, forcing you to go it alone. They all agreed to participate in a murder plot because— why? The chief is such a nice guy? He gives them cigars?"

"Scubbetts is a master of manipulation and intimidation. You'd be surprised what he can force people to do."

"And the trigger man, Earl Tarburn. The chief just asks him out of the blue, hey, Tarburn, I need you to kill somebody. And Tarburn, a cop with a distinguished and unblemished record says, sure, Chief, no problem. Right?"

Voros frowned. "The two of them . . . there's some strange connection there. Haven't figured it out yet."

"Strange connection?"

"I know that Tarburn has had numerous closed-door meetings with Scubbetts. Not sure how much you understand hierarchical organization, but that's highly irregular. In formal hierarchies, you talk to the next layer up or down, your immediate supervisor and your immediate subordinate, if you have one. The guy at the top having intense regular private discussions with someone at the bottom—that just doesn't happen. That's something I still need to nail down."

"So you don't have all the answers yet."

"I have the ones that matter," she said.

Jommers walked back to his desk table and picked up the photo that Reverend Truly had brought, the one with Earl Tarburn showing his son how to operate a telescope. He took it over to Voros and showed her.

"Does this guy look like an assassin to you?"

Her face went through several phase changes as she looked at the picture. First was curiosity. Then, briefly, anxiety, as if she entertained the possibility she might be wrong—but only for a moment. The final phase was a pouty-faced defiance as she turned away from it.

"That means nothing," she said. "Most fathers love their sons, including gangsters, dictators, drug lords, murderers . . . do you think I can be so easily manipulated by something like that?"

"I had thought we were making progress," he said, "but now I don't know."

"Your definition of progress is different from mine."

"There was something else I wanted to tell you," Jommers said, "something I was in a moral quandary over, because I'd promised not to tell anyone. I was almost willing to break that promise with the hope and expectation that it would help you. Now I'm not so sure."

"Tell me what?"

"Hold on, I'm still thinking if it's even a good idea."

"What, damn it? What? If it concerns me, I need to know."

"Oh, it definitely concerns you," he said. "But you tend not to believe anything I say that contradicts your view of things. So I don't know if I should violate a confidence."

"What? What? Do you want some guarantee I believe it before you tell it? How can I do that when I haven't heard it?"

"You see, that's the thing. It's not about believing *it*, whatever *it* is. It's about believing me. If you honestly feel I would lie to you to suit my own purposes, after all the conversations we've had, then I don't know what we have to gain by talking any further. Do you trust me or not?"

"I don't know who to trust," she said. "I don't know whose side you're on. I'm in survival mode. Do you understand what that means, survival mode? You're a psychologist, I hope you would. Can you possibly stop trying to torment me always and start trying to help me? Isn't that what you're supposed to do?"

"Yes," he said. "But it's getting increasingly difficult to know how."

She groaned in exasperation and turned away from him, looking back out the window. He rubbed his forehead for a few moments in thought.

"Oh, what the hell," he said. "You'll find out anyway when Force Review releases its report. Just promise me you won't tell anyone I told you early."

"Fine. Yes. Fine."

"Okay, then. You presumably know how Homicide examines a shooting scene, looking for all the slugs, all the shells, charting trajectories, looking for relevant—"

"Yes, yes, yes. Get on with it!"

"Well, when they examined the scene at Crone Point, you know, where you shot Earl Tarburn . . ."

"Yes, damn it! I know where it happened!"

"They found something curious there. Specifically, a dead rat. It had been shot. Twice. They dug up the two slugs that had gone through it. Then they found two more slugs close by. The rat had been shot at four times, with two hits and two misses. And when they did ballistics on them, they found that all four slugs came from the gun of Earl Tarburn. And, as you know, he only fired four rounds that night. So, as it now turns out, Tarburn's shots weren't fired at you, but at a rat."

"No, no, no! That's stupid. You're lying again. Why would he shoot a rat? That makes no sense."

"As previously noted, the man was experiencing a psychotic episode, which is why you and your partner were dispatched to pick him up and get him to the hospital. By definition, people in that state of mind do not behave in rational fashion. There is no sense in their behavior."

"I don't believe this. No, I don't accept this."

"Again, as previously noted, this will all come out in the report from Force Review. So I would have nothing to gain by lying to you, as my lie would be soon exposed."

"Even if it were true, which it can't be, but even if . . . what possible benefit could be derived from telling me I shot a man for no reason? Why on earth would you tell me such a thing? How is that supposed to make me feel better?"

"I'm not trying to make you feel better. I'm trying to free you from a delusion."

"I'm not delusional!"

"On this particular issue, you are," he said. "I can't help but notice that whenever we talk about this, you avoid mentioning Tarburn's name. You call him the hit man, the 5122, the target, the whatever. This reluctance tells me that at some level, you're distressed that you had to take another man's life. And that's a good thing. It tells me you have some humanity in you. But your response to that pain is not a good thing. Rather than accept and deal with that pain, you have chosen to distance yourself from it. Bury it. And you've achieved that by dehumanizing Tarburn to make the act less troubling. Your inner moviemaker goes to work revising your inner docudrama. The goal of the revision is to rewrite the role for Earl Tarburn. Instead of a good man having an unexplained psychotic episode, a man in urgent need of medical assistance, you recast him as a cold-blooded assassin. With that recasting, there's no need to feel bad about killing him. You didn't kill a man, you killed an animal. You're a hero! Ah, now that feels much better now, doesn't it?"

"You're warping and twisting this, making up stories, that's what you do. You throw things at people to get them off-balance so that you can manipulate them, denigrate them. That's what you're really about. You don't help people, you're just in this for the bullying. You get off on it."

"You see," he said, "you just did it again. Rewrote my role. Dehumanized me, too. You going to shoot me, too?"

"Stop it! I did what I had to do. He was trying kill me."

"No, he wasn't."

"Yes, he was. For whatever reason, psycho or assassin, it doesn't matter. He was trying to kill me."

"No. He wasn't."

"I don't accept that. I'm not buying all these stories. They make no sense."

"Settle down and listen to me," he said. "Listen to me closely. You've been around guns a long while. You're familiar with the sight and sound of them. That night, the position and shape of the muzzle flashes in the dark, the sound propagation profile—on an intuitive level, they would have indicated directionality of fire. More importantly, for you to have struck him in the head and neck, you must have clearly seen his silhouette in the dark. Which means you would have seen his arms pointing downward, not upward at you. But you didn't have time to process all that. You were in pursuit. Adrenaline was pumping. Shots were fired. You reacted immediately and instinctively as you were trained to do. You were not at fault for what happened. But even in all the excitement, something discordant about it all would have lodged in part of your brain somewhere. And afterward, the incongruity bothered you down at some foggy level. So your inner moviemaker went to work producing the docudrama version, and in that version you cleaned it all up, removed the fog, corrected the sights and sounds so that Tarburn appeared to fire in the more logical direction, toward you. But for a brief flicker of a moment, you were vaguely aware that he was not shooting at you. You suspected it then, and you know it now."

Voros was troubled and confused, and her twisted face showed it. She paced unsteadily across the room, as if treading across marshy earth. After a few laps of this, she then sat down in a rocker. At first she hung her head down, then she leaned back and looked up at the twirling ceiling fan. The fan wobbled slightly when on, and there was a short length of chain hanging from the center of it, which, by pulling, would change the direction of fan rotation. The wobbling of the fan caused the chain to sway gently and rhythmically back and forth.

As she sat staring at the wagging chain, her eyes widened and her body slumped, as if she were putting herself into a trance, replaying the images from that night in her inner theater. Jommers chose not to interrupt, letting it play out in its own way.

After a few minutes of this passed, she spoke again, very weakly, moving minimally.

"It was so weird, so weird. I wasn't expecting that to happen. Not prepared at all. When I'm running after him, all I'm thinking is how big he is. How am I going to wrestle cuffs on him alone? I'm imagining him beating me to a pulp. It didn't even occur to me that there would be shooting. It was dark on the point, but the city lights were reflecting off the river, creating this sort of back glow, so, yeah, I could see his outline. So weird. You train by shooting at fake silhouettes. Then the one time you have to do it for real, it's a real silhouette. I was so surprised that he would shoot, I almost dropped my gun going for it. Then the reflexes took over. I aimed for center body mass, like you're supposed to. I got the centerline right, but in my panic, didn't control the kick, so the shots went high. First two missed. With the two hits, I wasn't trying for the head and neck—I lied about that—it's just where they went. I wouldn't have seen the rat in the weeds. I wouldn't have seen it after either. I was afraid to go near him. I don't mean afraid in the danger sense. I could tell he was dead. I was just afraid to look. I know I was supposed to go over. At the very least check his pulse. But everything that I was, my sense of being, just left me. I couldn't move my feet. I just stood there trembling in the darkness. I was so alone."

She paused.

"I couldn't grasp what happened. It was so fast. I felt detached, out of time, like my brain was behind me, still trying to catch up. Suddenly I realized I was soaking wet, and I panicked, because I couldn't remember how I got that way. I thought maybe I was hit and bleeding. But it was just sweat. It was hot and I'd been running. That's how disoriented I was—surprised by my own sweat. It felt like forever before help arrived. Forever."

She fell silent again, eyes still fixed on the wagging fan chain above her. After another minute or so, she slowly turned her face back toward Jommers.

"So what really happened that night?" she asked.

"We just went through what happened," he said.

"No," she said. "There's more. There's another layer. You're right. It wasn't about me. But it was about something. I know it. I feel it."

"No," he said. "There is no other layer. Stop trying to embed a larger meaning into it. There is none. Sometimes bad things happen randomly. There are six billion of us running around this planet. We're going to bump into each other in unpredictable ways. You need to stop looking for intention behind everything. Stop seeing patterns where none exist."

"You're trained to see certain things, and I'm trained to see other things. And you're not seeing what I'm seeing. This was no accident. There's way too many coincidences. Biederbach conveniently on the ground. But if it wasn't about me, then it had to be about him, Tarburn. And if that's the case, then it means that I'm the assassin, and that everything happened like it was supposed to."

"Stop it," he said. "Stop it right now. I won't let you replace one delusion with another."

"Everything happened according to Scubbetts's plan," she said. "The only question now is why. Why would Scubbetts want Tarburn gone? What were their private meetings about? How did Tarburn cross the chief?"

"Stop it! Listen to me. I talked to Tarburn that night. I'm the one who recommended Tarburn be taken to the hospital. I wanted him to be picked up in a safe place to minimize the danger to bystanders if something happened. I'm the one who directed him to the bridge house. So if there was a plot, then I have to be part of it. Do you honestly believe that?"

A look of shock came over her face.

"Oh my God!"

"What?"

"It just popped into my head for a second," she said. "The bridge house. That's where I saw him with it."

"Saw what?"

"The bag. He was carrying a dark blue kit bag as he took off running. Now I remember thinking at that moment—how strange. This guy is on the run but won't drop the bag. What's so important about the bag? Then, after everything happened, that little fact just flew out my mind—until now."

"Let it go," Jommers said.

"No," she said. "That's it! Whatever this is all about was in that bag. But where is it now? Did the scene team find it? Did he toss it in the river? Did he hide it? I have to know what was in that bag. How can I find out what was in that bag?"

Jommers groaned and put his face into his hands, shaking his head in exasperation. He'd won the battle but lost the war. He wanted to end the session, but still had something big on his agenda. Really big. He had to change the tack.

"You know," he said, "your partner, Balzer, is genuinely injured. Busted up in several places. He's in severe pain. He's facing months of disability and rehab. He may never work as a cop again. Have you even visited him?"

"We didn't get along."

"It doesn't matter," he said. "He was your partner. He's a human being and he's hurt bad. Visiting him is the human thing to do. It's the non-asshole thing to do."

"Oh, my. You're normally more reserved. Did I cause this?"

"Some days are more challenging than others, and I'm just a human, too."

"Am I the worst?"

"No. But you're up there."

"I'm sorry. If it helps, I do trust you."

"Wonderful," he said. "Thank you."

"So where does this go?"

"I want you to meet Becca Tarburn, widow Tarburn."

"What? Oh, no. I can't. When?"

"Now," he said.

"Now? You mean, right now?"

"She and her pastor are down at Landing Park, just a few minutes away. They're waiting for my call."

"Oh, no. You can't just spring that on me. I have no time to prepare."

"Prepare what? A script?"

"That's not fair."

"You don't have to do it. I'm giving you a choice. You can handle it, like the self-assured person you pretend to be, or you can run away from it."

"And that's not fair either, putting it that way."

"At the end of this day, your inner moviemaker will shoot the docudrama segment about the things that happened and how you handled them. How do you want your role to play? How do you want to carry this day in your head?"

She walked over to the table desk and picked up the photo of Tarburn and his son. She looked at it long and hard.

"Okay. Make the call."

⁓

BECCA TARBURN WORE a long, traditional collared gray dress with a modest ladies' hat of matching color. She also wore black dress shoes and carried a small black handbag that she clutched at waist level with both hands. She was solemn, prim and proper, as if heading off to Good Friday church services.

Introductions were polite, but cold and formal. There were no handshakes, only nods. Reverend Truly stood near the widow, but slightly behind, a balanced position that was supportive but not intrusive. This wasn't his show. Jommers detected a look of apprehension on Truly's face. The pastor had reluctantly agreed to the idea, but was not entirely comfortable with it.

In an unintended bit of symmetry, Voros also struck a stiff, formal pose, hands clasped in front, with Jommers standing a few steps behind her, supportive but not intrusive. It wasn't his show either. The moment belonged to the women.

"So, you're the one," Becca Tarburn said softly.

"Yes, ma'am," Voros answered.

"Let me be clear. I don't want your condolences. I don't want your justifications. I just want to know exactly what happened. I've been given vague overviews, but nobody has shown the courtesy to provide me any details. I have a right to know how my husband died."

"Yes, ma'am, you do."

"Then can you please tell me what happened?"

"I can tell you my part in it, which is all I know at the moment. I'm currently on administrative leave, which is standard department policy, so I'm not involved in the investigation of prior events and circumstances. I have no way to know what they've learned since."

"I'll take whatever I can get. Something is better than nothing."

Voros delivered a detailed, but official play-by-play recap of her role in the evening's events. Just the facts, dispassionately presented without interpretative commentary. She left out the part about the rat, which she was not supposed to know. She left out her suspicions of plots and omitted any mention of her own emotional reactions.

"Can you tell me if he suffered long?" the widow asked.

"No, ma'am. He perished instantly."

"So there were no last words."

"No, ma'am."

"Can you look me in the eye and swear that you had no other choice?"

"Yes, ma'am, I can."

"You realize that wasn't him. That wasn't my Earl you encountered that night. My Earl was an honest, upright, God-fearing man. For him to be that way . . . something must have taken hold of him, possessed him. I don't know what. Nobody seems to know."

"Yes, ma'am, that seems to be the case. And when I am allowed to return to duty, I promise to do whatever I can to make sense of this tragedy. And I know you don't want my condolences, but I cannot in good conscience refrain from offering them. I can't pretend to understand the depth of your grief. And there is nothing I can say to diminish it. But you should know that he was respected and revered by his peers, and his presence among them will be sorely missed."

"Thank you."

In turning to leave, Becca Tarburn stopped and leveled a stern gaze at Jommers. She didn't utter a word and didn't need to—her eyes did all the talking. Her sharp, silent stare queried: And what, Mr. Jommers, do you have for me? When will I learn what you know?

After the widow and the pastor departed, Voros sighed to Jommers.

"That didn't go well, did it?"

"I didn't expect it to go well," he answered. "There's no way it could have."

"Then what was the point?"

"At my end, the point was to see how you handled it. You had two choices. You could make it about yourself, act defensively, use the time to justify your actions, or you could make it about her, think about what would she want to hear. And I was pleased to see you chose the latter course. You respected her grief and anger. You exhibited sincere sympathy in measured fashion, devoid of artificial sentiments. And that contributes to my assessment."

"So where do we go from here?" she asked.

Jommers took a deep breath, then spoke in an even tone.

"I want you to listen to me carefully here," he said. "Emotional states generally cannot be described in black-and-white terms. It's not like saying your ankle is broken or your ankle is not broken. Mental health issues distribute across a spectrum. When we first talked, I was surprised and concerned over your lack of emotional response at having to shoot a fellow police officer. I was concerned that you might be suffering from an antisocial personality disorder. After subsequent discussions, I've come to understand the reasons for your response, and I no longer suspect that condition. However, in my judgment, you do you have significant emotional problems for which you should pursue professional counseling."

"I called her, the woman therapist you gave me. I made an appointment."

"Very good. I'm pleased to hear that. If you would mention to her my opinions, I think your experiences have contributed to a persecution complex and a propensity to falsely attribute malevolent human intention behind coincidences and random acts. However, if we canned everybody in the country who believed in some flavor of conspiracy theory, we would likely have a sixty-percent unemployment rate. So, while you do have problems that need addressing, in my professional opinion, the nature and severity of those problems are not of sufficient magnitude to interfere with the proper execution of your duties as specifically enumerated in your job description. Therefore, I intend to officially disagree with the HR recommendation that you should be terminated for psychological reasons."

"You're clearing me to go back to work."

"Yes, I am. But bear in mind you are only being cleared at my end of things. You're still on administrative leave until Force Review delivers its report, at which point it will be up to the chief and HR to decide whether and when to bring you back. If they're determined to fire you, they may try a straight-up performance review or some other angle that doesn't involve psychological assessment. So you're not out of the woods. They may still get rid of you, but they won't get any help from me in the process."

"Thank you."

"I'm just doing my job, trying to be fair as I can, which is exactly what I promised you at the outset. You won't need to come back here. But I would like to make one more recommendation to you. I'm going to give you the name of a woman who teaches cultural anthropology over at Grayton State who I think you should meet. She's a friend of mine, and she'll be happy to talk to you."

"You think I need courses in cultural anthropology?"

"No," he said. "She's a Muslim from Jordan, and she wears the traditional attire, including the hijab. You wouldn't believe the amount of harassment she has endured since 9/11. The threats. The daily insults. Yet she is the most serene person you will ever meet, lacking even a trace of bitterness. She has developed her own coping strategies, and I think you could learn a few things from her. But, it's up to you. Just a thought."

"Thanks."

"One last bit of advice," Jommers said. "Stay out of it."

"What do you mean?"

"You know what I mean. I can tell by your face. Now that you have a new theory about what happened, you're itching to investigate it. Don't do it. If you do any investigating while on admin leave, that would be a direct, unambiguous violation of department policy. You would be handing him the ammunition he needs to discharge you. You would destroy any hope of going back."

"I have friends," she said. "I'm not the only woman in Grayton PD, and not the only one who's been harassed. We have an informal network. We help out each other. There are things I can do remotely, indirectly."

"Don't do it. Resist the temptation. Take a vacation somewhere. Mackinac Island is nice this time of year. Or take a train ride in Canada. Or stay at home, read a book, learn some new piano works. Just stay out of it, for your own sake. Stay out of it."

"I'll be careful."

A discouraged Jommers shook his head with disapproval, then raised his hands in a gesture of resignation. "We're done here."

PEOPLE ARE STRANGE

Eavesdropping over lunch at Spreckels Tavern, Jommers heard two grit blasters talking about their work on the Charter Building near Public Square. They looked like they could use some blast cleaning themselves. During the course of their work, they had many opportunities to also blast pigeons and considered it a public service to do so. They were now arguing about who had blasted more of the birds and whether there should be a prize, one involving some quantity of beer.

At another table, two men were discussing lottery tickets.

"You sure you don't mind stopping on the way back?"

"Not at all. Happy to do it."

"Happy? I thought you didn't approve."

"Only for myself. But I'm all for you buying them."

"I don't get it."

"The lottery is basically a voluntary state tax that I choose not to pay. If everybody took my position, there would be a severe budget shortfall and they would then have to raise the mandatory taxes on everybody. So when you buy lottery tickets, you're helping to keep my taxes lower, and I thank you. Please buy as many as you can afford."

About then, Connor Quirke, the criminal defense attorney, sat down next to Jommers and ordered a beer.

"Counselor," Jommers said. "Good to see you. Though I must say you're looking a bit vexed."

"I'm in the middle of this murder trial, okay? The other day, I go down to the courthouse cafeteria to grab something quick. I see a woman down there who I recognize—she's on my jury. While eating her lunch, she's reading this tabloid. And I can see the headline. It's about someone finding a mini-mermaid in a tuna fish salad. And she isn't just reading the article, she's consuming it. She's drinking it in like a tall, cold one on the veranda. Eyes wide open, jaw dropping. Clearly believing every word of it. So it's been bugging the hell out of me. Having to sit there in court and look at her, listening so attentively, behaving so studiously, as if she's the most judicious person on earth. But I know her secret. And I know that in a few days I must make my closing argument to her and the others, and try to plant a reasonable doubt in the mind of someone who is neither reasonable nor capable of doubt."

"If I might suggest, resist the temptation to mention either mermaids or tuna fish in your closing argument. Also, avoid eye contact with her. She'll know that you know and resent you for it."

"And so this woman gets me thinking," Quirke said, "what about the rest of them? The other eleven, are they much better? Someone in your business, you probably know the statistics better than I do. It's damn scary. Half of Americans believe in ESP and more than a third say, yes, there are ghosts. Close to a third think we've been visited by extraterrestrials. Slightly less than a third accept the premise of astrology. And about a quarter believe in witches. I could go on . . ."

"No need."

"So, if my jury is a representative sample, there's a good chance that at least half or more live in the same place as the mermaid lady. So I've got this complex case, with a ton of complicated forensic evidence, dueling scientific experts attacking each other's credibility, and the jury that is charged with sorting this all out is likely half-bonkers."

"I feel your pain. Trust me, I do."

"So what do I do?" Quirke asked. "How do I get people who believe in ET and witches to believe my client is innocent?"

"From what I know of your clients, those propositions are of equivalent credibility."

"Objection! The observation is not relevant."

"Sustained."

"Understand," Quirke said, "it's not just about keeping this guy or that guy out of the cage, it's about keeping the system honest. Making them prove it every time, every day. But you need competent juries to make it work right. How does that happen when half of them dwell in ditzy world?"

"Your observations pose a larger question," Jommers said. "How do you make a democracy work right if half your electorate dwells in ditzy world?"

"Oh, thanks. When I came in, I was only moderately depressed. Now—how did it get this way? Isn't education supposed to be the antidote to all this crap?"

"In theory. And there are many who suggest that we should add mandatory courses in critical thinking and skepticism in high school and college."

"Sounds like a good idea to me."

"It probably couldn't hurt," Jommers said, "but that assumes the problem is intellectual and not psychological. Would knowing physics or math protect you from depression or anxiety? No. Then why would critical thinking protect you from delusional beliefs?"

"You ever served on a jury?"

"No. Been called up several times, but I always get bumped in selection by peremptory challenge."

"And it's the prosecutor who bumps you, right?"

"Yeah. Why is that?"

"Because you're smart, single, and childless. Smart people are more likely to question the prosecutor's evidence. Also, jurors with children are more worried about crime and, therefore, more eager to send defendants to jail."

"So, as with politics, it's like making sausage."

"Yes, and in a capital case, the sausage can be fatal."

⌒

PATROLMAN NEFFERS WAS A MAN who liked to talk. Unfortunately, the most recent thing he had to talk about was the fact that he had shot a man the evening before. He was off duty at the time, but it was still considered an official act and required a critical incident review by Jommers. Neffers was the last appointment Jommers had for the day.

Generally speaking, a man should be somewhat reflective, maybe pensive after shooting somebody, and Neffers exhibited that, only in a verbose and digressive manner. He was a fit, energetic fifty-nine-year-old man who started talking even before he sat down, launching into his commentary unbidden.

"Well, I'll tell you, I'm just glad it was pierogi day and the wife didn't have to see or hear any of it. She was still at the church. You see, the church we go to, St. Vlad's, sells pierogi on Fridays to help fund its programs, and they have this group of women that spends all day Thursday making all of it. And my wife is part of the group, and this was early evening, about seven or so, so some of the pierogi ladies were still there waiting for the last batch to cool and doing the after cleanup. And I don't mean to say it that way—the pierogi ladies—because it makes it sound like a chitchat club, which is what I once thought it was until one time I actually went there to watch and couldn't believe my eyes. They're all business about it and organized like it, too. Commercial appliances with big pots steaming away. They got the tables set up in different cells doing different things, and the different cells all feed into the final assembly cell, because, you know, they make six different kinds. I mean, I'll tell you, if Henry Ford was looking down on these ladies, he'd be weeping with pride, weeping with pride. And they're all intense like, working fast and hard. Like they're on a mission, which I suppose they are. And when the day is done, they've built a mountain of bagged pierogi, and not a small mountain, a big mountain. And I looked at it and said no way, no way they can possibly sell that much pierogi. That's just crazy. They must have gone batty to make that much. Then Friday comes. The cars start rolling in the drive late morning. First a slow trickle. Then it picks up early afternoon. By late afternoon it's a steady stream. By six o'clock, the mountain is gone. Every last one of them is gone. If I hadn't seen it with my own eyes, I wouldn't have believed it. It's the most amazing thing."

"Let's talk about the shooting," Jommers said.

"Oh, yeah, right. Well, like I said, just glad the wife wasn't home. I'm sitting there watching TV. Drinking a beer and eating pretzels. Well, not regular pretzels, the nugget kind that you can pop in your mouth whole without making a whole lot of crumbs because the wife, she doesn't like pretzel crumbs in the chair. It was a new kind, too. Honey mustard, I think. Anyway, I'm watching TV. It's one of those shows about fixing up old houses. I like to watch those because I live in an old house and it seems like I'm always having to fix something. And they're talking about toilets—toilet flanges, actually. How you know if there's a leak and whether it's the wax ring or the flange, and whether you should repair the flange or replace the flange, which is harder, but a better long-term solution. And I thought I noticed some water on the floor the other day, which I thought was just condensation dripping off the tank, but the more I think about it, it's probably a leak, so this is an issue I'm going to have to deal with soon."

"The shooting."

"Right, sorry. So right at the part where they're talking about why you should never caulk around the toilet because it will contain the leak and you'll never see it and know it's leaking—unless, of course, you just caulk the front and sides but leave the back uncaulked so that a leak could show up there—but, right at that point, I hear some pop, pop, pop, you know, coming from outside. Maybe five or six pops. And you want to think firecrackers, because firecracker people always got some left over from the Fourth and they'll use them up over the course of the summer, though usually more on the weekend rather than a weekday. But when you do what I do for a long time, your mind is subconsciously analyzing everything, because you know from experience there's a difference in the sequence, the spaces between the pops, a difference between random and deliberate, because a human can't duplicate random, even if you tried, because the deliberation is always there. You recognize it in the spacing. The sequence. And you just know. That was a gun. And so I know, in a second, right there in the middle of the caulk talk, I have to go. When you're a cop, on duty or off, you hear that sound, whatever it's about, it owns the next chunk of your life."

"Right."

"So I run into the bedroom and grab my service pistol, then run outside. I'm not even thinking at this point, just on autopilot. Instinctively, I'm heading across the street. Somebody was having a party. I already knew that from the music and the cars in the drive and on the street. So you kind of figure, if something bad's happening, that's likely the place. And there's a guy casually walking away from the house, toward the street, real casual, like he's headed out for a stroll. So my logical mind tells me this can't be the guy, he's too casual. Then he sees me. He raises his right arm. He's got a gun. This is the guy."

"And you're in range?" Jommers asked.

"I honestly don't remember how close I was. Just seeing the muzzle flash and realizing, okay, this is it, this is where it happens, right where you are. Right now. I drop into the crouch, both hands on my pistol, returning fire. And that's when I felt this kind of strange split. There was this one part of me acting instinctively, immediately in real time. Then there was this other me who was consciously thinking about what was happening. And the thinking me was about a few milliseconds behind the instinctive me. Just a few milliseconds. But that was enough to make it feel like it was two different me's. And the thinking me is trying to talk to the instinctive me, trying to get his attention. And the thinking me is saying, look, that guy you're shooting at, he's not going down, you haven't hit him, you're firing wild, and you just brought your gun with the mag that's in it, you didn't bring an extra, and so if he's still standing when you're empty, you're toast. You got to slow down. You got to merge. You got to think. You got to aim. You got to make the next ones count, because there aren't many next ones left. And this conversation is taking place in milliseconds. And it's just not possible to have a conversation in milliseconds, but that's just what's happening. And the message somehow gets through, because the next two shots hit, and the guy goes down, and it's a good thing, because those two were the last two."

"How did you feel immediately after that?" Jommers asked.

"Feel? How did I feel? I didn't feel anything right then. I'd left my feelings back in the easy chair. They were back in the house, still watching the toilet video. I was just numb. No, I take that back. There was one thing I felt. Something hard and dry in the back of my throat. It scared me because I didn't know what it was. Thought I was going to choke on it. I panicked, coughed it out as fast as I could. It was a couple of pretzel nuggets. I had tossed a couple in my mouth right before the pop-pop-pop, and just acted so fast I forgot to spit them out. It happened all so fast. I mean, from toilet caulking to shooting somebody, maybe less than a minute. It didn't even register with me what happened. I'm not sure it has yet."

"How do you feel now?"

"How do I feel now? I don't know. You don't want to have to shoot somebody. Most of us will go through our whole career without having to do it. I thought that's how it would go for me too, being so close and all. Been on the force thirty-four years. Never had to do it. But you do what you have to do. What you're trained to do. It's not something you want to do, but if you have no choice, well, then that's what you do. I don't feel bad for me, I feel bad for him."

"What do you mean?"

"He was a young man. It was all so pointless, so stupid. I found out after the fact what was going on. He knew the people going to the party, but he hadn't been invited. So he was indignant about it. So he showed up with a gun and started shooting the place up, just because he wasn't invited to a party. What the hell's the matter with people today? How do you justify shooting at people over something so trivial? Fortunately for them, and for me, he was a bad shot. A room full of people and only one person got hit—in the leg. But him, the shooter, he's dead. Surrendered the whole rest of his life over this. For what? For nothing. When I was starting out as a cop, a man got shot over one of three reasons: money, drugs, or women. That was it. Today, people get shot over nothing. And I don't get it, don't get what's going on. Every day you read a new story about some rage incident. You didn't see those stories thirty or forty years ago. Something's changed, and nobody is connecting the dots. It's like something is collapsing."

"How do you feel about taking some time off? You're going to be out at least a week or two with admin leave while Force Review does its work. But how do you feel about taking some vacation time after? Stay out longer. I see in your file you've accumulated a lot."

"Yeah, I know," Neffers said. "I'm not one of those guys saving it up for the big payout. I just been afraid to take it."

"Afraid?"

"Yeah. Afraid that if I step away from it, even for a little bit, I won't want to come back."

"Have you considered that option? You got your time in for full bennies. You can walk anytime you want."

"Yeah, I know," Neffers said. "Thing is, though, it's a one-way walk. You don't take it lightly."

"Have you thought about what you might do on the other side?"

"Oh, yeah. The wife and I bat that around all the time. She says I should have a plan before I do it. You don't go through a door without knowing what's on the other side, not if you can help it that is. Sounds like a cop herself sometimes."

"You have a plan?"

"Not an actual plan yet, just some leanings is all. I could see myself as a tour guide at some historical site, like Fort Sumter or Williamsburg, someplace like that where I would get to tell stories. Also, you know, after years of dealing with folks in trouble, it would be a nice change of pace to deal with folks having a good time. But it would have to be someplace that wasn't too hot and didn't have too many skeeters. Can't stand skeeters. Which reminds me, they're getting in the porch now because the finches poked holes in all the screens. They're after the threads. They try to pull them out to use as nesting material. That didn't happen in the old days, when they made screens out of metal instead of crappy fibers. Anyway, I figure I got to do something about that, so I go up to the home center to get some new screen material, and this woman up there was real helpful. She reminded me I would need new spline to install the screen in the frame and that I would need a spline tool if I didn't already have one. Showed me how it's done. And I thought about that afterwards, you know, that's not a bad way to spend your day, helping people get the stuff they need to get stuff done. Get to talk to different people every day. I think I could be happy doing that. Really could."

"I think you could, too," Jommers said.

"Well, anyway, they told me you were going to give me some kind of quiz or something."

"Well, let's just say I already gave it, and you passed."

"I don't mind taking it. I like seeing how things work. How other people do things."

"It's okay. You're good."

"I don't mind answering questions."

"No, really. You're good."

GHOST WOLF JOURNEY

As usual, Biederbach had keys to everything, except the one for unlocking the mysteries of his own mind. The place he opened this evening was a small brick building more than a century old. It had originally served as a fire engine house, then later as an armory for the city's militia. The structure had enjoyed multiple lives since those old days, including repair shop, factory, gym, boutique and restaurant. Now it had assumed its final role—another vacant ruin in the Bends.

What a shame, Jommers thought. It was gorgeous. Built in a Romanesque style, the three-story red brick building projected an immensity beyond its proportion through its design and use of materials. Massive stone arches framed the top of the two ground floor wagon portals and also the second-story windows. Brooding overhangs from the roof added to its dimensionality, but its most striking feature was a square turret rising above the right front corner. As with many old fire stations, the tower served as a lookout post for spotting fires in the distance.

He always was amazed how much art and expense was put into utilitarian architecture in the old days. Even the old power station in the Bends, which had once supplied juice for the streetcars, that structure too, was a thing of beauty. He lamented the passing of the old styles, their replacement by the sterile modern aesthetic, which just happened to coincide with cheap.

The two men noticed a stink to the place as soon as they entered, and when they got to the third floor, they found its source—an extensive soufflé of bat guano slow-cooked by stifling summer heat in an enclosed space. Both men pulled their shirts up over their noses.

"Ever wonder how bats shit while hanging upside down?" Biederbach asked.

"Never have," Jommers said. "But I'll be sure and ask Larry over at Spreckels. That sounds right up his alley."

They continued climbing stairs until they got up into the tower, which was open to air. It solved the stink problem, but did little to diminish the heat rising off the building. The view, however, was pleasant. The time of evening allowed them to catch the tail end of a colorful sunset. The apricot clouds hugging the horizon almost suggested a distant wildfire.

"My turn, right?" Biederbach asked.

"Yes, your turn."

"You questioned the authenticity of my sources last time. Just so you know, one of the key people I'm communicating with is an army vet who served in Iraq and also in the Gulf War. So he knows things."

"You mean that he identifies himself as an army vet online. In actuality, you don't know anything about him."

"He says he worked with RDECOM, which is the army's R and D. So he knows what goes on there. Said he was one of the first to test a new shoulder-mount weapon that fires thermobaric rounds, how one shot can turn a structure into rubble. The fact that he knows about such things that the general media has not yet written about. You can only find mention of this in obscure military journals."

"Define the word obscure in the age of Google," Jommers said.

"If you're going to knee-jerk reject everything I say, then what's the point of this?"

"Fine. Continue."

"So, recapping from last time, we got Zoran the ex-KGB chemist coming to America after the Soviet breakup, where he then works for the army, refining a fear-inducing chemical he developed, the Ghost Wolf formula, GW-37, but not for the reasons you might first suspect. You recall the Persian Gulf War in '91, which is happening right about the same time the chemist is approaching our government. Stormin' Norman launches Operation Desert Sabre. Everyone is shocked how fast it all goes down. Ground gained at lightning speed. Iraqi soldiers surrendering in droves. The Army's VII Corps captures some twenty-two thousand prisoners. It's all over in a hundred hours. So that was one of the issues the army examined in the aftermath—how do you control massive numbers of prisoners taken quickly? What if they riot, try to escape, or otherwise raise hell behind your lines?"

"So you're suggesting the army originally wanted this chemical to control prisoners in time of war?"

"Correct. Now, do you smell the Grayton connection yet?"

"I do not," Jommers said.

"Responsibility for guarding prisoners of war rests with the military police. Derle Scubbetts served in the Gulf War in '91 as a lieutenant colonel in command of an MP battalion, so he has firsthand knowledge of the issue. A year later, in '92, he gets assigned an MP training battalion at Fort Leonard Wood, Missouri. He becomes part of a project to explore new methods for controlling prisoners, which then evolves into a special unit. This unit gets sent to Aberdeen Proving Grounds to test experimental technologies, including GW-37. You see how this makes perfect sense. Put a little bit of the scare stuff in the prisoners' gruel, and they become afraid to escape, afraid of the guards. A small number of guards can then control a large number of prisoners. And this is how and where Scubbetts meets Zoran, during these tests. But eventually the army loses interest. Everyone imagines we're done with ground wars. Zoran is disappointed and starts thinking about possible civilian uses for his formula. Starts work on a paper for technical conference. Now skip to the late '90s, and Lieutenant Colonel Scubbetts, who has put his time in, is thinking about retiring from the army. At the same time, a city in Ohio is looking for a new police chief to impose order on a department with discipline issues. Cronyism is part of the problem, so the city looks for an outsider who can restore control. A military man who commanded an MP battalion fits the bill quite nicely."

"Okay," Jommers said. "Say I accept all that. It explains how Scubbetts gets to Grayton, but not the chemical. You don't exactly get to take stuff home as a souvenir."

"I'm getting to that, don't jump ahead," Biederbach said. "So now we advance to 2003. The Drawling Doofus is going after the mustachio that tried to blow up Daddy. And just like that, we're back in the ground war business. But for Kid Doofus, war isn't quite the piece of cake that Daddy's war was. The first part goes smooth, but then the insurgency starts, and that brings up the whole classic urban warfare problem. How do you destroy your enemy without taking out a whole mess of civilians? You just can't go in and blow the shit out of everything like in the good old days. You see, we have the greatest weapons systems in the world, but we have an Achilles heel—our reluctance to kill civilians. The bad guys can set off a car bomb that kills dozens of civilians in an instant, and the world yawns. But if we shoot a taxi driver who doesn't stop for a barricade, then everybody screams how we're the Great Satan. So the insurgency suddenly makes the army interested in GW-37 again. If this stuff works, then you can pacify the occupants of a building without having to kill everybody inside."

"I thought you said that the Soviets already proved that it works."

"Yes, under controlled conditions. The Soviet psychiatrists were directly injecting it into the dissidents in captivity. In a combat arena, you can't exactly ask your enemy to please roll up his sleeve. So you've got to develop delivery systems. Figure out the best way to aerosolize it, either as a solid powder or liquid vapor. How many parts per million in ambient air do you need for it to be effective? How much is too much? Is a cloud of it combustible if someone in it fires a weapon? This is the kind of stuff you need to nail down. The devil is in the details, as they say."

"Among other places."

"So the army reconnects with the people involved in the original experiments. Zoran gets a call. He's told to withdraw the conference paper and keep quiet about the formula. Scubbetts gets a call, too. And with him they get a twofer. Not only is he familiar with the chemical and the original experiments, he's now in a position to help test it. Because if you're going to terrify your enemy, you need to know what he'll be afraid of. If he's afraid to die, he'll surrender. If he's afraid of capture, he'll fight to the death. You can't test that emotional response in a lab. You have to test it in the real world. Scubbetts is in a perfect position to do that. As a police chief, he can secretly test it on criminals in real situations and report back. Even better, the gas man on SWAT is an ex-army man and Gulf War vet who's ready to serve his country again in different fashion."

"Tarburn," Jommers said.

"Correct," Biederbach said. "A good man whose hierarchy of loyalty will place service to country over adherence to municipal ordinances and PD protocol. He believes his actions are patriotic at first. And that's how we got the disaster at Eggers Court. GW-37 makes the meth heads afraid of a tire store inflatable. They then shoot at it and inadvertently kill bystanders. And this happens because the people behind this experiment haven't yet figured out how to control the front-end part."

"Which is?"

"Implanting the object of fear," Biederbach said. "If you chemically induce fear into someone without first implanting an object for that fear, they will latch on to the first thing they see. In the case of Eggers Court, it was an inflatable mascot bobbing over a tire store. In the Juneberry Jumper case, it was weird fish in an aquarium. If you want to control people, it's not enough to make them afraid, you have to provide them something specific to fear. Implanting the object of fear must come first."

"Okay," Jommers said, "let's just say for the moment that all that is true. I'm not yet seeing anything very nefarious here. A police chief is going to test something on scumbag criminals that will ultimately help save lives of American soldiers in the field. Why should that bother me?"

"I'm not finished yet."

"Sorry."

"It should concern you because during all the high-level discussions, Homeland Security gets wind of the chemical, because they're tapped into all the intelligence services, even military. And Homeland Security, under the auspices of the war on terror, will be the vehicle by which the government federalizes municipal police departments and county sheriff departments."

"I was wondering when you'd get back to that."

"The test data that Scubbetts gathers on the effects of the chemical will be fed back to both army and Homeland Security. And they will use that information in the final formulation of their plan to subsume local law enforcement in the near future—Operation Cobalt Quell, which I mentioned previously."

"You see, this is where you lose me," Jommers said. "Up to this point, what you said almost sounded logical. Almost. But now, it's like you're jumping the tracks. So you still believe that this fear-inducing chemical will be used on cops who resist federal takeover?"

"Well, I've scaled that back a bit."

"Oh?"

"I don't think it will be broadly used on large numbers of people. Delivery and implementation without discovery would be too difficult. I think now that the chemical will be selectively used on particular influential individuals to get them to fall in line. Used in a smaller, private environment."

"Explain."

"You assemble a city's mayor, city council members, police chief and police commanders, police union officials, newspaper editors, civic leaders, you get them in a room together to explain your plans and why they are necessary. And while they're listening to your presentation, then you secretly expose them to the chemical. The presentation tells them what they should fear, the chemical covertly makes them actually afraid. A one-two punch. They fall in line, get on board with whatever you're spouting. And when the population of a city sees its authority figures and movers and shakers all embracing something, then everybody else buys it. It's a more efficient way of getting it done."

"And Tarburn? He's okay with the feds taking over police?"

"He doesn't know the endgame," Biederbach said. "They sold him with the first part, while withholding the second part. They told him that the experiment would save lives of soldiers, and as a former soldier himself, he was all for it. Another opportunity to serve his country. Then somehow he got wind of the second part—the plan to federalize the police. He threatened to leak it. They needed to eliminate that threat, and being a bunch of cold, calculating bastards, they chose to take him out in a way that would give them more data. They exposed him to the chemical so he would go crazy with fear and get himself killed, which he did. And now they have more information on how it affects a particular person of known personality."

"Interesting," Jommers said.

"That's all you have to say? Interesting? You should be totally blown away by this. Outraged. Ready to revolt."

"I'm going to be honest with you. I've got mixed feelings here. I'm happy that you've reduced the scope of your conspiracy theory a little bit in terms of how many people would be exposed to this chemical. It gives me hope that we can shrink it still further. On the other hand, I'm troubled by the ease at which you accept an incredible proposition, namely, that the U.S. Army, the Department of Homeland Security, and the chief of police had together conspired to murder Patrolman Earl Tarburn in order to conceal a scheme by which the federal government takes over city police departments."

"It is what it is. I didn't build it. I'm just giving you the tour."

"It's a bizarre explanation of events," Jommers said.

"The problem is not with my explanation, but your complacency. You're placing trust in institutions that have repeatedly demonstrated that they do not deserve such trust. They're conning you every minute of every day. I'm totally dumbfounded why people aren't storming the barricades. We are now worse than sheep—we're sheep taking orders from wolves who no longer bother to wear disguises. I don't even have a name for it."

⌒

JOMMERS WALKED AWAY from the meeting trying to mitigate his discouragement. He was making progress with Biederbach in their therapy sessions, but those daylight discussions were not penetrating the dark evening rants. Positively, Biederbach admitted he had problems. Negatively, he refused to link those problems to his worldview.

Jommers cautioned himself about unreasonable expectations. He'd only known Biederbach for less than two weeks. It was not realistic to expect that a patient's irrational fears could be magically dispelled with a few waves of the therapist's wand. The proper model was not wizard, but personal trainer at a health club, where progress was achieved incrementally. But trainers and therapists shared a common necessity—success was contingent upon the client continuing to show up.

A larger concern for Jommers was the number of years and emotional intensity that Biederbach had invested in his worldview, which raised the issue of loss aversion theory. In economics it's known as the sunk cost fallacy, where someone irrationally throws good money after bad because of an inherent reluctance to waste unrecoverable costs. As loss aversion, it has broader application to relationships, careers, and ideologies. People can't bear to see their emotional investment wasted. They need to walk away, but can't.

And given that people derive meaning from their relationships, careers, and ideologies, loss aversion must also be considered from an existential perspective. To jettison commitments negates the meaning once found in them. It deletes a piece of personal history by rendering it pointless. It is, in a sense, an amputation. Seen in that light, it is amazing that people can change at all.

DAY THIRTEEN

FOILING A GAS ATTACK

Things did not go well for the crow, just as Jommers had expected. In the graffiti fable's progress over the course of the last day, the crow had wondered about water world, then dove into the river to investigate. Underwater, he complained about not being able to see anything and that the dirty water stung his eyes. He griped that his wings were not well suited for swimming. He also grumbled about the inconvenience of being unable to breathe. So he flopped his way to shore. With his eyes blinded by polluted water, he could not see the cat waiting to pounce. His wings were too wet to fly anyway. Chomp, chomp. The final scene of the episode was the smiling cat spitting a feather out his mouth.

As it was Saturday, there were no appointments and no noise in the shop below. It was a good day for Jommers to catch up on chores, maybe relax some. More importantly, it was a good day to set aside the tragedy at Crone Point and all the characters who were haunting his thoughts. Unfortunately, the replay in his head was not a TV show that could be flicked off. And the early phone call made it harder.

"Good morning, Chief. Was not expecting to hear from you."

"I'm on my way in to the station," Scubbetts said, "but I'm going to stop over your place first. Some things we need to discuss. Called to make sure you're present."

"Present."

In preparation for the chief's visit, Jommers grabbed a particular old magazine from a file cabinet, opened it to a certain feature story, and then laid it out on his desk table. The story was about people who abandon houses in foreclosure and leave their pets behind to starve to death. The article contained graphic, heartrending photos of emaciated dogs and cats. Heartrending, that is, for a normal person.

His intent was to covertly test Scubbetts for an aspect of sociopathy—insensitivity and lack of emotion. There were more formal and established methods for such inquiry, but impossible to perform without consent of the subject.

To further disguise the test, Jommers grabbed some magazines from his waiting area, placing them into two piles on either side of the open magazine. He would then claim to be sorting out the old magazines while happening to come across this article.

He already knew how it would go, but he was hoping it might trigger something revealing, an insight into the chief's oddness. Now that Voros suggested that Scubbetts had orchestrated the death of Earl Tarburn, the need to comprehend the chief's mind seemed more urgent.

Scubbetts shared many of the antisocial traits of sociopaths, but Jommers had always found ways to dismiss them. The chief spent a career as an officer in the military, where there are different traditions of social interaction with perceived subordinates. Scubbetts was also an outsider in a new environment where those around him resented his presence. He'd been brought in to impose discipline and order on an unruly department, efforts which disgruntled nearly everybody. He was an isolated man who needed to establish his authority in short order. On top of all that, he had been raised in the boonies by relatives who didn't want him, a situation not likely to confer social graces. Manners did not necessarily reveal morals.

These were the excuses Jommers used to justify Scubbetts's strange and often belligerent behavior. But lately, Jommers had to admit, the excuses were wearing thin. There was just something not right about this guy.

Still, even if he was a sociopath, that would not make him a killer. The vast majority of sociopaths are nonviolent. Instead of assaulting with deadly weapons, they injure with more mundane devices: lying, cheating, stealing, conning, betraying, slandering, verbal abuse, manipulation and exploitation, anger, meanness, hostile driving, boorish behavior, and so forth. The threat they posed was not in a dagger to the heart, but rather in the millions of small but bleeding cuts they collectively inflicted on the social body as a whole. If Scubbetts was the violent, dangerous type of sociopath, then Jommers would need more evidence of it, evidence he had no way of obtaining.

After arranging the magazines on his desk table, Jommers then put on some blues, knowing that Scubbetts despised the music. Perhaps it might shorten the length of the visit. At the very least it would annoy him.

Jommers wondered what music the chief liked, if any. Some researchers theorized that sociopaths were unable to appreciate art or music on an emotional level. Even if true, other neuroscience researchers had found that music could be appreciated on a purely physiological level, that it could stimulate pleasure centers in the brain in the same fashion as sex, food, and drugs. Getting high on music. The famous poem "The Lost Chord" may well have been referring to this phenomenon.

So, what music might have instilled euphoria into a young Derle Scubbetts, a boy raised on a poor chicken farm and headed towards a military career? Mountain banjo music? The famous march from the movie *Bridge on the River Kwai*? Or maybe "Yakety Sax" by Boots Randolph? The young man would probably have preferred instrumental music to avoid dealing with the emotional content of romantic lyrics.

Sociopaths typically craved stimulation, hence their love of risk and conflict. What music might Scubbetts have found stimulating? Fast polkas? Sousa marches? "Wipe Out" by the Surfaris?

On the other hand, sociopaths often experiment with pain when they are young, and Jommers had noticed some old, straight line scars on Scubbetts's arms, suggestive of self-cutting in his younger days. So maybe boy Scubbetts had listened to music so awful that it was painful. Like maybe Brian Hyland's "Itsy Bitsy Teeny Weeny Yellow Polka Dot Bikini," or anything by Alvin and the Chipmunks.

When Scubbetts finally arrived, he strutted into the room, contemptuously surveyed the surroundings, then ceremoniously lighted one of his big black cigars. This was his standard manner of seizing the space.

"Still listening to that cotton-picking music, I see," Scubbetts said.

"It's relaxing. It is Saturday."

"I find it too dark for my tastes, if you know what I mean."

"And what kind of music do you listen to, Chief?"

Scubbetts shot Jommers an indignant look. People in authority asked questions, they didn't answer them. But after a few moments, he did anyway.

"I like 'Baby Elephant Walk,' the Lawrence Welk version. It's all I listen to."

Jommers smiled politely without comment. It was, of course, absurd to think that a man would listen to only one song his whole life, and that one in particular. But Scubbetts was a weird man who said weird things, sometimes obliviously, sometimes deliberately to gauge the effect, like someone throwing a rock in a pond to see what it stirs up. Jommers ignored it and moved on.

"I was cleaning up the waiting area before," Jommers said. "I made a promise to myself I'd never have more old magazines out here than my dentist, and I think I broke it. As I was going through them, I found this disturbing story about people abandoning their pets in foreclosed houses."

Jommers opened the magazine to a picture of a pitiful-looking, emaciated dog, just barely alive, then turned the image toward Scubbetts's direction. The chief remained impassive.

"You know they eat dog in Asia," Scubbetts said. "You can go to the markets there and see skinned puppies hanging on hooks in a row. If it were legal here, then you wouldn't see people abandoning dogs. They could sell them for cash to the market. We could empty the dog pound tomorrow."

"Interesting observation," Jommers said. "Anyways, you said we needed to talk about something."

"Yes. I have an idea for one of those training sessions you give down at the station."

"Love to hear it."

"The number of police officers killed on duty in vehicle-related accidents now exceeds the number killed by criminals. This also takes a heavy toll on equipment. I have a collection of videos that have captured people being killed or maimed in car accidents. Some of them are pretty good, quality-wise. If you were to show these to the ranks while delivering lectures on safe driving, it might make them more cautious. More attentive to the issue."

"Intriguing idea," Jommers said. "There are some high schools that do something similar before prom week. However, it does raise the issue of desensitization. We treat phobias by repeatedly exposing a person to the thing they fear. So does repeated exposure to images of road mayhem make people more or less afraid of it? But that's not what you actually came to talk about, is it?"

"She was here yesterday," Scubbetts said. "I want to know what she said about me."

"I assume you mean Detective Voros."

"What did she say about me?"

"She didn't say anything about you."

"You're lying. I know she's talking about me. I know it."

"She may be, but not here," Jommers said.

"She lies to cover her own ass. She makes up stories to deflect attention away from her own incompetence, her recklessness, her impulsive and erratic behavior. She's lying about what happened that night to save herself. She puts the blame on everyone but herself. She's a character assassin. A despicable, self-justifying neurotic who would destroy anybody or anything to protect herself. I know she blames me and her more immediate superiors. I know she blames her partner. I know she blames everybody but herself. I want to know her version of events that night. What her wild tale is."

"As I have repeatedly noted, I don't do operational debriefing. I do psychological assessment. I don't study the storm. I examine the damage it leaves behind."

"How do you do one without the other?"

"Very skillfully, as I have lots of experience at it."

"You can't tell me she doesn't feed you the same line she feeds everybody else."

"What line?" Jommers asked.

"How she's persecuted. Oppressed. How she's this valiant knight in pursuit of justice, thwarted by dark forces of evil. She lives in a fantasy world with dragons and monsters and wizards. She shouldn't even be on the streets, much less on a police force."

"I didn't get that impression."

"Then you're an idiot. Or she's outwitting you. Or both. She's a rogue. A cancer. Spreading her disease."

"What do you mean, spreading?"

"She's got others believing her bullshit. She's recruiting others to her delusional cause. Particularly other females on the force. Some of them are buying into it. I'm afraid she's developing some type of rebellious cult within the department. Undermining authority. Disrupting command. Spreading chaos."

"Is this a suspicion on your part? Or has she actually done something specific to warrant that accusation?"

"She is actively undermining my command."

"How exactly is she doing that? She's not even on duty now."

"She uses her cult."

"Her cult?"

"The other women."

"To do what? I don't understand."

"Prowling, snooping, planting, infiltrating, undermining . . ."

"You've lost me. I still don't—"

"What the fuck don't you understand about prowling? They were seen, damn it."

"Who?"

"Members of her cult, in the Second District. Surreptitiously digging through files they have no authorized access to. Being somewhere they weren't supposed to be. Doing it on the sly. Looking for ways to undermine command."

"Second District. That would be run by Commander Mungfreud. You're saying she has a cult that wants to undermine Commander Mungfreud?"

Upon hearing Jommers mention the commander's name, Scubbetts, who had been on a reeling, roiling rant, abruptly stopped, as if realizing he'd said too much. There was a long silence, with Scubbetts smoking, staring, studying. Then back to a more formal tone.

"So, where do you stand with her?" he asked. "Your assessment. How soon can we get the ball rolling to get her booted?"

"Well, I'll tell you where I stand," Jommers said. "My initial concern with her was her lack of emotional response to the experience of having to shoot a fellow police officer. It made me concerned about her mental state. In due course, after several sessions with her, I realized what was happening. She was experiencing a delayed reaction. She was emotionally numb about what happened, in a state of denial. Eventually, I was able to break through to her, get her to experience the normal range of emotions expected after the horror of such an unfortunate tragedy. This incident will trouble her for a long time to come, but I think she can handle it. I don't think it will interfere with her duties. I don't see any psychological deficiencies that warrant keeping her off the job. I don't see any reason to prolong the assessment any further. Early next week, I will submit to HR my paperwork clearing her to return to duty."

"What?" Scubbetts slammed his hand down on Jommers's desk table as he shouted his response. "Are you crazy? Did you look at the file I gave you?"

"Yes."

"Did you read it?"

"Yes."

"Then how can you ignore repeated acts of insubordination, repeated violations of protocol and regulations, repeated confrontations with colleagues, repeated acts of dishonesty, repeated breaches of confidentiality, repeated—"

"Yes, yes, yes. But those are all performance issues, not psychological issues. You'll have to deal with those at your end, and, of course, deal with her union rep—"

"Fuck the union rep."

"In addition, I'd have a hard time declaring that she can't perform her job function when her rate of successful case resolution is higher than her peers in the unit."

"She is a fucking psycho bitch."

"You're half right. She's not a psycho. As for the bitch part, again, that's at your end to handle."

"This is your job—"

"It's not my job."

"She's obnoxious, arrogant, insubordinate, disruptive."

"Again, conduct issues at your end. Not indicative of psychological disorders at my end."

"Her ability to function properly is—"

"Her ability to function is quantifiable in this case," Jommers said. "And by department records, she outperforms her peers. Under those circumstances, I can't make a case that her ability to do her job is impaired."

"How the hell can you fail to grasp the importance of discipline in a hierarchical organization?"

"I grasp it perfectly."

"The need for adherence to protocols and procedures."

"I agree wholeheartedly."

"Then how the hell—"

"Again," Jommers said, "procedures and protocols are policy issues, not psychological issues. You need to address her problems at your end. If you want to terminate her over discipline issues, it sounds to me like you have a good case, but it's your case to make, not mine."

"This is bullshit. Pure bullshit."

"Look, Chief, I'm not saying she's the ideal detective. And frankly, I wouldn't want her on my police force either. All I'm saying is that there are no psychological grounds for her dismissal, and that single narrow criterion is all I'm permitted to consider under the policies and protocols defined by the regulations of your department. I pride myself on strict adherence to those policies and protocols, as should you."

Scubbetts slammed his hand on the desk table again. "You don't tell me what to do. You don't get to tell me anything. You're a fucking contractor. You're the fucking window washer, the floor polisher, the guy who fixes the crappers. You don't get to tell me anything."

Scubbetts exhaled a plume of smoke and glared silently for the next half minute or so, the raging dragon wreathed in his own smoke. The conversation had gone circular long ago, so Jommers saw no point in responding. He simply stared back at Scubbetts impassively, declining to react to the insults, yet refusing to look away.

"Were you surprised when I gave you the business in the beginning?" Scubbetts asked. "You should have been. I knew you were a slacker from the get-go. But I was fighting battles on multiple fronts back then. I knew that a slacker is too ambivalent to take sides. A slacker doesn't take up arms and join crusades. I figured a slacker in this position would make one less enemy to fight. In retrospect, I should have been more discriminating. I will obviously reconsider that decision now. In light of your ingratitude. In light of your betrayal. I will definitely reconsider."

"You do whatever you have to do, Chief. As will I."

"Aren't you the cocky, complacent bastard? None of this worries you. What does scare you, Jommers? What makes you tremble?"

"Not much into trembling, Chief. Sorry."

"But you fancy yourself some kind of healer. So you must care about other people. That whole thing about do no harm. Do you want to see people get hurt? Get hurt because of your actions. Do you?"

"Detective Voros's response to the firing of Patrolman Tarburn's weapon was entirely appropriate given her perception of the situation at the time. I don't perceive her to be a threat."

"I'm not talking about her specifically," Scubbetts said.

"Then I don't know what you're talking about."

"I'm talking about unleashing chaos, damn it."

"I still don't follow."

In the course of the conversation, Scubbetts's cigar had gone out. He groped for his lighter and attempted to relight the stogie, but the lighter didn't work. Unperturbed, he simply tossed the lighter on the floor.

"These piezo lighters are nice when they work, but they're too damn finicky. They don't like being dropped."

The chief then launched into a murky, ominous ramble about the consequences of unleashing the dark forces of chaos, the suffering of innocent people, perhaps even those who are close, loved ones hurt by random menace, and so on. But Jommers wasn't listening. He was focused on the lighter that the chief had tossed on the floor.

The move was surprising for a number of reasons. One, Scubbetts had drawn the lighter from a different pocket then when he had originally lit the cigar after entering, meaning that it was a different lighter. Two, one does not discard an expensive lighter simply because its electrode needs cleaning or adjustment. Three, one does not normally carry two separate lighters in case one breaks. And, four, most importantly, the lighter on the floor was emitting a peculiar, unfamiliar chemical odor.

A leaky butane lighter should stink. Odorants consisting of mercaptans and sulfides are added to the butane so that people can detect leakage by their sense of smell, as is done with natural gas. But Jommers knew that smell, which lay somewhere between garlic and rotten eggs. And this wasn't it. This was something else. Something astringent, like isopropyl alcohol, but different.

Jommers didn't wait to find out what. He briskly, though calmly, arose from his chair, picked up the lighter and nonchalantly tossed it out the open window.

"Smelled like it was leaking butane," Jommers said. "Not good for you to breathe that stuff."

Jommers remained standing, standing the way one does when expecting a guest to leave. Scubbetts, unaccustomed to occupying a lower position, also stood up, giving Jommers the chief's famous laser stare.

"You know the term loose cannon, right? Its origins?" Scubbetts asked.

"Yes," Jommers said.

"When I was in officer school, an instructor made us read an old sea story by some frog writer describing a sailing ship's cannon breaking loose in rough seas, how it rolled around this way and that, killing and maiming and wrecking the ship, almost sinking it. The difficulty of capturing it, not knowing which way it will roll next. The gun captain bravely corrals the thing, for which he's given an award of valor. Then the gun captain is hanged for failing to properly secure the cannon in the first place."

"The army teaches French literature. Who would have guessed?"

"The point of the story was to drive home the lesson on responsibility and the consequences of negligence. You are about to set something loose, something with unpredictable consequences. Whatever happens next will be on you. If somebody gets hurt, regardless of who, it's on you. Now, you still have time to change your mind. I suggest you think long and hard about what you do next."

"Enjoy your weekend, Chief. Thanks for stopping by."

A half minute after Scubbetts left the room, Jommers walked over to the window where he'd tossed the lighter. A few seconds later, Scubbetts came into view, walking over to retrieve the lighter. As he walked away, he stopped, turned around and looked up at Jommers in the window. Jommers smiled and waved, then Scubbetts kept on walking.

JOMMERS WAS SURPRISED by the chief's nuclear reaction to clearing Voros. The response lent credence to her claim that she was about to take him down. And the loss of Grayton PD business would also take Jommers down.

While he had no intention of capitulating, he considered temporarily delaying the submission of his report on Voros. The delay wouldn't hurt her, since she was still on admin leave anyway. It could also serve as a feigned retreat. Make Scubbetts think he'd won. Buy some time. But buy time for what? Who or what would be coming to rescue the situation?

He put that question aside as another one quickly popped into his head. Should he tell Voros that Scubbetts knew she was covertly working on his case? She was no longer a patient. No longer Jommers's problem. She was an intelligent woman capable of making her own choices. He'd warned her to stay out of it. It was her choice. She must bear the consequences. Regardless of outcome, a war between an off-duty Internal Affairs detective and a rotten police chief was still an intradepartmental matter. There were no grounds for him to be involved.

The only compelling justification for Jommers to call her was if he genuinely believed she was in danger. And to accept that, he would have to admit to himself that she was right, that her conspiratorial view was valid, a view he had tried to shoot down. How could he embrace that contradiction? What was his responsibility as a therapist? As a person?

He made the call.

"He knows," Jommers said.

"Knows what?" Voros asked.

"Whatever you did yesterday, or had a friend do in the Second District station—he knows about it."

"How do you know?"

"Never mind how I know. I warned you to stay out of it."

"I can't," she said.

"Wait till you're back on duty," he said. "Then at least you're covered legally. By doing this on leave, you're operating outside the law. You have no cover."

"There's no time to wait. I don't know when they'll let me back, if ever. Things are happening. I sense it."

"You're going to ruin your career, maybe get yourself in jail. And maybe do the same for your friends. Let somebody else handle it."

"That's just it," she said. "There isn't anybody else. Wifflyn doesn't have the balls. If I don't do it, then it doesn't get done."

"You've been warned," Jommers said. "He knows every move you make. Whatever happens to you will be your own fault. And that's all I have to say. You won't hear from me again."

⌒

THE LUNCH-HOUR PACE at Spreckels was much slower on a Saturday, so Larry had more time than usual to chat.

"So, Karl, let me ask you something. I come home the other night and there's this little plastic bag of ads hanging on the door. Okay? And it's a clear bag, so I can see the top one right away. And it's got a big picture of this really scary-looking prickly creature with big eyes and antennae, like a giant bug monster or something. And it says something about how this thing is at loose in my house and it's going to hurt me. So I grab a crowbar from the garage and go looking for it. And I don't find it. So I go back to the ad and look at the fine print, and it says that this is a picture of a dust mite taken by an electron microscope and blown up like a gazillion times. So I think, okay, I'm probably not going to need the crowbar. But I'm still worried about the damn thing because it looks so menacing."

"And you don't have a microscopic crowbar."

"Exactly. So I pull the ad out of the bag and see that it's from this vacuum cleaner store, wanting to sell me a certain type of vacuum cleaner. I read more fine print and find out that it's not actually the micro bug monster going to get me, it's the micro shit that it leaves behind. So I was a little pissed off by them scaring me with the monster picture."

"Images of micro-monster poop would not have gotten your attention in the same way. The scary bug got you to read the ad."

"Yeah. And it says I got this micro shit all over my house and it's going to give me asthma if I don't vacuum it all up with some supersonic megapower deep-drilling g-force micro-crud vacuum extraction device with pico filtration."

"Which is now on sale for a limited time only," Jommers said.

"So you got the ad, too?"

"No. Just a lucky guess."

"So does it work? Do I need it? Or are they just trying to scare me into buying something?"

"Not being an engineer, I can't address the mechanical performance of the device in question, and the medical mysteries of asthma are also a bit outside my bailiwick. However, as to the thesis that micro-monster poop causes asthma, I would offer an observation and a question. In the old days, people cleaned their carpets with a corn broom. And if they were the diligent type, and had rugs that rolled up, come springtime they might hang it on a line outside and beat it with a stick. So, given those crude methods of cleaning, you would expect that this era would yield maximum quantities of micro-monster poop. Then in the late 1800s, they invent various types of manual vacuum cleaners with rotating brushes, and in the early 1900s you get the first electric motorized vacuum cleaners. Over the years these things become more powerful. Somewhere along the line you get the electric motorized beater bar attachment and filters, and later on, high-efficiency filters. So over the years, the quantity of micro-monster poop in your carpet should have been declining steadily and sharply, and by now should be at its lowest level ever. So if that stuff is the cause of asthma, then asthma, too, should be at its lowest level ever. In reality, asthma cases have been skyrocketing over that same period. So how do they explain the negative correlation?"

"You see," Larry said, "this is why I like talking to you. The comments you always have."

"I would also point out that your skills at risk assessment could use some polishing, given that the cigarette in your mouth is exponentially more dangerous to your respiratory system than anything in your carpet."

"You see, this is why I don't like talking to you. The comments you always have."

SUNDAY, AUGUST 19, 2007

DAY FOURTEEN

THE BIRDS AND VERTIGO

The chipmunk was positioned at the bottom of a utility pole, staring upward at a gull resting atop it. The succeeding thought bubbles over its head revealed the rodent's curiosity about how much more it might see at a higher elevation, how much wiser it could become by having a greater perspective. He wondered about life in sky world.

Jommers was surprised to see Graffiti Girl working hard early Sunday morning, but apparently she was serious about her appointment with immortality, by way of getting her graffiti animation posted on YouTube.

Looking through the binoculars, Jommers laughed at the chipmunk's interest in a higher perch. "Don't do it, pal. Don't climb that pole. Stay grounded. Always stay grounded."

His murmured counsel to the chipmunk was interrupted by the sound of a vehicle entering the parking lot below. Nobody should be working downstairs, and this corner of the Bends would normally be quiet and unfrequented on a Sunday morning.

He went down to investigate and found Lieutenant Augie Dallabaco, SWAT commander, leaning against his black Ford Explorer.

"Shouldn't you be at church with your family?" Jommers asked.

"The wife handles that part, which, today, will be the easier part. Afterward, I'll be taking them out to Cedar Point one last time for the season. One last time to hit all the rides. They're starting school next week. Still can't get used to that, starting in August. You didn't start until after Labor Day when we were kids, remember? Anyway, wanted to give you a heads-up on something. We had to shoot some dumb bastard Friday, so you'll be seeing some of my guys tomorrow or Tuesday for that critical incident review bullshit you do, and your fast-tracking of said bullshit will be appreciated."

"I did hear something about it on the news," Jommers said. "Wasn't clear what happened."

"One of those screwy Louie head cases with the heebie-jeebies who thinks the government is after him. So he's got these high-voltage power lines behind his backyard. The power company inspects all these lines regularly with a helicopter. So you have a technician in an open doorway operating an infrared detection device, looking for hot spots on the line, places where corona discharge has degraded the insulation. So this quaky flaky looks out his window and sees this helicopter hovering out back with a guy aiming something out the doorway and thinks that this is it, the big one, his own personal D-day. So the numbnuts grabs a semiauto carbine and starts taking potshots at the chopper. Fortunately, he's a shitty shot. The guys in the chopper don't even know what's going on. It's the neighbors who call 911. We get there and the tizzy starts popping at us before our feet even hit the ground. So we had no choice but to introduce him to his ancestors. Honest to God, what is it these days? I don't remember there being so many foil hats when I was young. Now they're all over, acting like backwoods moonshiners. You're the witch doctor. What the fuck is going on? Is it something in the water?"

"They're not necessarily more numerous, they're just more connected thanks to technology, and that's made them bolder and more intense. Positive feedback leading to a chain reaction. Your backwoods moonshiner metaphor is apt. In both cases you have someone socially detached, hostile to authority and government, mistrustful of other people. He feels the sting of social disapproval and has a victim mentality."

"That's a contradiction, isn't it? If he got that way by being detached, then connecting with others should make him better, right?"

"That would be true if he connected with normal people. But if they just connect with their own kind, then they just reinforce each other's bad attitude. Like a clowder of feral cats, isolated together, hostile together. But you didn't come down to the Bends early Sunday morning to talk about the decline of mental health in this country. And there's a reason you waited for me to come down rather than come up, a reason you prefer to talk outside rather than inside."

"Maybe I just happened to be in the area and thought I'd drop by for some small talk. And maybe I prefer to talk out here because your office smells a bit mildewy. You do know that, right?"

"What kind of small talk?"

"How do you feel about Alfred Hitchcock?" Dallabaco asked.

"An overrated creepy artist lucky enough to have lived in a culture that idolizes creepy artists."

"Not a fan."

"No."

"How about *The Birds*?"

"Second-rate horror schlock," Jommers said.

"Really? It's considered a classic."

"Call me old-fashioned, but stories should make sense. There's no rhyme or reason for why the birds start attacking or why they stop or who they target. The behavior of the characters seems equally random. Like the screenplay was written by a stoner with ADD."

"How about *Vertigo?*"

"A cop with acrophobia," Jommers said. "Obviously more interesting from my place."

"A professional interest."

"Yes, but more than that. In spite of its old-time movie style, convoluted plot, and this Hollywood thing of showing strangers fall deeply in love implausibly quickly, *Vertigo* still has a classical structure. Actions result from motivations. Things happen because of the behavior of the characters, propelled by their strengths and their weaknesses. And the best part is how the cop overcomes his fright. In the early section, he's unable to go up the bell tower stairs. He surrenders to his fear of heights. But at the end, his quest for answers overcomes it, and he charges up those same stairs, the hunger for truth conquering his fear. I like that."

"I like that, too," Dallabaco said. "You know, the part about questing for answers, having a hunger for truth. We should all be like that."

"You know, I never imagined the two of us standing around pleasantly chatting about old movies."

"Yeah, well, don't get all warm and fuzzy over it. This goes dark quick."

"I suspected as much."

"So let me pose a hypothetical."

"Which almost certainly isn't," Jommers said.

"Say you're involved in something shady and there's someone else in it with you. Your partner in crime calls you. He needs to meet with you urgently. Things are unraveling. There's a need to strategize. But the two of you can't be seen together. So he suggests meeting up in the bell tower of a closed church, like, say, St. Bartholomew on the West Side on Seneca Avenue, a grand, century-old stone church with a bell tower over two hundred feet high. And while you're up there, you smoke a cigar your partner gives you, because it's kind of a tradition with this guy, something he insists upon. Only this time, your cigar is spiked with something, a drug that will make you inexplicably terrified. And he leaves you stuck up there in the bell tower. You're stuck because the drug has made you afraid of heights, afraid to go back down the stairs, because it's a very high stairway, narrow, winding, and only one side has a railing, and they're those metal grate kind of stairs that you can see through, and they're all corroded, and some of them got holes rusted through. You with me?"

"Scary stairs. Got it."

"So you're not real eager to go down those stairs. But you've got another problem, all the goddamn birds in the bell tower. And your partner has spread a whole bunch of birdseed around so the birds are all over, seems like a gazillion of them. And they're those ballsy city pigeons who aren't afraid of humans. And they're making that fluttery cooing sound, which, under the influence of the drug, sounds extremely menacing. And they're scratching and pecking and flapping and cooing and looking at you, getting closer and closer, and they are just totally scaring the shit out of you, and you want to get the hell out of there. But you're scared of going down the stairs. What do you do? You're trapped between two terrors. Which one seems worse? Do you stay? Or do you go?"

"Well, if I'm still capable of rational threat assessment, I'm staying put, because the stairs are genuinely dangerous in my condition, but the birds are not. But if I'm in a highly charged emotional state resulting from a psychoactive drug and I'm not thinking clearly, then I'm living in the moment and I'm more worried about the threat that I perceive to be more immediate, even though it isn't real. I'm more scared of the birds."

"Like Tarburn stopping to shoot a rat while being chased."

"Exactly."

"So you're going down the rickety rusty stairs, and given the effect of your panicky state on your neuromuscular control, there's a good chance you're going to fall."

"A very good chance," Jommers said. "So who are we talking about?"

"Commander Mungfreud, Second District. His body was found at the bottom of the stairs to the bell tower at St. Bartholomew. He apparently did some screaming for help before making the attempt to descend. Some neighbors heard it and called 911, but not in time."

"So how much of your lead-up was observable fact versus speculation? If you're finding him after the fact, all you have is an eccentric guy who accidentally falls down some bell tower stairs after feeding some birds."

"Which is exactly what it was supposed to look like," Dallabaco said. "Something that would barely make the news. Something that would not prompt any further inquiry and not add any additional scrutiny to Grayton PD."

"And the grounds for your suspicion?"

"Nothing syncs here. First off, Mungfreud is not known as an eccentric who would be feeding birds in the bell tower of a closed church. An avid hunter, he'd rather shoot birds than feed them. More importantly, he and his wife had plans to have dinner with another couple, longtime friends, at some fancy restaurant. Just before they head out the door, he gets a call on his cell phone. He goes outside to have the conversation. He comes back in and tells his wife he can't make the dinner, that's there's trouble at the Second District station house requiring his immediate attention. But he never shows there, and no one there called him about any problems. So how does he end up at the bell tower? Who called him? Who sprinkled the birdseed they found up there?"

"Did they find his cell phone?" Jommers asked.

"Excellent question. No, they didn't. Which means it was taken from him. They're contacting the cell phone service provider for information on the source of the call, but it will likely turn out to be a burner phone, which still leaves you nowhere."

"So how do you see Scubbetts behind this?"

"Two ways. One, who else has the authority to order Mungfreud to skip his dinner plans? The only person over a commander is the chief. Two, my friend in Homicide, we've been talking, so he jumps on it. He goes up in the bell tower, forces himself to inspect every square inch of caked-on bird shit. And when he does, he finds cigar ashes in two separate places. Two people were up there smoking cigars. But there's no cigar butts. They've been picked up. Oh yeah, he finds cigar ash one more place. At the bottom, near the stairs. The cocky son of a bitch just waited there, waited to make sure his plan worked. That's cold. Robot cold."

"Okay, let's say your hypothesis nails the who, what, when, where, and how. There's still the why."

"You see, this is what frustrates me," Dallabaco said. "That troubled look on your face when I mentioned his name tells me you already know the why. Yet here you are, trying to act all casual, like you don't know shit about anything. Do you understand why I get so fucking pissed off at you? It's disrespect. You know how cops feel about disrespect, don't you? Now, we can continue to have a serious discussion where we both contribute insights and observations, or I can be on my way."

Jommers put his hands in his pockets, turned and strolled a few paces away, where he stopped to look off in the direction of Crone Point. He wondered why he was so reluctant to confide in Dallabaco. Was it just the therapist habit of maintaining confidentiality? Was it that he simply disliked an obnoxious man? Or was he afraid of what the hothead might do?

He turned back toward Dallabaco.

"Detective Voros has a theory that she was pursuing, that Scubbetts and Mungfreud were secretly running a security business on the side, against the rules. Scubbetts discovered that she was still looking into it, even though she's on admin leave. But I don't see how that kind of rule-breaking would lead to people getting killed, unless I'm missing something."

"You don't find the parallel with Tarburn significant? Both people who may possess secret information about Scubbetts. Each of those two people on separate occasions has a secret meeting with the chief, after which each of those two people exhibit strange behavior and end up dead."

"You're suggesting that the chief of police arranged to eliminate two people in his command for reasons we don't yet know."

"You have an alternative perspective? You can't possibly see all of this as a coincidence at this point. How do you assess the situation?"

"I see it as encrapulated."

"Encrapulated?"

Jommers nodded in the direction of the shop. "That's Pete Gerzny's term for when the head of a bolt or screw is so rusted that you can't get a tool on it to unscrew it."

"Well, then, you drill it out, then, don't you? Things are coming to a head here. It's time to grab your drill, Jommers. It's time to get it done." Dallabaco looked at his watch. "My tour group awaits their driver. We'll talk again soon, right?"

"Just out of curiosity, what's your favorite ride at Cedar Point?"

"I don't have the stomach for the thrill rides the kids like. Some of those things they got now—I'd be puking like a fountain. My body kind of likes to have its feet on the ground. So I just follow the kids around and watch. Cup of warm beer in one hand, cup of cold French fries in the other." He paused. "Wait a second. How can the beer be warm and the fries be cold when they're both the same temperature?"

"Our rendering of reality is governed by our expectations."

"I expected you to say that."

⌒

As much as Jommers disliked Dallabaco's pushy personality and blustery manner, the therapist still appreciated the SWAT commander's refreshing lack of ambiguity. While Voros, Biederbach, and Scubbetts were all ciphers that required decoding, Dallabaco was transparent. There was a certain respect owed to people who don't wear masks, people who were exactly what they appeared to be. And that gave him pause to reflect on Dallabaco's assertions. When a straight-up, down-to-earth, no-nonsense guy like that got suspicious, you took him more seriously than fretful souls who traded in portents and omens like baseball cards.

At what point do you begin to doubt your doubts? As a therapist who was trained to relieve patients of baseless anxieties and unwarranted fears, Jommers had an inherent predisposition against reading things into coincidences, the drawing of imaginary lines between disconnected events, creating earthbound constellations. But what if that reluctance was in itself a type of bias error that blinded him to ligatures that were palpable?

Real things were clearly happening, but the various interpretations seemed incredible. The situation was like a hologram of a rock garden projected onto a real rock garden. How the hell did you walk through that?

But an even larger question hung over it all. So what? What if he did see everything clearly? What if he knew exactly what was going on? What could he do about it?

Nothing. So there was no point in fussing over it. The matter remained for others to handle. He was not a man standing at the crossroads. He was a man standing on the scenic overlook staring down at the crossroads, watching other people approach it. Just an observer, not a participant.

Right?

THE SHADOW EVERYWHERE

Mr. Yellowlegs gave Jommers a quizzical look, which Jommers returned in kind. They were both strangers here on the Dike. Jommers because he was a human in a wild place. Mr. Yellowlegs because he was from out of town.

The shorebird's long yellow legs normally plied the shallow waters of streams, lakes, and marshes in Northern Canada. His presence here in Northern Ohio meant one thing. The great migration had already begun. Somewhere, way up north, the armies of winter had started their slow march south, beating the bushes ahead of them, shooing off native birds to their winter home abroad.

It was hard to believe during this spell of stifling heat that Mr. Yellowlegs, and other interlopers soon to follow, were the harbingers of cooler weather coming, the evidence of things not yet seen. And weeks later, when the air eventually turned damp and nippy, people would have something new to complain about.

Mr. Yellowlegs would rest a while after his long flight across the lake. Then he would fly off looking for a beach or mudflat to catch some chow. Had to be real hungry, not having had any in-flight meal.

In keeping with his Sunday afternoon habit, Jommers had lugged a bag of journals to the Dike with the intent of catching up on his reading. But, unable to concentrate, he didn't get far into them. He blamed the morning conversation with Dallabaco for the distraction, but the oppressive weather didn't help either.

Earlier in the season, the lake waters had looked so tantalizing that he'd fantasized about being a gull gliding over the water, then splashing down and bobbing around for a while. The weather had been pleasant back then, the air clean, the waters still cool. Then the unrelenting, breezeless scorcher had set in. The water had warmed and the algae had bloomed, and Erie had slowly turned from inviting to off-putting. A giant slow-cooker producing a sick-smelling stew.

The odor, along with the blistering heat, the dusty earth beneath his feet, and the sight of brown, crisp vegetation all around made his secret hideaway seem less an idyllic sanctuary and more a bleak outpost in harsh territory. He felt uncomfortable, itchy, and irritable. Even the dragonflies buzzing about appeared intent on annoying him. This was not a good time to reflect meaningfully upon the mysteries of the human psyche.

So he closed his eyes, pulled his bucket hat low over his brow and tried to take a nap. After repeatedly brushing off this or that insect from his arms, he realized that wasn't going to work either. So he decided to go back home. He pushed his hat back and stood up to leave.

And that was when he noticed the boat.

It was a small stern-drive powerboat with a blue hull, which was the only reason he'd noticed it the first time, since most of the other boats he'd seen that day were white. It had passed by earlier, several hundred yards out, traveling east. A while later, it had passed back traveling west, slightly closer in. And now it was back, and closer. Only this time, it slowed down and made a circle directly north of him.

The boat then turned its bow in his direction, creeping slowly closer, almost as if the boater knew he was there. And that didn't seem possible. With tall reed grass to the left and right of him, someone would have to be looking his way through binoculars precisely at the brief moment he would be in line of sight. Someone would have to be looking for him. Someone would have to know he would be there.

The boat inched closer carefully. Whoever was at the wheel surely knew that the giant blocks of stone that formed the Dike's perimeter were not stacked simply like a vertical wall, that the bulkhead sloped downward into the water in stepped fashion like an Aztec pyramid. And with lake level low, you couldn't be sure exactly how close to the surface the stone blocks were.

No doubt with that in mind, the boater stopped a few hundred feet out, its bow still pointed directly at Jommers's position. And that was when he heard the music. It was too faint to make out. The boater was obviously playing the music loudly, but it wasn't coming from good speakers, and the open air sucked up most of the sound's energy, so the music wasn't recognizable.

Jommers cocked his left ear in that direction, and in doing so was able to discern a sense of familiarity with the music, but it still wasn't clear enough to identify. Lower frequencies traversed distance better than higher ones, and notes held longer were easier to discern than those played quickly in succession. So he was getting fragments. It was like trying to guess the phrase on *Wheel of Fortune*, with some letters there but others missing. This went on for about a minute or so until the boat turned away and sped off westward, and Jommers began the long trudge back to his car.

Musical recognition is a funny thing. One hears a song in a drugstore or dentist's office without consciously noting it. Then hours later, it sneaks onto one's mental jukebox and plays itself, and the person, forced to listen, then wonders— where the hell did that just come from? And this happened to Jommers just as he was loading his stuff back into his car, his mental jukebox mysteriously kicked on. And just as mysteriously, it was playing "Baby Elephant Walk."

He didn't have long to think about it, though. By the time he opened the driver's-side door, his cell phone was ringing. Reverend Truly wanting to know if they could have a chat. He was still at the church. Jommers noted that he was not far away and offered to stop by on the way home.

WHEN JOMMERS ENTERED the Evergreen Baptist Church, he found Reverend Truly playing a hymn on the church piano. When Truly saw Jommers enter, the pastor smiled and launched into a boogie-woogie number that lasted several minutes.

"That was a more spirited version of 'Just a Closer Walk with Thee,'" Truly said. "Sometimes you have to jazz up the old stuff."

"Praising the Lord with barrelhouse blues," Jommers said. "I'm surprised at you, Reverend."

"Well, Jesus took it on the road, you know, took it to them. Didn't just wait for them to drop by."

"Ah, so it's not a vice, it's outreach."

"Maybe a virtual vice. This lets me go to the juke joint without stepping outside the house. But don't credit me for that version. I heard it down in New Orleans years ago. Folks down there sometimes have their own take on spreading the word. Whatever it takes, you know? If you want to preach to people, you have to preach in their language."

"But you like it, though," Jommers said. "It's not just strategy. You're a closet blues man."

Truly laughed. "I have to confess, when no one else is around, I like to bring by my bad company, my old friends, Albert Ammons, Pete Johnson, Lux Lewis, Jimmy Yancey, Speckled Red . . . I know you mostly take your blues with guitar—how about the eighty-eights?"

"Oh, yeah," Jommers said. "Got to love Otis Spann. And Memphis Slim. That version of 'Key to the Highway' he did with Jazz Gillum . . . maybe the best one out there. Then Booker T. Laury. Hard to find his stuff. Champion Jack Dupree . . ."

"Dupree wrote some raunchy stuff. I have to be careful what I keep lying about."

"Like that one where he wants her to take out her false teeth and—"

"That's far enough."

"So Reverend Truly has a secret life."

"Musically only. I think the real reason I keep it secret is that I don't want anyone to hear how bad I play."

"I thought you played pretty good," Jommers said.

"Spoken like a true mental health professional. Now if I could just figure out how to do a sermon as entertaining as boogie-woogie. We don't have A/C here, as you can tell. It's hard enough to hold their attention under normal circumstances. So when you get the devil's heat like this, making that connection is a mountain to climb. When I'm standing out there in front, looking out at them, I can see them looking back in my direction, but I'm not sure whether they're looking at me or through me. Sometimes I feel like an invisible watchman who can see but cannot be heard, that I'm both present and absent at the same time."

"I know that feeling. I surely do."

"As long as we are briefly on the same page, I wonder if I might pose a question on professional behavior, counselor to counselor."

"Sure," Jommers said. "Go ahead."

"Do you ever let a patient hug you?"

"Hell, no."

"Why is that?" Truly asked.

"A certain level of detachment is required for me to be effective. I know that sounds counterintuitive, since I'm coaxing people to bare their souls, but the anonymity of a stranger paradoxically makes that easier to do. As an analogy, think of a digital prostate exam. It's uncomfortable both physically and psychologically. But the psychological discomfort is mitigated by the fact that it's being performed by a stranger. Now imagine that being done by your best friend, or a member of your family."

"Ooh."

"Right. Really, really awkward. So, similarly, if I'm going to go poking around someone's head . . ."

"Yes, I see your point," Truly said. "Here's why I ask. We have a tradition in our church, like many, where, at the end of the service, I stand by the exit and the congregants file by, shake my hand, offer greetings, and so forth. Lately, some people have taken it upon themselves to offer a hug instead of a handshake."

"Ick."

"I confess, that was my initial reaction, also. But then thinking about it after, I felt guilty about it. You see, I preach love, and here is a person trying to express it. Why should I find that uncomfortable? Yet, on a gut level I do. But, I can't find words to illuminate the conflict."

"Well, Reverend, trust your gut on this one. Because what your gut is reminding you is that intimate gestures should be reserved for intimate relationships, that when you hug someone you know only casually or not at all, it's inappropriate and phony, and that when you participate in such phoniness, you compromise your integrity. That's why you are instinctively uncomfortable with it, and rightly so."

"I take your point. But if I refuse the hug for those reasons, isn't that a bit stiff, a bit starchy? Shouldn't a person in my vocation be more forgiving?"

"No," Jommers said. "In this case, you should be less forgiving. In your business, as mine, integrity is more important than affection. People don't have to like us, but they do have to respect and trust us. Acquiescing to falseness degrades both respect and trust."

"You stake out an uncompromising moral position. Have you considered becoming a Baptist?"

"You must draw a line in the sand here. If you don't put the kibosh on the phony hug, then a bit down the road, it gets worse."

"You mean . . ."

"Yes, the phony kiss."

"Ugh," Truly said. "I definitely could not handle that. I would have to leave the ministry."

"Then you have to nip it in the bud now."

"But what can I do? Pretend I have a cold? Put up a sign that says please don't hug the pastor?"

"You can make a moral case for it. Turn it into a sermon. Observe how in modern life, artificial sentimentality is increasingly replacing genuine compassion and benevolence, that the cheesy, mawkish greeting cards that people send serve as a compensatory strategy to disguise growing materialistic self-absorption. That to participate in this charade is deceitful."

"Oh, I like that," Truly said.

"Then you can wrap it up by noting the difference between those who put on a noisy show about love and charity, and those who quietly live out those principles through discreet action."

"I like that a lot. It ties in perfectly with Mathew, Chapter 6, Verse 6, which elevates private prayer over the posturing of public prayer."

"Okay, then, here's your closer. You say to them, if you're so eager to show your kindness and humanity by embracing someone, then how about embracing the poor, the sick, the lonely, the hopeless, the abandoned. Why do you presume to hug me, but turn your back to them?"

"Good stuff!" Truly said. "Very good. I think you could do this job."

"No, no, not me. I'd be too much the hypocrite. I'm the type whose loudest sermon would be the one I most need to hear."

"We're all that type."

They both laughed. Then Truly turned serious.

"I had a chance to sit down and talk with Becca Tarburn today after services."

"I assume you discussed her meeting with Detective Voros," Jommers said.

"Indeed."

"Did she derive anything beneficial from it?"

"To be honest, I cannot tell you that it was transformational in the way I had hoped, but I do feel that answering some questions has moved her closer to a place of acceptance. She is still angry and in pain, but no longer angry at the person who did it. Becca is a woman with great empathy and insight. She sensed that Detective Voros herself was in pain. Becca does not blame the detective. At the same time, there are disturbing questions that remain unanswered. And those questions persist as open festering wounds."

"You mean, of course, why Earl displayed peculiar behavior that day, behavior that was so uncharacteristic of him."

"Yes, that would be the big one," Truly said.

"More specifically, you, and she, want to know whether that behavior had some random inexplicable cause, or whether there was a human agent behind it, someone who deliberately caused it to happen."

"You're reading my mind."

"I can tell you honestly that I do not at this time have a definitive answer to that question, and that there are aspects that could lead you to either conclusion, but nothing that would qualify as evidence. I do know that Earl smoked a cigar with Chief Scubbetts that day, and that Earl started behaving strangely after that. I don't know what, if anything, was in that cigar. There are other recent examples of people behaving inexplicably strangely, exhibiting a similar paranoia without direct cause. The chief may be connected to those incidents as well. But, again, there is no proof."

"We, of course, Becca and myself, believe Chief Scubbetts to be that agent you speak of. We are absolutely convinced of it. As we are convinced of his evil nature."

"I now share your opinion of him," Jommers said. "I also have come to believe he is evil, not in the supernatural sense you have, but in the psychological sense of being sociopathic. But that's an informal opinion, not a formal diagnosis. He's a paradox in some ways, simultaneously reckless and careful. His shadow is everywhere, his fingerprints nowhere. If you know what I mean."

"I do. That is precisely how the Prince of Darkness operates."

"I don't have more to give you at this point. More troubling is that I don't know how to get more. I'm not a detective. I'm an outsider. There's a limit on how much I can ascertain. There is a vortex in motion here, but I'm at the periphery of it. My vision is limited from that position. I'd love to promise you more. Really, I would. But I won't lie to you. I don't know how much more I'm going to get on this. I know that's not satisfactory to you or her, but I'm being honest with you."

"I believe you. And regardless of your beliefs, my prayers are with you. You may no longer have faith, but I can see the residue of transcendence."

"I'm not sure what I believe anymore, but I appreciate your confidence."

"Sometimes we must accept unsolved mysteries, not allow them to be obstacles. Still, I can't stop wondering what choices Earl made that led him to that fateful night. Where did he pass the point of no return? There's that haunting line in 'House of the Rising Sun,' you know it, one foot on the platform, one foot on the train. The last chance to turn back . . ."

Truly hung his head down as he began to play the melody of the song on the piano. Played it slow tempo, like a dirge. He kept his right foot on the sustain pedal the whole time, tickling all the piano strings with sympathetic vibrations that reverberated gently off the hard surfaces of the church, conjuring the sound of a chorus quietly humming in the background. And he held the pedal down long after striking the final notes, until the last hint of hum crept away.

ON THE WAY HOME from the church, Jommers stopped in Spreckels for a quick one, and Larry had another nature story to tell, derived from the tube as always.

"So I'm watching this animal show today, and I'm telling you, it just blew my mind."

"I don't see how that's possible," Jommers said. "I would think at this point, you would know everything there is to know, zoologically speaking, that is."

"I haven't even scratched the surface. But let's say I did. They're always finding out new stuff. So you're always behind. And today, wow. Just wow."

"So what blew your mind today?"

"Okay," Larry said, "so you know how we shot all the wolves in this country and then didn't have any."

"Right."

"So, the naturalists watching Yellowstone National Park find that the elk there are getting out of control population-wise, because there's no wolves to eat them anymore. And all these elk do a number on all the trees there, chowing down on the saplings, strutting around out in the open, going wherever they want like they own the place, because they got nothing to worry about. They're safe. So then back in the '90s, they bring some wolves down from Canada and reintroduce them back into Yellowstone, and everything changes because the elk know that the wolves are back. They can smell the wolves in the air. So there's fear in the air, literally. And that changes the elk behavior. They avoid the fields where most of the food is and stick to the woods, which is safer, but then they have less food to chow on. And the decrease in food knocks down the birth rate. So the elk population declines, but not just because wolves are eating them again, but because of their fearful behavior. And so now a whole lot more trees survive without elk eating them early. And with more trees, they got more beavers, and with more beavers, they got more beaver dams, which makes more fish and amphibians and birds and, well, the whole ecology of the place has changed—because of fear."

"You're right, that is mind-blowing."

"But wait, it gets better. Listen to this. There were these other researchers experimenting with birds that they divided up into two groups and played various animal sounds to over speakers. The one group heard sounds of harmless animals, the other heard sounds of predators. The latter group laid fewer eggs, and fewer of them hatched, and of those that hatched, fewer of them survived. So even a fake nonexistent threat changes everything. The fear messes with the head, the body, the offspring, the whole damn population. That's pretty freaky, huh? So what about us? Would it mess with us, too?"

"Unlike birds and elk, we have the power of reason to combat our fears. That is, when we choose to use it."

WILLIE, TOM, AND HAMLET

Not long after Jommers got home, he received a call from his ex-wife Rachel, who lived in the Cincinnati area. Also a therapist, she specialized in marriage counseling. She typically called Jommers about two or three times a year, always under pretense of wanting advice on some patient or professional issue, but the conversation always drifted toward the same place, a reflection on their marriage, or more specifically, its end.

No, reflection wasn't the word. Campaign was more like it. A long-running crusade of disputation in which she tried to persuade him into accepting her interpretation of their personal history. And her interpretation differed from his. But after all these years apart, what did it matter? Why did she still fight to capture that flag, the symbol of victory? Why did she still feel the need to say, I am right and you are wrong about what happened?

He found it tragicomic, though he knew it was not uncommon. It was like someone fighting to obtain a posthumous exoneration of a dead relative. A symbolic thing, but for some, an important, all-consuming thing. Pursuing the chimera of closure.

She would never totally cut him off until she got what she wanted. And so he wondered why he repeatedly refused to give it to her. Was it ornery impishness? A matter of principle? Or maybe, he just didn't want her to stop calling. Maybe having a bad connection with her was better than none.

"How are you, Karl?"

"I'm doing fine, Rachel. How about yourself?"

"Doing well, thanks."

"Good. I'm happy to hear that."

"How's business?"

"Could be better," he said. "I'm sure you're aware of trends, health insurance companies pushing people away from therapy and toward pharmaceutical solutions."

"Yes."

"You picked a good specialty. They don't have a chill pill for marital problems yet. I think you're safe for a while."

"Did you get your website up yet?"

"Not yet. I'm still mulling over what I should do with it, the image I want to convey. Then I have to find the right guy to do it. There's a million guys out there calling themselves website designers, some of whom may or may not know what they're doing. Like remodeling contractors. You have to do your homework."

"Of course," she said. "You still have the police business?"

"Yes. That's holding steady, fortunately. For now, anyway."

"Well, that's good. It kind of relates to why I'm calling. I'm advising a couple now where the husband is a longtime police officer and where his occupation is connected to their issues. So anyway, I was wondering if you'd be willing to offer some insights to help me better understand them better, you know, where that job is the issue."

"Sure," he said. "I'd be happy to. Though I should start by warning you that sometimes they use the job as a convenient excuse for troubles that exist independently of the job, troubles they don't want to recognize. In a situation like that, if all you talk about is the job, you end up talking around the real problem."

"Interesting. That's a good tip. Though in this case, it definitely seems to be the job."

"Okay. Tell me about it."

"He was recently involved in a questionable shooting of a suspect—you know, was the use of lethal force actually necessary? And the thing is, it isn't the first time. There have been several other similar incidents in his history. So naturally he became part of the local news cycle for a while. And that's what's stressing the marriage, the notoriety."

"What you mean to say is that the notoriety is stressing the wife."

"Well, yes. You know, she has to deal with people looking at her, in the store, walking down the street, or the dentist's office, whatever, and knowing they're all whispering, oh, that's her, the wife."

"But he's oblivious to her embarrassment."

"Yes," she said. "And that irritates her all the more."

"So the problem is not the notoriety per se, but the fact that he's unsympathetic about her having to deal with it."

"Yes."

"So it's more about him not caring about her feelings, which likely extends to other areas beyond the notoriety issue."

"That's a good point. One that neither has raised yet."

"What's his response?"

"What you might expect. That not every job is a simple nine-to-five office job. That unique jobs require unique forbearance on the part of a spouse. A politician has to be out constantly campaigning, a real estate agent frequently has to spend evenings and weekends showing houses, healthcare workers have to do shift work, military personnel are away for long periods, sales reps have to travel a lot . . .”

“And her response to that?”

“She’s willing to demonstrate such forbearance, but wants it appreciated.”

“So it’s not about his job, it’s about her not feeling appreciated.”

“Yes,” Rachel said, “but it’s still about the job, because she feels that the job is the reason she’s not appreciated. That he has more interest in the job than her. That the job has made him colder. That she doesn’t know who he is anymore.”

“Elaborate on the last one. Who he is anymore.”

“Well, there’s an ambiguity about him. He has this history of questionable use of force. But he also has a history of bravery and heroism, undaunted in the face of danger, daring rescues, and so on. So there are two contradictory narratives out there on him. Blue knight versus rogue cop. And she wants to know which one she’s married to.”

“The narratives are contradictory only on a moral plane,” he said, “but not necessarily on a psychological plane.”

“What do you mean?”

“I can only speculate here because I don’t know the guy. But let’s say he has a strong appetite for risk. Let’s say he gets high on it. That he gravitates toward risk at every opportunity. For a guy like that, an unjustified engagement looks the same as a justified engagement, an opportunity for risk-taking. He’s not making judgments on a moral spectrum, but strictly to satisfy a need. He’s not thinking about being either a hero or the villain. He’s craving the action in either case. In his own mind, there is no ambiguity. He is internally consistent.”

“So you’re suggesting he could be a sociopath.”

“Not necessarily. Base jumpers, race car drivers, extreme skiers and snow-boarders, they all have a high appetite for risk, but that doesn’t make them so-ciopaths. You would have to look for other indicators of antisocial personality disorder.”

“Base jumpers don’t kill people.”

“True. But if you’re married to a risk-seeker, sociopath or not, you have to be able to deal with it.”

“So you’re with him,” she said, “throwing it all on her. She needs to stop whining and accept it.”

“No. I’m saying you need to know who you’re married to and decide wheth-er you’re okay with living with that person. Let me ask you a little more about his history. The incidents that put him in the news cycle. Have some of these incidents happened while he was off duty?”

“Yes,” she said. “Many of them.”

"And for those incidents, he claims that he just happened to be where the crime was taking place, even when it's not in his own neighborhood."

"Yes."

"So he just happens to be where the action is. A lot."

"Yes," she said.

"Okay, here's what's actually happening. He tells her he's going up to the home center for picture hooks or something, or out to have a beer with a buddy, but what he's really doing is cruising around with his scanner on, hoping for something to go down in the area. And when he hears something, he races toward the scene, hoping to get there before a patrol car, hoping to be in a position where he gets to deal with it all by himself, hoping for that opportunity to enjoy another risk rush. Now then, if this is the kind of guy he is, you need to ask yourself whether this a marriage you really want to save. Do you honestly want that woman to stay married to that guy?"

"Does a guy like that even belong on the force?" she asked.

"Probably not," he said. "The best thing that could happen for him and the public at large is that he wins the lottery, quits the force, spends the rest of his life climbing cliffs and racing motorcycles. A win-win for everybody."

"So you don't think I can change his behavior?"

"Not unless you have magic powers. At this point in his life, he is what he is. If I were you, I'd be telling the wife to put on her walking shoes."

"That's not what I do normally," she said.

"I know. But it's something you need to learn to do. You need to think less about what's best for your batting average and more about what's best for the two human beings sitting in front you. And in some cases, it is best for one of them to get the hell away from the other as fast and as far as possible. Their failure is their failure. It's not about you."

"I was afraid we'd end up here."

"I know, you're going to give me all those statistics again about the benefits of marriage. How people live longer, live healthier, have higher quality of life, commit less crimes, exhibit fewer emotional problems, less substance abuse . . ."

"All true, of course," she said. "Thank you for making my argument."

"True on average, but not true for everyone in particular. And certainly not true for a woman married to a complete asshole."

"I'm so happy to hear that you're concerned about the woman, and that's my concern, too. It's the woman who suffers most from a divorce economically. In this case, the woman has no college education and no technical skills. She works part-time retail for minimum wage. She leads a middle-class life strictly because she's married to a cop with a good wage and benefits package. Her quality of life would suffer tremendously with a divorce."

"So you've expanded your professional mandate," he said. "You don't just save marriages, you preserve lifestyles. Because in the end, what matters most in life is that you have upscale appliances."

"Dropping a middle-aged woman into a near-poverty existence after she's lived middle class for decades is devastating. Traumatic. All the more so because she's dealing with the trauma alone."

"Life is about choices," he said. "And sometimes you don't always get good ones."

"It shouldn't have to be about choosing the lesser of evils. If you can change the behavior of the people in a marriage, one or both, such that you make the marriage satisfactory again, then you avoid the hard choice. And that's the proper objective."

"The operative word being *if*."

"Honest to God, how do you function as a therapist if you don't believe in the possibility of changing someone's behavior? This is what the cops have done to you, isn't it? Corroded your belief that people can change. Belief in change is kind of important to the job of therapist, don't you think? Maybe this is why your business suffers."

"I was afraid we'd end up here," he said.

"Sorry. I didn't intend it to."

"No, I think you did. You see, I think I've finally figured out why you make these calls occasionally. You know, where you pretend to want my advice, which you know in advance you won't agree with. Then the conversation rolls down to the same place, like BBs rolling around in a funnel. I imagine it begins in a coffee shop somewhere. You know, one of those trendy places with ridiculously over-priced bitter coffee that tastes like steamy mulch water, where people sit and look at their laptops earnestly like they're doing something important when they're really just watching funny cat videos. And you're in there, and you just happen to see a happy couple all goo-goo eyes and giggly smiles, and the irony starts to creep up on you like a hairy spider on your back—that you're a divorced mar-riage counselor. You have this irrational belief that all marriages can and should be saved, but you were unable to save your own. And you have to resolve that contradiction. And you ask yourself, could I have done more? Was there any hope unexplored? So you make the call to find the answer. Then you push it to the point where you can say to yourself, nope, Karl is still an asshole. There never was any hope. And then you feel so much better about yourself."

"I do believe most marriages can be saved," she said, "because unlike your-self, I think it's necessary to believe in what you do. If you don't have faith in what you do, and you continue to do it, then you're a phony, a hypocrite. Which is ironic in your case because you're so quick to illuminate hypocrisy in others. But I think that therapists may be the exception to the rule. So predisposed to lay bare maladaptive behavior, unable to turn off the scrutiny. Two therapists can't possibly stay married."

"That's just your easy out," he said. "Some therapists can and do stay married. But they have to actually like each other. Respect each other. Yet, even with us, you refuse to chalk up the loss. Blaming externalities, blaming our profession. But it wasn't our profession. It was us. It was our failure. We own it."

"We liked each other once," she said. "Maybe too much. We suffered from hubris. We presumed that because of our training, we could never fall into the trap of allowing passion to blind us to someone else's flaws."

"And it's back to flaws," he said. "BBs in a funnel."

"You talked about my calling to reaffirm the decision—my God, you did that right in the first ten seconds. You haven't got a website up yet because you're still doing your homework on it. How hard it was not to laugh when you said that. Or cry. Thinking back, how you couldn't act on anything unless you had perfect information. Which, of course, is never available. The joint article we never wrote because more research was needed. The house we never bought. The vacation we never took. Then the coffeemaker—geez, that should have been the tipoff. Six weeks after the coffeemaker breaks, you're still investigating all the possible replacement options."

"You knew me before you married me," he said.

"No, I didn't, honestly. I misread. I thought that whole laid-back shtick was cool when I first met you. I thought I was getting Willie Nelson in Tom Selleck's body. Wow! Am I a lucky girl or what! But I didn't get Willie or Tom. I got Hamlet. When I first raised the divorce option, and I saw you give a ponderous nod, I knew immediately that I would have to be the one to initiate it."

"And I thank you."

"You're welcome."

DAY FIFTEEN

Over the course of the previous day, the chipmunk had climbed to the top of the utility pole to enjoy a better view of the world. He was disappointed to find out that nature had not designed his vision for long distance. "I can see everything and nothing," he complained. More unsettling to him was that sky world offered no holes in which to hide. So on Monday morning, when the chipmunk spied a red-tailed hawk, he thought it best to head back down to earth. At the bottom of the pole, the cat was waiting.

Jommers's monitoring of GG's graffiti animation was interrupted by Claire Maroun rushing in the room and plopping down in one of the rockers, a distressed look on her face.

"You okay?" he asked.

"Not really," she said. "I can't calm down, I can't reset. I feel like I'm going to throw up."

"What happened?"

"One of those road rage things. I don't even know what I did to make him mad. Don't even remember seeing his car. But suddenly, there he is, behind me, doing that charging thing, you know, where they race up to your back end like they're going to ram you, then slow at the last second, then do it over and over. Then he pulled up alongside, swearing at me, giving me that murderous look."

"Did you call 911 on your cell?"

"I was too scared to even think. He was so close, like he was going to run me off the road. My hands were locked on the wheel. It was all I could do to breathe. It went on for a few minutes, but seemed like forever. Finally he turns off. And no, I wasn't able to remember his license number. I was too flustered. I wouldn't be able to tell you my own phone number at that point. I had to pull off the road, I was shaking so bad. I just don't understand why . . ."

"Don't try to understand it," Jommers said. "There is no sense to it. It's nothing you did. It was a random encounter with something bad in the environment. Like an angry dog in the park. It wasn't about you. Okay? If you had left five minutes earlier or five minutes later, the dog would have chased someone else.

But it doesn't matter. The dog is gone. It's over. You're safe now. It's over. So we want to start detaching from it now. Start sliding it over the side. Okay? So, I want you to lean back and close your eyes. Start taking long, slow breaths. Then rock back and forth very slowly. We're going to replace the jangle with the quiet, step by step. Inch by inch. Start with your toes. I want you to relax your toes. Concentrate on relaxing your toes. Put all other thoughts out of your head. Focus only on your toes. Relax your toes. Keep rocking. Keep breathing. Slowly. Gently. Let it go. Now your toes are relaxed. You can feel the quiet moving from your toes into your feet. A small, relaxing wave of quiet. And your foot is starting to relax, like someone was giving you a foot massage. Think about how that would feel, how relaxing that is. Feel how the quiet is moving up into your ankles . . ."

He kept talking to her, slowly and gently for several more minutes until she became more relaxed. He let things stay quiet for a while. After a few minutes, she opened her eyes.

"Thank you."

He smiled and nodded. As he walked her back toward the door, he gave her some advice.

"Before the day is over," he said, "you'll be tempted to fuss over this. Don't let it poke at you. Refuse. You tell yourself, it was just a wild dog, and now it's gone, and I won't ever see it again. It can't hurt me anymore. Okay? Say that every time you feel it coming back at you."

"Okay," she said. "I'll try." Before leaving the room, she shook her head with a perplexed look. "You know, there was one other very weird thing about it all."

"What's that?"

"You know how some of these jerks play music super loud? Like hip-hop or heavy metal, or whatever?"

"Yeah. All my favorite things."

"Well, this guy had his system cranked up a gazillion decibels, too, only he's playing 'Baby Elephant Walk.' Like he was psycho or something."

Jommers barely had a chance to process the comment when Ilona Voros showed up at the doorway.

"I was hoping you had a minute," Voros said.

Claire gave Jommers a small wave. "I'll talk to you later. Thanks again," she said as she scooted down the stairs.

"Actually, no," Jommers said to Voros, as coldly as possible. "I have interviews scheduled at Central."

"I just need a minute."

"I haven't done your paperwork yet, but I'll get to it before—"

"It's not about that," Voros said. "I was wondering if you heard anything about Commander Mungfreud."

"I heard about his accident. That's all."

"I meant have you heard anything from your connections about it. There are rumors . . ."

"I don't know anything about it. And you overestimate my connections. Now if that's all . . ."

"You're angry," she said. "You blame me for his death, which we both know wasn't an accident."

"There's no reason for you to be here. You are no longer a patient. And since you are still on admin leave, you have no business investigating anything or asking anybody any questions. You should be home watching TV, catching up on celebrities, cooking tips, and miracle foods that boost energy and remove wrinkles. Now if you'll excuse me . . ."

"Wait, just one more. Do you know anybody in Grayton on the Grow?"

"What's that?"

"The chamber of commerce group. Changed their name from Go Go Grayton."

"No, I don't know anyone there. That it?"

"Aren't you curious why I ask?"

"No," he said.

"Chief Scubbetts supposedly gave a talk to them not long ago about how everyone needs to be vigilant about terrorist activity. He told them about how he and the Department of Homeland Security had thwarted a terrorist plot to poison the city of Grayton water supply."

"You said supposedly, meaning you don't know what he said at this meeting or even if such a meeting actually happened."

"Supposedly after the talk he had a Q and A and someone, probably a plant of his, asked if he could recommend any security consultants to help them protect their businesses. And he supposedly tossed out a name of a security firm with expertise in that area. I'm trying to find out the name, because it almost certainly was the name of the firm he's running on the side illegally. I mean, this is how ballsy this guy is. Giving a scare talk to the chamber of commerce with the express purpose of steering business to his illegal enterprise. So I'm trying to find someone who was there."

"Someone who was at a meeting which may or may not have even taken place, since it appears all you have is a rumor of it. You're still chasing whispers and phantoms."

"What is with you? That's how investigators work. Most of our leads come from hearsay. And then you track those paths back to original sources, people who know. That's how it's done. Questions fuel the inquiry. Answers don't get delivered to you in packages. You hunt for them. We don't use doubts as an excuse for sitting on our ass. Uncertainties propel us into action. How could you work with cops for so long and not understand that?"

"This is all good stuff," he said. "I'll be sure and jot it all down later. But I've got to run now."

"You're not even trying to hide how mad you are. That's not like you. Oh, of course, now I get it. You told him. Told Scubbetts you were going to clear me. And he pulled the police business in retaliation. And now you blame me. Well, I'm sorry. I'm sorry some of this clipped you. But this is much more important than your business deals. There are people who have been killed here. Major crimes have been committed. There is rot at the top of the police department. There is action required. Justice that needs to be served. So I'm sorry if your business suffers, but this isn't about you. You need to stop being so self-centered and start seeing the bigger picture."

"Even more handy advice. Can you put all that on a coffee mug for me and give it to me at Christmastime? You know, just in case I forget. Now, if you'll excuse me. I've got to go talk to some cops who shot a guy who was shooting at a helicopter. I've got to go deal with the real."

SHE WAS RIGHT about the anger. He was mad as hell. But not necessarily at her. He was mad about all the crazy crap that was happening around him, bizarre, baffling crap that he didn't understand and couldn't control. And she was absolutely right—when bad things went down, you were supposed to find out why. He just wasn't in the mood for a lecture. Not from her, anyway. Maybe not from anybody. Even himself.

He was frustrated and flummoxed. He was an investigator all right, but licensed to prowl only that delimited territory that lay between the ears. Everything beyond that was outside his jurisdiction and skill set. In this new situation, he was a man at sea. But if you are at sea—well, then, that's where you are. And you do something about it. You look for firmament.

Right now, though, it was time to head over to the hole, the unused office in the basement of police headquarters where closed files were kept. It was dank, poorly lit, and smelled of mildewy boxes and unpainted concrete. But using the hole was an efficient means for conducting multiple interviews in succession.

The morning was scheduled for him to perform post-critical-incident interviews for SWAT team members involved in last Friday's engagement, the one where they'd had to take down the paranoid gunner who was shooting at the power company helicopter. Jommers had seen many of the same guys just two weeks ago after the Eggers Court raid. Seen them right there in the hole.

Only this time, he shared their feelings of futility in the exercise. He planned to hurry through it without bothering with the checklist of questions that they already knew by heart. He simply asked them if they were feeling okay, then sent them on their way. Each one was in and out in a few minutes.

There was no banter or joking around. Their expressions ranged narrowly from grim to glum, which shouldn't have been surprising. They didn't live in a vacuum. They were hearing things, too. If Dallabaco, their leader, believed things were rotten at the top and that it somehow factored into the death of their comrade, Tarburn, then they probably believed likewise. Only the last SWAT guy on the ticket had something to say.

"You know, we're hearing a lot of weird shit," he said.

"Yeah, me too," Jommers answered.

"And we don't know what to make of it. What to do about it."

"Me neither."

"Well, let me just say this. I know you and the lieutenant don't see eye to eye on things, like this shit right here we have to do every time, but you should know that he's a good man. And I don't mean good like warm, but like dependable. If you're going into the fray, he's the guy you want next to you. Remember that."

"I will. Thanks."

⌒◦

AFTER THE LAST ONE LEFT, Jommers spent another twenty to thirty minutes doing the paperwork, wanting to finish it up and drop it off to HR before going back. And just as he was wrapping it up, he smelled cigar smoke. He looked up from his desk and saw a furl of tobacco fume slowly twisting in the doorway, its source unseen but easily inferred. It was the dragon, theatrically presaging his presence to properly set an ominous tone.

Jommers remained silent, refusing to acknowledge the cheesy overture to a clumsy entrance by a third-rate dragon. This nonresponse forced the reptile to make the next move, which he did, stepping in front of the doorway, standing astride the opening with a wide stance, exhibiting an overweening cartoonish cockiness that might have been comical in someone else who wasn't a sociopath with power.

The smoke-shrouded saurian didn't speak. He simply stood there, staring Jommers down. The chief had not come down to converse, but to reconnoiter. Like a general riding to the top of a hill to survey the field of battle, he had come hoping to view a scene of his enemy's defeat.

Jommers first impulse was to casually walk over and throttle the lizard, stomp it into the rough concrete floor until it was unrecognizable as animal matter. This, of course, was inadvisable for numerous reasons, not the least of which was the scaly one's sidearm. Instead, Jommers delivered a performance of his own.

Jommers was not a student of military history, but was aware of the common ploy in warfare where one feigns a retreat, then prepares an ambush trap to snare an overeager pursuer. With that in mind, Jommers presented Scubbetts with the appearance of defeat that the chief had come down to see: a doleful, downcast expression, slumped shoulders, a motionless quietude that conveyed weakness and submission.

Scubbetts soaked it in. Savored every bit of it. He responded silently with the cruel smile of an unforgiving victor as he slowly walked away.

It galled Jommers to put on such an act, but he didn't have time to fret over it. He had already planned a busy day for himself. As he left the police station, he was already thinking about the next task. He was living in the moment. Yet, as he cast a backward glance at the hulking stone building, he was dimly aware that he was about to cross the line. Aware that things would never be the same again.

And it was at this pivotal moment, where he was about to step past a point of no return, that his thoughts turned to ice cream.

Specifically, Jommers thought about Vermeer's Old World Ice Cream, whose cartons boasted: Every Flavor a Masterpiece!

He had lied to Ilona Voros earlier that morning when she asked whether he knew any members of the chamber of commerce group, Grayton on the Grow. Lied because he was angry. In fact, he did know a member—Dusty Presbee. A man with the best job in the world. He owned an ice cream factory.

Presbee's paternal grandfather, Dobroslaw Przybysz, had started the business as an ice cream parlor during Prohibition, when the closing of taverns prompted people to seek alternative gathering places. When the arrival of commercial refrigeration enabled large-scale production and retailing of ice cream, the family business expanded by establishing a small ice cream factory for local distribution.

Dusty Presbee, however, grew up dreaming of being a legendary blues-rock guitarist in the mold of Eric Clapton, Jeff Beck, and Jimmy Page. Jommers had become friends with Presbee long ago when the guitarist was with a popular local band called Febryle, a group perpetually hovering at the edge of breakout. When Presbee's father suddenly died, the bluesman found himself standing at the crossroads—the blues or ice cream.

He asked one of his friends, a young psychologist, for advice. Jommers declined to sway the musician one way or the other, but instead advised him to honestly dissect the key drivers behind his dream. Was it devotion to the music itself, or the pursuit of fame, fortune, and the rock-star lifestyle?

While Jommers readily acknowledged Presbee's musical virtuosity, the psychologist candidly noted that the genre had peaked a while back, that popular music was splintering in different directions. Presbee's idols had caught the wave at the right moment. So even though the guitarist might someday match his heroes in talent, he could never equal their place in history. The moment had passed.

Presbee chose to preserve the family's heritage and assume control of the business. In a nod to his jettisoned dream, he introduced a new flavor—Blues Berry Blast, a mix of blueberry, boysenberry, and black raspberry.

Not long after, Presbee asked Jommers for advice of a different sort. He was expanding his workforce and wanted tips on how to recognize people who might have obsessive-compulsive disorder. Jommers obliged, but added that he didn't think it fair to exclude such people as candidates for employment.

"Oh, I'm not going to weed them out," Presbee said. "They're going to the top of the list. When you run an ice cream factory, you need to be obsessed with cleanliness and purity. I need people who can relate to that."

Jommers smiled as he remembered that long-ago conversation, because when he pulled into the company's parking lot, the first thing he noticed was how neatly the cars were parked between the lines, all perfectly spaced. But he hadn't come to see his old pal to talk about old times.

The air inside the ice cream plant smelled minty and sweet. The crew was making a batch of mint chocolate chip. Dusty Presbee had lost some hair and gained some weight since his blues band days, but still exhibited the same intensity, the kind where one is completely focused on the task at hand, however large or small, where opening mail merits the same concentration as wrestling with the devil.

He had one of those unfortunate, peculiar, and distinctly male physiques where fat accumulated viscerally, but not subcutaneously. So he had a very big belly, while still maintaining skinny hips, skinny thighs, skinny ass, skinny arms, and so on, making him look like someone who had swallowed a beach ball. It is very difficult for such men to buy pants. One must buy a large enough waist size to accommodate the circumference, but with little mass on the backside, the superfluous trailing fabric tends to flap and flutter like a flag in a breeze.

The behemoth belly was no doubt an occupational hazard for someone in the ice cream business, but also an inadvertent marketing message. The man obviously loves his product, so it must be good.

"Nice and cool in here," Jommers noted.

"Yes," Presbee said. "And it's a very costly cool this time of year."

"Oh, come on, man, you're the ice cream wizard, the duke of dessert. Doctor Sweet, come to cure you with his frozen treat. You just got to love summer."

"Yeah, I love summer from a business standpoint. But it's the most miserable time of year for someone who gets hit with hay fever. The ragweed now, it's like my archenemy. Out to get me. I'm good in here because of the purification system. But I know it's out there, the pollen enemy, hovering in the air, waiting to get me. The alien swarm. I step out that door, it's like beaming down to some strange planet with a toxic atmosphere, and I'm like yelling, Scotty, get me out of here, now! But there's no escape, because it's my planet. And I have to live here, even though it hates me."

"Yikes. That's pretty harsh. I assume you take something for it."

"Yeah, my doc got me on some pills. Hydroxy something."

"Hydroxyzine?"

"Yeah. You know it?"

"It's an interesting multiuse drug," Jommers said. "It's an antihistamine, which is why it helps with your allergy. But it also has a tranquilizing effect, so it's used for treating anxiety and psychosis."

"Hey, maybe that's why I'm such a mellow dude."

"Nah. I think it's the ice cream."

"So what's up?" Presbee asked. "You were kind of mysterious on the phone."

"Well, I heard this incredible rumor. Disturbing rumor. That there was a terrorist cell operating here in Grayton, and that Grayton PD, working with Homeland Security, had thwarted some kind of attack on the water treatment plant. That the whole matter was being kept under wraps because they haven't yet rounded everyone up. It was difficult for me to believe. But then the source of this rumor tells me that there was this secret meeting, where the chief of police met with civic leaders and businessmen and shared the information, warned them to be on watch. So now I can't stop thinking about it. So I drive around the Bends, and every time I go over a bridge I'm looking to see if there are any odd characters hanging out nearby, and, well, you know the Bends, there's always odd characters hanging out. So it's bugging me. Then it hit me. I remembered that you were a member of that chamber of commerce thing. So I thought maybe you might know something about it. So . . ."

Presbee didn't answer, but he frowned slightly and rubbed his chin contemplatively. Jommers noted that and smiled.

"Okay," Jommers said. "I can see that you do know something about it, but you're not allowed to say anything. That's fine. I don't want you to compromise any promises you made. I was just curious. I mean, who wouldn't be?"

Jommers got up to leave, but Presbee waved him back.

"You're right, Karl," he said. "I did make a promise. But I'm going to break it. One, because you're an old friend. Two, because I think it's all a bunch of bullshit."

"Oh."

"Here's what happened. The head of our group, Grayton on the Grow, invited us to a meeting with the police chief. *Invited* isn't the word, actually. Lot of arm-twisting going on. There was about, I don't know, maybe twenty or so of us. He wanted to reach out to the business community in small groups at a time, control the interaction, I guess. That's what they said, anyway. We had to swear not to repeat anything we heard, which struck me as odd. I mean, if you want to warn people about something, then you publicize it, right? So that contradiction, right off the bat, makes it all fishy to me. We had to put our cell phones and computers on a table. Anything electronic. So the chief starts talking to us. And this guy is big-time bizarro strange. No social skills whatsoever. He's detached and distant, but arrogant and condescending at the same time. It's like you programmed a robot to be a dickhead."

"Yeah, I know him," Jommers said. "That's a good description."

"So he gives us this story, just like you heard. That there was this terrorist cell planning to poison the water supply, but they don't want the cat out of the bag yet because they haven't rounded them all up yet. But he's doing us a favor by tipping us off so we can increase our vigilance and security. Then when he's done, someone pipes up and says that he's not on top of all this security stuff and can the chief recommend a consultant to bring him up to speed. And, of course, the chief rattles off a name for him. Talks about how this consultant is an ex-FBI guy with a lot of expertise. And all this is sounding way too scripted to me."

"Like the chief is a shill for the security consultant."

"Exactly," Presbee said. "So I don't even write the name down because I'm not buying the show. And even if I did believe it, I'm not worried. I got things under control here."

"Meaning . . ."

"I'm very traditional when it comes to the product. Gramps would be proud of this ice cream. It's got the same old-world quality and ingredients, eighteen percent butterfat in my premium brand. And I'm very state-of-the-art when it comes to protecting the product. Start with threat prevention. I've got a high-tech, monitored surveillance system with multiple cameras inside and out. It includes laser-based tripwires, acoustic sensors, chemical sensors, and combination motion sensors, meaning they incorporate both infrared and ultrasonic sensing. Then there's product quality protection. I have my own internal water and air purification systems. And the air is important, because you have to beat air into ice cream to make it soft enough to eat. Otherwise it would be like trying to eat an ice cube. So air is a key ingredient. My premium is twenty-five percent air, and the contract stuff I make for a local drugstore brand is fifty percent air. So air quality is a big deal. You may have noticed a breeze blowing past you when you walked in the door. That's because I maintain inside air pressure higher than outside ambient air pressure. So when a door opens, air blows out, never in. It minimizes the potential for contamination coming in. Then, obviously, I'm concerned about maintaining freezer temperature. So I have natural-gas-powered backup generators that will kick on in milliseconds if the power goes out. They reside in a concrete blockhouse so no one can mess with them. Freezer temperature is monitored and logged constantly. Let's say it's three in the morning and freezer temp goes out of spec. The control system would automatically place a phone call to me, the plant manager, and the maintenance supervisor. We can then remotely access the system to diagnose it, see how far the temp went out of spec and for how long. I deliver the product in my own fleet of trucks, and they're all monitored and networked. I can go on that computer right now and tell you exactly where every truck is and the exact temp in its storage compartment. Also, as a final check, I use the batch method. When a batch is finished, samples are taken and sent out to a lab, and that batch sits in cold storage until we get the results. Not an ounce ships until we get the green light. So you won't ever see any of my ice cream being recalled. Not ever."

"So you didn't write down the name or contact info for the security consultant that the chief recommended?"

"No," Dusty said. "Didn't the second time either, though I probably should have just so I could complain to someone."

"Second time?"

"Yeah. The son of bitch comes out here on a cold call, no appointment, trying to pitch me."

"You mean the security consultant, he came out here?"

"Yeah. Pissed me off, too. Because now I knew for sure that the whole meeting with the chief thing was all just a setup. I mean, it's not a coincidence he shows up here unannounced, right?"

"So you talked to him," Jommers said.

"Briefly. Like I said, I was pissed off. So I didn't let him get past the reception area. I just went out and talked to him there. Real slimecake. You know the type. Slick, smooth, pushy, all at the same time. He launches into his spiel about all his areas of expertise, how he can provide a turnkey package with this and that, and I'm trying to explain how I don't need anything he's got because what I got is way better. But he doesn't listen. He launches into to the whole air quality thing, how he can monitor and protect it, how critical that is to a food business, like I don't already know that, and before I even know what's happening, he pulls this meter-like contraption out of his attaché case and says he's going to sample my air quality and tell me what's wrong with it. And as soon as he does that, I smell a strange odor in the room. And I realize he's not sampling my air, he's releasing something into my air. So now I am ultra, ultra pissed. I grab him by the arm and literally drag him out the door. I swear at him for a few seconds, tell him what body parts will get broken if I ever see him here again, which you know is not my style. So I come back inside and see that in the melee, the contraption thing fell to the floor and it's still there emitting something stinky. I pick it up, walk outside, and pitch it at him like a fastball. Nailed him pretty good, too. I come back in again. I look at Nadine, the receptionist, and she's shaking like a leaf, right? I say what's the matter? She says she feels scared. And I can't calm her down. After an hour, she's still the same, so I just send her home, told her to take the rest of day off. So I don't know whether it was the slimecake who scared her, the odor in the air, or both, I don't know. It was just incredibly weird."

"But you didn't feel scared," Jommers said.

"No, I was just pissed."

"So I don't need to worry about terrorists in Grayton."

"I think it's all a scam," Presbee said. "I think the police chief is crooked. Which shouldn't surprise me. Just about everybody in local government here is crooked. I don't know how it even functions. Everybody knows it. Nobody seems to care."

"Well, I guess that answers my question. Sorry to bother you."

"No problem, Karl. It was good to see you again."

"So, hey. You still play?"

"Not a lot of time for it. I used to squeeze in a little bit on Sunday, but I got kids now, and that's the only chance to spend time with them. But I still perform twice a year. At the company picnic and the Christmas party."

"Captive audience."

"Exactly. And you better clap when the beer is free."

"So you're happy with the way things worked out."

"I guess so. I don't think about it. I mean, you know, happiness is like air or water, something you only worry about when you don't have it. So if I'm not thinking about it, then that means I probably have it, right?"

"Sounds good to me," Jommers said.

"You know, I never told you, but you were right back in the day, back when I had to choose. I didn't just dream of success, I wanted to be a trailblazer. But you can't be that when the trail has already been cut and paved. I would have spent my life chasing a designation that was unobtainable. Somehow you saw that. You're a lucky man, having a job where you can help people find their way."

"No, you got the great job. You get to sell joy in a box. How can anyone top that?"

⌐

It made perfect sense for the security sales rep to call on an ice cream plant. If a terrorist cell wanted to blow up a grommet factory, it would affect the relatively small number of people who worked there. But the surreptitious contamination of a consumable product would have the potential to harm thousands.

So Jommers pondered what other consumable products might make potential targets for the mysterious sales rep. Local producers of various food and beverages would be obvious subjects, including confectioners, makers of bread and other baked goods, bottlers of milk and soft drinks, local growers of fruits and vegetables, butchers and sausage makers, and so on. There were also plants in Grayton that made pierogi, spaetzle, pasta sauce, BBQ sauce, and specialty mustards. The city had a fish processor and coffee blender, too. But the first product that popped into his head was beer, and not only because it was near and dear to him. He knew a guy just a short hop away who owned a small craft brewery-restaurant operation.

ZACK SWEETAPPLE HAD BEEN a successful, highly paid regional sales manager for a medical equipment distributor when he was inspired to chuck it all and immerse himself in the craft beer business. He later opened the Bends Brewing Company in an old brick warehouse perched on a bluff overlooking a patch of riverbank known as the Jungle, a dense green thicket of untamed wild growth. There were many such patches in the Bends, but none bigger than the Jungle. The riverbank there rose up at such a steep incline that no one had ever found it practicable to build on it or put a road through it. When you viewed the Jungle from a boat, you could imagine yourself cruising the Amazon.

The Bends Brewing Company stood at the upper edge of the Jungle, where the land leveled out slightly before rising again. The location provided patrons with a spectacular view. In warm weather, guests sitting out on the patio could hear the chatter of birds and hum of insects. And in the late spring they could smell the flowering of linden and poplar.

Sweetapple gave his brews colorful names with occupational themes: Stone Cutter Lager, Bargeman Bohemian Pilsner, Switchman India Pale Ale, Harbormaster Irish Red Ale, Bridge Tender Brown Ale, Lock Keeper Stout, Tug Skipper Porter, and so on.

That pattern carried over to the menu, which offered dressed-up versions of old-fashioned classics such as meatloaf, chicken paprikash, pork chops, bratwurst, mac and cheese, grilled cheese sandwiches, and a variety of chicken sandwiches and gourmet burgers, though Sweetapple refused to call them by that name. He found "gourmet burger" an oxymoronic construction that ranked with artisanal potato chips. Instead, he called them spiffy burgers. *Spiffy* was a term used by his mother to compliment his bricklayer father when he dragged out his only suit for a wedding or funeral. *Spiffy* implied better than usual while avoiding highfalutin overreach, and Sweetapple was exactly the kind of guy who could ponder such nuances at length.

Regardless of nomenclature, Jommers thought the spiffy burgers were pretty damn good, and way better than Larry's over at Spreckels, though he would never dare to utter such blasphemy in a public place. As it was almost near lunchtime, Jommers found himself thinking of the Black Bread Burger, a paprika-sprinkled patty topped with Swiss cheese, green onions, and hot mustard, layered between two thick, dense slices of pumpernickel bread. Grabbing one of those burgers would also provide an opportunity to maybe grab a minute of the proprietor's time to see if he'd met any suspicious characters selling security services.

The Bends Brewing Company displayed a clean, simple, tasteful style, mercifully free of the mass-produced ersatz antique bric-a-brac that has become standard restaurant and tavern decor these days. Sweetapple himself displayed a similar forthright crispness, unencumbered by pretentiousness. He was a tall, slender man with a studious expression and meticulous manner that could just as easily peg him as a pharmacist or microbiologist. Fortunately, he was aware of his reserved image and compensated by hiring gregarious staff.

Jommers's timing was propitious. At around eleven thirty, the lunch crowd was but a trickle, but would soon swell. He told Sweetapple about his friend Dusty Presbee being approached by a slick sales rep who said some pretty alarming things, and that his friend was rattled by it, wondering if it was for real or part of some scam. For that reason, Jommers said he was curious about it, asking other business operators he knew if they'd had similar experiences.

"Yes, I know exactly who you're talking about," Sweetapple said. "He explained how easy it would be for a terrorist cell to poison my products. It got my attention for a moment, because I bottle for local retail now. I'm in a lot of the beverage stores and groceries in the area. But you're right, scam was the first thing that entered my mind when he showed up."

"Was it the way he looked, talked . . . things he said?"

"He was trying to sound like an expert in areas where he clearly had no expertise. Pure bluffery."

"Like?"

"Like chemistry. In raising the possibilities of contamination, he's tossing out chemical terms. But they don't jibe, you know? You have to study a lot of chemistry if you want to open a brewery. So I like to think I know my stuff. If you were interested, I could give you a talk on how the photodegradation of isohumulones in hops leads to the formation of MBT, 3-methyl-2-butene-1-thiol, which causes—"

"Skunky beer."

"I gave you that talk already, didn't I?"

"Yes, but I could use a refresher at some point."

"Anyway, you know how some old fifties or sixties comedian, Jerry Lewis type, would go for laughs using some kind of fake foreign language, you know, talking fake French or fake Japanese? Well, this guy is talking to me like in fake chemist. And it might actually work on a layman, but to me it was just nonsense."

"He's bogus from the get-go," Jommers said.

"Most definitely. Now then, everyone knows I can occasionally be brusque, but I'm rarely hostile. So I figure I'll let him run on for a bit before I run him off. A weakness, perhaps. But then he brings out this contraption. Says it's an air quality analyzer, that he's going to sample my air and tell me what's wrong with it. As soon as it he presses something on it, I smell a peculiar odor, sharp, astringent, and I realize this thing isn't drawing in air, it's emitting some type of chemical. I start yelling at him to get out, which he initially ignores. Fortunately, Jake, my chef, kind of had an ear tuned to it all, and he runs out holding a butcher knife, and, well, that was kind of the exclamation point on my order to vamoose."

"Let me ask you an odd question," Jommers said. "At any point in that conversation, did you feel afraid?"

"Yes, right after he pulled out the contraption thingy."

"Was it a generalized fear, or were you afraid of something specific?"

"I was afraid of him. It was like some movie where some ordinary-looking person turns into a demon or an alien or something. He didn't physically look different, but I saw him as evil, threatening. It was so weird. I was actually trembling."

"Before you chased him out, did he by any chance leave a business card or literature?"

"Yes. He tossed a card on the bar. You want it?"

Jommers's morning travels had given him a lot to digest besides the enormous Black Bread Burger, but there wasn't time. He had to prepare for Dwayne Biederbach, scheduled for the first afternoon slot. Jommers had already determined that this would be the last formal in-office therapy session for the patrolman. There was little left to say about his perspective that had not already been said. If Biederbach was going to reform, it would be by his own choice and effort or as a result of changing circumstance, not as a result of further insightful argument.

His thoughts about Biederbach were interrupted when he got back to the office, as he found Yolanda Arroyo, the police reporter, waiting for him.

"I missed you at Spreckels," she said.

"I didn't know we had an appointment."

"I assumed it was your regular lunch place."

"I'm expanding my horizons," Jommers said.

"I saw a UFO early this morning while I was jogging," she said.

"I'm happy for you."

"You're not going to try and explain it to me?"

"No."

"It was a bright light that just appeared in the sky out of nowhere. It moved across the sky for about twenty seconds, then just disappeared."

"Sounds like an iridium flare," Jommers said.

"What's that?"

"Look it up."

"You're more curt than usual. Are you stressed out about something?"

"I have a patient coming in shortly. I need to prepare."

"I'll just be a minute," she said. "I presume you heard about the strange accident that killed Commander Mungfreud of the Second District. Just wondering if you had any thoughts on it."

"Why do you call it strange? Seems rather ordinary. Check the CDC stats. Deaths by accidental falls are way higher than deaths by homicide. So you got all these people buying guns when they should be buying handrails."

"What I meant was that it's strange because of some chatter I heard from certain sources."

"By chatter, you mean unsubstantiated rumors from people with no first-hand experience with the event in question."

"Yes," she said.

"But when you look at the hard, verifiable facts, you have a common, everyday type of accident."

"Are you trying to convince me, or yourself? You have to admit, lot of weird things happening in cop world these days."

"Maybe it's the heat, or the taste of the algae in the water, driving everybody crazy. Or maybe it's the UFO emitting brain disruption rays."

"You think I'm some tabloid hack who wants to sensationalize this."

"Look, my beef is not with you personally," Jommers said. "You seem like a decent, conscientious person. My issue is with media in general, the way they promote every outlandish, weird story that comes down the pike, when they should be shooting it down. And I don't just mean news media, but all of them, movies, television, publishing . . . I mean, you have a gazillion books out there promoting different flavors of JFK conspiracies and less than a handful debunking them. Why? Because crap sells. And those companies are carnival hucksters scamming the public. We have an epidemic of looniness in this country, and the media biz is Typhoid Mary."

"You know, the sad thing here is that we're both on the same side, both trying to get at the truth. I don't know why you can't see that. At some point you'll have to."

"Perhaps. But not today."

BIEDERBACH ENTERED THE ROOM with a touch of swagger, his expression betraying a hint of gloat, the bearing of a man who had just won a bet and had come to collect.

"I suppose you heard about Commander Mungfreud," he said.

"Yes," Jommers said. "It's unfortunate. He'd served the department a long time."

"I was going to ask if you also heard the rumors about it, but I'm fairly certain you have, and I don't want to put you in the uncomfortable position of pretending you haven't."

"And if I had, so what?"

"You look different today. Less condescending. Like a man who knows a whole lot more today than he did yesterday and isn't too happy about it."

"I thought we'd gotten past this opening dance, the dance of defiance. I thought we had made progress."

"This must be an awkward moment for you. All this time you invested in trying to debunk my theories, and just when you think you've succeeded, that's when you find out I'm right. It's clear that you now know that something shady is going on here. Shady in high places."

"Yes, definitely something sinister," Jommers said. "But then this is Grayton, Ohio, isn't it? There's always something sinister lurking in high places. If there wasn't, I'd think I'd been shuttled to a parallel universe. Given the history of this city, we can assume that at this very moment, somebody somewhere is taking a bribe or a kickback or doing something else crooked. So, no, I don't find it an awkward moment. I find it an opportune moment, an instructional moment, one where we can distinguish between garden-variety graft involving petty players, which is common in this city as elsewhere, and grand, pervasive conspiracies promulgated by powerful malevolent forces, which are rare."

"Curious place you run here, where smoking is allowed, but reality isn't."

"We had a deal. Debating facts and their meaning would be something that occurred informally off-site at places of your choosing, but our encounters in this office would be about therapy."

"If my view of things is correct, then therapy is unnecessary."

"Therapy isn't a jury trial examining the probable correctness of assertions. Therapy is an examination of how you view reality through a distorted lens and what we can do to correct the distortion."

"Your comment is circular. If my view is correct, then there is no distortion in need of correction. Or are you suggesting that truth and reality have no role in therapy?"

"The focus of these sessions is not on specific recent incidents. The focus is on your lifelong predisposition to see pervasive malevolent agents behind all events, to envision connections where no such connections exist. So, even if you were accidentally correct about recent events, which is not likely, but even if you were, it wouldn't change the fact that, for most of your life, you have been wrong about things, and that if your predisposition goes uncorrected, you will spend the rest of your life being wrong about things. So this therapy is not about the little picture, the minutia of the moment—it's about the big picture, how you view the world for the rest of your life."

"You're afraid of the truth, aren't you? You're afraid that if I'm right, it undercuts everything you try to do here. Negates your utility, dissolves your sense of purpose, your reason for being what you are. You're filled with existential terror right now. That's why you can't bring yourself to acknowledge anything I've presented to you. If I put a mountain of physical evidence and documentation in front of you right now, it wouldn't make a bit of difference. You would still reject it. You're no longer operating from a place of rationality, but from a place of fear. And it's made you immune to the facts."

"Your semantic legerdemain is quite good," Jommers said. "You can certainly get a job as a press secretary for a politician if you ever leave the force. Forgive me for pointing out, however, that you have not yet provided any verifiable facts, and that you haven't provided even a thimble's worth of evidence or documentation, much less a mountain. Your rants are always quite clever, because you're a very smart man. I acknowledged that on day one. It's regrettable that you choose to use your intelligence to construct defenses of your worldview, rather than using that intelligence to honestly reexamine your worldview. But you're partly right about wanting to validate my efforts. Everyone wants to be successful in their endeavors. That's perfectly normal. And sometimes, when I'm unsuccessful, I feel like a juggler on the radio. But I carry on. Keep stepping up to the plate because the occasional hits make it all worthwhile. And I had hoped you might become one of those hits. The only reason I agreed to this arrangement was because I sensed a glimmer inside you, a tiny bit of recognition that there was a dissonance that needed mending, a small spark of desire for change. And that's critical, because I can't change you. You must change yourself. That's why I wouldn't bother with an extremist who doesn't recognize any need for change. There is no access. There is no hope. They will not be affected by anything I say to them. They can only be changed by some future emotional event in their lives that opens the door. The door must open from the inside. I can't open it from the outside. So this is what it comes down to. Was I right? Do you at some level recognize a need for an attitude adjustment? If not, there's no point in us discussing it any further."

"Radio juggler. That would be a good name for a band."

"I'll take that as a yes," Jommers said. "So let's dispense with the dance and resume where we left off. Did you make a list of things that interest you, like I asked?"

"I tried, but all I could come up with was guns."

"That's fine, that's something. Now then, there are healthy ways and unhealthy ways of expressing that interest. Healthy ways would be hunting, target shooting, joining a gun club, collecting antique guns, and so on. On the other hand, stockpiling assault rifles and crates of ammunition in preparation for an apocalyptic showdown with the *federales* would be an unhealthy way of expressing that interest. I know a guy who restores antique guns, I can put you in touch if you'd like to meet him."

"Let me think about it."

"All right, then let's move on to today's topic. Today I want to talk about the Hollywood in your head."

"Not the inner movie thing again. I hate sequels."

"Yes, that again. Previously we discussed simply being aware of them, and how they're reactive, responses to personal experiences. But awareness is just the first part. The next step is taking control of them. You can't stop the inner movies, but you can rewrite them. But let's revisit the reactive aspect briefly, how these inner dramas are often compensations to life's emasculating frustrations. They provide victory, where real life has delivered defeat. They provide the opportunity for resolution and rebuttal, where real life does not. And whether these compensations are positive or negative is important, because the replaying of an inner movie is analogous to the repetition involved with memory. The more it goes around the track, the more it wears a groove. And these grooves define you, become the rehearsals for your life. The inner roles break out of the mind's theater and leap onto the stage of reality. The body performs what the mind has practiced. The guy who shoots his boss, the guy who becomes a dark alley rapist or highway sniper—none of them act out of the blue. Their deeds have been mentally rehearsed a hundred times."

"I have enough self-discipline to avoid becoming one of those guys," Biederbach said.

"Today. What about tomorrow? If you maintain this frame of mind, where will you be five years from now? Ten years from now? Last Friday, you probably heard, SWAT took out a guy shooting at a helicopter. That guy didn't get that way overnight. Somewhere in his past, he was likely a normal person who got on the wrong path. His inner movies got darker, and darker, until he was staging life-and-death battles. And Friday he staged the last of them."

"Again, I won't ever get that bad."

"Maybe. But the issue isn't a dichotomy, that you are positive or negative, up or down. It's a continuum. And where you fall on the continuum determines how much poison courses through your system. So you're confident you don't have enough poison to be fatal. That's good. But why would you want any poison at all? Wouldn't you rather live clean and free?"

"Yes, with the operative word being *free*. You're good with your analogies, but what you're advising is surrender. That the key to serenity is apathy and submission."

"No. You should keep fighting for what you believe in, but in the proper way, both externally and internally. In the real world, you should be like Atticus Finch in *To Kill a Mockingbird*, fighting boldly against injustice, against overwhelming odds, using courage, intellect, the law and the truth. And that's also what you want playing at your inner cinema, with square-jawed, tenacious Gregory Peck in the lead, playing the stand-up guy. That should be your model, inside and out. Unfortunately what happens in life is that our injured ego leads us into the wrong theater. One playing film noir, something with a creepy Peter Lorre character, a simpering man simmering with misanthropic malevolence. So you have to recognize when that happens. Because when that guy spends too much time in your head, he changes you. The outer actor follows the inner actor. So you need to take control of the movie. Show the one with the hero you should be, the man you once wanted to be before you got hurt."

"Well, that all sounds nice, cheery and easy, but some of us are just hard-wired to see things a certain way," Biederbach said. "When you come down the chute, you don't get to pick out your personality like picking out a shirt. You get what you get, and one guy gets peachy, another guy gets midnight blue."

"You know, I'm not a big fan of that phrase, hard-wired. Many in my field like to make a distinction between conditions and personality traits, suggesting that conditions are acquired and alterable but that traits are immutable. They see it as binary, that your behavior is due to a condition or a trait. I see it as more of a continuum. More specifically, I reject the notion that inherent traits are immutable. I have seen many people undergo changes in their personality as a result of life experiences. Some of these changes were sought after, some imposed by circumstance. Some have been positive, some negative. For example, I've seen different responses to adversity over my career. In some, it weakens, destroys, embitters. In others it strengthens, enlightens, emboldens. In still others, the experience passes through like an undigested seed with no effect at all. People in my business can argue into the wee hours about how much of that variance is due to inherent predisposition, how much to upbringing, and how much due to personal choice. But regardless of proportion, the choice component is always there. Always. There are those who say we have no free will, that we are powerless in the grasp of natural forces. And that is a load of crap. If that were true, then no one would ever change their life, when in fact it happens all the time. More specifically to my field, I have personally witnessed patients exerting their will to overcome phobias, substance abuse, depression, anger issues, and more. You have a choice as to how you will respond to life experience. And as long as you have consciousness, you will always have that choice."

"It's not like flipping a switch, you know."

"No, it's not. And thank you for making my final point. You can't just walk out of here and say from now on I'm a new man. It will take work. Like building muscle, rehabbing an injury, or learning a new skill, it takes practice over time. And this work must consist of concrete actions. You must pick a time of day to reflect on this. And every day when that time rolls around, you grab a notebook, a journal, or whatever, and you record how your inner movies played that day. What happened in them. How you can rewrite them turn out differently tomorrow. And at the end of every one of these, you write the following reminder—the outer actor follows the inner actor. Make that a daily habit."

"And that'll work."

"If you want it to. You have to harness your discontent and channel it into motivation, make it an agent of change. Look, I don't expect you to become Mr. Sunshine. That's not going to happen. But you can transform your poisonous resentment into the ordinary frustration of a normal person. Accept your imperfect world, accept your imperfect self. Cast off the boiling sense of grievance. Get on with life. And that's it. We're done."

"What do you mean, we're done?"

"We've explored how you got where you are and where you need to go. The rest of the journey is yours. I've done all I can do. While I'll still be happy to talk to you informally, here or elsewhere, this marks the end of our formal therapy sessions. Your movie and your life are now in your hands. And whatever you do, please don't give it a crappy soundtrack. Good luck."

PROTECT THE PORK RINDS

It was midafternoon by the time Biederbach departed, and Jommers had no other sessions scheduled for the remainder of day. Again. Realizing there was time for another reconnoiter, Jommers got back in his old Taurus and drove over to Meatland on the near West Side.

In the days before refrigerated railcars became the customary method for shipping animal carcasses, every city by necessity had its own slaughterhouses. Live animals were transported in ventilated rail cars, then slaughtered at the destination. Trains with livestock cars were a common sight back then. There was nothing unusual about seeing such cars pass by at a railroad crossing and seeing animal snouts pressed against the slits, sniffing for air.

It was also typical for affiliated downstream businesses such as meat processors and fat renderers to locate near a slaughterhouse, creating a district that often acquired a distinct and descriptive moniker, in addition to its distinct odor. In Grayton, that neighborhood was known as Meatland.

Meatland's slaughterhouses were long gone, but the old folks who grew up nearby could still remember the odious stench they generated, especially in the heat of summer. It was the odor of death. The fetid reek of blood, viscera, and unused body parts rotting in a holding area while awaiting proper disposal, which was not frequent, and not likely proper.

The nauseating stink blew thick as foam, and those unfortunate enough to live nearby found that the omnipresent smell permeated everything they owned, infused their very being. It soaked into carpeting and drapes, upholstery and clothes, even flesh and hair. Wherever you went, everyone recognized your distinct cologne, *Eau d'Abattoir*. Everyone knew you lived in Meatland.

The last abandoned slaughterhouse had been torn down years ago, but some of the affiliated businesses it spawned still remained in the district. There was a meat processor with an established local brand for bologna, wieners, and Polish-style sausage. There was a producer of canned dog food. And there was a snack food company whose flagship product was pork rinds.

Jommers's earlier visit to The Bends Brewing Company had been enlightening on several levels, but the big bonanza was the business card that Zack Sweetapple had given to Jommers, the card left by the slimy security salesman.

And that man was Wolf N. Stonecipher, president of Pike Square Security. The logo for the company was a drawing of the famous fifteenth-century Swiss pike square deployed in its "porcupine" formation, allowing it to defend from all four directions simultaneously. The firm's motto was "Providing protection from all angles."

Jommers smiled when he looked again at the card, not just because of the clever marketing it displayed. The flexible and nimble pike square had been transformative, helping to end the era of heavily armored knights. But Jommers smiled because he knew that security companies always finagled a way to get their name and logo displayed on the client's property. A sign stuck out front by the evergreen shrubs, or a decal in the front door, and so on. Now he knew what to look for.

Knowing that Stonecipher had already targeted a brewery and an ice cream plant, Jommers had a hunch the salesman would pursue other such businesses selling consumables. His goal in Meatland, then, was to simply to drive around and look for the security firm's logo. He was only about ten minutes into his mission when and he found the logo plastered on the front door of MPP Corporation.

The letters were an abbreviation for the company's original name, Micklewhite Pork Products, back when bacon had been its primary focus. As the popularity of its pork rinds had grown, the company had dropped the bacon and leveraged its brand into a snack food company, adding potato chips and cheese puffs. But Micklewhite's Deluxe Pork Rinds remained the flagship product, and seasoned varieties were eventually added, including BBQ, Cajun Spice, Cinnamon Spice, Honey Mustard, and Italian Herb. Though packaging graphics had been updated, the product's longtime slogan still adorned every bag—The Fluffy Crunch!

Jommers could personally attest to that, as Micklewhite snacks were heavily featured in the vending machine down in Pete's repair shop. And on occasions where Jommers missed his midday sojourn to Spreckels, he found that a bag of Micklewhite's Deluxe Pork Rinds would tide him through the afternoon quite nicely. And he agreed with the assessment. It was indeed a fluffy crunch.

He had found what he sought so quickly that it only then dawned on him that he didn't have a plan. The owners of the ice cream plant and microbrewery were both acquaintances. But the head honcho at MPP would be a total stranger. What excuse would he give for coming here and asking questions?

Jommers had lots of vices, but lying to people wasn't among them. He was about to acquire a new skill. On the fly. But first he had to get in. The front door was controlled by an electronic lock, so he had to state his business into an intercom. He explained to the receptionist-gatekeeper that he had been approached by a sales rep for a security firm, and upon noticing that this company was a client, he was wondering if the boss would be willing to recommend the security agency as a reliable firm.

She told him to wait a minute, and in roughly that amount of time, she buzzed him in. He stepped inside the lobby, where an armed security guard wearing the same Pike Square Security logo patch smiled and pointed to the receptionist. Jommers then gave the receptionist his card, and she disappeared down a long hallway. A minute later she returned, with the boss man right behind.

The boss was a heavyset sixtyish man with curly brown hair and a broad, genial smile on his rubbery face. He walked with vigor and purpose, and with each step, the large coil of fat that surrounded his torso jounced up and down like pudding in a balloon. He smiled amiably and offered a firm handshake.

"Archie Micklewhite, president of MPP."

"Karl Jommers, pleased to meet you."

"You know, when I was in college, getting my business degree, I took every psychology course I could squeeze in the program. You want to know why?"

"You wanted to learn how to communicate the importance of the fluffy crunch."

Micklewhite beamed and laughed. "You see, I knew as soon as I saw you, this is a man I want to talk to. Come on back my friend."

Micklewhite had a deep but lilting voice, like the narrator of a children's nature show. His gregarious personality suggested he might well talk with anyone who happened to walk through the door, just for the joy of conversing.

"Why do people do the things they do?" Micklewhite asked. "It's the most fascinating question, isn't it? And the more interesting subset of that is, why do smart people do stupid things? You see it every day. They can't really be that stupid, or we all couldn't have gotten this far, could we? And yet, the stupid things you see every day just boggle the mind. It's like there's some kind of push/pull thing going on inside the head, and understanding what's the push and what's the pull, I mean, that's like the big mystery, isn't it? If I hadn't been preparing to enter the family business, I would have definitely gone into psychology somehow, probably on the research side. It's got to be the most interesting job in the world."

"You're right," Jommers said. "It is the most fascinating question, but it can also be the most troubling when you can't answer it and need to. People want it to be like medicine, where you can say an infection is this bug or that bug, or you broke this or that particular bone, but it's not like that. And that's where it gets sticky. How do you precisely define a remedy, when you can't precisely define the ailment?"

"That does sound sticky, and I hate sticky. So I guess I'm better off where I am."

As they walked down the hallway, Jommers noticed that the walls were lined with framed movie posters, and that every one of them featured the actor Michael Caine. And each framed poster had a little light over it, as if they were works of art. Jommers was curious but held his tongue, not wanting to digress from his purpose.

"So Mr. Stonecipher has got you thinking about security?" Micklewhite asked.

"Yes, belatedly," Jommers said.

"Your concern, then, is personal security."

"No, actually, I was thinking about my files."

"Ah."

"I have case files on a number of locally prominent people, some who are current patients, some previous patients, and it occurred to me that if unscrupulous individuals should get their hands on these files, it could seriously damage the careers and reputations of these patients, maybe even expose them to extortion attempts."

"That's the new national pastime, isn't it? Sandbagging people. Makes me sick."

"Me, too. And I don't want to see it happen to any of my patients, and I certainly don't want it to happen because I failed to properly secure those files. I have a responsibility here that I'm embarrassed to admit I haven't taken seriously enough in the past. Especially in light of my office location, which is in an area not frequented by anyone after hours. You could take a sledgehammer to my front door at ten o'clock in the evening and there would literally be no one around to hear or see you."

"You definitely need some security arrangements, my friend, definitely."

"Yes, I realized that as Mr. Stonecipher was talking to me. He has a way of commanding your attention."

"He certainly does," Micklewhite said. "And that's a good thing, too."

"So he's there in my office and sees this half-eaten bag of pork rinds on my desk and he smiles and points to it, says you're a good customer, someone he's helped. So I thought, what the heck, I'll take a chance and drive over and see if you were willing to put in a good word for him. I apologize for just barging on in like this."

"Not a problem. I'm happy to give you my two cents. And I'll tell you flat out, upfront that man probably saved my business."

"That right?"

"Absolutely. I get a visit from a police detective one morning. He tells me that two men were trying to break into the plant here the night before. A passing police cruiser on patrol just happened by at the right moment and interrupted them. The patrolman gave chase on foot but lost them in the dark.

The detective took me out back and showed me the pry marks on the door by the loading dock. Another few minutes and they would have gotten in. And then comes the shocker. He gives me a photo print from the cruiser's dash cam video that got a few seconds' worth of images before they took off. Here . . ."

Micklewhite opened up a desk drawer and removed a file folder. He reached in the folder and took out a grainy photo of two men looking surprised while standing at the plant's back door. One was holding a crowbar, the other a duffel bag.

"Well, that's an eye-opener, isn't it?" Jommers said.

"To say the least. And you can't help but notice the most unsettling thing of all."

"Which is?"

"They're both clearly of Middle Eastern descent."

"Oh, right."

"And you notice that the duffel bag appears full of something, not empty."

"Meaning?"

"Meaning they intended to bring something in, not take something out. This wasn't a robbery attempt, this was a sabotage attempt."

"You mean a bomb?" Jommers asked.

"Worse, likely. The detective told me some things confidentially, but since you're a fellow businessman I think it's fair to let you in on it. Homeland Security is tracking a terrorist cell operating here in Grayton."

"Here? In Grayton, Ohio?"

"According to their assessment, major cities in the US have beefed up security so much that al-Qaeda is shifting its strategy toward midsize cities where there's more complacency. Just like your reaction indicates. What? Here? No way. They're going for the big guys. They're not coming here. Not to Ohio. And that attitude is what makes us easy targets. We're in the crosshairs, my friend, and no one here even realizes it."

"But if it's not a bomb, then what?" Jommers asked.

"Look, you blow something up, you can kill a few hundred people. But if you poison something that's widely distributed, you can kill thousands, maybe tens of thousands. That's part of their new strategy. The detective said that they foiled a plot to poison the city's water system, but they now believe the cell is going after other chemical sabotage opportunities, like suppliers of foods and beverages. And that's almost certainly what was being attempted here. If they had succeeded, thousands of people in the area could have been affected, and this business would have been extinct in no time. He told me I needed to take security more seriously, and, well, he didn't need to tell me twice."

"No way! Seriously? I had no idea about any of this."

"Me neither, my friend. Me neither. Fortunately, I'm just smart enough to know when I'm clueless. So I asked the detective if he could recommend someone on the security side to help bring me up to speed fast. And he's the one who steered me to Stonecipher. He said that Stonecipher, in addition to being the smartest son of a bitch he'd ever met, was triple-connected. Had ins at local PD, FBI, and DHS. The guy knows what's going on everywhere at all levels. Well, I called Stonecipher the same day. And I tell you what, the detective was right. That guy is the smartest son of a bitch you'll ever meet. And the stories he can tell you about what's going on. Hell, if people out there had any idea about the things they don't know, they'd never leave the house in the morning."

"Wow," Jommers said. "This definitely sounds like a guy you want on board."

"Without question. And the other thing about this guy, he's totally on top of cutting-edge technology. And not just surveillance stuff, either. He knows all about monitoring air and water quality and biohazard sensors and all that stuff. In fact, while he was here, he takes out this portable air quality analyzer, and, you won't believe this, but he was able to tell me everything I had in the air here by percentage and ppm. And not just chemical content either, but microorganisms, too. He impressed the hell out of me. Just totally blew me away."

"Sounds like you were mesmerized," Jommers said.

"Totally. How could you not be when someone lifts the veil like that?"

"So you contracted with him for services."

"Absolutely. He offered different packages of services, and even an a la carte menu, so to speak, but I went whole hog with the gold package, and I'm glad I did. I get armed guards, all kinds of surveillance, air and water monitoring, background checks on my employees, consulting services, and a monthly security threat report customized for my particular needs."

"Sounds like you got a good deal."

"Well, it isn't cheap, I can tell you that, and when you're dealing with the Rolls-Royce of security, you're going to pay the Rolls rate. But what's the alternative? Have a newspaper headline saying that thousands of people are dead from eating Micklewhite's pork rinds? How do you put a price on preventing that?"

"That's an excellent point."

"I feel safe now. Secure. When I realized what was going on out there, how vulnerable I was, I literally trembled. Thought I would pee my pants. But I put my trust in Mr. Stonecipher, and he delivered me from fear. And he can do the same for you."

The two men talked about security a few more minutes, then Micklewhite offered Jommers a quick look around at plant operations.

The concentration of any odor can be overwhelming. The smoky scent of a small campfire is evocative, but the stinging smog from a burning house is noxious. And so it was with pork rinds. Jommers found the aroma of their preparation mildly appetizing from a distance, but once inside the building, the smell got uncomfortably stronger to an unpleasant degree, while still tolerable. But when the door to the plant area was opened, it was like a nuclear attack on his olfactory system. The acrid, stifling vapors coming off giant kettles of frying pork skin stormed Jommers's nostrils, roared up into his sinuses, and stabbed his brain. It took every bit of his willpower to suppress a gagging reflex. He felt those stomach muscles tightening, the familiar prelims for a puke. How the hell did anyone actually work in there? He desperately hoped that he was being offered only a peek and not a tour, and the Fates granted his wish.

"I'd love to give you the full tour, but I'd have to fit you with non-skid shoes, safety glasses, a hairnet, and another net for your mustache, and I don't want to put you through all that. Unless you want to."

"No, no, that's fine. I understand."

Micklewhite then started walking Jommers back down the long hallway toward the reception area. After achieving his objective, Jommers then decided to inquire about the movie posters, all featuring Michael Caine.

Micklewhite laughed.

"I was wondering when you would notice. Do you happen to know Sir Michael's real name?"

"I do not."

"Maurice Joseph Micklewhite."

"Seriously?"

"Absolutely seriously."

"A distant relation?"

"I'm fairly sure. It's not a common name."

"Have you researched it?" Jommers asked.

"I never actually got around to that, but people in my family have been claiming it for so long, I figure, you know, if enough people say it, well, then it must be true. Where there's smoke, there's fire, right?" Micklewhite stopped at one poster that appeared a tad crooked, and then lovingly straightened it. "Besides, when I look at that face, stare into his eyes, I just feel something, feel the connection on a gut level. It has to be. We are so proud of his achievements. It's an honor to be a splash from his gene pool, however remotely."

"He's had a quite a run," Jommers said.

"Yes, indeed, and he's not done yet. He won't stop until the director up there says cut. It's just that work ethic he has, which, of course, has hurt him at times."

"Meaning?"

"Meaning he sometimes made stinkers for which he took a lot of guff. You know, stuff like *The Swarm* or *Blame it on Rio*. But you see, no matter what, you have to keep working in order to stay in the game, because in that business, staying in the game is the game. You get too picky and they forget your name.

Staying in the game is what put him in a position down the road to play some of his finest roles, such as in *Cider House Rules* and *The Quiet American*, which is my favorite. It was the best and most nuanced role of his career."

"You won't get an argument from me," Jommers said. "The concept of taking work where you can get it is something I understand intimately."

"Oh, let me show you this one over here. It's my favorite from his early years." Micklewhite led Jommers over to the poster for *The Ipcress File*.

"I don't remember this one," Jommers said.

"Well, you don't look old enough to have seen it at the theater. It came out in sixty-five. But if you ever get a chance to see it on cable or find the out-of-print DVD, you definitely have to see it. It's right up your alley."

"My alley?"

"Oh, yeah. It's one of those Cold War spy flicks that deals with brainwashing and psychological stuff."

"Interesting. How'd it go?"

"Well, Sir Michael plays this guy named Harry Palmer detailed to some British counterspy bureau where he's assigned to dig into this plot to brainwash scientists. The name *Ipcress* is actually an acronym made from the title of a book they find in the movie that explains the brainwashing process, which is called *Induction of Psychoneuroses by Conditioned Reflex under Stress*. It involves sleep and food deprivation and a sensory bombardment of bright lights and loud electronic noises and somebody repeating instructions over and over."

"Hmm," Jommers said. "Sounds similar to the psychic driving experiments."

"The what?"

"There was a scientist named Cameron who was paid by the CIA to perform mind-control experiments on unwitting, innocent mental patients as part of the agency's MKULTRA program. His procedure was called psychic driving. First the person was injected with paralytic drugs, then the immobilized patient was subjected to tape loops of noise or repeated verbal phrases. Sometimes hundreds of thousands of repetitions. In one case, a person was forced to listen to a repetitive message continuously for more than a hundred days. Cameron also experimented with something he called depatterning, which involved giving subjects massive doses of hallucinogenic drugs, then administering massive doses of electroconvulsive therapy, electroshocks, thirty to forty times the normal power levels."

"Holy moley! You mean this kind of stuff actually happened? It wasn't just movie stuff? That's unbelievable."

"To paraphrase Mark Twain, truth is stranger than fiction. Fiction has to be plausible. The truth doesn't. The scary part about the project is that was done by our guys, the good guys, on innocent people."

"Wow!" Micklewhite said. "That's a nut grabber. Anyway, in the movie, Harry Palmer, Sir Michael's character, gets captured by the bad guy and is subjected to this process, whatever you call it. Only he finds a bent nail somewhere, so while he's getting the treatment, he jams the nail into his hand, hoping that the pain will disrupt the conditioning. But eventually he's broken, and then the bad guy drills this trigger phrase into Palmer's brain, so that whenever Palmer hears the phrase, he'll obey any command that comes after it."

"Ah, yes," Jommers said. "The old trigger technique. They used that in *The Manchurian Candidate*, too, remember? Laurence Harvey and Frank Sinatra? When the character would be shown the queen of diamonds, he would obey whatever command he heard next."

"Yes, yes, absolutely. Another classic spy flick with brainwashing. Anyway, in *Ipcress*, the final scene has Sir Michael's character, who has escaped, pointing a gun at two men. One is his good guy boss, the other is the bad guy, and the good guy is telling Palmer about the bad guy, but the bad guy is using the trigger phrase to get Palmer to shoot the good guy, and so Palmer's brain is like arguing with itself, and—you know, I really shouldn't spoil this for you. You need to track it down and see it."

"I will. I promise."

"So what's your favorite?"

"I'm with you. *The Quiet American*. The way his weary face showed the angst of moral quandary, worrying whether action or inaction is the greater offense."

"No, I meant what's your favorite flavor?"

"Oh. The Cajun, without a doubt."

"You got it."

Micklewhite disappeared behind a door for a minute and returned with a carton containing a dozen snack-size bags of Micklewhite's Deluxe Cajun Spice pork rinds.

"This is terrific," Jommers said. "Thank you so much."

"The reward for pleasant conversation."

RECONFIGURATION

When Jommers got back to the shop and parked his car, he gathered up the bags of pork rinds he'd been given and could smell them through the bag. To his surprise, he found their scent repulsive. During that brief time he had poked his head inside the plant where they were made, the intense smell had sickened him so much it had poisoned his mind, rewired his brain. While carrying the bags inside, he felt nauseous, and he realized he would never eat another pork rind as long as he lived. So he took the bags into the shop and placed them atop the vending machine, confident that the mechanics would scarf the free snacks quickly. His decades-long affection for pork rinds had just been erased by one seriously intense malodorous moment.

Jommers had learned a lot over the course of the day, and now he had to sit down and make sense of it. He grabbed a notepad and a pen and wrote down several words on the page, deliberately not on the lines. He put them in different places in no particular order, then circled them so that they presented as free-floating planets.

> *Motivation.*
> *Fear.*
> *Object.*
> *Trigger.*
> *Reaction.*

Then at the bottom of the page he scribbled down a metaphoric observation he'd composed some years ago:

> *The fox runs away from the coyote out of fear of becoming a meal.*
> *The fox runs after the turkey out of fear of losing a meal.*
> *So if you tell a fox to run, you must specify the fear so it knows which*
> *way to go.*

It had been entertaining reminiscing with Archie Micklewhite about old spy movies, and how those flicks with brainwashing plots typically employed a sensory input to trigger the conditioning and induce a certain mental state.

Jommers hated to admit it, but something Biederbach had said a while back now seemed on the mark—if you want to manipulate somebody through fear, you must first implant the object of fear. It now struck Jommers that this very concept had likely been used on Patrolman Earl Tarburn the day of his demise—the nickname Early Bear.

When Jommers had visited Moe Balzer in the hospital, Ilona Voros's partner had said that they were instructed to use the nickname Early Bear when confronting Tarburn. The friendly nickname would help keep him calm, make him think he was being approached by friends. But when Balzer had used the nickname, the exact opposite reaction had occurred. Tarburn had burst out the bridge house door in a state of terror. When Jommers had asked Becca Tarburn and Augie Dallabaco about the nickname, neither had ever heard it before.

Jommers was now convinced that it never was a real nickname, but an invented phrase designed to trigger a terror response in Tarburn. Jommers couldn't make sense of what Tarburn was saying that night outside the Lousy Pirate bar, but Jommers had jotted down what he could remember after the fact. Tarburn said something about people chasing him to clean up a mess, and that they knew his code name.

Tarburn obviously believed that Early Bear was his code name for the experiments, and the "mess" clearly referred to the shooting of bystanders during the raid at Eggers Court. So when he heard the name, he felt his pursuers had found him and meant to kill him. And that's why he bolted in a panic.

But how did the code name get implanted into Tarburn's head as an object of fear?

When Tarburn had first called Jommers that day, the SWAT team sharpshooter had mentioned that he felt strange after smoking a cigar with Chief Scubbetts. It now seemed likely that the fake code name and the fictional hit team had been planted in Tarburn's head during this session, and that Tarburn's cigar was likely spiked with the fear-inducing chemical. It was all designed to ensure that Tarburn would get into a shootout with the Internal Affairs officers trying to take him into custody. Designed to end with him dead.

For Jommers to accept this theory, he also had to finally accept that the fear-inducing drug actually existed, and after a few minutes on his computer, that was easy to do. The pharmaceutical industry had both identified and created classes of anxiety-inducing substances called anxiogens and panic-inducing substances called panicogens for legitimate research purposes. The reason was simple. In order to test the efficacy of pharmacological treatments for anxiety or panic, one must first be able to induce those states into the test subject to see if the tranquilizer drug works. One must first be able to create the problem to test the solution.

So it was clear that such drugs existed. It also was probable that such a substance was being surreptitiously used on business operators to sell security services. But Jommers refused to accept Biederbach's notion that the chemical was some nefarious Ghost Wolf formula developed by the KGB and obtained by Scubbetts from military intelligence.

But it still left the question of how a police chief in Ohio had been able to obtain a pharmaceutical material unavailable to the general public and kept in monitored guarded supply. One thing now less puzzling was how the drug functioned. The conversations with the three business owners were revealing. All three had had similar encounters with the security sales consultant Wolf N. Stonecipher, but each encounter had produced a different result.

At each location, Stonecipher was clearly releasing a chemical into the air by means of a portable device he claimed was an air quality analyzer. When Stonecipher released the chemical in the reception area of the ice cream factory, Dusty Presbee was unaffected, but the receptionist was found trembling in fear. Jommers found this seeming contradiction easily explainable.

Presbee took hydroxyzine for his allergic rhinitis, and the antihistamine also had both anxiolytic and antipsychotic properties. That also suggested an explanation for how Stonecipher himself appeared unaffected by the release of the chemical—he took something to counteract its effects.

Brewmaster Zack Sweetapple had a different experience, but one that was also instructive. The fear-inducing agent worked well on him. He felt afraid in Stonecipher's presence. But the security salesman had failed to effectively implant an object of fear for Sweetapple to focus on. In an effort to understand his fear, Sweetapple had seized on Stonecipher as the object, the thing to be feared, and promptly expelled the salesman.

When the fear was instilled first, the mind struggled to interpret the feeling, identify a reason. At the Eggers Court raid, the chemical fired into the building by Earl Tarburn had made the meth cooks afraid, but they didn't know why. When their addled brains searched for an answer, they found it in a giant inflatable mascot bobbing over a tire store. They filled it full of holes, and in the process killed and injured bystanders in the apartment building behind it.

When the jilted lover holed up in a second-story apartment on Juneberry was exposed to the chemical, he, too, became inexplicably afraid. His mind, searching for an explanation, turned to the fish in the aquarium. He started shooting at the fish, bursting the aquarium. And when they started flopping on the floor, he jumped out the window in terror.

And when Tarburn himself was exposed to the chemical he'd fired at others, his final act was to shoot a rat, too afraid to realize that the shot would be misinterpreted by his pursuer.

There is ample psychological research that human brains work this way in general, in the same sequence. Feelings first and explanations second. We arrive at perspectives on an emotional path, then plant the rationalizing signposts after the fact.

Belatedly, but eventually, Stonecipher had acquired this insight, so that by the time he'd visited the snack food factory, he had refined his technique. First present the object of fear, *then* induce the fear. With that approach, the subject's mind need not struggle to interpret the feeling. The explanation had already been provided.

The one-two punch had worked perfectly on Archie Micklewhite. He was told that terrorists were trying to break into his plant. Next he was hit with the chemical, which he couldn't possibly detect over the stink of frying pork rinds. Without hesitation, he'd bought the gold package of security services. Ka-ching!

However, the Micklewhite example did provoke one important question. No matter how much of the chemical was inhaled by Micklewhite, at some point later, the drug would be completely metabolized by the liver and the metabolites eventually filtered and excreted. So why wouldn't the man come to his senses after the drug wore off?

Jommers hypothesized a two-part explanation. The first part concerned unawareness of the influence. A stoner knows when he is stoned and why. And so when it wears off, he knows to blow off anything unusual he'd felt, thought, or done while stoned. It wasn't him, it was the THC. By contrast, someone surreptitiously drugged, with no awareness of the influence, must develop reality-based explanations. And absent any subsequent discovery of the covert offense, those explanations would persist uncontested.

The second part related to the role of emotion in memory formation, how emotion colored the memory of an experience and determined its intensity and long-term impact. For example, research had shown that the emotional state of someone during and immediately after a traumatic experience significantly affected the probability of developing post-traumatic stress disorder.

The coupling of intense emotion with experience formed an intense memory, such that a single experience could have the long-term effect similar to that of repeated conditioning. Or, as Mark Twain observed, a cat that sits down on a hot stove-lid, will never sit down on a hot stove-lid again, but it will never again sit down on a cold stove-lid either. Once connections were vividly made, they persisted. A pattern imprinted on memory. And that was how Micklewhite's interpretation of events persisted long after the drug had worn off.

The hidden face in the drawing, once seen, cannot be unseen. Once three random stars are proclaimed to be Orion's belt, they remain so unalterably.

And that got Jommers thinking about Paraguay.

He had once created an analogy to describe how people assessed the truth, in which he'd noted that he was not one hundred percent certain about the existence of Paraguay. He'd never been there, and you could only be completely certain of things you'd personally observed or experienced. Most of the acquired knowledge we hold in our heads comes from external sources, not personal experience. So how do we know what we know?

A reasonable person judges the reliability of externally provided information by assessing the credibility of the sources. Are the sources in position to know? Do they have expertise? Do they have a history of reliability? Do they have any incentive to lie? Are there alternative sources refuting the reliability? If so, what is their credibility?

After answering those questions, the reasonable person temporarily assigns a level of probability to the assertion. There is a fifty percent chance this is true, or there is a seventy-five percent chance, or ninety percent, and so on. And all notions lie somewhere on that scale of probabilities. And these assignments are made temporarily because, when new information arises pertaining to a particular notion, the reasonable person determines whether the new information should move the needle up or down on the probability scale.

Sometimes new information comes slowly or not at all. Jommers was 99.9 percent sure that Paraguay existed. Given that no one was contesting the notion, the needle would not move downward. But given that he had no plans to fly there and see it for himself, the needle would never take that last little click upward either.

On other occasions, new information arrives quickly and demands nimble processing.

You're playing center field when the batter hits a fly ball. Crack! In the first few milliseconds, responsibility must be determined. Is it a short pop fly, the domain of infielders? Or is it headed to the outfield? And if so, to left, right, or center? Who is responsible for grabbing it? Someone else, or me? With each passing millisecond, the ball's new position yields updates about its ultimate destination. Even before apogee, you know it's yours. You lock your eyes on the ball, scanning its trajectory for guidance. But it is constantly changing its position. And you can't predict, even if your mind had a trigonometric processor, because this isn't happening in a math problem, but in reality, and you don't know hard it was hit, which way it's spinning, how it will be affected by the breeze, whether the breeze up there is the same as the breeze down here. All you can do is observe, analyze, adjust.

Observe, analyze, adjust. You do it a thousand times, right up to that last moment of truth when ball hits glove. Thwack!

On this particular summer evening, after a long and interesting day, Jommers found himself in center field, running fast, mitt out in front of him, desperate to catch a fly ball.

His career training had predisposed him to be suspicious of fantastic notions, but he was a reasonable man. The day had yielded new information. It was time to move the needle. And after doing so, this was where it stood.

The notion that Chief Scubbetts was using some unknown anxiogen to manipulate people for personal gain now appeared highly probable. The notion that larger government forces were behind this activity still appeared improbable.

He now felt that he better understood what the hell was happening, but he was still uncertain what to do about it. There were three people with whom he could share his insights: Ilona Voros, Dwayne Biederbach, and Augie Dallabaco. He had to consider who could do the most with it, but also their ability to protect themselves. The sharing would be a dubious gift, as it would come with a target.

He rubbed his temples and sighed wearily while walking over to the window to stretch. While there, he picked up his binoculars to see where GG stood with her graffiti animation.

Previously, the stalking cat had eaten the carp, the crow, and the chipmunk, each of whom had become vulnerable after wandering into the other's domain. The cat was now lying back like a human in a recliner, its belly full, a big satisfied smile on its face. At its feet lay the bones and inedible remnants of all three of its victims.

GG had said it would be a fable. If so, then all that remained was the posting of the moral.

DAY SIXTEEN

Curiosity fills the cat.

Jommers groaned. It had been a good wait for a bad pun, the ultimate moral of GG's graffiti animation and its last frame. Of course, in YouTube time, the moral would arrive in minutes rather than days, and would probably seem funnier. In any event, she would have made her mark, achieved her virtual immortality. At the very least, he had to give her an A for effort. The step-by-step, frame-by-frame painting had been a staggering amount of work that had consumed countless hours. They were, regrettably, unpaid hours, but at least you could say she was dedicated to her art.

Jommers turned his attention away from the graffiti in the distance and toward the problem at hand. It was Tuesday morning, and the things he'd learned the day before convinced him that the time for contemplation had passed, and the time for action had arrived. Limited action.

Of the three people he could trust, who best to confide in? Biederbach was only a patrolman, powerless to do anything. Dallabaco, by contrast, was a lieutenant. He had authority and lots of connections in the department, lots of colleagues he could trust. But he lacked the disposition to probe the situation with any finesse or secrecy. He would be as subtle as a bull wearing bells. Voros, for all her other issues, was an experienced investigator who, by her own initiative, was already on the case. But Jommers had just scolded her for nosing around while on admin leave. He would look like a hypocrite for urging her onward now. But what choice did he have? It wasn't about him.

Jommers picked up the phone to call her, but then stopped, wondering if his line might be tapped or his office bugged. Biederbach had bugged the place easily at their first meeting. The chief had been here since then. So had Dallabaco. And who else might have been in here while he was out? Maybe the place was full of bugs. He found this new wariness irritating, that he was thinking like one of his patients. But circumstances had changed, and he had to change with them.

He stepped outside and made the call.

"I didn't expect to hear from you again," Voros said.

"I'm going to ask you a question," Jommers said. "I want you to answer yes or no without saying another word in addition. Okay?"

He spoke with as much graveness as he could muster, hoping she would understand the seriousness, not think it a game or a joke. There was a long pause on the line as she struggled to comprehend, which she ultimately did.

"Yes," she said.

"The second time you were here, you referred to a man who endured life as a prisoner by drawing strength from stoic philosophers. Do you remember his name? Don't say it, just yes or no."

"Yes."

"Good. Now I want you to go downtown to the Grayton Public Library. Find that book he wrote in the stacks, then wait there by it. I'll meet you there. Can you do that now?"

"Yes."

⁓

SHE WAS SITTING on the floor in the aisle between two rows of bookshelves, her back against one. Stockdale's book was open in her lap. Jommers sat down on the floor, too, facing her, his back against the other row. She looked up with a disconcerted expression.

"I'd forgotten the part about his trying to commit suicide by slashing his wrists," she said.

"Philosophy can take you only so far. It's not an anesthetic. Wisdom can't start until the screaming stops."

"So what's going on?" she asked.

"I was wrong about that night at Crone Point. I now agree that it was a setup. I think you were meant to shoot Earl Tarburn."

"Lot of rigmarole for an apology."

"It's not an apology, actually," he said. "Just an observation."

"Oh, my mistake. Your remorseless tone should have been the clue."

"I regret the error, but my remorse over it is mitigated by the knowledge that I'm among the dwindling segment of the population still capable of conceding error."

"You're quite a guy, Jommers. The only one I know who's cocky enough to compliment himself for admitting a mistake."

"Here's an idea. Why don't we skip the usual sparring and get to business?"

"Fine. What is the business?"

He proceeded to tell her about his visits to the ice cream plant, microbrewery, and snack food factory. What he'd learned, what he'd surmised. That her suspicions about Chief Scubbetts running the security business on the side were probably correct, and that Stonecipher was either a business partner or a hired hand serving as the proxy face of the operation. There likely existed a chemical capable of inducing fear and anxiety in those exposed to it, and Tarburn had been used to test the chemical at SWAT standoffs. When Tarburn had felt guilty about his loyalty being exploited, he'd presumably confronted Chief Scubbetts over it. The chemical was then used on Tarburn with the intent that he would get himself killed. The false nickname given to IA to calm Tarburn was in fact a trigger created to push him over the edge. The chemical was almost certainly being employed by Stonecipher to scare up customers for the security firm.

Jommers deliberately omitted a few things. He declined to note that Dallabaco and Biederbach had similar suspicions and that Biederbach had a questionable offbeat theory on the origins of the chemical. He left out his suspicions that Biederbach possessed shotgun shells containing the chemical that he had gotten from Tarburn the night of his death. Jommers didn't want her distracted by digressions. He wanted her to focus on the foremost problem—how to take down Scubbetts as quickly as possible.

"I'm sitting on your paperwork until Force Review clears you," Jommers said. "I need to keep Scubbetts off my back as long as possible, so I can do my own little bit of recon without his scrutiny. As soon as they clear you, I will immediately follow suit. Now then, you had to turn in your service weapon when going on admin leave. I assume you also have a personal weapon for your protection until you get your official service gun back."

"Baby G," she said.

"Glock 26."

"Right. Gives me ten."

"Good," he said. "It's imperative that you act with extreme caution and prudence."

"I'm investigating my chief while officially on leave without backup and without the knowledge of my superiors. I think we can safely say that prudence flew out the window a while ago."

"Agreed. But don't let caution flee with it. Now, on the off chance that you should ever get surreptitiously exposed to this chemical, I want you to understand how it works. You will be suddenly overcome with strong feelings of anxiety and fear, complete with accompanying physiological symptoms. Trembling, rapid heartbeat and breathing. But you won't know why. At some level, you will recognize something strange about those feelings, that they're unwarranted or disproportionate to the situation. You will find that confusing. Your anxiety will be more intense than you have likely experienced before. You won't understand why, but they may supply an explanation in order to manipulate you. Absent that, you may seize any explanation that's immediate and handy, the way Tarburn in his final moments thought that the thing he needed to fear the most was a rat. If you find such feelings coming over you inexplicably, you must remember this conversation. You must fight the feeling. Exert your intellect over your emotions. Repeat to yourself over and over, this isn't real. This isn't me. It's just a drug. It will pass. I refuse to do what they want me to do. I am in total control of my actions. You follow me?"

"Understood."

Jommers then took out a small notebook and suggested that, for purposes of future meetings, they compose a list of coded locations that they were both familiar with. It was the same idea he had found comical when Biederbach had suggested it. She agreed, and when the list was completed, he scribbled out a second copy and handed it to her.

"If we need to meet again, whether you're calling me or vice versa, we meet at one of these places and refer to it on the phone only by its code number. Understood?"

"Got it," she said, then snickered. "This must feel odd for you. I mean, you spend your days telling people how to chill out, and here you are handing me a coded list of secret meeting places in case our phones are tapped."

"The word *odd* doesn't begin to cover it," he said, rising to his feet.

"Before you go, I want to thank you for putting me in touch with your friend Fahmida. We had lunch together the other day. She's an amazing person."

"That she is," he said.

"I suppose you know what she endures wearing the hijab in a place like Grayton. The looks, the comments. Yet she remains cheerful, optimistic, and loves America. She remembers what things were like where she came from. There's a big difference between getting a snotty look and having your father seized in the night, never to be seen again. She'll take snotty looks any day."

"Sounds like you hit it off."

"We did," Voros said. "She also gave me a lot of sage advice. She warned me not to presume everyone around you hates you, just because some do. Study your environment. Identify people who have the potential to become an ally or friend, and understand the difference between an ally and a friend."

"That's good advice."

"I guess it's obvious for most, but for me, the way I've lived, it was like an epiphany. So afterward, I thought about it, did some brainstorming. I came up with an idea. Did something impetuous. I called Councilwoman Elvira Birdsong. Know her?"

"She represents Ward Seven. More importantly, she chairs the Safety Committee, which oversees police, fire and EMS."

"Exactly."

"And because she holds that title, by ordinance, that puts her on the Force Review Committee, which is now in the process of determining whether to reinstate you."

"Right again."

"Which means it would be a conflict of interest for her to speak with you."

"Totally, but she did anyway. And guess what?" Voros stood up and brushed some dust off her slacks. "She's always thought Chief Scubbetts was a corrupt bastard who needs to go, but never had a confidante with whom she could share that opinion. So boom! Just like that, I've got an ally. All I had to do was look. I'm seeing things differently now. That couldn't have happened without our sessions. However this ends, I will always owe you that."

"Good luck, Ilona. Stay healthy. Be stealthy."

It was late morning by the time Jommers returned to the shop. Claire Maroun waved to beckon him.

"There was a guy here to see you," she said. "Said he'd stop by again later."

"Yeah? What did he look like?"

"Like someone who could whisk me away."

"Oh. So he looked like an ambulance driver for a psychiatric hospital."

"Funny, funny. Here, he left this."

She handed him a business card—Wolf N. Stonecipher, Pike Square Security Consultants.

Jommers was intrigued. Enough so that he skipped his usual trek to Spreckels Tavern for fear of missing the mystery man's return visit. If Stonecipher was the chief's man, there could only be two reasons for the visit: a recon to gauge the direction of Jommers's loyalties, or to reinforce the chief's threat. Or both.

The other obvious and crucial question—would Stonecipher expose Jommers to the fear-inducing agent? And, if so, would Jommers's knowledge of it be sufficient to combat its effects?

Jommers weighed his possible strategies while periodically gazing out the window with anticipation. It was early afternoon when a new, shiny metallic gold Cadillac Escalade raced down Nickel Plate Road toward the shop. The point man had arrived.

Stonecipher strode into the room with a commanding air, like an officer come to inspect recruit barracks. He was tall, brawny, and fit. He could have been a tight end on an NFL team but for his age, likely mid-fifties. He had short white hair and a broad, sturdy face with an anvil chin. His skin was weathered and tan, his gaze intense. He shook hands with a bearlike grip and introduced himself with a deep, gravelly voice.

He wore an expensive tailored taupe suit with a shiny gold tie. His teeth were white and perfect. His manicured nails displayed a clear sheen. All in all it conveyed a refined ruggedness, the power and affluence of a gold-plated tank.

But his imposing features and manner were contrasted by a warm smile and jocular tone, like a tough guy who had mastered the art of urbanity. Stonecipher apologized for not making an appointment and politely asked if Jommers had a few minutes to spare.

"Just to put you at ease, Karl, I'm not trying to sell you anything. I'm here to offer you a business opportunity. I was referred to you by Chief Scubbetts, who speaks very highly of you and your capabilities. And the chief is not generally the type to make recommendations."

Jommers was initially confused by the comment, given that he was at odds with Scubbetts over the Voros assessment. Then it hit him. Scubbetts was clumsily employing the carrot-and-stick approach. The indirect but unsubtle threats that arrived accompanied by "Baby Elephant Walk" represented the stick. And Stonecipher was here to offer the carrot. Jommers had no idea what the carrot might be, but would feign an interest in taking a bite of it, if only to buy more time. The friendly overture also suggested that Jommers need not worry about exposure to the chemical, which was a relief. The mysterious portable air analyzer would not make an appearance.

Jommers welcomed the visitor and the two men sat down in the rocking chairs, turned so that they faced each other.

"So how do you know the chief?" Jommers asked.

"It's imperative for people in private security to maintain close ties to those in public security. I have relationships with local law enforcement, both PD and sheriff's office. At state level, I work with the troopers and BCI. I also interact with appropriate federal agencies, FBI, Homeland Security, Marshals, ATF, and others. And it works both ways. Private and public helping each other. Extra eyes and ears. We're all fighting the same battle, just from different foxholes."

"Sounds like a good practice."

"And that's what it's all about, Karl, good practices. In any business. Doing the right thing as a matter of habit and regular procedure to maintain continuous optimal performance. You don't want to be like one of those restaurants that's good only three nights a week. You need to be at the top of your game every day in every way. I'm sure you feel the same."

"Absolutely," Jommers said. "Consistency is everything. Clients aren't looking for adventure when they go to a service provider. They want a well-planned comfortable cruise, not a crazy-ass jaunt down a whitewater river."

"That's a terrific way of putting it. Scubbetts was right about you, Karl, about your insights. The way you perfectly grasp the situation at hand."

"I try."

"So I'm assuming you guys get along well, based on what he says."

"Mostly. Sure."

"Yet, there are occasions where there's a little friction, perhaps?"

"Naturally," Jommers said, "but that's going to happen in any kind of relationship, personal or business. You deal with it and move on."

"You don't go nuclear and blow it all up."

"Exactly."

"Because you understand that some relationships are worth preserving, even when they seem difficult."

"Precisely."

"But at the same time, you wish the chief would put in a little more effort into making things work. Just a skosh."

"Sometimes, yes," Jommers said.

"Is there some aspect or area in particular that you think he should be more aware of?"

"I guess so."

"His manner, right? Always the hard-ass army officer."

"That would be it," Jommers said. "I mean, I understand his background, and I respect that, but—"

"But he needs to give it a rest."

"Yeah."

"You're willing to work with him, but you just want some respect. You're a human being like anyone else. You want to be treated with respect."

"Who doesn't?"

"So if you could send him a subliminal message somehow on how to improve the relationship, it would be something like, you need to reframe your posture, get away from this superior/subordinate thing. Karl Jommers is an accomplished, successful professional. You should treat him like a partner or an associate, not like a goldbricking private. Karl Jommers is not Beetle Bailey."

"Exactly so."

"And that's a perfectly legitimate expectation," Stonecipher said. "And I think he's coming around to that idea finally. I think you'll see some positive changes in the future. But you can be patient, right?"

"Sure."

"You don't let some petty resentment screw up a good deal."

"No," Jommers said. "But you know, it's not about the deal. Not about the business. I genuinely care about the cops. I like helping them. They're out there every day, out on the front lines. And I see myself as a support function, helping to keep them out there, helping them to do a good job. I feel like I'm part of the team. I don't want to lose that."

"That's terrific. That's absolutely the right attitude to have. You're above all the bureaucratic crap. You serve a higher calling. You do the right thing because, well, damn it, it's the right thing to do. And you don't expect anyone to throw you a parade or give you a medal. But at the same time, it would be nice if someone recognized your efforts once in a while. Not something big, just in some small way, somebody saying, hey, thanks for all your hard work. Wouldn't it?"

"Sure," Jommers said. "Everyone likes to be recognized."

"Of course. So if a recommendation could bring a little extra business your way, you'd be okay with that. I mean, guy like you, top of your game, probably doing gangbuster business here. Everything under control. Everybody knows you're the go-to guy. But, hey, we're not selling hamburgers here. This is a service business, and like every other service business, it has cycles, ups and downs. So we could all use a little extra cushion to help even things out, make it a smoother ride. You can relate to that."

"Oh, yeah. Definitely."

"Of course. So, at the end of the day, you're still a businessman, and you have to take care of business. You can't help anyone if your shop is closed."

"Very true."

"So, Karl, how do you feel about the security consulting business?"

"Well, I hadn't actually thought about it much."

"You probably think we go around scaring the shit out of people to sell our services. That's how you picture it."

"It would be a concern, obviously."

"And it should be," Stonecipher said. "You spend your time trying to relieve people of their anxieties, you don't want to be implanting more of them. At the same time, you're a health care professional. If you discerned a particular affliction or disorder in a patient, it would be your ethical duty to point that out, wouldn't it? You wouldn't lie to him and tell him everything's hunky-dory. You can't propose a solution without first identifying the problem."

"True. But I'm also very wary about overstating a diagnosis."

"And that is precisely the issue, proportionality. You nailed it. Say you're a truck owner-operator. You bring your rig downstairs to have the brakes checked. You want the mechanic to be specific about where things stand. If the pads are worn but still functional, he tells you to get this handled within the next couple of months. But if they're shot down to the shoes, then you want him to be straight with you. If you go back on the road with this, you're toast. You scale the warning to the threat. And we're professionals, we know how to do that."

"Absolutely," Jommers said. "But aren't you occasionally tempted to sell a bit more than necessary? I'm not saying you do. But the temptation arises, does it not?"

"How should we define that phrase? More than necessary. Do we look at it from a simple statistical perspective? The overwhelming majority of people will live out their entire lives without ever experiencing a house fire. So should a smoke detector be considered more than necessary? Am I a shyster for selling you a smoke detector? No, because it's not just about probabilities, it's about assigning values to possible outcomes for different decision paths. The cost of a smoke detector is low. The cost of a house fire is high. So even though the probability of a fire is low, installing smoke detectors is still the prudent thing to do. It's about big-picture thinking. And that's what we bring to the table, our expertise in big-picture thinking. And understand, it isn't just about protecting the business in the abstract, it's about protecting people. Both the employees and the customers of that business. The owner has a moral responsibility to protect all those people and not just his bottom line. We help him see that. We help him do that."

"So you essentially approach it as a formal risk analysis."

"That's exactly right," Stonecipher said. "Probably not much different than how you handle things. You don't scare the piss out of your patients, you just tell them matter-of-factly, look, pal, you got some issues, and here's how to handle them. That's all."

"Well, it sounds like you're taking the proper approach. Certainly one I'd be comfortable with. Didn't mean to sound like an interrogator . . ."

"You asked all the right questions. It demonstrates thoroughness and proficiency. Someone who pays attention to the details. Exactly the kind of guy I'm looking for."

"To do what?"

"You saw the card I left, right? The line about all the angles covered. That's not a hundred percent true at the moment. There is one gap in my menu of services. Preemployment evaluation."

"Ah."

"It seems like every day now that we read about some guy getting pissed off over a poor performance review or because he was disciplined for being late, whatever. Boom, he snaps. Maybe he sabotages the product or the equipment. Maybe he shoots up the place, with the boss first in line. And as you know better than I, this just doesn't come out of the blue. The potential was there all along. It's resident, because he's got a victim mentality, a persecution complex. He's a land mine just waiting to be stepped on."

"Good way of putting it."

"But these people don't wear signs," Stonecipher said. "And the problem doesn't reveal itself in the job interview because the interviewer isn't looking for it. The interviewer is focused on assessing the candidate's qualifications for the job. And that's important, but it's objective, impersonal. If you concentrate on that alone, you overlook the personality, which is critical. And that's how you make mistakes."

"Indeed."

"A plumber walks into a bar, okay? And inside the bar the plumber sees this pissant little dipshit giving him a snotty goading look. That in-your-face kind of look, right? But the plumber ignores it. He figures a shrimp dick like that isn't going to dare try anything. Now the plumber is not necessarily built like The Arnold, but on the other hand, he's got to lug hot water tanks up and down basement stairs every day. If you have the beef to do that, you don't worry about handling a situation. So the plumber doesn't pay attention to the puny dipshit, takes his eyes away. And then suddenly the little prick swings and sucker-punches the plumber. The wallop sends him to the deck, and now the plumber's reeling on the floor, and runt is kicking the shit out of him, and just before the plumber blacks out, he asks himself, how did I let this happen? And the answer is this. The plumber was appraising the runt's capabilities instead of determining his intentions. It's a common mistake. Focusing on the objective attributes while ignoring the subjective characteristics. But guys like you get it. That's your thing. That's your business. You know what to look for. Right?"

"Yes," Jommers said, "yes, I do."

"Okay. So here's the deal. As an additional service, I start offering my clients psychological evaluation of job candidates to help them weed out bad apples before they get inside the barrel. You will perform this function for me. And since it's your business, you determine the best way to handle it. Tests, interviews, a combination, whatever. I'm not going to tell you how to do your job. You'd work as an independent contractor. That way you don't have to take any shit from me and you can walk away anytime you want. I can pay you by the hour or by the job, whichever you prefer. Either way it will be generous. And if you want to leave a stack of your business cards with the client's HR person, that's fine, too. So, I get to fill a gap in my service package, and you get to pick some extra revenue without sacrificing any independence. What do you think?"

"Sounds like a win-win scenario to me."

"That's terrific," Stonecipher said. "I was hoping you'd say that. I'll send over some paperwork later. It won't be a formal contract, per se, more of memorandum of understanding, so that we're both on the same page. That work for you?"

"Yes, sir, it does."

"I have to tell you, Karl, I love these chairs."

"Thanks."

"More importantly, I like the way you use them. You sit down in the same chair as your guest, the same level, face-to-face as an equal, looking me straight in the eye the whole time. That tells me I'm dealing with an honest broker. A man who's got it together. You know, I go into some places, and the executive, some douche bag who doesn't deserve his pay or title, he's sitting in some oversized leather chair behind an oversized desk, and he makes his guests sit in some ratty, cheesy little side chair with coffee stains. Why does he do that? Because he wants to project power over the other person, the guest. That whole superior-subordinate thing—you know what I'm talking about, right? The guy doesn't have the gravitas to project strength with his persona, so he tries to fake it with furniture. Only it doesn't work. It just makes him look like the squirrelly little shit picker that he is. But you don't play any games. A guy like you doesn't need to. I think we're going to get along just fine."

"I hope so."

As they were finishing up the conversation, the acrid odor of solvent fumes crept up from the shop below and Jommers apologized for the stink.

"I barely noticed it," Stonecipher said. "Thought maybe you had a gal Friday around the corner putting on nail polish."

"It's this goopy sealant they use down in the shop when they fix a trailer roof."

"So trailer roofs leak, too?"

"Well, what happens is the roof gets damaged going under a low bridge. Sometime they even get stuck. Surprisingly, it's a good chunk of Pete's business."

"Well, now that's fascinating," Stonecipher said. "Because I can't help but notice that bridge heights are usually posted. Don't truck drivers look for that?"

"They do, but here's the thing. If you got a heavy load, it depresses the springs and the trailer sits lower. So the driver sees the sign, looks at the load weight on his manifest, does a quick mental calculation. He doesn't want to take the long way around."

"Truck drivers engaging in risk assessment. I love it. You see, this is why I like being out in the field, hearing stories, learning things. Life is a never-ending classroom. Karl, this has been a pleasure. I look forward to working with you."

"Likewise."

AFTER STONECIPHER LEFT, Jommers stretched and took a deep breath. He was impressed by his newly discovered acting ability, yet at the same time troubled that it came so easily. It was disconcerting to realize that, if he so desired, he could be a Wolf N. Stonecipher. He shook off the thought with a shudder.

Jommers was now confident that, as a result of this conversation, Chief Scubbetts would stay off his back for another day or two, assuming nothing new came up. And given the events of the past two weeks, that was a big assumption.

At that moment, his belly growled. Feed me. Heeding the call, he walked down to the shop, intending to get something from the vending machines. As soon as he got there, his eyes fixed immediately on a bag of Micklewhite's Deluxe Pork Rinds. While he couldn't actually smell them through the bag and vendor glass front, the mere sight of the bag triggered the memory of the concentrated odor of pork rinds frying at the MPP plant. He felt a sudden queasiness in his stomach, and just like that, he wasn't hungry anymore. After years of eating pork rinds, he could no longer bear to even look at a sealed bag of them through a pane of glass.

He trudged back upstairs empty-handed. The odor of the solvent fumes lingered in the air. It smelled kind of sweet.

MONEY TO THE WRONG POCKET

It was late afternoon when a mysterious, well-dressed young man quietly entered Jommers's office without saying a word. Jommers had been reflecting on the strange proposition made by Stonecipher, musing about what strange thing might happen next. The young man carried an envelope that held the answer.

"Hello, can I help you?" Jommers asked.

The young man put his right index finger to his lips, the universal shush sign, then handed Jommers the envelope. Inside was a handwritten note on the official letterhead of Elvira Birdsong, Councilwoman, Ward Seven, Grayton City Council:

> *Dear Mr. Jommers,*
>
> *I apologize for this peculiar approach, but these are peculiar times. I wonder if it is possible for you to meet me immediately for a brief, but critical conversation about matters concerning the Grayton Police Department.*
>
> *If so, please accompany the messenger bearing this letter. If now is not a convenient moment, please write down a better time on this page and the messenger will return later. Thank you for your consideration.*
>
> *Sincerely,*
> *Elvira Birdsong*

Jommers nodded silently in the affirmative, and then he went for a ride.

⌒

THE MESSENGER DROVE a mile west over to West Shore Lakefront Park, then took the bumpy access road over to Banshee Horn, a small peninsula near the mouth of the Claybank River. The strip of land had been named in the 1800s by the Irish stevedores who lived and labored there, but it wasn't clear whether the name referred to the shrieking wind that roared off the frozen lake in winter or merely the daily tragedy of ordinary life in an era where poverty and disease saw to it that one in four children perished before the age of ten.

Banshee Horn was actually part of the Bends topographically, but the circuitous route was necessary for want of a proper railroad crossing. The messenger drove slowly over the rutted road to avoid busting an axle or denting the rims. Eventually they arrived at their destination, the end of Lighthouse Service Drive. The name of the short road had become ironic, since the old lighthouse no longer required servicing for a couple of reasons. As with many such places, radio beacons and navigation electronics rendered the old lighthouse obsolete, with distant ships no longer needing its light to find their way to the Port of Grayton.

The short stretch of narrow road was more of a pier that led out to an irregular-shaped platform that supported the lighthouse and its adjacent structure. Both pier and platform were buttressed around the perimeter by giant blocks of stone, fortress walls to protect from Erie's angry waves.

Years ago, during an especially fierce early winter storm, before the lake had frozen, towering, thunderous waves had battered the shoreline and hammered the thin lighthouse promontory. The storm's duration and intense agitation of the water had undermined the footing of the stone blocks on the front face, causing them to lean forward with a slight sink, leaving the foundation of the lighthouse platform exposed and vulnerable to Erie's next fulmination.

After the storm, preservationists and editorials from the *Ledger* had demanded that the city take immediate action to shore up the platform and protect the old lighthouse. The newspaper ran a long feature story collecting the reminiscences of recreational boaters, commercial fishermen, and ore-ship captains all recounting what the lighthouse meant to them. The story included comments from an old Czech woman who lived nearby. She recalled how when the old foghorn bellowed and groaned, the resonant vibrations caused the crystal wineglasses in her china cabinet to sing and dance across the glass shelves that held them.

Unfortunately, the situation arose in a spell of budget cuts and police layoffs. At the same time, the city's ongoing history of racial politics and conflict was at its vitriolic peak. This was evident in the response of the mayor at the time: "If all those white people who fled the city for the burbs are so damn nostalgic about the damn lighthouse, then they can raise the funds to save it. I will be happy to take their money."

A fund drive was launched, but quickly petered out. Reinforcements for the lighthouse never arrived. And so, about a half dozen storms later, the old lighthouse tipped over into the lake.

With no lighthouse to maintain, the city no longer bothered to maintain the service drive either. Its concrete was broken, jagged, and heaved in places. Intertwined thickets of water-polished driftwood draped in green scum hugged the pier on either side.

Jommers trod carefully as he walked out to the platform. Once he got there, he found Councilwoman Birdsong standing on a slab of crumbling concrete, wide stance, hands on her hips, staring with disapproval at the fallen lighthouse, its head dunked in the water but its base still ashore, conveying the image of a beached leviathan.

She was a slender woman, and appeared to be in her late thirties or so. Her posture exuded a sense of strength and primed stillness, like a hurdler waiting for the starting gun. She wore an ivory pantsuit with cocoa blouse and short necklace of faceted garnets. Her shoulder-length black hair was coiled in natural tight curls.

As Jommers came near, she gestured toward the ruins.

"This is the flag of our surrender, the banner of a city crippled by disunity." She spoke with the gravity and lyrical cadence of an advocate, which one expected from a lawyer in politics. "If preserved monuments trumpet the high spirit of the past, then fallen monuments betray the broken spirit of the present. And we don't even have the decency to remove the remains."

Jommers nodded in agreement. "Definitely not postcard material."

"We need to change how we do things here," she said, "but reform efforts get devoured like meat in a shark tank. Progress demands a burying of hatchets, but the elders have built their houses upon such hatchets, and will not surrender them. I have tried to reach out, be a bridge, but have been disowned for my efforts. The masters of the old game send the hounds after those who refuse to play it. The men who were my heroes are now my enemies. The aging freedom riders who would now rein me in." She paused and sighed. "But that's another battle for another day. The fight at hand is more than enough for the moment. I recently had the pleasure of meeting Detective Ilona Voros, with the police department's Internal Affairs Unit. As you are intimately familiar with her situation, there's no need to rehash that here. When we spoke, I was surprised to discover she and I held something important in common—a belief that Chief Scubbetts is corrupt and ruthless, and has likely committed numerous criminal acts. She revealed the grounds for her suspicions and I gave her mine, which I will now share with you. May I trust you to keep this confidential for now?"

"Yes, ma'am. You may."

"As you are no doubt aware, in the wake of 9/11, the federal government enacted the Patriot Act and created the Department of Homeland Security. You may be less aware that the government began distributing funds to municipalities across the country with the objective of increasing the capability of local law enforcement agencies to detect and prevent terrorist acts in their jurisdictions. The funds were also intended to improve interoperability and communications among emergency responders. The amounts varied by the size of the city, but even smaller cities got millions."

"How much did Grayton get, if I may ask?"

"Your question points to the problem," she said. "Under our city charter, city council must authorize expenditures from the general fund: money raised through taxes, fees, and fines. But direct federal grants carrying specific designations go straight to the executive branch, the mayor's office. Such funds do not get allocated by city council. And due to deficiencies in the charter's language, it is not even required that we approve acceptance and usage of the grant. Realizing that a significant amount of DHS money was coming Grayton's way, council requested that the mayor's office involve our body in the distribution of these funds. Our request was rebuffed. Not only does Mayor Cheeks decline our input, but he also refuses to report to us on how it's being spent or even on how much the city got. We're totally in the dark on it. For reasons not clear to us, Mayor Cheeks has chosen to make Chief Scubbetts the exclusive advisor on where this money goes. And they're both extremely secretive about the whole matter. It is my belief, for which I do not yet have evidence, that a good portion of this money is being funneled into a private security consulting firm that is secretly owned and run by the chief."

"In other words," Jommers said, "millions of dollars of federal grant money could be going directly into the chief's pocket."

"Correct."

"Wow."

"That would be the polite exclamation," she said. "I can think of others more expressive. So, it was comforting and inspiring to learn recently that a detective from Internal Affairs was already quietly investigating Chief Scubbetts, albeit without authorization. So she's alone, out on a limb, putting herself and her career at risk. It is therefore imperative that she be returned to duty as quickly as possible so that she can act in an official capacity and legally carry a weapon. To that end, I privately persuaded most of my fellow members of the Force Review Committee to expedite the review process regarding the shooting of Patrolman Earl Tarburn. When Chief Scubbetts was informed of our desire to fast-track it, he strongly objected. We met anyway, and he was outvoted. He exploded. He angrily vowed that Detective Voros would never again carry the badge, saying that she was psychologically unfit for duty and he would keep her off the force on those grounds. My subsequent inquiry into those comments has led me to you. Since I've been candid with you, I was hoping you would be candid with me. Is that true? Are you judging her unfit for duty?"

"No, ma'am. The chief misjudges the situation."

"Where do you stand with her evaluation?"

"I'm finished," Jommers said. "She's good to go. I was only waiting for your committee to finish up before turning in the paperwork."

"Our paperwork will be submitted to PD Human Resources first thing tomorrow morning."

"In that case, mine will be there the same time."

Birdsong smiled for the first time, though fleetingly. "It was a pleasure meeting you, Mr. Jommers."

"Likewise."

AFTER BEING DELIVERED back to the shop, Jommers drove up the hill to hit the Old Town Market. He needed food, but given the steamy weather, he wanted items that would not require cooking, an activity he disliked even in cooler weather. So first on his list was smoked sausage that could be eaten cold or with the chill taken off by a few seconds of nuking. He picked up some kielbasa with garlic, Andouille, and some brats made with onion and green pepper. He grabbed some cheese, too, both Swiss and pepper jack. To that he added a loaf of Russian rye bread, a jar of stuffed green olives, some hot mustard, cottage cheese, potato salad, and rotini pasta salad. He also bought some tomatoes, green peppers and a container of fresh-cut pineapple. And this time of year, strawberries were both luscious and inexpensive. He could toss those in the cottage cheese with some pineapple, and that would be a cool meal right there.

On his way out with his purchases, he smiled and nodded to the uniformed security guard at the door. About twenty feet out the door, he stopped in his tracks, a delayed reaction to something his eyes had seen but his brain not yet registered. He turned around and looked back at the security guard. The shoulder patch emblem on his shirt was the logo for Pike Square Security.

The Old Town Market was owned and operated by the City of Grayton, with the stalls leased to the various vendors. So somebody at city hall must have made the decision to contract with Pike Square for the market's security. The enlightening moment resonated with what he'd just heard from Councilwoman Birdsong, her suspicions about Chief Scubbetts having influence over Mayor Cheeks. And that made Jommers wonder about how Scubbetts had pulled it off. How could this socially awkward man, who was definitely not a people person, have such influence over his superior?

The obvious answer was so improbable that Jommers immediately dismissed it. Yet it kept springing back up. Enough so that he had to seriously pose the question to himself. Was Scubbetts ballsy enough to use the fear-inducing chemical on the mayor? Was that in fact possible? And not for the first or last time did he ask himself, at what point do you begin to doubt your doubts?

After Jommers got home and put his food away, he popped open a can of beer and put some blues on the CD player and switched it through the old Philco cathedral cabinet. And while drinking and listening to the music, he let his thoughts race and collide at will. Somewhere in the course of the evening, he heard a train song. Maybe it was "B&O Blues No. 2" by Blind Willie McTell, or something in that vein. And that caused him to recall the night at the old railroad roundhouse where Biederbach had shot the wild dog that was about to attack. And he remembered how Biederbach had spoken of the dogs that get dumped and become wild.

And that stirred him to think about the City Kennel, the dog pound, which was in the Bends not far away. And that prompted him to remember an article he'd read in the *Ledger* about political patronage in the current administration. Something about the mayor's brother-in-law being hired as the animal warden in charge of the kennel. And as that story darted through his head, it plowed into the image of the Pike Square Security guard at the city-owned Old Town Market and careened into the theories of Councilwoman Birdsong. By the time the pileup was over, Jommers knew exactly where he was going in the morning.

DAY SEVENTEEN

FINDING IN THE HELLMOUTH

The door for the City Kennel was essentially a hellmouth, a portal from the normal world to a wretched netherworld. From the outside, the kennel looked no different than any other grimy brick building in the Bends. Only after entering did it reveal itself as an infernal region.

The odor gripped Jommers first, enveloping him like an invisible poisonous fog. Feces, urine, vomit, unwashed fur, black mold—all steam-cooked by a swampy summer besieging an unventilated building. Just one whiff made him nauseous.

The noise walloped him next. It wasn't ordinary dog yelping and yapping, but a fierce cacophony infused with violence, panic, and madness. The wild commotion incited a primal response of terror, causing the hair on his neck to stand up. The dogs were all in cages, and a twelve-foot chain-link fence separated the offices from the area where the animals were held, so there was technically nothing to fear, but Jommers felt his heart pumping faster, adrenaline oozing into his bloodstream. The massive weight of auditory threat signals was overwhelming the visual certitude of safety. Yet he pressed on.

Jommers had already crossed the border of his domain with the research he'd performed on Monday, so coming over to scope out the situation at the kennel didn't seem like a big deal. And after his performance for Wolf Stonecipher the day before, he felt strangely comfortable as he mentally prepared to once again lie about his intentions.

Perhaps it was yesterday's talk with Councilwoman Birdsong that inspired him. Perhaps it was his realization that once the paperwork on Ilona Voros got to police headquarters, things would never be the same. He had called a messenger service to deliver the papers for him. Not that he feared encountering Scubbetts at the station, he simply didn't want to be distracted from his morning mission—kennel recon.

Even with the chain-link fence protection, Nate Paver, director of Animal Control, kept the door to his office locked with two deadbolts, only one of them keyed from the outside. The lanky, lumpy man toddled over and looked out the window nervously before unlocking it, seeming less concerned with who was there and more concerned that there were no dogs behind him. The windows in the door and office were made of old-fashioned chicken wire glass. Paver quickly shut and locked the door after letting Jommers inside, at which point Jommers notice that Paver wore a semiautomatic sidearm on his right hip.

Paver relaxed once back in his chair, sitting with an uneasy slouch that was both world-weary and tense, a jittery man feigning poise. That same discordance played over his face with its sardonic, assured smile betrayed by wide anxious eyes. This was a man who would cockily tell a dirty joke in the graveyard at night, then look over his shoulder to ensure no ghosts were offended.

He was smoking a cheap, overly sweet aromatic cigarillo, most likely in a futile attempt to counter the ambient stink. There was a glass of dark liquid on his desk. Jommers cast his eyes around the room and noticed a bottle of dark rum and bottle of Dr. Pepper on a table in the corner. It was barely past nine thirty in the morning.

Jommers introduced himself and presented his card. He mentioned how he was providing counseling services to the police department, helping officers cope with occupational-induced stress and depression. He then inquired whether staff at the kennel might also benefit from similar counseling, given the emotional toll of the job. He phrased it as a question, but intoned it as more of a suggestion. Paver nodded in a way that implied he understood the proposition, but did not necessarily agree with it.

Jommers pointed his thumb backward over his shoulder.

"Interesting environment," Jommers said.

Paver responded with a dismissive chortle. "The word *interesting* would be a weak accounting of it. The word *interesting* does not fully relate the situation. Try *nightmarish, barbarous, unearthly, horrific*. A relentless brutal barrage upon your senses, all the ones you know, and some you didn't even know you had. That at least gets you in the ballpark. So, leading off is that stench, which you notice, rising off their watery putrescence, simmering in this infernal heat. Inhaling that all day long is enough by itself to crush your will and make you want to cross the river sooner rather than later. But what really gets in your head is the noise. You do hear that, don't you? They start that barking like that, you know, rage barking, start as soon as you get here and keep at it until you go. They're letting you know how badly they want to shred you into jerky strips. They keep it up until their throats get raw and all they can do is emit this low, demon growl, a hellhole creature sound, like it was the end of the world. And when they can't do that anymore, they're still talking at you with their eyes, giving you that murder stare. Still letting you know. They never stop letting you know what they'll do if they get the chance. So what you get in your stomach is that hurly feeling, like you're dangling off a skyscraper flagpole, staring down.

Get me? You feel that hour after hour. That's my day. My wife knows not to ask me. Nate, how was your day? So, no, *interesting* is not the word for it. And I don't have the word either. Maybe that Italian guy who wrote about all the different layers of hell, maybe he's got the word for it. I surely do not."

Paver took a gulp from his glass, swished it around his mouth, then swallowed it. He was already a patient, in the care of a liquid therapist. Jommers understood.

"Well, I guess that affirms my reason for coming," Jommers said. "I've had good success in helping people cope with stressful occupations, as my years of experience with police officers indicates. In particular, I frequently help officers deal with the emotional aftermath of having to use force or engage in violent encounters. In a similar vein, I'm sure your staff experiences some anxiety, if not distress, over having to put down animals. I can guide them on how to best handle those feelings."

Paver again let out a dismissive chortle, only this time it was more of a scoff.

"Let me tell you something. My people are not distressed about killing these monsters. My people are distressed that they are not allowed to kill every one of the motherfuckers on the spot. They're distressed that they're required to risk life and limb by wrestling a crazed psycho beast into a cage and then bringing it in. We got to follow the rules. Get me? Bring them in first, hold on to them in case someone wants to adopt one, like anyone in their right mind is going to adopt a maniacal hellhound who wants to eat your liver. We only get to kill them when all the cages are full, which they always are. So it's first-in, first-out inventory control. For every new one coming in warm, we send an old one out cold. And doing it isn't as easy as you might think because, again, we got rules. If it was up to me, we'd machine-gun the motherfuckers in their cages. But the rules say we got to put them down all nice and gentle like so they don't feel any pain. So we inject them with sodium pentobarbital. We've got these long-handled syringes so we don't have to take them out of the cage. Needle on a stick. But these motherfuckers got dictator-type brains. They're crazy evil, but they're not stupid. They see you coming with one of these, and they know what's up. Don't ask me how. They just know. So as soon as you poke the needle on a stick into the cage, the beast flanks you. Pivots to the side and clamps down on the handle. Yanks it out of your hand. Pulls it inside. Then it gives you that look. Oh, this here your stick? You want it back? Then come on in and get it. So we got to use two people coming at the motherfucker from opposite sides, both of them got a stick. You know, what you call on the battlefield a pincher movement."

"Pincer," Jommers corrected.

"Right, okay, pincer. Whatever. The beast gets stuck one way or the other. And I don't take any chances. I load up those syringes. That thing isn't getting the doggie dose. That motherfucker getting the dinosaur dose. Even then, after it goes limp, I make my people use this mirror on a stick, position it in front of the thing's nose to make sure it's not breathing. And even then I worry that the devil going to breathe life back into it just for fun, because the devil knows its own. My nerves don't stand down till it's in the bag. So that's how it is down here. That's not what you expected to hear, was it?"

"No," Jommers said. "I guess I'm out of touch on all this."

"You got that right. Let me tell you how things changed. There was a time when we were about the name, Animal Control. We'd come get your skunks, raccoons, bats or your whatever. We don't have time for that shit anymore. Raccoons aren't ripping people's feet off. What we're about now is dogs. Period. Your standard city rippers, to be specific. Yeah, if some stupid shit asshole dumps his python or his alligator, we still got to go get that. But it's mostly the dogs now. So if you call me about a raccoon, I'm going to give you two recommendations. One, where to buy a good trap. Two, where to buy a good metal baseball bat. And don't even bother to call me about cats. Just fucking handle it. See recommendation number two. And when I say dogs, I'm not talking Lassie getting lost or poodles that crawled under the fence. I'm not talking wiener dogs or chee-hooah-hooahs either. Get me? Those are suburban dogs. I'm talking city dogs. Ripper dogs. I'm talking pits, Rotts, Dobermans . . . I'm talking motherfucking flesh eaters. Killer curs. Hounds from hell. And it's not just the strays, though those are bad enough. And *stray* isn't the right word either. The thing didn't just wander off. It was dumped by someone who got tired of it after getting bit. You see, when they get these things, it's all about the gangsta-tude. Don't mess with me. The same with their badass slouchy strut and that pissy, goading look they give you. You just try messing with me. You just try. So when you get a dog that's a nasty rip-ass motherfucker, it's all part of the show. You're saying I'm a nasty rip-ass motherfucker, too. Then one day your nasty rip-ass motherfucker dog bites you in the ass and you say, fuck that shit. This dog got to go. Get me? So then you drive it somewhere and turn it loose. So it's not a stray, it's a dump. But, like I was saying, it's not the dumps, it's their brood. Because their offspring are feral. You know that word, right?"

"Yes," Jommers said. "They have no experience with human contact. They don't act domesticated."

"That's exactly right. They act wild. Like lions and tigers in the bush wild. Only worse. They act like lions and tigers on PCP. Bad PCP. And then they form into packs. And once they're in the pack, they get all cocky, defiant. Now then, as you also know, these things are carnivores. They're not looking for fallen apples or acorns. They're not looking to steal Big Rocco's tomatoes. They want meat. Only this is the city. We don't have herds of elk and caribou for them to chow down on. What we got is people. And in the eyes of the beast, people is just meat with shoes. And when they get the kids, that's what really pisses me off. The kids suffer worse. They're smaller, they're weaker, and they're closer to the ground. Let me tell you, if it happens to you, don't go to ground. Just don't, because then they get to your head and neck. Stay up as long as you can. You can still live without feet and hands. You can't live without a neck. You get me?"

"Got it. Keep standing."

"You came with suggestions, but I'll tell you what we really need. You know them cracker boys that like to go hunting in the woods? I mean the hardcore ones. The ones who'll take on a wild boar with a crossbow. You bring some of those cracker boys to the city with their crossbows, cammie jammies and whatnot. You give them fifty dollars a dog head, no questions asked. They'll get it done. They'll take care of business."

"That's a bleak picture," Jommers said. "You're obviously under a lot of pressure here. Forgive my asking, but you might wish to ponder whether you personally could benefit from some counseling, maybe just someone to listen, like I'm doing now."

"You're not going to send me a bill now, are you? You're the one who came to see me."

Both men laughed. Paver took another gulp from his glass. He ground out the butt of his expended cigarillo and lit up another. In the quiet pause, Jommers's mind raced, desperately wondering how to subtly shift the conversation over to his real topic of interest. And just then, Paver fortuitously did exactly that.

"I'll tell you who could use some talking to. Lonnie."

"Lonnie Cheeks," Jommers said. "The mayor. Your brother-in-law."

"That's right, my brother-in-law. I know the newspaper likes to make a big deal about that. But this job is real and someone's got to do it. And I'm not getting any more money than the last guy, and I'm doing real work. Not like his cousin Estelle. Sitting in some air-conditioned office, filing a few papers, then taking home fifty G. Strutting around like she's some queen of the roost or something."

"What makes you think the mayor has some issue that requires addressing?"

"He's been acting real squirrelly lately. Antsy. Looking over his shoulder. Like he's been fishing in someone else's pond. And that's not the way he is. You've seen him on TV. You know what he's like. Backslapping and glad-handing. Jazzed up and jive-ass. I come off a shy boy standing next to him. Used to be anyway. Now he's all pulled in, huddled up, like a tornado coming or something. Like now. This is the time of year where you got all those ethnic festivals going—the Greek Festival, the Serb Festival, the Ukarainians and Cromanians and the what-the-hell-ever-manians. And Lonnie used to hit all of those, because that's what you do, how you play the game. He would try all their funky foods and throw his head back and rave about it like he was receiving the Holy Ghost. Even when that shit tastes like old basement, which is most of the time.

Like . . . what's that yellow-brown Middle Eastern goop look like baby shit?"

"Hummus," Jommers said.

"Yeah, hummus. Look like baby shit, taste like baby shit, too. But Lonnie never blinked. He would eat that shit, smile, and go mmm, mmm, mmm. You know? Because that's what you do. That's local politics. Eat shit and smile. But this year, he hasn't gone to a single one of them. Not one. Something's not right with him."

"Was this a gradual or sudden change in him? What do you think caused it?"

"I think he's listening to the wrong people, getting some bad advice. He needs to trust his own instincts, which used to be pretty keen."

"Anyone in particular giving bad advice?" Jommers asked.

"The hoodoo man."

"And that would be?"

"Chief Scubbetts."

"Why do you call him that?"

"He got the black cat bone or something. People spend any time behind his door come out with the worries."

"Like the mayor."

"Yeah. And I'm hesitating here. I know you work with PD. I don't want to trash your main man or nothing."

"I hardly know him," Jommers said. "I work with HR mostly. So don't worry."

"In that case . . . I think Scubbetts is messing with Lonnie's head. Making him think terrorists are coming to Grayton. Maybe already here. And Lonnie is getting all panicky about it."

"Terrorists? In Grayton?"

"Yeah. That's what I said. I mean, yeah, we were all freaked out after 9/11, but then we all settled down and got back to business. Right? Because we know that you're more likely to get mashed in your car than get blown up by a rag-head. And those people aren't coming to Grayton, get me? They like the big stage. If they're fixing to put on another show, it's going to be in a big-city opera house, not the Moldy Oaks Community Theater."

"Does Scubbetts have any grounds for his assertion? Or is he just speculating?"

"This is supposed to be top secret, okay? But frankly, that's illogical. If it's all horseshit, which it is, then how can it be secret? How do you hide something that isn't there? Get me? But all the same . . ."

"Understood."

"Now I'm hearing this from Lonnie, who heard it from Scubbetts, that terrorists supposedly tried to sneak in the water treatment plant planning to poison the water supply. They got found out in the nick of time, but managed to get away somehow. Well, now. I work in city government. I know a lot other people in city government. And none of them heard a word about it. And Lonnie himself got a nephew Antoine over there at Water. And I talked to Antoine, and guess what? He doesn't know a thing about it. So how the hell does something big like that happen at Water and a guy who works at Water knows nothing about it? You get me?"

"Right," Jommers said. "But then that raises the question, why would Scubbetts concoct such a story?"

"I think someone is hot in the biscuit for a piece of that DHS kitty, and I think I know who."

"You lost me."

"Which part?"

"All parts."

"Okay. You know DHS?"

"Department of Homeland Security."

"That's right," Paver said. "So after they got done looking at everything that went wrong at Twin Towers, DHS starts sending money out to cities to help them prepare for something like that. Better yet, prevent something like that. And one of the big problems they had, if you remember, was communications. All the different units of first responders trying to talk to each other. No one with the big picture of what was going on. So the first thing on everybody's wish list when this money starts flowing like honey is new communications equipment so they can deal with that whole issue. So Lonnie gets these fancy, high-tech radios that are supposed to improve interdepartment communication. These things were crazy-ass expensive, like five thousand dollars apiece or something like that. And everyone in a first-responder position got one. They even gave some to me and my people, too, you know, just in case there was a stampede of flaming animals somewhere, and we'd need to get both PD and FD involved. And these things were software-driven, you know, where you got to navigate menus and shit. Damn things came with a hundred-and-seventy-eight-page instruction manual. And worse, it was written in Engrish. You know Engrish, right?"

"A bad translation from Japanese to English, commonly found in consumer electronics instruction manuals."

"That's right. Only in this case, the word *bad* doesn't tell it. It was like Japanese translated to Bulgarian translated to Martian and then to English. So the radios never got used because no one could ever figure the fuckers out. Then somewhere down the line, the company tells us we need to upgrade the software because the version we got has bugs in it. In other words, even if you were that Rain Man guy and memorized the entire hundred-and-seventy-eight-page instruction manual, you still wouldn't have been able to work the motherfucker because of all the glitches in it."

"Not exactly a prudent purchasing decision," Jommers said.

"You got that right. Now, you know, I love Lonnie. I have a great deal of respect for the man. He's smart in a lot of things. He can play politics the way Little Richard played piano, like a wild man in total control. But we all got the weak heel, right? And Lonnie's is . . . well, he just doesn't know how to buy shit. Which is why half the garbage trucks don't work right now. But eventually he gets it, understands he's going to need some good advice with all the money pouring in. And everybody is eager to give it, especially Chief Scubbetts. Now Lonnie was pretty savvy about seeing when someone had an angle to work, because that's pretty much everybody when you're the mayor. Get me? So anything Scubbetts threw at him, Lonnie took with a pinch of salt. Then something changed. Somehow Scubbetts got Lonnie's ear and never let go. So now Lonnie is all, Chief suggests this, Chief suggests that—like Scubbetts is his fucking guru or something. And that's bad enough, but the fishiest thing about it is this other guy that Scubbetts brings around, someone in the private security business. So then it's like tag team, with both of them working Lonnie over."

"What's this guy's name?" Jommers asked.

"Stonestuffer or something. Supposed to be a consultant, but sounds more like a salesman. Slicker than snot on a doorknob. This guy could steal your goddamn balls without you noticing them gone till later. That kind, you know?"

"So you met this guy?"

"Oh, yeah. Lonnie called a meeting, just the four of us, about improving security here at the kennel. And I could see the way Scubbetts and Stonestuffer were riffing off each other that they were in cahoots somehow. Like maybe Chief getting kickbacks for greasing the sale. Seemed pretty obvious to me. I don't know why Lonnie couldn't see it. Like I said, he used to be pretty good at reading that."

"They think someone's going to bomb your dogs?"

"I wish. So long as I'm not here at the time. But, no. Stonestuffer starts throwing out this wacked-out theory how they're going to sneak in here at night and infect the dogs with some kind of weaponized microbe. Then when people adopt the dogs, they get this fatal and contagious disease, then pass it on to their families, coworkers and all that. He said he heard this from his connections in the intelligence sector. And they got it from monitoring phone calls. So then he lays out this comprehensive plan for how to transform this place into a more secure area. And when I say comprehensive, I mean big ticket. The kind where you got to write the zeroes real small so they all fit in the box on the check. So, I'm sitting there and I can't believe Lonnie is sucking this all in with a straight face. Trying to spread some kind of disease roundabout way using pound dogs is just ass-brain. You'd be better off taking a job in fast-food joint. You could infect a couple hundred people a day there. And even if they did give something to these dogs, it wouldn't matter. I don't care if it was fucking Ebola. Anyone gump enough to take home one of these curs doesn't ever have to worry about getting sick, because that motherfucker will chew your fucking head off before the germ gets a chance to put his suitcase down. You'd get the chomp before you get the chills."

"So the mayor bought it?"

"Oh, yeah, he bought it. That package is in the works. I'm not allowed to punch a hole in the wall to install a fucking room air conditioner for my office, but I'm going to get a security system better than Fort Knox. What I don't get is how Scubbetts pulled it off, getting Lonnie's ear like that. I mean, at first, Lonnie's got no use for that peckerwood. Original plan was just bring him in to clean up PD and fuck with the union. And once that was done, Lonnie was going to give him the gate. Then everything changed after that meeting. You should have seen him in there, shivering like the hawk was out. Can't figure out how they did that. You got the gypsy eye. You tell me how."

"The chief is obviously playing on common fears," Jommers said, "and fear is a powerful influence. It alters your perception. Sometimes for the better, sometimes for the worse. Fear can induce clarity and focus, but it can also create distortion and hysteria. And if the influence of fear persists for an extended period of time, it makes an imprint. It rewires the brain. Makes you a different person."

"Well, how do you un-rewire that brain? How do we get the old Lonnie back?"

"Give him my card. Maybe I can help."

"I'll do that, but here's the thing, though. People get like that can't see what they got, you know? Like trying to catch your eyeballs move while looking in the mirror."

"Well, what you do is—"

The conversation was interrupted by some commotion out on the floor. Paver jumped out of his chair and moved over to the window, and Jommers followed. An Animal Control van had backed into the loading dock, and two Animal Control officers were attempting to remove a large, agitated dog from the van cage with the intent of transferring it into a kennel cage.

"Fuck," Paver grunted. "A monster mastiff, two hundred and fifty pounds at least. Motherfucker could tow a barge. And it's injured. See the hind? This won't go well."

The two men on the floor were using common catchpoles to take control of the dog. The poles were aluminum shafts that looked about five feet long. They had rubber grips at the handle end. At the business end was a loop of cable that the user slung over the dog's head, then tightened by pulling the cable at the handle end.

Both men were successful in getting their loops over the dog's head and cinching them. They pulled the dog out of the van cage onto the floor, and that was when all hell broke loose. The dog tried to bolt. And given its size and strength, it pulled both men to the floor and started dragging them. The men struggled to get up, only to be pulled down again as the big dog ran crazily around, yelping and snapping the whole time.

Paver tensed up and put his hand on his sidearm, eyes wide, face taut. He whispered slowly, barely audibly.

"Just . . . fucking . . . shoot it."

Several other men quickly appeared on the scene, adding their hands to the catchpoles. With the extra muscle, the dog's movement was restricted, but it was still an intense struggle to get the dog into a cage, a process that took an agonizing ten minutes of wild chaos.

When the battle was over, Paver relaxed, walked over to his desk, then gulped down the rest of his drink.

Jommers smiled politely and decided it was an opportune moment for an exit.

"Well, I should probably let you get back to work. I appreciate your time."

"Yeah, sure," Paver said. "Good talking to you."

Before Jommers got out the door, Paver was already mixing himself another drink.

JOMMERS WAS STUNNED. So stunned he couldn't remember where he'd parked his car and wandered around blankly for a few moments like a man lost in the desert. He turned around and realized he'd been so lost in thought he'd walked right by his car.

What stunned him was not the sensory experience of the visit, but the realization that Scubbetts and Stonecipher were using the fear-inducing chemical on the city's mayor in order to divert massive amounts of money into their pockets, money from federal funds granted to the city.

It was brazen beyond belief. And it confirmed his opinions about Scubbetts. No ordinary criminal could be so coolly cocksure.

As he recalled Paver's description of the meeting, it was clear that Mayor Cheeks was under the influence of something, but Jommers wondered why it hadn't affected Paver similarly. Maybe because Paver was full of rum at the time, oblivious to other influences. Or maybe, knowing that Cheeks was the decision-maker, the chemical was somehow directed only towards him. It didn't matter. It was all clear now. Except for one thing. What next?

THE CHIEF EXPLODES

Jommers knew that Chief Scubbetts would call after finding out that Detective Ilona Voros had been cleared. His initial impulse was to avoid the expected rant. No reason to endure it. The PD business would be lost regardless, at least for now. Maybe, if Scubbetts got the axe, the next chief might restore the business. Maybe not.

On second thought, Jommers changed his mind. He was, after all, a professional psychologist. He might learn something about this particular type of personality, gain insights that could prove useful with future patients. Engaging the chief as a subject of study, then, could be educational, even if briefly uncomfortable.

Yet he also understood that, in any such engagement, he must avoid making any accusations or suggesting he had any knowledge of wrongdoing. Doing so might encourage Scubbetts to destroy evidence and otherwise interfere with Voros's investigation. So Jommers knew he must restrain himself, confine the conversation to their professional relationship and nothing more. He even rehearsed how it might go. So when the call inevitably came, he was ready. Ready to deal with it, and ready to record it.

"WHAT THE FUCK are you doing? What the fuck are you doing? What? What? What?" Scubbetts's enraged voice was barely recognizable. He was yelling loudly from the deepest part of his lungs. Bellowing slowly, he extended the notes of each syllable into a predator's roar, rhythmically accentuating the beginning of each, hammering them, his voice beating the words, as if language itself was a thing that could be tortured and punished. "What the fuck are you doing? What? What?"

"What's your point, Chief?"

"What's my point? What's my fucking point? What are you doing? Are you insane? Delusional? Suicidal? You are a fucking mouse in a cat's mouth. And you do this? You defy the cat to bite? To sink its teeth? Do you think you're protected? That a cavalry somewhere is coming to your rescue? Are you fucking crazy? What? Tell me, what? I can't see what you're seeing. What? Tell me."

"Are you referring to the paperwork I submitted on Detective Voros?"

"What the fuck you think I'm talking about? You juked me. You fucking juked me. You did exactly what I ordered you not to do. You did exactly what you promised not to do. You fucking backstabbing traitor. You think you can get away with that? Do you? Do you think I will let you get away with that? You think you're that smart? That you can get away with it? You're not smart. You are fucking stupid. You will see. You will see what happens."

"I had no choice. The requirements of my profession."

"Fuck you and your choice. Don't talk to me about choice. It's about dictates, and I dictate to you."

"No. That's not how it works."

"Yes, that's exactly how it works, you fucking dumb shit. I don't understand this. I don't understand. I was good to you. Supported you. Treated you like a fucking regal concubine. This is how you repay me? This is my thanks? You fucking ungrateful cocksucker. You exploit me, then double-cross me? This is what you do? This? What?"

Jommers refused to respond to the invective in kind or even acknowledge its intensity. He let the insults roll off. He declined to elevate his voice or escalate emotion. He carried on the conversation calmly with a casual tone, as if he were confirming a pizza order.

"You know, Chief, this isn't about you, or me, or our relationship. It's just business. And my business has certain standards that I must follow. There's no reason for you to make this personal."

"It is absolutely fucking personal, goddamn it. Don't tell me it's not personal. I did for you. I did for you. And you fucking owe me. You owe me gratitude. You owe me loyalty. You owe me everything. But what do I get? Fucking stabbed in the back."

There was a slight tremor in Scubbetts's voice and the sound of hurried footsteps in the background, suggesting that the chief was pacing furiously while yelling into the phone.

"So, yes, it is personal. A knife in the back is most definitely fucking personal, you fucking cockbite."

"Gratitude and loyalty are fine concepts, Chief, but they're contingent concepts. The value of loyalty is contingent upon its object. It's not about loyalty per se, but who or what one is loyal to. There's a hierarchy. And at the top is ethics. One's highest loyalty is to ethics."

"Fuck your pussy ethics."

"What I did was the right thing to do."

"The right thing? The right thing?"

Jommers heard a loud whack in the background, quickly followed by a few more. *Whack. Whack. Whack.* At first, Jommers wondered what it could be. Then he remembered the last time he was in Scubbetts's office, seeing the Civil War saber in the umbrella stand and the gouges on the chief's wooden desk. Scubbetts was murdering his furniture, his legendary rage apparently not an act, but for real.

"You don't get to decide the right thing. I decide the right thing. That's the fucking hierarchy. That's the way it works. The people in charge decide the right thing. The people with the big picture decide the right thing. That's why they're in charge. They're on the horse, on the hill. They see the field. You don't see shit. You're a grunt in the mud. Your face in the ass of the grunt in front of you. What do you see? You see ass and mud, that's all. You see nothing, you know nothing. You're a dumb fuck. You don't know the right thing. I tell you the right thing."

Scubbetts was breathing heavily, his frantic yelling and pacing and saber-whacking all competing for oxygen. "I tell you the right thing."

"Sorry, Chief. That's not the way it works with me. I'm not in your army."

Whack. Whack. Whack. "Fuck you. You are in my army. You work for me. You are in my army. You take from me. You are in my fucking army."

"No."

"Where is this coming from? How did this happen? Did she turn you? Are you fucking her? Where is this coming from? Is that all it takes? A stump grinder? I could have got you some high-class clapper that looks better than her. Is that all it takes to betray your cause? Betray your protectors? Is that all it takes?"

"Again, you're not getting it. You're not listening. There is no betrayal where there is no presumption of allegiance. You're personalizing this."

"There was a presumption, goddamn it. You misled me. You used to listen to me, like a cocksucker, like a bootlicker. You exploited me. Like a goddamn parasite. A parasitic ass-worm eating my shit crust. You scum-sucking . . ." Scubbetts was now panting and gasping, struggling to maintain the force of his voice. "You pretended to respect me. You juked me. Used me. Fucking faker. Liar. User . . ."

"No, Chief. That's wrong."

"I am not wrong. You signed on. You signed on. You pretended to respect . . ."

"There was no pretense. Whatever respect I exhibited was simply a business-person behaving in a professional manner. Like a lawyer or a dentist—even if they hate you, they're going to treat you in a professional manner. That's all it was. I didn't mislead you. You misread the situation."

"You kissed my ass. Don't tell me you didn't."

"No."

"You licked my boots."

"No. I tolerated you. But compared to other responses, you might have perceived that as kindness."

"You what? You tolerated me? What the fuck does that mean? You tolerated me."

"I gave you the benefit of the doubt. I considered your upbringing in an isolated rural area, and then going from that straight into the army, how under those circumstances, you might not have had the opportunity to develop proper social skills. So I attributed your adversarial propensity and awkwardness as—"

"My what? My awkwardness? What the fuck do—"

"Yes, your awkwardness. Or what I perceived as mere awkwardness. So I didn't take it as seriously as I should have. But now I understand better what's happening. I understand your behavior now that—"

"What do you mean you understand me? What do you mean? What? You don't understand me. You—"

"You had an inherent neurological predisposition that was catalyzed by the environment of a peculiar upbringing. You—"

"Cata-what? What the fuck are you talking about?"

"Call it a potential that was activated by circumstance. Nature planted the device and nurture, or rather lack of it, triggered it."

"What the fuck are you—"

"The seed of your antisocial personality disorder was cultivated by the experience of isolation, being raised under brutal conditions, in a house where you weren't wanted. It was held in check by your military life, the rules and regimentation, your superiors—all that kept you in line. Then you came here, landed in a socially hostile situation, but where there's no constraints, and where you're in charge. And that combination unlocks the thing. The check valve blows. Your condition erupts. And there's no one to rein you in. No one to recognize the symptoms. No one but me. And I failed to."

"Symptoms? Of what? What the fuck are spewing about? What?"

"But it's not too late, maybe. Maybe not too late to get help."

"Too late for what? What are you talking about?" He was roaring again. Each syllable hit like a drum, then drew out into a loud yowl.

"Therapy, Chief. It's possible therapy can get you back on track, back to a normalcy you probably never knew."

"Therapy?" *Whack.* "Therapy?" *Whack.* "You calling me a psych section?" *Whack, whack, whack.* "You calling me mental?" *Whack, whack, whack.* "You have the fucking gall to taunt me like this?" *Whack. Whack.* "You dare to taunt me, you motherfucking son of a bitch? I will fucking gut you. I will fucking gut you and throw you in the chicken shit pond with the rest. You motherfucking son of a bitch."

"Your behavior right now is indicative of—"

"Don't you dare taunt me, you motherfucker. You insolent, insubordinate, motherfucking son of a bitch. Don't you dare taunt me. I will fucking gut you. I will—"

"I'm just trying to be honest with you, Chief. I don't want to fail you the way I failed Tarburn."

"In the pond with you. In the pond. You insubordinate motherfucking son of a bitch."

"I'm looking at Tarburn's picture right now. It's a photo of him showing his son how to operate a telescope. He was a good man. A good father. A good husband. Good cop. Good soldier. And the last part, the good soldier part, that's what got him into trouble. Trying to figure out just what that means. Trying to understand the hierarchy of loyalties . . ."

"Fuck you and fuck Tarburn. He got the jellies when things got hot. Just like you. Two of a kind. With your jelly-nut whimpering and moralizing. That's not what real men do. That's not what good soldiers do. Real men, real soldiers, they act upon command. They stand tall. They don't whimper and whine. They do their duty. Accept the call to action. They stand tall. They stand proud."

"Earl Tarburn stood taller than you can ever hope to. You don't come up to the top of his boots."

"You fucking insubordinate asshole. I will fucking gut you. Put you in the pond. You have no right to turn your back on me. You have no right—"

"If you seek help now, I mean formally, with notice to HR, it will look better for you down the road. If things should fall apart, the fact that you sought help—you will be credited for that. I have some open slots if you'd like to make an appointment now."

"Fuck you." *Whack.* "In the pond." *Whack.* "Fuck you." *Whack.* "In the pond." *Whack.* "Fuck you."

The cursing and the whacking continued for short bit, though it seemed much longer in emotional time. When finally, it ended, all Jommers could hear was an exhausted Scubbetts wheezing and gasping for breath. Then, after a long silence, Scubbetts spoke again in a calmer, but more chilling voice, a voice so hoarse from screaming that it was reduced to an unearthly growl.

"Everything that happens next is on you. Remember that. When you see it happen, you own it. It's yours. So when you look at it in shock and horror, remember, you did it. Remember that it was you. You pulled the trigger."

Click.

JOMMERS DEBATED HOW SERIOUSLY to take Scubbetts's threats. If the chief was behind the deaths of Tarburn and Commander Mungfreud, then Scubbetts was certainly morally capable of eliminating other people without qualms. Yet in both cases, the manner of dispatch was deliberately indirect and impersonal. That approach suggested that, in spite of Scubbetts's rash rant, he was still cautious enough to avoid committing an equally rash act.

Also, with the business relationship severed and Voros cleared, Jommers was no longer in a position to impede or imperil the chief, so there would be no rational reason for Scubbetts to retaliate, assuming that Scubbetts was a rational player.

Jommers was reassured by his conclusion. But was it an act of reasoning, or an act of self-persuasion disconnected from reality?

He called Ilona Voros, saying they needed to talk urgently. Using their pre-arranged code system, they agreed to meet on the fishing pier at West Shore Lakefront Park in a half hour.

UPON ARRIVING, Jommers saw her already out on the pier. But before walking out to join her, he stopped at the concession stand service window.

"So, how much longer?" he asked.

The young woman at the window laughed at the question.

"If you're asking about the pumpkin custard again, it's not coming till around October first. Same as I told you last week when you asked."

"Here's what I don't understand," Jommers said. "You can get pumpkin pie all year round. Why can't you get pumpkin custard all year round?"

"I don't know. You'll have to ask someone higher up the ice cream chain."

"So what are my options?"

"Same as last week. Vanilla, chocolate, or the swirl."

"Well, I need to ponder that a minute."

"That's what you always say. Then you get the swirl."

"You know, I think I'll go with the swirl today."

After obtaining his frozen treat, he walked up the concrete steps, then out to the end of the pier where Voros was waiting, looking out across the lake. The men who were fishing paid no notice, as was their penchant. Sitting in their rickety folding lawn chairs, with their battered tackle boxes at their feet, they maintained an almost worship-like focus on the water below. A man in a gorilla suit would not likely turn a single head.

Approaching Voros, he held up his cone.

"Want some? I haven't touched it yet."

"No, thanks," she said. "I avoid sugary stuff. And I just ate a handful of grapes."

In spite of the scorching heat, she was wearing a lightweight beige blazer. It was worn loosely, maybe a size too large. And that meant one thing. They had returned her service weapon and badge and she was carrying both. Things had moved quickly.

"So you're back," he said.

"Yes," she smiled. "And thank you."

"Have you discussed the situation with your boss, Captain Wifflyn?"

"Yes."

"And?"

"He's a decent man, mostly. He got in this job to do good. But he suffers from Bureaucrat Syndrome, calculating how his actions will impact his position. So instead of debating the right thing to do, he's wondering who wins, me or Scubbetts. He doesn't want to be caught on the losing end. So he's stuck in a paralytic dithering. Not willing to give me more unit support, but not telling me to back off either. He wants to pretend the conversation never took place."

"His inner crusader checked by his inner mouse."

"That would be it. When I left him, he was rubbing his temples, mumbling about wanting to be away on an island somewhere."

She looked out over the lake, where the persistent lack of breeze kept the water still, and the layer of algae floating on top gave it a thick look. She was gazing at the Water Department's intake crib off in the distance, which had a small houselike structure atop it.

"I guess we all dream of islands at some point."

"The romantic escape from our problems."

"And you?" she asked. "You have a dream island, too?"

"No. Islands don't interest me. They typically have lots of bugs and generally lack beverage stores."

"So what do you dream of?"

"I dream of discovering budget-priced air conditioning."

"Always the practical, down-to-earth man. Or is it more that, as a psychologist, you think romantics are neurotics?"

"Romanticism is like ice cream. Nothing wrong with an occasional indulgence. But if you consume large quantities of it, you're going to get sick."

"So we should stick more with the carrots and apples of life."

"Yes."

"He says, wildly slurping a giant ice cream cone."

"Normally I'm more dainty, but this is melting fast."

"So what's up?"

"I went down to the dog pound this morning."

"Oh? And did you find something cute you wanted to take home?"

"Not exactly. But I did find some interesting answers as to what the hell is going on."

Jommers told her about his recent conversations, first with Stonecipher, then with Nate Paver down at the kennel, and how the latter suggested that Scubbetts and Stonecipher had used the fear-inducing chemical agent on Mayor Cheeks to get the stream of DHS funds flowing toward Pike Square Security, how the cumulative amount of money could be in the millions.

"Unbelievable," she said. "The incredible, mind-boggling gall of it. That nervy bastard."

"I'm tempted to portray it as a classic example of criminal escalation," he said. "You get away with something at one level, then you crank it up a notch, take it to the next level. But this is so rash it defies the model."

"This means he already has enough resources to disappear at a moment's notice," she said. "I no longer have the luxury of time."

"It also tells you what an amoral creature he is, that he would shaft the mayor, the guy who gave him the job and the power. It shows you he has no loyalty to anyone or anything but himself. And just to give you a clearer picture of who you're dealing with . . ."

Jommers then went on to recount his last conversation with Scubbetts, including the rage, the threats, and the chilling references to having disposed of people in the chicken shit pond. When he was finished, she looked concerned.

"Now you have me worried about your safety," she said.

"Well, you shouldn't be. I think it was mostly performance. He wanted me to know how pissed off he was. There's nothing more I can do to hinder him. He has nothing to gain by coming after me."

"I'm totally shocked to hear you say that," she said.

"Why?"

"Why? You're assuming he's going to act rationally, right after he's demonstrated how irrational he is. I know his mindset. You see it with the mob, with gangs. The idea that a lesson must be taught, an example must be made. It's a core principle with those types. You're evaluating the advisability of his options when you should be heeding his clearly stated intentions. It's a naive mistake a psychologist shouldn't make."

"I'll be careful."

"Look," she said, "I know you equate your laid-back attitude with good mental health and all, but there's such a thing as underreacting. If a car is about to hit you, then you need to leap, not stroll, out of the way."

"I'll be fine."

"I know you prefer to give advice rather than take it, but try a role reversal just this once. I'm very grateful for what you did today. You've helped me a lot. But if I can ask you one more favor—take a road trip. Go somewhere interesting for a week. The world's biggest cuckoo clock is only a few hours' drive. Seneca Caverns is even closer. Or go watch the trains in Fostoria. Or somewhere else. Just don't tell anyone where. Don't call anyone. Don't write to anyone. Just have fun. And have it away from here. Please."

"I'll be fine."

She let out a grouchy groan of frustration and slapped her hands on the tubular railing in front of them. She yelped and jerked her hands back when she discovered that the metal railings were iron-skillet hot.

None of the fishermen batted an eye.

⁓

On the way back to the shop, Jommers stopped by the building that was the host for the GG's graffiti animation project. He'd hoped to take one last look at the final frame and its horrible pun: "Curiosity Fills the Cat." But upon arriving, he found that the artist had already painted over it. True to her word, she had restored the wall to its original appearance, carefully matching the blackish-brown color to the other exterior walls of the grimy brown brick building. She had cleaned up after, also, carefully picking up her own litter, while not disturbing litter left by others. No evidence of the crime. Not even a single spray-can cap remained as a clue.

It was like she had never been there at all.

THE CORRECTOR GETS CORRECTED

Jommers arrived at the shop shortly after quitting time. The crew had left for the day and Pete Gerzny was inspecting a recently completed semitrailer leaf-spring replacement job. Satisfied that the repair was done correctly, Pete hooked up the tractor and pulled the trailer out of the garage and parked it in the yard outside.

As was often the case with undercarriage work, the task left a thick layer of rust flakes and grit on the floor. Jommers knew that Pete would not go home until the mess was swept up, so Jommers hung around downstairs to help. The two men grabbed push brooms and attacked the deposit of brownish-orange metallic dirt from opposite sides.

"You always were a good kid, Karl," Pete said. "I mean, yeah, you were a lippy smart-ass sometimes, but when things needed to be done, you always pitched in without being asked. Come crunch time, you always did the right thing."

As the two men swept the pile of powdery crud toward the open garage doors, they kicked up a vast cloud of dust that swirled and furled in slow motion in the heavy, humid air. When they got the mess out the door, they swept it off to the side of the lot, over onto the gravel, then quickly moved away from the settling dust cloud.

Given the muggy weather, just that short burst of physical activity was enough to make both men sweat, and the dust, clinging to their wetness, had painted both of them with streaks of muddy brown. Pete joked that the look was probably an improvement. The two men leaned on their brooms, waiting for the cinnamon-colored dust cloud to creep away, but the grungy beast lurking in the air was in no hurry to leave. Jommers smiled.

"You know, I remember when I was kid, the old man took me down here to show me the mills and furnaces. I wanted to see where he worked."

"It was busier back then," Pete said. "What, maybe eight or nine blast furnaces still cooking. Remember how they lit up the sky at night?"

"Yeah, yeah. And it looked so weird when you had clouds at night. The underside of low dark clouds glowing orange. Like upside-down lava in the sky."

"Yep. It was up that way that one of the furnaces helped kick off the big fire."

"You mean the burning river thing."

"Yep. Was before your time."

"What happened?"

"You know how a storm sends tree branches and debris sailing down the river?"

"Right."

"Well a mess of that stuff had piled up against the pylons of a railroad bridge that was used to ferry molten pig iron from the blast furnace to the oxygen furnace on the other side of river. So then you get this refinery spill upstream that sent down a huge floating oil slick that gets trapped by the flotsam barrier. Not long after, a torpedo car full of molten pig iron goes across the bridge with sparks of molten droplets shooting out the top. The falling sparks ignite the oil-soaked flotsam below. Then the whole burning shebang breaks loose and floats downstream. A bit later, it bumps up against a wooden railroad trestle and sets it on fire. That's when it got noticed."

"The way I heard it, the river just spontaneously combusted."

"People always tell the better tale, even when it's wrong."

"So, anyway, I'd been nagging Dad for a long time to bring me down and he finally gives in. And it must have been before they had the pollution controls, because there was all this red dust in the air and on everything."

"Ferric oxide," Pete said. "They would have probably had the precipitators by then, but they frequently just blew by them to open stack if they could get away with it, which they usually could. Even if they got caught, fines were pretty low back then. They wouldn't try that today."

"Right, right. So when he finally gets around to it, bringing me down here, it was winter and snowing. And the snow on the ground was reddish brown, all around, and the snow coming down was the same, and being just a kid not knowing any better, I thought that was cool. Red snow. I was so excited, I yelled out, 'Dad, Dad, look, we're on Mars!' And he just keeps looking straight ahead, all glum like. And says something like, 'You got that right, son. You got that right.' I think it was somewhere around then I realized his head was in a different place."

"Yep. He had the cloud all right. He tried to hide it, but you could see it. You couldn't talk about it, though. Not with a guy like that. Rough and tough steelworker. Motorcycle rider. Not going to admit it. Not back then. I don't know, has that changed any?"

"A little. Not enough. A lot of the guys I see, you know, the cops, kind of the same. Keep it in the pocket. Don't let anybody see."

"Yep."

"Some of them just not cut out for the work. A different job gives you a different perspective. Maybe that's all some of them need. I think Dad . . . if only he had a different job."

"What do you mean?"

"Well, you know, how he hated that job . . ."

"Where'd you get that?" Pete asked. "Did he ever say that?"

"No, I guess I just kind of assumed. I mean it was a hard, crappy job."

"Oh, yeah," Pete said. "It definitely was crappy, tenaciously crappy. You couldn't pay me enough to do it. But your dad, he loved it. Loved it more than anything."

"Seriously?"

"Oh, yeah. He worked at the furnace. Hellish job. Like working inside an active volcano. But it's all about how you look at things. And your dad, he looked at it like an adventure. The job he had, I don't remember exactly, I think he was a sample-taker, but whatever, it was something where he had to get close to it, close to the cauldron, or whatever they call it, the thing filled with all the molten metal. You're talking about getting close to something that's a couple thousand degrees. And so he had to wear one of those insulated fireproof moon suit things because it was unbelievably hot, skin-blistering hot. He would tell me about taking off that suit, how the sweat would just pour out of it like you were emptying a bucket. So you had to drink a lot of water, take salt pills—they had these salt pill dispensers all over. And, obviously, it was dangerous, too. You make a mistake, you don't pay attention, and you're toast. Literally toast. So, like I said, you couldn't pay me enough to do it. But for your dad, it was like being a fighter pilot, cliff climber, and alligator wrestler all rolled into one. It was his way of grabbing the world by the balls. We had this thing, this routine, where he'd come in the bar, sit in his usual spot at the right end, all stinky gritty like the rest of them, and I'd bring him a shot and a cold beer and say, 'So, what did you do today?' And he would smile, this big ear-to-ear grin, and say, 'Today I stole hellfire from the devil and used it to make steel. And I got out alive. And tomorrow, I'm going to do it again.' So that black dog he had, it never followed him to work. The furnace was the one place he was free of it, the one place he was happy. But that dog, it was waiting for him when he got home."

"I had no idea," Jommers said. "This totally blows me away. I just assumed . . ."

"A lot of them liked it. College boys like you don't understand—when you're blue collar, you're not thinking about whether this or that job is your true calling and all that horseshit. You're thinking about how to make a good living, provide for your family, pay for your house. And back then, steel was the best you could do blue collar. Best pay, best bennies. You felt lucky to have it. And you would just jump at the chance for some time-and-a-half OT. Kill for double-time Sundays. And guys who had something less, they would envy you. They would say, there goes Joe, he's a lucky guy, he got in at the mill. And your dad, well, he felt lucky, too. When he was there, that is. The job gave him meaning and purpose.

But when he was away from it, for some reason, he was like a man lost. He lived in two different worlds, one light, one dark. I just wish . . . wish I . . ."

Pete never finished the sentence, but Jommers guessed how it might go, and immediately refuted the unstated self-incrimination.

"Pete, you've got to let that go. I know you served him that last drink before he did it, but you know, I know, and everyone else knows, Dad had an appointment with that bridge, an appointment he made long before. It had nothing to do with that drink. It had nothing to do with you. It would have all happened the same regardless. You know that. So you need to let that go. Just let it go."

Pete stayed silent for a long time before answering.

"You always were a good kid, Karl."

JOMMERS WENT UPSTAIRS and took a shower. Then he headed over to the CZ Bar, still hashing over his conversation with Pete. Except for several changes in ownership, virtually nothing about the CZ Bar had changed from the time Jommers's old man drank there decades ago. The same old rusted metal sign displayed the bar's name along with the logo for a long-defunct local brewery. Same old battered, warped wooden screen door. Same old gravel parking lot with cars parked every which way.

Inside was the same dim light and nondescript decor. The same old ugly speckled linoleum floor whose tiles sported dents, chipped corners, cigarette burns, and scary stains you don't ask about. The same old bar, surfaced with ugly speckled laminate, which also sported chips, burns, and scary stains you don't ask about. And sitting at that bar, the same clientele—blue-collar guys who did the kind of work that the body remembers long after the mind forgets. Guys who, after a long day in overdrive, need to kick it down so something doesn't blow.

Jommers sat down near the end of the bar and ordered a beer. Then, on second thought, in honor of his old man, he ordered a shot of cheap whiskey to go with the beer.

He looked over at the stool where his old man had once sat, then held the shot glass up in the air—a toast to a ghost—then gulped the whiskey down. As the whiskey's heat warmed his gut, he imagined Pete behind the bar serving his old man. Jommers struggled to envision his usually glum father grinning broadly and bragging to Pete. "Today I stole hellfire from the devil and used it to make steel . . ." But the apparitions declined to appear. Just as well. He hadn't come for phantoms anyway.

He'd come to consider the corrective revelation just received from Pete. Jommers's old man hadn't hated his job. He'd loved it. How could the son have spent most of his life being wrong about his father? Where had the notion come from? And when?

It wasn't only a personal question, but a professional one, as well. After all, the better part of his job was correcting a patient's misperception of reality. Now someone had just corrected his.

He cast his mind back to his boyhood and teenage years trying to solve the puzzle. But it was so long ago. It was hard enough to remember tangible things that happened. How the hell do you remember something as fuzzy as when a particular thought enters your head? Especially a thought that likely crept in gradually rather than noisily charging in.

He certainly remembered feeling confused after the old man had crashed the TR6 motorcycle into the bridge counterweight. How could that happen on a route the old man took all the time? Yeah, he drank a lot. But there was always a line. He got lit up, but never totally plastered. The booze didn't drive him into the bridge. Everyone suspected it was deliberate, which simply created a new set of questions. Why would he do that?

For young boy Jommers, the question had hung in the air for a long time. When he got a bit older, he encountered psychological terms, including one called depression. But the kid, like many adults, had difficulty grasping the idea of depression coming out of nowhere, like a cold or the flu. It must have an external cause, right? So that was the new foggy puzzle that floated around with nothing solid to be found in it.

And yet, strangely, that was tolerable, even if unsettling. It was okay back then to have an unsolved mystery. Because when you're still a kid, life is full of unanswered questions. The whole world is a puzzlement. You can't possibly grasp everything that is going on. So what's one more riddle, when you are already beset by a million?

The poet John Keats referred to it as negative capability: "when a man is capable of being in uncertainties, mysteries, doubts, without any irritable reaching after fact and reason." Children have this capability by nature, but it is harder to maintain as an adult, and after a certain age, it's found only in those few not disturbed by an unfinished symphony or an open-ended tale.

As Jommers remembered from personal experience, and from studies in developmental psychology, when people reach their late teens or young adult years, they start demanding answers. Keats's negative capability disappears in most.

And so, when a question persists after a certain age, it becomes an itch that must be scratched. A fill-in-the-blank test question that must be filled in. The compulsion to have an immediate answer becomes greater than the desire for an accurate answer. The emotional need for a quick satisfactory explanation trumps the more arduous intellectual quest for truth.

This is why kids are less likely to believe in weird notions such as conspiracy theories. The predisposition is an age-acquired trait.

And so it was for a young Karl Jommers. One summer between college semesters, he worked at a car wash, and went home with aching shoulders from having washed the inside of windshields on countless cars, a task requiring the arm to be held an unnatural and uncomfortable position. So he naturally concluded at the end of the day that physical labor was a lousy way to make a living. And after a number of such days, it occurred to him that working in a hellish steel mill must have been even worse. And from that followed the conclusion that the old man must have hated his job. And once accepting that, it was a short step to explaining the old man's depression and suicide. It was all so logical.

And so there it was. A young man reaching an age where questions must be answered, mysteries must be solved, combined with having to work a crappy summer job. And by summer's end, he was certain about what had happened to his old man and why. Absolutely certain, but without a single bit of evidence.

He eventually learned in his studies that many people, for reasons not fully understood, suffered from nameless depression with no apparent external experiential cause. But by then it was too late to alter his certainty. The idea that his father had been depressed because he'd hated his job had been run around the mind's track enough times to have worn a groove. It was no longer viewed as a theory. It was deemed a memory. And, as a memory, it had remained firmly entrenched for years. Right up until a little over an hour ago, when Pete had yanked it out like a dentist extracting a tooth. And even though Jommers was shaken by the experience, he felt lucky. Most people did not have access to such a mental dentist, someone who was a reliable witness to their own past.

So as Jommers walked out of the CZ Bar, he felt simultaneously wiser and less certain. The discovery of his perception error made him think of the guy with Charles Bonnet syndrome who saw a gorilla with a tuba in his backyard. The guy wasn't crazy. It was a vision system problem. But how could a therapist offer relief? Yes, you see a gorilla that isn't actually there. And, no, you're not crazy. But, yes, you're going to keep seeing it. How do you correct a perception error that refuses to leave? How do you train someone to ignore a gorilla with a tuba?

As Jommers drove out of the bar's parking lot contemplating his error, he wondered if he might also be wrong about the old man's suicide. Everyone assumed his father's collision with the bridge counterweight had been deliberate. Young Karl had, too. But was that conclusion based on his own observations, or was he only going with the whispered consensus? Could it have possibly been an accident? Too much booze clouding judgment and awareness of the bridge position? Alcohol inhibiting reflexes and neuromuscular control?

Jommers was a bit woozy from sucking down a beer and whiskey on an empty stomach. Just woozy enough to trip on the gravel and drop his keys on the way to the car as he left the bar. Woozy enough to do something impulsive. Something stupid. Like performing a crazy experiment to answer a question, test an assumption.

Once out of the parking lot and on the road, he accelerated sharply, driving as fast as he could while still maintaining control of the car. He roared down Gate Road toward Trammel Street and its lift bridge. He barely made the turn without losing control. As luck would have it—good or bad yet to be determined—the bridge was up, the counterweight down. Now about three hundred yards away from it, he put the accelerator to the floor and raced toward it.

Was there any remote chance that his old man, dead drunk, could not notice the bridge up in the time it took to reach the bridge after the turn?

After the sharp turn, it was a straight shot to the bridge. Nothing to obstruct the view. Even before Jommers got near it, he could see the flashing lights, see the shine of his headlights on the high-visibility orange reflective gate that was down. And he could clearly hear the loud clanging of the bells. Sure, the old man's TR6 motorcycle could accelerate faster than an old Taurus, but the sharp turn from Gate Road onto Trammel Street was more than ninety degrees, more like a hundred and twenty. You had to really slow down to make it. If the old man was so drunk he couldn't see flashing lights and hear the clanging bells, then there was no way he was making a high-speed hundred-and-twenty-degree turn on a motorcycle, especially given how the road was littered with sand and loose stones falling off the gravel trucks that went by there every day. He would have wiped out at the intersection, long before he got to the bridge.

Jommers slammed on the brakes at the last possible moment, and the Taurus screeched to a sliding halt just shy of the gate, at a slight angle. He shut off the car and got out immediately, looking back at the straightway, the bridge bells pounding his ears.

Experiment concluded. No, it was no accident. No way. At least he was right about that part. He stared back at the turn. Imagining his old man parked there, waiting for the opportunity, waiting for the bridge to go up. He tried to imagine that icicle in the brain that is depression, the biting inner cold that blots out everything else. Tried to imagine the old man arriving at the decision. Tonight's the night. Tonight it's over.

Jommers again studied the counterweight hanging inches above the road. Stared at it as he had done so many times before, hoping it might yield some insight. But none was to be had. Decades ago, a man who had been depressed for inexplicable reasons had taken his own life for inexplicable reasons. There was nothing more to be wrung from it. And never would be.

And it was at that moment Jommers resolved that he would not come to this place again. The shrine he had visited so often had nothing to offer. It never did. Some questions in life can't be answered. And whatever answers are discoverable, they will not be found in a block of concrete. He no longer needed to ponder the past. He needed now to consider the future.

He turned and looked down at the river. A familiar tour boat was passing by. In the daytime, it provided narrated tours of the river and its history. The boat also offered nighttime dance cruises, where people dined, drank, and danced the night away while plying the river. And that was the boat's business this evening as it passed under the raised bridge. Fun and music on the water. As he listened to the music and laughter float up, he envied their enjoyment, realizing that, for all the time he spent in the Bends, he'd never been on that boat. Why was that? Was it too uncool for a native to behave like a tourist? Or had he subconsciously sentenced himself to a life of unexpressed angst?

The boat passed, the bridge came down. Jommers turned his back on the decommissioned shrine and went home.

DAY EIGHTEEN

Early Thursday morning, Jommers was still obsessing over the revelation that his old man had loved his steelworker job. It was almost impossible to accept after assuming the opposite for decades. He would not have even believed the surprising disclosure had it come from someone other than Pete. He better understood now the difficulty of correcting a false connection. Once a mystery seems solved, it's hard for the mind to reclassify it back to unsolved. No wonder you can't ever convince a cop that his intuition about someone's guilt was wrong. No wonder prosecutors stoutly resist reopening cases of innocent men they put away.

Like pattern recognition. Once you perceive a face in something, it's impossible not to see it thereafter. And that holds true whether the face is serendipitous, like the famous Mother Teresa cinnamon bun, or intentional, like the familiar illusion known as the Boring figure, which appears as either a young girl or old woman. The recognition imprints itself as memory. And that insight had implications for dealing with Patrolman Dwayne Biederbach. Once you perceive a malevolent face in the textured fabric of government, is it possible not to see that face thereafter? Once you draw unseen connections, can you ever erase them?

Just as Jommers posed that question, he received a text message from the man himself: "My turn, right?" This was followed by one of their prearranged codes for a meeting place.

A little more than two weeks ago, the two men had made a deal to have a dual track of meetings where each would attempt to change the other's perspective. But they had never discussed the endgame. How it would conclude. How it would be scored. How to determine who had won.

After the last session in Jommers's office, the therapist had discharged the patrolman as a formal patient. Jommers had presumed the game over after that, but apparently Biederbach wanted to get in the last word. Fine. Bring it to resolution. So the therapist texted back a confirmation.

Jommers found it curious to see Biederbach schedule the meeting for late morning. All his previous arranged contacts had been in evening hours, mostly after dark. Was that a good sign or bad sign? Was he less anxious, or more urgent?

Jommers drove his beater Taurus south toward Marsh Cross Road, where he could cross over to the East Side of the river and get to the meeting place. Halfway down Marsh Cross, he approached a railway crossing just as the flashers and bells kicked on. He looked to his left and saw a familiar sight, a 1968 EMD SW1500 diesel-electric switcher painted bright yellow with an overlaid black chevron pattern. It was chugging along at less than ten miles per hour and pulling three empty hoppers, all of which represented the better part of the rolling assets of the Claybank River Railroad.

With no crossing gate, Jommers could have easily continued across the tracks and avoided being delayed by the slow-moving train. Instead, he pulled off the road, got out, and waved toward the locomotive. A stout engineer, wearing a navy-blue ball cap and a fluorescent green hi-vis vest, leaned out the locomotive cab window and waved back.

Roone Sweelinck, the man leaning out, wasn't just the locomotive engineer for the railroad, he was also the president and CEO, VP of finance, operations manager, sales manager, and maintenance chief, which included the unromantic task of walking the tracks with a sprayer and tank of weed killer on his back.

The Claybank River Railroad was a short line with several miles of track and two lift bridges. Operating in the Bends, the line provided a linkage between the two mainlines that passed through the area, and also connected various industrial operations with those mainlines. Typical loads included ore, stone, and various steel products. But Sweelinck's long-term goal was to extend the line up to the Port of Grayton docks and to build a rail-to-truck transfer facility that would allow him to handle container business, which would represent a giant leap for the line.

When the window of the locomotive cab got within shouting distance, Sweelinck yelled out to Jommers.

"Hey! Just found seven hundred yards of track I didn't know I had. Overgrown spur. Once I rehab it, I can get into Bellwin Steel Products, and they're interested."

"So how much you got now?" Jommers yelled back.

"It'll give me almost nine miles."

"Nine miles! You're a goddamn railroad baron!"

"That's right. That's right. I'm the Baron of the Bends."

Sweelinck sounded a brief blast on the locomotive's air horn. Jommers raised his hands in the air and let out an appreciative whoop. He stayed by the tracks and watched as the empty hoppers creaked, rattled and rocked in their slow transit past. He mused upon the phrase—Baron of the Bends. Perfect! From then on, that was what he would call the man, the Baron of the Bends.

Sweelinck had been hooked on trains ever since he was a kid, but it wasn't until the age of fifty-nine that he had become a real railroad man by selling his fast-lube franchises and buying the short line. Many warned him that it was a foolhardy move, and not just because of his lack of railroad experience. Nobody else actually wanted the line. The contraction of steel operations had significantly reduced the business, rendering the line unprofitable. Maintenance had been deferred for years, so the track was in poor condition. The two mainlines that ran through the Bends both said they needed the short line for connections, but neither wanted to assume the responsibility for running it. So Sweelinck got a good deal on the purchase, and ended up acquiring the biggest challenge of his life.

He obtained loans to rehab track and unused spurs and also repaired an inoperative lift bridge, which allowed him to cross the river at a second beneficial location, enabling access to more potential customers. Within several years, he had turned the short line back into a profitable enterprise.

Like many successful entrepreneurs Jommers knew, Sweelinck had that enigmatic power core, an inner something that combined energy, tenacity, patience, and focus. The will to do whatever it takes, for however long it takes, to get something done. In addition, he was amiable, jocular, and contented. Longtime acquaintances said the man had always been that way, even when he was in high school working evenings at a gas station.

Sweelinck carried that inner light with the same constancy that he carried his old Hamilton 992B Railway Special watch. And that made psychologist Jommers wonder what part of that jaunty personality was inherent and how much was owed to upbringing and experience? To what extent was it a matter of personal choice and conscious effort?

Further rumination would have to wait. Jommers had to meet a man on a boat.

THE MEETING LOCATION suggested by Biederbach was an inactive commercial dock on the lakefront a half mile east of the river mouth. The slot was occupied by the SS *Gavin D. Fitzwilliam*, a six-hundred-foot decommissioned ore boat built in the twenties to fetch iron ore from the iron ranges of Minnesota and bring it down to the steel mills. As massive as the ship appeared up close, it was only a little kid brother compared to the one-thousand-foot ore carriers that plied the Great Lakes today.

It was named after an executive of the mining company that had once owned the ship. It was decommissioned in the seventies, but instead of being sold for scrap, the usual fate, it was donated to a historical society that hoped to turn the ship into a floating museum, but the group had yet to scrounge up the necessary funds. And so the rusting, hulking relic sat there, a mute ghost waiting to be reincarnated as a troubadour, eager to sing its tales.

Access to the dock was restricted by a chain-link fence with a locked gate. As always, Biederbach had a key and unlocked the gate as soon as Jommers arrived. There was a large flock of gulls resting quietly on the dock, their white feathers positively glowing in the sunlight. The birds did not stir, preferring to ignore the arrival of the two interlopers.

"I wasn't sure you'd come," Biederbach said.

"I had the first word, so you get the last word. Fair is fair. A deal is a deal."

"It's going to be hot. Big hunk of steel sitting and roasting in the sun."

"I can handle it," Jommers said. "I assume since we're meeting here instead of, say a diner that you still see the need to be secretive."

"Maybe. Even if not, the ship is pretty damn cool, especially if you've never been on one. You could spend all day in the engine room alone trying to figure it all out."

The only way to board the ghost ship was a narrow metal gangway ramp at the stern, leading to a hatch where crew and galley supplies had once been taken aboard. The hatch had a lock on it, but Biederbach had the key.

Biederbach showed Jommers the oak-paneled officers' mess. The wood was all charred. "Some bums got in here one winter. They started a fire to keep warm." He pointed to a small chalkboard on the wall. "That's the menu board. It's still there, the last meal before the last stop. Roast pork loin, bread dumplings, braised red cabbage, sautéed apples, German potato salad, and cucumber salad. Those guys ate pretty good."

They walked forward across the main deck, past the long row of telescoping hatches for the holds that once carried the ore. Invisible waves of heat rippled up around them as the late-morning sun transformed the steel deck into a hotplate. They passed a set of mooring winches near the forward cabins, then climbed the narrow metal ladder that led to the ship's wheelhouse, which held a commanding view. Right as they entered, the flock of gulls on the dock inexplicably took flight, launching into a furious vortex and producing a clamor of agitated squeals and whistles. After a half minute or so of this display, they settled down and fluttered back down to the dock.

Biederbach hiked up his pants.

"Before we start—are you open to constructive criticism?" he asked.

"Sure," Jommers said. "Feedback is always welcome."

"Well, my suggestion is that you might want to use more contemporary allusions in your spiels, or whatever you call them. That last talk we had in your office—you were taking the movie tack, asking me if I want to be more like Gregory Peck or Peter Lorre. First thing to strike me. If you were laying that on some thirty-year-old, instead of your message resonating with him, the poor son of a bitch is sitting there thinking, who the hell is Peter Lorre? So you either have to update your patter or limit your clientele to a certain older generation. You see my point?"

"I do. And it's a valid one. I appreciate it."

"No problem. Now then, as to the status of the situation. The last time you characterized all this shady business as merely garden-variety local corruption. So let me say that I still believe that Scubbetts possesses and has used some type of fear-inducing drug for some nefarious purpose. And I still believe that he used that drug to bring about the death of Tarburn and Commander Mungfreud. That said, I have to admit, this is looking more and more like just a local graft thing, a Scubbetts thing. So you're probably right on that part."

"Well, as long as we're in confession mode here, you're right about the drug. I'm almost certain now that Scubbetts has an anxiety-instilling agent and that he's using it to scare up customers for an illegal security business he's running on the side. And he's not just using it on private business managers, he's using it on city officials to get city contracts. And like you, I also believe he used it on Tarburn and Mungfreud. You were right on that."

"Hmm. This is an interesting turn. You and me agreeing on things. I didn't expect that."

"Me neither," Jommers said. "You've reduced the scope of your theory, and I've been forced to expand mine. It appears that we've met in the middle somewhere and somehow ended up on the same page. At least for the moment, anyway."

"Then we should savor the moment. Let it hang in the air a bit. I suspect it won't last long."

Jommers smiled and nodded.

"Step behind the wheel," Biederbach suggested. "Tell me what you see."

Jommers walked over to a small platform in the center of the pilothouse, surrounded by a badly tarnished brass rail. He stepped up to the wooden helm and looked at the binnacle directly in front of him.

"I see a broken compass."

"I mean outside."

"What am I looking for?"

"Imagine you're trying to steer this thing."

"Oh," Jommers said. "It's what I don't see."

"Exactly."

"I can't see the front end of the boat."

"It's called the bow."

"Right."

"So that's why they stuck that steering pole on it," Biederbach said. "See it? That's what you had to go by."

"Kind of like those monster Caddies in the '70s where you had to steer by the hood ornament."

"Yeah, exactly like that, only totally different."

"Kind of like life," Jommers said. "Never truly seeing where we're headed, but somehow getting there anyway."

"That's a bit sappy for you, but I suppose you could use it on the touchy-feely types. They'd probably lap it up. Just leave Peter Lorre out of it."

"Will do. All right, then. Now that we're in agreement that this is a localized case of corruption within the Grayton Police Department, it's time for you to step away from it. Let Internal Affairs handle it. Detective Voros is back on duty, and she's well aware of the situation. Any further ideas or insights you have should be shared with her. More importantly, it's time to stop pretending you don't have the bag with the shotgun shells that Tarburn carried that night. And it's time for you to turn them in. The chemical inside those shells is the only physical evidence available to support the theory. And analyzing the chemical will help determine the source of it. It's time."

"I don't think going to her is a good idea," Biederbach said.

"Why is that? Don't you trust her?"

"I trust her integrity, but doubt her competence. She doesn't understand the concept of stealth. She makes a lot of noise when she pokes around, like a raccoon knocking over a metal garbage can in the middle of the night."

"Well, maybe you can give her some pointers."

"I don't think she'll be around long enough. Scubbetts eliminated Tarburn and Mungfreud. What makes you think he won't take her out? You want my honest opinion? She's toast. More likely sooner than later."

"She can handle herself," Jommers said. "She's very smart and has superior skills."

"Yeah, sure. And if we were having this conversation a couple of weeks ago, you could have said the same thing about Earl Tarburn."

"She grasps the situation."

"She's got tunnel vision. Sees only what's in front of her at the moment. I see the bigger picture. That's why I have to follow through."

"What do you mean, follow through?" Jommers asked.

"The source of the drug. That's the key to nailing the whole thing, and nailing Scubbetts. We now agree on what's happened and why, but it's still all speculation. We need something hard. We need the source. The person who knows all and can tell all."

"You know, I'm very gratified to witness your newfound appreciation for facts over fanciful conjecture. But in this particular instance, obtaining those facts is outside your area of responsibility. You're a patrolman on vacation. This is the proper business of Internal Affairs. If the source is the key to prosecution, then IA is in the best position to find it, not you. You should know that there are legitimate research uses for such a drug, which is normally used to measure the efficacy of tranquilizers. The source is very likely a researcher at a pharmaceutical company or a medical school. Trained detectives are much better equipped to track down that individual than you."

"Except that I already have," Biederbach said.

"Already have what?"

"Tracked down the source."

"What do you mean?"

"You remember my theory about the source being a former KGB chemist who came over to work for our side?"

"Yes, that's what I was referring to when I used the phrase *fanciful conjecture*."

"Then you'll find it inconvenient to learn that he's here."

"Who?"

"Zoran, the chemist."

"What do you mean he's here?"

"Living in the area. Over in Carnelian. Maybe an hour's drive away. Kind of a coincidence, don't you think?"

"How do you know this?" Jommers asked.

"As I mentioned previously, I got his name from a paper he had submitted to a neuropharmacology conference in 2002, a paper that perfectly describes the drug we're talking about. And when I started looking for him, I found someone with that name living in Maryland near Army's Edgewood Area, where they research chemical warfare. So I had a hunch. If Scubbetts contacted him about testing the drug here on a long-term trial, Zoran might want to move near here, at least temporarily, rather than going back and forth to Maryland. So I used a department computer to do a BMV search on the chance that he's been here long enough to need new plates. That's how I found him. Since he doesn't realize he's involved in something illegitimate, he's not trying to hide."

"Those are interesting connections, but don't prove anything. There are millions of Russian Americans. So one of them happens to move from Maryland to Ohio. So what? You don't know anything about this guy, whether he's a chemist, or if he created the drug."

"Yeah, actually, I do," Biederbach said.

"How do you know?"

"I've talked to him."

"You what?"

"I wrote him a letter and asked him to call me. He did."

"This is crazy," Jommers said. "This is totally crazy."

"You want to hear about it or not?"

"No! Yes! I don't know. This totally crazy. I can't believe you did this."

"I'll just proceed while you figure out if you want to hear. So I write Zoran a letter on some fake letterhead I made. I pretend to be a researcher for a pharmaceutical company. I tell him that I found an online reference to the paper he wrote and that I was intrigued by it because my company is pursuing that very line of research. I tell him my company has made a lot of money selling boner toner, but when the patents expire and they go generic, we're screwed. We need a new rainmaker. So I tell him about a brainstorm we came up with at my fictional company. Our idea is to create a drug that would make someone more reluctant to commit a crime by making them more afraid of getting caught. It would also reduce other assorted risky behaviors like drunk driving, getting in fights, unsafe sex, taking drugs . . ."

"Smoking."

"And, as you know better than me, the willingness to take risks can be defined as the absence of fear. So I suggested that if there were a drug that could induce anxiety in a controlled fashion, it could reduce risk-seeking behavior in individuals where that was an identified or diagnosed problem. So I told him in the letter we were pursuing a solution that maybe he already had, that maybe he might want to work with us or for us."

"That's actually a brilliant ruse," Jommers said. "I'm impressed."

"Thank you."

"It's also reckless and totally irresponsible. You are way out of your element here. You can't pursue this any further."

"It's too late," Biederbach said. "He responded to the letter. He called me and was quite interested in getting together discuss it further. We're going to meet tomorrow out in Quarryville. A small restaurant that used to be a train station. Veil Street Depot. Then I'm going to show him my badge and tell him what's really going on."

"And you think that after that, he'll just want to open up on everything and cooperate?"

"Yes. He'll want to come clean."

"And what's your reason for thinking that?"

"We talked a while. I got a sense of the man. He wasn't specific about his past, but ventured enough for me to make some inferences."

"As you are prone to do."

"Here's my take. When Zoran worked for the KGB's Lab 12, he felt he was just being a good citizen. He initially invents this drug for the same reason that Kalashnikov invented his famous rifle, to serve and protect his country. Remember, the scorched-earth tactics of the Nazis laid waste to half the Soviet Union and killed more than twenty million civilians. That tends to inspire some nationalism in people, regardless of how they felt about communist ideology. So Zoran initially sees himself as a patriot. That's how it always begins. The flag becomes the curtain behind which you can justify anything. And one doesn't object, because dissidents are traitors and traitors are the enemy and the enemy has no rights.

Keep your eye on that logic because we're halfway there already. But Zoran has a remnant of morality. He feels guilty that his invention is being used on his own people instead of enemy spies. He invented something for the good, and it is being used for the bad. So when the Soviet Union falls apart, he comes to America with his invention, hoping it'll be used for the good instead of bad. It doesn't quite work out that way. Again he's disappointed and dispirited. Then one day he's contacted by a former military police officer he met at Edgewood who is now a police chief. This police chief remembers the drug, says he wants to experiment with it as a way of getting criminals to surrender without gunfire and shootouts. It has the potential to save lives. Zoran is excited. He's got one final opportunity to find a constructive use for the Ghost Wolf formula. One last chance to turn sword into plowshare. So Zoran is eager to help this police chief, not knowing that, once again, it will be used for sinister purposes. You see, what Zoran really wants is redemption. He desperately wants his evil thing put to good use before he dies so that he can die a good man, instead of a bad man. This is why my ruse worked so well. It exploited his desperate need for redemption."

"And he told you all this?" Jommers asked.

"Well, no, not in so many words. Like I said, I inferred a lot of this from his tone."

"Holy crap. You need to take this stuff to Detective Voros immediately. This is totally freaking nuts for you to be out there playing secret agent with an ex-KGB guy, if in fact that's really the case. You do not go to that meeting without first contacting Voros and determining what she wants to do about it."

"You have an awful lot of confidence in someone you were previously treating as loopy loons."

"She has the authority and experience to handle this, and the connections to bring in other law enforcement agencies as necessary."

"Perhaps," Biederbach said, "but there is some urgency here. We have to get to Zoran before someone else does."

"If you think Zoran is in danger, that Scubbetts will go after him, then that's all the more reason for you to contact Detective Voros immediately, so she can arrange protection."

"Oh, he's definitely in danger. But not from Scubbetts."

"What do you mean?"

"I'm sensing a third force here."

"A what?"

"Another player," Biederbach said. "A bigger player with more to lose. One that wants to keep all this quiet. They've sent a cleanup crew to contain this. Eliminate anyone who knows anything about it. So Zoran is a target. Scubbetts, too. Maybe me, and maybe you."

"I know I'm going to regret asking, but here goes—who might this cleanup crew represent?"

"Well, it's kind of obvious, don't you think? This whole business originates with army research. Who knows what they plan to do with this stuff? They sure as hell don't want anybody to know about it. They're going to make sure that nobody does."

"So you're telling me the army is operating here in Grayton."

"Its military intelligence arm, to be specific," Biederbach said. "They don't actually have authority to operate domestically, but we know from experience they do whatever they feel needs to be done, wherever it needs to be done."

"So we're back to that," Jommers said. "Government putting the hammer down."

"Well, if you wish to phrase it that way, then yes, given that the army is a branch of the federal government."

"I thought we'd moved past this. Made progress. But here we are, back to square one."

"Yes, indeed, which is precisely where we belong. Because it is at square one where Tarburn gets shot at Crone Point. It's at square one where he tells me right before about a cleanup crew sent to wipe out traces of something gone wrong. It's square one where he tells me that MI is to blame, MI being the abbreviation for military intelligence. So, while, yes, I think Scubbetts is crooked and using the formula for personal gain, it's still critical to establish the source of it. Because if this stuff does have military origins, then the military has a natural incentive to want to keep it secret. And they're here, right now, doing exactly that. Maybe those army trainers who work with SWAT on tactics are part of it. Dallabaco is good buds with those guys. So maybe Dallabaco is part of it, too. Maybe he just plays dumb with you to keep track of what you know. There's all kinds of possible scenarios here. You can't see that because you've got the tunnel vision, like her. So that's why I have to handle it."

Jommers emitted a long sigh of disappointment and shook his head. "I was an idiot to think I could change you. No, it was vanity. I overestimated my ability to reach your kind. Well, I know better now. Lesson learned. So let me tell you this up front so you can't accuse me of deceit or backstabbing. This private investigation of yours, this quixotic adventure, is over. As soon as I leave here, I'm going to call Detective Voros and relate every conversation I've had with you, including this one. And I'm going to include my suspicion that you're harboring evidence, the shotgun shells that Tarburn carried in his kit bag that night. I'm going to tell her everything. She will come after you. Consider yourself warned."

"No problem. I figured it would come to this. I've already relocated. I've got it under control."

"I'm done with you, Dwayne. I did my best for you, but I failed. It happens." Jommers reached into his pocket and took out the list of coded meeting places that Biederbach had provided, crumpled it into a ball and tossed it. "I'm getting back to my own business, my own domain. Don't call me again."

"Funny thing about the whole domain issue. It's kind of like the ocean. You can make up different names for different parts, you know, the sea of this, the bay of that, the straits of whatever, but it's all connected, it's all the same water. The waters don't know their names or compartments. They just flow together."

"Sorry. I'm done with this. It's over."

"So you think. Like they say, it ain't over till the plus-sized lady sings."

～

Jommers left the ship discouraged. He dearly wanted to suck down a couple of beers at Spreckels, but he had a doctor's appointment in the early afternoon and figured a temporary abstinence might be in order.

Instead he went down to West Shore Lakefront Park to review his interactions with Patrolman Biederbach. The therapist debated what he might have done differently and whether it would have mattered. He now doubted the wisdom of even accepting Biederbach's challenge to begin with. The one thought he refused to entertain was Biederbach's notion of a third force in town, a military intelligence cleanup crew sent to eradicate evidence of the fear-inducing drug. And even as he found that reflexive thought-suppression perfectly reasonable, he could almost hear a rebuking Biederbach snidely remarking something about the therapist's rigid adherence to his worldview.

Feeling hungry after leaving the park, Jommers headed over to Metzel's, a small greasy spoon on the way to nowhere, but a major destination for its blue-collar regulars who shoveled food into their maws with a mission-like focus, as if they were about to depart on a long voyage and not eat again in days.

The ramshackle clapboard joint faced a riverside lot that was piled with discarded tires from heavy-duty earth-moving equipment. Here and elsewhere along the riverbank, the gigantic tires enjoyed a second life as dock bumpers.

Jommers sat down at the counter and ordered a lemonade and a grilled cheese sandwich, which, like most everything else at Metzel's, automatically came with a side of hash brown potatoes. He suspected that if he had ordered nothing but a piece of cherry pie, it would also come with hash browns, but he hadn't the gumption to test the theory.

He was lucky enough to arrive just in time to observe a fresh batch started. A stout woman effortlessly picked up an enormous bag of frozen potatoes and emptied it on the griddle. Then, like a harmonious blacksmith, she hammered down the irregular chunks to establish a flat blanket. Next she picked up a five-gallon can of cooking oil and liberally doused the frozen mat of shredded tubers with the slick, golden liquid. The combination of heat, oil and frost created a fierce crackling-sizzling-hissing that resembled the sound of rough ocean surf.

Jommers smiled at the spectacle, reassured that the most important people in the world were being fed, the people who make things and fix things, the unheralded stalwarts who perform the unseen, unglamorous work that keeps the machinery of civilization turning, who skin their knuckles and strain their backs doing all the hard things that need to be done, whose resolutely dark-tipped fingernails testify to their tasks.

On the way back to the shop, he drove along Overlook Drive on the west bank to check on a rumor that the Sentinel Bluff project had broken ground.

Affirmative. At the site of the abandoned truck terminal that had once been Lagerstern Freight Lines, an excavator was dismantling the structure. A leasing sign on the lot confirmed the long-circulated speculation. The Sentinel Bluff condo-retail project was going forward. If it proved successful, it would herald a new era in this part of the Bends. Previous projects in this section had involved rehabbing and adapting existing old structures. This would be the first new construction in decades, maybe even a century.

He paused for a while, watching the monstrous yellow machine munch away at the old building, with each new bite launching billows of dark, demolition dust that rose explosively, then settled leisurely. He felt ambiguous about the project, with his distrust of developers matched only by his disdain for decay. But he knew Connor Quirke was right—the Bends had reached a tipping point. Things would get better, or things would get worse. But they would never be the same again.

When he arrived back at the shop, he found Yolanda Arroyo, the police reporter, waiting for him. She was off to the side, taking shelter from the sun in the shade of a scrappy box elder tree and talking on her cell phone. When Jommers arrived, she ended her conversation and strolled toward him.

"Hi, how are you?" she asked.

"Fine," he said. "How you doing?"

"Good, thanks. Did you happen to read the story I wrote about city council seeking a federal grant to get some security cameras set up in Ward Three to help cut crime?"

"I did. It was very interesting."

"Yeah, but what's more interesting is that the people in that ward, instead of getting behind the cams, don't want them, which I found curious, since it's all to their benefit. Anyway, I was wondering if you might offer me some insight on their reaction, you know, just on background. I would use your thoughts, but not your name."

"Sure."

"Seriously? I thought you'd tell me to hit the road."

"I just had a really good grilled cheese sandwich. It put me in a good mood."

"So that's all it takes?"

"Sometimes it's the little things that make a big difference."

"So why are they hyper about the cameras?" she asked. "I mean, I understand the whole Big Brother thing, but they have serious problems in that ward. Why wouldn't you want it?"

"Do you have any candles in your place?"

"Um, yes. Why?"

"If I were a purely rational being, utterly devoid of emotion, I would not understand why you have candles. I would not understand why candles even still exist, because in the age of electric lighting, candles have no functional value. And yet, candles are found in seven out of ten homes. They represent a two-billion-dollar-a-year industry. Why is that? Because they provide a positive emotional value that outweighs their lack of functional value. And all things, including security cameras, have both a functional value and emotional value. And in the case of the cams, the negative emotional value often outweighs the positive functional value. From a purely functional standpoint, security cams are no different from having a beat cop on the corner. Yet we're spooked by the cams, but find the beat cop nostalgic and comforting. The difference is the emotional content. The monitoring of the cams is distant, impersonal, while being omnipresent. Those same characteristics explain people's negative view of federal government, even though their negative interactions with government are more likely to be with local entities—speed traps, zoning restrictions, rising property taxes, and so on. They distrust the distant powers that protect and benefit them, but idealize the local powers that punish and constrain them. It's all about the emotional connection."

"Okay, that's interesting. Now let's say they came to you and asked your advice, you know, those who want the cams. What would you suggest to make them more acceptable?"

"Well, first of all, instead of trying to make the cams inconspicuous by concealment, I would make them obvious and prominent, eliminate the secretive aspect. You could make the information flow two-way. Put a display beneath the cam that gives useful information such as time, temperature, traffic conditions, weather forecasts, sports scores, so on, so they're giving something back, not just taking. You could also have an open house at the place where the cams will be monitored. Anyone could come see the operation. The tour would be conducted by a gregarious potbellied cop named Officer Duffy. There would be free cookies and soda pop. People could play with the cam controls, aiming them this way and that, zooming in and out. Let them have fun. Meanwhile, Officer Duffy explains how this all will help protect their children from harm. And you leave thinking it will be Officer Duffy sitting in the control room watching the camera monitors. Even better, you get a basset hound. Give him a cute name, say, Sorley. And Sorley is there at the open house where everybody can pet him. Then you place an image of Sorley on every cam. Maybe Sorley holds the display that gives the time and temperature. So you associate the cams with a cute dog who's looking out for you. And better yet, give the cams microphones, so if you walk by one and say 'Hi, Sorley,' this will be heard in the control room and Officer Duffy will push a button and the image of Sorley with the cam will emit a friendly woof to answer you back."

"I never know when you're being real or messing with me," Arroyo said.

"You mean like you coming here to ask me about security cams when you most certainly have other things you want to address after you've captured my attention."

"This is not about me, you know. This is not some ego trip. I'm not out to be any journalistic hero or anything. I genuinely see myself serving the citizens of Grayton. I know you don't believe that. But it's true. And if their police department, the entity that's supposed to protect them from harm, is somehow imploding, they need to know that. They need to do something about it. But they can't solve the problem if they don't know about it. You understand? It's for them, not me. I honestly want to do the right thing. I am not a bad person trying to hurt you. I am a good person trying to help the place where I live. I know that sounds corny to you, but—"

"I don't mistrust your motives," Jommers said. "I believe you to be a sincere and diligent professional."

"Thank you."

"But you suffer from occupational bias, just like everybody else."

"What do you mean?"

"Let's say you have an area in your backyard where the grass doesn't grow and you want to do something different with it. A carpenter will suggest a deck. A concrete guy will suggest a stamped-concrete patio. A landscaper will give you ideas for an exotic Japanese garden. When all you have is a hammer, everything looks like a nail."

"Okay. You're doing the Yoda thing. You're trying to tell me something here."

"Am I?"

"You're saying that there are other people looking into this."

"I didn't say that, but it would seem logical. There are checks and balances in the system. Players who oversee what PD does. Both external and internal."

"By external you mean the mayor's office and city council. And internal you mean Internal Affairs Unit. The woman cop who shot the guy cop at Crone Point, she was Internal Affairs. And the Force Review Committee just cleared her to return to duty in what I'm told is record time. So you're saying she's on top of this."

"I didn't say that. And I would have no way to know that. But let's just suppose for the moment that Internal Affairs is in fact looking into these events. I would assume that such an investigation, like most, would be discreet. They would avoid tipping off the subjects so that they could gather evidence before it can be concealed. So if you were to publish a story that apprised a bird about a cat sneaking up behind it . . ."

"Okay so you're telling me that I should back off to avoid screwing up an ongoing investigation. But here's the thing, I don't know that there is one. My usual sources don't know anything about what's going on. I can't just sit and do nothing."

"Maybe you should broaden your range of sources."

"You have any suggestions?" she asked.

"Well, I don't know anything about journalism. Only what I saw in that movie long time ago. What was it? Something about some little scandal involving Nixon."

"*All the President's Men.*"

"Yeah, right, that's it. Great flick. And there was this line in there that became a famous catchphrase. What was that again?"

"Follow the money."

"Right, right. That's it."

"Okay, okay. Cops and money. I'd look at salaries, overtime, bribes . . ."

"Yes, of course you would look at it from the micro level, but as a thorough reporter you would also look at it from the macro level."

"Macro, macro. You mean department level. Okay, that would be the money PD gets from the city, operational funds, and grants from state and federal government. What am I looking for?"

"The players and the process."

"Um, the mayor would propose a budget, then negotiate with city council to get it passed. And, and . . ."

"The players and the process."

"And it would first have to come out of the Safety Committee on council, which oversees police, fire, and EMS."

"The players and the process."

"And the Safety Committee is chaired by Councilwoman Birdsong. Who also happens to be on the Force Review Committee. You're telling me I should talk to Birdsong."

"I said nothing of the kind. I was merely quizzing you on the operations of municipal government."

At that moment, her cell phone emitted a ring tone. She looked at the phone and quickly answered.

"This is Yolanda." Pause. "Where did they find it?" Pause. "So it was definitely a carjacking?" Pause. "So now you can ID the victim." Pause. "Can I come see you?" Pause. "Thanks."

She disconnected the call and turned back to Jommers.

"I have to run. Carjacking homicide. But thanks for your help. I hope we can talk again soon. Maybe we can talk about some of your other favorite movies."

"Sure. There's a few with Michael Caine I like."

Blood out the ass is never a good thing, though it's not always a critical thing either. The first time Jommers saw it, he assumed it was just hemorrhoids and didn't get too excited about it. He did find it curious, however, given that he never experienced constipation, the typical cause of the unwelcome veinal visitors. Still, he was in his late forties now. Stuff happens. He resolved to eat more fiber, drink more water, and get back to the running, presuming that would be enough to make it go away.

It didn't.

He hadn't been to a doctor in years and the last one he'd seen was retired. So he had to start from scratch, asking for recommendations from acquaintances. He picked the one who could squeeze him in the earliest, rather than the one who was closest. Unfortunately, it meant a long drive out to a southwestern suburb, terra incognita for a guy who lives, works, and plays in the Bends. In preparation for the visit, the doctor wrote an order for a standard blood work up and instructed Jommers to have it done at least a week before the visit, enough time for the results to be sent over beforehand.

Jommers had also been instructed to arrive fifteen minutes early to fill out the standard patient information sheet and medical history. He gave similar instructions to his own patients. And the questions themselves were similar. And when he was finished filling out the form, he looked it over and realized he'd skipped a question.

It wasn't an accident. It was the alcohol question. How many drinks per day. How many per week. It was more than a question. It was a reckoning. A moment of truth. Or lie.

His pen hovered over the page, frozen in hesitation. What's the big deal? Not like the doctor is going to tell anyone. Was he afraid of seeing the number? Or was he just reluctant about receiving the inevitable lecture? Just put something moderate down. What does it matter? What does alcohol have to do with blood out the ass? Probably nothing. Or possibly everything.

Patients lie. They lie a lot. It's one of the biggest obstacles in health care. He thought about how often his own patients lied to him, how it irritated him, how it delayed resolution of issues. No one wants to admit their flaws. He had always known that. But now, for the first time, he understood it. Did he now want to be one of them?

The pen hovered, held aloft by the tension between the interrogator and the subject. Screw it. Just get it over with. What does it matter?

He answered the two questions honestly. Then grimaced when he saw the numbers he had written down.

Wow. Seriously? Wow.

It wasn't like he didn't know. He simply had never added it up like that. So while he was vaguely aware how much he was drinking, he had gotten in the habit of ignoring it. Like a leaky roof making water stains on your ceiling. Yeah. I see it. I'll deal with it later. I'm busy now. And then one day, a big chunk of ceiling falls on the middle of the floor. And there it is. There's no ignoring it anymore. There is no later. There is only now. The situation is out of hand.

Dr. Krokos appeared to be in his fifties. He was short with a bit of a belly. Borderline pudgy. Slightly balding with curly gray hair creeping over the tops of his ears. He had big brown hound dog eyes and a droopy face with a double chin. He sported a goatee beard in need of a trim. He didn't wear the traditional white coat, but rather a French blue dress shirt with sleeves rolled up and no tie. He lacked that severe crispness and hurried manner one typically associates with doctors. In addition to his casual appearance and manner, he hummed. Not anything recognizable, just random melodic snippets. The vocal equivalent of doodling.

He asked a lot of intensely personal questions, as every good doctor should. But the tone was informal, like a service manager asking you where the noise was coming from on your car and whether you heard it at all speeds. He kept his eyes on his clipboard, and through it all, he hummed. And when the questions were finished, he performed a brief physical exam. And hummed. And when the exam was over, he put down his clipboard and stethoscope and rolled his little wheeled stool closer, folded his hands, and looked straight into Jommers's eyes. And the humming stopped.

"Okay. We're going to need some more tests to nail this down, but I already have a hunch based on your lab and your self-reported alcohol consumption. Your triglycerides are sky-high and you are drinking way too much, which I hope you realize."

"Yes."

"So here's what I think is happening. You probably have a fatty liver, and that is probably causing portal vein hypertension. And I'll explain that in layman terms. Your drinking has gunked up your liver, and all the gunk is putting the squeeze on an important vein that goes through the liver. Like stepping on a hose. It creates a backpressure. And that backpressure is causing nearby veins to swell and distend. And that includes the veins in your anus, which are nearby on the same circuit. This, in and of itself, is a bad thing. But a fatty liver can also be a precursor to cirrhosis, which can be a fatal thing. So this isn't just about the discomfort of hemorrhoids. This is about your future. It's about saving your life. You need to quit. Or, at the very least, cut back to a moderate two per day. I'm guessing you already came to that conclusion, but like everybody else with a problem, you said to yourself, yes, I need to deal with this. Tomorrow. Right?"

"Yes."

"I know this feels awkward for you being on the other side of it, receiving instruction instead of giving it. But you need to put that aside for a moment. I think you would benefit from counseling from someone in your own field. I'm sure you have a lot of contacts, but if you're not comfortable going to someone you know, if you prefer the anonymity of a stranger, I can give you some names."

"Yes. I'd prefer that."

"And I'm sure you're smart enough to avoid the prevailing folklore and stick with evidence-based methods of cutting back."

"Yes."

"If for some reason, the therapy by itself is insufficient, I can prescribe naltrexone for you. It's helped a lot of people reduce their cravings. And if the naltrexone doesn't work, there are some newer alternatives available that have been proven equally effective. In other words, this is an absolutely solvable problem when evidence-based methods are employed against it. You will beat it one way or another."

"Understood."

"Finally, do not go home and beat yourself up over this. That won't be helpful. Do not be dumbfounded that this could happen to you of all people, someone in your profession. Working in healthcare does not confer immunity. We're still just people. We get sick like everybody else, and we get emotional and behavioral issues like everybody else. I'm going to tell you something personal I wouldn't ordinarily tell a patient. I used to be a smoker. Crazy, right? A smoking doctor. But they exist, and I was one of them. There's this big gray metal box behind the building, part of the air-conditioning system. It's about six feet high. I would sneak out there and hide behind it to smoke. Sometimes I needed a smoke so bad, I would go out there even when I had patients waiting in the chairs. I imagined that nobody saw me, that nobody knew. But somebody always knows. Whatever your weakness, whatever flaw you think you've concealed, somebody knows. And with smokers, everybody knows. There's the odor, the brown-stained tooth, the yellow finger, the bit of ash on the shirt. So one day I sneak out there, go behind the big gray thingy, and there's this piece of paper taped to the back of it. And somebody had written on it with a broad felt-tip marker, real big letters. 'Just stop. Please stop.' My eyes froze on it. I was shocked. Not so much that somebody knew, but that somebody cared. The word *please* was underlined. My eyes watered. I never found out who did it, though I suspect someone on my staff. And this is an important point—you need to seek out people who care. To crawl out of the hole all by yourself is very tough. You need helping hands. These issues are as much social as they are personal. And I know that you already know that on an intellectual level, but you need to internalize it, grasp it at the emotional level. Anyway, the day I saw that sign, that day was the beginning of the end. It wasn't quick or easy. It was a long battle. But eventually I won, and now I'm free. So you must understand that you're in for a fight, and you can't win it until you start it. You can beat it in time, and time starts now."

Time starts now.

A lot of men go through a youthful Superman phase, which can often last well into middle age, or for the very lucky, even longer. Not Superman in the sense of believing they are extraordinarily strong and can perform great feats, but in the quiet, subconscious sense of feeling invincible healthwise. Sure, they see and hear about bad things happening to other guys, and they understand on an abstract level that anything can happen to anybody at any time. But on a personal level, someone with the Superman complex feels that all that crappy stuff happening to other guys won't happen to him. He's special. He's in the zone. He never actually articulates this notion, but feels it on a gut level. Those bullets flying around will miss me.

And then one day it happens. Something forces the realization, which arrives like a Kryptonite arrow, and the world never looks the same again.

As he walked outside the building, Jommers moved slowly, taking small, careful steps, as if he was made of glass and didn't want to break anything. He wasn't thinking about what had just transpired. He wasn't thinking at all. He strolled right past his car and wandered dazed onto the front lawn of the nondescript medical building.

It was a typical small suburban office structure—blocky, ugly, gray, adorned with some low-cost architectural details that were meant to disguise the drab concrete blockhouse it actually was. It was located in a typical suburban commercial area, with other similarly ugly office buildings, retail strip centers strung together, and lots of well-known chain stores and chain restaurants. It was a scene familiar to most Americans, but less so for a guy who rarely left the Bends, who shopped for groceries up the hill at the market, bought other stuff online or out of catalogs to avoid going shopping. So for Jommers, a trip to the burbs was voyage to another planet.

As he approached the curb, he looked up at the stream of traffic zipping by him, then past it. As he fixed his gaze at the businesses across the street, he didn't even recognize some of the names on the chain outlets. And with one of them, not sure whether it was Greek or Mexican or even how it might be pronounced.

He mused to himself—this is what it must feel like to get released from prison.

There was no safe way to cross the fast-paced four-lane road. So he turned to his right and continued his wandering by walking parallel to the thoroughfare along its edge. There were no sidewalks, as this was not a planet designed for pedestrians. After ambling along for a couple of minutes, he approached a bus stop.

No sidewalks. Yet, strangely, bus stops.

A young man and a young woman were waiting for a bus back toward the city, judging by the route number on the sign. Each wore a uniform suggesting they were fast-food workers, though for different chains. As it was late afternoon, they were likely headed home after their shifts. The two commuters greeted Jommers warmly, as if he were a member of their tribe—the clan of the car-less.

Jommers stopped to chat a moment. He asked how they were holding up under the brutally hot sun, given that the bus stop offered no shade, consisting only of a sign on a rusted metal pole. He expected them to echo the grumble about the weather, and was surprised when they didn't.

"Oh, I'll take it," the young man said. "It's bad, but the winter's worse. When you get snow, it's a whole lot worse. When the plows come by, they throw up a three-foot wave of black, salty slush, and you don't want to be standing here, because they don't lift the plow for you. And after they go by, it'll be knee-deep right here. And it'll be the same other side where we get off. So you're coming in, and the bus door opens, that's it, that's what you jump into, a three-foot pile of black slush. And the drivers, they won't cut you any break by pulling down to a driveway somewhere. This is your stop, this is where you get off. Nothing you can do but step right in it. So then you show up at the job, and you look all grungy wet from the knees down, they yell at you, because you're supposed to show up looking clean and right."

"That's right," the woman chimed in. "They get nasty on you if you don't look clean. But they don't give you a locker or anything. No place to change. So you have to wear it in. No choice. Then they holler when it isn't clean."

"Maybe get that rubber pants and boots thing," the young man said. "You know, like those guys who stand in the river fishing."

"Waders," Jommers said.

"Yeah," the young man echoed. "Waders. Get some of those. But even if I did, nowhere to put them once I got in. They don't give you any space for anything."

"You're just supposed to magically appear without any stuff, like coming in on some spaceship transporter beam or something," the young woman said. "They don't know what it takes to get here every day. To get home. The adventure. Different buses, none of them on time."

"Like going to Katmandu every day. But they don't know. And they don't care."

"The snow makes the bus late, they yell at you. You don't get paid for missed time."

"They threaten you," he said. "Don't let it happen again. Like I control the weather. Like I control the buses. So, yeah, I'll definitely take this over winter."

"Definitely," she echoed. "The heat is uncomfortable, but it doesn't mess with your time or your pay."

"And the sweat doesn't make you dirty. You get to show up clean."

"That's right."

Wisdom from the lower bracket. When life runs the gamut from bad to miserable, then simply bad is okay, the best you'll get.

But Jommers didn't have much time to ponder it. His cell phone received a text message from Ilona Voros. She was requesting a meeting, using one of the location codes they had previously agreed upon. It was followed by the question: Soon?

He answered yes.

SLICK GETS HIT

The Grayton Hungarian Cultural Center was an old two-story brown brick building, rectangular and undistinguished, save for its sooty stone cornice. An enclosed walkway linked the structure to a shuttered church next door, made of the same brown brick, but whose gothic windows were boarded up and whose bell tower conspicuously lacked a bell.

Inside the center's entrance were two short sets of stairs. One led down to the kitchen and dining hall, which was slightly below ground level. The other stairs led to the upper hall, which appeared to be designed for entertainment activities. The floor was mostly open, with rows of small tables running alongside the walls, and there was a small stage at the end opposite the doorway. An American flag stood draped on a pole on the right front corner of the stage and a Hungarian flag adorned the left.

The original dark stain finish on the red oak floor was mostly worn off except around the edges. The walls were covered with wide vertical planks of mahogany-stained knotty pine. On the back wall of the stage was a faded painted mural depicting a lake in a rural setting with a flat-topped mountain on the lake's far shore. Lake Balaton, Jommers presumed.

Near the right wall of the stage was an upright piano that Ilona Voros was playing. Jommers heard the music as soon as he opened the door, so he entered quietly so as not to interrupt her. Not being a fan of classical music, he could not identify the piece, but he placed it as twentieth-century music, discerning its departure from traditional tonality.

His unfamiliarity and dislike of the work made it impossible to judge how well she played it. He intuitively sensed, however, perhaps by her manner and the look of preoccupation on her face, that she was not exploring the music so much as hiding in it. More escape than love. When she finished the piece, she gazed downward and sighed deeply with dissatisfaction.

"That was very nice," he said.

"Yes," she said. "The composition, that is, not my rendering of it."

"I didn't recognize it. Not that I would."

"It was by Zoltán Kodály, Dances of Marosszék. It was based on traditional folk tunes he'd collected in the countryside. He wrote it for the piano, though it was later arranged for orchestra, which is the more popular version. He and Béla Bartók both did that sort of thing, adapting folk tunes with classical interpretation. This is from Bartók's Sonatina on Romanian folk tunes."

She resumed playing for another couple of minutes, but stopped before finishing the piece.

"That was also later orchestrated, though renamed as Transylvanian Dances," she said. "I often wonder if Bartók or Kodály ever went back out into the field, to some village where they had recorded a folk tune, and then played their version of it. And, if so, what did old peasants think of what they heard? Would they pleased with the homage, or regard it as some awful, bastardized thing? Vandalism of their heritage. What would you guess, being a social scientist?"

"Hard to say," Jommers said. "Back in the old days, here or wherever, the music of the people was just part of everyday culture, like attire, recipes, stories—just part of the landscape of life that belonged to everybody and nobody. Borrowing was commonplace. Ownership doesn't become a big deal until the music starts making money. I would have to guess that the peasants would have had more concern with the tonality issues rather than the idea of appropriation per se."

"Okay, let me put it this way. Say you had this aging Delta blues man, some poor farmer who just plays the music for its own sake, then somebody from the city shows up and records him, and then his music becomes well known, then a particular piece of it gets adapted into a piece of classical music with a modern take, then you take him to hear it played by a symphony orchestra—what would he think of it?"

"Well, my guess is that he would scrunch up his face like someone who's eaten a rotten nut. Then he'd go looking for some whiskey to get the taste out of his mouth."

She laughed. "I think maybe you just answered my question."

"Maybe."

"So just now, when you said I played very nice, you were just being polite. In fact, you hated it."

"Well, let's just say that particular piece wouldn't be my cup of tea and leave it at that. Nothing to do with your performance of it."

"So this is a different side of you. The ordinary person who tells white lies in the service of civility. The opposite of the brutally honest therapist. Which role do you prefer?"

"There's a place for everything," he said. "There are a lot of people—therapists, prosecutors, cops—who must play a certain role on the job, but need to learn how to leave it at the office in order to have a life. To have friends."

"So your behavior now, that means you're not here as a therapist, you're here as a friend."

"Yes, I am."

"That's good. I could use a friend now."

"So what exactly is this place?"

"It used to be Saint Laszlo Hall, part of the church, which had always let the association use the hall. But then when they closed the church, the association raised the money to buy the property. They wanted to keep using the hall and prevent the church from being torn down. But they don't have the money to restore it. I've been coming here since I was a kid. I was even part of the Csárdás Dance Troupe Youth Ensemble for a while. Dressing up in the costumes, dancing to the old music, the whole bit. I can still remember this guy Sándor who played a blazing cimbalom, usually set up right over there. And then there was this fiddler in a cape, darting and dancing around without missing a note, as if the fiddle was playing itself. I have fond memories in retrospect, but, to be honest, I didn't fully appreciate it all back then. Eventually the musicians grew old and passed away, so the dancers turned to recordings. Then, interest in the dancing waned. The group slowly shrank until it disbanded a few years ago. I was so sad."

"They still do things here, though."

"Oh, yes, there are still various activities, dinners, dances, but they're getting fewer and farther between, and fewer attending."

"Well, that's the other side of the melting pot, isn't it?"

"Yes," she said, "but it's not only assimilation by itself, it's all the mixing. If you're third or fourth generation from those who came over on the boat, the connection to heritage isn't automatic. You have to consciously seek it. I mean, if all four of your grandparents have different ethnic backgrounds, what are you? Do you even pose the question? I suppose it's good in one sense, not having an identity thrust on you. You get to choose. But then it's not quite the same, is it? Shopping for an identity as if it were a toaster. It's less authentic that way, don't you think? I guess that's why I've stayed a member of the club. I need an anchor to something that's real. Otherwise I'll just float away, like an ash ascending from a campfire."

Her face changed from wistful to worried as she bowed her head toward the piano and clasped her hands tightly.

"You look stressed," he said. "You get a lot thrown at you when you returned to work?"

"I'm not so much stressed as distressed," she said.

"By?"

"Remember that guy who visited you, Stonecipher? The guy supposedly heading up Pike Square Security, the guy we think was just serving as front man for the chief?"

"Yes."

"He's dead."

"How?"

"Officially? A carjacking. His body was found late morning on a side street of Toledo Avenue next to a vacant factory building. Head shot. Left side. Consistent with a surprise carjack. No vehicle, no wallet. Got his identity from the business cards in the suit coat pocket. He's also wearing a holster, but the gun is gone. So they run his name through BMV to get make, model and license on his vehicle, then put it out to patrol. Early afternoon, a zone car spots the Escalade and lights up. There's a brief chase. The driver hits something and bails, but they run him down. He's got Stonecipher's credit cards in his pocket and Stonecipher's gun is still in the Escalade. He admits to stealing the vehicle, but denies shooting the driver. Says the ride was just sitting there with the keys inside the ignition, nowhere near the scene of the murder."

"And you believe the suspect?" Jommers asked.

"Yes, I do. Otherwise, it's all too neat, and the timing all too coincidental. And where it happened, low-traffic street with abandoned industrial buildings. Not the kind of place a carjacker is hanging around waiting for a nice car to show up. More like a place where two people who don't want to be seen together would go to meet. Besides, a security consultant getting surprised like that. Someone who's always got his guard up. This doesn't fit. But if he was approached by someone he knew . . ."

"Like?"

"Like Scubbetts."

"Does it make sense that Scubbetts would take out his own man?" Jommers asked.

"It does if he thought I was closing in. Think about it. What would be an obvious strategy for me? Get something on Stonecipher to turn him. Make a deal in return for testifying. Scubbetts would know that. So he gets rid of the one guy left who can bring him down. And if I'm right, then it means I'm running out of time. I have to get him before he eliminates all other evidence or just disappears. I need a breakthrough, fast. I need to get something on him. Anything at all. Something to hold him in place."

Jommers intended to share with her at some point his conversations with Biederbach and Dallabaco, but after hearing her news, he thought that sooner might be better than later. He told her everything, including Biederbach's theory on the Russian chemist and their planned meeting. Jommers also shared his suspicion that Biederbach possessed the kit bag that Tarburn had carried the night he died, a bag that very likely contained physical evidence of the chemical.

While she took careful note of everything he said, she oddly did not seem very curious about it.

"You don't look too excited about all that," he said. "You don't find it useful?"

"Oh, it's all good stuff," she said. "But it's down-the-road, case-building stuff. I need something for right now. I need to arrest him before he's gone. Like soon."

"You seem to have something specific in mind."

"I mentioned to you before this high-end prostitute that Scubbetts exploits. Freebies in return for protection. Raven. She has acknowledged it with me non-verbally, nods and winks, but won't articulate it, and is afraid to file a complaint. I've been working on her slowly, didn't want to be the heavy-handed cop leaning on her. I sympathize with her position. She's a victim. I understand that. She's afraid. I understand that, too. So I was trying to gently coax her into cooperating, gain her trust. I was making slow progress, but now I have no choice but to push her, and push her hard. And it it's making me sick. I have to be the pushy asshole cop, just as I was learning not to be the pushy asshole cop. You understand?"

"I do."

"That's why I'm distressed."

"I can't tell you how to do your job," he said, "but let me state the obvious. If the call girl is the only angle left, then Scubbetts is also aware of that. He already knows your next move. And he may lay a trap for you. If he in fact brazenly murdered Stonecipher in broad daylight, then it would confirm my estimate of him as a sociopath, making him remorseless, amoral, and fearless. And I don't mean fearless in the sense of being brave, I mean in the literal sense of lacking fear, not recognizing risk. And that means he is capable of surprising you, doing something unexpectedly bold, something that an ordinary criminal would never try. At the same time, this characteristic is also his weakness. He's cautious only on an intellectual level, but not on an emotional level. He can be simultaneously clever and stupid. You need to think about that. What details might such a man overlook? Where might he be overconfident? Paradoxically, while he can surprise you with his impetuousness, he may also lean to the repetitive. Meaning that, if there is a problem-solving method that has worked in the past, he is highly likely to use it again. They don't like reinventing the wheel. Finally, he'll be acting tactically rather than strategically, reacting to current situations rather than imagining future ones. He thinks one move ahead, but not two. Maybe you can use that to box him in."

"Thanks," she said. "Those are helpful insights about him."

"Good. Now let me give you some insights about you. You are a smart, capable, well-seasoned cop, and like other smart, confident, well-seasoned cops, you rely heavily on experience-based intuition. And that's a good thing in familiar situations. Like a veteran quarterback seeing a linebacker leaning a slightly different way and sensing a blitz. He changes the play at the line of scrimmage, then exploits the blitz. But relying on experience-based intuition can be a handicap in an unfamiliar situation. You try an old solution for a new problem and you get burned. Right now, you're dealing with a situation you never dealt with before. Your experience may be of little use to you. You should calculate every move as if it were your first day on the job. Think about everything that can possibly go wrong."

"I appreciate the advice," she said. "But I am good at what I do. Better than most. I've got catlike reflexes and stone-steady aim. I can take out the flame on a candle in a jack-o'-lantern without ruining its smile."

"Tarburn was a good shot, too. But his fate was sealed the moment he lit up a cigar. It's the decisions—"

"I understand the risk. But I have to take it. This is what I am. This is what I do."

"Don't emotionalize it. Don't make it an existential quest. That's how you make mistakes. Leave out your past, leave out your issues. Think dispassionately, like a mercenary general or a chess master. Think about what he's thinking."

"He's thinking about taking flight, and I have to stop him. But my point in calling you—before he goes, he may retaliate against you first. If he killed his own man, he won't hesitate to kill you. Please go away somewhere. Whatever you do, don't go home. Please. Do not go home."

LATE FOR A MURDER

Triggers, rituals, denials—the tripod support of bad habits. The conditioned response to stress becomes the ritual. To establish a new ritual, one must create a new response. You can't just eliminate the old thing, you must replace it with a new thing. Something must fill the gap. So it's more complicated than merely stopping a bad habit. One must change the lifestyle that bred the habit and cultivate alternative good habits. So it's much more than restraint—it's a creative project, one that requires planning, procedures, targets. All of which is easy to articulate, but difficult to implement.

How often had Jommers given this lecture to patients? Now he understood how overwhelmed they felt upon hearing it. Because now he stood outside the door of Spreckels Tavern, staring inside, hearing the music and the murmurs, the chuckles and the chatter, all beckoning like the mythic Sirens. The hum of humanity offering its warm embrace. And competing against the senses was a speech playing in his head, the one about triggers, rituals, denial. Emotion versus intellect.

Finally, he surrendered to the song and went inside, promising himself—no, challenging himself—to have just one beer. Yet the news he'd heard from Ilona Voros made him want to swallow it in a gulp. She had suggested that Scubbetts murdered Stonecipher directly in broad daylight. Was that even possible? Was he that bold? On the other hand, was it possible that the chief's right-hand man coincidentally becomes a carjacking victim just as an Internal Affairs detective is about to bring the hammer down on the chief? Which interpretation was more incredible?

And then, against his will, the third possibility intruded into Jommers's internal discussion, as unstoppable as noise. Biederbach's dark muttering about a cleanup crew working behind the scenes to eliminate evidence of a government experiment gone bad. The same notion Tarburn had raved about in his final hour. Jommers quickly tried to spit it out, like a hard piece of nutshell that had found its way into a nut roll.

Forget it, he told himself. It doesn't matter anymore. Not to him anyway. He was done with it. By confiding everything he knew to Voros, he had no more decisions to make, no more actions to take. He no longer had any influence over events. The whole matter was now in the hands of other people, which was where it had belonged all along. It was time to return to his own world and his own problems, which had mushroomed. There was his health issue that he'd learned about that afternoon. And then the matter of Scubbetts taking away police department business, the primary source of Jommers's revenue. He would have to reinvent his business model and market the hell out of it or find another way to make income.

At that moment, he felt like someone with acrophobia walking a wire over a canyon. How would it be possible to have only one beer? He grimaced, clenched his teeth, and summoned every last bit of will he could muster. He stood up from the barstool and put some money on the bar.

"Hey!" Larry shouted. "You leaving already?"

"Yeah, I got some things to do," Jommers said.

"Well, can you hold on a minute? I got something to tell you."

"Sure."

"I'll get you another. On me."

"Okay."

Jommers slumped back down on the barstool and rested his face on his left hand, sighing in defeat. The new day, which absolutely had to begin today, would begin tomorrow.

Larry brought another beer, but was immediately distracted by other customers needing refills. Five or ten minutes later, Larry finally got back to Jommers.

"So, earlier this week," Larry started, "I'm shooting the breeze with these two young lawyers. Well, they're in their thirties, but that's young to me now."

"Me, too."

"Anyways, they're pissing and moaning about how the law business has changed. How they're working longer hours but making less money than lawyers in the old days. But the worst part, there's no longer that guarantee of making partner just by putting in your time. You can spend years doing all the standard associate drudge work, paying your dues, and then they tell you bye-bye. So these two are asking me about the bar business, what's it's like and all, because they're thinking of just walking away from the whole law thing altogether and opening a bar. And so, half-joking, I say, hey, you want to buy Spreckels? And their jaws drop open like I was offering some famous diamond or something, the same way my jaw dropped open when Old Man Kaz said the exact same thing to me. So we talk about it, but I don't take it serious because they've been drinking and bitching all night long. It's just bullshit talking. Right? So, then, the next day they come by before lunch, and they ask me, was I serious, because they are. And I pause for a moment, then say yes. I was serious. Even though I didn't realize it the night before, I realized the day after. Something inside me wanted out. Something that's been there for a long time. So we talked more, and then some more. Hashing out the details, like, you know, I want them to keep as many of my people as they can, at least for a while anyway. Stuff like that. Anyway, we're pretty much there. And so now they're going to write up a contract. I'll run it by my lawyer to make sure I'm not getting screwed, but, barring unforeseen obstacles, it's going to happen. I'm going to walk away. Get a life. So, I wanted you to know."

"Well, I'm going to miss our conversations, Larry. I've really enjoyed them."

"We can still talk. And still talk here. Only difference is I'll be sitting on the stool next to you instead of being on the other side of the bar."

"Sounds like a plan to me."

"All right, then."

"All right, then."

As Jommers sipped the second beer, he and Larry reminisced about some of the strange characters that passed through Spreckels and the interesting things that happened there. And as Jommers got near the end of that beer, Larry, without being asked, brought him another, and the storytelling continued a little longer.

BY THE TIME JOMMERS LEFT the tavern, the sun had set and darkness had descended on the Bends. And that made the flashing lights ahead all the more prominent when he turned onto Nickel Plate Road.

When he got to the lot outside the truck repair shop, he found a fire truck and three police cars, two black-and-whites and an unmarked. Shop owner Pete Gerzny was talking to a detective that Jommers recognized from previous encounters. Even in the poor light, the short man's bald head and pencil mustache announced him.

As Jommers got out of the car, a firefighter approached him.

"You the guy who lives upstairs?"

"Yeah."

"Well, you're sleeping somewhere else tonight."

"What's going on?"

"The place is filled with toxic, flammable fumes. We opened all the windows, but we don't want to energize the garage doors and set something off. So we disconnected them from the chains and we're going to try and winch them open from the outside because they're too heavy to lift manually."

"So what happened?"

"I'll let Detective Yopko explain it. He's been waiting for you."

By this point, Yopko had spied Jommers and was already strolling over with his notebook.

"Hey, Jommers."

"Detective Yopko."

"Who do you know that really hates your guts?"

"That would be virtually everybody in Grayton PD who's had to go through my office involuntarily, including you."

"That's not exactly correct. I don't hate your guts per se. I hate the process of having to see you. The shit I gave you, I would have given to anyone sitting in that chair. So it wasn't personal."

"I feel so much better."

"You shouldn't. Somebody wanted you dead tonight."

"What's the story here?"

Detective Yopko started flipping through the pages in his little notebook. "Okay, bear with me. This gets complicated. It starts with a 911 call. Woman says she's jogging in the Bends and smells chemical fumes coming out of a truck repair shop and there's no one there. So they send FD to check it out. When they arrive, the woman is still here. She warns them that something doesn't look right. She was looking in the windows and tells them to be careful how and where they enter. So they take her advice. And after looking through the windows themselves, they break one and put in this remote control thingy on wheels, looks like something you'd give a kid for Christmas, only it's special-made with a camera, sensors, sealed construction, and other stuff. So while they're focused on what they're doing, they're not paying attention to the woman. And she slips away into the darkness. They never see her again."

"What did she look like?"

"She was young, say early twenties, skinny, short dark hair, denim shorts, black T-shirt with paint on it, like she'd been painting something."

"I don't think she was a jogger. She sounds like this graffiti artist I've seen around here lately."

"That could explain her disappearing act. Doesn't want to explain that she was really doing something illegal."

"Possibly. So what did the remote control thingy on wheels find?"

"All kinds of shit, and none of it good. First, there was this fifty-five-gallon drum of sealant that someone overturned after removing the lid. The owner, Gerzny, says they use it when fixing the roofs on trailers."

"Yeah, I know it. It's this silvery sticky goop that stinks. I can smell it upstairs whenever they use it."

"Part of what you're smelling is the solvent in it, toluene, which is nasty stuff, both toxic and flammable."

"Not possibly an accident? You know, the drum knocked over somehow."

"A nearly full fifty-five-gallon drum is pretty goddamn heavy to just accidentally knock over. Besides, there's more. Whoever did it, they then went and opened the valves on all the welders' tanks, filling up the place with oxygen and acetylene."

"Holy crap."

"Yeah, and I'm not even to the best part. You familiar with the air compressor unit?"

"Yes," Jommers said. "They use air power tools because they're lighter and smaller. They got air lines running to every work bay. The compressor charges a reservoir tank up to a certain PSI so that there's always maximum pressure available. Then it kicks off. When they use the air tools, they bleed the tank, and when the pressure drops to a certain threshold, the compressor kicks on to charge it back up."

"Very good," Yopko said. "Then you'll understand the next part fine. So here's what the intruder did in sequence. First, he runs an air line up to your apartment entry door on the second floor. He cuts off the connector on the end of the hose, then closes the door on the cut end, pinching the hose closed. Then he turns on the compressor and wait till the tank is charged and the compressor shuts off. Next he tips the sealant drum and opens the oxygen and acetylene tanks."

"So when I come home and open my door, I unpinch the hose and air starts flowing out of it. When the tank pressure drops, the compressor kicks on, creating momentary sparks across the contactors. Then ignition."

"And bam," Yopko said, "you're blown to flaming unidentifiable crispy bits that come down a quarter mile away. It would take us a week to find your teeth, assuming we felt it was worth the effort."

"Sounds a bit exotic way to get things done," Jommers said. "I wonder if it was actually intended to work, or just make me think it would. It would be hard to predict the proper stoichiometric ratio necessary—"

"The wha'? Look, be happy you didn't have to find out the hard way."

"The intruder must have prior familiarity with this place and everything in it. You don't come here on a lark and put this together on the fly."

"The shop owner, Gerzny, thinks the hillbilly did it."

"Who's that?" Jommers asked.

"He says there's this hick he hired little over a week ago. Looked like he knew what he was doing, but turned out to be a slacker. Always listening to some old pocket radio with an earphone. Gerzny said he chewed the guy out several times about it, then today, had enough. Fired him right after lunch."

"Well, that gives you motive and familiarity," Jommers said. "Case solved."

"Except for one little hitch—the air line to your door that makes you the trigger. If the mechanic just wanted to destroy the place, he could have set up a delayed blaze with a candle or a cigarette, like arsonists do. It would have been a lot simpler. My gut tells me this is all about you somehow."

"Your gut. Experienced-based intuition. A hunch."

"My hunches are usually pretty good," Yopko said. "Which takes us back to the start. Who hates your guts enough to do this?"

"Well, there is this one guy I pissed off recently."

"What's his name?"

"Derle Scubbetts," Jommers said.

"Derle Scubbetts. That's the same name as—are you fucking with me? Don't fuck with me, Jommers. This is serious shit."

"I'm not messing with you, Yopko. I'm serious. Chief and I just had a falling out. There was this detective he wanted declared psychologically unfit for duty. Instead, I cleared her to return to work."

"Big Red."

"Word travels fast."

"Oh, yeah. Especially about her."

"So Chief calls me up, rips me a new one. Made direct threats, too. I recorded it, so as soon as we get access, I can play it for you."

"Jesus H. Christ, what the fuck am I supposed to do with this? What? Just drop by his office? Hey, Chief, mind if I ask you a few questions? First off, where were you last night?"

"Toss it over to Internal Affairs where it belongs. Call Big Red."

"Fuck, fuck, fuck . . ."

"Hey, you don't like that angle, then go chase down the mechanic before he gets back to Weirton."

"Fuck, fuck, fuck . . ."

At that point, Jommers's cell phone rang. It was Claire.

"Karl, you okay? I just heard from Pete."

"Yeah, I'm fine thanks."

"Pete thinks it was the new guy he just fired."

"Yeah, most likely."

"I had a bad feeling about that guy from the get-go. I told Pete that. But he hired him anyway."

"I guess he should have listened to you."

"Lot of people should listen to me," she said.

"I'm not going to ask for names on that one."

"So Pete says you can't stay there tonight."

"Right."

"Well, if you want, you can sleep on my couch. It's not all that comfortable, but at least you won't have to go hunting for a motel."

"You know, I think I'll take you up on that."
"Okay, then. You know I don't have A/C."
"It'll be just like home."

A DREAM DEFERRED

The call was providential. After hearing how the shop was rigged to explode, Jommers became concerned about Claire's safety. He had planned to discreetly park on her street and spend the night watching over her from inside his car. Now, with the sofa invitation, he could watch over her more directly and comfortably.

She lived in an old neighborhood on the near West Side not far from the Bends. It was once known as Little Lviv because of all the Ukrainian mill workers who lived there. In the sixties and seventies the area declined along with many such urban neighborhoods as better-off people migrated to the suburbs.

Recently, fortunes had begun to improve for the neighborhood with the opening of some trendy nightspots and the rehabbing of some older buildings. That in turn started attracting some young professionals who worked downtown. The resultant spotty efforts at gentrification had transformed the neighborhood into a hodgepodge of incongruous juxtapositions, where a bustling boutique bakery prospered near a busy check-cashing/payday loan operation, where an upscale eatery and jazz club stood opposite a thrift shop run by nuns, and where the sidewalks carried both the fashionably offbeat and the working poor, coursing past each other with neither friction nor mixing, like oil and water.

The strangeness of the whole scene was ideal for Claire, who saw the diversity as some type of social adventure, an escape from the tedious tasks of billing and bookkeeping. She had no desire to appear fashionable, and in her attire she certainly wasn't. She just liked the fresh air of the unexpected.

When Jommers arrived at her house, they immediately talked about the incident down at the shop. Like Pete, she believed that the disgruntled mechanic had caused all the trouble. Jommers was disinclined to offer the alternative theory, that he himself had been the target. He preferred instead to have a normal conversation with her, one that did not involve talk of murder, sociopaths, and conspiracies. He did not want her to worry about him. Fishing around his brain for a more mundane topic, he recounted his recent conversation with Roone Sweelinck, who ran the short-line railroad in the Bends, and how Sweelinck was one of the few people he knew who'd achieved his dream.

Her response took him by surprise.

"And when will you get back to pursuing your dream?"

He pretended to stare at her dumbly for a moment, though he knew exactly what she meant, as she had brought it up before. Back when he was young and enthused about his career, he had often told her about his plans to transform therapy for blue-collar men and find ways for them to overcome their resistance to it. And once he had accumulated enough case histories and success stories in doing that, he would start writing papers for peer-reviewed journals. Once he got those published, he would consolidate the sum of his experience into a textbook that would be referenced by clinical psychologists for generations to come.

He had even codified the goal into a great line, one she'd found so apt that she had written it down. And now, decades later, she retrieved the little piece of notepaper that held his words:

"When I look at blue-collar male culture in America, I feel like a medic flying over a disaster area with no place to land. I've got the ability to help, but not the access. I've got to change that."

The small bungalow lacked a formal dining room, so they were talking at a small table in the corner of the kitchen. She was old-school about straight talk and the best place to conduct it. Face-to-face at the kitchen table. She was also an old friend who'd known him since they were both kids. There would be no playing sphinx at Claire's kitchen table.

"So," she asked, "what happened to all that?"

"It's common for young people to have ambitious goals, big and bold ideas. And that's fine. But dreams have to reconciled with reality. Capabilities measured against limitations. Opportunities against constraints. So when people get older and have more encounters with the real world, they learn to scale down those goals to more achievable levels. It's a perfectly normal process. Somewhere out there is a person who studied architecture hoping to design stunning skyscrapers and art museums, but instead ended up drafting plans for self-storage facilities. Somewhere out there is a person who studied law with dreams of trying cases before the Supreme Court and changing legal precedent, but instead spends his days drawing up franchise agreements for fried-bologna-on-a-stick outlets. And that's okay. It's a tough world. You do what you have to do to survive. And sometimes that means adjusting expectations. It's a prudent adaptive behavior. It's what sensible people do."

"So that's what you teach your patients, surrender? Go belly up, be happy?"

"I teach them how to deal with reality, because the detachment from reality in all its various forms is the root of most psychological problems. People need to discard the fantasies that pop culture sells them, that life is just like some smarmy movie where if you just try hard enough all your dreams all come true.

Life gives you line fences and a certain amount of running room within them. You have to figure out your running room."

"Yeah, but who builds the fences? I understand a gatekeeper telling you no. I don't understand when it's you telling yourself no. Is there someone preventing you from trying? Are there any dire consequences if you attempt and fail? Look, I understand better than anybody about dreams getting shot down. But what I don't get is letting your dreams nosedive without a single shot being fired. Explain that to me."

"It's complicated."

"Is it? Or so simple you can't see it?"

"You apparently do."

"It's obvious to me, and to Pete, too, by the way. You spend day after day talking to burned-out cops. Guys who started out idealistic, wanting to do good, but then got disillusioned and cynical. And attitudes are contagious, which you should know better than anybody. You caught their disease. You have their sickness, but you can't see it."

"That's an interesting theory, but incorrect."

"Then give me a better one."

"Survival," he said.

"Okay, you lost me."

"As you know, both my parents died fairly young. And with Dad, well, it's very likely he was the agent of his own demise. So, as you might imagine, I spent a great deal of time contemplating the concept of survival, both emotional and physical. More specifically, how to ensure my own. And there was this one night where things crystallized. You remember when I was just starting out, I was doing some volunteer work at the free clinic. Couple nights a week. Substance abuse counseling, mostly. And this one night I was there, a young doctor who was on duty grabs me and asks me to look at someone. There was this homeless guy who somebody dropped off. His face was banged up and bloody. They weren't sure whether he was assaulted or just fell down face-first, as he was clearly drunk. Staggeringly drunk. He was behaving erratically and resisting treatment. They wanted me to take a quick look to determine whether he was psychotic in addition to being drunk, in which case they were going to run him over to the psych ward at Saint Bridget's. I came into the room, the guy was bellowing, 'Let me show you, let me show you.' And he was standing funny, in a pose, his right fist held in his left hand under his chin. He jerked his head from left to right, like looking for somebody, but he did it without moving his shoulders. The young doctor didn't know what to make of it. He was foreign born and—"

"Came from a country without baseball."

"Exactly. So I explained that the guy was imitating a pitcher in the set position, keeping an eye on the base runners. He wanted to show us his pickoff move, or his fastball, or whatever. And when he got the chance, he promptly fell down on his face, which explained his injuries. So I tried talking to him, tried to calm him down enough for them to clean and bandage his abrasions. I kept him occupied with conversation while they worked on him. And in the course of this, I get a brief glimpse into his past. His dad had gotten him throwing the ball almost as soon as he could walk. So his dream of being a major league pitcher begins early in childhood. But with him, it's more than a dream, it's a feeling of destiny. He awes them in high school, then later wows them in the minors, and soon he gets called up. Then it goes south. Says he got some bad advice and he ended up overworking the arm, injuring it. Says he got more bad advice on how long to rest it. Bottom line, he blows out his arm before his first season in the majors even ends."

"So his career is over before it actually begins."

"Not just his career, but his perceived destiny. He viewed it in mythic terms and had invested his entire sense of purpose in this aspiration, and then it's snatched away. He falls without a net. And never stops falling. So, anyway, the clinic staff gets him patched up and, since there was nothing else seriously wrong with him, they send him out the door. He staggers off into the night, looking for a place to sleep with his demons. The image of him standing like that, on his imaginary mound, haunted me. I can still see it, like it was just this morning. And I remember saying to myself, I don't ever want to be that guy. I don't ever want to be that guy. America preaches to its children, chase that dream, don't stop believing, and all that crap, but there's little guidance offered for how to handle that nasty little business of falling short. So realizing that too much fire in the belly can incinerate you, I erred on the side of too little. And I know what you're going to say, that the story is nothing but a justification for a natural inclination, and if that night had never happened, I would have lived the same. And you may be right. I'll never know. But this is where I am now."

"But it's not where you have to stay," she said. "You just told me about a guy who bought a railroad at age fifty-nine, which is twelve years older than you are now. And he makes it work. There are plenty of other people like him who have started entirely new careers at an age older than you. Remember Colonel Sanders?"

"Please, not the Colonel's story. Too much inspiration makes me swoon."

"You don't even have to go that far, starting a new career like him. All you need to do is move your existing career up out of first gear. And you could start that tomorrow."

"Yes. Tomorrow."

DAY NINETEEN

It was a comfortable couch, but Jommers hadn't slept much. He'd spent too much time glancing out the window at every car that went by, jumping to alertness with every sound. The motorcycles unnerved him the most. Their loudness bursting through the stillness. Who the hell rides motorcycles in the middle of the night? Where the hell are they going?

And just when the night grew quiet enough to get some shut-eye, the sun rose. The opportunity had passed.

He put his shoes back on, but before quietly slipping out the door, he left a note for Claire on the kitchen table. "Thanks for being a port in the storm."

He found an open diner and filled his belly with eggs and coffee, then headed back to the shop. Pete was already there cleaning up the half-dried muck of spilled sealant. He'd been there since first morning light. The firefighters had winched open the bay doors before leaving, and that, along with the open windows, had cleared out the dangerous fumes, though it was clearly going to stink for a while.

"Crazy son of a bitch," Pete scowled, referring to the departed mechanic. "You get fired, you just go. What the hell is the matter with people today?"

"It's a messy world, Pete. Things don't always end neatly."

"I guess I shouldn't bitch. We got lucky. If it wasn't for that jogger, this place would be gone now. You, too."

"The former being more important than the latter."

"I wasn't going to say it, but as long as you did . . ."

They both laughed.

Once Pete got done grumbling, he would get back to business, make sure nothing fell between the cracks. That was his most enviable trait, that innate old-timer ability to carry on through adversity. Things happen. You keep working. You keep moving.

Satisfied that Pete had matters under control, Jommers promptly called Ilona Voros and requested an urgent meeting using their prearranged location codes. She was available.

And as soon as he got off the phone with her, an uninvited thought jabbed him—should he start carrying the gun?

He hadn't bought the gun for protection, and had been reluctant to get it at all. He was aware of the stats regarding gun use in the home. For every single incident in which a gun in the home was used for self-defense, there were four accidental shootings and eleven attempted or successful suicides.

He'd bought the gun to comprehend the gun. To experience it. The feel and weight of it. The sound and kick of it. The surprising heat it generated. The unforgiving lethal power of it. He wanted to grasp its influence on the mind of a person carrying it.

This was back when he'd first started working with Grayton PD and he'd wanted to better understand a cop's perspective. So he went on ride-alongs in cruisers to see what they saw. Experience what they experienced. But he also wanted to know what it was like to carry this iconic thing, this strange mechanical contraption whose sole purpose was to take the life of another human being. How does that change you?

When he first mentioned the notion to some cops, they were eager to offer purchasing advice. Unsurprisingly, many cops are gun enthusiasts, with some a bit too enthused. The latter type tend to equate guns with artillery—the bigger the better. The more sober-minded gun expert will tell you that the best gun is the one you can best use. There are ergonomic issues, like matching gun size to hand size, grip strength to recoil force, and so on. A small round in the target beats a big round in the ceiling.

But a guy who listens to old acoustic blues through a speaker in an antique Philco cathedral style radio already knows what gun he wants. He wants Andy's gun, the Colt Official Police revolver. In the old TV series, the sheriff of Mayberry rarely carried his gun, keeping it at home most of the time, unloaded on top of a china cabinet. He explained in one episode that he wanted the good people of Mayberry to respect him, not fear his gun. Law and order should be about respect, not fear.

Though production of the legendary .38 Special six-shooter ceased back in '69, it was not hard to find a decent used one, as it was one of the best-selling handguns ever made and widely used by police everywhere during its time. While a mint one could go for over a thousand smackers, a used one with a worn finish and grip could be had for a couple hundred.

After buying his Sheriff Andy gun, Jommers signed up for a training course that would allow him to apply for a concealed carry permit.

The people who teach such courses vary in their level of expertise, dedication and soundness of judgment. With the help of recommendations, Jommers made sure he found himself a good one.

The portly, elderly and highly experienced instructor conveyed a quiet gravitas, like a Zen master. He compelled your attention with seriousness of tone rather than loudness of voice. He began the course with a lecture on gun-owner responsibility. He noted that in a high percentage of crimes involving a gun, the gun in question turns out to be stolen.

People who leave the house with a gun sitting in a nightstand or dresser drawer, the first places burglars look, are stupid and irresponsible. Such people are unintentionally the biggest suppliers of guns on the streets. And the grand prize for stupid goes to the morons who put a sign in their front window that says something like "This Home Protected by Smith & Wesson."

Announcing to all the would-be burglars of the world that you keep guns in your house is just as dumb as a posting a sign announcing that you collect rare coins and antique jewelry, which are also typically and stupidly kept in the top dresser drawer. If you're that eager to be robbed, you might as well send out invitations, the master advised. Responsible gun-owners keep their weapons in gun safes.

He then got into the nuts and bolts of the course, types of guns and ammunition options, gun operation and safety, and shooting techniques, which included a discussion of the common shooting stances—the Isosceles, the Weaver, the Chapman, and the Fighting.

Throughout the course, the instructor served up helpings of common sense, wisdom, and even game theory. For example, if you intend to carry the weapon, you need to practice with the weapon. People who carry but don't practice end up with their guns being taken from them during a confrontation. You end up supplying the bad guy with a gun he gratefully uses on you.

Jommers paid close attention to the instructor's advice, but at the same time, the psychologist couldn't avoid observing his fellow classmates, especially at the breaks, where he often covertly eavesdropped on their conversations. He wanted to know why they were there.

There were two women, one who worked as a cleaner and the other as a barmaid. They both worked nights and had already experienced close encounters of the bad kind and wanted to be ready for the next one. There was the barber who owned rental properties in iffy neighborhoods and often had to collect rent in person when payment was overdue. Then there were a couple of guys like Larry, guys who ran a cash business and, after closing time, had to make the scary run to a night deposit with a bag of cash.

More than half the enrollees, however, seemed to be there for cultural reasons. Affluent residents of outer suburbs whose probability of being engaged in mortal combat was comparable to that of getting hit by lightning. Their desire to pack a piece was more of a political statement reflecting their worldview. There were at least two attendees who actively fantasized about having the big encounter—shooting a bad guy. They intuitively recognized each other right off the bat, and their conversations were disturbing. They wanted it to happen. They wanted the opportunity to shoot someone. It was then Jommers realized that a psychological evaluation should also be a prerequisite to obtaining a concealed carry permit, but in the present political climate, such a notion would never even be suggested, much less enacted into law.

The master ended the course with a heartfelt bit of counsel consisting of six words.

Be safe. Be smart. Be sane.

Everyone was out the door before the last part.

Jommers had started packing as soon as he'd received his permit. The gun was heavier than he'd imagined and harder to conceal than he'd envisioned. It altered his gait and affected what clothes he wore and how he wore them. And when rushing across the street or walking fast for any reason, he found himself instinctively putting his hand over the gun to keep it from shifting. So initially, it was more of a pain in the ass than an object of awe and contemplation. But he eventually got used to it.

He followed the instructor's advice and practiced regularly, though not always legally. Most of the time he practiced at a gun range, but other times he was less formal about it. There were any number of places down in the Bends that were deserted on a Sunday morning. Places where you could shoot at beer cans using a brick wall or slag pile as a backstop. Places where there was nobody to see, hear or care.

Over time, his practice sessions, legal and otherwise, diminished in frequency. This, too, was prophesized by the master: "You purchase your weapon with a sincere level of commitment that you don't realize is fleeting. And eventually your weapon becomes like the twice-used inscrutable bread maker in the attic, the wobbly budget-model elliptical trainer getting webby in the basement. A tucked-away thing that you bought with the best of intentions but that you no longer know how to use, assuming you can even find it."

With reduced practice came less frequent carrying. The first time Jommers left it behind was because he was late and in a hurry. The second time was because his knee hurt. The third time was because it was too hot, or maybe too cold. He didn't remember. But by and by, as the master predicted, the gun became that tucked-away thing. Out of sight, out of mind.

And now, with Jommers feeling under threat, the gun popped up in his mind. Should he start packing it when he went out?

He recalled one more bit of deflating sagacity tossed out by the instructor: "Do not imagine that carrying a gun puts up a force field around you, that it imparts any invincibility. I'm sorry to tell you that, in most cases, it won't help you at all. That's because the upper hand is always with the attacker, who has the advantage of surprise. He knows what's about to happen before you do. Even an alert, well-trained police officer approaching a traffic stop with hand on weapon can still end up dead when the criminal's weapon is already drawn because seconds make the difference. So don't be deceived or complacent. Carrying the gun may make you feel safer, but it doesn't change reality. Cowboy movies are fantasies, but they get one thing right. At close range, the guy who draws first usually wins. And it won't be you. Because you won't know you're at a gunfight until it's over."

Reflecting on that observation, Jommers realized that carrying a gun was even less effective when you were a planned target. A real-life hit wasn't like the movies, where your assassin approaches from the front and engages in banter beforehand. In reality, if someone has targeted you specifically, you won't see or hear it coming. There will be a sudden, sharp, inexplicable pain. And you'll think, briefly, what the hell is that, gallstones? A moment of puzzlement followed by darkness. Then it's over. Your fingertips won't get anywhere near your gun because your mind won't even have the chance to figure out what's happening.

So after that brief deliberation, he left the gun behind.

***

IN LATE SUMMER and early autumn down in the Bends, it was not uncommon for a light, low-lying ground fog to develop during the night, especially during humid weather. Usually, it was quickly burned away by morning sun, but could linger a bit longer in shaded areas and tunnels, including the meeting spot with Ilona Voros.

In the late 1800s, there had been a stone viaduct that took traffic over the Bends and its river, but its future had been doomed by a low passage height that could not handle larger ships. Most of the bridge had been dismantled in the early 1900s during the river-widening project, and all that remained was a span on the west bank with three high arches, broad enough to permit vehicle traffic underneath. From below, the massive stone arches conveyed a sense of grandeur, even with the drapes of bug-eaten, weedy vines. A grand ruin, like an ancient Roman aqueduct, maybe. On top, though, the truncated viaduct was just another dead-end street, which was used as a parking lot. Another item of Bends refuse, only on a slightly larger scale.

Coursing underneath the west end of the viaduct were two side-by-side arched railroad tunnels that allowed north-south passage of trains under the bridge. The trains carried materials southward from the docks on the lakeshore. The railroad that had once run through those tunnels was long defunct and the tracks long ago removed, the only remnants being the black soot deposited on the tunnel ceilings by the coal-burning steamers that passed through.

The twin tunnels, with their segmented arches, were more functional in design, being just wide and tall enough to handle the passage of trains. Scrub trees and brush almost obscured the openings, rendering them more sinister, tomblike. For a few feet inside, ferns prospered in the shade, imparting a beguiling, mysterious appearance. But deeper in, things were less enchanting, as the tunnels contained the typical detritus of secret places—empty beer cans, broken beer bottles, snack food wrappers, cigarette butts, used condoms, and the ubiquitous flattened boxes used by the homeless as beds. A detached abandoned backseat from a car likely served a similar purpose.

Voros had no trouble finding the place, and appeared familiar with it when she arrived.

"I suppose this is a fitting place for us to meet," she said. "A tunnel to nowhere under a bridge to nowhere."

"Been here before?" Jommers asked.

"Back in my patrol days. Got a call to come here. A body. Woman had been bound, raped, then had her throat cut." She paused to look around. "She was lying right over there. I can still see her. She was my first. Body, that is. I was horrified, yet transfixed by her face. Desiccation had tightened it, pulled the flesh back to expose the teeth, creating this ghastly expression. Nature programs your mind to interpret faces. Hostile or friendly. Honest or deceitful. Happy or sad. So, on first encounter, the mind doesn't know what to make of this new face. It doesn't register. It has nothing to reveal but the obvious. I'm dead. When you're growing up, the only place you see bodies is in funeral homes, where the look of serenity on the face has been carefully crafted by a mortician. When you don't know better, that's what you expect to see. But when you see the stark face of death for real for the first time, it's like a thorn in the eye. And you never forget it."

"Yes," he said. "And I just narrowly avoided the opportunity to acquire that look."

"What do you mean?"

"You were right. I was wrong. I should have gone to see the world's biggest cuckoo clock."

Jommers told her about how the shop had been rigged to explode when he arrived home and suggested she contact Detective Yopko, who was on the scene.

"So now you've got someone to work with on this," he said. "There's no need for you to play the lone ranger."

"Somebody to work with, maybe. But somebody to trust? I don't know. You don't fully grasp how much I'm despised. Most of them would only be too happy to see Scubbetts liquidate me."

"You need to get past all that now. These guys are still cops. They still understand good versus evil."

"Do they? If you'd seen the cases I've worked on, you wouldn't be so confident about that. Anyway, it doesn't matter. I talked to the prostitute again last night. She's ready. I'm going to see her this afternoon. I've got a friend I can trust, she gets off patrol shift early afternoon. She's agreed to go with me, back me up. So I won't be the lone ranger."

"This doesn't sound right," he said. "It's too easy. I'm starting to get a feel for Scubbetts now. I underestimated him. Both his capabilities and his intentions. You need more than an off-duty cop going with you. You need the cavalry. This smells like a trap to me."

"Now who's the paranoid? This is what I do, Jommers. I bust bad cops. And I'm going to bust this son of a bitch big-time. By nightfall, Scubbetts will be in cuffs. And I'll make sure it hurts."

"I guess I shouldn't have expected that you could shed your narcissism as easily as tossing an old pair of shoes in the Goodwill bin. You need to drop the whole Xena Warrior Princess thing for a moment. Think clearly about the risk here."

"Well, isn't this classic. A man takes a risk, he's brave and heroic. Woman takes a risk, she's being foolish. Imprudent. Needs some sense slapped into her."

"That's not where I was going."

"But it's where you went."

"No. What I meant was—"

"Displays of courage are for men, the ladies should mind their place. And if one should dare to be bold, well, then, she's clearly hysterical. Probably having her period or something. Give her some pills to calm her down."

"No. You're getting me wrong—again."

"No. I'm getting you perfectly right—again—like I did on day one. A guy who deals with other guys, but doesn't know any more about women than he does particle physics. You don't know me. You don't know anything about me, what runs through me. I told you my father was a 56er. So while other kids got lectures on manners, or on finishing their plate because there are hungry people in Africa, I got lectures on courage. He would say, never forget what beats inside you, never forget your Magyar heart."

"I'm not discounting your courage, merely advising it be supplemented with wisdom. When you romanticize heroism, the smart part often gets left out. He's counting on that with you. He's going to exploit it. Sucker you. Because he knows you better than you know yourself."

"A minute ago, you admitted that I was right about something and you were wrong. And now you don't even consider the possibility you might be wrong again. But I'm the narcissist."

"This won't end well. Not well at all."

"Stick to your job. And I will stick to mine. We're done here."

THE TRAP

Jommers returned to his office distraught and unsure what to do about it. He tried calling Detective Yopko, but all he got was voice mail. He left a message, expressing his concern that Detective Voros might be headed into a dangerous trap and needed either backup or dissuasion.

He flopped down in one of the rockers and rocked nervously, considering what else he could do. After a minute, it occurred to him to call Captain Wifflyn, Voros's superior at Internal Affairs. Ironically, just as he was reaching for the phone, Captain Wifflyn called him.

"Jommers! Did you or did you not clear Detective Voros to return to duty?"

"I did."

"Then why the fuck is she acting so loony? She's pestering me with some bizarre cockamamie story about Chief Scubbetts committing murder, that the chief has some mystery drug that he uses on people to get some voodoo-like control over them, including the fucking mayor! How the fuck do you clear someone who has totally lost it? Did she give you a slow slobber knobber? Was it that good?"

"Listen to me, she intends to see a prostitute for a statement this afternoon, but it's likely a trap. You either must provide her with backup or prevent her from going. One or the other."

"I'll tell you what the fuck I'm going to do. I'm going to get her the fuck out of here. She has gone totally rogue. Total and complete insubordination. If I can't get her fired, then I will get her transferred to Traffic, where she can pass the days writing tickets, and hopefully not fuck it up."

"No, listen—"

Wifflyn disconnected before Jommers could say any more.

Jommers resumed rocking, trying to brainstorm another option. Not long after, Claire came up to talk. She apologized for confronting him the night before about his career.

"It's okay," he said. "Your candor is always appreciated, if not immediately, then in retrospect. When you stop being frank with me, then I'm lost for sure."

They chatted a few more minutes, getting back to the fired mechanic and the awful things he'd done before leaving, and how she was willing to personally drive to Weirton and track him down if the cops failed to do so.

When she went back to work downstairs, Jommers returned to rocking and ruminating. It was impossible to do anything else.

Then Ilona Voros called him.

"What the hell are you doing?" she yelled over the phone.

"What?"

"You know what. You called Captain Wifflyn and told him to stop me. You called Detective Yopko and told him to stop me. So why are you trying to sabotage me right when I'm about to win? I thought you were on my side. I thought I could trust you."

"I am on your side. I'm trying to save your goddamn life."

"I don't need you butting in. I know what I'm doing. So stay out of it."

"Listen—"

"No. I'm done listening to you. It doesn't matter anyway. I've got to move now. Out of time."

"What do you mean, move now?"

"Raven just called me."

"The prostitute."

"Yes. She's suddenly all panicky. Said she's seeing strange people around the apartment where she lives. She thinks something is going to happen to her soon. She says she wants my protection right now or she's going to run, leave town, in which case I wouldn't ever see her again. I have to move things up."

"What about your friend?"

"She can't get off this early. Too much going on. I can't wait. I have to go alone or I'll lose this."

"No. You can't. This is exactly what I warned you about."

"I'm not asking your advice. I'm telling you what I'm going to do. So don't call me anymore. Don't call my boss anymore. Don't call anybody about me anymore. I am done with you. Goodbye."

"Ilona, please—"

She disconnected the call. He tried calling back, but she refused to answer. He was out of options.

He had often advised patients to let go of things beyond their control, but acceptance is easier after something bad has already happened, and almost impossible when the bad thing is about to happen, when you feel an urgent need to prevent something but cannot find a means to do so.

Like watching a funnel cloud form in the sky and not knowing if, when, and where it will come down as a tornado. How do you not fixate on it?

Jommers's cell phone sat on his desk table next to his landline phone. One or both would notify him of the tragedy and its particulars. He sat quietly and stared at them, the funnel cloud on his desk.

A short while later, Ilona Voros called back. He was relieved, but only briefly.

"Have you ever heard of the Markos?" she asked.

"The what?"

"I just got a weird call on my cell. Man's voice. No name. Said that Tarburn was part of a subgroup within SWAT called the Markos, short for marksmen. Said that I've been set up. That the Markos are coming to kill me. Take revenge for my shooting Tarburn, one of their own. This doesn't make sense. How would they even know where I am?"

"I never heard that term," Jommers said. "Where are you?"

"I'm at her place. She's dead. Someone got here first."

"You mean Raven, the prostitute?"

"Yes," she said.

"Is there a chemical smell in the air?"

"Yes. She . . . her head . . . it's stuck in a pail. Smells like some kind of glue . . ."

"Get out of the room, Ilona. Right now. This second. Get outside. Fresh air now. Get out of the room. Now."

"I don't understand what's happening . . . can't think . . ."

"Ilona, listen to me. You've been set up for a confrontation with SWAT, the same way Tarburn was set up for a confrontation with you. You are now breathing the chemical I warned you about. It will take complete control of you in seconds. And when they arrive, that word Markos will be the trigger. Just like the nickname they told you to use on Tarburn. Do you understand? You need to get out now. Outside. Fresh air. Now."

"Can't think . . . Why can't I think? My hands trembling, like they're cold . . . But it's not . . . I don't understand . . . What's going on? I'm just so . . ."

"Ilona, please, go outside now. Go outside now. Outside. Now."

"Oh my God, they're here."

"Who?"

"SWAT. They're here to get me. Just like the call said. There's no way out. I don't know what to do . . ."

"Go outside now. Go outside now. Go—"

"I can't talk anymore. Have to think. Have to think . . ."

She disconnected the call and didn't answer when he tried to call back. He put the phone back down and stared at it with desperate frustration, as if it held some inaccessible magic, requiring a secret code he did not have.

The funnel cloud had just touched down.

In an ideal world, one could control and dial in the optimal quantity of anxiety dripping into one's system, set it like a computer-controlled medical device. Anxiety has utility in its power to command attention. As Samuel Johnson famously noted, "When a man knows he is to be hanged in a fortnight, it concentrates his mind wonderfully." But an excess of anxiety paralyzes the mind. The fight-or-flight response was beneficial on some distant primal plain, but in modern times interferes with problem-solving, where the imagination must be engaged to generate options and reason employed to weigh them.

And so the imperturbable sphinx found himself being tested. Was the unfruffled persona a fundamentally solid aspect of his character, or just an affectation, loosely worn like a cheap bucket hat? It's easy to play the unflappable Sherpa when exploring somebody else's problems, but what happens to composure when you're caught up in your very own personal vortex from hell?

Initially, Jommers saw his poise snatched up into the air like a cheesy plastic lawn chair seized by a storm gust. He stood there with a blank, helpless expression, his body not so much frozen as simply disconnected from his brain. The flywheel was turning, but the clutch was slipping. And all was revealed. The sage of the Bends was an ordinary human after all.

The minutes that passed next were lost time. Lost in two senses. Time wasted on stalling when action was required. And the measure of time lost while the mind floats detached. When his sensibility finally returned to firmament, he had no idea how long he'd been away. But he had returned with an idea. There remained one option.

He called the SWAT commander, Lieutenant Augie Dallabaco.

The call went to voice mail. Perhaps it was too late. SWAT was already on the scene, responding to reports of a crazy red-haired woman waving a gun. Jommers left a message, desperately hoping Dallabaco would check it.

"Dallabaco, this is Jommers. Listen carefully. You are being set up to take out Ilona Voros the same way she was set up to take out Earl Tarburn. She's been exposed to a chemical that will induce a paranoid psychotic state. In addition, she's been told you are coming to kill her. Do not use the word Markos under any circumstances. This is all designed to trigger a fatal firefight upon your arrival. Scubbetts is using you to eliminate her. Don't do it. Don't be suckered. Don't be Scubbetts's gun."

After leaving the message, he resumed staring at the phone. Only now his look was intense, determined, his fists clenched. None of which mattered to the phone. The panic response evolved for action, not phone calls. Your adrenaline does not affect the intensity of someone's message indicator. Your heavy breathing and pounding heart are not noticed by the communications network. And yet, he remained focused on the phone, as if the sheer force of his will could compel it to respond. And roughly ten minutes later, the phone complied.

"Got your message, Jommers," Dallabaco said. "And, jeez, I don't really know what to make of it. It was so wild, bizarre, and complicated. So much stuff in there. I suppose I could make sense of it if you had kept me in the loop on things, you know, like we agreed. But with all this coming at me out of the blue, I don't know how to process it all, even if I had time, which I don't."

"I'll explain," Jommers said.

"Maybe later. I've a crisis to deal with here. Dangerous situation. My duty is to act decisively and quickly to protect the public. Eliminate the threat. Do what I have to do. The time for chatting has passed."

"Where are you? I need to be there."

"That's probably not workable. I can't afford to put a civilian at risk. I'm still in trouble about the bystanders hurt at Eggers Court. I'm sure you understand."

"Crisis negotiations fall within my job description, a fact you know but rarely avail yourself of because you traditionally prefer to shoot first and talk later. In any event, I have a signed release on file with the city wherein I assume the risk in such situations. If something happens to me, it's on me, not you."

"Well, I don't know if there's a whole lot of time for all that talky kind of stuff. I got a red-haired psycho bitch waving a gun. She's shot out a window and screamed maniacally at us to go away. She fired a warning shot over our heads. The only reason we haven't gone all shock-and-awe on her already is that she might have someone else up there. A call girl, I believe. And as you know, if this city is ever going to make a comeback, we're going to need all our high-class hookers, so I don't want to put one at risk. So my imperative here is pretty straightforward. If my sharpshooter sees a clear shot, I got to let him take it."

"Dallabaco, you know what's going on here. God damn it, you know. Tell me where you are."

"I don't know anything, because a certain somebody I trusted kept me in the dark."

"Tell me where you are."

There was a long pause. Dallabaco trying to mess with Jommers as much as possible. Then, finally . . .

"Tennyson Place Apartments, Breakers Drive, in Shore View."

"I'm on my way."

THE GAMBLE

Tennyson Place was a nine-story tan brick building with a broad front and two wings set off at about a forty-five-degree angle on each side. In the 1920s, when it was built, it was the grandest luxury apartment around, as suggested by extensive stonework on the first floor, especially around the entrance. In a different old neighborhood, the apartment would have long ago slipped into the low rent category, but its commanding view of the lake kept rents high enough for the owners to maintain the building's condition and its display of vintage elegance, conveyed by the crisp, newish burgundy canopy shading the front entrance area.

It only took twenty minutes for Jommers to drive there, but the police had blocked traffic on Breakers Drive a quarter mile in each direction of the building. So Jommers had to park some distance away and hoof it. Once there, he had to wait at the yellow-tape police line while a patrolman contacted Dallabaco on the radio.

By the time Jommers got to Dallabaco, more than forty minutes had passed since they had last spoken, but the situation on the scene had not changed.

"Anything further happen?" Jommers asked.

"Not much," Dallabaco said. "I got a hold of her on her cell briefly."

"And?"

"She was hard to understand. She's marginally coherent and highly agitated. The best I could make of it was that she was not going to let the Markos kill her and that they would die trying. And this is kind of discombobulates me because, you see, I never heard that word before in my life. Then, strangely, I hear three times in less than an hour. Once from a weird phone call I get from Central. Two, on your phone message. And three, from her."

"Who called you from Central?"

"He identified himself as Koda with Internal Affairs. The number he was calling from was definitely a police line inside the station, I checked it. But I didn't recognize the name. No one else did either. Called HR, and they had no record of such a person."

"The caller advised you to use the word Markos when approaching her, told you it would calm her down."

"Yeah," Dallabaco said. "He said it was the name of some kind of Hungarian club that she belonged to. Said that by identifying ourselves that way she would think we were her friends, we could gain her trust. But how would you know that?"

"This was the same method used on Tarburn. Remember when I asked you if Tarburn had a nickname, Early Bear, and you said you never heard of it? He was told that he was being hunted by assassins. That their code name for him was Early Bear. At the same time, Voros and Balzer, who were sent to bring him in, were told that Early Bear was a friendly nickname used by his buddies on SWAT, so they should use that name to make him think they were friends. So when they followed that advice, used the name, it made him panic, thinking his killers were at hand. Scubbetts is trying the same thing here, using a trigger word to incite a gun battle that results in her death. It worked the first time. You can prevent it from working a second time."

"Fascinating stuff, but it suggests you know a whole lot more than you were sharing with me, you know, like we agreed. I'm disappointed to say the least. I can't help but wonder if this whole situation here could have been prevented if you'd been straight with me. So if this turns into a clusterfuck, is it on me, or you?"

"We should probably be talking about preventing that. Focus on the moment."

"Good idea. So what do you want to do? Try getting her on the phone? Use the bullhorn? Not a lot of options here."

"I want to go up," Jommers said. "Talk to her face-to-face."

"She will shoot you on sight. Not that you don't deserve it. But I'm kind of supposed to prevent that shit. So you're putting me in a predicament here."

"You're negotiating. Again."

"Am I? Jeez, what could I possibly want?"

"You want to know what I know."

"You're damn fucking right I want to know what you know. Everything you know, everything you don't know but wish you knew. Everything you believe, suspect, or fear. Everything you heard, saw, felt, or dreamed. If you saw a vision in your farts, I want to know about that, too. Understand?"

"Deal," Jommers said.

"Okay, then."

"One more thing—when it's over, you take her to the hospital, not to jail."

"Done."

"And someone protects her until she's back to her senses."

"Done."

"Okay, then. Let's do it."

"I got to put a vest and a radio on you. SOP."

"Understood," Jommers said. "Does the vest work?"

"If you are asking me if it will stop a slug from the gun she's carrying, yes. But since she will clearly see that you are wearing it, she will aim for your head, and she's an excellent shot. But you got to wear it anyway. Now the radio I'm putting on you, I'm going to lock it open. So I'll hear everything at your end, but you won't hear anything at mine."

"Understood."

"I'm going to give you a code word in case things turn to shit up there," Dallabaco said. "Crackerjack. When you say that word, I'll know you're in trouble and we'll come rushing up."

"Crackerjack?"

"Yeah. It has to be distinctive, something you wouldn't accidentally use in conversation. Plus it has hard consonants, so I'll pick it up. So you say something like, let's go, there's a crackerjack team out there waiting to help, or you're a crackerjack detective, or whatever, you're a college boy, good with words, I'm sure you can figure a way to use it."

"Sure."

"Good luck, Jommers. You got stones. I would've never guessed."

"I need the room number."

"Four sixteen. Right wing."

"Got it."

"Remember, the code word is—"

"Sashay."

"Okay. That'll work. Whatever."

Once in the building, Jommers decided not to take the elevator, knowing it would likely make some kind of ping to announce its arrival on the floor. He didn't want that to set her off. So he chose to slog up the fire stairs. And as soon as he got in the stairwell, he took off the radio setup and the bullet-resistant vest and placed them both on the floor. If he had any hope of getting through to her, he had to seem as nonthreatening as possible. Trust was essential.

When he got to apartment 416, he stood near the door, but to one side, in case she shot through it. He called out to her.

"Ilona? Are you okay?"

"Go away."

"This is Karl Jommers. You recognize my voice?"

"Go away or I'll shoot you."

"I can't go away. We have to talk. I need to come in."

"If you come in, I will shoot you."

Her voice was tense and strained. The words spurted out of her like yelps. Jommers tried to reassure her.

"I'm not going to hurt you. I'm not armed. I won't approach you. But I need to come inside."

"I will shoot you."

"I want to help you. You know that. But I have to come in."

"Do not come through that door. Do not."

"I'm coming inside, Ilona. I will come in very slowly."

"Do not. Do not. You will die."

"I'm coming in."

Without stepping in front of the door, Jommers reached over and turned the doorknob slowly, then slowly pushed it open a few inches. He stepped over to the other side of the door, the hinge side. There he could push the door all the way open without actually standing directly outside it. He did so.

He put his hands in the air and took a deep breath. Then he cautiously stepped in the doorway.

The room was dark. She had closed the blinds over the windows and kept the lights off. Though he couldn't see her, he knew that he was fully visible in the light of the hallway.

The room reeked with the pungent odor of a chemical solvent. Strangely, there was another scent, not as strong, but still palpable and recognizable. Lavender.

The air flow from the air conditioner vents were rocking a set of vertical blinds back and forth, allowing small slivers of light to enter and sweep an arc in the room with the reciprocating rhythm of a metronome. And she was within the arc as it swept over the back of her, displaying slices of her silhouette. He could hear her rapid breathing, close to hyperventilating.

He needed light.

He took step inside the door. There was a double switch on the wall just to the left.

"Ilona, I am going to turn on some light."

"Don't do it. I will shoot you. Don't do it."

He reached over and flipped up both switches. One activated an overhead light just inside the door, the other lit a ceiling fixture in the living room. And there she was. Both arms outstretched, hands grasping her service pistol, a Glock 19, shakily pointing it at him. If she intended to shoot, she would do it now.

She didn't. But the trembling hands were worrisome, as her twitching might cause her to inadvertently pull the trigger on the cocked weapon.

With the lights on, Jommers noticed a woman's body on the floor, presumably the prostitute. She was naked and in an awkward position, hunched over with her face in a plastic bucket. Nearby was an open gallon can of contact cement.

Jommers immediately suspected that this was not the only source of the chemical odor in the space, that it, in fact, was meant to disguise the other source. As his eyes rapidly scanned the room, he spied a device sitting on a corner end table. He couldn't read the graphics on it, but its appearance and slight hum, along with the lavender scent in the air, tipped him off. It was likely an ultrasonic aromatherapy mister-diffuser.

The device was almost certainly generating the anxiogenic compound affecting Voros's mental state. And, importantly, if the machine was still spewing the compound, that meant Jommers was now breathing it as well. If that suspicion was correct, then in a few minutes, he would be just as paranoid as her. Whatever he was going to do needed to be done quickly.

He still kept his arms up slightly, not like a suspect being arrested, but halfway, palms facing upward in a welcoming posture, like he was carrying an invisible cake.

"Ilona, listen to me. You know what's happening here."

"Yes. You're going to trick me into coming outside so the Markos can pick me off once I'm in their sights."

"Nobody wants to shoot you. We all want to help you. I want you to trust me."

"Trust you? Trust you? You're one of them. One of the boys. You have been the whole time. All this time. Priming me for this moment. Steering me for this. One of them. The band of brothers out to kill little sister. But it's not going to work. I'm not falling for it. You're the one who's going to die today. Not me. Not me."

"That's all wrong. And you know it."

"No. It's exactly right. It's been there all along, like a big sign. Why didn't I see it? You fooled me. But that ends now. You won't fool me anymore."

"Ilona, pay attention to what I'm saying. Everything that's happening to you now, I warned you about it. Remember? I tried to prevent this. You know that. You are in the grip of chemical substance, a mind-altering compound inducing your panic. Part of you understands that. Another part does not. There are two voices in your head now. One is a screaming frightened child. She is wailing so loud that the other voice cannot be heard. But the strong quiet voice is still there, and you need to listen to it. Listen to the quiet voice behind the noise. It is the voice of a calm, confident woman who wants to put you back in control. She is telling you the truth about what is happening, the truth that I warned you about. The truth that you know. Listen to the quiet voice."

"Stop attacking me. I am not crazy. I am not hearing voices. I am not crazy."

"That's not what I meant. I agree with you. You are not crazy. You are just frightened and upset. You want to be back in control, and you don't know how to get there. So I'm going to help you."

"I don't need your help. I am not crazy. I am not crazy."

"No, you're not crazy. You are struggling for control. And I am going to show you how."

"I am not crazy."

"You have an old friend, one who has never let you down. And that old friend, your music, is going to help you now. Your music will put you back in charge."

"I am not crazy."

"I want you to think about your music. Think about playing the piano."

"Stop trying to trick me."

"Don't think about me. Don't think about this. Think only about your music. The music you grew up with, the old friend that was always there for you. The music won't trick you. It's the only thing you trust. Trust the music."

"Stop it. Stop it."

"When you play the piano, the commander part of your brain has to take control. It takes control of your thoughts and emotions, takes control of your actions. Takes control of your memory. Takes control of your hands, your feet, your breath, your everything. Everything must submit to the music. When you play, all distractions must be banished. You don't think, hear, see, feel anything but the music. The music is in charge."

"Stop it. Stop it."

"Remember that piece of music you told me about? The one that was hard to play? What was it, a Hungarian Rhapsody or something? You said you could play it perfectly in your head, but your fingers couldn't keep up. I want you to play it now. Play it perfectly in your head, the way you used to. Focus all your being on playing that piece of music. Exert control. Banish distraction. Banish fear. Play the music. Play it now. Let it fill your head. Let it flow down through your body, your arms, your hands, and most importantly, your fingers. Focus on the music only. Play that piece now, Ilona. Play it now. Play it better than you have ever played it before. Play it as if the entire fate of the universe depended on it."

She shook her head defiantly and glared back at him with an angry, pouty face. The gun was quivering more now as her tired arms struggled to hold it up.

"You don't know me," she said, breaking into sobs. "Don't pretend you know me. You're just . . . just . . . a thing. A thing that stabs and slashes. A reckless thing that makes pain. Broken glass at the beach . . . lying in wait to hurt . . ."

"Play it, Ilona. Play it now. Imagine that you have mastered that piece and that you could go back in time. Imagine that you are in that room where your mother held those tea parties—"

"Shut up. Shut up."

"The ladies are smiling at you adoringly. You are eager to play this new piece you have mastered."

"Shut up."

"Your mother is beaming with pride as she introduces you—"

"Shut up."

"And now young Ilona will play the Hungarian Rhapsody."

"Shut up."

"And now young Ilona will play . . ."

Her eyes grew watery and she gently squeezed them closed, as if in pain, releasing a trickle of tears that descended fitfully around the contours of her face. Slowly, her head began to droop until her chin came to rest on her breastbone. Then, her outstretched arms started to wilt under the weight of the gun, gradually slanting downward until the gun was pointing at the floor. After a long minute or so, her hands weakened, and the gun slipped free, falling to the carpet. He could have charged her right then, done the cop thing and dived for the gun. Instead, he did the therapist thing. He remained still and quiet, watching her head bob slightly to music he could not hear.

He was not familiar with the piece he'd just asked her to play, so he had no idea how long it was. Though he assumed one would play it faster in the head than in real time. He chose to wait until she was finished.

And when it was over, she opened her eyes and looked at him. He held out his hand toward her, offering to take hers, lead her to safety. She stepped toward him, then walked right by him out into the hallway. She wrapped her arms around herself as if wearing an invisible straightjacket, and walked briskly with her head down. He followed about ten to fifteen paces behind her, as an unacknowledged shadow, down the hall, down the stairs, through the lobby, and out the door.

Once outside, she paused a moment to take in the scene. Upon seeing the EMS wagon with its open doors, she immediately strode toward it, as if intuiting the script. Jommers kept following, until interrupted by Dallabaco, who had jogged over.

"What's up with the hostage?" he asked.

"The prostitute was already dead when Voros arrived here."

"How?"

"Head held in a bucket of contact cement," Jommers said.

"That's a new one."

"Probably intended to make her look like a huffer who died accidentally. The odor of the glue was meant to mask the odor of something else. When your crime scene team gets here, the first two places they'll want to look for prints is the can of contact cement and an ultrasonic aromatherapy device. Then they'll want to run those prints through a federal database, one that contains military personnel. Also, whatever's in the aromatherapy device, make sure it gets analyzed and saved as evidence."

"You never cease to fascinate me, Jommers. I can hardly wait for our little confab. Unfortunately, I got a lot of shit to do here, then I got debriefing and paperwork back at Central. So we're looking at later this evening probably."

"You got my number."

"I sure do."

Jommers climbed into the ambulance to accompany Voros to the hospital. She kept her head down and shivered the whole way. She didn't utter a single word.

AT SAINT BRIDGET'S ER, Jommers immediately got into an argument with medical staff. He suspected that Voros had been subjected to an anxiogen and suggested that she be given a sedative to calm her down. The suggestion was problematic for two reasons. One, physicians do not generally appreciate advice from non-physicians, sharing the same tribal trait as cops in regard to respecting opinions of non-members.

In addition, a detective back at the scene, wanting to be helpful, had phoned the ER and suggested that Voros might be suffering from exposure to toluene, the solvent in the contact cement found in the prostitute's apartment. Given that toluene acts as a depressant on the central nervous system, you wouldn't administer a tranquilizer to someone exposed to it. In the case of short-term inhalation exposure, you would maybe give oxygen and fluids, but otherwise wait for it the exposure to resolve itself.

It didn't help that she smelled of toluene. And it didn't help that Jommers could not identify the alleged anxiogen or even credibly explain why he suspected one.

So he first exhorted them to carefully observe her physiological and psychological symptoms, which were more consistent with some type of stimulant psychosis than exposure to a CNS depressant.

He then urged them to perform a particular type of urine analysis that looked for the metabolites of toluene, which would then prove that toluene wasn't the problem. As the argument grew heated, he was then ushered into a waiting area. Instead of sitting down, he stood defiantly near the doorway, hands on hips, staring at everyone who passed through, making sure everyone knew he was there.

At some point later, a nurse approached him and advised him that Voros had been given a sedative and was responding nicely. About the same time, two of Dallabaco's men had arrived to guard Voros. Confident that the situation was under control, Jommers left. As he walked outside the hospital, a woman's voice addressed him.

"You need a ride?"

Yolanda Arroyo, the police reporter for the *Ledger*, had been at the scene, watching from the police line and taking notes. She followed the EMS ambulance to the hospital, hoping for the chance to talk to Jommers.

Given that his car was still back near the Tennyson Apartments, he accepted her offer, while warning her that he couldn't say much about what happened, that she would have to get the story from official sources.

"Yeah, I figured you'd say that," she said. "But I'll give you a ride anyway. Looks like you had a bad day."

"Appreciate it."

When they arrived at his beater Taurus, he smiled and thanked her.

"Sure," she said. "I owe you."

"For what?"

"The tip. Councilwoman Birdsong. We had an interesting conversation earlier today."

"Glad to hear it." He paused. "Things are coming to a head."

"No kidding."

"I think we might be able to talk more about it soon."

"You can call me at any time, day or night," she said.

"Understood. Thanks again for the lift."

He hoped to avoid stopping at Spreckels Tavern, which was his reflexive response to a bad day, and also his reflexive response to a good day. But staring down the barrel of a gun and coming out alive was probably the best excuse he would ever have for violating a new regimen he had yet to begin. The new day would once again be put off until tomorrow.

"You okay?" Larry asked.

"Yeah, why?"

"You look all frazzled. Shell-shocked."

"Eh, just a long day, that's all. You know how that goes."

"Yeah. I was hoping you'd drop by earlier. I had another one of those flakes who spout crazy shit. And I was thinking, boy, I wish Karl was here to shoot down this asshole."

"What's his story?"

"Well, first off, he was going on about some giant serpent that some people supposedly saw out in the lake."

"South Bay Bessie. The Lake Erie monster."

"Yeah, exactly. Bullshit, right?"

"You can't prove the negative, but you can make a case. A few points. Nature predisposes animals to conserve energy, which is why we are inherently lazy, and why well-fed pets mostly sleep. When you hear people describe serpentlike water monsters, it's always with a long neck sticking in the air and the serpent body undulating vertically, loops in the air above the water. It is highly unlikely any such creature would move through water this way, as it would be very strenuous and inefficient. When you look at a snake swimming on the water, the locomotion is by lateral undulation, same as on land. Or look at a crocodile swimming, keeping as little of its mass as possible above the water line, just enough for the eyes and snout. And his tail, again, whipping side to side to propel itself. If there were a giant reptile out there in the water, that's how it would move, not like in the legends. More importantly, for such a species to survive over time, there would have to be more than one. In fact, you would need to meet a minimum population threshold to avoid extinction. Below the threshold, you get inbreeding effects that inhibit survival and reproduction."

"In other words, for there to be one, there would have to be dozens," Larry said.

"Exactly. And if there were dozens, we'd be seeing them all the time, what with all the commercial fishing boats, ore boats, and pleasure boats. But I think the biggest argument is right here." Jommers pulled out his cell phone and laid it on the bar.

"A cell phone?"

"More specifically," Jommers said, "a cell phone with integrated camera. Just about everybody carries one now. If there were monsters, flying saucers, or whatever, we should have images out the wazoo by this point. But we don't. We got zip. So why is that? Did all these strange things suddenly start to hide after the invention of the cell phone camera? Or, more likely, did they never exist at all?"

"See, I knew you would have the answer. You always do. So anyways, after that, he said that one evening back in April, he was at the lakefront park out in Lake Ridge taking pictures of the sunset, and he realized something weird was going on with the lake, and that he was able to see Canada from where he was standing. Obviously more bullshit."

"Yes, under normal conditions. But in certain types of weather conditions, it might be possible."

"Seriously?"

"Seriously."

"So you mean like if it's a super clear day then you can see super far, even all the way to Canada."

"No," Jommers said. "The distance to Canada—roughly fifty miles here— that's not the main issue. What matters is the distance to the horizon line, which is determined geometrically by the curvature of the earth, but can be influenced visually by atmospheric conditions. So this guy at the park, if he's standing at the water's edge, he's limited to seeing about three miles out because that's where the horizon line is, depending on how tall he is, because height makes a difference. But if he's standing on the promenade, which is several feet above the water's edge, that gives him an extra mile or two of visibility. Now if he's standing up on the bluff, that would extend his visual range to maybe fifteen miles or so. But he still can't see the Canadian shoreline because that's still behind and below the horizon line under normal conditions. Now then, there's a situation known as a thermal inversion that can change the picture, literally. That happens when you have a layer of warm, less dense air, sitting above a layer of colder, denser air. The lower layer of denser air increases light refraction and bends the light downward in an arc. And if the cold layer is high enough, and if the air is very still, it can create a refraction phenomenon called looming. When looming occurs, objects can seem closer, bigger and higher in your field of vision than they actually are. More importantly, looming can allow you to see something that's normally beyond the horizon line. The phenomenon is more common in arctic regions, but has been observed many times in the Great Lakes, particularly when the lake waters are cold. You said this guy had the experience back in April—well, that would be an ideal time of year for this to happen."

"So he maybe wasn't bullshitting me on that one."

"Maybe not."

"So every once in a while, something that sounds like crazy shit at first glance can turn out not to be crazy shit after all."

"I might put it more elegantly," Jommers said, "but you have the gist of it. Ball lightning would be another illustration of something falling under your earthy maxim. You can't go by your gut. You have to do the homework."

IT WAS SEVERAL HOURS LATER before Dallabaco finally called. He sounded tired. Jommers offered to reschedule for the next day, but Dallabaco wanted to talk as soon as possible.

"Wild horses couldn't drag me away," he said.

They met at Roman Roads, a hole-in-the-wall place on the East Side that focused on pizza, calzones, stromboli, and meatball subs. The exterior signage featured the head of a Roman soldier that was so crudely rendered that the helmet looked like some janitorial device. There was a small dining area inside, but most of the business was takeout. Illumination was dim, provided mostly by imitation torch wall sconces with flicker-flame lightbulbs. The stained wall coverings featured a fake stucco pattern. Off in one corner was a plastic bust of an unidentified dead Roman, which meant he could be anyone you wanted him to be, including your uncle Dom. The laminate tabletops were imprinted with a red-and-white checker pattern, meant to emulate a tablecloth.

Back in the kitchen, the Russian owner barked orders to his mostly Russian staff, causing Jommers to joke, "I feel like I've been transported to Naples."

"It's the same old story," Dallabaco said. "Kids not interested in their old man's business. So they sold it. Thing is, though, this Russian guy, he didn't just buy the place and the name, he bought the recipes, too. So everything still tastes the same. And he got the beer and wine license, also."

Dallabaco had obviously had a busy day, too busy to eat. He wolfed down a couple of meatball subs as fast as someone else might eat a couple crackers. Washed them down with a few beers. Then, once his primal needs had been met, he leaned back and relaxed.

"So, you got a story to tell me, right?"

Jommers nodded. Keeping the promise he'd made to save Voros's life, Jommers told Dallabaco everything. Everything he'd heard from Voros, everything from Biederbach, everything from Stonecipher, and everything he'd learned on his own at the ice cream plant, the craft brewery, and the pork rinds factory. He included conversations with Chief Scubbetts, the attempt on his life, and his own theories about what might be going on.

It took a while.

And when Jommers was finished, he was surprised to find that Dallabaco shared something in common with Ilona Voros: a curious disinterest in the big picture, the grand scheme. Like Voros, he cared more about the personal angle. There was an evil person that needed taking down. How would that be accomplished? Throughout the conversation, Dallabaco was focused on how he had lost a good man, Earl Tarburn, and how that would be avenged.

So when Jommers had completed the overview, Dallabaco, the man of action, had but one simple question.

"What do we do about this?"

"Bad cops is IA," Jommers answered. "Scubbetts being top cop doesn't change that. Voros is on it. That's why she was there. Once her head clears, she'll be back to it. You can offer her your assistance, but what else can you do?"

"You never got detention, did you?"

"What?"

"When you were a kid, in school, you never got detention, because you never broke the rules. And if you were ever bullied, you'd report it to a teacher instead of handling things after, right?"

"I don't remember that far back, but that sounds about right. Yeah."

"A goody two-shoes kid."

"Not that so much," Jommers said, "just an early recognition that the rules hold it all together. You start making your own rules, then the other guy does, too. Then you're all back in the jungle, one crazy tribe attacking another crazy tribe. Like certain places in the Mideast. No good guys either side. No progress. No order."

"Yeah, right. That all looks good on paper. But, you know, I grew up in a jungle. And I don't mean a Tarzan jungle with vines and screaming monkeys and shit. Where I grew up, looked like an ordinary neighborhood. Houses with lights in the windows and cars in the driveway. An outwardly civilized place. But in terms of people behaving, it was a jungle. Tribes with long pants and indoor plumbing. Know what I mean?"

"Yeah."

"The experience of that, it teaches you. Stuff you maybe didn't want to learn, but it goes into you all the same."

"Yet you wear the badge," Jommers said, "and the whole point of that badge is to transcend that jungle stuff. Put all that away."

"Yeah. But what do you do when that whole transcend thing doesn't work? What do you do when something needs done urgently, and the process, the civilized process, isn't capable of getting it done?"

"You wait until the process catches up with necessity."

"That's it?" Dallabaco asked. "You just wait? That's your answer?"

"It's the proper thing to do."

"Here's your problem, Jommers. You're too quick to hesitate. You sneer at the impulsive. You think restraint is always superior because it's reversible. But you're wrong. Sometimes all you get is just one shot. And if you don't take it, the consequences are irreversible. There are times where you can't afford to blink."

⌁

IT WAS NIGHT by the time the two finished talking, and after everything that had happened, Jommers was uneasy about going home, not knowing what might be waiting for him. So he found a quiet spot in the Bends to sleep. He drove down Tankfield Road toward Anvil Bend, stopping on the south side of the anvil, where there was a small marina and boat repair shop.

He parked in the gravel lot of the marina and removed from his trunk a cheapo aluminum-frame plastic-web reclining lawn chair. He walked toward the north side of the anvil, a deserted patch of earth with rectangular foundations left over from demolished warehouses. The area was crosshatched with short drives to nowhere, exhibiting the familiar geometry of urban desertion, broken and heaved asphalt yielding to splotchy eruptions of weeds and scrub shrubs, which were ugly enough when green, but looked worse now when burnt crisp by drought.

And so it was crunch, crunch, crunch, as he walked toward the specific spot he had in mind, a rectangular plot of concrete near the river's edge. It had once been the foundation for oil storage tanks dismantled long ago. Because the foundation ran deep to support the weight of the tanks, the concrete remained flat and unbroken. But for the surface dirt and grit, you could bowl on it.

He set up the lawn chair parallel to the river, pointing in the direction he'd come. There were advantages here. No one would likely see him here in the semidarkness. Even though the half-lit moon in the sky cast a pale glow, in such dim light he would appear as no more than a strange silhouette from a distance, and no one could possibly guess he'd be here. And since there was no practical point of destination near where he sat, if in the night he should see someone coming his way, he would have no doubt they were coming for him. There was nowhere else to go. Of course, as Earl Tarburn had learned a little over two weeks ago, there was one big disadvantage to hiding out on a peninsula—there was nowhere to run.

Once settled in the chair, he watched a boat putter on by as it headed back to the marina. Men and women were laughing and chattering, their words undistinguishable over the light jazz that spilled across the river. A woman's voice exclaimed something loudly and it was followed by wicked laughter.

After the boat had passed from sight and its wake of party noise had faded away, Jommers's eyes and ears turned to activity on the opposite bank of the river—the late-night illegal drag racing on Flagstone Road. It was a good street for the bad thing, being one of the few in the Bends with a long, level straightway. Most other roads in the area were short, zigzaggy, or hilly. Flagstone Road also ran through an area with no bars or second-shift operations, so night traffic was virtually nonexistent, which meant cops had no reason to patrol that stretch either. Night shift zone cars had more than enough to keep them busy watching over the bars on Old Levee Road and the projects up the hill.

But it was also a bad street for a race, because it ended with a sharp curve delineated by a concrete wall. This altered the tail end of the run, often creating a secondary competition, a dangerous game of chicken. Who would brake first?

He'd long been aware of the street races, usually happening on Friday and Saturday nights, but had never come over to watch them before, even though it was barely a mile from the shop. So at first he watched and listened with a tourist's fascination. A couple dozen rowdy spectators milling near the starting line created a party atmosphere, laughing, drinking, and smoking, while Latin hip-hop music shot through the air like aural fireworks, occasionally overpowered by the roar of revving engines and the squeal of spinning tires.

At one point, a collective shriek of concern rose up after one driver narrowly avoided the wall at the end. Jommers then shifted back to the vantage of social scientist, considering the motives of the young male drivers putting themselves at risk for no good reason, motives not too mysterious. They were male peacocks with tricked-out cars taking the place of tail feathers. The macho mindset, the performance of manhood, the very thing he'd initially hoped to address in his career. And here it all was, playing out before him across the river.

Was there ever really any hope of dealing with a trait so ingrained in the culture?

And that's when Biederbach's ruse popped into his head. Biederbach claimed to have lured the Russian chemist into a meeting by proposing a potentially socially useful purpose for the anxiogenic formula, creating a potion to keep trouble-making young males in line by decreasing their appetite for risk.

Was that a crazy-ass idea? Or a crazy-ass brilliant idea?

It was at least tenable that one could plot a good chunk of human behavior on an anxiety axis, with paranoids having too much and sociopaths too little. Is prudence merely low-grade anxiety? Is normative responsible social behavior actually derived from reason and virtue, or is it simply possessing the proper level of anxiety? Would it be ethical to chemically induce anxiety in people who lacked a normative amount of it? And why would that be ethically any different than using chemicals to reduce anxiety? What if it eliminated crime? War?

He found himself laughing out loud at this. Him entertaining a pharmaceutical answer to humanity's perpetual problems, the very thing he railed against repeatedly, a solution that would make his profession obsolete. His amusement turned to unease as he thought again of Biederbach. Today was the day Biederbach was to meet the Russian, and the patrolman had not called to say how that had gone. Jommers's last conversation with the man had ended badly, the therapist voicing his exasperation. The exact words were still fresh. "I'm done with you, Dwayne."

That could be one reason Biederbach had not called. In light of the day's events, there could be worse reasons, too. There was no way to know, and nothing left to be done with a day that had already passed. Nothing but let it go. And with that thought, he turned his attention to the river that lay before him.

On most nights, lights reflecting off the river twinkled and glimmered, animated by the water's peppy shimmy shake. But not tonight. The still, humid air refused to even nudge the water's surface, and the long dry spell had damped the river's momentum, rendering it calm as an unruffled millpond. So on this night, the lights did not shimmy. Instead, they gently swayed, like dreamy, druggy dancers. And as he stared at them, he absorbed their tranquility, embraced their hypnotic effect.

And soon, an old favorite song faded in on his mental jukebox. Mississippi John Hurt singing Lead Belly's "Goodnight, Irene." He preferred Hurt's muted mellow version, which was often the case when he had a choice of a song. Too many bluesmen had rough and jagged voices, like the bad end of a beer bottle with the neck broken off. But Hurt displayed the opposite. His was a gentle voice, the kind you could leave your children with. Hurt never growled his way into your head space. Instead, he tiptoed in and discreetly took a seat without making a fuss. And that was why the man was always welcome.

Eventually, the gentle song in his head and the water's swaying reflections conspired together to snatch Jommers into slumber.

SATURDAY, AUGUST 25, 2007

DAY TWENTY

PERSUASION WITHOUT A HAMMER

The eastward-facing position of the cheapo reclining lawn chair ensured that dawn's first arrow of light would pierce Jommers's eyelids with a jolt, waking him earlier than he normally rose. Roused before sufficient rest, he hurried home, hoping to squeeze in an extra hour in the comfort of his own bed. That didn't work out, and daylight wasn't the problem. It was all the wondering.

What was Ilona Voros's condition in the hospital? What happened with Dwayne Biederbach and the Russian chemist? What was Augie Dallabaco up to now that he knew everything? What will Derle Scubbetts do next after failing to eliminate his nemesis? When's the right time to talk to that reporter woman, if ever? Am I out of danger? Should I fetch the gun? Or should I just go for a long drive in the country? And should I make it maybe a three-day drive in the country? Or maybe a three-week drive in the country?

The world's largest cuckoo clock is in Ohio, down in Amish country. He could browse around the furniture stores while in Holmes County. Maybe come back with a new oak rocker. Or look into buying a custom-made freestanding oak coatrack with antique brass hooks and an integrated umbrella stand. He'd always wanted one of those, even though he didn't own an umbrella. It was just something a civilized person should have. No question. And maybe a boot bench, too. Hell, yeah. Everyone needs a boot bench. How had he managed to survive so long without one?

And so, in this fashion, did he pile up Amish furniture against the door of consciousness in an effort to keep out thoughts of murder and mayhem. It was strenuous work that was not conducive to sleep. And so he just stewed. Later, he went for a run, hoping the sheer discomfort would be distracting. It wasn't. He came back, showered, and stewed some more.

At some point in the morning, his fretting was interrupted by a call from Reverend Elvis Truly, who wanted to ask Jommers a few questions. Jommers eagerly agreed to drive over to the church, hoping to leave his worries behind him.

As Jommers walked into the Evergreen Baptist Church, he found Truly playing a hymn on the church piano. Upon finishing, the pastor nodded at Jommers, then launched into a pretty decent version of "Saint James Infirmary Blues."

"Good stuff," Jommers said afterward. "But shouldn't you be working on your sermon for tomorrow?"

"Normally, I would be. Or at least polishing it. But after our last talk, you know, about the whole hugging thing, the idea for a sermon sort of flowed into me and I had to write it all down then lest I forget it. Probably the first Saturday in ages I'm not working on a sermon."

"Glad I could help. So you get to spend today at the beach?"

"I wish. Plenty of other things to work on. It's a time-consuming occupation. Two Sunday services to hold and prepare for. Marriages, baptisms, funerals. Teaching Bible study classes. Driving all over to visit shut-ins. Counseling couples and others with problems. Managing the volunteer committees, which have high turnover, by the way. Managing finance and maintenance. Various fund-raising activities. Reporting to and consulting with the board of elders that employ me. There's not much downtime. Definitely no beach time. I also have to find time to meditate on modern questions for which the Bible provides no easy answers. For example, the other day, someone asked me if belief in vampires was compatible with Baptist theology. Have to say, was not ready for that one. Was not addressed in seminary."

"Young woman?"

"Yes. Their thing, I suppose."

"Mostly," Jommers said.

"And I assume your profession would see it as connected to sexual repression. The penetration of teeth as the surrogate for sex."

"That would seem an obvious interpretation. The problem is that there's not a whole lot of repression of sexuality in this day and age. Not much repression of anything. Substitution seems superfluous."

"Agreed," Truly said. "Which suggests, then, it's simply part of the general prevailing wackadoo."

"Or perhaps a new twist on the allure of the outlier. If Brando and James Dean were starting out today, they might very well be biting necks rather than riding motorcycles. But your wackadoo theory has merit, also. Reality seems to have fallen out of favor, which obviously troubles me. Disconnection from reality is how we define insanity."

"Troubles me, too. I assume that in your various psychology readings, you have come across the Jung essay regarding the UFO craze?"

"Yes."

"He saw the increased sightings of UFOs and growing belief in the paranormal as symptomatic of a decline in the historical Christian perspective on things.

When you lose one supernatural interpretation of things, you simply replace it with another supernatural interpretation. The need remains, so you look for alternate means of fulfilling it. So all the peculiar things that people believe these days may just be alternative dogmas for those who got bored with existing ones."

"Research supports the idea of some inherent need to believe in something out there, and that if religion seems too old-fashioned for your tastes, you'll find something else to fill the hole."

"In some derivatives, it seems like a revival of primitivism," Truly said. "Looking for answers in exotic foods and potions that will cure your diseases, make you smarter, and defy aging. Looking to nature for magic. A kind of neo-paganism."

"Minus the blood sacrifices."

"So far."

"I'm thinking of the witches in *Macbeth*," Jommers said. "Eye of newt and toe of frog, wool of bat and tongue of dog—today those witches could have their own daytime TV show and toll-free order number."

"But why does snake oil sell better than ever precisely at a time when it should be disappearing?" Truly asked. "You see, I'm looking at this from a spiritual perspective. As people become more materialistic, they increasingly envision salvation and doom played out in corporeal terms. In the New Age, angels and demons no longer appear out of the ether, they arrive in spacecraft or emerge from foodstuffs."

"True. People get a better science education today than at any other time in history, yet it doesn't seem to provide any immunity. In fact, research suggests that college-educated people are more likely to believe in aliens and UFOs than the less educated."

"Yes," Truly said, "and if I'm not mistaken, it was Francis Crick, the codiscoverer of DNA, Nobel Prize–winning scientist, promoting the idea that life on earth was deliberately seeded by aliens doing some Johnny Appleseed thing. And today we have the pop-gods of science, the astrophysicists, simultaneously mocking religion while zealously searching for signs of extraterrestrial intelligence that almost certainly does not exist. Does that really differ much from hunting for wood nymphs?"

"I'm not sure the people behind SETI see it that way, but one thing's for certain, the zeal to believe tends to remain a constant across time and geography. All that changes is the object."

"Like water flowing downhill. You cannot stop it, only channel it."

"And that's the history of us, isn't it?" Jommers said. "Competing approaches to that channeling. Which is why the skeptics argue that the zeal should simply be quashed, that it is a vestigial characteristic that has outlived its purpose and needs to be excised."

"I would obviously view it differently, seeing all the lives that have been reclaimed by faith, all the lives ruined by its absence. I think even if I were an atheist, I could make a case for the benefits of religion based on its positive effects alone. The sociological research suggests—"

"Yes," Jommers said, "though the skeptics would bring up inconvenient facts about religious conflicts and oppression—"

"Yes, yes, yes. Let us all hear yet again about the Inquisition, the Crusades and whatnot. Interesting how the skeptics adore using the very confirmation bias tactics they supposedly deplore. Forgive me, but I do not see many people in America being burned at the stake or stretched on the rack. But I do see legions of Americans victimized by violence, substance abuse, suicide, and numerous other social ills, and I cannot help but wonder how much of that could be mitigated by more people taking a spiritual approach to life. And even if you consider religion to be the placebo of the masses, it still raises an interesting question: if the placebo works, is it ethical to take it away?"

"Well," Jommers said, "we could debate this well into the night, but I suspect you called me to discuss other matters. Yes?"

"All the hubbub at the Tennyson Place Apartments yesterday. You were probably too preoccupied to notice the TV crews at the edge of the police line. You likely didn't know you were on the evening news, even if at a distance. But I recognized you. And I recognized her. More importantly, I recognized the similarity in circumstances, what was happening there and what happened to Earl Tarburn. And a chill went up my spine. So I couldn't help but wonder if you had something new to report on the matter. Something that I could perhaps share with Becca Tarburn."

"I'm limited in the specifics of what I can tell you for a couple of reasons. For one, I'm not actively involved in the investigation. So while I may have a closer view of it all, I'm still an outsider looking in. Secondly, what you just said, your desire to share information with others. I can't jeopardize official inquiries by leaking confidential information. But I can tell you this. Your assumptions about Chief Scubbetts's character are largely correct. The appropriate people are actively pursuing the matter. His Waterloo is at hand."

"I am glad to hear that," Truly said. "I look forward to hearing more. I hope we can stay in touch."

"I'm not sure when I'll acquire more specifics. I'm not in the loop, so to speak."

"Understood. But let's stay in touch anyway. I've come to enjoy our conversations."

"Me, too."

"I think we share some conundrums in common," Truly said. "For example, a bit ago we both laughed condescendingly at those who believe in aliens, monsters, miracle berries from Tibet, or whatever. But that mocking attitude we just exhibited, isn't that part of our problem?"

"We could laugh here because no one else was present and because we have a common view of such things. In a different social context . . ."

"Yes," Truly said, "we would have both refrained. But our outward social graces would not have changed our inner attitudes, that the person in our presence was a fool to be mocked."

"We share a common frustration," Jommers said, "wanting to transform people, but frequently failing because we don't understand how they got where they are. We don't know how to walk them back."

"But it's our failure. In Christian life, we seek to reject sin while embracing the sinner. And that's real easy to say, but living it . . ."

"I understand where you're going. In secular terms, I might use the example of obesity or smoking. How do you discourage a behavior without attacking the person exhibiting the behavior, which then makes them defensive and combative, severing the interaction?"

"Like trying to remove a tentacled brain tumor without injuring the patient."

"Maybe sometimes it's not possible."

"Perhaps," Truly said, "but you don't instill wisdom into a man's head with a hammer. But, here, I think our metaphors are failing us. In our passion to transform, we forget that persuasion requires humility. We are all broken, in need of grace. Those we would change must be approached with the compassion of a healer, not the anger of a combatant. The answer is terrifyingly simple as it is artlessly trite—all we need is love."

"Like you said before, easy to say . . ."

"But we can work harder. It's about the posture, the tone. Those are things we can practice."

"I agree," Jommers said. "I'm as guilty as anyone. As hard as I try to be non-judgmental, I'm still human. It's a challenge."

"More than we realize, I think. I have an elderly aunt who is hard of hearing, but won't use hearing aids—the way they amplify certain sounds, music in particular, such that they make sound irritating. So without hearing aids, when I speak to her in a normal tone of voice, she can't understand what I'm saying. But if I raise my voice to be understood, she thinks I am yelling at her and starts crying. So how am I supposed to communicate?"

"Yes," Jommers said. "That's it right there. Finding that razor-thin space between silence and scolding."

"You know, there is the obvious canyon that separates us, you and me, skeptics and clergy in general, yet, at the same time, you cannot deny the areas of shared purpose. Certain myths and fallacies we both fight. Do you foresee any possibility of us standing side by side in common endeavor?"

"Well, if the river floods someday and they need volunteers to stack sand-bags, I suppose it would be possible for skeptics and preachers to find them-selves standing side by side in common endeavor, but beyond that . . ."

They both laughed.

"Well, then," Truly said, "we should seize opportunities for collaboration whenever they arise."

With that, Truly turned back to the piano keyboard and started playing "Key to the Highway." He sang it like a pro, his sonorous voice honed by years of hymn-singing. After a few bars, Jommers joined in with his own god-awful singing voice. Sadly, the man who loved music so much could not hit the right note any more than he could hit the moon with a stone. And when they were finished, the two had a good laugh over it.

On the way back from the church, Jommers stopped at the hospital to check on Ilona Voros. At first he was glad to find out she was no longer there. It suggested that she had recovered quickly. But he found it curious that the hospital's computer system showed no evidence of her being formally discharged, so nobody knew when it had actually happened, as it was a different shift of staff. They're probably just behind in updating the system, he was told. The computers are often taken offline at night for maintenance procedures. Nothing to worry about.

He tried calling her cell phone, but it was turned off. He then tried calling Augie Dallabaco, since his men were supposed to be protecting her while she was down. He got Dallabaco's voice mail and left a message.

He tried to forestall any sense of foreboding. He convinced himself that there were likely reasonable explanations for all of it, until he got a panicky call from Dwayne Biederbach.

"It's all hitting the fan. We need to talk. Like now."

"Okay. Where?"

"I'm not going to give a location on a line that is most certainly being monitored. And if you recall our last meeting, you got pissed off and tossed your copy of the coded meeting locations we had. And I have to say, that was extremely unprofessional for someone in your business, in addition to being imprudent."

"Yeah," Jommers said. "Thanks for the review. Okay. Give me a minute to think."

"Make it a short minute. Things are closing in."

"All right. Let me think." Jommers paused a bit. "Okay. I'm going to say two words. Then you tell me if you understand. Okay?"

"Understood."

"Taconite. Grasshopper."

"Oh, so now you want me to make weird connections."

"Yes."

"Got it. Make sure you're not followed."

J OMMERS DROVE BACK HOME, put on some old jeans, a faded burgundy T-shirt, a weathered khaki bucket hat, and a pair of sunglasses. He then grabbed his Huffy cruiser bicycle and set off in a lazy fashion, like someone out riding around on a nice day with no particular place to go.

It would be difficult for some malevolent person in a vehicle to inconspicuously tail a bicycle, given the speed difference. Also, there were also numerous shortcuts in the Bends that could accommodate a bike, but not a car. And, ironically, the bicycle might even get him to his destination faster.

He was headed to Hulett Park on the lake side of Banshee Horn, a small curved peninsula running parallel to the natural shoreline and whose eastern tip served as the west bank of the river's mouth. Geographically part of the Bends, the park was near as the crow flies, but distant travel-wise. That was because the south border of the park was bounded by a set of east-west railroad tracks with no crossing and the railroad had erected chain-link fencing on the north side to keep park and marina visitors off the tracks.

By car, the only way to the park from the Bends was to drive a few miles west to West Shore Lakefront Park, the first available place to cross over the tracks, then look for an unmarked access road that backtracked to the Bends, only at a much slower pace. The narrow, bumpy access road was untended and had spectacular craters that the moon could only envy. So there was only one way in and out of the park. But if you knew about the tunnels, then you had another option.

There was a north-south rail spur that served the bulk transfer docks on the north side of Banshee Horn. The spur coursed through a tunnel under the east-west tracks to avoid interference. If you knew where the tunnels were, you could get to Hulett Park from the Bends without making the long, looping trip west. To reach the tunnels, Jommers first rode his bike over to Willow Street and crossed the swing bridge, then went down Willow to Hook Road, then over the Hook Road lift bridge that crossed Old Channel Cove and onto Banshee Horn.

At this corner of the Horn, towering piles of sand glistened in the sunlight, making it look otherworldly, like a moonscape. He wheeled the bicycle around the backside of the piles and over near the tracks. A narrow strip of wild growth ran parallel to the rails, including a thicket of sumac bordered by a spread of goldenrod in full bloom that glowed in the sun. It was too rough to ride over this part, so he dismounted and walked the bike the rest of the way over to the underpass that would take him under the tracks.

Once he got to the north side of Banshee Horn, he pushed his bike up an embankment, up to the access road. He looked at the vehicles heading to and from the marina and the park, wondering if he could have been followed. It was possible, but even if someone had followed him over the Hook Road bridge and figured out where he was heading, they would have to hoof it after him, or drive around the long way, which would take a good fifteen minutes or more. He paused a few moments until he was sure no one had followed on foot. Then he mounted up and continued cycling east down the access road.

Jommers was always surprised how many people found their way to the park, given its problematic access. Maybe it was the water, or maybe just it was being a hidden green space in an otherwise gritty industrial area. A tucked-away Eden in the last place you would look for it.

It was busy when he arrived there—people jogging, picnicking, grilling, playing volleyball, exercising their dogs—partly because it was Saturday, and partly because summer was playing its last act, and everyone instinctively knew that a cold curtain would fall before long. Out on the water, boaters were also capitalizing on the waning days of good weather. Behind the boats, a humid haze obscured the horizon line.

Arriving on bicycle, attired in weekend casual grunge, Jommers blended in with everybody else, which was his intent. After passing through the tunnels, he knew he had not been followed, but he had no idea what might be happening at Biederbach's end. He walked his bike across the dusty gravel parking lot, then over to the stamped-concrete promenade at the water's edge, where a bronze plaque on a boulder explained the history of the place.

Hulett Park was named after the Hulett ore unloaders that had once operated on the site at the water's edge. The giant steel contraptions were designed to reach down into an ore boat hold and scoop out the taconite it contained. Then, after moving backward, the unloader bucket dropped its load into a waiting hopper rail car. The operator guided the whole process from a small cab perched above the bucket. Patented by George Hulett in 1898, the unloading machines replaced more labor-intensive methods, reducing the time to unload a ship from days to hours. About seventy-five Hulett unloaders were built, with most of them installed on the southern shore of Lake Erie and used to unload ore coming down from mining sites around Lake Superior.

From a distance, the Huletts looked like mammoth grasshopper legs, and legend had it that George Hulett's inspiration for the invention came to him while idly gazing at a grasshopper. True or not, anyone who remembered the Huletts also remembered the tale.

Over time, new generations of ore boats were designed with self-unloading equipment and conveyor booms that made the Huletts unnecessary and eventually obsolete. The conveyors in a modern ore boom could move a ton of ore per second. One innovation replacing another.

Jommers reminisced how, when he was a boy, his father had brought him down here to watch the Huletts in action. He looked across the open space where the black steel behemoths had once stood, groaning, screeching, clanking as they worked, remembering how they'd created a brief metallic thunder when the bucket dropped a ten-ton scoop of ore pellets into a hopper car, sending a cloud of taconite dust into the air. On dark, drizzly days, the Huletts had all their running lights on, and their motions in the mist looked almost magical. He recalled how those monstrous mechanical marvels had filled him with awe.

Jommers's reverie was interrupted by the arrival of Biederbach in an old dirty white Ford E-Series cargo van, instead of his usual aging Crown Vic. The van had some kind of brackets mounted on the roof, suggesting its former owner was a contractor. Biederbach stayed in the van a few minutes, presumably scanning the park for anything or anyone suspicious, not realizing that by doing so, he was the one who looked suspicious.

Eventually he emerged wearing khaki cargo pants and an untucked green polo shirt instead of his usual navy-blue outfit, what was essentially a patch-less uniform. He also wore gray athletic shoes and an olive-green baseball cap with the brim pulled low. He was clearly exhibiting a new persona, one designed to blend in with the everyday environment around him. But for Biederbach, trying to look normal was a disguise he couldn't really bring off convincingly. The clothes were new and oversized for the skinny man, but the real giveaway was his recognizable bearing. His uneasy manner. His stiff, awkward gait. Things that would betray him even if he was wearing a hooded monk's robe.

Biederbach was tense and jittery, and Jommers could tell that the man was packing at both the waist and the right ankle.

"Were you trying to find the most conspicuous place possible?" Biederbach asked.

"Had it occurred to you that all the previous places we met were deserted and off-limits to the public and that we were conspicuous as hell by being there? Sometimes the best place to hide is in a crowd."

Biederbach looked out at the still waters of the lake. "All those boats. Every one of them has a clean, clear shot."

"We only talked twenty minutes ago. Even if someone was listening and could figure out where we were meeting, they would have to first drive to a marina, launch a boat, sail on over here, get in position—all in twenty minutes."

"You won't be sounding so cocksure when I tell you what happened yesterday."

Just then, a soccer ball rolled in their direction. Jommers smiled, picked it up and tossed it back to the teenage boy who was chasing it.

Biederbach moved his hand over the bulge at his waist and gave the kid a menacing look, as if the soccer ball had been a grenade or something. He pointed at a less populated patch in the park.

"Let's move over there."

They walked slowly, Jommers taking his bike along. When they got to a certain spot near the water's edge, Biederbach stopped and looked around.

"It was right about here, I recall."

"What?" Jommers asked.

"The last one. The last Hulett."

"Oh, yeah. I think you're right."

"One of my first arrests, too."

"Was it eventful?"

"No," Biederbach said, "but still memorable. You remember that preservation group that wanted to save it for posterity. But they couldn't raise the money or figure out a place to put it if they did. So the day it was scheduled to start being dismantled, the people from this group had chained themselves to it in protest. Of course, the city knew that was going to happen, so we were given a special briefing on how to be extra super nice and gentle arresting them because the TV crews would all be there. It started out kind of comic weird. We'd only brought one set of bolt cutters, and the blade in it broke on the first try, so someone had to run over to a hardware store to get a set of replacement blades. So we're all kind of standing around, cops, protestors, reporters, twiddling our thumbs waiting for someone to come back from the hardware store. So I'm standing by this young woman in chains and we start talking. She says, 'This is wrong, what they're doing.' And I says, 'Yeah, they do a lot of things wrong. But if you waste all your energy fighting the little ones, you won't have any left to fight the big ones. You have to choose your battles.' And she looks at me with a sort of wonder, as if I'd said something profound. Then she suggests we meet for coffee later."

He paused a few moments while reflecting on the past, then continued.

"You know the whole left-right linear thing is oversimplified. There's a whole other dimension. People concerned with preserving liberty all down the line. And there's this odd overlappy space where the line curls around at the ends and all these different people can find a common ground. So, amazingly, we hit it off. And things went well for a while. It was fun. But that odd overlappy space—it's kind of small. We could only dance in it for so long before falling out."

He paused again. "We parted amicably, which I thought was important at the time. But what does it matter? Done is done. Gone is gone."

Biederbach's jitteriness receded for a brief spell as he stared into space with wistful eyes, recalling what was likely his only encounter with romantic love. Out of respect, Jommers remained quiet, not wanting to intrude on the man's memories. After a half minute or so, Biederbach twitched like someone awakened from a nap, and in a snap, his jitters were back in control.

"We need to get out of Grayton," Biederbach said. "Or we're dead."

"What happened yesterday with Zoran the chemist?"

"So I told you how I lured him into meeting, pretending I was a pharmaceutical company interested in a beneficial use for his anxiety-producing compound, as a way of treating individuals whose risk-seeking behavior gets them into trouble. He was very excited about the prospect. So we meet at the Veil Street Depot in Quarryville—"

"That's the restaurant that was a train station."

"Yeah. So I start off by trying to get him to confirm the origins of the chemical and that he'd originally created it for the KGB for the purpose of tormenting dissidents. And he kind of confirms that, but doesn't want to dwell on it. Nods and waves it off. You can see he's ashamed of it, that he's eager to absolve the invention by imbuing it with moral purpose. He wants redemption before he dies. So that's when I reveal myself. Pull out the badge, though I lie a little bit. Tell him I'm with Grayton Police Internal Affairs, investigating Chief Scubbetts. So I tell him about the Juneberry Jumper where the guy shot the fish, and the Eggers Court incident, where the meth heads shot up a tire store inflatable. I tell him we think Scubbetts is using the stuff to scam people into buying security services, and all of it. And Zoran, he's totally crestfallen, like you sucker-punched his soul. He says he suspected something wasn't right, but was afraid to think about it."

"So he confirmed that he was supplying this stuff to Scubbetts?" Jommers asked.

"He didn't actually say that. Only that he suspected something wasn't right. So I'm inferring here, because he didn't disagree. He didn't ask me who the hell is Chief Scubbetts. So I'm guessing he knew. And while I'm telling him all this, he stops a waitress, orders a double shot of vodka. Not once, but twice. He tells me that he's terribly depressed. That he so much wanted to make things right. He wanted desperately to do good instead of bad, he wanted to be able to die knowing that he had done so. And now that wasn't going to happen. He hung his face into his hands, then when he looked up, he acted like he'd seen something out the window. I asked him what. He said he felt that he was being watched by strangers recently. He said he initially dismissed it as just his imagination, but now, after what I told him, he thought otherwise. He suddenly looked very afraid. He said we couldn't continue this conversation in a public place with people around to hear. He told me to meet him forty-five minutes later at the Scorn Falls Scenic Overlook, which wasn't far away. Said that once we were alone, he would tell me everything. That I could record it. But that once we were done, he would have to disappear."

"Did he show up?" Jommers asked.

"You could say he was there, but not there."

"What do you mean?"

"We were to meet on the wooden platform at the overlook," Biederbach said. "It extends out over the river so that you can get a good view of the falls. So I'm standing there waiting for him for a long time. I figure he's not going to show. But before I leave, I look down at the river. And there he is, facedown on the rocks. Body twisted, head broken, dirty water flowing over him. Definitely dead. They had obviously gotten there first, tossed him over the side rail."

"How do you know it was him, the guy you just met? You said the body was facedown in dirty water a hundred feet down and away from you."

"Who else would it be? If it wasn't him, then why didn't he show up?"

"Did you call it in?"

"Hell, no. I hauled ass out of there. I call it in, then they know for sure I know things. Then I'm next."

"Who's they?" Jommers asked.

"You don't even listen to me when I talk, do you? I told you last time there was a behind-the-scenes player here, a third force. And that's what Tarburn was babbling about before he got it, a cleanup crew chasing him, wanting to cover up the experiment gone wrong so no one would know the government was involved. He referred to MI, military intelligence."

"Okay, hold on here a second. You don't know that this Russian guy was killed. You just said he was both drunk and depressed. So he could have fallen accidentally, or jumped deliberately. Aren't those possibilities?"

"Kind of big coincidence for either of those to happen right when he thinks someone is watching him, right when it's all hitting the fan."

"You confronted him with his failure, implicated him in crime, and stole his last chance at redemption. So maybe you incited his suicide. Have you thought of that?"

"Oh, yeah. This is all my fault somehow. Give me a break."

Biederbach turned and looked nervously at the boats out on the water, as if one of them might launch something lethal in his direction.

At this point, Jommers faced an ethical dilemma. As a psychologist speaking with a former patient who suffers from paranoid thinking, the therapist's first concern should be the patient's long-term mental health, extricating the man from his distorted perspective. Extinguish anxieties. Play down threats.

Yet there were threats. Bad things were happening, and Jommers couldn't deny that. Under the circumstances, was it ethical to tell a potential target that his fears were imaginary and encourage him to let his guard down? What if Biederbach ended up dead as a result? Was that okay so long as he died mentally healthy?

Jommers had only seconds to decide the matter.

As far as Jommers could discern, all the bad events happening stemmed from a corrupt police chief trying to cover his ass. In the last few conversations Jommers had had with Scubbetts, the chief had never mentioned Biederbach, never hinted that Biederbach might be a threat. Scubbetts was definitely going after his enemies, but was oblivious to the fact that Biederbach might be among them. With that thought in mind, Jommers determined that Biederbach was not in danger, and that all efforts should be directed to diminishing his fears rather than fueling them.

Decision made.

"Have you ever heard of the novella titled *Futility*, written by Morgan Robertson?" Jommers asked.

"No. What the hell does that got to do with anything?"

"Well, in the story, there's this enormous triple-propeller cruise ship called the *Titan*, which was deemed to be unsinkable. But on a cold night in April, while in the North Atlantic, it strikes an iceberg on the starboard side and sinks about four hundred nautical miles from Newfoundland. And because it has less than half the lifeboats needed, more than half the passengers drown."

"Sounds like a fictionalized account of the *Titanic*," Biederbach said. "What's your point?"

"It does sound like the *Titanic*. Just one problem. The story was written fourteen years before the *Titanic* sank, ten years before the *Titanic* was even designed or named."

"So what are you saying, fiction predicts reality?"

"No," Jommers said. "I'm saying that weird coincidences happen. In a world with billions of people doing billions of things, it would be way weirder if coincidences never happened."

"Isolated coincidences maybe happen. But when you get a whole mess of them, and they're all connected like pearls on a string—seriously, count it all up now. You got Tarburn going inexplicably bonkers and getting shot by Voros. You get Commander Mungfreud inexplicably falling down bell tower stairs. You get Wolf Stonecipher, a security consultant who carries a gun, getting killed in a supposed carjacking. And don't think I don't know how you saved Voros's ass yesterday, and about the dead hooker who was affluent enough to buy any drug of choice but supposedly died huffing a can of contact cement. And then the Russian who says he's being watched and ends up dead right after I meet with him. But you want me to think he just slipped and fell? You gave me a lecture on probabilities at one point, how the probabilities sharply decline when multiple things have to be true at the same time. You want it to be true that all these things are coincidences, even though they're all connected and happened within a short time frame. You need to give yourself a lecture right about now."

"Okay," Jommers said. "Let's stipulate for the moment that they aren't coincidences, that they're all planned murders. It would be fairly obvious to even a casual observer that the string running through all these pearls is Derle Scubbetts, a corrupt police chief who's going to be taken down in the very near future. There is absolutely no evidence supporting your sinister third force theory. The idea that U.S. military intelligence operatives are murdering American citizens to cover up some failed experiment—it's simply not plausible. And you don't have a shred of evidence to suggest otherwise. Not everything bad that happens is a government conspiracy."

"Scubbetts isn't smart enough or competent enough to do all that. He may be evil, but he's no genius. He's a rube boob who accidentally ended up in a position of power. It happens a lot in this country. Remember Gerry Ford? You're also ignoring timing issues here. My Russian chemist is getting killed right about the same time the hooker gets it. Does Scubbetts have a doppelganger?"

"Look, he's a criminal. And criminals have associates, cronies who do things for them. That's SOP. He doesn't have to do everything himself. He doesn't have to leave the office. And you know that."

"You know what?" Biederbach said. "You're the one who's delusional. You're the one who needs therapy. The reality on the ground here conflicts with your established philosophy, your reflexive posture. So you refuse to accept the reality. You're knowingly blind to imminent danger because it doesn't fit your worldview. You're willfully ignorant. And I can't help you with that. I only called to warn you, to try and save your life. You're pretty lame as a psychologist, but as a person, you're a decent straight-shooter who means well, so I thought I owed you the warning. Anyone and everyone who knows anything about this whole matter is going to disappear shortly, one way or the other. Scubbetts, you, me, Voros, Dallabaco. Everyone. Total erasure. So I've fulfilled my ethical obligation by warning you, but now I'm done with you. It's time to fly away."

"What do you mean?"

"I always knew this day would come. That they would find an excuse to come after me. That I would have to disappear on my terms, rather than theirs. I've cultivated an active alternative identity for years. I have all the necessary documents. Kept that van in some old lady's garage I rented. Tires got flat spots from the sitting, but that'll work out on the road. I got it all planned. Where to go, how to get there. I prepared for this moment."

"Look, I know you got one foot on the train here, but you don't have to do this."

"Yes, I do."

"It's not necessary to throw away your life," Jommers said. "Just think about it a moment. You can disappear temporarily, then come back when it's all over, which will likely be in a week or two. Maybe less. Take a brief road trip and pay for motel rooms in cash, or sleep in the back of the van at highway rest stops. Visit Seneca Caverns. Or go to the world's largest cuckoo clock, which is right here in Ohio. You don't even need to go away to disappear. There's a thousand places you could hide in an urban area like Grayton. A hundred in the Bends alone."

"You still don't get it. I'm not running from Bruno the shark who wants to pipe my knee because I haven't paid the vig. I'm talking government here, and I mean all of them, because they're all tied into the same surveillance web, local, state, Fed, Interpol, UN. You don't have a clue as to how local law enforcement is complicit in all this. The automatic OCR scans of license plates that go into a Fed computer for cross-check, which is connected to other intel computers with communications data, satellite data, financial transactions data . . . you don't have any idea. The systems in place right now make Orwell's 1984 scenario look primitive by comparison. Someday it will all come out and everyone will have a piss fit over it, but by then it'll be too late to dismantle. I understand it. So I know how to beat it."

"This is so unnecessary. To throw away the life you built here, such as it is. Aside from the financial security and benefits of established routine, Grayton PD is the only family you have. The only roots you have. A life on the run for a man with your issues—totally alone and feeling besieged—it'll be highly detrimental to your mental health. You will spiral down quickly."

"Will life on the run suck? Hell, yes, it will suck big-time. From now on, I will most definitely lead a piss-poor life. But you know what? It beats surrendering to a piss-poor death. So I'm out of here. Good to know you."

"Wait," Jommers said. "The shells. The shotgun shells that were in the kit bag that Tarburn carried that night. I know you have them. You need to leave them with me. It'll be the only physical evidence of the chemical. Without them, we'll never know what it was or where it came from. Your Ghost Wolf formula remains just that, a ghost. It's critical to have them here. Admit to me now that Tarburn gave them to you, then I can testify how you gave them to me, then we have something resembling a chain of possession for legal purposes."

"I never said I had them."

"Stop it, damn it. I know you do. I saw you fish them out of the river at Crone Point the morning after. There's absolutely no sensible reason for you to take them with you."

"No? Right now, the system thinks those shells are at the bottom of the river. They're not sure what I know or don't know. But if I admitted I had the shells like you want, then I'd move to the top of their target list. They would spare no resources."

"That's a nonsensical answer. I know the real reason you want to keep them. The shells are your Shroud of Turin. The evidence of things unseen. Wherever you end up, you'll turn those shells into a shrine. You'll look at them every day, smile and say to yourself, see? I was right about everything. I was always right. That's the real reason, isn't it?"

"Don't worry, Jommers. I'll always do my homework."

With that, Biederbach hiked up his pants, gave a quick forefinger salute, then walked back to his white van and drove away.

Jommers felt certain he would never see the man again. He also felt a failure, that all his time spent with Biederbach had amounted to nothing. Maybe Big Pharm and its psychiatrist toadies are right, that talk therapy is pointless, that it's all about the drugs. Maybe all Biederbach needed was some tranqs to mellow out. Maybe it is all a continuum and we all need our own personalized pill to either crank up or wind down our anxieties to the optimal level.

A feeling of emptiness overcame him as he rode his bicycle homeward. He was going through the railroad tunnel when a realization struck him. The whole time he had spent with Biederbach at Hulett Park, the man had not once puffed on a cigarette. Jommers sighed plaintively. The therapist had helped a conspiracy theorist to stop smoking, but nothing more. The consolation prize for someone who juggles on the radio.

FOR MOST OF THE WAY BACK, Jommers kept his eyes down on the road. The potholes in the Bends could pop the bead on a car wheel, separating the tire from rim, so they could do a lot worse to a bicycle tire. He looked up only at intersections. And when he raised his gaze at the intersection of Riveredge and Nickel Plate, about a quarter mile from the shop, he noticed a shiny black car in the lot. He impulsively swerved off the road and stopped to hide behind some high brush. There shouldn't be any cars in the lot on a Saturday, except his. Trucks and trailers awaiting repair, but no cars. And it didn't belong to Pete or Claire either.

So who was it? Why were they there? They had to be there for him, because he would be the only one expected there on a weekend. So who was looking for him? And why?

In a flash, Biederbach was in his head answering the question, going on about the cleanup crew. "Total erasure." Jommers shook his head, trying to dislodge the words, like someone with water in his ear. It didn't work.

This was nuts. If someone wanted to kill him, they wouldn't be so audacious as to park in the front lot, would they? Then again, why not? There was nobody around this area on a Saturday. Nobody to see or hear anything. And what about Stonecipher? He had gotten hit in broad daylight. That was pretty brazen.

Jommers was spooked and irritated. Specifically, irritated that he was spooked. He stayed hiding behind the brush, feeling both anxious and stupid, surveilling his own place, uncertain whether it was safe to go home. The more he vacillated, the more annoyed he became with himself. The issue soon resolved itself when the mysterious black car pulled out of the lot.

As the car headed toward the intersection, Jommers sequestered himself further in the brush, crouching down. As the car turned onto Riveredge, he pushed aside some scraggle enough to peek through at the car as it passed. The vehicle was a brand-new Chevy Impala, all black, with black steel wheels, tinted windows and tinted license plate covers. The kind of trim package you expect to see on unmarked law enforcement vehicles. But it couldn't be Grayton PD, because all they had was ancient Crown Vics that were beat to hell.

After the mysterious black Impala drove off, he waited behind the brush another minute or so to make sure it wasn't coming right back. Then he went home.

Remembering how the place had been rigged to explode the other night, he paused at the door after unlocking the deadbolt, his hand hovering over the doorknob. Again irritated by his newly discovered capacity for anxiety, he shook it off and went in.

The first thing he did was grab his copy of the *Ledger*, then flip through the pages to see if there was a story about a body found in the river below the Scorn Falls Overlook. He found it on page four. The Quarryville police were treating it as an accident and were asking help from the public in identifying the man, as he was not carrying any identification and no one had been reported missing in the area. The police believed he lived within walking distance, given the lack of any abandoned vehicles in the nearby parking lot.

Jommers now wished he'd gotten the full name of the man Biederbach had called Zoran. But at the time, Jommers hadn't believed that the purported Russian chemist actually existed. He wanted to call the Quarryville police, but realized he had nothing to offer them. He had no proof that the body in the river was a chemist, Russian or otherwise, and no evidence that the dead guy was involved with Chief Scubbetts. In fact, it was entirely possible that the working theory of the Quarryville police was correct, that the body was just some old guy who lived alone in the neighborhood, someone with poor balance and possible partial dementia, who'd wandered off and met an accidental tragic end.

Jommers again tried unsuccessfully to reach Ilona Voros, even tried leaving a message on her office voice mail.

He tried again to reach Augie Dallabaco, also unsuccessfully. He left another message, demanding to know where Voros was, given that he'd promised his crew would protect her. Jommers wanted to interpret the lack of responses as meaning that everything was under control, but Biederbach was still ranting in his head about how they would all be eliminated. Maybe Voros and Dallabaco were already finished. Maybe Jommers was the last target standing.

He shook his head again, trying to get Biederbach out of it. The cleanup crew theory just wasn't possible. Was it?

He was a reasonable man, so what was the next reasonable course of action?

How did one make an informed decision in the absence of solid information? Who else could he call? Was there anyone out there in a position act?

He could call Captain Wifflyn, Voros's supervisor in IA. But he had already angrily shown a disinterest in the accusations. Wifflyn thought that Voros was nuts, and that Jommers was nuts for clearing her.

He could call Detective Yopko, who had shown up the night the shop was rigged to explode. But Yopko was also disinterested in wild stories about Scubbetts being a corrupt murderer.

So who was left? Was there anyone at all who wouldn't think Jommers a nutcase?

Just one. Maybe. Yolanda Arroyo, the police reporter for the *Ledger*. If she wrote about it in the paper, publicized the whole affair, then things would have to happen. Inquiries would be launched, actions taken.

In his typical deliberative fashion, Jommers weighed the pros and cons of calling the reporter. There was an obvious potential downside to placing such a call. If Voros was right now planning some operation against Scubbetts, any publicity could scuttle the plan.

On the other hand, in the unlikely event that Voros and Dallabaco were already dead, then Jommers was the only person left able to tell the tale. And if he was also on the hit list, he wouldn't have much time left to tell it.

He chose to wait a little longer. That surely was reasonable and prudent, wasn't it? Yet, at the same time, he could hear his ex-wife Rachel mocking him as a dithering Hamlet. He could almost see her in the room, shaking her head in disgust, calling him names. The duke of dilly-dally. An irresolute lump.

Yet he was in good company. He knew from research that when both action and inaction offered potentially bad consequences, most people prefered inaction. The reason was self-interest, the avoidance of blame. If you take action and it ends badly, it's your fault. If you refrain from action and bad things happen, it is the fault of circumstance. The ego tips the scales toward restraint. A truly selfless person removes the subjective weight of blame and weighs only the outcomes. Which path offers the most good, or the least harm?

He knew all that. And he knew also that he was human, just like everybody else. Being a psychologist helps you understand emotions, but it does not relieve you of having them. The more time that passed without any word, the more his sense of foreboding grew. His mental jukebox began playing "You Got to Move." It was the Fred McDowell version, of course. He thought the more famous Rolling Stones version sounded like moaning prisoners with sinusitis being tortured.

Eventually, a growing sense of urgency demanded a halt to deliberations. Yolanda Arroyo was a newspaper reporter with a hard deadline. Maybe Dallabaco was right. Take the shot while you have it.

He called Arroyo's cell phone number and got her right away. Told her he had a long story to tell and that he wanted to tell it now. She asked if it could wait until Monday. It was clear she had the weekend off. There were voices and music in the background. She was obviously at some kind of party. Maybe a late-summer barbecue. A final outdoor fling. He responded by tossing some Biederbach-style melodrama into the pot.

"I'm not sure I'll still be around on Monday," he said.

The drama cinched the deal, and they agreed to meet at Fleck's Diner. With that decision out of the way, he had only one more to make. Should he take the gun? He'd deliberated this question the day before and had chosen not to. He went over all the arguments again, then came to the same conclusion. Stone-cipher had a gun, along with a warrior attitude, and a vigilant stance. It hadn't saved him. Some things are out of your hands. If you're toast, you're toast. Focus on the mission at hand. Whatever happens, happens.

It was already afternoon when Jommers met Yolanda Arroyo downtown at Fleck's Diner, near the newspaper's office. He realized that she didn't have a lot of time to put together a long piece for Sunday's paper, so initially he thought about giving her some condensed version of events to increase the probability of it getting published the next day. But he changed his mind. He would give her everything and trust her judgment on what to use. He had underrated her because of her age. One of the problems of growing older is that you perceive young people as little more than teenagers, and you assume a teenager's inexperience. But she was an adult, and a smart one. He would have to respect that in order for their talk to be fruitful.

As this was a Saturday, the downtown diner lacked its usual weekday bustle and buzz, which made it a good place to talk.

"We had a joke about this place," Arroyo said, "you know, about the sign saying everything is fried in butter. That even the salads are fried in butter. But the joke's on us. They don't even sell salads."

"Are there any new homicides you're aware of, or any new bodies found anywhere?" Jommers asked.

She was taken aback by the question. "Well, that's an interesting way to start a conversation. No. No new homicides. The only body report is from down in Quarryville, which we ran today. Some old guy slipped off the scenic overlook platform at Scorn Falls, and they're trying to figure out who he is because there was no ID." She paused. "Are you going to tell me something weird here, weirder than I even imagined?"

"Yes," he said. "Almost certainly. You know that old saying, be careful what you wish for."

"I don't know what your expectations are for when this would run, but I don't have a lot of time left to get in a big story by deadline for tomorrow. First, I have to sit here and listen to your story, then, depending on what you tell me, try and confirm important details with other sources, then write it, then run it by my editor, who may or may not think it's urgent. Long stories tend to get planned. Breaking news is mostly shorter pieces, like fires, crimes, accidents, speeches . . ."

"Right."

"Just so you know."

"Understood."

"And just to be clear," she said, "everything here is on the record. Anything you say, I am free to use."

"Understood."

She took out a notebook and a pen, then pulled out a pocket recorder that placed it between them. "You have any problem with my recording the conversation?"

"No. In fact, I encourage it."

"All right, then. Giddyup."

Jommers began with that fateful Monday, the day of the Eggers Court raid and Tarburn's shooting. He told her everything he had discovered since then, and everything he conjectured. At the moment, he was not terribly concerned about repeating things heard from Biederbach or Voros. Biederbach was long gone and Voros was probably dead.

In the middle of the talk, a couple of cops that Jommers knew walked in to grab a bite on their break. They stopped when they saw him. One of them had the classic Liberty Bell shape, where the belt undercuts belly and waist fat. And it was this one who had the nerve to be snarky.

"Jesus, Jommers, she's young enough to be your daughter. Only rich guys get to do that. You come into money or something?"

Mildly annoyed, Jommers fired back. "You really ought to upgrade that belt you're wearing so it doesn't hurt anybody when it snaps. I'm thinking steel cables."

The other cop chimed in. "He actually had one of those. It snapped at Mc-Greevy's last week and took out half the room. So he's upgraded to titanium."

Both cops laughed and headed over to the counter.

Jommers looked back at Arroyo. "Sorry."

"Don't worry about it," she said. "You should hear what I get down at the station."

"I'll bet."

"Been doing this only little over a year," she said, "and already feel ten years older."

Jommers continued with his narrative, noticing how often she repeated certain questions:

"How do you know that?"

"Do you know that for sure?"

"Do you have any evidence for that?"

"What's your source for that?"

She was a good reporter, determinedly seeking evidence for various suppositions. So when the long tale was finally finished, she looked frustrated and crestfallen. He had expected her to be excited.

"You don't seem too fired up about this," he said.

"Let me be blunt," she said. "You've given me a lot of interpretation and speculation, but very few hard facts. You've given me pudding where I need rocks. We're not talking about a garbage man stealing a pink flamingo from someone's garden. You're accusing the chief of police of corruption and multiple murders. And when it comes to proof, you got zip."

"I thought you guys were less fussy about that these days."

"You're thinking of mebby webby world, where they post first and ask questions later, and mebby it's true and mebby it isn't. They can toss out whatever they want— they can divine entrails for their source material—it doesn't matter. Because if it turns out wrong, they just take it down and pretend it was never there. I live in good old-fashioned print world, where stuff has to be nailed down before you run with it. And I've got a good old-fashioned print world editor who wants it nailed down like it's on a sailboat heading into a typhoon. Know what I'm saying? I give him this, he goes flamethrower on me. Then I'm that little burnt potato chip at the bottom of the bag. So this isn't running anytime soon. Something this sensational, I'd have to corroborate every detail before he'd let the readers get even a whiff of it. We're talking weeks' worth of investigation here before it runs. And if I can't find enough to support it, maybe it never runs. So while I'm grateful for the lead—it's terrific if it pans out—you shouldn't have any great expectations. I'm sorry."

"I understand," he said. "I had to give it a shot. And if something happens to me, at least there's someone else now who has a clue about it."

"You're serious about that, aren't you? I thought you were just giving me a bait line on the phone. But you've been anxious the whole time, looking over your shoulder. Never saw you like that before. You think this is for real?"

"I don't know what to think anymore. I felt an obligation to get it on record. And an urgency to do so. Regardless of whether I'm at risk, you can be sure that Chief Scubbetts is doing his best as we speak to cover his tracks and destroy evidence. So all you'll ever have is the disappearing whiff of it. Nothing more. So you're probably right. This never runs. He wins."

She frowned at that thought. "Let's not cave too quick here. Maybe there's another angle. Work with me. Let's brainstorm." She looked off in the distance while tapping her pen nervously on the notepad, making a rat-a-tat noise. It appeared to help her think. "The tape on the latch," she said.

"What?"

"The other day, we talked Watergate. Remember how it all began? A security guard finds a piece of tape on a door latch. Some little bitty thing that leads to bigger things, then to humongous things. Two years later, the president of the United States resigns for the first and only time in history. That's what we need. Some little thing that turns on the spotlight. Then, once he's under scrutiny, other stuff starts trickling out. People start coming forward. Momentum builds. The little thing doesn't even have to relate to what we just talked about. It could be anything so long as it's real. Anything that turns on the light. Of course, the verifiability issue remains. It would have to be something you can personally attest to."

"In other words, wrongdoing that I was personally aware of or personally involved in."

"Exactly."

"Sink myself to sink him."

"This was your idea, remember. How bad do you want it?"

He reflected for a moment. He knew exactly the story to tell her. What gave him pause was not a reluctance to suffer the consequences, but an inexplicable eagerness to suffer them. He wanted to do the right thing here, but he wanted it to be the wise thing, not an impulsive desire to commit hara-kiri to assuage his guilt, because just then, at that very moment, he fully realized how long he'd been suppressing feelings of guilt over the death of Earl Tarburn. If only he had handled things differently that night, Tarburn might be still alive. But self-immolation would not bring Tarburn back. Maybe he should think it over. He could get up and go home right now. Sleep on it. Get back to the reporter sometime later. There's no rush.

"There was this cop named Nitchenko," Jommers said. "I helped Scubbetts toss the guy overboard. I screwed up. And then I kept quiet about it."

Jommers told her the story about Patrolman Nitchenko, who had beaten up a deaf guy who hadn't responded to commands or questions for the obvious reason. The incident became a big story, fueled by a city councilman who was the victim's uncle. The cop and the victim gave differing accounts and there were no witnesses, so the case promised to drag on and remain in the spotlight for a long time, given that the patrolman's union was defending the officer's actions.

It threatened to embarrass Chief Scubbetts, the outsider who had been tapped to reestablish discipline in the ranks and restore the image of the Grayton PD. So Scubbetts turned to Jommers for help.

Under the terms of the union contract, as well as the municipal code, the PD could terminate a cop for health or medical reasons with nothing more than the professional opinion of an accredited expert in the field. And psychological problems fell under the heading of health or medical. This meant that Scubbetts could sack Nitchenko immediately with nothing more than a letter from Jommers saying that the patrolman was psychologically unfit for duty. One letter and the cop was gone. Then Scubbetts would look like a decisive, strong leader, a man who lived up to expectations. All he needed was to get the department's official psychologist on board.

"So Scubbetts brings me this file thick with citizen complaints against the cop. At this point, I have no reason to be suspicious about it. No reason to distrust the chief. I mean, yeah, he was a difficult person, harsh and imperious, but I attributed that to his military background, his being an army officer. I perceived it initially as a fault in style, not a flaw in character. Temperament doesn't always neatly mesh with morality. There are plenty of evil people who are charming, and there are plenty of virtuous people who are assholes. He struck me as the latter. I thought he was a genuine reformer, so I wanted to help him clean up the department, make it more professional. And if that meant getting rid of some bad apples, then so be it. Still, I insisted on performing an evaluation. So Nitchenko shows up like he's supposed to, but with a monster bad attitude. No matter what I say or ask, he responds the same. 'Fuck you.' That's it. Those are the only two words I can get out of him. Now we're supposed to exhibit professional detachment, right? But still, we're human beings. Somebody screams 'fuck you' at you thirty times, well, it's going to affect you, like it or not."

"Sounds like a no-brainer to me," she said. "You write the letter."

"Right. And I do. And the cop is booted. And I think it's all done and over. In the ensuing months, we do this a few more times, using the psych eval to boot a cop Scubbetts wants gone, short-circuiting the normal disciplinary process. And it all seems legit at first, like each one really deserves it. Each time I'm prepped with a fat complaint file. So I think I'm doing the right thing. But here's the point. I don't discuss the specific complaints during my interviews, because it's not a hearing, only an evaluation, so they don't know what I've seen, how I am already predisposed. We don't discuss the specific details of complaints, because I'm just supposed to evaluate their personality, and they all give me a hostile attitude that conforms with my prepping. It's only later I find out that these complaints may be fabricated, not actual citizen complaints, but no one knows because I'm the only one who sees them besides Scubbetts."

"Then how did you find out?"

"There was a secretary who worked for him and quit. Didn't like the way she was being treated. Wanted to get back at him. She contacts Nitchenko about the fabricated complaints in his file. She knows because she was the one who typed them up for the chief. So after Nitchenko hears this, he comes to see me."

"I assume he was even more PO'd than the first time."

"No, actually. He was dispirited, enervated. Totally defeated. He didn't come to blame me, but to let me know how I'd been used. He told me that all the complaints in the file were concocted, except for the one."

"So he really did beat up a deaf guy."

"Yeah. He admitted blowing up that day, but swore that his record had been spotless up to that point."

"So what made him lose it that day?"

"There was a lot going on in his life at the time. None of it good. His marriage was falling apart, his kid was in trouble at school, and his dad was declining with Alzheimer's. On top of all that, he was starting to hate the job. So he's on the edge. And he's on patrol and sees what looks like an attempted break-in at a house. Young guy at a side window holding some kind of tool. So the cop comes up behind the guy and orders him to turn around and drop the tool. The guy doesn't know the cop is there because the guy is deaf. And the guy isn't breaking into the house, because it's his house. He's scraping old caulk from around the window so he can put some new caulk in. So Nitchenko is yelling at a guy who's ignoring him, because the guy doesn't know the cop is there, and the cop is getting increasingly agitated about being ignored. So Nitchenko blows, starts seriously wailing on the guy, and the guy has no idea what is happening to him or why. And when the reality of the situation finally dawns on the cop, he realizes he has to cover his ass. So he makes up the story that the deaf guy attacked him with the scraping tool, which was nonsense. Your predecessor covering the police beat writes a story about an evil, sadistic, out-of-control cop that needs to go, and then the TV stations pile on, too. So at this point, Nitchenko is ready to blow his brains out. So when he comes to me for the evaluation, he doesn't care anymore. He wants to get fired. He wants to run away from it all. And so he curses at me repeatedly to get it all over with as quickly as possible."

"But you don't know any of this when you write the letter recommending dismissal. So you didn't do anything deliberately wrong up to that point. You were tricked."

"Yes, but it's what I did afterwards that was unpardonable. After Nitchenko came back to me months later, after he told me about the falsified record and his personal situation."

"What did you do?"

"I did nothing."

"Nothing? Absolutely nothing?"

"I offered to reopen the case with the department. He wasn't interested. Said it was too late. He could never go back. Said he hadn't come back for justice or retribution. He only wanted me to know the truth. He said to me, and I've never forgotten it, that 'the truth matters even when it can no longer change anything.' At which point he got up and left. And I didn't stop him. And I didn't mention it to anyone."

"What should you have done?"

"A number of things. I should have confronted Scubbetts over it. I didn't. I became less gullible and less pliable after that, but never called him on it. I should have made an issue of rehabilitating Nitchenko's record for purposes of future employment. I should have called your predecessor at the paper and told him he needed to update his story about the bad cop. But most importantly, I should have reached out to Nitchenko, offered gratis counseling, helped rescue him from the pit of despair he was in. My failure to do that was my biggest sin."

"So just like him, you were basically a good guy who did a bad thing. You gave me his excuse, what's yours?"

"I guess on a subconscious level I wanted to hold on to the business. I was enthused about being a police psychologist. I wanted to stay one. It jibed with my reasons for becoming a psychologist to begin with. You see, there's this justification process that afflicts people in health care, law enforcement, politics, probably your journalism business, too. The calculation goes something like this. I got into this business to do good things, to help people, to help make the world a better place. But now I've made a mistake. If I let this mistake ruin my career, it will negate all the potential good I can do down the road. In the end, all the good I'm yet to do will certainly outweigh this one little mistake I made. So even if it's wrong in the short run to sweep it under the rug, in the long run it's for the higher good, which is all the good I'll do in the future. You see how that works? How easy it is to roll it over into a positive? So I was happy to see him go, to disappear. I wanted it behind me. Pretend it was never there. Move on."

"What will happen to you when this story gets out?"

"I'll probably never again work as a police psychologist. And there's a high probability that the state certification board will suspend or revoke my license."

"Meaning you can't work as a psychologist."

"Without the therapy license, I wouldn't be allowed to practice clinical psychology, be a therapist who diagnoses and treats people. I could still do psychological research or teaching, I could serve as a social worker, or as a last resort, I could retreat to that occupation where many psychology majors end up."

"Bartender."

"Correct."

She frowned and shook her head. "It's not fair that you should have to go down with him. You made some mistakes in judgment, but in a world full of creeps and corruption, you seem like a decent guy who means well."

"Perhaps," Jommers said. "But we're all responsible for our mistakes, aren't we?"

She paused for a few moments, tapping her pen while thinking. Rat-a-tat-tat. Rat-a-tat-tat. "If I offered you the chance to forget past few minutes, erase that part of the tape . . ."

"No," he said. "We had a deal. Everything on the record. Do what you have to do."

"Okay, but I have to put myself in my readers' heads now. And they're asking the obvious question. This happened some years ago, why are you just now coming forward with this story? Remember, there won't be anything about all this mysterious chemical business. So your reason has to be something real and current."

"Right. I can say, quite honestly, that this all came back to me during a recent similar situation, where I was being pressured by Chief Scubbetts to prevent Detective Ilona Voros from returning to duty. As in the past, he wanted me to use the psychological evaluation as a tool for getting rid of a cop he doesn't like. This recent incident has forced me to reflect on my years of interaction with Chief Scubbetts, in which I have observed a pattern of inappropriate and unprofessional conduct. He has a vindictive personality and he verbally abuses his subordinates. He has created an atmosphere of fear that has devastated morale within the department. He can also be sadistic. Recently, he forced a captain with paruresis, shy bladder syndrome, to drink several cups of coffee, then attempt to urinate in front of an audience. The man, Captain Allomint, required medical treatment afterward. Another thing, when I defied the chief by approving Detective Voros to return to duty, he launched into an enraged rant that was borderline psychotic, a rant in which he threatened to kill me. And I have that recorded, by the way. So, it's my professional opinion that Chief Scubbetts is psychologically unfit for command, and unfit for law enforcement in any capacity. I believe that Mayor Cheeks should terminate the chief immediately."

"Perfect!" she said. "Absolutely perfect! This will definitely turn on the spotlight. Now then, just so you know, the very next thing I must do is contact everyone you mentioned and try to get a comment. Most importantly, I have to give Chief Scubbetts an opportunity to respond to your charges. You understand that?"

"Understood."

"Okay. Just one more thing, I need to get a shot of you in case we're not able to send a photographer over in time." She pulled a digital camera out of her purse, took a few shots and grinned while reviewing them on the camera's screen. "Hmmm. That's interesting."

"What?"

"Funny, I just noticed. Did you know you look a bit like Tom Selleck in his younger days? You know, the mustache thing."

"Actually, I was going for Carlos Santana."

"I'd love to hear more about that, but I suddenly have a whole lot of work to do and not a whole lot of time to do it."

"Good luck."

Jommers stayed in the diner for a few minutes after she'd gone, then, as he was rising to leave, he was approached by a young cop in uniform.

"Hey, aren't you that shrink guy who gives the training sessions?"

"Yep, that would be me."

"Cool. Glad I ran into you. I want to tell you, the one that I was at, you gave some of the best advice I ever got."

"No kidding? Which one was it?"

"The one on tone, you know, speaking. You talked about how people in an emotional state or an altered state are not cognitively processing what I'm saying, they're only perceiving the tone of voice that I'm using to say it. Like babies and pets. They don't understand the words, just the tone. So whenever I'm in that position, you said I should first think about what I'm trying to accomplish, then choose a tone that will convey that. Communicate with the tone because they aren't hearing the words. And that was just so on the money. I can't tell you how many situations I've been in where that helped me. That was a really good pointer."

"That's good to hear. I appreciate your stopping to tell me."

"No problem. Take it easy."

As Jommers drove home, Arroyo's warning belatedly resonated, that her first priority was to seek a response from Scubbetts. How would the hot-tempered, vindictive man react?

That question bobbed around like something fallen in your coffee, floating just beneath the surface. It's there, then gone, then back again. When he looked in the rearview mirror, he felt that the car behind was tailgating. After it turned off, the next one behind appeared to follow even closer. When he arrived back at the shop parking lot, he saw a mysterious dark object in the field behind the shop. He started walking through the brown, crunchy knee-high weeds toward the strange thing. He'd gotten only a few feet when he recognized it as a rotting, jagged-topped tree stump that had been there for years.

Why had it been briefly unrecognizable, this thing he saw all the time? Was it the weird shadows created by the setting sun? Or had he just caught sight of it at an unfamiliar angle?

While standing there, he caught a whiff of something peculiar. Instead of the field's normal musty dead weed smell hovering over the ground, an acrid odor rose out of the earth, a smoky scent where there was no smoke. A hint of fire with no sign of flame. He noticed his skin felt clammy, even though the air around him was still muggier than a sauna.

Just then he heard a horrible shriek. He wheeled around to see a gull winging by, making a sound he heard every single day. Why did it sound so startling at that moment?

There was an inexplicable strangeness about everything. The familiar had become alien. Even the silences appeared sinister. The ground had shifted without moving. The landscape had changed while staying the same. He had traveled to a different dimension without having gone anywhere. He had become that thing he'd never fully understood—the fearful man.

He trudged slowly out of the field, then upstairs to his apartment. Once there, he put on a CD with some slice-and-dice bottleneck blues, then grabbed a beer. He wanted to float away, banish all contemplation, but couldn't stop brooding about the career he'd just flushed down the drain.

He hadn't accomplished all that he had hoped. Who does? He had made some mistakes. Who hasn't? He was confident he had helped many over the years. Some of them came back and thanked him for being pulled back from the edge. But it was the others that haunted him, those that had gone over the edge without having ever sought help.

That was the one nut he'd never cracked. Figuring out how to make counseling appear acceptable in cop land, a macho world where seeking help is viewed as weakness, where most handle problems by self-medicating with alcohol or painkillers. That's cop culture. Keep it a secret. Hide the pain. Don't let anyone see you cry. An outsider will never change that. Cop culture has to change from within, and the change has to come from the top down. Until that happens, too many will suffer in silence.

There was another riddle that had gnawed at him over the years. Why did some get PTSD and others don't, even when they'd been through the same experiences? Why were some more emotionally resilient than others? Was it an inherent, hard-wired difference? Luck of the draw? Was it the presence or absence of a social support structure? Education? Upbringing? Religion? More importantly, could resilience be taught? Could you prepare someone for trauma and reduce its aftereffects?

He had intended to perform original research to help answer those questions, but he'd never gotten around to it, like so many other things. Like the pictures leaning against the wall on the floor in the corner, still awaiting hanging.

As he looked around the room, he deliberately avoided looking at the one thing that required reflection more than any other, even though it was right in front of him. That cold can of frothy liquid in his hand. Just like the cops, he was self-medicating. And just like the cops, it had never occurred to him to seek help. How can you solve others' problems when you have yet to face your own?

He picked up the photo of Earl Tarburn, the one where the father was showing his son how to use a telescope. Jommers stared at it for a minute until interrupted by the sound of raccoons fighting outside. Screeching, growling, grunting, the severity of their savagery sounded disproportionate to their size. The sound of menace snatched his mind back to Biederbach world. Could there actually be a dark force out there cleaning up the mess, eliminating both evidence and people? It was now evening, and neither Dallabaco nor Voros had returned calls made in the morning. Were they dead? Was he next? Or was he loony for posing the question?

In the midst of uncertainty, he could at least exercise caution, spend the night somewhere else. Or move some furniture in front of the door and grab the Andy gun, keeping it pointed at the door.

No. He refused. In the event that these were his final hours, he would not spend them living in fear. He walked over to the door, unlocked and opened it, leaving it slightly ajar. He turned up the music loud. He made some microwave popcorn and grabbed some more beer. He closed his eyes and leaned back. Savoring the moment. Savoring life, whatever its length. Lousy popcorn and all.

SHORTLY AFTER ELEVEN O'CLOCK, he was jarred out of his reverie by a phone call from Yolanda Arroyo.

"Here's what's happening," she said. "I thought my editor was going to give his famous rotten-pistachio sneer for bringing him this without warning. Instead, he was totally psyched up about it. He said he always felt in his gut that there was something crooked about Scubbetts and that he dreamed of the day I would stumble upon it. So he goes into like full mobilization mode. He tells me to start writing, focus on that. He pulls people off other projects to do the follow-up contacts. Has someone to dig up the original Nitchenko story. He personally calls Sergeant Piebalgs, the PD public affairs officer, requesting comments from the chief. Gives him a deadline. So Sergeant Piebalgs gets back to my editor and confirms that he relayed the message to the chief and if there's going to be a response, the chief personally will contact us. But the chief never calls. So when the witching hour arrives, my editor decides calls Piebalgs again to confirm Scubbetts got the message, and he says yes. So my editor tells him he's going to run it regardless, that the chief had been given several hours to reply and hadn't, so that's the equivalent of declining to respond. We couldn't locate Detective Voros, but we got nearly everybody else. We got Nitchenko, got the shy bladder guy, even got the secretary who typed the fake complaints. It's so crazy amazing how we pulled it all together in like five or six hours. I am so wired right now, I need a mojito to power down. Multiple mojitos. Anyway, wanted you to know—it's front page, tomorrow morning."

"Appreciate the call," he mumbled. "Look forward to reading it. Sort of. You know."

"Yeah, sure."

Only half-awake, he thought about what she'd said, wondered why the arrogant, overbearing police chief had not responded with a tirade, his usual response to challenge. But his musing did not last long, as he quickly nodded off.

DAY TWENTY-ONE

CONSEQUENCES

When garnering the truth, most prefer it served up simple and solid. The steak over the stew. But in the mess hall of life, you take what you get. And too often, what you get is some oily ground mystery meat in some greenish gelatinous glop pretending to be gravy. And even though you find it revolting, you hold your nose and scarf it down anyway, because it's all you're going to get, and it's better than nothing.

When Jommers woke up Sunday morning, he still had no idea what the hell was going on. Well, actually, he knew one thing. He had woken up alive rather than dead, and that was a plus. So far, anyway. The day was young.

He vaguely remembered a long conversation with a reporter that would irrevocably alter his future. Alter as in totally trash it. Or was that just a bad dream? So his first order of business was to head down to the parking lot in front of the shop and hunt for the morning paper, which was ingeniously tossed in different place every day.

He couldn't find it at first. The carrier was getting more creative. This morning the paper was tossed so that it had slid under Jommers's battered Taurus. It rested almost exactly in the middle, so that Jommers had to lie down on the gravel and reach with his arm to grab it. And while lying in that position, he observed a car on Nickel Plate Road coming toward the shop. It was a new black Chevy Impala with black steel wheels, tinted windows and tinted license plate covers. Just like the one he'd seen sitting in the lot yesterday.

There had once been a time in journalism's heyday that the Sunday morning paper had been heavy enough to beat a man with. But times had changed. Today's Sunday edition of the *Ledger* might be used to dispatch a pesky fly, but not much else. So Jommers got up calmly and stoically, awaiting whatever fate might be arriving in a shiny black new Impala with tinted windows.

The car pulled in the lot slowly and right next to him. The driver door opened slowly, and out stepped Detective Yopko, his bald head shining in the oblique rays of the morning sun.

"Yopko," Jommers yelled. "Where the hell you steal that? I thought all you guys had was Crown Vic beaters."

"Yeah. The Vics are falling apart all right, and you can't keep them on the road with the service situation. We're not allowed to take them to a dealer to be fixed. They have to go over to the city garage on Plover and wait in line with garbage trucks, dump trucks and anything else the city owns that has wheels. They're backed up out the wazoo, but whenever you go over there they're all sitting around drinking coffee and shooting the shit. You drop off a unit with a bad starter motor and you don't get it back for three or four weeks. Three weeks for a goddamn starter. Bunch of fucking numbnuts over there. So anyway, city is going with a phased replacement since it doesn't have the cash for whole new fleet. So every time a Vic bites the dust, it's replaced with an Impala 9C3."

"You like it?"

"Oh, hell yeah. Handles really nice. Got all this stabilizer shit on it, traction control, nice trim package, and other stuff. Only a V-6, but you still get over three hundred horse out of the sucker. Rocket acceleration. You just blow out the gate with it. Plus it's nice being in something new and more modern styling. Fits in on the street. You can actually do a serious tail or stakeout with these. With the battleships, that stakeout is a joke. Everybody knows."

"Sounds good."

"Oh, yeah. At shift change, we actually race down to the pool to get one before they're gone."

"Now there's an image for the imagination, detectives racing. I didn't even know detectives could run."

"Sure, we can run. You know, when there's an incentive."

"Right."

"Anyway, I stopped by to see you yesterday, but I guess you were out for a walk or something. Saw your car still here, so waited a while."

"I was out riding my bike."

"Okay, anyway, the other night, you know, when someone rigged this place to be a time bomb meant for you, and you pointed the finger at Scubbetts—I thought you were yanking my crank. So when I tell my lieutenant about it, I'm half-expecting him to bust up. But he ain't laughing. He gets all tense like I just pissed in his coffee. He takes me over to the captain to repeat it. And the captain, he gets the same look, like I pissed in his coffee, too. He tells me to dump it on Captain Wifflyn at IA, and says when I'm done, let it go. Don't touch it, don't talk about it, don't think about it. And so I take it to Wifflyn, and he ain't laughing either. He's rubbing his temples like he's trying to teleport himself to Tahiti. And then I realize, this shit's for real. Jommers wasn't jerking me after all. Okay, so I'm done. But I'm pulling a weekender, I figure what the hell, can't hurt to stop by and ask you a few more questions I forgot to ask that night."

"I'll be happy to rehash anything you want," Jommers said.

"It doesn't matter now. That's what I came by to tell you, that you can relax now."

"How so?"

"Somewhere around five thirty this morning, a jogger is taking a run over in Nike Beach Park by the lake. He notices something on the beach by the water and checks it out. It's a police uniform all neatly folded, hat, skivvies, everything. Sidearm, wallet and badge, too."

"Scubbetts."

"Yeah. Looks like he took the long, one-way swim. So in no time, every cop who hears it is calling every other cop he knows with the news. It's time for dancing in the streets. I'm surprised the phone system didn't crash. Not long after that, the *Ledger* hits the streets, with your mug and story on page one. And the phones go crazy again. Everybody calling everybody. And they all think the obvious, that your story drove Scubbetts to take the plunge. And now everybody on the force wants to buy you a beer, send you a fruit basket. But then it slowly dawns on us. A guy who carries a piece on his hip doesn't check out by taking a swim. He bites the barrel. Quick one in the stem. Right?"

"Right."

"So now we're thinking it's staged. He skips, but we don't go looking for him because we think he's waltzing with the walleye. Plus there's the joke part to it, too. Ex-army guy faking a suicide at a former army base. It's called Nike Beach Park because in the fifties it was an army Nike missile site. They had anti-aircraft missiles that were supposed to shoot down the Soviet bombers flying down over Lake Erie to bomb Grayton. So Scubbetts gets in one last laugh on us. Oh, yeah, the cincher. No cigars or lighter with the uniform. Everybody knows he always carried both, and you can't smoke in the water. Cocky son of a bitch too cheap to leave his expensive cigars behind and thinks we're too stupid not to notice."

"So what's next?"

"For us? Probably not much. If he's skipped Grayton, he'll just keep going out of state, which means we toss it to the feds. He's probably headed back to where he came from, backwoods in the Ozarks. If he makes it back there, they'll never find him. So you're probably safe now. Thought you'd want to know."

"Appreciate it."

After Yopko left, Jommers finally took the newspaper out of its plastic bag and grimaced. It was an odd feeling seeing his face on the front page. The weirdness of it, that everyone in the city now knows you. Every waitress and bartender. Every cashier in every store. The postal carrier. And now they all know how you screwed up. And the people who you already knew, but who knew nothing of your business, they also now know how you screwed up. Your professional peers and personal acquaintances. Larry the bartender. Claire.

Pete. The guys in the shop. The psychology majors you spoke to at GSU. Your dentist. Every cop who ever sat in your rockers. They all know your sins now. They will never look at you the same again.

Yet, for all the magnitude of that insight, it blew through his head like a bottle rocket as he focused on his photo. *Holy crap.* Do I look that bad now? Does my face really look like an old shoe? Maybe it is time to just roll over and die.

When he finished obsessing over his photo, he read the story that Arroyo had written. And he experienced the usual shock every source feels upon seeing a lengthy conversation condensed to its essentials. It's much like a politician looking at an editorial cartoon and being taken aback by how his large his ears and nose appear. He felt abused. Yet when he read the story for the third time, he could find nothing factually wrong with it. It simply felt wrong when the bare facts were stripped of mitigating context. But that's journalism. He should have known.

He should also have guessed his actions would have consequences. Sergeant Piebalgs, the public affairs officer, had confirmed to the editor of the *Ledger* that he'd gotten through to Scubbetts early Saturday evening. That meant that Scubbetts's flight was made subsequent to the contact, and most likely as a result of the contact. And Jommers talk with the reporter had initiated that chain of events, for better or for worse. The better—the son of a bitch was gone. The worse—he had taken his secrets with him.

And it was the latter part that Detective Ilona Voros zeroed in on when she roared into the lot minutes later, almost running him over as he stood there reading the paper.

"You idiot!" she screamed, leaping out of the car. "You goddamn, stupid idiot. What the hell were you thinking?"

"Good morning," Jommers said, "I'm happy to see you're okay. I was worried about you."

"I had him, damn it. I had him by the balls. I went to arrest him last night. But he was gone. He'd apparently gotten a call from a reporter about a story. After that, he split. Vanished. Nobody knows where. All because you felt a sudden, inexplicable, urgent need to flagellate yourself. Why? Why did you do that? What the hell is the matter with you?"

"The circumstances at the time—"

"What circumstances? You were drunk? A piano fell on your head? You were drunk *and* a piano fell on your head? Tell me. I want to know."

"As I was saying—"

"You blew my case. My collar. He's gone. We'll never get him. Because of you. We'll never have answers. Because of you. Why? Why? Why have you dedicated your life to undermining me?"

"When you're finished, let me know, then I can explain."

"I am so frustrated now I just want to put something through a wall. You! Put you through a wall. Then knock the building down on top of you. Then set it on fire. Goddamn you."

"Just let me know—"

"All right. Fine. Talk."

"After the incident at the Tennyson Place Apartments—you know, the place I told you not to go but you went anyway, the place where I prevented Dallabaco's men from turning you into a cheese grater, which was their preferred course of action, after—"

"Yeah. Let's talk about those guys while we're at it. Did you know—"

"Let me finish," he said.

"Then do it."

"After that incident, I was concerned about your safety, particularly since you would be confined to a hospital room in a vulnerable state of mind, without your weapon to defend yourself and with a certain police chief still wanting to eliminate you. So I arranged with Dallabaco to have someone stand watch over you until you were in a position to defend yourself."

"Yes," she said. "Brilliant idea. I had just been primed to believe these very men were coming to assassinate me, and you arrange to have them stand outside my hospital room staring at me, the very men I thought came to kill me. Brilliant! You must be a genius or something."

"Let me finish," he said.

"Then finish already."

"So I try to check on you yesterday at the hospital, see how you're doing. Only you're gone, and nobody at the hospital knows where, because there was no official discharge. You just disappeared. I try to reach you, but can't. I try to reach Dallabaco, but can't. I'm concerned that something bad has happened to you. Hours go by. And still no response from either you or Dallabaco. I don't know what to make of it. I fear the worst at this point. There are some other things that get me thinking about my own safety. You recall that someone, likely Scubbetts, arranged to have me blown up the other night. That was still very fresh in my mind. So I had to ask myself, if you're gone, and I'm about to go, who is left to tell the story? Who will know what happened to any of us? As the day wore on with no word from anybody, I felt a sense of urgency to deposit the story with someone while I was still in a position to do so. Someone who could pursue it further and not think me nuts. The reporter was the only person I could think of that fit the bill. Based on the information I had, and the information I lacked, I felt it was a reasonable response to a reasonable fear. If only you had called."

"Stop blaming me for your stupidity," she said. "You don't know what I was going through, the scary place my head was at."

"Okay. Tell me what happened."

"You know the state I was in."

"Yes," he said.

"And you say it was one thing, and they say it was another thing, but it doesn't matter. Something foreign was in me, and it was making me terrified without having any sense of what I'm terrified about. My mind is flailing around for an answer. Then these two SWAT guys stroll in, the guys who were supposed to be protecting me. And they're looking at me, muttering quietly to each other, snickering. And now I have something specific to be afraid of. Them. I hit the call button, and while I'm waiting for the nurse to show, one of them says, 'You know, I had you in my sights, just waiting for the green light, then the asshole shows up, and I have to wait. I should have just got itchy, you know? Maybe next time.' He makes a motion with his hand like he's pulling a trigger. At this point I am totally freaking like you can't believe. Ready to jump out the window. Finally the nurse comes. I tell her I need a bedpan, make the guys leave. She does and closes the door. Then I grab the phone and call my friend, Kendra, ask her to come get me as soon as possible. Tell her what's happening. So when she gets there, she shows her badge to the two SWAT guys, tells them they're being relieved and can go. They're confused, but don't question it. They're happy to get out of there. As soon as they round the corner, Kendra unhooks me from the tubes and wires, helps me dress, and we run down the fire stairs and out of there. She takes me to her place where I can finally relax and breathe. She recommends that I don't take or make any calls, so that no one will know where I am. I agree. I need time to get it together. So we just relax, listen to music. And I know I shouldn't drink anything. Alcohol on top of unknown chemicals in my system—not a good idea. But I do anyways. It seems to help. And it helps me fall asleep."

"So that's where you were the whole time, why I couldn't reach you."

"Yes," she said. "So I sleep late. I'm feeling better. Whatever was in me seems to be gone. Kendra runs out to Szell's Pastry for some Napoleons, the last place in town you can get them. Then she comes back and makes a pot of coffee, and we're just sitting there in her little dinette area, having a divinely decadent breakfast at this small round dinette table. And the scene reminds me of a painting in Raven's apartment."

"Raven the prostitute."

"Yes. I don't know if you remember her apartment much, but it was furnished and decorated like an upscale chain hotel—contemporary, with neutral earth tones, sparsely furnished, bland abstract art on the walls. The master bedroom was like that, too, you know, the work room. But it was a two-bedroom apartment, and the smaller bedroom was completely unlike the rest of the place. This was her personal space, where she slept when alone, where she spent her time when not entertaining clients. And this room was like some eccentric little curio shop with lots of interesting things. Antiques, folk art, classical art repros—cluttered, but with style. It was in this room she had this nicely framed print of a painting by Giovanni Boldini called *Conversation at the Cafe*. It depicts two well-dressed women sitting and drinking at small round table on the terrace of a cafe. And they're smiling and looking off to the right of the frame at something or someone outside the scene. An unseen player. One presumes a man. Anyway, I remember how a few days ago, when I'm working on her to tell me about Scubbetts exploiting her, she takes me in this room for the first time. Like sharing her sanctuary with me. And she shows me the painting. Makes a point of it. And she says, 'If anything ever happens to me, come and take the Boldini.' And I find that very odd."

"Because you're not really a friend," he said. "You're a cop pressuring her to testify."

"Exactly. So why would she want to leave me anything? And the phrasing was odd, too. Not, 'I want you to have this.' But rather, 'Come take this.' She's telling me something, but I don't get it at the time. And so yesterday morning, I'm sitting with Kendra at her little round table, we're stuffing our face with pastry, smiling, it reminds me of the two women in the Boldini. And I remember Raven saying: 'come take this.' I immediately call up the Homicide detective on the case, ask him if he looked behind that painting. He says no, that they had found a wall safe behind a kitchen clock, that it contained cash, jewels, and her little black book with client names. They figured they'd found all her secrets and didn't look much further. I give him an earful, and he gives me one back. I realize I need to go there immediately. Kendra comes with me. I'm excited, hoping to find something. I take the Boldini off the wall, and there's a metal door behind it. I open the door, and it's just an old-style fuse box, you know, threaded-base fuses. I look at the print again, the way the women are looking at something out of frame to the right. What are they watching? What are they telling me? I look back at the fuse box. I slip my fingernails under the right edge of the metal plate surrounding the frame, and I pull. It opens. It's a fake fuse box on a hinge—a door. Behind it is a wall safe with a combination lock. Now I'm so excited I can't even think. I'm officially off duty. How am I going to get a crew out to drill it? Then Kendra smiles, points at the fuses. There's nine of them in three rows. The sequence of amperage ratings is the same in each row—fifteen, twenty, twenty-five. That's the combination! We get inside and there's an active laptop computer. Turns out there are mini cams hidden throughout the apartment and she's recording everything on the laptop."

"Was she blackmailing clients?"

"Maybe. I don't know. Maybe it was just for her own protection. You know, in case someone hurt her, she could prove what happened and who did it. And the setup certainly achieved that."

"Scubbetts."

"Yes," she said. "When we looked at the most recent video, it was astounding. There he was, coming in with the big can of contact cement. Knocking her around. Holding her face in the bucket until she went unconscious. It was horrifying. Sickening. Yet it was also inciting. Because now I had him. And the disgusting grin on his face as he killed her. He wasn't just going to get prison, he would get the needle for this. So I call—"

"Wait a sec," he said. "On the video, when he entered, did he bring in anything else besides the contact cement?"

"Yes. Some kind of contraption. Couldn't tell. But he sets it up and plugs it in after he kills her."

"Was it still there when you went back there yesterday?"

"No, now that you mention it, but it doesn't matter. Like I said, we had him, right there on video, committing murder. So I call up Captain Wifflyn, tell him what I found. He doesn't believe me, thinks I'm hallucinating. I tell him, then get your ass over here and look at it. And he does. And he can't believe it. But it's real, and he knows it. And he reawakens to his duty, shakes off the shilly-shally. He wants to move, but he doesn't want to blow the collar by doing it half-ass, and he obviously can't involve dispatch. Can't have it go over radio. So he calls up half a dozen IA detectives, so that we can cordon off any escape hatch. But this obviously kills time—critical time, it turns out, because we don't know, at the same time, a certain psychologist is talking to a newspaper reporter who will shortly call the police chief about allegations. By the time we get it together, make the assault, Scubbetts is gone. We find out about the call he got from Sergeant Piebalgs. He disappears right after that. We had him. But just missed him. Because of you."

"I'm sorry," Jommers said. "I had no way to know what was going on at your end. I didn't know whether you were even alive. And I was—"

"Scared shitless and wondering how you could save your sorry ass. Mister mellow. Always taking the philosopher's pose. Condescendingly instructing lesser lights how to jettison their anxieties, but when the shit hits the fan for you, you piss your pants like a schoolboy. You understand now, don't you? You understand how fear changes the calculation. If you felt afraid, you should have just gone away for a while like I suggested instead of interfering."

"I made the best decision I could with available inputs at the time, irrespective of any emotional influence."

"Who the hell are you to be making decisions? This was police business, not your business. For all intents and purposes, what you did constitutes obstruction."

"I sensed the need for urgency, for action."

"It wasn't your place to divine a sense of urgency. You should have held off until you heard from me."

"We can argue this all day, but it won't change anything. I assume you know about them finding his uniform at Nike Beach Park."

"Whoa! You really are tied in with the boys gang, aren't you? This early in the morning, and you already know the details—maybe that's what's going on here. Maybe you're not that incompetent. Maybe you were part of the plan. Help Scubbetts get away while helping the boys thwart me yet again."

"If you really believe that, then I suggest that whatever chemicals were put in your system have not yet been fully metabolized and you need to drink another pot of coffee until you piss it all out."

"Damn it, stop telling me I'm sick just because I see things differently than you. I've had different experiences than you, and experiences shape our perceptions. You're supposed to understand that. I am not sick. I'm just different. Stop saying I'm sick whenever I disagree with you."

"I don't know if it will make any difference, but at some point you might want to search the residence of Patrolman Biederbach. He claimed to have a lot of information on all this."

"Yes," she said. "Thank you for your brilliant insights. I'd already thought of that. His personnel file listed an address on Hawkmoth Avenue, but when we go there, it turned out to be a cemetery. We have no idea where he actually lived. No idea where he went. So, without him, and without Scubbetts, we have nothing, nowhere to go. You can't make bricks from fog. It's just done. Over. And somewhere out there, Scubbetts is laughing at me. Laughing while smoking one of his big black cigars. I'm sure your cronies told you, in spite of the ruse with the uniform, the smug son of a bitch took his cigars with him."

"Back to Biederbach for a moment," Jommers said. "I told you that he had arranged a meeting with this Russian guy, who was found dead in a river down in Quarryville."

"Yes," she said, "I had not forgotten, thank you. But we don't have any way to know if the body found in the river was a Russian guy. Dead men don't have accents. He had no ID. No abandoned vehicles nearby. No fingerprints on file. No missing person reports matching his description. Nobody coming forward to claim the body. We have no idea who the hell he was, no way to know whether he fell, jumped or was pushed. No way to know if he even relates to any of this or whether his demise was just a coincidence. Biederbach might have just invented the chemist to make his theory sound more believable to you."

"Why would he go to meet a nonexistent person?"

"We don't know that he did, don't know that he was even there. Maybe he heard about a body being found on the scanner, decided to work it into his tale for you. We don't know. All we have is fog."

"Well, maybe the feds can get a bead on Scubbetts," Jommers said. "They'll have access to his military records showing where he came from. They'll have his prints on file."

"Oh, yes," she said. "Thanks for bringing that up. We checked in with the feds first thing. And they just got back to us. The military has no record of him. So, either he fabricated his military history and the mayor just failed to perform any background check, or the military records somehow got lost."

"Or deleted."

"Lost, deleted, whatever, it doesn't matter. It's not there. And neither is he. Like some stupid TV show where a character wakes up and everything you've been watching turns out to be a dream."

"Except for the dead people," he said. "They're still dead. And that's not a dream."

"No, it's not. But we'll never know any more about their demise than we do now. The bridge is out. We can't go any farther."

"I'm sorry," he said. "I didn't want it to end this way any more than you. Everything I did from beginning to end was an attempt to get answers."

"Well, we don't have them, do we? And now we never will." She leaned over and snatched the section of newspaper he was reading with his story and smacked it with the back of her hand. "And why in the hell are you apologizing for tossing a few psycho cops? They were sickos who never should have gotten in to begin with. Your biggest sin was not tossing more of them. But of course, I do understand the problem. If you weed out all the misfits, racists, and sadists, you wouldn't have enough cops left to field a softball team, much less cover the zones. You know what? Here's what we need. Term limits for cops. Maximum term of service. Ten years and you're out. You get on with the rest of your life, whatever that is. Because it's the internal cop culture that's the problem. I've seen it. I've seen good ones come in, but then they get corrupted by the culture, the peer pressure. To survive socially, they have no choice but to adopt the same attitudes, drink the poison. It's like . . . like a machine. A humongous stamping press. And the new guy is just a thin piece of sheet metal. And the press comes down on him, and it deforms him, shapes him. He can't resist, no matter how pure he once was. The machine is too strong. Resurrect Saint Francis of Assisi, give him a badge, and in ten years he's an asshole, too. The machine will not be denied. And that's your problem, too. You meant well. You wanted to understand them, but you got too close and fell into the press. And then you got deformed. Instead of changing them, they changed you. And that's why you didn't bounce more of them. Because you became one of them."

"If so, you won't have to worry about it anymore," he said. "I'll have to look for new line after this. Kind of reached my own term limit."

"I could use a new line, too," she said. "Why do I put myself through this?

Working for lunkhead bureaucrats, chasing down a never-ending parade of brutes and slime cakes. Dwelling in the sewer. I don't need this aggravation. I could be teaching children how to play the piano. I'm good enough for that. I could have a fulfilling life, a peaceful, rewarding, civilized life."

"That sounds like your mother talking."

"Yes, and I should have listened. Become a proper lady. But, as you noted, events sent me on a detour."

"Maybe I was wrong about that," he said.

"What do you mean?"

"There's the other voice in your head, the 56er who fought against a totalitarian regime, who was followed by the secret police. The man who gave you lectures on justice and liberty. Maybe your father steered you down the path that led you to become an Internal Affairs detective. Maybe it wasn't a detour after all."

"It's weird you say that. After I escaped the hospital, afraid of those two SWAT guys, things my father said about police started popping into my head. The overwhelming and pervasive fear of police under the communists, the paralyzing dread, how leaving all that behind was the most important thing about coming to America, more important than opportunity or anything else. The first freedom is the freedom from fear. No innocent person should never have to fear the law. You need police to protect you from criminals and gangs, but they have to be honest and fair. Otherwise they become just a gang with a dress code. Nothing made my father more irate than reading a story about a bad cop abusing his authority. That's not supposed to happen here, he yelled. This is America. Oh my God, how this is all coming back to me now. I just assumed I ended up where I am because of my experiences. But you're right. He drove me here. Drove me where I was meant to be. I am not a victim of events. I have been my true self all along."

She paused and let out a long sigh while looking off in the distance. Her shoulders slumped weakly and her jaw slacked while things rearranged themselves in her head. Then, after a few moments, with things properly reordered, she quickly straightened up and displayed a look of determination, a sense of renewal.

"I have to go. I've got work to do." She spun around back towards her vehicle.

Jommers smiled. "Stay healthy, Ilona. Keep eating those apples."

She gave him a nonchalant backhand wave and drove off. He was pretty sure he'd never see her again. They had nothing left to say.

He had yet to shower or shave that morning, but priority one was to brush his teeth and swish some mouthwash to remove the stale, cottony taste in his mouth. But it would have to wait. Before he even got back in the door, another vehicle, a black Ford Explorer, turned onto Nickel Plate and made its way toward the shop and into the lot.

Lieutenant Augie Dallabaco stepped out of the driver's side slowly, looking a bit tired. Once out, he stretched his arms like someone who'd just gotten up. He walked toward Jommers in a relaxed manner, lacking his usual intensity. He smiled, another atypical feature.

"Jommers, how the hell are you?"

"Vertical and breathing. Old guys count that as a good day."

"Me, too. Anyway, I wanted to apologize for not getting back to you yesterday. Had a hellaciously busy day, both with official business and personal business. Hope it didn't create a problem for you. But to answer your question about Detective Voros, a friend of hers showed up at the hospital—I guess that's what you call her, a friend—anyway, she's on the force, a patrol officer. She showed her badge to my guys and told them they were relieved. They presumed everything was copacetic. By the time they got hold of me, the ladies were gone, and so there was nothing more I could do because I had no idea where they went. So I don't want you to think I didn't uphold my end of the deal."

"Understood."

At this point, Dallabaco drew out a large black cigar from his shirt pocket. He lit it theatrically, using a flamethrower of a lighter, one that looked familiar to Jommers.

"I don't remember you being a cigar smoker," Jommers said.

"I just happened to come into some, you know, what's the word, sara-something . . ."

"Serendipitously."

"Yeah, that's it. So I thought I'd give it a try. You want one?"

"No, thanks. I've got enough vices."

"It's a beautiful day, don't you think? We should take advantage of it. That nasty chilly shit weather is right around the corner. Before you know it, all this will be a memory. We should seize the day."

"You seem in unusually good spirits today," Jommers said.

"Yeah, well, you know, we all have our moods, don't we? And today, well, my mood is optimistic. I think things have turned a corner with Grayton PD. I think we're going to have a new dawn."

"If I'm not mistaken, all dawns are new."

Dallabaco laughed. "Always thinking. Always analyzing. And that's good. You know, to a point. We need thinkers like you, but we also need guys who— what's that guy, the ancient guy and that business with the knot . . ."

"Alexander the Great. When faced with the complex problem of untying the Gordian Knot, he just whacked it with his sword."

"Yeah, yeah, that guy. Sometimes you need a guy like that, someone who just cuts through the shit and gets it done. You know? Because sometimes, you just don't have the time to untangle something complicated. You just have to get it done. You know?"

"Sure. Sometimes."

"I'm happy to hear you say that. We don't often agree on things. It's good to see you being agreeable." Then Dallabaco took a deep puff of his cigar, and exhaled it slowly. He smiled as he watched the thick, whitish, acrid cloud swirl and unfurl slowly in the humid morning air, like ink in water. "You know, you should take one of these anyway. Every man should experience a high-class cigar once, just to know what they're like. And who knows, you might have a reason to celebrate later."

Dallabaco walked over and tucked into Jommers's T-shirt pocket a round metal cigar tube. Jommers initially recoiled from it, but relented to avoid jostling over it.

"Relax, it's okay," Dallabaco said. "Sometimes a cigar is just a cigar."

He chuckled, walked back to his Explorer, and drove off.

Jommers walked inside, picked up a clean shop rag, then used it to extract the cigar tube from his shirt pocket. He wrapped the rag around the tube, being careful not to touch it, all the while quietly fuming. The unwanted gift presented Jommers with yet another unwanted dilemma—the complicity of silence. The cocky cop was overconfident about the outcome.

Jommers went up to his apartment and secured the cigar tube in a safe place. While doing so, he wondered about the millions of dollars the city had steered to the chief's security firm and where that money was now. He wondered if Dallabaco had the answer. And then he wondered if one more conversation might be necessary with a certain red-haired detective in Internal Affairs.

But first he needed to grab a sledge.

ABSOLUTION

It had been three weeks since the peculiar incidents at Eggers Court and Crone Point. The people connected to those incidents had swept into Jommers's life like a summer storm. And now, just as quickly as they'd come, they were gone, leaving behind downed things in their wake. Damage assessment was required. But Jommers had only one thought—*I need to whack metal.*

Jommers had originated the concept years ago as a means to overcome his patients' traditional male hesitance to open up about emotional issues. Down in the shop, there were a few old eight-pound sledgehammers with three-foot hickory handles. The mechanics occasionally used them to dislodge brake drums and other heavily corroded truck parts that stubbornly resisted removal. The sledge was an effective persuader of balky parts, so long as you could access the part at an angle that permitted a decent swing.

Behind the shop was a pile of metal scrap—bent tire rims, worn brake drums, busted leaf springs, crunched trailer bumpers, trailer body crossbeams, and various pieces of jagged sheet metal torn from damaged trailers.

The theory was simple. Inhibiting speech requires firm executive control—concentration. Presenting the brain with something else to focus on diminishes that control. And given that no one wants to drive an eight-pound sledge into their foot, the use of the tool requires some attention. Thus, asking a man questions while he's whacking metal makes it harder for him to hold back his thoughts and feelings. So the sledge, whose main purpose was to loosen recalcitrant truck parts, could also be used to loosen reluctant tongues.

Jommers also discovered that the practice helped with one of his own difficulties. He frequently found himself pondering a problem that was too complex to solve. Occasionally such a problem persisted in its demand for attention, putting his brain into runaway train mode. He found that his runaway brain could be derailed by whacking metal. And after Dallabaco's departure, some definite derailing was required.

Jommers located a sledge, then walked out back. His first whack at the scrap pile yielded a surprise—a pissed-off snake jumping out and striking his ankle. There is an innate primal response upon being suddenly attacked by a snake, and Jommers's first impulse was to pancake the reptile. The sledge was already in motion, prepared to do exactly that. But in the intervening milliseconds, Jommers noticed the long yellow head-to-tail stripes on the snake's dark green body and realized it was only a harmless garter snake. And at the last moment, he was able to divert the head of hammer slightly to the right of the snake, just missing it. The second impact of the sledgehammer inspired the serpent to reconsider the advisability of combat, whereupon it beat a strategic retreat and slithered off into the brush.

Jommers returned his attention to the scrap pile, and upon poking around, was pleased to find a nice heavy-duty brake drum. Being more than a foot in diameter and almost a foot in depth, this baby would ring out like a bell when struck. He yanked it out and set it up front, then started whacking away. The loud clanging brought forth a smile, made him feel like John Henry laying rail. Bong! Bong! Bong! He found himself humming that old folk song, "Take This Hammer." The joyful noise did not last long, however, as the brittle iron eventually cracked and broke in the face of repeated bashing. Then, as he surveyed the pile for another target, he sensed a presence off to his right.

"That wouldn't have worked much for me," Nitchenko said. "I was too caught up in the vortex."

Jommers tossed the sledge to the ground. "I guess I should have expected a visit. I'm sure you didn't appreciate seeing it all rehashed in the paper this morning. Having it all run up the pole again for everyone to see. You want to lay into me, you got the right."

"Nah. I didn't come here for that. And while you're right, I was not crazy about seeing it all hung out there again, I came down here to tell you that it's okay. I mean, what you did back then."

"You lost me," Jommers said.

"People are suited for different things, which I guess you already know. Say you work in a hospital emergency room. You show up for your shift, and you have absolutely no clue what you're going to face that day. You have to be ready for anything, able to fly by the seat of your pants. And able to like it, too. And that particular thing, it's something that a cop needs. But I didn't have it. I didn't realize it at the time, but I'm someone who needs more structure to my life. I'm not the guy for improvisation, the long guitar solo. If I played music, I'd need all the notes written down. What I'm supposed to play and how to play them. And the next time like the last time. I guess in the extreme you call that OCD."

"Right."

"I maybe didn't have it to the extreme," Nitchenko said, "but it was definitely there. It wasn't a problem in the beginning because I was in the Traffic Unit, which is not exactly a boiling cauldron, you know, emotionally. But then I get transferred to zone patrol in the First District, which is the worst. And I got the worst part of it, the Terrell Avenue neighborhood. Terrible Terry they call it. And every shift was just mass chaos from the get-go. Shootings, stabbings, rapes, robberies, wife beaters, drug dealers, hookers—same stuff over and over, day after day, no progress—and the discomfort, the irritation, it slowly grows inside you. It's like some twinge you get, where you know something is wrong inside your body, but you don't want to deal with it. So you pretend it will go away. But it doesn't. Know what I mean?"

"Yeah, I know that twinge."

"So this one night I'm assigned to block traffic around where firefighters are trying to put out a blazing carpet store. Should be an easy gig. But the fire, it's ferocious. Frightening. You know, carpet, it's just oil basically. There's nothing you can do. So it's like a hell mouth opened up. I'm a couple hundred yards away and I can feel the heat smacking me, roasting me. And there's three engines there pumping water on it. And it's like nothing. All the water turns to steam as soon as it hits. And there's all this soot coming down out of the air all around. My hands look like I was playing with charcoal. My black-and-white cruiser is turning all black. And then something happened inside me, everything went cold and empty, like you pulled out all my guts. Because I just then realized, that's my job, what I'm watching, an exercise in futility. My zone's out of control and I'm supposed to be doing something about it, but I'm not making a damn bit of difference. Zip. Nada. Nothing. A wasted life. And that's when the depression set in. Then all the rest of it comes down the pike, problems with the kid, my wife, my dad slowly losing his mind—and I told you all that when I came to see you after."

"Yeah, you did," Jommers said. "And I didn't listen like I should have."

"What I didn't tell you then, not sure I should tell you now even, how close I came to killing that guy, you know, the deaf guy I beat on. There's this scary thing you should understand—maybe you already do. It's like momentum, only in your head. I only started hitting him to take control of the situation. I thought he was defying me. I didn't know he was deaf. But once I started, I couldn't stop. It's not something I do, yet there I am doing it. So your mind asks why, and your mind has to answer. If you're doing something bad, then the only possible answer is that you are bad. And if you're bad, then there's no reason to stop what you're doing. You embrace it. Or maybe it embraces you. But there you are. And you absolutely know that what you are doing is totally fucking crazy, but you can't stop. You can't stop because it has to make sense. And keeping at it is the only thing that explains having started it. And I know that sounds totally fucking illogical, and it is. But it happens. You need to understand that, because it's not just me."

Nitchenko paused for a few moments, looking off. "I almost killed him. But the worst part is that I wanted to kill him. And for no other reason than he ignored me. After that day, I knew it was over. I could never be a cop again. Should never. So you did the right thing by getting me canned. It had to be."

"I should have reached out to you," Jommers said. "Should have tried to help you."

"Yeah, you should have, though I'm not sure it would have made a difference, not sure I would have answered. I was in a bad place. After the news stories, my name still fresh in everybody's head, I couldn't even get a job washing dishes. And after the divorce, I was living in my car for a while. At least as an ex-cop, I knew the best place to park it. Every other day I'd drive over the Baldwin Avenue Bridge and ask myself, is today the day I should just pull over and jump. No, I'll give it one more day. Decide tomorrow. Then I caught a break. My cousin Stan was working for a deck builder. It was springtime, when the business takes off. The guy needed some extra help. My cousin vouched for me. And it was while doing that when I got this big insight, there's a fancy word for that, you know, what they use in church."

"Epiphany."

"Yeah, one of those. I found out I liked working with wood. No, I loved working with wood. See, once you understand the wood, you can control the wood. You can make what you want out of it. That feeling, I can't explain, it was like going home. You know that feeling? So one day a customer asks for something different with the balusters—didn't want the same old standard row of two-by-two verticals. And the boss, he was ready to walk away, didn't want to deal with it. He was more like, do the basic setup, jump in, get it done, get out. So I suggested a radial pattern, like a rising sun thing, and told him I could do it. And the customer loved it. So after that, it became available as an added option. Then later I suggested to the boss that there's a lot of other design things I could do because the balusters aren't structural, you know? But he didn't want to hear it. Didn't want too many ideas mucking up the operation. Weird, but you get guys like that, guys who see innovation as contaminating their business model. So I took a leap. Set myself up as a subcontractor specializing in railings and balusters. I sub out to deck builders. They build the structure, then I come in at the end and do the baluster work. I could show you my brochure displaying all the designs I can do, but I don't want to bore you. The main thing is this. I'm doing good. Not getting rich or anything, but I'm happy what I'm doing. And that's the next best thing to being rich. Maybe better."

"I'm glad to hear that."

"And on top of all that, I got a new woman in my life, and that's going great, too."

"That's all wonderful news," Jommers said. "Happy that it's all on track for you."

"The bottom line, the reason I came down here, to let you know that everything is fine now. That you don't need to beat yourself up over it. That you can let it go. Just let it go."

"I appreciate that. I really do. I don't know where I'm going or how I'm going to get there, but you just took a whole bunch of miles off the trip."

"We all got our mess. We all got to learn how to cut some slack."

"Yeah."

"Take it easy, Jommers. Don't hurt yourself with that damn thing."

"Thanks."

After Nitchenko left, Jommers stood dumbfounded, trying to process what had just happened. And as his brain started slipping into runaway train mode, he thought it best to pick up the sledge again.

The morning sun was higher now, so he took off his shirt. He planned to stay at it for a while. He started in on an old truck axle, with each thwack making a dull ka-thunk. He didn't stay on the axle for too long, as the impacts on the unyielding mass sent unpleasant shock waves up the hickory handle and into his wrist bones.

So he switched his attention to a large section of a trailer side panel that still had portions of aluminum supports attached. He found he could make a grand resounding racket by whacking the posts. Each impact sent a shock through the sheet metal, generating a harsh clang, like the crashing of giant defective cymbals. It sounded just right. And so he kept at it, swinging rhythmically with purpose, a deranged percussionist making strange music. And the sharp, ringing claps boomed through the air down to the river and beyond, reverberating around the Bends, echoing like the sound of gunshots.